"Too many military SF novels ignore the essential unevenness and tragedy of war. John Dalmas knows better. His *Soldiers* have both courage and heart."
—**David Brin**

"Rich, inventive world-building and a good solid story from an outstanding writer."
—**C. J. Cherryh**

"Slam bang action . . . with a heart and soul."
—**William C. Dietz**

BAEN BOOKS by JOHN DALMAS

Soldiers

The Regiment
The White Regiment
The Regiment's War
The Three Cornered War

The Lion of Farside
The Bavarian Gate

The Lizard War

To Donna & Clint

SOLDIERS

JOHN DALMAS

John Dalmas

SOLDIERS

This is a work of fiction. All the characters and events portrayed in this book are fictional, and any resemblance to real people or incidents is purely coincidental.

A Baen Books Original

Baen Publishing Enterprises
P.O. Box 1403
Riverdale, NY 10471
www.baen.com

ISBN: 0-671-31987-6

Cover art by David Mattingly

First printing, May 2001

Distributed by Simon & Schuster
1230 Avenue of the Americas
New York, NY 10020

Production by Windhaven Press, Auburn, NH
Printed in the United States of America

This novel is dedicated to gamers,
and particularly to Rod Martin,
Cory Rueb and Bill Cooper.

And to an extraordinary warrior
Bill Ashby

ACKNOWLEDGEMENTS

My thanks to novelists David Brin
and Jim Glass for their critiques
of an early draft of this novel.
To the Spokane Word Weavers
for reading critical chapters
in preliminary form.
And to Gail, who as usual,
read and commented on the
very first, very rough draft.

Chapter 1
The Wyzhñyñy

Grand Admiral Quanshûk shu-Gorlak waited. "Thirty-nine," the ship counted. "Thirty-eight, thirty-seven . . ." *After eleven years in hyperspace,* Quanshûk asked himself, *how can these final seconds seem so long?* Eleven years of wondering what he'd find. Probably, hopefully, nothing basically unfamiliar.

Most of his people had spent the entire eleven years in a sleep so profound that aging was suspended; even he'd spent alternate months in a stasis chamber. Eleven years of hyperspace, mostly between spiral arms. On the screen's display of the F-space potentiality, there'd been whole months without the matric distortion of a single star. Only today had they seen two on a watch, both clearly unsuitable. And now a third. Judging by its mass not a promising third, but it was time to emerge, examine the starscape.

" . . . twenty-four, twenty-three, twenty-two . . ."

He glanced around at the bridge watch, all of them tense. Not so much as an ear flicked. But Quanshûk was not deceived. Those long brain cases harbored thoughts. Anticipation. Apprehension.

" . . . thirteen, twelve, eleven, ten . . ."

1

The word "ten" focused him. His eyes gripped the matric distortion caused by the massive stellar object, with a lesser distortion showing "nearby." Unexpectedly he too was gripped by apprehension. Intense apprehension. His bowel wanted to void right there on the bridge.

" . . . five, four, three, two, one . . ."

Stars exploded onto the screen, glorious, a panoply of brilliant points almost stunning in their collective beauty. For a moment Quanshûk's emotions soared, then responsibility took command. Responsibility for 26 million people. What would they find in this distant place, or what would find them? Every earlier swarm, over the centuries, had expanded the empire's existing boundaries into space already probed by scouts. But this—was territory totally unknown.

The brightest star was brilliant blazing red, the primary of this system. Ten degrees to its left was the next brightest, a planet orbiting it.

Reaching, Quanshûk pressed a key, and on the screen, reality was replaced with a system mechanics simulation, and a data menu. Already navcomp was identifying and computing provisional orbits for the system's planets, along with their masses, spectra, solar constants . . . Perhaps one of them would prove habitable despite the red giant primary.

Shipsmind would inform him promptly of any technically produced electronics.

The living gas bag was both ancient and young, had identity without a label, and thought without words. For its kind, language had long since become not only needless, but pointless. It floated in the uppermost atmosphere of a Jovian giant, enjoying the radiation—the sunshine—on its huge balloon-like body. Meanwhile it composed/produced what, for lack of a more suitable label, might be termed music. An activity carried out jointly with its play companion, fifteen degrees of arc—10,000 miles—distant on the same latitude.

A sudden awareness interrupted their activity— interrupted the activities of all the gas bags around the planet. Something else sentient—some sapient presence—

had manifested within their perception. An armada was not part of their experience, but the concept intuited within the group mind, and expanded to comprehend the beings operating the ships.

Together, the thousands of great globules contemplated this new phenomenon, among other things perceiving its reason for coming there, its purpose and intentions.

They made a decision.

What happened next intensified the newcomers' earlier apprehension. For brief minutes they'd been in a planetary system which their navcomp made perfect sense of. A locatable system in real space, F-space. Even now, ships-mind could tell Quanshûk where that system was, relative to their home sector. Even though they were thousands of parsecs from it—11.26 hyperspace *years,* rounding off.

Then for a moment the navcomp had blacked out so to speak, as the Wyzhñyñy had. They had completely lost orientation—and Quanshûk's armada was suddenly at a different location. A location without any recognizable reference point.

The ship insisted that the change had occurred in zero elapsed time, and that they had not left F-space. They'd simply—translocated. Instantaneously. Meanwhile Quanshûk and most of the bridge watch stood frozen, transfixed. Only one had lost consciousness, and toppled to the deck.

For a full half minute—a half minute with millions of star reads and trillions of computations—the navcomp labored to determine their new location. Without success. What it was able to do was begin creating a new star chart, centered on current ship position. Which was effectively stationary, relative to galactic coordinates. Clearly they were not in the outermost fringe of a spiral arm, as they had been moments earlier. They were well within whatever galaxy this was.

Acknowledging that was the first step in recovery. Quanshûk's muscles twitched. Tremors flowed across his hide. His hair bristled from nape to withers to tail. Bypassing the ship's captain, who still stood cataleptic, Quanshûk called the flagship's medical center and ordered the fallen crewman tended to. Then he ordered the ship to generate hyperspace and proceed to the vicinity of the nearest promising star.

To give that order had taken a major effort of will, but he was grand admiral, with all the responsibilities thereof. He tried not to wonder what might happen next, or what it might mean to this migration, this outswarming he led.

Chapter 2
Pirate Base

The planet had no official name; its system hadn't yet been visited by a Survey ship. Unofficially it was called "Tagus"—short for Tagus Cove—by the only humans who knew it existed. Actually, the small part of the planet they were interested in didn't look at all like the historical Tagus Cove, which lay on the west shore of Terra's Isla Isabela, in the Galapagos Archipelago. But both were, or had been, pirate hangouts.

Also like the Terran Tagus Cove, this deep-space location was equatorial and volcanic, though the vulcanism had long been dormant. But the base itself was twelve miles from the planetary ocean, and had no shortage of drinking water. Instead of scrub, it bore magnificent rainforest, with towering trees, lush green foliage, and colorful darting birds—red, yellow, blue—even more vivid than the flowers.

And numerous technological improvements: a system of tunnels and chambers cut deep behind the craggy wall of a basaltic plateau. These tunnels accessed, among other things, comfortable dormitories and mess halls for raiders, and both family-style and bachelor lodgings for base keepers. Caverns sheltered and concealed the fighting craft and "bag ships," whose long absences provided the reason and wherewithal for the base. Entrances were inconspicuous, opening into a narrow gorge eroded into one flank of the plateau. The excavation rubble was visible from overhead, of course, but resembled natural rockfall.

Everything at the base was designed to elude detection from both space and atmospheric reconnaissance. Even the geogravitic power converter, that provided the base's energy, was too deep to be detected. As was the emergence wave detector. Hyperspace emergence waves pass through rock as freely as neutrinos.

Not everything could be concealed, of course, but what couldn't was designed to mislead. The electronics scanners had been installed in the roofs of what looked like a fishing resort, on the coast twenty miles from base. There, except for the scanners, everything was exposed: lush lawns and gardens, tennis courts, comfortable cottages and cabañas, dining hall, large pool, boat houses . . . There were almost always off-duty base personnel and crewmen there, who came on anti-grav scooters to enjoy their free time.

An innocent vacation spot with little to hide, a secluded, low-gravity stop for the space-touring wealthy. Though it was a long way to go for a vacation.

All in all, Tagus seemed a harmless place, without so much as a pod beacon in the system's fringe.

Henry Morgan was Tagus's founder and (often *in absentia*) ruler. He'd borrowed his name from a 17th century Welsh buccaneer, and it was the only name he admitted to. Like the original, this latter-day Henry Morgan was Welsh, born in Swansea, but he'd grown up in the North American city of Omaha. Remarkably, his birth name was Edward Teach, a name he shared with an 18th century pirate, but the earlier Teach was more barbaric than his namesake cared for. In fact, this latter-day Morgan and his personnel were generally civilized, even amiable, with a leaning toward nonconformity and adventure. Morgan thought of his crew and himself as gentlemen adventurers—daring, risk-taking, colorful. An attitude shared vicariously by many "good Commonwealth citizens." On Terra, from time to time, pirate dramas were popular, in the form of books, videos, and cinemas.

Henry Morgan was eating lunch in his living quarters when his yeoman knocked, audibly agitated. "Commodore," he said, "come quick!"

Morgan stopped his fork in mid course. "What stung your ass, Jerzy?" he called back.

"Sir, it's emergence waves, sir! All over hell, sir!"

Frowning, Morgan lay down his fork, with its morsel of sea turtle fried in nut oil, got to his feet and left, hurrying down the corridor. In his forties and moderately overweight, he still moved well. The wall screen in his office showed a three-dimensional coordinate model of the local solar system and environs. And thousands of hyperspace emergence loci! A footer said 16,297.

Sixteen thousand spacecraft! And Jerzy's "all over hell" summarized the situation nicely: the loci formed a diffuse lenticular swarm in the Tagus System's far-side fringe. Some were out—hell!—close to 5 billion miles, according to the grid. Others were less than 2 billion. Allowing for distance, the size of each locus indicated the mass of the emergent ship, and virtually all were larger than anything his two small squadrons of corsairs had. Larger than anything the Commonwealth admiralty had, excepting a handful of prototypes.

For just a moment Morgan stared, then sat down on his command seat and pecked at his key pad. An overlay, a chart, popped onto the screen, its numbers telling him more than he cared to know. Centuries of galactic radio monitoring had turned up nothing remotely convincing— threatening or otherwise—in the way of alien radio traffic. But in his youth, Morgan had read disreputable novels in which the Commonwealth was invaded by aliens. So the concept of alien invasion was familiar to him, and it seemed the only possible explanation of what he was looking at. Sixteen thousand alien ships! While the Commonwealth had half a dozen squadrons—frigates and (mostly) corvettes— for piracy suppression. That was the sum of its space defenses.

Sixteen thousand! And unless their hyperspace navigation was incredibly poor, they'd come a *very* long way; otherwise they wouldn't be so dispersed. After—what?

Years? After years in hyperspace, it seemed likely they'd explore a bit before moving on. Look over the neighborhood, establish references.

Morgan frowned. "It's going to take them weeks to re-form formations," he said thoughtfully. "Days even to form up an assault group, if they're interested." He turned grinning to his yeoman. "Tell me, Jerzy, if you were me, what would you do about this?"

The young man blinked. "Why, sir," he said, "I'd order all hands to prepare for evacuation. In case the intruders move insystem."

Morgan laughed. "Sounds like a winner. Let's do it."

Preparing ships would take a day or so. The onworld squadron parked in the hangar caverns had recently returned from a long sweep. The loot was still being transferred to the bag ships, and Morgan was short on AG cargo handlers. And till now there'd been no hurry.

The only data he had on intruder ship positions was when the instantaneous hyperspace emergence waves were received. The emergence loci were an unchanging record of something that had already happened. They told him nothing of subsequent ship movements. Equally important, Morgan was unfamiliar with either the intruders' intentions or procedures, and his working assumptions were incorrect. Nor, of course, could his sensors see into warpspace, to detect ship movements there.

He left his office and strode back to his apartment. He was someone who didn't hesitate when something was necessary, however unpleasant, and he was about to throw away a secure base he'd developed over a dozen years. Entering his younger brother's room, he stepped into a fragrance much like Terran night jasmine. An orderly on an AG scooter had collected them from the forest roof; she collected some fragrant species or other every morning. It was more than a duty. It was an expression of fondness for Robert Teach. Robert was a pudgy, disarmingly sunny man, a thirty-one-year-old child liked by everyone. Beginning with his older brother, who'd rescued him after their mother suicided.

Just now, Robert was sitting at his computer terminal, playing with the ephemeris for Epsilon Indi. He could compute in his head—if compute was the word—the moment-to-moment positions of the planets of every inhabited system in the Commonwealth, for any moment you'd care to give him. What he could not do was read above the primary level, or write at all beyond a carefully lettered "signature." He even had trouble buttoning his shirt. Med-tech Connie Phamonyong did that for him. Robert didn't like Press Close or pullovers. He liked buttons. They were nicer.

"Hi, Robert," Morgan greeted. Robert didn't reply. The words hadn't registered; he was utterly engrossed. Connie came out of the kitchenette and gave her commodore a hug and kiss. A fond, familiar kiss. They'd been together for fifteen years.

Morgan nodded toward Robert. "I need his help," he told her. "I need to contact the prime minister and the Admiralty."

Her eyes widened, but she asked no question, simply nodded. Turning, she spoke to Robert, the words a command hypnotically programed years earlier. He didn't hesitate, didn't even blink, simply turned his chair, got up, stepped to a nearby couch (it once had graced a yacht owner's saloon) and lay down. Connie pulled the computer chair over to it and sat, then looked questioningly at Morgan.

"Just the two for now," he said, "the PM and the Admiralty."

She turned to Robert, and spoke with a calm she did not feel, a standard prolog to whatever the message would be. Then she looked again at Morgan, and briefly they waited.

On Terra, in the palace penthouse at Kunming, a young man not basically unlike Robert Teach sat at a keyboard, playing a flowing improvisation based on a Chopin nocturne. Abruptly he stopped, and turned to his attendant. "It is something for Mr. Peixoto," he said. Then getting to his feet, he stepped to a nearby lounge and lay down. The attendant clicked a switch on his belt and sat down beside the young savant.

At the same moment, half a mile away, a tiny aging woman at a computer screen broke off her inspection of a commercial freight schedules at the Kinshasa terminal; she could have recited it verbatim, it and numerous others. Turning, she spoke to her attendant, not a frequent event. When a communication triggered a trance, her speech was quite clear, not at all like her usual lisping voice that resembled a three-year-old's. Her attendant helped her to her couch; the old woman couldn't walk unassisted. She'd never been able to.

When the two communicators on Terra had responded, Robert Teach spoke again. "They are ready," he said. Then his elder brother began to dictate, identifying himself by both his legal name and pseudonym, Robert passing them on precisely, mentally. Instantaneously. Without a qualm, Morgan gave his galactic coordinates, then described what his emergence wave detector had shown. Those same emergence waves had reached Terra at the same instant, of course, but at that distance—hundreds of parsecs—they'd been far too slight to register.

It would be an historic event: the first planetary capture by the Seventh Wyzhñyñy Swarm. The flagship's bridge was bright with officers of the exalted genders, their fur blue, except for the ridge of cardinal that began at the withers, and in the master gender culminated in a cranial crest. Amongst the tan or reddish-brown of the crew and subordinate officers, they were vividly dominant.

Their flagship was equipped with the best sensory system the empire could provide. Within minutes, the grand admiral knew the location and approximate orbits of all the system's planets, and their first-order environmental parameters—mass, solar constant, magnetic field, surface temperature, approximate atmospheric composition . . . Also the presence of technical electronics—that had been recorded almost at once—and the curious absence of any apparent pod beacon.

With those data established, Grand Admiral Quanshûk shu-Gorlak had ordered the fleet of one preselected tribe—transports, cargo ships, armed escorts—to head insystem.

While inbound, all colonists were to be revived; all but the matrons were soldiers. The bombardment ships and ground-assault craft would emerge from warpspace close to the inhabited planet, move in, and wipe out all military installations and population concentrations. That accomplished, ground forces would seek and destroy all remaining native sophonts. With mop-up under way, they would commence base construction.

Nothing was said about prisoners. The only prisoners the Wyzhñyñy ever took were for interrogation, and only as ordered by their high command. Without such an order, all alien sophonts would be killed. Of course.

The tribal fleet, or most of it, emerged from warpspace and approached quickly in gravdrive. Its scouts quickly found the sole source of technical electronics—the "resort." Eight miles out, Support Force Commander Kraloqt stood on the bridge of his flagship, frowning. Was this all? The place didn't appear dangerous. He ordered a single pulse fired, adequate to obliterate the central building, hopefully drawing fire from any defense forces.

It did the first but not the second.

Perhaps the defenders were in subsurface installations. Kraloqt ordered a spray burst, each pulse more powerful than the single first shot. The resort site exploded, lofting a large cloud of smoke and dust, leaving a twenty-acre crater field.

He then ordered in an elite infantry battalion, to scout the surrounding forest and flush out the enemy. The first assault lander had barely put down when a small spacecraft emerged unexpectedly at the surface, twenty miles east-northeast of the landing zone, accelerating outbound as strongly as its crew could tolerate. Another quickly followed, then a third, a fourth. By that time the first had generated warpspace on the run, and was essentially out of harm's way. The others followed suit.

Kraloqt's battlecomp had peripheral attention better than any living organism's; it was never distracted. In the same moment that its alarm system squalled, his flagship fired a series of pulses at the location from which the alien craft had appeared. Kraloqt ordered a bombardment ship into action.

To hunt fleeing craft in warpspace was impractical, and at any rate not Kraloqt's responsibility. His job was to destroy the planet's surface defenses and prepare it for occupation. He radioed a report to the grand admiral (it would take a dozen hours to reach him), then ordered another elite battalion to the site of the alien launch. In less than a minute, the battalion's armored assault landers were on their way, with gunships flying cover.

When the resort's electronics reported bogies entering F-space only 90,000 miles out, the surprised Morgan had ordered all base personnel to board their assigned ships for evacuation. They were to be fully secured for flight within ten minutes, and depart on his command. His own yacht would leave after the others were clear.

But again the invaders surprised him. While the transports and cargo ships entered F-space 90,000 miles out, the assault force had continued in warpspace, and emerged unexpectedly overhead at only 63,000 feet.

Despite his surprise, the intruders' haste grabbed Morgan's curiosity, which at times could be stronger than his good judgement. Thus, though Connie and Robert were still in his apartment, he was reluctant to leave his office. The intruders might try to communicate via computer. It seemed probable.

Before the ten minutes were up, communication with the resort was cut off. Two minutes later the shock wave of its destruction hit the subterranean pirate base, and Morgan's hopes crashed and burned. He knew at once there'd be no negotiation, or even an ultimatum, just destruction. A touch on his key pad showed he still had communication within the base. Biting the words out, he called Flight Control. "Drago, it's time to vamoose. Are all ships secured and ready?"

"All but yours, boss."

"Leave without me. Now! No delay! I'll follow when I can. Till then, you're in charge."

"You're the boss, boss." Drago paused. Morgan could hear him talking laconically to someone else—Hideo Pienaar, Morgan's own first officer, who would serve as launch control till Morgan boarded the *Delight* with Robert and Connie.

Then Drago was speaking through the base communication system. "Emergency evacuation! Emergency evacuation! Standard rendezvous! Standard rendezvous! All cradles except the commodore's yacht cradle will power up to launch. NOW!" There was a brief lapse, then Pienaar was speaking. "Launch one!" Pause. "Launch two!" Pause. "Launch three." Pause. "Launch four."

Morgan felt the rock shudder much more severely than before, a series of heavy shock pulses hammering the plateau top directly overhead, and the upper face of the gorge. He hadn't imagined such a quick response. His hands clenched the arms of his chair. Objects fell from shelves. A vase waltzed briefly and toppled, spilling flowers and water across the surface of his desk, wetting his lap. He swore. Jabbing a key on his pad, he called, "Damage report!"

"Boss, this is Hideo. Ships one through four got out. Then we took multiple hits, and a lot of rock came down. Both ports are blocked by rockfall. Doesn't seem to be any interior damage though."

Thank God for any favors, Morgan thought. "How long will it take to clear the ports?"

"An hour at least. Likely four or five. We need to get the dozer running."

"Okay, do it."

It was as if the invader had been listening. There was another, longer series of shocks, and Morgan's line with damage control cut off. *Along with any prospect of getting the ports cleared at all,* he told himself.

Opening a desk drawer, he took out a remote control and shoved it into a pocket. He had no doubt intruder scouts would be along soon, checking the target area. *We'll really be in the soup then,* he told himself, *unless the ports are so thoroughly blocked, the bastards don't notice them. We'll likely have their version of marines in the tunnels with us.* Or worse, some explosive aerosol that would blow the base all to hell from the inside out.

Defense was out of the question. Moving more quickly than he had for years, Morgan headed for his apartment, to find Connie standing round-eyed with worry, Robert beside her. Pointing at Morgan, Robert laughed. "You wet your pants!"

Morgan looked down where the water from the vase had spilled on him. "Well, I'll be darned," he said. "Look at that." Then he stepped to the phone and keyed base security. That line was working. The speaker was on, and Connie and Robert listened.

"Prieto," a voice answered.

"Have we got visitors yet, Léon?"

"They just landed. They will be knocking at our door in a few minutes. Our monitor eyes are all inop, but I have men peeking over the rubble blocking the work port." Prieto laughed. "Maglie says they are the centaurs from hell. Then he said no, they are centaurs from the Jurassic." Léon paused, then continued: "I think they will blast their way in."

"Look, Léon," Morgan said, "if you think it's best, surrender to them. I'm giving you full authority. Meanwhile I need to get Robert out of their reach. One way or another."

"Got it, boss."

Morgan switched off. "Robert, Connie, let's go." They followed without questions. Nearby was a dead-end corridor. As they approached it, he took the remote from his pocket, and aiming it at what appeared to be solid rock; he touched the switch. Groaning, the rock slid aside about five feet, a steel panel with rock slab veneer. He gestured Connie and Robert through the gap ahead of him. "Hurry!" he said, and even Robert hurried. Then he pointed the remote again, and the gap closed.

The tunnel on the other side was narrow, crudely finished, and unlit. It smelled moist and fusty, as if not serviced by the base's ventilation system. Morgan pressed a second switch, and the remote became a flashlight. Turning, he directed the beam down the tunnel. Blackness swallowed it a hundred feet ahead.

"Morgan," Robert said, "I'm scared." His voice was a little boy's now, despite its tenor pitch.

"It's okay to be scared, but you'll be all right. I'm your brother; I take care of you." Gently he rumpled Robert's close-cut hair. "We're going to a *secret* place. The bad guys don't know about it. No one does except us three."

Then he led off along the tunnel.

❖   ❖   ❖

It went farther than Connie had expected. Half a mile at least, she decided, and except for the first hundred yards or so, it climbed. Not steeply, but enough that Robert got a bit querulous. "You'll make it, brother," Morgan told him. "You're doing great. Our father used to climb mountains, and we inherited his legs, you and I."

"Really? What mountains?"

"He used to climb Mount Snowden every chance he had. When I was little, back in Wales. A couple of times he even went to Scotland to climb; he climbed Ben Nevis there, and Ben Macdhui. Once, after we moved to Nebraska, he took Mother and me to Colorado, where there were even bigger mountains. He climbed one of them, too. I wanted to go with him, but I was too . . ."

A faint tremor shivered the rock beneath their feet, interrupting Morgan's recitation. He didn't get back to it, simply walked faster.

Connie's knowledge of Terran geography pretty much ended with what was taught in middle school, and in high school in connection with history. It didn't go much beyond the more important places and historical events. Her mind couldn't create an image of Wales on the map, but she was pretty sure it was part of Great Britain. Scotland she could image. On the map it looked like the profile of a dowager, with a feathered hat from some far-back time—the 20th or 21st century. Before "the Troubles." As for Colorado—she'd heard of it. It was in North America.

She wondered if Henry was telling Robert the truth. She'd never known him to kid his brother, but over the years she'd learned he could lie when it suited him.

After what might have been twenty minutes, the flashlight picked up a steel door ahead, with what looked like a wheel on it. Like much else in the base, it was from a waylaid ship—the security vault door of a luxury cruise ship. It wasn't locked; Henry simply spun the wheel and pulled, then ushered them in and closed it after them.

He didn't take time to show them around. Leaving them in the dark, he disappeared through another door. Half a minute later she could hear humming from wherever the machinery resided that provided the utilities—a small geogravitic power converter, water pump, sump pump, air circulation . . . Lights turned on. Seconds later she heard water running.

After Henry returned, the rock shuddered again, this time more strongly than in the tunnel, though nothing like they'd felt in the apartment. He went back into the machinery room, and while he was gone, the shudder repeated strongly enough to worry her.

They made love that night for the first time in a week. Afterward, over brandy—short drinks; they needed to be frugal with it—Henry told her more about what had happened. Including the tremor in the tunnel, and those they'd felt since then. The first, he believed, was the intruders blasting their way into the base. The second was the use of concussion to kill everyone inside. "And the third—" He exhaled gustily through pursed lips. "If the alien charges didn't collapse the base, I wouldn't want them to find this place. And years ago I had charges set to bring down the corridor leading here."

He reached, and patted her hand. "There's a way out though, and enough food to keep the three of us for a couple of years if need be. Meanwhile I'll be doing things, finding things out, and you and Robert can help me communicate what I learn to Terra." *Though what it might be,* he told himself, *or what good it might do them, God only knows. Sixteen thousand, for godssake!*

Chapter 3

Chang Lung-Chi and Foster Peixoto

President Chang Lung-Chi's chauffeur had let him off three hundred yards from the palace. Three hundred esthetic yards, pregnant with history. A long, initially turbulent history. After the Troubles, the Commonwealth of Worlds had undertaken to recognize and honor its diverse roots. And for Chang, walking through Peace Garden was to celebrate those roots. He strode briskly between vivid red and white flowerbeds, past the tall, crystalline Fountain of the Heroes, then across Unity Square, to mount the broad, low marble stairs of the Palace of Worlds. There he entered through the Portal of Admiral Gavril Apraxin.

The president was a man of less-than-ordinary height; without exception his bodyguards were taller. They didn't march, didn't even keep to any particular configuration. They could almost have been walking together by chance. And if you watched them, not knowing who they were, it would be Chang Lung-Chi your eyes would follow. His somewhat portly sixty-year-old form was straight-backed, and he had presence.

17

The vast lobby was busy, though the senate and assembly would not be called to order for two more hours. Staff members bustled on errands. Bureaucrats and members of parliament sauntered in conversation. Families and other early sightseers circulated, examining displays and memorials, or gazing at the shafts of colored light from reflectors overhead.

Security was inconspicuous but excellent. Concealed surveillance cameras recorded everything. They were not sapient, of course, but they were programmed to notice—and correlate—face and form, bearing and demeanor, clues subtle as well as overt. And to inform as appropriate.

The president passed the broad corridor that led to both senate and assembly, proceeding instead to a secure express tube to the next-to-top floor, where his offices and apartment were. When he stepped out into the eighty-sixth floor's east elevator bay, the prime minister was waiting for him; the surveillance system had more than just security functions.

"Mr. President!" the prime minister said. "Something has come up which urgently requires our joint attention."

Chang Lung-Chi raised his eyebrows. "Well then," he said, without asking what. It seemed to him he could guess.

Foster Peixoto had already turned, starting down the corridor to his own wing, which was larger than the president's. It was not a matter of rank or prestige. The prime minister was head of government, which in the Commonwealth meant its director of planning and operations. He required a larger staff. The president was head of state: its spokesman, setter of directions and goals, co-setter of policies and priorities.

Physically they were not at all alike. Peixoto had lived the first fourteen years of his life on Luna. Not surprisingly he was nearly seven feet tall, though weighing less than the president. And their differences went beyond body type, yet they'd been friends at first meeting, and close friends almost as quickly. They even complemented one another. Peixoto was an analytical thinker who dealt well with details. The president was intuitive. His mind cut quickly to the core of a problem.

Peixoto's office was spare, and strictly utilitarian. The few art pieces had been supplied by the General Services

Administration. Folding his long body onto his desk chair, he rested his hand by his key pad. The president, a frequent visitor, seated himself.

"The alien armada has attacked another world," Peixoto said. "This time the Gem of the Prophet. My communicator learned of it only minutes ago. You'd already left the airport, so I decided to wait." He tapped a short sequence of keys. A picture lit a wall screen, of a youth, a savant lying in trance. President Chang knew the young man, whose talents went far beyond his musical virtuosity. He lay in a penthouse apartment overhead, but his words originated on a world so distant, its sun was not visible to the naked eye.

The savant spoke in Terran, in the first person. After identifying the system, he began the message. "Two hours ago," he said, "bombardment craft, parked out of sight overhead, began to destroy our towns. They ignored our attempts to communicate. Now not a town remains standing. After you forwarded the report of Morgan the pirate, this unit was ordered to the Mountain of the Poet, where the invaders have not yet found us."

So, Peixoto thought, *the aliens, the intrusion, are real. This leaves no doubt.*

The words continued. "They have landed ground forces at numerous locations. Video signals show their soldiers as having six limbs, and like the mythical centaur, they walk on four of them. The other two, the arms, are on an upright torso that rises from the withers. The head looks reptilian, despite fur and external ears, and the tail is like that of an ass. They wear no clothing, only a harness to which their gear is attached. They run briskly, and even ignoring the upright torso, their body appears larger than the largest dog.

"They attack fiercely, and have rejected, or failed to understand, offers of surrender. They simply kill, the unarmed as well as the armed."

There was a long pause. "They have detected us. Our . . ." Briefly the savant shifted on the couch, then lay quiet. His attendant moved into camera view. "Ramesh has lost contact," he said. "We will continue to record further communication, if there is any."

Peixoto touched a key and the screen went blank. Chang's head had bowed as they'd listened. Now it raised. "Faith has gotten itself tangled in the thorn hedge again," he said. The Faith Party was small but sometimes pivotal. When the report from Tagus had been released, Faith had been vocally upset with it. Their pacifism had been threatened, and they'd denied vehemently that there was such an armada. It was impossible, a pirate ruse.

They'd have a hard time calling this report a pirate ruse. And Faith depended on the perception that their positions and statements came to them from the deity. "Faith will lose more than face," Chang went on. "To the eight hundred million Muslims on Terra, traditional and reformed, the Gem of the Prophet has been the crown jewel of their colonies. Now Salam will disassociate itself from Faith." His gaze sought Peixoto's. "This will help you get a war powers act through."

Peixoto nodded absently; a thought had taken his attention. "We must somehow establish communication with these . . . centaurs. Negotiate with them."

The comment took the president by surprise. "Of course," he said. "But meanwhile we'll promote a war powers proposal to parliament. Rearming will require immense focus, unswerving determination—and discipline." Chang paused, peering carefully at his friend. "Do you actually suppose these creatures might negotiate?"

Peixoto shook his head reluctantly. "I hope, but I do not expect. We must try."

The president nodded. "I agree, my friend, we must try." He frowned, then gestured at the wall screen. "Call up a space chart. Centered on the azimuth of Gem."

Peixoto's forehead furrowed, and he tapped keys. A three-dimensional star chart appeared on the screen, with a thin green line that extended from Terra through the Gem of the Prophet. "Now show me where Tagus is," the president said.

Peixoto's lips framed a silent "oh" of realization, and he tapped keys again. The primary of the Tagus System showed a pulsing red. It was not far off the azimuth that ran through Gem.

"Now show the Gem-Tagus bearing, enlarged."

Peixoto's fingers busied. The image jumped, showing a line from Tagus to Gem. Several labeled systems lay near it; one had a colony. A touch of the arrow gave its name: the Star of Hibernia.

"Does our embassy there have a communicator office?"

All colonial embassies were authorized one, but there were more embassies than there were suitable savants. Once more Peixoto's fingers tapped, and names appeared. "Yes," he said.

"Contact them, right now. We must know."

"Of course, Mr. President." Peixoto phoned his communicator's apartment, and gave quick instructions. Then they waited. It took a few minutes; Ramesh had gone to the roof garden with his attendant, to enjoy the flowers. It was something he did daily at about this time. Like most idiot savants, he was happier, and healthier, when his workday was organized around things pleasant and predictable. Meanwhile the prime minister and the president waited without a word, Peixoto wondering how he and his staff had managed to overlook the Star of Hibernia. Finally Ramesh was back on his couch. Peixoto told the attendant what he wanted, and the attendant instructed the savant.

Chang was not surprised when the embassy on Star did not respond. "Burhan, is there any possiblity that their communicator is engaged in something that prevents his answering?"

"None that I'm aware of, Your Excellency," the attendant said. "There should be at least an autonomic response, even if asleep, or deeply engaged in something."

"Ask Ramesh if he gets any sense of how things are on Star."

Burhan passed the question to his ward while the two executives watched the screen. The tranced savant did not reply.

"As you see," the attendant said, "he says nothing. But I can sense his distress. Something bad has happened there."

Peixoto nodded. "Thank you, Burhan. And if it seems appropriate to you, thank Ramesh for me. For myself and the president."

The slender, youthful-looking attendant nodded soberly. "I will forward your excellencies' appreciation to Ramesh."

Peixoto broke the connection. "*I can sense his distress,*" Burhan had said. It could well be true, but it was a frail basis for decisions. He looked at Chang Lung-Chi, who looked back grimly.

"How," Chang asked, "could the intruder armada—the *invader* armada—have arrived at Star without our being notified of their emergence?"

"I can think of a possibility. It is the beginning of the rainy season at New Kerry. The whole planet celebrates, drinking intoxicants, squirting water on people . . . Perhaps no one was tending the detector at the time . . . Or the invader may never have emerged there. Their savant may simply be ill."

Chang's only comment was his wry expression. "Call a cabinet meeting," he said, "for ten hundred hours if possible, with Shin and Kulikov sitting in. Invite Thorkelsdóttir to sit in for Faith. By Faith standards she's a pragmatist; she will actually listen to what others say." *Against a set of 20th century preconceptions!* "We face the biggest threat in the history of the human species.

"We need a plan on how to contact the invaders, and a strategy for negotiation. Establish a peace committee; Thorkelsdóttir can be vice chair. Then keep it focused on specifics: how to contact the alien, how to communicate with them. How to begin learning their psychology. How! How! How! We must focus!"

As Chang spoke, the enormity of the task struck Peixoto.

"There will be a language problem," Chang went on. "And the invaders will travel in hyperspace. Probably in an invasion corridor centered on the Tagus-Gem axis. We'll have to predict where they'll emerge, and decide on how to intercept them."

The prime minister nodded, but his heart was a stone in his chest. The prospect of negotiation seemed zero.

"Meanwhile I'll meet with Diderot and Gordeenko. We need to plan the evacuation of colonists in and near that corridor." The president paused. "Sixteen thousand ships! Phew!" The number itself was overwhelming. "You realize what this means," he said.

Peixoto had no idea what Chang referred to, and waited for him to answer his own question.

"We may face a folk migration instead of simply a war."

Peixoto gnawed a lip; he could see the logic. "If that's true," he said, "the situation is less severe than it might be. Every transport means one fewer warship."

"Ah, but my friend, a folk migration suggests they do not have the option of returning home, wherever that may be. And they are a different life-form than we are. They may all be warriors. Born warriors. Then every transport is a troopship!"

Again the president paused, then the flow of words resumed, more measured now. "We must see to the requisition and conversion of all available shipping, to evacuate colonies. And expand our war and shipbuilding industries as rapidly as possible. Recruit and train armies! Build hundreds on hundreds of warships, and train crews for them! It will require complete and rapid mobilization of human and industrial resources—the biggest challenge in human history!"

The prime minister almost stared, attention fixed less on the enormity of the task than by the president's sudden energy. "With a population that hasn't fought for centuries," Peixoto pointed out. "Many with the conviction that to fight is immoral. That in the long run, the results of surrender are best. But seemingly this is an enemy that does not accept surrender."

Chang seemed not to hear. His mind was busy. "Evacuees will be our best source of recruits. Their lives will already have been disrupted." His focus returned to his prime minister. "We must approach negotiation as if there were no chance at all of winning a war, and we must prepare for war as if there were no chance of successful negotiation. In the meantime, victories in battle may give us leverage."

Chang Lung-Chi rubbed his hands.

Good God, the prime minister thought, *he is savoring the challenge!*

Peixoto watched the president leave, then breathed a deep sigh. *We have no actual defense forces at all, beyond a few squadrons to suppress pirates. Contingency plans and industrial mobilization plans—yes. A small cadre of warfolk, yes, some active, some retired, but none with combat experience. Trained on sophisticated electronic war games. Limited experience with prototype weapons and virtuality trainers. But armed forces? A war industry?*

We'll have to start with recruitment and industrial mobilization. He realized he didn't know enough to evaluate either the problems or the prospects realistically. *Kulikov and Shin will know as much about that as anyone,* he thought, and reaching, keyed his phone.

Chapter 4

Chief Scholar

Quanshûk shu-Gorlak touched keys on his* command panel, then spoke into his communicator. "Chief Scholar, please report to my quarters at once."

"As you command, Admiral."

Quanshûk turned and crossed the bridge, his dull claws inaudible on the acoustical surface. He was aware that his executive officer, Rear Admiral Tualurog, was following him with his eyes. *I have been brooding,* Quanshûk realized, *and now I will discuss my thoughts with Qonits instead of with him.* On a flagship, a certain tension was natural between the XO, who was operations officer, and the chief scholar, who was not military. It would rarely cause serious difficulties—the separation of functions was hardwired—but it could distract the XO. *I will,* Quanshûk decided, *set his mind at ease later. Somewhere other than on the bridge.*

When the grand admiral arrived at his suite, Qonits

---

* English doesn't provide pronouns to deal with the Wyzhñyñy genders. For simplicity, the masculine—he, him, his—will be used to cover them all.

zu-Kitku was waiting in the corridor. Quanshûk placed a palm on the security plate, then pushed the stateroom door open, and gestured. Both stepped inside, the door closing behind them. The admiral poured nuts into two bowls, handing one of them to Qonits with a brief, casual gesture of blessing. Then he lowered his hindquarters onto a cushion, much as a dog might sit.

Qonits followed his example, then ate several nuts. "How can I serve you, my lord?" he asked.

"I need your ears and your responses." Quanshûk paused, gathering his thoughts. "I have been analyzing our experience in this new region. It has troubling aspects."

"Ah."

"The three worlds we have taken were all occupied by the same species. And their ships generated strange-space, which almost certainly means they have hyperdrive.* Is that not so?"

"It is hard to imagine otherwise, your lordship, considering that the ships were small for faring deep space in warpdrive."

"Yet the sapient populations of all three worlds were very small. One was no more than an outpost. Correct?"

"Unarguably."

"Therefore they could not have been self-sustaining. They must have been part of an empire."

Qonits bobbed his torso from the waist, a formal Wyzhñyñy nod. "True."

"And clearly they were only recently colonized, so this is an expanding empire. But even so, within a month or two—three at most—we will reach their core worlds. And

---

* Strange-space is a collective term for two different phenomena—warpspace and hyperspace. Warpdrive utilizes warpspace, and hyperdrive utilizes hyperspace. The strange-space generator can generate both. The Terran term "warpdrive" grew out of a 20th century theory that four-dimensional space could be warped, permitting faster-than-light travel. Though the concept would prove unproductive, the term was familiarized by space fiction. Later, by extension, the first drive to actually bypass the speed of light was dubbed "warpdrive," though it has nothing to do with warping four-dimensional space.

with their technological level, they will no doubt defend themselves vigorously."

Qonits shrugged with his hands. "One would think so."

"Ours is the greatest swarm ever assembled, and far the most powerful. So we will continue in the traditional manner, neither hastening nor dawdling. Thrust into the heart of this empire like a great spear, pausing to put a tribe or tribes on every suitable world along the way. That should force their warfleet to come to us, away from the advantages of established defenses.

"And if they will not be drawn, we will continue. Eventually they must fight, and we will crush them. After that, the remainder of their worlds can be occupied without concern."

Qonits bowed deeply. "Your lordship," he said quietly, "you did not call me here to lecture me on the obvious."

"True. But it was necessary to set the table." Quanshûk's thick lids lowered to half-mast, a Wyzhñyñy frown. "But there are peculiarities in this situation, are there not? Why have these aliens not provided their outposts with meaningful defenses? Warships parked outside the radiation belts. Things to bleed us."

His fly-whisk tail waving slowly, Qonits considered the statement. "Who knows how these aliens think," he replied, "or what they value and do not value? Perhaps, my lord, they are sufficiently powerful, sufficiently dominant in this sector, that they did not foresee an invasion."

Quanshûk filed the reply and continued. "The rulers will soon know of our arrival, if they do not already. Ships escaped worlds one and three, and presumably world two as well. After a day or so, they would have emerged into F-space to launch message pods, warning their nearer colonies, the nearer core worlds, and their crown world." Absently Quanshûk nibbled nuts. "But . . ." His gaze intensified. "Does it not seem that on the worlds we captured, their ships escaped with remarkable alacrity? As if they already knew of us, and were prepared?"

"They could have acted on the basis of our hyperspace emergence waves, which surely they found alarming."

Quanshûk licked air in apprehension, a gesture that might have embarrassed him with someone other than

Qonits. "There should have been *some* defenses. Unless their rulers are indifferent to their outpost worlds."

"They may simply keep the core worlds strong and the outer weak, to ensure obedience. Depending on coercion instead of loyalty, in which case it must be a young empire. As dispersion grows, coercion becomes self-defeating." Qonits paused. "Or this life-form may be so remote, it doesn't recognize the danger."

Quanshûk considered the reply. "I must have information," he decided. "What are they like? How large is their empire? Their fleet? At the next world we capture, we will take prisoners. You will learn to question them and understand their answers. Shipsmind can develop a translation program. The Second and Fourth Swarms did it."

Again Qonits nodded. "True," he said. "But such a program requires much linguistic data, along with time and caution. Prisoners may lie. As for capturing them . . ." He paused, not liking to point out the obvious. "Enemy wounded are potentially dangerous. It is natural to kill them."

Quanshûk flicked a hand as if at a fly. "The physical presence of a commander enhances compliance. I will go insystem with the assault force, to demonstrate the seriousness of my order; they will feel constrained to abide by it."

Qonits' next bow expressed deference, but when he raised his torso, he did not avert his eyes. "You will be risking your life, Grand Admiral, and you would not easily be replaced. You were anointed by the emperor."

Quanshûk answered mildly. "We have yet to encounter meaningful resistance," he pointed out. "And if I deem the situation dangerous, I will stay away."

Qonits placed his palms together in a formal nod. Clearly the admiral would not be dissuaded. And the nature, extent and intensity of the system's technical electronics output would suggest the likely level of danger. "Of course, Grand Admiral. And if we gain no more than some insights into their psychology, they will be useful."

"Thank you, Chief Scholar." Quanshûk stepped to his small bar. "Will you drink with me before you leave?"

◈　　◈　　◈

After Qonits had left, Quanshûk poured another drink. He felt much better than he had. But even so, the situation had peculiarities.

The chief scholar settled himself at his terminal and turned his attention to the multifaceted entity known as shipsmind. "Librarian," he ordered. And a moment later, "Give me all you have on the interrogation of alien captives." It wouldn't be much, and who knew if any of it would be pertinent here. But it was a place to start. He watched the annotated source list form on the screen. *We might learn a great deal,* he told himself, *or we might harvest confusion and lies. But it will be interesting. I can monitor their brainwaves, their electrical fields . . .* He began to like the idea of prisoners.

✧   ✧   ✧

Chapter 5
Eric Padilla

When the Wyzhñyñy arrived at distant Tagus, few people on Terra had heard of Doctor Eric Padilla, humanity's pioneer in cyborg engineering. There weren't many experts. A one-handed man could count them on his fingers. But the technology had survived in old training cubes, and tangentially in the fields of neurosurgery and pseudo-organic engineering. In fact, given a two-week training intensive, numerous neurosurgeons and roboticists, working together, could function as cyborg engineers.

Unfortunately there were no such training intensives. Cyborg engineering had been proscribed by law, and abandoned by universities, and by science in general. Such thorough abandonment would have been impossible before the Troubles, but the drive to innovate, to search deeply and build daringly, had faded during that period. The Troubles: nearly a century of martial law, chaos, terrorism, and intermittent, cautiously tailored warfare. A period during which distrust of government, of corporate greed, of innovation and activism had all intensified. The result had been a combination of technological and business conservativism, and social liberalism. Over subsequent centuries these persisted, though somewhat changed in their expression.

There had also been growth toward a spirituality relatively free of boundaries and mostly of creeds. A growth abetted by the emigration of many unhappy sectarians to the stars. In the new spiritualism, the main approach to dogma lay in pacifism and human rights doctrines. And even these were mostly not zealous. Zeal was suspect. Combative idealism had become much less common. It had served its purpose. The public cynicism it helped sire had largely dissolved political, racial, and ethnic chauvinism in the Sol System, leaving occasional dull scums of prejudice and scattered, hard and bitter nodes of hatred, like social gallstones, to dissolve gradually, one by one, without surgery.

In the process, the cynicism too had faded.

Meanwhile, pacifism and the long peace had minimized and marginalized the military. Even military fiction had become socially disrespectable: a ghetto genre with a low profile. The child Eric Padilla had grown up in Denver, in the Colorado Prefecture. He'd been part of that ghetto. By age ten, his favorite reading had been regimental histories, novels set in historical wars, and especially yarns in which aliens invaded the human worlds. He rented them from private libraries, or bought them on the Ether, or borrowed them from friends, hiding them in his pocket reader.

His mother would have been prostrated, had she known. But she didn't snoop into his activities; unconsciously she feared what she might find. His father knew, and had reluctantly supported young Eric's habit, while trying to keep his wife from learning of it, and hoping his son would outgrow it.

Which in a sense Eric did. At age thirteen he announced to his parents an interest in neurosurgery. At the same time his grades surged from decent to excellent, allowing his selection into prep school, which was quite demanding. Three years later he qualified for university, and begged his parents to send him. University educations were expensive, but with loans and a scholarship, they'd managed.

They hadn't known his motive. His reading had stimulated the belief that aliens would in fact invade Terra someday. To his young mind it seemed inevitable; occasionally he even dreamt of it. And from this and playing war games, he'd developed a powerful interest in the concept of the military cyborg.

In fact, he intended to build one! In an era of peace and technological stagnation, he was a century and a half ahead of his time.

When he left for university, he knew that to be a neurosurgeon, one must first be an MD. But he hadn't realized how little latitude his scholarship left for courses outside premedicine. Over three years he managed to schedule only two courses in pseudo-organic engineering—courses focused on industrial applications and information technology. And having no interest in an actual medical career, he found himself impatient, and in danger of losing his scholarship.

All of that was to change. At a war-game "convention," in an old warehouse in Cheyenne, he met an officer from the small, low-profile Bureau of Commonwealth Defense. Colonel Roger Kaytennae sometimes visited such conventions, where he might quietly talk an especially promising youth into a military career.

Kaytennae had himself grown up in North America, in the Arizona Prefecture. Eventually he became director of the Defense Bureau's War Games Section, where the army prepared in virtual reality for what they believed was inevitable alien contact, quite possibly hostile. Impressed by young Padilla's intelligence, vision and dedication, Kaytennae hired him as a civilian intern, where he could observe his talent, adaptability, and judgement. Within a few weeks the colonel had decided, and contrived a scholarship for his young, fellow American, dipping into the Bureau's discretionary funds.

He then enrolled Eric in Kunming University. There, with Kaytennae's participation, a professor of neurological physiology, and another in pseudo-organics, tailored a curriculum for the young man. This put him close to his military sponsor, and far from his parents, who were relieved if uneasy about their son's education being financed by the government.

His scholastic performance proved exemplary, and the colonel was soon satisfied that the young man's potential was as good as he'd hoped. Kaytennae then approached a wealthy manufacturer he'd cultivated, and got him to finance several scholarships. From the ranks of games enthusiasts, he'd already recruited several youths to fill those scholarships. Because Eric Padilla would need skilled collaborators and assistants.

At age thirty-seven, Doctor Eric Padilla personally and successfully removed the living central nervous system— the CNS—of one Carlos O'Brien. O'Brien was a thirty-year-old ex-construction worker who'd lost both arms and his eyesight in an explosion. Removed and transferred his CNS live, into a bioelectronic interface unit (BEIU, or "bottle") where it underwent hormonal detraumatization. Then he successfully installed the "activated" bottle into a newly designed prototype infantry combat servo. When fitted with the activated bottle, the servo provided a ruggedly formidable, prototype fighting machine.

This epochal operation was carried out with great care for secrecy. For the human rights movement had gone full circle, and begun to eat its own tail: to protect human rights, it undertook to deny them.

Normally Padilla was calm, unflappable, but he found the operation nerve-wracking. Not because of any possible leak and criminal prosecution; he gave that scenario almost no attention. But because neither he nor anyone else had ever performed such an operation on a live human being, and no one knew with certainty what the result would be. Of necessity, the servo's inputs to the overall sensorium were extremely complex, and though analogous, were quite unlike any a human CNS had experienced before. And especially troublesome, the procedure was not reversible. The human core of the cyborg could not be put back in its original body.

To function effectively for an extended period, the CNS requires an integrated set of inputs from its new body. Inputs producing a broad spectrum of information and responses that include, among other things, esthetics, orientation, discomfort, even a modified sense of pain. In fact, pretty much the same spectrum provided by human bodies. Padilla and his collaborators had spent a great deal of time and care in designing, testing, and fine-tuning the servo's quasi-organic nervous system, along with the manifold neural connections of the bioelectronic interface.

But the tests had used devices, not the human brain. There was no way Padilla could know, really know, how Carlos O'Brien would find life as a cyborg.

That had been 157 years before the capture of Tagus Cove. Carlos O'Brien had wakened to life as a cyborg and found it mainly interesting, not traumatic. Certainly it was far better than his brief experience without arms or vision. Also it gave him a job—helping test the prototype. And the series of prototypes that followed, for if O'Brien could never wear a human body again, the bottle that held his CNS could be removed and installed in other servos. The more sensitive procedure had been installing the CNS into the bioelectronic interface unit, attaching pseudo-organic neuroconnectors to biological nerves.

Then someone blew the whistle. The Respect Movement was outraged, and bottling was made illegal. And of course, careers were ruined, among them Eric Padilla's.

Eventually the Wyzhñyñy arrived in the fringe of Commonwealth space, Henry Morgan's savanted message reached Kunming, and the news galvanized the Commonwealth. (Changing it forever, though just then no one gave "forever" much attention.) At that time, five manned servos existed, all secret. Five actual manned servos, but many virtual, generated in the computers that drove the Commonwealth military's virtual reality trainers.

Five manned servos, none of them military. That would quickly change. The Office of Industrial Mobilization would see to it.

Chapter 6
Maritimus

David MacDonald sat at the sun-deck table, wearing shorts and Sunsafe, and reading a task report from *Submersible 4*. From their office, his wife's voice interrupted, loud and agitated. "David!"

Afterward it seemed to him he should have known, given the reports from Morgan the Pirate and Gem of the Prophet. But his immediate thought was that she'd cut herself, badly. In an instant he was on his feet and through the door. "What is it?"

"It's happened." Her agitation was gone now, leaving anger and chagrin. She pointed at the wall screen. "The hyperspace emergence detector just kicked in. There are 16,212 blips on the screen."

He turned and stared. A vast display of icons—mostly of large ships—was spread across a perspective representation of the Maritimus System.* A footer gave the

---

* Normally, in the Commonwealth, when a system is settled, it is named for its first colonized planet. The exceptions are systems with well-known names of long standing.

number. Briefly he stared. "Good God," he muttered, then
shook his head. "At least we're prepared for them." Most
personnel, and all children but one, had been evacuated to
Terra. Those who'd stayed had a very simple plan: If invaders
arrive, get the hell out of F-space.

He turned to his wife. Yukiko Alegría Gavaldon—all five
feet three inches and 115 muscular pounds of her—stood
with hands on hips, face grim. They had eight years of work
and dreams invested in Maritimus. His fingers tapped
instructions on a key pad, and a klaxon began to blare over
the master comm system, both on Home Base and at work
locations—a sound that could waken the dead. He gave it
ten seconds before switching it off and speaking into the
microphone: "All personnel, this is Mac. All personnel, this
is Mac. This is *not* a drill; repeat, *not* a drill. We've got
sixteen thousand bogies in the fringe. That's sixteen thousand bogies. Carry out Plan 1-A promptly. Carry out Plan
1-A promptly." He gave them another five-second shot of
the klaxon, then repeated his announcement, followed by
a roll call.

The fourteen humans who'd remained on Maritimus had
told themselves the invaders might miss the system. But
they'd retained the hyperspace vessel *Cousteau,* moving it
to a cave that opened onto the sea, forty-one miles up the
coast from Home Base. They'd also restricted their studies to a travel radius of two hours from Cave Bay, and kept
their radios on at all times. Thus almost everyone responded
as he read off their names. The two who didn't were
accounted for. There were no questions.

His last order was to Dennis Bertrand: to message Terra
of the invaders' arrival. The project's communication savant
and her attendant lived aboard the *Cousteau.*

With roll call completed, Yukiko went to the spacious
bedroom she shared with her husband. They kept partly
packed bags in the closet; filling them would take only a
few minutes. David stepped back onto the sun deck to grab
his reader from the table, then went to help her.

First they finished packing. Then, Yukiko ran a computer
check on the status of the computer-destruct systems at the
various locations. The Emergency War Directorate on Terra
didn't want the invaders laying hands on a Commonwealth

database. Not that it was likely, if the invaders' penchant for indiscriminate destruction was as bad as reported. The checkout was a stepwise procedure, requiring that she confirm each step. She considered the human confirmation needless, but did it as prescribed.

When she'd finished, David rechecked all manned locations. Everyone was to meet at Cave Base, aboard the *Cousteau*. The Talacogons had already left North Bay, and the Mellstads had left Cleaver Station. Ngozi and Hogan were about to leave Atoll Station. At Home Base, Marcel Kwong was loading his scooter just two hundred yards up the inlet from the MacDonalds. His wife Jeanne had just arrived in a jet boat, from an aborted run to service plankton traps. They'd leave within ten minutes.

With that information in hand, David activated the remote timer program for the destruction of all but the base at Cave Bay. If they lucked out and the invaders bypassed them, he could cancel it. *Fat chance*, he told himself. Aloud he said, "That is the hardest thing I've ever had to do."

Yukiko nodded. "Let's hope they leave without moving insystem. Given the descriptions from Gem, they're not remotely an aquatic life-form. And if it's living space they're looking for, they won't find much here."

An exercise in false hope, she chided herself. Without a fly-by, the intruders wouldn't know that Maritimus was an ocean world without a single real continent. And if they came close enough for a flyby . . . Even parked a few billion miles out, they'd have picked up the base's electronics signature as soon as they emerged from hyperspace. They'd know there was technology here. And judging from Tagus and Gem, they'd come in with death and destruction on their minds.

"I'm going down and let the dolphs know," she said. "We can't leave without telling them."

"Go ahead," David answered, then turned and left the room. The house was cantilevered over the inlet, some fifty feet above the Tufftile dock where *Submersible 1* lay secured. The rear of the house, however, opened on the cliff top, where a three-walled shelter of deep-jade Tuffglass housed their travel scooter. He took their bags to it in two trips, loading them in the already half-filled luggage compartment.

On the first luggage trip, he saw the Kwongs' scooter start off across the inlet. Now everyone except himself and Yukiko were at or on their way to Cave Bay. After the second load, he returned to the deck and looked down through a Tuffglass panel at *Submersible 1*. Its hatch was open: Yukiko was still talking to the dolphs via the speaker. While waiting, he found himself fidgeting, and wondered why. It would take hours for invader ships to arrive by warpdrive. Finally Yukiko emerged, shut the hatch behind her, and started for the stairs. David went back to the scooter and activated the AG.

Two minutes later, she came out carrying a padded beverage basket. "Brandy," she said, holding it up. "In case we have something to celebrate, or for nightcaps if we don't." She put it in the luggage carrier, then climbed into the cab. Their weight, when they sat down, activated the restraint fields in their seats. David's fingers tapped a brief instruction, then at his practiced touch on the joystick, the scooter rose slightly, moving out of the shelter.

When they were clear, he accelerated, the scooter curving smoothly out over the inlet. Yukiko looked down past her feet at dark water. *So much to learn here,* she told herself, *and so much potential.* She wondered if they'd ever come back. It seemed to her she should have been incarnated a dolphin. Maybe next life.

So far they'd found no evidence that Maritimus had any sapient native life-form: terrestrial, aquatic, or avian. But they'd released thirty dolphins to assist in a survey of native marine life, and Yukiko was—or had been—in charge. Now she felt as if she were running out on them. But the dolphs were smart and resourceful, and they knew the situation.

The scooter had crossed the inlet, and they were low over Dolerite Point, when Yukiko became aware of the cold. She frowned. "David . . ." she began.

"I feel it," he answered, and tapped brief instructions to the scooter, his eyes on the resulting heads-up display. "It's the AG cooling system," he said. It was almost the only thing that went wrong with scooters.

"Can we make it to Cave Bay?"

"We'd better." He veered the scooter out over the ocean's edge. If the drive shut down, they wouldn't be able to stay aloft for long; they'd coast down on whatever azimuth they'd been flying, modified by the wind. With considerable momentum and no control at all. And if they were over the rugged coast when they hit, they'd likely be killed.

Yukiko switched her microphone on. "This is Yukiko," she said. "Dennis, we're on our way, but we're having AG trouble. We're on our way, but having AG trouble. Do you read me? Over."

Dennis Bertrand was their licensed hyperspace navigator, stationed at Cave Bay. His wife, Ju-Li, was the attendant of the project's savant, who was also her baby sister. "This is Bertrand," he said. "I read you, Yukiko, loud and clear. Marcel is about a dozen miles south of here. I'll have him turn back and follow you in, just in case. Over."

"Thank you, Dennis. Yukiko out."

David set a course that would keep them near the shore without taking them over land till they crossed Cedar Point. After Cedar Point they'd have a straight shot over water to the *Cousteau* in its cave. *If we get that far,* he thought. The cab was getting *really* chilly.

He'd barely thought it before the drive choked, nearly died, cutting back in just long enough that he initiated a turn shoreward. Then it cut out entirely, leaving the turn incomplete. Bracing himself, David opened the door on his side. He wanted to keep it open just a little, like an off-center drag chute, to complete his shoreward turn by air resistance. Which was stronger than he'd anticipated. He hadn't tightened his restraint field, and the door jerked him half out of the scooter. For a moment his joints turned to water. His mind knew that the restraint field, even lax as he'd left it, would keep him from being pulled out, but his body didn't believe it. Then the handle ripped free of his clutch, and the door banged back against the scooter's side. But not before nudging the craft almost directly toward the rocky shore. Heart still hammering, he tightened his restraint field.

They were losing elevation more rapidly now. Marcel

wouldn't get to them till well after they were in the drink, and with the decay of the scooter's residual AG, they wouldn't stay afloat long. Punching the fat mayday switch in front of him, David let anyone within range know they were about to crash. Some distance ahead, surf raised on a rocky shelf, to slam against massive basalt blocks fallen from the cliffs behind it. Ahead to their right, a low rocky islet stood just above the sea.

"Yukiko," David said, "open your door. And hang onto it as hard as you can!"

She realized what he had in mind, and didn't hesitate. She cracked the door, and instantly the air jerked it wide. Her seat restraint field held her securely if resiliently. The door jerked her shoulder muscles painfully before tearing from her grasp. Now they were headed almost toward the islet, though well short of it. "David," she said, "the seat cushions . . ."

She didn't finish; he already knew. Holding their breath, they stared at the onrushing water. David shut his eyes, felt the scooter hit, skip, hit again, skip again, and again, each skip shorter than the one before. One final time it struck, nosing into a swell, jarring hard, then stopped. Their restraint fields had eased the shock while pressing the breath out of them.

David's eyes had popped open, and he pushed his restraint release, then looked at Yukiko. She was already free of hers. Water was spilling in over their feet. A touch on the control panel slid the cab's tinted hood back. A swell lifted them. David rose from his seat, snatched up its cushion and thrust his arms into the straps. "Go!" he shouted, and jumped.

In the water, another swell raised them. Beside him and slightly ahead, the scooter lifted again, less buoyant now. His eyes found Yukiko perhaps fifteen feet away and slightly to his rear as the swell left them behind. When the next swell lifted them, they saw waves breaking on the point of the small islet, ahead and a little to their right. The scooter would be carried past it, toward the surf crashing on the rocks some three hundred yards ahead.

"Swim for the island!" he shouted. "Don't let yourself be

carried past it." Then he began kicking his feet, swimming toward it himself. *Marcel will find us,* he thought. *And if he doesn't, the surf may be less dangerous when the tide recedes.* Not that the tides amounted to much.

Marcel Kwong had received the mayday signal, but gotten only an azimuth, not a location. Not knowing of Yukiko's delay to message the dolphins, he assumed the two were somewhere north of Cedar Point. When he reached the point without spotting them, he turned back, flying higher to see more area.

After flying halfway back to where he'd received the mayday, Marcel consulted briefly again with Bertrand, then turned south once more, seriously anxious. The sun was low, cut off by the cliffs now. This time he crossed Cedar Point instead of stopping. Seventeen miles from Home Base, his wife spotted the twisted, surf-battered scooter on the rocks, each successive breaker compounding the destruction. Angling lower, they approached it at an altitude of twenty feet. Not surprisingly its cab was empty, its hood torn half off. He made two sweeps above the shelf, watching for bodies, and found none. That didn't surprise them either. There'd be an undertow here, and a south-flowing current offshore.

He switched on his microphone. "Dennis," he called, "this is Marcel. Dennis, this is Marcel. We've found the wreckage of a scooter on the shelf rock nine miles south of Cedar Point. But no bodies or survivors. We need help in finding either bodies or survivors. Over."

"Marcel, this is Bertrand. Elisio and Nona just arrived from North Bay, and Ngozi is on her way from the atoll. How badly was the scooter damaged? Over."

"It was utterly demolished, and I can't picture a human surviving the breakers here. There's shelf rock and lots of boulders. Over."

"All right, follow the offshore current south. They could be riding it on their seat cushions, watching for a gap. My chart shows a good-sized stream coming down off the plateau about four miles south of the wreck. There'll be a break in the boulder line there, and the outflow current should make the surf less dangerous. Over."

"Got it. We'll follow the offshore current south. Marcel out." He angled southward at about fifty feet above the waves.

He glanced at the time display: 1714 base time. It seemed to him they needed to find David and Yukiko today. Tomorrow would be too late.

Chapter 7

Reconnaissance

For a pirate, Henry Morgan was amiable. Almost always.

Seven years before the Wyzhñyñy arrived, his Squadron One had captured the hyperspace yacht *Guinevere*, whose owner/master was identified in the yacht's records as Gomer Colwyn—though Morgan at first didn't know that. Trapped in F-space and under the pirate's beamgun, Colwyn had asked for quarter, and Morgan, as always, granted the plea. In the case of merchantmen, his practice was to disarm the ship, then loot it before giving it back. But the *Guinevere* was well suited for use as a corsair. So when she hove to, Morgan decided to load her personnel and passengers aboard a lifeboat and send them off, then put a prize crew aboard the yacht to fly it to Tagus.

The yacht's master had other ideas. After accepting the pirate's clemency, Gomer Colwyn had drawn a blaster from inside his blouse. With shocking quickness and force, Morgan disarmed and disabled the man. Colwyn cursed him then—surely those were curses—in a language unfamiliar to the crew.

Morgan's face turned stony hard, and he replied in what sounded like the same language. Then he ordered all the

45

captives manacled, and told Colwyn to flip a coin for each of the twenty others the *Guinevere* had carried. Heads they lived, tails they died. Either that or choose ten to live. Colwyn wilted—he couldn't do either—so Morgan decided for him. One by one, ten of the yacht's eleven-male crew—stoic or struggling, pleading or praying or silent—were jettisoned out the trash lock. To float as corpsicles in the empty vastness between Not Worth Much and New Pecos. The yacht's second officer he spared.

Morgan's boarding party was stunned. A few were near mutiny.

The eight passengers remained. A broken Colwyn pleaded for their lives; one was his wife and another his daughter. After listening, Morgan had all eight loaded into the forty-foot lifeboat with the second officer, and let them go. When they were gone, he told Colwyn he'd had the lifeboat's strange-space generator disabled. It would take them decades to reach a habitable world. Except of course they couldn't; not alive. In a few months they'd run out of food.

At that, Colwyn went psychotic. Morgan had him strapped screaming into a workboat, personally disabled its drive, then set it adrift.

When it was gone, Morgan sagged. With the boarding party, he returned to his modest flagship, leaving only the six-man prize crew. Then he generated hyperspace, set course for Tagus, and retired to his suite.

What, if anything, he told Connie Phamonyong, none of his men knew. But after comparing notes, there was one thing they did know: their commodore had *not* had the lifeboat's strange-space generator disabled. Only the workboat had been sabotaged. The yacht owner's family and guests, and the second officer, were safely on their way to whatever world they'd chosen. In that, Morgan had been merciful. Not that it made up for murdering eleven people, only one of whom had done anything to earn it.

In his suite, Morgan told Connie nothing, simply opened a bottle of brandy, and drank from it. He *had* known Colwyn, but hadn't recognized him till Colwyn cursed him in Welsh. Then Morgan had identified himself. Morgan had been eleven the last time they'd seen each other, and Colwyn had been in his twenties—his father's first cousin, his own second cousin. Colwyn had always treated him badly, pouring sarcasm over him, sometimes slapping him around. Though never abusing him sexually. That right his father reserved for himself. As a young man, Morgan had suspected his father had sodomized Colwyn when *he* was a child, and that Colwyn took it out on him.

If he hadn't told Colwyn who he was, this wouldn't have happened. Not that he regretted deep-sixing him. What troubled him was having killed the ten crew members. Telling himself he'd been insane at the time hadn't helped.

An hour later, Morgan had moved into a vacant crew cabin. When he finally emerged again, three days later, he smelled of brandy. But although he may have been drunk much of the time, he lacked severe tremor, and showed no sign of hallucinating. So, two days drunk and one getting well, the crew concluded.

Meanwhile, even those who'd been most disturbed by their captain's actions aboard the *Guinevere* had recovered from their shock. Largely because of their commodore's reaction to his own deeds. It was agreed he must have known the yacht's skipper earlier in life.

After emerging from his isolation, Morgan began showing up for meals, saying something now and then, and sweating regularly in the workout room. His second continued to run the ship. He also moved back in with Connie and Robert. Long before they reached Tagus, Henry Morgan seemed normal once more, and the crew was at ease with him again.

All of that, though, had been seven years earlier, and seldom did anyone, including Morgan, think of it anymore.

The first night after the Wyzhñyñy arrived, Henry Morgan wakened from an ugly dream, its events remaining sharply in his mind. In the dream he'd been a little boy. His father had been flogging Morgan's mother with a large penis, like a horse's, while she'd cried bitterly. Then he'd turned to Morgan, raised the penis, and began to beat him too.

It was then Morgan had wakened, and discovered his face and pillow wet with tears. It had been a very long time since he'd revisited those days. The stories he told Robert were fictions. He wasn't entirely sure what Robert might have experienced or remembered. He himself had run away—escaped—at age fourteen.

Apparently he'd been crying aloud, or perhaps thrashing around, because Connie was awake, her eyes wide, and white by the nightlight. Without saying anything, he'd patted her shoulder reassuringly, then got up and went into the small kitchen, to drink himself into a stupor. Something he hadn't done since just after the *Guinivere*.

When next he awoke, it was in bed. Obviously he'd gotten there himself; Connie was too small to have managed it. His stomach was queasy, and there was a hard, heavy pain behind his forehead. Groaning, he found the bottle lying unstoppered on its side. It still held a shot or so, trapped by the bottle's shoulder, and he swallowed what was left. Then he asked Connie to make coffee. While he waited, he marched in place, raising his knees high and swinging his arms. When the coffee was ready, he had bread and jam with it, then read to Robert from the savant's favorite storycube.

Afterward he planned, as far as it made sense to. He would, he decided, remain holed up for four weeks. "The invaders will either leave or stay," he told Connie. "If they're going to leave, they should be gone by then. And if they stay, they'll have had time to decide there aren't any of us left."

Electric torch in one hand and a C-sized power slug in a pocket, he'd ventured up the tunnel and stairs that led to his bolt hole. He wasn't surprised that the first two hundred yards were intact. It was the last dozen he'd worried about, where the protective rock overhead thinned as he approached the tunnel's opening. The part that worried him most was the steel door. It had been installed to slide open and shut, and the bombardment might have deformed the rock, holding the door immovable. He installed the power slug in the door mechanism, and holding his breath, pressed the switch.

The door slid back smoothly, and the weight of the world lifted from Morgan's shoulders. Beyond the door were three more yards of tunnel, cut to resemble a natural break in the rock. It opened inconspicuously near the bottom of a draw, 0.7 mile from the gorge the invaders had pounded so severely. Cautiously he crept far enough to peer out. The bombardment had reached here, too; the forest was a shambles of broken trees.

Silently, thoughtfully, he withdrew back down the tunnel, and closed the steel door behind him. It seemed to him things were better than he deserved.

Henry Morgan tended to be a patient man, and he stuck to his decision to stay holed up for four weeks. Meanwhile he spent more time than usual with Robert, telling him stories that grew more outlandish with time, making the savant whoop with laughter. Some of them even made Connie laugh. She had a pleasant sense of humor, but wasn't much given to laughing out loud. They were remarkably happy for three people hiding in a tunnel thirty yards underground. Morgan wasn't sure if they were the happiest four weeks of his life, or whether he simply had more time to appreciate them. It occurred to him the two might go together.

He also inventoried their supplies. For some of them, the need had been foreseen. Others had been stashed "just in case." He worked up two ration schedules—one for twenty months and one for thirty—and a chart on which Connie could keep a record of use. It wasn't something he considered vital; if they were somehow rescued, it would likely be sooner than twenty months. And if they weren't, then sooner or later they'd have to surface anyway, and forage for their keep. So he'd chosen the twenty-month version; they could back off on it later if it seemed best.

There was also a box of aerial stereopairs he'd had taken of that entire end of the continent. From them, the base computer, now undoubtedly destroyed, had produced a set of large-scale topographic maps with the forest shaded green. There was little which wasn't forest: the "resort," and an occasional marsh or rocky prominence. The photography and maps had seemed like a good idea at the time. Now he was truly glad to have them.

Meanwhile he undertook to overhaul his body, for he was overweight and out of shape. He began to eat less, while following a modest kung fu regimen. He'd learned it as a youth and small-time criminal, at Kip Poi's Hall in Vancouver. Not that he imagined kung fu would prove effective against invader soldiers, but it improved his endurance and flexibility. He also did strength exercises that some spacers used in relatively confined quarters. Emphasizing his legs, because when he resurfaced, they'd be his only means of travel.

When finally he emerged beneath the sky, he carried a pack, binoculars, and a short-barrelled blaster with a fully-charged power slug and spares. *Now,* he told himself, *we'll see how effective that exercising was.* He marked the tunnel opening with a sort of mini-cairn, thirty yards away in the bottom of the draw: a thirty-pound chunk of stone atop a larger. It was something a snooping invader was unlikely to recognize as meaningful. Then he reshouldered his pack and headed on a compass course for the ex "resort."

For a hundred yards he picked his way through forest debris from the invader attack, the damage thinning as he went. Then he was out of it, in peaceful forest, where he settled for an easy pace and a short day. Exercising underground didn't prepare the feet for hiking in boots not well broken in, and blistered feet didn't fit his plans.

One of his maps showed a rocky knob less than three miles from the site of the old resort. On its top, the trees were sufficiently sparse and small that the computer had mapped it as bald. He climbed it late on the second day, and standing beneath a stubby, umbrellalike tree, trained his binoculars on the distant clearing where the resort had been.

A month earlier, he might not have seen the clearing from where he stood; certainly not much of it. It had been only twenty acres, and all but a very small part would have been screened by bordering forest. Now he guessed its area at perhaps a square mile. From its borders rose the haze of burnt-down fires, no doubt of woody debris from land clearing. Through the haze he made out buildings and activity. Tiny figures moved about on machinery and afoot, figures minute with distance, but clearly not human.

Morgan took a deep breath of relief. This part of the continent had always struck him as fertile enough, and the ancient volcanic surface was mostly not rugged. But the planet had what seemed to him more promising land for colonizing, much of it on other continents. He'd feared that when they'd destroyed what they could find of human settlement—this one tiny area—they might leave, and settle halfway across the planet. And that wouldn't have served his purpose.

His lightweight binoculars weren't powerful enough to show him much detail. As he watched what he could see, he plotted his next move. He would, he decided, approach the fringe of the opening that day, and lay up overnight. At dawn he'd move closer, and see what he could learn, then return to base and see if he could get inside through one of the hangar openings. Hopefully he could work his way to his yacht. There was something he very much wanted to get from it.

Chapter 8

A Scarce Resource

The voice on the phone was the prime minister's. "Mr. President," he said, "I have granted Dr. Farrukhi an audience, and you may want to be present. It is about the savant situation, of course."

"When?"

"At 11:30—in forty minutes. The hour will help him be brief. He called only moments ago." Peixoto chuckled. "He wanted to bring Ho and Sriharan. I told him to come by himself."

Chang glanced at the screen. On it was page 17 of a hypertext document on Masadan military training, and its applicability to the Commonwealth's new army. He was skeptical; the Masadan culture was far more homogeneous than the Terran. Unlike any other human world, Masada had maintained and cherished a tradition of compulsory military training. Through centuries without enemies. From a 30th century viewpoint, it was one of the more unlikely marvels of human social behavior.

"Eleven-thirty? I will be there," said the president, and

disconnected. Unlike himself, the prime minister preferred electronic conferencing. "People need not leave their desks," he'd explained. "And we are more concise. There is less protocol and small talk." Occasionally he asked someone to his office, especially if they were officed on the same wing and floor. But for those like Farrukhi, officed elsewhere, such requests were rare.

The president tapped an alarm instruction on his timer, giving himself thirty-five minutes, then returned his attention to the Masadan document, and continued reading as if he'd never been interrupted.

He arrived on the dot, to find Farrukhi there ahead of him, not yet seated. The psychologist was a thin man with an apologetic expression, and a fringe of black hair framing an expanse of bald brown head. If allowed to, his blue jaw would grow far more hair than his cranium. In other company he would have seemed tall, but in the same room with Foster Peixoto . . .

Farrukhi worked in the Office of Technical Recruitment. The previous afternoon, he'd sent Peixoto a brief description of a problem. Without suggesting possible action; a lack the prime minister despised. But the description seemed to say it all: War House had issued a confidential document outlining the intended conduct of the war. A description that, if carried out, required more than twelve hundred savant communicators. However, Farrukhi pointed out, only four hundred and forty seven suitable savants were known to exist. Nearly three hundred of them were at Commonwealth embassies on colony worlds, their only effective means of communication with Kunming.

The prime minister waved his two guests to chairs. "So," he said to Farrukhi, "what do you suggest?"

The man squirmed. Literally. "I hesitated to enter this into the system, but there are many verified savants in institutions, in very delicate health. Some have critically defective hearts or immune systems, some physiological processes that fluctuate beyond sustainable limits. Most die in childhood. If they could be transferred . . . their central nervous systems that is . . . " His dark face grew even darker with blood. "Transferred into mobile, life-support modules ... "

Say it, man, Chang thought. *The word is "bottled"!* But the idea was excellent. It was a solution.

"Unfortunately ... " Shrugging, Farrukhi spread his hands.

"I know," Peixoto finished. "Bottling is illegal. But with our new war powers, that will be changed by supper." To be followed by outrage, he added silently.

The psychologist nodded. "I am also aware of another at least potential source. Worldwide there are many ... 'defective' children not identified as savants. And most in fact are not, but surely some are. If we could screen them ... But ... "

"But unfortunately," Peixoto finished for him, "it will further outrage our watchdogs."

Again Farrukhi's head bobbed. "And equally important is the matter of finding suitable sensitives to serve as attendants, to manage their communication function."

"Surely there are more psychically sensitive persons than there are savants."

"I'm sure there are. But again, the problem is to identify them. Many will seem quite ordinary, and prefer to keep their sensitivity private."

The president spoke now. "How have they been identified in the past?"

"In the past, sensitives were hired who were already known to institutions researching the field."

"Ah!" said Chang. "But surely some of the anonymous sensitives associate with others. Identify such groups and their meeting places. Post notices on the Ether: 'good money and secure, satisfying jobs for qualified sensitives.' Make the wages suitably attractive, perhaps equivalent to a PS-12. Consult with the attendants of savants already in government service. Ask their advice."

Farrukhi's face brightened. He shifted to the edge of his seat, as if to dash out and get started.

"Doctor," the prime minister said, "the president and I thank you for your astute help. I want you to sketch out quickly—before you break for supper—a rough plan to carry all this out. Now, don't let me keep you from getting started."

Abdol Farrukhi's long legs raised him from his chair. "Thank you, Mr. Prime Minister," he said, then looked at Chang Lung-Chi. "Thank you, Mr. President."

When he had gone, Peixoto turned to Chang. "It distresses me," he said glumly, "to outrage the honest if mistaken scruples of so many people. It could lead to demonstrations."

Chang grunted; his own distress threshold was higher than the prime minister's. To him there were reasonable people, and there were problem people, the latter including the chronically indignant. "We do what we must," he said, "and when we've won the war, or lost it, any demonstrations will be forgotten."

"Nonetheless . . ." said his friend, and shrugged. "Why don't we have lunch together? On your balcony over the rotunda. We can talk about other things than problems."

The president agreed, and they did their best to talk about grandchildren, the food, and the weather. It wasn't much of a conversation, but they'd get plenty of practice before the war was over.

Chapter 9
Drago Draveç

The flood of early human migration to outsystem worlds was almost entirely atavistic—agrarian, ethnic, sectarian, or some combination of them. By the 26th century, however, humankind in the Sol System had evolved enough, socially, politically and spiritually, that sectarianism had greatly shrunken. Ethnic and racial mixing was widespread and accepted, chauvinism had lost its edge, and tolerance had far outgrown intolerance. As a result, colonization almost stopped; only nine new projects left Terra in the 26th century.

Colonization picked up strongly, though, in the 27th, with new projects directed largely at the Ultima Fornax Sector, to facilitate eventual intercolonial commerce—a factor ignored during the centuries when colonists sought isolation. Most of the new colonists wanted to expand financially, and felt inhibited by Terran legal and cultural restrictions, or by established competitors, or both. Or simply wanted to start over on a virgin planet, this time to "do it right." In any case they had the goal of creating interacting, high-tech societies, using Terran technology and experience.

As a result, by the 29th century, interplanetary commerce had become significant in the remote Ultima Fornax Sector.

Syllabus of Human History
Collegiate Books, Lyon, France

Sky Harbor was the political and commercial capital of Hart's Desire, and Drago Draveç, Henry Morgan's surrogate, knew it well. And while he had nothing to fence this trip, Morgan had done business there with Harlan Cheregian for more than a decade. And Cheregian, who knew everything and everybody worth knowing on Hart's Desire, also had the ear of government there.

The monsoon had arrived, hot and humid, and Drago Draveç set the *Minerva* down at the port of Sky Harbor in an afternoon deluge. (The squadron's other three ships had put down at Nuevo Oaxaca, far from Hart's central government. Summers at Nuevo Oaxaca were relatively cool and dry, the entertainment district less restricted, and the port authority more flexible. And Harlan Cheregian had a branch office there.)

A cabby had seen the *Minerva* land, and moved hopefully to her pad. Draveç sprinted the few unprotected yards to it, jumped in and slammed the door behind him, somewhat less than soaked.

"Where to?" asked the cabby.

"The roof of the Cheregian Building."

"They expecting you?"

"I wouldn't go if he wasn't."

He. The cabby nodded. The spacer was indifferently dressed, but he'd arrived in what appeared to be a very expensive yacht, and gave the impression of someone in charge. Cheregian probably did expect him. The cabby lifted his floater against the downpour, riding lights flashing a penetrating blue, then swung toward the commercial district, headed for the Cheregian Building. "You from offworld?"

"Yep."

"Did you hear about the alien invasion?"

"Yep."

The spacer's answers didn't inspire follow-ups. Minutes later the floater hovered inches above the Cheregian Building's passenger pad, as close to the canopy as the cabby could get it. A flunky in a suit waited with an umbrella. The cabby turned to Drago, expecting plastic, and wondering what sort of tipper the guy was. Instead of plastic, the spacer handed him a Commonwealth 50-credit note, and got out saying, "Keep the change." He'd hoped for more, but it wasn't too bad.

Drago had been to the Cheregian Building before, and remembered his umbrella-carrying guide, who asked his name but didn't request identification. They rode a drop tube down a single level to the seventh floor, then followed a clean-carpeted corridor to a suite. The suite and its furnishings were like the building, the corridor, the carpet—not imposing, but they indicated money and conservatism. A receptionist buzzed Cheregian and announced, "Mr. Draveç." Drago did not doubt that Cheregian was watching on a screen.

The receptionist looked up at Drago's guide. "Take Mr. Draveç in," she said.

The first thing Cheregian said was, "I presume you know about the aliens." Everyone on Hart's knew. The Gem of the Prophet had been captured, and apparently the Star of Hibernia. Darwin's World was also in the invasion corridor, not so far from Star. So the Commonwealth embassy there had evacuated to Hart's Desire, which seemed to be safely clear.

Drago nodded. "The aliens don't fool around. They started pounding Tagus the same day they arrived in the system."

"I suppose you have nothing to sell this time," Cheregian said.

"Right. What I'm looking for now is a favor."

Cheregian's rambunctious eyebrows rose. "I suppose you know that Commodore Morgan warned Kunming. A selfless act. What favor do you have in mind?"

Warned Kunming? This made things look more promising. "I want to use the Commonwealth embassy's savant, to propose something to Kunming. But if I simply knocked on their door, I'd probably end up in jail. So I hoped you'd refer me to them. Call me an ex-employee you haven't seen in years . . . "

"Hmm. And what is this proposal to Kunming?"

Draveç smiled wryly. "For three years I was a midshipman in the Space Academy. I want to scout the aliens. Sting them, see how they respond. Learn whether they have force shields, that sort of thing. Then duck into warpspace and let Kunming know by savant. Which means I'll need to take one with me."

"Aha. What do you suppose the odds are that the aliens will let you escape, after you've, ah, 'stung' them?"

"I've got four ships. I'll stand off, send them in and watch, then generate warpspace and report to Kunming. I've talked it out with my captains, at rendezvous." Drago paused. "The aliens moved in and started blasting without any communication whatever. As if they preferred killing to negotiation. So our prospects of survival—mine, the Commonwealth's, the human species'!—look rotten. And this just might help."

Cheregian nodded, thinking *sixteen thousand ships.* "I'll see what I can do," he said, then tapped keys and spoke to his phone. He was put on hold, but only for half a minute. Meanwhile he keyed the call to his desk speaker, so Draveç could hear both sides of the exchange.

A woman's voice spoke. "This is Ambassador Khai. What can I do for you, Mr. Cheregian?"

"I have a gentleman in my office, a Mr. Drago Draveç. He was referred to me by a business associate who feels I might have more influence with you than he would. Mr. Draveç would like to propose something to you regarding the alien intruders. And he seems to me worth listening to. He's one of Commodore Morgan's associates."

"Indeed! Well." There was a moment's silence. "The alien intruders." Another silence. "I'll send a car for him. It should arrive at your roof in—ten minutes. Considering what Commodore Morgan has done for humanity, we owe him that."

With eyebrows raised questioningly, Cheregian turned again to Drago, who nodded. "He'll be waiting," Cheregian said, then disconnected.

✧   ✧   ✧

Drago went to the embassy in the ambassador's chauffeured floater. The ambassador didn't ask many more questions than Harlan Cheregian had. She'd already alerted her savant's attendant. Now she talked her way to Admiralty Chief Fedor Tischendorf himself. With Tischendorf "on the line," she turned the session over to the pirate, prepared to assist if necessary.

Savant communicators duplicated not only the speakers' words, but their voice, tone, and emphasis, as nearly as their vocal equipment allowed. Which was nearer than a listener might think possible, given the typical savant's mental and physical difficulties. To Drago it was almost like listening to the admiral himself, who took him seriously, and definitely seemed interested. Tischendorf—famous for his recall—remembered Drago from twenty years past. The pirate had been a promising midshipman, till he'd been expelled for repeated unacceptable behavior while on pass. The Space Academy was fairly lenient about minor misbehavior on pass, but Draveç's had outgrown minor. His loyalty and command potential had never been questioned. His problem had been impulsive mischief or violence, usually inspired or aggravated by alcohol.

The admiral and the pirate rather quickly agreed on what Drago could reasonably hope to learn about the aliens, and how to approach the mission. Then Tischendorf spoke with Ambassador Khai again. "Madam Ambassador, I'd appreciate it if you'd arrange the transfer of Ambassador Rees's savant to—um—Commodore Draveç. And the savant's attendant, of course. Can you do that?"

Rees, Drago realized, had to be the Commonwealth's evacuee ambassador to Darwin's World.

"I'll propose it to Ambassador Rees."

"Do you expect him to balk?"

"I don't expect him to, no. He doesn't need a savant; he no longer has an embassy. And he's been an agreeable guest."

"Good. Let me know when it's arranged. And Drago, keep me informed of your progress."

Though she couldn't have said why, Ambassador Khai had felt a moment's misgiving when Tischendorf asked her to arrange the meeting with Rees. When she went to Rees's small embassy apartment and broached the matter, the man's face went—wooden was the best description. But he agreed to talk with Draveç.

Ten minutes later she brought Draveç to Rees's living room. "Mr. Ambassador," she said, "I'd like you to meet Commodore Drago Draveç. Commodore Draveç, this is Ambassador Llewellyn Gustavo Rees."

Now Rees's face was more stony than wooden. Drago realized something was seriously wrong, but extended his hand. "I'm pleased to meet you, Mr. Ambassador."

Rees's arms remained stiffly at his sides. "I had never," he said, "expected the pleasure of meeting one of Morgan's men under such—gratifying circumstances."

Drago frowned, his extended hand lowering. "It seems you don't like me," he said slowly. "Care to elaborate on that?"

"First let me say how pleased I am that your nest of hoodlums has been destroyed. And if you think I dislike you . . . I hate your master, Henry Morgan, with a passion you could never understand."

The pirate's gaze was mild, but it didn't soften Rees. "I got that," Drago said, hoping to get the meeting back on the subject. "And I suppose it's appropriate for you to hate him. And me. What do you think about the aliens?"

"I prefer them to you. They perform their atrocities against foreign life-forms. You perform yours against your own species."

Drago stood quietly, groping for a useful response, something that wouldn't torpedo his proposal. "Ah . . . Meanwhile the matter at hand is a reconnaissance of the alien armada. And I need your savant to make it work."

"You shall not have her, sir. First of all, you intend no reconnaissance. That is a cover, a sham. Your intention is to get hold of a savant for your own piratical purposes. And my savant is female—I'll wager you'd like that, wouldn't you?"

Drago's hands took them all by surprise. Quick as snakes they grabbed Llewellyn Rees by the shirt front and jerked him close, even as the seams split. The violence shattered the man, who began to babble. But to Drago the babbling made sense. "Do you remember the yacht *Guinevere*, Mister Pirate? Do you remember the officers and crew jettisoned out the trash lock? One of them was my younger brother! Murdered! Cold-bloodedly, without even being accused of anything! Our sister was Gomer Colwyn's niece, sent off in a lifeboat. It was she who told us what happened."

Rees was panting and trembling with repressed hysteria.

Drago stared and let him go. All he could say to the man was, "I'm sorry. I understand." To Ambassador Khai, he said "Let's go."

Two minutes later they were alone in her office. The emotional encounter had left her almost as shaken as Rees, but she'd remained oriented on Drago's mission. "You'll have your savant," she said. "I'll message Kunming, tell them I'm going to let you take Peng, and I'll take Lew's Lovisa to myself. I'm in charge here; I have the authority. And if they have misgivings, I'll refer them to Admiral Tischendorf."

She paused, looking at Drago, really seeing him for the first time. "Would you like a short drink before you return to your ship?"

"Yeah, I could stand a drink."

"I have several mild liqueurs . . . "

"Scotch and water if you have it."

She poured first for him, then for herself, and they sipped. "Lew really lost it this evening," she said.

"Ambassador Rees? Yes, he did."

"You handled it effectively."

Drago shrugged. "It's a good thing he didn't see the *Minerva*. My ship. She's the old *Guinevere*, renamed for the Roman goddess of martial prowess."

"Really!" She paused. "What is there to Llewellyn's story?"

He told her. He hadn't actually been there; as Morgan's principal captain, he'd been off with the other squadron, and heard the story after returning to Tagus. From the man who'd brought the *Guinevere* in as a prize.

"Morgan got back a month later," he went on. "The Morgan I knew, had known for years, was easy to get along with. The boss, but even-tempered. I'd seen him annoyed, but that was unusual. And I hadn't been able to reconcile the man I knew with the story I'd heard. So one evening over cognac I asked him about it."

Drago paused, pulling threads, retrieving memories. "And he told me. Things he'd never told anyone, he said, not even Connie. His father had been an abuser. Abused him sexually and generally. And the owner-master of the *Guinevere*—the ultimate in coincidence—was a cousin named Colwyn, maybe ten years older then Morgan." Drago fished for a moment and came up with the first name. "Gomer Colwyn. Morgan's dad had abused him, too, and Colwyn took it out on Morgan. They hadn't seen one another since Morgan ran away from home, barely in his teens. Made a living as a petty criminal, and worked up from there.

"Anyway Morgan recognized Colwyn, who tried to get the drop on him. The boss got the gun away from him, and things were said. In Welsh. Until Morgan totally lost control, and did what he did. Afterward, according to the crew, he locked himself in a cabin and stayed drunk for days."

Khai sighed gustily. "Gentle Buddha," she said, "the things people do to each other!" And wondered how Drago Draveç had wandered into piracy.

When they'd finished their drinks, her chauffeur took Drago back to the *Minerva*. She'd been tempted to invite him to spend the night. She was only forty-three, and her mirror told her she was still attractive. Drago Draveç was probably still short of forty, and the most vital man she'd seen since . . . ever, she decided. And she hadn't had a man in her bed since she'd left Terra. Her husband, the director of a major art museum, had refused to follow her off-world, and she'd never been seriously tempted to indulge herself in the opportunities on Hart's.

It's best not to this time, either, she'd told herself. *It would complicate things.*

She awoke to someone pounding on her bedroom door. A marine guard, a sergeant; she recognized the voice. "All right!" she called, "I'm awake! I'm awake!"

Muttering, she swung her legs out of bed; dawnlight filtered through one-way windows. Slipping into her robe, she went to the door and opened it. "What is it?" she demanded.

"Ma'am, it's Ambassador Rees! He's been found bound and gagged in a closet, with a lump on his head! When he woke up, he made enough noise, thumping around, to wake up his orderly."

Her eyes widened, then narrowed. *Draveç. It had to be Draveç.*

"And, ma'am, his savant is gone! And her attendant!"

Good grief! she thought. *And right under the noses of marine security.* The *Minerva* would be gone, too, from Sky Harbor and probably from F-space. The Ministry would cry bloody murder, and look for someone to blame. Her.

She looked at the situation. If War House backed her, it might not turn out too badly. In these times, War House would outweigh the Ministry. And Österdorf wasn't deputy minister for security anymore.

Security. She wondered if her marines had anything to do with this, then shook her head: surely not.

Chapter 10
Esau Wesley

The trees were tall for a heavyworld. Mostly their branches were strongly upsweeping, but remained subordinate to the strong central trunk.

This was old forest, the ground marked by fallen, "mossy" trunks of an older generation gradually converting to soil. Scattered patches of green shoots broke the sodden layer of last year's fallen leaves. Here and there were clusters of delicate pink—the first spring flowers.

Esau Wesley was adding his own dynamic to the ever-fluctuating system. He swung his ax again, and a chip flew from the steelwood tree. Then *chop!* and *chop!* and another flew. He continued, working his way around the tree without pause, cutting an unbroken ring through the hard bark and outermost layer of wood. Only then did he pause, removing his sweat-stained, lightweight leather hat and wiping his forehead on a homespun sleeve. It was early spring, and cool, but he was sweating. Steelwood was exceptionally dense and hard, even for New Jerusalem, but it favored the most fertile sites. And Esau was ambitious, and a bear for work.

He was also tall—five feet eight inches in his bare feet— and on Terra would have weighed a lean 227 pounds stripped. On the scale at the flour mill, however, he registered 322 pounds; gravity on New Jerusalem was 1.42 Terran-normal.

The years too were long. Esau was fourteen and a half by the calendar of New Jerusalem. On Terra he'd have been reckoned nearly nineteen. His frame was broad, his bones thick and dense, his heavy muscles powerful. And he was agile. Wrestling was a popular youth activity, and he was exceptionally good at it.

Thirty generations after the colonization of New Jerusalem, bodies more or less like Esau's were the rule. Bodies created by ruthless selection and strong gravity. And by the vigorous lives to which the colonists had been committed, in accordance with what the founders considered the Will of God.

The people of New Jerusalem were aware of space flight, and that their long-ago ancestors had come from distant Terra, where people lived ungodly lives, in technological sloth, and fought wars—the greatest evil of all—killing each other in droves. That was pretty much all the Jerusalemites knew about their ancestral world, and even that was incorrect. The last war on Terra had been fought before their forefathers left it.

The Commonwealth maintained a small embassy on New Jerusalem, though beyond the upper hierarchy, almost no Jerusalemites knew or cared anything at all about what went on there. Which wasn't much. Through the church hierarchy, the embassy purchased certain local products with silver and gold. The Jerries had no electronics, rejected paper money, and disapproved almost all proposed imports. All in all, the embassy had virtually no impact on the lives of New Jerusalem's citizens. Though it was about to. It had been put there mainly to confirm that New Jerusalem was part of the Commonwealth.

The Church of the Testaments taught its people to read scripture, write letters, and do basic cyphering. Nonbiblical history, even of their own world, was not taught, except as morality and precautionary tales. The only books were on paper—scripture, hymn books, prayer books, and Elder Hofer's *Commentaries on the Testaments*.

The Jerusalemites, of course, sinned like anyone else. They murdered, abused, lied, seduced, cuckolded—even occasionally blasphemed!—but rarely stole. Mostly, though, they were a law-abiding people who generally trusted the officials of their theocracy. Theirs was a peaceful, stagnant, patriarchal, and rather tolerant backwater. Occasionally someone went berserk—perhaps assaulted a family member or neighbor with ax or gun, or themselves with gun or rope. But there were no psychologists to point the finger at depression growing out of frustration. The preachers had their own explanation: the evildoer had been led astray by Satan. And whoever doubted, kept it to themselves.

The summer after his thirteenth birthday, by the New Jerusalem calendar, a youth took a farm. Unless, of course, he was in line to inherit one. With family help, he might buy one in his own neighborhood—complete with buildings and mortgage—if one was for sale. But more often he moved to the frontier, and claimed new, wild land at the edge of settlement. Land surveyed by the Church, which valued orderly ways. There, with the help of neighbors, he built a log house, a log barn, and sheds, and began life as an adult. He might bring a wife from his old community, or marry into the new, and over the years they'd produce a brood of their own, to repeat the cycle.

His first winter on his homestead, he'd hire himself out to an established neighbor, clearing land. And on his own holding, clear a garden patch, and "deaden" timber. The ax-girdled trees died a year later, and their roots and stumps didn't sprout. No one on New Jerusalem could explain why, physiologically, or felt any need to; it was simply a fact of life. Afterward, "grass" grew beneath the dead trees, providing pasture for livestock and attracting wild herbivores— wild meat. Certain food plants could even be grown in the much reduced shade. And by the time the deadened trees had been felled, cut up, dragged and burned, the roots were much decayed. The settler then had a field, hard won but ready to plow.

Thus the typical Jerusalemites were strong, tough, self-reliant. And subject to the authority of their physical environment and the hierarchy, both of which they accepted matter-of-factly. They were a matter-of-fact people.

Meanwhile they were unfamiliar with ethnic or religious diversity. Their immigrant ancestors had been fervent sectarians, "full of the spirit." On Terra, they'd been fearful and indignant toward a society abounding with subcultures, where political, social and religious varieties sometimes yammered, and occasionally squabbled. Despite which there was already widespread mixing, intermarrying, blending.

From the beginning, the goal of the founders had been emigration. It had taken courage, dedication, zeal, and pretty much all their earthly wealth to organize and incorporate a colonization company, lease emigrant ships, meet the requirements for the Commonwealth's approval to launch, and leave behind almost everything familiar except each other. Many families were divided, and some, when it came down to it, backed out.

Of those who'd followed through, the most common trait had been zeal.

Those born to New Jerusalem were different from their migrant ancestors, though they didn't know it. They'd been inculcated from infancy with, and only with, the dogmas, values and customs of those ancestors. As modified by the early experiences of life in a heavyworld wilderness. A world where the severe difficulties of heavyworld pregnancy, and gravity-induced, early deterioration of joints and organs, culled the early generations ruthlessly, shortening lives, and helping menfolk value their wives and daughters.

Whatever religious zeal they felt was seldom fervent. Like Esau Wesley and his wife Jael, they took their religion for granted. Its strictures seldom seemed onerous to them, and most were reasonably content with their lives.

Lives to be lived doing worthwhile things deemed pleasing to the Lord, finding satisfactions in farming, and in their offspring and each other. Given the effects of gravity on human physiology and anatomy, the Church had recently condoned the use, after five births, of a contraceptive herb known as lamb bane. This after three generations of earnest but confidential consideration and discussion at the highest hierarchical level.

The founders would have been horrified. But even given the generations of culling by New Jerusalem's gravity, deaths in childbirth left too many husbands alone on the farm with a brood of children to care for. And available widows were far fewer than widowers.

Esau Wesley rarely thought about such things. He was young, sure of himself, and found pleasure in work. After wiping sweat, he'd picked up his ax to assault another tree, when his hound Clancy began to bark. Esau knew from the tone that the dog sensed a human coming, not a predator. Someone the dog knew.

"Halloo!" the young man called. Then "Clancy! Shut up!" From a little distance came an answering halloo. A minute later, a man on horseback rode into sight among the trees: Speaker Martin Crosby from Sycamore Run,* one of Jael's uncles.

"What brings you, Speaker?" Esau asked. Crosby hadn't been there since the parish had raised Esau's house and barn the summer before, though he'd seen him at church often enough. The older man looked more serious than usual. Outside of church, he was inclined to joke and laugh a lot.

"Got news," he said. "Big news." From his face, it was bad.

"Such as?"

"Such as—a war."

"A war?" Esau was mystified rather than alarmed. War on New Jerusalem was impossible.

"Word just came from Terra."

"Terra? What's that got to do with us?"

The older farmer sighed gustily and shook his head. "Elder Fletcher is sending word to all the people." He paused, as if what followed was so unreal, he lacked the words. "Satan is coming through the worlds, with his demons. They've got the body of a donkey, with a sort of man stuck on where the neck ought to be, and a head like nothing you'd ever imagine."

---

* On New Jerusalem, "sycamore" was not an imported species of the Terran genus *Platanus*, nor the Eurasian *Acer pseudoplatanus*, but a native tree with pale smooth bark.

"You sure someone hasn't been japing you, Speaker Crosby?"

The man reached into a saddlebag, brought out a folder, and leaning down, handed Esau a piece of durable paper. A photocopy from the Commonwealth embassy, printed on both sides, with a picture. It had begun as a mental image, crossing the parsecs to Terra instantaneously, from a savant on a world called Maritimus. It was almost the last thing the water world's savant saw before blacking out, a strange phenomenon even for savants. From Terra the image had been forwarded to the embassy, and sketched by the savant there. Speaker Crosby knew none of that, of course. It was enough that Elder Fletcher accepted it.

"Keep it," Crosby said. "I've got more than enough. The demons know how to find people hiding, and got ways of killing them from the sky. That's what's said, anyway. There's sixteen thousand ships full of them, giant arks for flying between the stars. They've come to various worlds that's got folks living on them, worlds way far off, and killed everyone there, man, woman, and child. Butchered them, and wrecked everything."

Esau looked at the picture, then back at Crosby, still not convinced, but troubled. Speaker Crosby took out another folder, this time with sheets of writing in quill pen and ink, copied at the embassy by some Terran artifice.

"This one's written by Elder Fletcher, in his own hand, telling us what we might do. Not have to, but might. When you go up for supper, read them with Jael. See what you think. I got a bunch more of these to take around."

The older man turned his horse then—what passed for a horse on New Jerusalem—and trotted off. Esau stood where he was, and read what Elder Fletcher had written. When he was done, he felt a deep misgiving. Without ringing another tree, Esau Wesley picked up his ax and started home. It seemed to him his whole world was about to come down around his ears.

Chapter 11
The Task

João Gordeenko was not at his best. As deputy czar of resource allocation, he'd worked till 0320 that morning, then slept on his office couch till 0730. Which had left time for only a hasty shower and shave, a cup of strong coffee, and to get dressed before receiving his first visitor. Breakfast would wait, probably till lunch.

The visitor, a new staff assistant, was very pretty, very bright, and very sure of herself. And well recommended. He hoped that Sarah Asayama would prove as able as her recommender claimed, but he was skeptical. She spoke well, but she'd never had anything approaching the responsibility of her new position. There was a lot of that in the burgeoning war bureaucracy. It was unavoidable. There were too few people with the knowledge and experience needed. Some would learn successfully on the job, coping, innovating. Others would be replaced, sent elsewhere.

With Sarah Asayama's looks and personality, people tended to pull for her success, but as she talked, Gordeenko's misgivings grew like his work load. He wasn't surprised. This first assignment was in part a test of her readiness for it.

She sat six feet to his right, displaying her three-quarter profile as she spoke, while controlling the screen display with her pocket key pad. Under other circumstances he might have better appreciated her looks, but her words and the chart on his wall screen held his attention. "Unfortunately," she was saying, "the invaders' approach is taking them through a sector well populated with colonies, and on an approximate intersect with Terra."

Does she imagine I don't already know that? he wondered.

She switched charts. "Here is a list of the planets we need to evacuate, and their populations. The job will require a minimum of 2,900 ships, depending on the types selected." She turned, looking crisply professional. "I'm afraid it cuts rather heavily into the total."

Great Gautama! he thought. *An intelligence score of 123, and no concept whatever of the overall problem!*

Again she switched charts. "I've listed existing ships by types and classes, with their estimated capacity for stasis lockers. I realize this draft proposal requires review, and perhaps some modification, but given the colonial populations, we have little choice." Once more she turned to Gordeenko. "The less review time, the better. We need to refit the ships as quickly as possible, and get them under way."

Gordeenko nodded thoughtfully. It seemed to him he needed to make an impact on the young woman. *But be kind, João, be kind,* he reminded himself. "I agree," he told her. "The process must be expedited." He laid his hand on his desk key pad. "But first— First I need to clarify some things for you. I see now that you needed a much fuller briefing than you were given." His thick hairy fingers touched keys. The chart on the screen was displaced by another. "As you have implied, the number of merchant vessels in the Commonwealth is finite. As for warships— we have no fleet, as I'm sure you know. Only a limited array of prototypes. And of course a few score patrol ships, small, with utterly inadequate armament, designed only to discourage piracy. Just now, every shipyard in the Commonwealth has begun building *warships*, or is being overhauled in order to build *warships*."

The young woman interrupted, honestly confused, her

crispness gone. "But sir! I was talking about ships already built."

He raised a constraining hand. "I'll get to that, but first you must understand the problem. There are seventeen shipyards on Terra, eleven others scattered from Luna to Titan, and three each in the Epsilon Indi and Epsilon Eridani Systems. And that is all. In the entire Commonwealth! Not enough, Ms. Asayama! Not nearly enough!" Now Gordeenko began to apply the heat. "We are beginning or planning the construction of more than *a hundred* other shipyards, of which fifty must be operating inside of six months! Can you conceive of what that means? Everything must be done differently than ever before, if only because of the extreme shortage of shipwrights!"

"But sir . . . "

Gordeenko waved off her interjection. "And how will we provide the metals? Or transport the shipyard machinery?" His intensity caught and held her. "The demand on existing shipping will be extreme. Most of the new shipyards will be in space, in the belts of the various systems. And where will the workers live? In *ships*, Ms. Asayama! Hastily converted dormitory *ships*! The same is true for the thousands on thousands of new asteroid miners and smelter workers who will provide the metals!"

Sarah Asayama looked ready to collapse. She'd known that the Commonwealth was drastically unprepared for this war, but she'd never considered what dealing with it might involve. She'd given no attention to media discussions of such matters. On her brief internship her days had been long, spent on her own narrow duties. While away from the office, her attention had been on theater and young men. Thus Gordeenko's exposition had been overwhelming.

"That," he added quietly, "is a *very* brief summary. Very very brief. I'd assumed you'd ask questions, where you didn't know." It struck him then that she hadn't known she didn't know. "Like every other war activity," he went on, "we suffer a great lack of suitably prepared personnel. Thus we turn to persons like yourself: bright, energetic, patriotic . . . but with limited relevant experience, or none at all."

Reviewing the problems for her, he realized, had stirred his emotions—a mixture of repressed anxiety and dismay at the enormity of the task. Pausing, he inhaled deeply, and shifted gears. "We expect to evacuate not more than forty to fifty percent of the colonial populations in the invasion corridor. It may prove to be more, but we're starting with that estimate. Consider: most colonies grew from religious or ethnic groups or political dissidents who withdrew into space to live in their own narrow communities. And to a considerable degree, the original colonists have forwarded their beliefs through the generations. Thus we expect that many of their people will decide to stay at home. To take their chances where they are.

"Many colonies are so distant, the aliens will reach them before evacuation ships can. You've already allowed for that."

He exhaled heavily, and brushed back his thick pompadour. "Aim at fifteen hundred ships. Get with Al Vorselen, the director of transport; he knows what there are and where. Sort out the possibilities with him."

She stared. "But Mr. Gordeenko! We can't leave people out there! They'll be killed! We can't just abandon them!"

His gaze hardened, and his voice became crisp. "If you have a magic wand, Ms. Asayama, I grant you all the ships you can conjure out of nothing. Or better yet, conjure the aliens back to wherever they came from. Meanwhile, tell Vorselen that you and he must give me your final figures no later than tomorrow."

"*Tomorrow?*" she squeaked.

"By 1600 hours. And the figures must be realistic. Then I can start requisition proceedings. They'll go swiftly; I have the necessary authority." He made a shooing motion. "Go now."

As she reached for the door, he stopped her with a closing statement, his voice low and confidential. "And, Sarah, do not think of it as saving people. Because if the invader isn't stopped, we're all dead. The evacuees, you, me—all of us. Dead! So think of your ships as transports bringing military and labor recruits to Terra. But do NOT call them that, not to *anyone*. Not to your sister, your boyfriend—*anyone*. The evacuees are vital to us, my dear. Vital to the human species."

She paled and nodded, then hurried out. It seemed to

João Gordeenko that she really did understand. She might work out after all; he'd know tomorrow before supper.

He hadn't mentioned the problems of training qualified workers, qualified ship's crews, qualified fighting men. He hadn't wanted to shock her into coma. Looking at his own chart, still on the wall screen, Gordeenko felt overwhelm wash over him. Opening a desk drawer, he took out a small bottle of vodka flavored with *Vaccinium myrtillus*. For just a moment he hesitated, then removed the cap, took a swig, and felt the heat spread through his belly. With sudden resolve he stepped to his small sink and poured the rest down the drain. The solution to overwhelm was not alcohol. It was more sleep, and working smart. Starting today he would quit at midnight. Or . . . better make that one o'clock, then sleep till seven. And during the day take two twenty-minute naps. One at least.

He was fooling himself of course.

Chapter 12

Observations

On returning to his hidey-hole, Henry Morgan was welcomed tearfully by Connie Phamonyong. The tears took him by surprise. He'd recognized his scouting expedition was dangerous, but his imagination hadn't built on it. She'd managed not to infect Robert with her worries though; he greeted his older brother with casual cheer.

Almost the first thing Morgan did, with Connie and Robert, was message the prime minister and the defense office, newly named the Defense Ministry, or War House. Not that he had much to tell them, other than that the invaders had been clearing land. But he wanted them to know he was still alive, and intended further scouting.

This time he got more than brief acknowledgement; both the prime minister and War House thanked him for his efforts. They also told him about the Star of Hibernia and the Gem of the Prophet. But they didn't tell him about Drago Draveç reaching Hart's Desire; they'd wait till something had actually happened with that, besides a kidnapping.

Nor did they tell him to be careful. *Careful,* he thought wryly, *isn't what they need from me.*

The next morning he returned to the surface, this time headed for the gorge into which the hangar exits had opened. He set out with a blaster on his belt, and a lunch and heavy torch in his day pack. And a nervous stomach. Not because the invaders might have posted guards there; that seemed highly unlikely. His concern was that rockfall from the bombardment might keep him from getting inside.

Lack of rope was his first problem. Seen from the top, the gorge side appeared impossible to climb. Previously trees and shrubs had found rootholds on the precipitous slope, and where it had been bare, the rock had been solid. Now the trees and shrubs were mostly gone, and the surface rock extensively fractured. If he'd been an accomplished rock climber . . . but he wasn't.

He got around this literally, by hiking half a mile up the gorge, beyond the bombardment, picking his way down, then hiking back to a point from which he could size up the situation from the bottom. Hiking in the bottom wasn't easy, either. It held a lot more broken trees and rock than before. In places they'd impeded the streamflow, and he picked his way above the resulting pools.

A bloody mess, he told himself. *But war always is.* When he got there, the depth of destruction was worse than he'd foreseen. The gorge wall had been destroyed back nearly to the hangars themselves, and overlying rock had collapsed into the openings. The mass of rubble had one apparent opening, but from the bottom he couldn't tell if it went all the way through. *Hell,* he thought, *the hangar roofs might even have collapsed.*

The great pile of debris at the gorge bottom provided a start up; it required tricky scrambling, but not scaling. Above that it became more difficult. A couple of times it seemed to him he'd cliffed out, but each time he found handholds, a place to put a boot, and somewhere to go from there. After a bit, scratched and sweaty, he reached the opening, widened by invaders removing fallen rocks. The hangars had not collapsed.

"Centaurs?" Morgan muttered. Nothing horselike had climbed this. *They must have used AG boats,* he thought, *or be more like goats than horses.*

Inside was dark, and musty with the smell of old death—of bodies scavenged and dessicated—and dried animal excrement. But his torch beam found no carnivores. They'd been there, done what they did, and left. Bones and tattered cloth were abundant, and all the bones were human. And the spacecraft had open hatches; the people aboard them had come out to fight.

He went directly to his yacht, the *Delight*. She hadn't been destroyed, merely killed. The invaders had slapped magnetic "bombs" on the command panels of her bridge and engineering section, and fried her "brains." They'd also dug through all cabinets and lockers, but except for weapons, which were gone, they'd left the rest strewn around. Mostly they hadn't even taken the trouble to vandalize. Apparently if it didn't look dangerous, any damage was incidental.

He entered his suite with concern, saw the carrying case opened and empty on the deck, and felt sharp fear. Then his torch beam found the telescope itself on the bed, where it had been tossed. He carried it out, set it up, and tried it. It was all right.

Now to find some cordage, he thought. Putting the scope back in its case, he left with it.

He spent the next day with Connie and Robert. Then he left again, this time with eight days' rations in his pack, the scope in its case slung on one shoulder, and, of course, a blaster on his hip. The scope weighed far more than all the rest of it, and was awkward. He'd take a break every hour, he told himself.

He felt cheerful about the situation, and after leaving the zone of bombardment damage, made good progress. On the second afternoon he reached the prominence he'd climbed before, and started up the side away from the alien clearing. At the top, he selected the same scrubby tree he'd sheltered beneath before, and set up the scope in its shade. Here lay a certain risk. He'd brought his belt recorder, and both it and the scope were powered by power slugs. If the invaders were monitoring the electronic environment, they might just possibly detect them, though it seemed doubtful.

Setting the scope at 10X, he focused on the distant opening. It had rained, enough to soak out the fires and lay the dust. He began scanning, increasing and decreasing magnification as needed, pausing to describe anything that seemed worthwhile. His voice activated the recorder. Building construction continued. Here and there large machines—crawler tractors!—moved across the clearing, apparently cutting the coarse root network of the cleared forest. The activity left little question: the aliens planned to stay, and grow crops.

He focused on one who appeared to be a supervisor. It stood sideways to the telescope, watching builders at work, seeming to comment to a recorder of its own. The long head had upright ears, and overall it had reddish-brown fur. Prieto had said they looked like "centaurs from the Jurassic." *He should have said Miocene,* Morgan thought, *or whatever period it was when Terran mammals were trying out bizarre body forms.* He was pretty sure, though, that there'd been no six-limbed mammalian species in Terra's history.

It hadn't occurred to him to bring a vid. He didn't realize he could let Connie view the cube, and the prime minister's savant would see what she was seeing, via Robert.

So he described the alien in words, portraying the features of face and harness, the articulation of the limbs, and the four fingers and two thumbs on each hand. The feet were obscured by vegetation. From what he could see, the teeth were "cone-shaped and not particularly large," but the back teeth could be different.

Then the creature strolled to one of the buildings being assembled, and disappeared inside. Morgan shifted focus to another alien then, this one the color of wet sand. It stood on a gently sloping roof, using what appeared to be some sort of spot-welder. The feet had two splayed toes, suggesting a camel's but with heavy claws. *Blunt claws,* he thought, *for traction instead of fighting.*

He thought of measuring its height, but that required knowing its distance, and this was not the place to use his range finder. *Use your map, and estimate,* he decided. His computer made the worker's height twenty-eight inches at the withers. He couldn't get a figure for height to the top of the long skull; torso and neck were bent forward, eyes on its work.

"Not as big as I thought," he said, "and not horselike at all." Again reducing magnification for scanning, he found a dozer piling sections of fallen trees. As Morgan watched, the operator began flailing its arms, and jumped from the driver's platform with the dozer still running. Its legs gave as it hit, but it was back on its feet in an instant, arms still flailing, hind feet kicking.

Morgan stared. The machine, he realized, had disturbed a nest of Tagus's version of hornets. The operator's dance became extreme, then it fell, limbs thrashing. Quickly Morgan increased magnification till he could glimpse the hornets, big as his thumb joint, strafing the invader until its limbs went slack, and its head flopped sideways on the ground.

"Jesus!" Morgan murmured. He'd been stung a few times himself—twice just the day before; presumably he'd gotten too near a nest. It hurt like hell when they hit, but it hadn't laid him low like that. Of course, from what he could see, the alien had gotten stung a lot more than twice. But still . . .

He cut magnification, and scanned for reactions by other workers who might have seen it happen. Two had left their machines, each holding what might have been a spray can, but instead of running to help their comrade, they watched from a distance, moving nervously, apparently anxious, as if they wanted to move in, but were afraid. Morgan reported that, too.

He continued scanning and recording for another half hour, feeling increasingly edgy. Abruptly then he made a decision, and after disassembling the scope, packed it in its padded case. Then he loaded his gear on his back and picked his way carefully down the knob. At the bottom he stashed scope and case beneath the trunk of a large fallen tree, and set out for home.

If I hike till deep dusk, and get an early start in the morning, I can get back to Robert and Connie by noon, he thought. *And debrief myself to the PM and the military.*

It seemed very important.

Chapter 13

Language Lesson

David MacDonald heartily disliked the awkward commode they were expected to use. It was ill-suited for humans: a dry ceramic box perhaps sixteen inches high, and wide enough for two of the alien invaders to back up to at once. He sluiced it clean with the hose provided, then in lieu of paper, hosed his behind with a needle-spray setting. He wondered how the aliens managed to hose their rears. Probably they didn't, he decided. Their arms were too short. And horses got by without it, and dogs.

Fortunately, alien hygiene arrangements included soft soap in bowls, and he made use of it now. He didn't particularly like making a spectacle of himself for the multilens monitor that left no part of their cell unobserved. When they'd wakened on the shuttle that had brought them to this—station? ship?—they were naked. But of course their captors were naked too, except for equipment harness.

He looked at Yukiko, sitting cross-legged on the other side of the room on a sort of futon. Annika lay still and pale, her head cradled on his wife's lap. Yukiko stroked the girl's short, blond, cap-cut hair, crooning softly to her. That the savant had been captured told him that even with no exposed structures, the Cave Bay station had been discovered. Probably from its electronics signature. And the *Cousteau* had obviously not gotten offworld, because Annika would have been on it.

Ju-Li would have fought a squad of hyenas to protect her, so the others must be dead, he thought. Yukiko agreed. Probably Dennis had sent the others out hunting for them, when they all should have been headed outsystem in warpdrive.

David shook his head. He and Yukiko were together, and when they'd been put aboard the shuttle, Annika had been given into their care. If any of the others had been taken alive, it seemed to him they'd all be together. The only apparent alternative was for each human to be held in solitary, and obviously they weren't.

"How's she doing?" he asked.

"Fine," Yukiko answered. Her attention remained on Annika. "Just fine. Annika knows we're with her, taking care of her. Don't you, darling?" she crooned, and continued to stroke. "She's just resting her eyes. She looked at me a minute ago."

David didn't take his wife's words at face value. She'd said what she had at least partly to sooth Annika, reassure her. It might take quite a bit of that before the child came out of whatever state she was in: a coma or stupor—whatever. The child. It occurred to him he didn't know how old Annika was. Eleven or twelve, he guessed, but mentally equivalent to four or five. If "equivalent" meant anything in cases like this.

A sound caught David's attention, and he turned. The door was sliding open, and two aliens looked in from the corridor, sidearms in hand, long reptilian jaws closed. The eyes were squarely in front, presumably providing binocular vision.

The weapons, David guessed, were stunners of some sort. But not the variety familiar from crime dramas; he and Yukiko had been stunned while being picked up on the islet, and there'd been no hangover. "Look who's here," David said. "The hyena twins, Ugly and Uglier." His eyes were intent on their faces, which he could not read. But he got an impression of wariness, as unlikely as it seemed. The two walked through the door, then stepped aside. A third one, larger, walked in between them, seemingly unarmed. The first two were reddish brown. This one had vivid blue sides; the upright torso and head were teal blue. The face was marked with red, and the seemingly clipped crest was scarlet. To David's eyes the colors seemed natural. Its own eyes intent on David, the latecomer spoke, the words recognizable despite very approximate pronunciations. "How do you feel?" it said. The eff sound was approximate.

It's got no lips, David realized. The alien's eyes were on him, and for a moment David thought the creature wanted to know. But then it answered its own question. "I felt vetter."

Before he got it all out, the creature's gaze had moved to Yukiko. "How do you *suffose* I feel?" it said, then answered its own question. "Cratty." It looked from one human to the other, then made what might have been a smile, and touched its upright torso where its heart might might have been but almost certainly wasn't. "Qonits," it added. "Qonits!"

"Yukiko," Yukiko answered promptly, and touched her chest.

Ah-ha. It's begun, David thought. He remembered now: the first sentence had been what he'd asked Yukiko when she'd wakened—"How do you feel?"—and the follow-up had been her reply. "Cratty" was as close as their interrogator could come to "crappy." The aliens had been monitoring more than their movements. They'd recorded their words, run an audio analysis, then this one had practiced the Terran phonemes, words, and sentences. They wanted to learn the language.

The chain of realizations had been more rapid than speech; the oceanographer didn't miss a beat. "David," he said, touching his thatched chest.

It was indeed the beginning. There was a wall table in the room, its height suitable for an alien to work at, but too low for a standing human; David and Yukiko would have to kneel. Qonits stepped to it and gestured. Gently Yukiko laid Annika's head down on the futon, and whispered to her. Then she and David joined the alien, who promptly walked the four fingers of one hand along the table's surface, and made a sound. Probably the word for walk, David decided. He repeated it back as best he could, and walked two of his own fingers on the table, human-style. "Walk," he said.

The alien repeated the word he'd used, and both adult humans tried to duplicate it. The alien's eyes were unreadable. Again David's two human fingers walked along the table. "Walk!" he repeated, forcefully this time. "Walk! Walk!"

The alien tried it again, and David glowered deliberately, wondering what, if anything, the alien made of human facial expressions. Shaking his head, he galloped his fingers along the surface. "Run! Run! Run!" he barked.

The alien stared, appraisingly it seemed, then walked his fingers again. "Wahk," he said. "Wahk. Wahk."

David didn't let him get by with that. "Walk!" he snarled, "not *wahk!* You're not a duck, you're a goddamn . . . " He paused. "Hyena!"

When Qonits left, some while later, he'd learned not only run and walk, but hungry, eat, drink, scratch, wash, bathe, breathe, heart, urinate, and defecate. He could also count to ten. And considering the undoubted differences in his vocal apparatus, approximated the sounds rather well.

He'd also proven a quick study, which did not greatly cheer the oceanographer. David had no doubt the words were recorded in the ship's computer, but what it might make of them, he had no idea. *Not much*, he guessed. *Not yet.* It lacked the workhorse words: *is* and *are* and *were*; *you* and *me*; *but* and *and*; *here* and *there* . . . But it was a beginning. Meanwhile, he'd established a kind of fragile dominance, though what good it might be, he had no idea.

Chapter 14

Goosing the Tiger

Drago Draveç had learned something: that a near-suicide mission weeks away can be planned more or less matter-of-factly, but close at hand it was a meaner breed of cat. Not that *he* was thinking of backing out. But here he was, newly emerged in the far fringe of the Hibernia System—in its cometary cloud—with only two of his three other ships. Several minutes had passed with no sign of Indio Fuentes and the *Aztec,* and even after one minute, the odds of their showing had become microscopic.

That son of a bitch! he thought, but without heat. Fuentes, a skilled captain, had been with them eight hyper-space hours earlier, when they'd emerged to compute their approach shot. Now he wasn't.

So they'd do it without him. Drago realized how lucky he was that *Bachelor* and *Ludmilla* had hung tough. He was asking a hell of a lot.

Drago pulled his attention to his sensor reads. He was always better at disconnecting from his emotions than at dealing with them. From time to time they'd pop up later, unbidden and out of context. That was a major reason even he was sometimes surprised by his actions; even jerked by them.

He tended to cherish those unexplained surprises. He'd told himself more than once they kept life interesting. He'd even told his probation counselor that once, at the Academy. The guy's comeback had been, "Don't fall in love with your faults, Drago. It's like sleeping with rattlesnakes." But Drago hadn't taken the psych seriously. He felt confident in his intentions, and in his ability to make things turn out right.

The main thing that had gotten him in trouble over the years was liquor, and he'd become good at refusing drinks. He'd said more than once, "A couple of drinks and even I don't know what the hell I might do." He didn't allow booze aboard ship, except for his crew's rum ration—three ounces at supper, actually 50/50 rum and water. And he left even that alone. Didn't even keep a bottle in his room back at Tagus, though he'd sometimes share a drink with Lu, his base wife.

His sensors showed him the location of the aliens' system defense force, in the planetary fringe roughly 90 degrees from the primary, some 11 billion miles insystem. While close to the colony was a smaller force, probably a planetary guard flotilla. Unless they had more sensitive hyperspace emergence detectors than human technology had come up with, which seemed doubtful, there was a good chance they hadn't picked up the emergence of his own three small craft.

And his EM signature wouldn't arrive with them for seventeen hours, so he radioed his other two commanders.

"Fuentes isn't going to show," he said, "so we'll do it without him. Give me your location fixes on the system defense force."

They did. Both agreed with his.

"Okay. I'm going to let Kunming know we're here and set to go. Then, on my count, we'll move in, just as we planned. And good luck. A lot depends on us."

He counted, then jumped.

If warpspace emergence produced waves, no human devices had ever detected them. But from this close, the three pirates' electromagnetic signatures reached the aliens in microseconds. They'd already be icons on the alien screens. That's why they'd jumped to emerge between the system defense force and the Star of Hibernia. Hopefully they'd be mistaken for small members of the aliens' planetary guard.

Drago had no way of knowing how close to the system defense force he'd be on emergence—100 miles, 500, 1,000 . . . It turned out to be 83. As planned, the pirate ships didn't pause to size things up. They could do that on the move. Nor did they break radio silence. Instead, as agreed earlier, the two subordinate pirate vessels began at once to move in gravdrive toward the alien battle group, neither hurriedly nor hesitently, as if this were routine. Drago followed more slowly, letting them open a larger gap. To sit motionless at a distance might bring questions he could neither answer nor read. Meanwhile *he* had the savant, and the responsibility to let War House know what he learned. Otherwise the mission would be wasted effort, and any lives lost, thrown away.

On emergence, the *Minerva's* sensors and her ships-mind had begun recording everything they could perceive about the enemy. Not everything a warship would perceive, but a lot. On his screen, the alien formation showed as an array of icons. He locked his sensors on one of the five largest, its mass not greatly less than a loaded ore carrier. Surely a battleship. He called for an actual image, and magnified it against a scaling grid. She was huge! By comparison, the pride of the Admiralty, the prototype cruiser *Yangtse,* was a dwarf. Of the aliens' outriggers, the only one Drago could identify with confidence was the strange-space navigational sensor array. Others, less conspicuous, might or might not be communication equipment and targeting locks.

His own small, base-made torpedoes were designed mainly as threats, though they could easily disable or kill a merchantman.

So far his sensors had detected no changes in the alien radio traffic. To Drago even their code sounded somehow laconic. Hopefully this meant they'd accepted his three small craft as normal.

The pirates slowed their approach now, as if to join the battle group, intending to come alongside one or more of the large ships. Drago's fists and belly had clenched. "Not yet," he muttered, "not yet . . . NOW!"

It was as if the *Bachelor*'s master had heard him; less than a mile from the nearest cruiser, he released three torpedoes. A moment later there was a great flash, the explosion driving the cruiser sideways. Magnified on his bridge screen, Drago saw flame and debris vent from the breached hull. Even as he'd fired, the *Bachelor*'s skipper had activated his strange-space generator. A second later the pirate vessel winked into warpspace.

Drago emitted a single explosive "Yeah!" Then his gaze fixed on the *Ludmilla*, intense again. She'd been trailing the *Bachelor* by about two miles. This was a delicate moment. Kunming's most urgent question was whether the aliens had force shields. The *Ludmilla*'s skipper was to hold his fire until they'd had time to generate shields, if any. *Then* they'd surely generate them, if they had them.

Seconds passed—dragged—three, four, five . . . No shields. It seemed to Drago they'd had abundant time. Meanwhile the *Ludmilla* had slowed to avoid overrunning her target. "Not yet," he muttered. "Not yet. Not . . ." Then, faintly luminous in the blackness, shields began to form. "Now!" he shouted. At that instant the *Ludmilla* launched her salvo. Almost as quickly the battleship's war beam hit her, and seconds later the pirate's unarmored hull blew apart in a widening sphere of gassed metal and debris.

Time to leave! The *Minerva* had half-closed the gap. As Drago activated the strange-space generator, her light hull resonated to an alien target lock. Had it been a torpedo lock, he'd have been in warpspace before the torpedoes reached him. As it was, a war beam began its non-explosive but sustained and intense energy transfer an instant before the *Minerva* left F-space.

An instant too short for human reaction, though the temperature increased. Then Drago stared at his screen. It showed not the indigo blue his shipsmind used to represent warpspace, but the restful yellow it showed for hyperspace.

"Gracious god," he breathed. He knew exactly what had

happened. In the moment when warpspace was generating—in that small fraction of a second—the beam had corrupted his warpdrive, and he'd entered hyperspace instead.

His first officer too sat staring, then finally spoke. "Looks like we're screwed," he said softly.

"Screwed, rolled over, and screwed again," Drago answered, then paused. "Take the helm. I've got a report to make." Getting up, he started aft to the cabin shared by his savant and her attendant.

It had been evening in Kunming when Drago Draveç notified War House of his emergence in the Hibernia System's cometary cloud. So instead of going to his apartment to sleep, Admiralty Chief Fedor Tischendorf had lain down on the couch in his office, just a few strides down the corridor from his savant's suite. When Drago's next savanted contact arrived, the admiral's night yeoman woke him. The admiral was off his couch instantly, wide awake and energized, and reached the savant's couch in under a minute, his shoes on but unsecured.

The savanted exchange was recorded and backed up on War House's AI. And on the admiral's powerful mind, where it instantly began to make connections, tying it into the extensive interconnected matrix that was his understanding of reality—his personal, internal version of the universe.

The session took nearly an hour, the information sometimes coming slowly: the size of the system defense force and the planetary guard flotilla; their distances from Star; descriptions of the enemy warships; the masses of the battleships and cruisers, their outriggers . . . and of course their shields, beam locks and radio frequencies. Important stuff.

Tischendorf imagined the pirate screening his cube—visuals and data—deciding what was meaningful and what wasn't. And when in doubt, telling it. Better the error of excess than to leave something out that might prove important. Invaluable.

The admiral wasn't surprised that one of the corsairs had funked out. He wouldn't have been shocked if none had carried it through.

The last thing Draveç mentioned was being scorched by a war beam in the moment of escape.

"Did you take damage?"

"It knocked out my warpdrive and FSP dish. So I can't use the F-space potentiality to navigate, and I can't use dead reckoning like I could in warpspace. I'll pop into F-space from time to time though, if I can, and see if I can figure out where I am and what direction I've been going. Ever hear of anyone making it back like that?"

The admiral pursed his lips, then answered. "No, Drago, I haven't. But I'll put someone on it; see if we can come up with something useful for you. Maybe we can. We've been performing wonders on industrial mobilization. We've got the beginnings of a real fleet under construction, and your information will be extremely useful. All of it. We'd hoped the aliens hadn't developed shield technology—it would have given us an important advantage—but just knowing it will help us plan, and save lives and ships."

He paused. "And, Drago, check in with us from time to time, just so I know you're alive. For what it's worth, I wish you well. If you make it back, and if you're interested . . . the fleet can always use more good officers."

A very long way off, in another, very different universe, Drago Draveç grimaced at Tischendorf's words. If Henry Morgan was dead, and he just about had to be, then Drago owed loyalty to no one but his crew. They'd waited three long days at rendezvous, and Morgan hadn't shown. While *Minerva*, *Bachelor*, *Ludmilla* and *Aztec* had arrived within minutes of each other. Presumably Morgan was dead.

"I'll think about it, Admiral," Drago said. "Meanwhile, do me a favor: pass along my apologies to Ambassador Khai." Only now did he realize he didn't know her first name. "I expect I made a lot of trouble for her. And she's quite a person, quite a lady. Maybe I should have let her handle things, but I didn't trust that bastard Rees. Basically he's psychotic."

They wound up the session then. War House's master artificial intelligence had not only backed up the recording of the session in real time, it had uploaded a copy to the prime minister. Meanwhile, for Tischendorf, it was less than two hours before time to get up, so he simply took off his shoes and lay down on his couch again.

Where he dreamed of drifting derelict in hyperspace.

Chapter 15

Recruits

Bulk carriers were well suited for conversion to "snooze ships"—stasis ships—for evacuating colonies. They were extremely large, and their holds readily segmented by decks, dividing them into numerous levels.

In Esau Wesley's broad, low-ceilinged compartment, the aisles between the stasis lockers were packed with men; the sexes had been separated when they'd come aboard. Which left Esau uneasy, because he didn't know where his wife was. Women and men, they'd been told, needed to be put in separate holds for prestasis processing. "Processing," he discovered, meant getting ready for three and a half months of stasis; a kind of deep sleep, they'd been told. "Standard" months, whatever that meant. They'd also been told they wouldn't get any older in stasis. He'd wondered if that meant setting back their birthdays three months, but hadn't asked. The man who'd told them things had one answer for all questions: the single word "later."

They hadn't even been fed since the night before boarding the ship. By then they'd had to show their nakedness to what he supposed were physicians, who among other things had stuck them with needles, drawn blood, looked at their teeth, and shamelessly examined their private parts.

After that they'd been given a thin, soft, snug-fitting, one-piece suit to wear "for while you're in stasis." There were no seams except in front, where they'd been open from throat to crotch. Like winter underwear but without buttons or a trapdoor. After they'd got into the sleep suits, men had shown them how to fasten the seams by pressing. He hadn't known the whys for any of it. Then, at their command, he'd rolled up his homespuns, tied them with a tape they'd provided, and fastened his high-cut moccasins to the bundle with another tape. All the while wondering if he'd ever see his real clothes again; they were a lot better than what he'd been given.

When he wakened, the lid was open on his stasis locker, and there was a faint smell in his nose, mildly sharp. He wasn't groggy, but he was briefly confused. Then he remembered. Meanwhile his bundle lay on his belly, moccasins included. At least the Terrans didn't seem to be thieves.

Then a whistle had blown, and a loud voice had bellowed instructions. Esau had climbed from his locker and changed into his own clothes, he and all the other men in his compartment. They filled the aisles. Nobody had said much, and most who spoke, spoke quietly. His stomach growled, and he felt strange.

The whistle shrilled again, cutting off the soft refugee murmur. Again the loud voice spoke, seeming to come from all around them. "ATTENTION ALL PASSENGERS! ATTENTION ALL PASSENGERS! YOU ARE ABOUT TO BE DISEMBARKED. YOU ARE ABOUT TO BE DISEMBARKED. STAY ALERT AND FOLLOW INSTRUCTIONS. STAY ALERT AND FOLLOW INSTRUCTIONS. WHEN ORDERED, FILE OUT IN AN ORDERLY MANNER. DO NOT PUSH. WE DO NOT WANT ANYONE CRUSHED, OR KNOCKED DOWN AND TRAMPLED. WHEN YOU GET OUTSIDE, LISTEN FOR YOUR NAME. WHEN YOU GET OUTSIDE, LISTEN FOR YOUR NAME."

Esau was pretty sure the voice wasn't human. They'd been warned that Terrans used machines to do all sorts of things for them; apparently that could include talking. As for "disembarked"—he supposed that meant getting off the ship. And they'd be calling off names! He'd listen for Jael's, and go to her regardless of anything. Anyone got in his way, too bad for them.

Meanwhile he waited. He didn't know whether three and a half months had passed, like they'd said, or three weeks, but he was pretty sure it was less than three years and more than three days. There was a vague sense of time having passed, and an even vaguer sense of having dreamt. But however long it had been, they seemed to have arrived, presumably on Terra.

Somewhere, someone must have given an order, because now the packed humanity in his aisle began to move. It was a main aisle, leading directly to an open door, toward which they moved slowly under the scowling gaze of a very tall man. He held what the refugees took to be a hand weapon of some sort. Esau's column flowed rather smoothly, out the door into a wide corridor. Like an aisle-wide subcurrent in a river of humanity, some of whose currents were female.

"You got a wife here somewhere?" asked a voice beside him. It belonged to another youth, a bit shorter but similarly built.

"I sure hope so. I did when I got on this thing."

"I wonder what it'll be like outside."

Esau had no reply for that. Just now his attention was on how he felt physically—light-footed, even light-headed. "Do you feel like I feel?" he asked.

"Might be. How's that?"

"Kind of strange. Light."

From behind them another voice spoke. "We all feel it. Things weigh less on Terra, including us. Back home I weighed three hundred and thirty pounds. Here I weigh two hundred and thirty."

Esau looked back at the man, a man about his own age. And like himself, rather tall by the standards of New Jerusalem. But not as strong-looking as most; he didn't have the look of a farmer. Also, he wore eyeglasses. Esau decided he must be a speaker of the books. Or judging by his age, a student speaker.

"How could that be?" Esau asked. "We don't look any thinner than we used to."

"Because the gravity is different here. A pound at home only weighs point-seven pounds here."

Esau wondered what a "point" had to do with it. And grabbity? "What's 'grabbity'?" he asked.

"Gravity," the fellow said soberly, "is what God created for things to weigh differently on different worlds."

Esau didn't ask anything more. He didn't think much of the answers he'd already gotten. Besides, they were spilling down a ramp now, into a cold drizzle. It had been early summer when they'd left home. Here it felt like fall. *Three months then,* he told himself, *or a little more. Seems like they told the truth about that.* Combined with not stealing his clothes, it made the Terrans out to be not so bad as he'd feared. Maybe they'd changed over the centuries.

He was glad he had his homespuns on again, and not the thin Terran clothes he'd slept in. Wool would keep off the drizzle better. At the foot of the ramp, tall men dressed like the armed guards in the corridor directed them into separate columns of twos. There was a certain amount of confusion, and the guards had to do some pulling and pushing. When one of them pulled on Esau, he didn't seem very strong, just tall. Esau told himself he could take the guy down and sit on him if need be. But it went all right, though one of the guards cursed way worse than Esau had ever heard in his life. The columns separated somewhat, eight or ten feet apart. Then someone up ahead shouted "halt" in another really loud voice, and after some jostling and piling up, the columns got themselves stopped.

Looking sideways down the gap between his column and the next, Esau saw a man talking into something he held in one hand. The words came out loud enough; it seemed to Esau he could have heard them a quarter mile. The man said that when their name was called, they should go to a flag that someone up ahead was waving in the air. Then a bunch of names were called, some of men, some of women. After a bit they got to the W's—there was even a Wesley—but no Esau or Jael. Then the process started over again at a different flag.

Esau stood there in the rain through several rounds of that, while the drizzle started to soak through. The column had got a lot thinner before his name was called—his followed by Jael's—and he took off at a trot. Running was so easy, he began to believe in grabbity. Jael had already been somewhere up near the flag; now he could see her standing by it. She'd seen him, too, and was waving her arms overhead.

Their group was led to a large sort of tent, the biggest he'd ever seen. Light passed through it, but he couldn't actually see through it. There they were given a kind of food—crunchy flatbread that tasted decent enough—and water to wash it down. Then they'd been lined up, each line leading to a different man at a different table. He and Jael stayed together now, determined not to be separated again, Esau first, Jael close behind. These lines also moved slowly; another kind of "processing," Esau decided. The people doing it to them wore clothes just alike, as far as he could tell: greenish-brown. When he reached the table for their line, the man sitting there had him say his name to a small box.

"Esau Wesley," Esau said, then gestured. "Hers is Jael Wesley."

The man ignored the last part. "Esau Wesley, you need to make a decision now, the one they told you about before you left New Jerusalem. There are two kinds of jobs available to you. You can either be a soldier, and protect humankind from the invaders, or you can be a laborer. The choice is yours. But I must tell you that if we get too few soldiers, the invaders will win, and kill us all."

Esau's jaw jutted. "I'll be a soldier if my wife can be. We've got to stay together."

"No problem," the corporal said. "Now I'm going to give you instructions. Answer when I tell you to. And speak clearly." He paused. "Do you, Esau Wesley, understand that you are volunteering to be in the Commonwealth Armed Forces? And that you will be subject to all military rules and regulations? Please answer now, yes or no."

Esau wasn't entirely sure what "military" meant, but "rules and regulations" was clear enough. "Yes," he said.

"Good. Congratulations, Recruit Esau Wesley." The corporal was supposed to shake Esau's hand then, but shaking the hand of one Jerrie had been more than enough. He simply pointed. "Get in line behind sign *C* over there. To get your physical exam and army clothes." He knew from an earlier shipment that some off-worlders didn't know the word *uniform*.

Esau frowned at him without moving. "I'll wait for her," he said, gesturing at Jael. "We'll go together."

The man's face and voice turned impatient. "Recruit Wesley, that is not possible. You'll be naked for your physical exam, so it's men with men and women with women. You can be together later. Now go get in line *C*."

Reluctantly Esau left. Then the corporal repeated the procedure with Jael.

Jael felt mildly anxious that she couldn't spot her husband. Though not as anxious as she'd been aboard ship, and that had worked out all right. There were lines of one sort or another all over the huge tent, and she'd been directed to one consisting solely of women. Most, like herself, were young, and either single or childless, she supposed. It seemed unlikely that soldiers could take care of their children. Surely not in a war. Within thirty minutes, she'd been checked out by medics, inoculated, and issued a uniform. After changing clothes, she was directed to a mixed line. Esau wasn't there, either. *He's still waiting for his physical exam,* she told herself, but again anxiety gnawed her gut.

That line took her through the drizzle to a large nearby tent called a mustering shed, where she still couldn't see Esau. Here there were quite a few women, and most of the men appeared older. Her anxiety grew. Again names were called alphabetically, recruits gathering behind a man called ensign something. Something outlandish. When a company had received its complement of newly processed recruits, it left. Then a new ensign replaced the old, and the process repeated, starting with *A* again. When at last

Jael's name was called, she fell in as instructed. And now she felt the beginning of panic, because Esau's name wasn't called. Hers followed Warner, and after it came Whitney, Wilcox, Williams and Yancy.

After the name Yancy, the ensign called, "All right, follow me!" and led off toward an exit, another man following to herd stragglers. Jael stepped out of line and ran to catch up with the ensign. "Sir," she said, "my husband isn't here!"

He glowered but did not slow. He was the tallest man she'd seen, even among the Terrans, a lantern-jawed giant. His skin was brown, his arms and hands long, and his eyes were hooded by thick slanting lids. "Soldier," he ordered, "get back in line. If you've got a problem, it can be handled at the waiting shed. We'll be there in a minute."

Not relieved, she fell in immediately behind him. In two minutes they arrived at another large tent, where a lot of people waited. The ensign told his charges to sit down on a block of empty benches he pointed to. They all did except Jael. She stood determinedly.

"All right, soldier, what's your complaint?"

Briefly she explained. Without answering her, he took a phone from his belt. "Provost Station, this is Ensign Adrup Gompo, 3rd Processing Company, at Station E. I have a recruit with a beef. This one needs an arbiter." He put the phone back on his belt and looked at Jael again. "Sit down, soldier. That's an order. Someone will come to take you to an arbiter. He'll fix what needs fixing."

She stood half numb. She'd only half understood what he'd said. A runner arrived, and led her to one end of the tent, to a room walled by plastic curtains hung on wires. Inside sat a burly, middle-aged man. A placard on his desk read SGT. MAJOR NGUVA. His skin was almost black, his short salt-and-pepper hair formed tiny tight curls, and he wore a plug in one ear. There was a chair a few feet from his, but he left her standing.

"Your name, soldier?" He asked it amiably, while aiming a microphone toward her, then watched the monitor on his terminal while she answered. Next he tapped something on his key pad, before looking back at her. "What's your complaint?"

Again she described it. He tapped an instruction, then frowned, listening to something she couldn't hear. Now his fingers tapped a longer instruction. From a box came Esau's voice, then the corporal's who'd sworn them in, and finally her own. The sergeant major cut it off.

"Corporal DeSoto misinformed you," he said. "He told you one thing and did something else. Your husband has been assigned to Company B, 587th Infantry Training Regiment. You have been assigned to Company G, 249th Fighting Vehicle Training Regiment."

Her breath stopped, trapped in her lungs.

"For whatever satisfaction it may provide you, Corporal DeSoto will be reprimanded before the recruiting staff, assigned punishment, and perhaps demoted.

"After you have completed your basic and specialist training, which will require several months, both you and your husband will be assigned to a corps consisting of your own people. Meanwhile you will train in different camps. On the same planet, but he in an infantry center, you in a fighting vehicle center."

Her guts shriveled.

"Or," the sergeant major went on, "you can choose to transfer to the infantry. In that case, considering how you were misled, you and your husband can be in the same platoon and squad. But there are serious disadvantages in that."

Again he paused, observing her relief. "You can also have your enlistments cancelled, on the grounds of Corporal DeSoto's deliberate misrepresentation. In that case you will find yourselves in a civilian labor battalion." He paused. "Perhaps on a colony world, building fortifications. If the invaders arrive there, and the fighting goes badly, an effort will be made to evacuate our fighting units, but it is difficult to imagine a situation in which labor battalions can be salvaged."

He leaned forward, forearms on the table, his tone detached but not unfriendly. "The army is no bed of roses," he went on. "The Commonwealth is in serious danger of being overrun, and the human species eradicated. That includes you and me, small children, old people—everyone. So in the army—or in the labor battalions—the purpose of existence is not pleasure, comfort, or convenience. It is to stop the invader. Defeat him and drive him out. Bloody him so badly he will never return."

She stared round-eyed, understanding enough to get his meaning.

"That is what your training will be about, whether you are an armor jockey, or in your husband's infantry squad. One is about as dangerous as the other. In the infantry, however, the purely muscular exhaustion is much greater. The need for muscular strength results in female recruits being routinely assigned to fighting vehicles, but exceptions can be made." He eyed the wide-bodied, broad-handed young woman before him, clearly from a heavyworld, and wondered how many Terran men were as strong. "You will almost certainly be the only woman in your company," he went on, "and probably in your regiment. And ancient experience has shown that few young women can long stand such isolation from female companionship.

"Meanwhile you would not be sharing your husband's bed. Private moments of any sort would be few.

"As an armor jockey, on the other hand, the exhaustion is more of the nerves, and fighting vehicle regiments have many women."

He leaned back slightly in his chair. "You must decide now: armored vehicle training, your husband's infantry platoon, or a labor battalion."

Her eyes met his, and her voice, though quiet, was firm. "I want to be with my husband."

Sergeant Major Nguva smiled. "Good," he said, getting to his feet, and held out a large black hand with a pink palm. Hesitantly she shook it. "Congratulate your husband for me," he said, "on his good fortune in having so steadfast a wife."

Chapter 16
Puzzles

The two Wyzhñyñy sat in the grand admiral's office, talking. "Our progress?" the chief scholar said. "It is accelerating. We exchange limited sentences now, on a growing number of subjects."

Grand Admiral Quanshûk shu-Gorlak nodded without enthusiasm. "And what of the questions and topics I have listed?"

"I have not broached them yet. They . . . "

"None of them?!"

The interruption was discourteous and its tone accusatory, but Chief Scholar Qonits zu-Kitku did not lower his eyes. He was the leading scholar in their mutual and extensive tribe, and in this galaxy without a gender peer. But given certain enigmas in the operating situation, he understood the grand admiral's concern. "Your Excellency," he answered, "the subjects I am able to discuss with the aliens deal with everyday experiences, largely physical. I must have a much broader vocabulary, and refine what I already have, before I can even present the questions you ask. Let alone understand any answers.

"But each day we learn more. As you know, I now spend most of my waking time at the task." He might have added, but didn't, that he'd warned it would take time. Instead he gestured now, palms out and open. "And as I said, progress is accelerating."

Quanshûk nodded. The chief scholar's reply had been as much lecture as answer, but his own impatience had brought it on. Qonits was exalted in more than gender, and due both courtesy and high respect. Pique, impatience, and gender prejudice were inappropriate between them.

"Meanwhile," Qonits was saying, "the ship runs semantic correlations, and presents me with strategical areas to explore." He changed the subject. "It seems that among the aliens there are two parent genders, not one, each gender with fixed sexuality. You can imagine how such personal—incompleteness—might affect the individual, and that a mated pair might therefore bond very strongly.

"The two larger aliens are a mated pair. The smaller one, who does not speak, seems to be a member of their kin group, and is mentally and physically defective. It was being cared for by a servant—apparently of the nanny gender—when the marines captured it. The bond between servant and child had become profound, and killing the servant traumatized the child severely."

"Ah." This was something Admiral Quanshûk could understand. It was easy to overlook that aliens had lives and feelings of their own. *It would be wise,* he told himself drily, *not to dwell on that.*

Prior to the invasion, Prime Minister Foster Peixoto and President Chang Lung-Chi had routinely met late in the morning, in the president's office. But seldom at lunch, which they'd agreed was a time for relaxation. Government had not been as crisis-laden and stressful, nor politics as consuming and ruthless, as they'd been a millennium earlier. Society was less overwrought. Socially and psychologically, the human species had truly evolved and advanced. Stagnated, their remote ancestors would have said. Lost their fire.

But since the invasion, crisis and stress were endemic in government. The prime minister and president had met routinely for lunch and often for supper, specifically to talk business. Time was too precious for relaxed eating. Usually they met in Peixoto's office, and ate at an AG table guided in by an orderly.

Chang Lung-Chi would not have changed jobs with his prime minister for anything. The demands on Peixoto's time and energy were more stringent than Chang liked to think about.

Meanwhile, it was Chang who'd come down with the latest new viral pneumonia, quite dangerous, and been confined to the palace infirmary for twelve days. Now Peixoto was updating him on some of the less worrisome matters of interest.

"You may recall my giving Bekr the task of learning where the 'messages' are coming from," the prime minister was saying. "He has it sorted out now. The Julie mentioned in their conversations can only be a sensitive named Ju-Li Hamilton-Gävle, the wife of a Dennis Bertrand. She is, or was, the attendant of her half sister, a preadolescent female savant named Annika Pedersen." He paused meaningfully, then finished: "Assigned on Maritimus. The people now looking after her—the Yukiko and David on the cube—are a marine biologist and an oceanographer, Yukiko Gavaldon and David MacDonald respectively. MacDonald was also chief of station on Maritimus. Apparently Hamilton-Gävle and Bertrand were killed by the aliens, and Gavaldon and MacDonald, not being trained sensitives, don't know how to control the savant. Bekr is convinced they don't know she's channeling. They think she's simply comatose."

Thoughtfully the president ate a spoonful of cream custard. "How," he wondered aloud, "does Bekr explain a comatose savant who channels automatically? Or could it be on her own volition, at some subconscious level?"

Frowning, the prime minister sipped thick Iranian coffee. "Bekr has said nothing about volition," he answered, "but you raise an interesting question. Each savant communicator is hypno-conditioned to react to a 'psychic touch' by another communicator. *Any* other communicator. Or to make such a touch, directed by the savant's attendant through a hyp-notically pre-installed . . . 'switch,' Bekr calls it.

"Judging from the date that Maritimus was captured, Annika did not channel at all for some weeks afterward. Perhaps she was too deeply comatose, and began when her level of consciousness rose to some threshold . . . which brings up the possibility that she may stop channeling as her level of consciousness continues to climb. I need to ask Bekr about this."

The president raised another spoonful of custard. "Without an attendant to direct her, how is it her messages get to Ramesh, instead of to someone else?"

"Bekr has an explanation for that. Hamilton-Gävle reported the aliens' arrival in the Maritimus System through Ramesh and Chloë. Via Annika, of course. That much we know. Then obviously the aliens caught the mission's base ship before it could escape. Presumably when they stormed it, Annika's attendant made another contact, seemingly cut short either by her death or Annika's injury before our savants here could react. Then, when Annika recovered sufficiently, the latent contact activated. Now, in the absence of an attendant able to direct her, she channels whatever is said in her presence. At least when she is sufficiently receptive; Bekr believes that within her coma she sometimes descends below functionality." Peixoto shrugged. "A sort of sleep within a sleep."

Absently he raised a morsel of preserved pear to his mouth, to be chewed and swallowed. "I have a new savant covering Ramesh's past duties," he went on. "Bekr has set the replacement up in the Lavender Suite. Ramesh is now available only to Annika. As Chloë is at War House."

Chang Lung-Chi nodded. "And what have we learned from this connection, besides a few words in the alien tongue? And their name: the Wyzhñyñy."

"Primarily we are gaining added insights into the aliens—learning what sort of beings they are, while they concentrate on learning our language. Which I, at least, find encouraging. War House's AI is working on theirs, but so far lacks a useful key. I'll inform you when we have a significant breakthrough.

"MacDonald and Gabaldon don't discuss their situation.

They are undoubtedly monitored and recorded, and careful of what they say to each other. Otherwise, when the aliens have an effective translation program . . . " Peixoto's long expressive hands gestured vague unpleasantness.

"Bekr feels sure the MacDonalds don't realize Annika is channeling. If they suspected, they'd have informed us covertly—given us some sort of hint. I've had Burhan undertake to pass an innocuous comment through Annika, to alert the MacDonalds without attracting alien suspicion. It didn't work. Bekr believes Annika is operating as a one-way relay—them to us. Yukiko Gavaldon is clearly not a sensitive, let alone a trained attendant, so that is not really surprising."

He paused. "In fact, as you suggested, we may lose even that one-way contact. Annika no longer has to be helped to use the sanitary facility, and she holds her own drinking cup."

"Without disconnecting?"

"So far."

Hmm. Chang wondered if her present state qualified as coma. He frowned. He definitely did not want that connection lost, but there seemed nothing to be done about it.

He changed the subject. "Has Special Projects had anything to report?"

"No, Mr. President, they have not. Dosado has promised a preliminary report no later than Threeday. The know-how exists; it has for a very long time. The difficulty is, we know next to nothing about invader physiology. Which does not preclude following through, of course. It simply leaves the result very much in doubt."

Chapter 17
The Home Front

The marchers ranged from elderly to children in arms, and wore no uniforms. They filled the boulevard from curb to curb, and the night with their drums and bagpipes. And they chanted Peace Front slogans, in every accent on Terra, some even in the tongues of ethnic forebears. Their weapons were banners, placards, and the Commonwealth flag. And though they threw up no barricades, they paralyzed traffic quite effectively, for they numbered an estimated hundred thousand. The din could be heard for more than a mile.

The demonstration was not remotely spontaneous. It had been carefully planned, and its contingents were rather well coordinated. The great majority who marched believed sincerely that the Commonwealth and its safety lay exclusively in the hands of God. That if the invaders were received by humankind in peace and love, their alien hearts would hear God whispering. And hearing, they'd move on to regions of space unoccupied by humans. So the various peace sects and persuasions had smoked the calumet, the pipe of peace—literally smoked it—agreeing that the important thing was to end Commonwealth defense activities. That only then would God act to save humankind.

Remarkably, the scores of thousands of marchers drew rather few spectators, and these were watched closely from police floaters. The government wanted no incidents that might cause an eruption of violence. Nor did the Peace Front, for the media were there in numbers, along the sidewalks, within the marching ranks, and in floaters keeping the legally required distance, recording with electronic eyes. Any violence would be witnessed worldwide, and video and holo cubes would be podded throughout the Core Worlds. If the marchers became violent, even in self-defense, the Peace Front would be seen as hypocritical, and so large a demonstration would itself be considered provocation.

If spectators sparked an incident, the government would be blamed for failure to police the demonstration properly. But if government force was seen as less than highly restrained, the demonstrators next time might be twice as many.

At length the marchers flowed onto the vast pavement of Wellesley Square, which was large enough to hold them all. Flowed onto and across it, their skirling, booming, chanting current carrying them to the force field that, activated for the event, encircled the huge capital complex—a city embedded in a city. There the current stopped, the marchers flooding to both sides to fill the square.

Near one side, this sea of humanity contained an island—"Martyr's Hill"—a large grassy mound with steps, topped by a platform, which tonight was topped in turn by a microphone connected to Wellesley Square's sound system. Martyr's Hill was 742 years old, an enduring memorial to the demonstrators whose battle and massacre on this very square had led to a military coup, and the overthrow of the old Terran war government. Ending the long Troubles—94 years of economic warfare, embargoes, sabotage, terrorism, guerrilla actions, and now and then formal space fights between Terra, on the one hand, and her insystem colonies on the other. The mound had held various impassioned speakers over subsequent centuries, but there had not been so many listeners for a very long time.

Paddy Davies was a small man, so with his companion he'd climbed a few steps up on the side of the mound, to see over the crowd. The demonstration monitors allowed it, for the two were the principal members of the coordinating committee. Paddy gestured toward the executive tower, a mile away within the Complex. "What would you bet the bean pole is watching?" He shouted it, to be heard over the din.

"Of course he is," Jaromir Horvath shouted back. "In person, from a balcony. And Chang with him." Even shouted, his words were tinged with scorn. Horvath had founded, and at age sixty-four still led, the quasi-religious Party of the Holy Universe. An organization nominally inclusive, but politically narrow and dogmatic.

So far as anyone knew, joy was foreign to Horvath.

Paddy Davies was an idealist, and a mostly cheerful young man—the executive director of the People of the Glorious Creator. At age thirty-two, he could pass for twenty-five. "The People" was an ecumenical, nontheological religious umbrella beneath which various churches and sects—and any individuals who felt inclined—could merge to pursue common objectives. These days the overwhelming objective was peace. Paddy found joy in political conflict, and had many opponents but not so many enemies.

He didn't trust Jaromir Horvath, nor did Horvath trust him, but they had smoked the calumet, and united two of the more effective activist groups on Terra into a Peace Front. Which they directed, though reckless splinter groups might force their hands.

Together they watched Fritjof Ignatiev climb to the platform atop the mound. Ignatiev was the third leg of the Horvath-Davies-Ignatiev tripod. Horvath was all intellect and bile, a theorist and planner as bitter as Karl Marx, and with far less justification. He might convince, but he seldom inspired. While Paddy was charming and bright, but lacked charisma.

Ignatiev, on the other hand—tall, blond, and messianically sure of himself—had a compelling charisma that worked well on crowds. He radiated power, spirituality, and certainty, and his eloquence never ceased to impress. His intelligence, however, was less than ordinary. He listened closely to more powerful minds—notably those of Jaromir

Horvath and Paddy Davies—and imprinted their arguments. His grasp of those arguments was often weak, but he delivered them as gospel, and Wellesley Square this night held a sea of true believers, eager to hear.

Simply standing by the microphone and raising his long arms, Ignatiev caused the clamor to fade, the drums to stop. The bagpipes groaned to a halt. He had a magnificent voice. He didn't test the sound system, didn't think about what he was going to say. He simply lowered his arms, opened his mouth, and began.

When he finished, thirty minutes later, the crowd cheered their heads off. Nothing he'd said had differed in substance from what they'd heard before. Afterward one of the major news anchors termed it "the same tired old bunkum." But Ignatiev had given it a sense of higher truth. And if it did not specify new efforts, it bathed the demonstrators in a pool of righteousness, strengthened their sense of unity in the cause, and inspired new fervor. While undoubtedly, some among those who watched and listened on television were converted. At least temporarily.

It was, Paddy thought, up to himself and others now to capitalize on it. Create and implement projects that would make a difference. Projects already prepared, that together would change the flow, turn public opinion around, and end this dedication to war. He left uplifted, less by Ignatiev's thirty-minute oration than by its effect on the crowd.

Jaromir Horvath had not been inspired. His cynicism left no room for that. Instead he returned sour-faced to his small grim apartment to plan and write, and channel the movement's efforts. Rarely did he imagine success—the war effort abandoned, the Infinite Soul triumphant, the Wyzhñyñy invasion turned aside. But he would persist. It seemed to him that in another twenty years he'd be dead one way or another. And whether or not the Front prevailed in its struggle with a blind and perverse government, the all-creative, all-seeing Infinite Soul would take him into its loving arms.

Basically, Horvath was really rather orthodox.

Foster Peixoto had watched from his apartment high in the executive tower, as Jaromir Horvath had supposed.

But he'd watched alone, and via television, not from his balcony, which was much too far from the scene. When Fritjof Ignatiev had finished, and the cheering had finally faded, only then did the prime minister switch off the set and step onto the balcony. There his tall form was susceptible to a marksman with a long-range weapon, but that was not the sort of thing that worried him. In such matters he was a fatalist.

He considered the Peace Front an annoyance of limited potential. It could produce mischief, but not revolution. Nothing Ignatiev had said had changed his mind on that. An overwhelming majority of Terrans found the Front's position seriously unconvincing. If history had done nothing else, he told himself, it had demonstrated the creator's disinclination to meddle in human affairs. Humankind would live or die by its own efforts.

Presumably the Front didn't expect to convert the broad public to its point of view. And surely its members were contemplating more than demonstrations. Even now, extremist splinters would be planning serious terrorism and sabotage. Or efforts to lever the political and theological primitivism of refugee labor battalions into strikes and uprisings. That had been his reason for setting up a government cable channel—for and restricted to—refugee labor camps. A channel with mostly entertainment, and educational/propaganda programming that would not offend refugee ethno-religious sensitivities.

But a certain risk remained: benign, well-intentioned civic organizations had begun inviting groups of refugee laborers to members' homes on Sevendays. One could cautiously vet such organizations in advance, but they could not be controlled without stirring up civic resentment and uproar. Thus Peace Front agents could infiltrate, as Internal Security agents had. Fortunately, the damage the Front might accomplish through such groups seemed limited. His main worry was that the media might fan small flames into something more troublesome.

Foster, he chided, *you have taken steps; let IntSec do the worrying. If they uncover anything, act accordingly. Otherwise do not tire yourself over these matters.*

❖   ❖   ❖

Chang Lung-Chi had watched the video in his living room, from the comfort of his recliner. When the cheering had died, he switched off the set. *Such delicious self-righteousness,* he thought ironically, then grunted. *In their imaginations, they no doubt say the same of me.* He hoped devoutly they did not create serious problems. Neither he nor Foster believed they would. History showed that *Homo sapiens* had come a long way: it was far less susceptible to having its emotions hijacked by agitators. Though there was still room for worry. So they'd agreed: let the Front march and rant as long as their resistance didn't seriously impair the war effort. Since the Troubles, martial law was anathema. It would do more damage than a hundred Ignatievs. He was willing to tolerate even a certain amount of activist destructiveness, if it came to that.

But if it became serious . . . Then the trick would be to take countermeasures that met with broad public acceptance.

Chapter 18

Camp Mudhole

The *Madam Jao*—another converted bulk carrier—
emerged from warpspace less than two hundred thousand
miles off Pastor Lüneburger's World. Brigadier Pyong Pak
Singh had been waiting in his cabin to witness the event.
Pak, his staff, his regimental commanders and their staffs,
and their company commanders had made the trip from
Terra "live," sixteen days in hyperspace, then a half-dozen
hours in equally featureless warpspace. In between there'd
been perhaps a minute in familiar F-space, but he'd been
sleeping, and missed it.

They'd hardly noticed the lack of scenery. They'd spent
six hours a day in class, reviewing the cube of *New Ground
Tactics*, produced by War House staff. Each day ended with
another six of discussion and simulation exercises.

They needed to know the stuff cold, and see that their
troops did. Because if things came together as planned—
ship-building, fleet training, weapons delivery, and their own
preparation—in nine months they'd take this now utterly
green division to its home world, New Jerusalem, to wrest
it back from the invaders. Whether or not they succeeded,
it would be the Commonwealth's first ground campaign;

War House had decided to start ground warfare—not defending but attacking. And in the process, for better or worse, they'd learn a lot, both War House and his task force. Though War House wouldn't pay for it the way his people would.

Of course, Pak mused, *that assumes the invaders have gotten that far by then.* Given their progress to date, and the lack of resistance, they should, easily. But who could be sure about the behavior of an unfamiliar alien life-form? And how large a battle force they'd leave behind in the New Jerusalem System was anyone's guess. Guesses! He'd take Kulikov's and Sarrufs's guesses over anyone's, but still . . .

Pastor Lüneburger's World now occupied all but a corner of his screen. Seen from this distance it showed no sign of humanity. It was almost a core world—an inhabited planet within ten parsecs of Terra. It had been Terra's third outsystem colony, and the first and nearest of the first dispersion. But like most worlds of the first dispersion, it had been settled by an agrarian sect, in this case United Mennonites. Even after the century of Troubles had ended, and Terra had finally begun reconnecting with the worlds of the dispersion, acceptance of technology had been slow and selective on Lüneburger's world.

Not as slow as some, he reminded himself, thinking specifically of New Jerusalem. Before leaving Terra, he and his entire staff, down to platoon sergeants, had studied a cube on the planet their recruits were from. The ethnologist who'd done the narration had called New Jerusalem an unintentional reconstruction of the United States in the early 1800s.

Pak could feel the ship slowing under gravdrive. They must, he decided, be getting close to the F_1 layer. The view before him was probably centered on the gravitic vector they were riding down. Much of the surface was dominated by forest, with the larger rivers visible, and to one side, ocean. He couldn't make out towns yet, but they were there. Pastor Lüneburger's World held some 200 million humans, nearly twenty percent of them townsfolk. Leaving plenty of partially cleared and semiwild tracts on the fringes of settlement, areas well suited for training.

Somewhere down there was Camp Woldemars Stenders. They'd studied a cube on it, too, showing the Terran 4th Infantry Division in training there. The Terrans had dubbed it "Camp Mudhole." *Within the hour,* the brigadier thought, *I'll see it live.*

In the real world, Pak had never commanded anything larger than a battalion before—no one on Terra had—and under the circumstances it was natural to feel misgivings. But in sim training he'd commanded a corps, so his misgivings were mild.

The *Madam Jao* sat on an AG cushion five inches above the surface. Herded by officers and sergeants, the disembarking Jerries saw a world looking not greatly unlike New Jerusalem or Terra: the sky was blue, the vegetation green. It had rained not long before, and things even smelled more or less familiar.

Esau was disappointed. It seemed to him a different planet should look, smell and, in general, feel more different. He could as well have felt that way when he'd disembarked on Terra, but he'd been too uprooted and anxious then to pay much attention. Now, by contrast, he had a new and major stable element in his life—the army—and some idea of what the future held for him: training. Though what training would be like, he hadn't tried to imagine.

Once on the ground, the recruits formed ranks—they'd learned to do that much on Terra—and were led down a graveled road toward camp, lugging their duffel bags, and sweating.

Camp Stenders was unlike the temporary wartime camps on Terra. Basically it consisted of low-tech huts and sheds—concrete slabs, lumber, and linoleum—though with Plastosil panels from a newly built local factory. War House had earlier provided the camp's administrative staff—the bureaucrats who were an essential if not always appreciated part of the system. They'd kept the place running while the 4th Terran Infantry Division got its basic and advanced training there, then had sent them off to Camp Chu Teh, for unit training exercises with the Terran 3rd Armored.

Most of the key administrative elements were "retreads," retired military personnel from the marines or the small, pre-war, Terran planetary defense force. The company clerks, supply clerks, cooks and flunkies were conscripts not considered suitable for combat. They'd been rushed through three weeks of mini-basic, then enough specialist training to function, and learned the rest of their duties on the job.

The second-tier training cadre were holdovers from the 4th Terran, mature men who'd completed their basic and advanced training right there at Stenders, and earned a stripe or two. They would help the first-tier cadre train the recruits.

Esau and Jael Wesley knew nothing of all that. They did know the name of the world they were on, and the camp; reception center personnel had told them that much before loading them onto a snooze ship. The time of day they could only guess—somewhere in the middle, because the sun was high.

They didn't talk as they hiked—no one had told them they could—but there was lots of observing and more than a little wondering. It seemed to Esau that a pound wouldn't weigh a pound here, either, but closer to it than on Terra; apparently Lüneburger's World had grabbity, too. Meanwhile he was hungry. They'd each been given an energy bar and a carton of apple juice when they'd been wakened, but it hadn't been enough, for him at least. The road brought them to camp, a broad featureless area of featureless shedlike buildings. Companies began to peel off from the column, moving into company hutments. Shortly, B Company, 2nd Regiment halted on what they would learn was their company drill field and mustering ground.

The second-tier cadre, who'd marched them in, formed up to one side. All wore at least one chevron on their sleeves. In front of the recruits stood the company's firsttier cadre—commissioned and noncommissioned officers. Like the recruits, they'd just arrived, but been bussed to the company area. A step in front of them stood a large, thick-bellied, fiftyish marine retread, with three stripes and three rockers on his sleeve. "All right, recruits," he bellowed, "listen up. I am Master Sergeant Henkel. To you I am god. You are not part of the 587th Infantry *Training*

Regiment, as originally informed. Instead you are Company B, 2nd Infantry Regiment, First New Jerusalem Infantry Division. If any of you goddamn sonsabitches can't remember that when asked, you're in deep shit. So I'll repeat it once: this is B Company . . . 2nd Infantry Regiment . . . 1st New Jerusalem Infantry Division."

A voice called from the ranks, loud, clear, and righteous. It was the student speaker of the books, Esau realized, the guy who'd told him about grabbity. "Master Sergeant Henkel, sir," the youth called, "in addressing us, you have twice taken God's name in vain and used several obscenities. Offending everyone, and more serious, offending God. You—"

The sergeant interrupted, his voice soft but easily heard, and dominating. "What's your name, recruit?"

"Isaiah Vernon, sir."

"Come up here, Recruit Vernon."

The young man did so.

"Do you know what pushups are, soldier?"

"Yessir."

"Good. Drop down and give me fifty."

"Fifty, sir?" Vernon sounded unbelieving. He'd never been much for sports or exercise.

"Make that a hundred, for backflash."

"For . . . but . . . I can't do a hundred!"

The voice almost purred. "Make that a hundred and fifty, and start NOW!"

Suddenly realizing his situation, Vernon dropped to the ground and started. In Lüneburger's relatively modest gravity—1.25 gees compared to New Jerusalem's 1.42—he managed to squeeze out fifteen, then collapsed. To lie there looking up at Henkel. The sergeant's voice became almost kindly.

"Recruit Vernon, you are guilty of backflash, disrespecting a superior, and refusing an order. Considering how green you are, I can overlook your ignorance. But not your stupidity. Common sense should tell you you don't mouth off like that to a superior. And here, anyone with a stripe on his sleeve or an insignia on his collar is your superior. Tonight, report to the orderly room at 2200 hours, to receive company punishment. Now, on your feet."

Pale-faced, Vernon struggled to his feet while Henkel scanned the recruits. When the sergeant spoke again, his voice was no longer soft. "Look at you!" he bellowed. "You look like some goddamn dog shit you out! STAND STRAIGHT!"

Every recruit straightened. Esau's eyes sized the sergeant up. He could, he told himself, throw down the big tub of lard and sit on him, but he doubted the satisfaction would be worth the punishment.

The sergeant turned sharply to the company commander and saluted. "Sir," he said, "with your permission, I will have the men shown to their quarters."

"Do so," the captain said mildly.

Before getting a break, they were shown to their huts, two squads per hut; assigned cots and open-faced wall lockers; given a guided, familiarization tour of the company area while marching in ranks; then issued bedding, field uniforms, and boots. Finally they were taken to the drill field, where they practiced close-order drill for an hour. Esau wondered what possible good close-order drill was.

Finally they were released to use the latrine and wash for supper. The company latrine was a shed with two long parallel rooms, one with two rows of washbowls and mirrors, the other with a row of commodes, and long, trough-like urinals. At one end of the building was the shower room, about twenty by thirty feet, with showerheads at thirty-inch intervals all the way around, and wooden duckboards on the floor.

Most of the recruits headed directly for the latrine. Others went first to the huts, to get towels and soap. Jael went to their platoon sergeant, above whose left shirt pocket "SFC Hawkins, A." was indelibly printed. What SFC meant, she didn't know, but she already knew the three chevrons, and guessed that the two rockers below them stood for increased authority. "Sergeant," she said hesitantly, "where do I go?"

"Go?"

"To—relieve myself."

He regarded her mildly. "There is only the latrine," he answered. "If you are willing, you can use it when the others do. Otherwise you can wait till they're done."

She looked at him with dismay. Dismay and pain, it seemed to him. He made a decision. "Come with me," he said, turning, and led her to the orderly room. There Master Sergeant Henkel ruled. When Sergeant Hawkins stepped to his desk, Henkel looked up at him. "What can I do for you, Sergeant?" he asked.

"Sergeant, I need to speak with the company commander."

"Bypassing your platoon leader?"

Hawkins' voice took an edge. "This is urgent."

Henkel gestured. "Go ahead."

The plaque on the door read CO. Hawkins went to it and knocked, leaving Jael standing in the middle of the orderly room. Through the door, a voice called, "Come in." Hawkins went in and closed the door behind him.

"Sir," he said, "something has come up that needs your attention."

"And what is that?"

Hawkins explained.

Captain Martin Mulvaney Singh's red eyebrows rose. "You've already presented her the options, such as they are, but it's not really practical for her to wait. She'll just have to use the latrine when the men do."

"I realize that, sir. But these Jerries are fundamentalist Christians. It may require some setting up. To lessen embarrassment and avoid incidents."

Mulvaney frowned. His briefing on the Jerries hadn't covered situations like this. "Being a Jerrie, she'll find it embarrassing enough anyway," he said, then paused. "Call her in." Hawkins opened the door to the orderly room and ordered her in. She stood before the captain sturdy but forlorn, and with pain that was more than psychological.

I wonder how old she is, Mulvaney thought. *Seventeen? Eighteen?* "Sergeant Hawkins explained your difficulty to me," he said mildly. "He has already told you the alternatives, such as they are. But it will seldom be practical for you to wait, so for the most part you'll have to use it when the men do. However, the company will muster before supper, and I will set certain rules of behavior. Which—" His face turned stern. "Which they will obey, as you will, or receive company punishment."

She nodded. Her answer was little more than a whisper. "Yes, sir."

He gestured to a door in the back of the room. "Meanwhile, just this one time, you may use mine if you wish."

"Thank you, sir," she repeated. Her gratitude was too heartfelt to be hidden by her embarrassment.

When she'd entered his little toilet and closed the door behind her, the captain spoke quietly to Sergeant Hawkins. "What is she doing in this company?"

"Sir, there's another Wesley in the platoon. Recruit Esau Wesley. I believe they're husband and wife."

"Ah. What does he look like?"

"Bigger than most Jerries, sir, and looks—like no one to fool with."

"Um-hmm. Good. And Jerries are supposed to be pretty straitlaced. All right, stay here till she comes out. Then take her outside and dismiss her."

Shortly afterward she emerged, and left with Sergeant Hawkins. Which reminded Captain Mulvaney of something he needed to do. Getting to his feet, he stepped to the orderly room door. "Sergeant Henkel," he said, "come in here please," then returned to his desk and sat down.

Henkel came in and stood at attention. He'd spent thirty years around officers. He could smell when something was wrong. "Yes, sir?"

"Sergeant Henkel, the Sikh style of command is different than yours. Therefore I am reassigning your command duties. That will give you more time for your administrative tasks, which in any case have been very much your main duties."

He paused.

"Yessir," Henkel said, but his eyes made it clear that his "yessir" was acknowledgement, not agreement. "You're aware, sir, that my duties are prescribed in our TO."

Their eyes met, the sergeant's resentful, the captain's mild. But behind that mildness was no give at all. "An old marine gunnery sergeant like yourself," he said, "doesn't need to be reminded of my authority. And the appeal authority is back on Terra. Pod time each way is fourteen days. I have no idea how long the turnaround time is at

War House, in times like these, but I'm sure things are prioritized by importance.

"Meanwhile, War House has seen fit to provide field commanders with extraordinary authority. The army, the fleet—even the Corps are re-creating themselves, doing things in new ways, to fit the time and resources available. And War House is giving us elbow room to do it."

Henkel's resentment was fading. He'd never had a CO like this one before, and there was something about the man he liked.

"Look around," Mulvaney went on. "The two-tier cadre system itself is new, a necessary response to the enormous training load, and the lack of experienced personnel."

Again the captain paused, then spoke with fresh crispness. "Field Sergeant Fossberg will carry out the command duties that you would otherwise carry. Tomorrow, you and he will go over your job description, write up the changes, and give them to me for approval. By 1700 hours."

The old marine saluted sharply. "Yessir, Captain," he said. "By 1700 hours tomorrow." He still was less than happy with this surprising development, but it would make life easier; he'd mellowed with age, and the captain held a handful of aces.

The company stood in ranks in the slanting rays of an evening sun, facing the company commander and Field Sergeant Kirpal Fossberg Singh.

"Men," Mulvaney said, "when I call you men, I include the sole woman in the company. It has been brought to my attention that among the people of New Jerusalem, men and women do not bathe together or use a latrine together. However, we do not have separate facilities for the two genders, and during duty hours, the opportunities to relieve yourselves are few and crowded.

"Therefore, it will be necessary that men and women use the latrine together. And the shower." He paused. The company stood at ease, but furtive glances flicked, largely avoiding Jael, who stood fiery faced.

Mulvaney went on. "I have consulted with Recruit Spieler about this. For any who don't know him, Spieler is a speaker of the books. He tells me that your religion forbids people to show themselves naked to others. That means men to men, as well as women to men and vice versa. So using the showers with the other gender should be no worse a religious misdemeanor than using it with others of your own gender.

"Some of you will also be sharing a hut with your female comrade. At appropriate times you'll be changing clothes there. So—" He paused, then raised his voice. "LISTEN UP! When someone of the other gender is naked in your presence, you will not stare, you will not make comments or gestures, you will not touch them, even accidentally! If you do, you will receive company punishment! Which is whatever I say it is, or whatever Sergeant Fossberg says it is, or your platoon leader or platoon sergeant!"

Again the captain paused. "You are in the army now, and you'll find many things different than you're used to. If you have difficulties with this, talk to Recruit Spieler about it. I've appointed him the company's religious advisor.

"Now! Back to business! The mess hall opens for supper at 1730 hours. That's in fifteen minutes. It closes at 1815. At 1900 you will muster here in field uniform for an evening speed march."

He turned to his field sergeant. "Sergeant Fossberg, the company is yours."

Fossberg nodded. "Thank you, sir." He turned back to the recruits. "Company," he bellowed, "dismissed!"

That evening the company learned what speed march meant, at least to Sergeant Fossberg, at least on that day. They jogged an easy quarter mile, then walked another, alternating the two for an hour and a half in the warm humid summer evening. And on Pastor Lüneburger's World, the hours, minutes, days, were 1.13 times as long as Terran standard. As they ran, they were joined by the local version of mosquitoes, which came out in force about sundown. And though the recruits had lost essentially zero conditioning during stasis, few had had distance running as an important part of their life-style at home. At 2100 hours they were dismissed, slick with sweat. Knowing intuitively that the experience had been just a foretaste of the weeks to come.

Then they headed for the showers. The most difficult thing Jael Wesley had ever done was go to the shower room with no more than a towel wrapped around her. Wrapped around her chest, it was not adequate to hide her loins, while around her waist it left her breasts exposed. She draped it around her waist, and with a truculent-looking Esau glowering beside her, walked to the shower room. Then of course came the new most difficult: she had to remove the towel to shower. Esau stayed by her, his scowl daring anyone to say or do or perhaps think anything out of line. If they did, they hid it. Any erections were concealed by turning away.

After a few days, mixed showering would seem routine, though Jael was never totally comfortable with it.

At 2200 hours the Charge of Quarters threw a switch, and the lights went off throughout the trainees' huts. But the night was clear, and rich in stars, and after a minute, Esau's eyes adjusted. Dimly he could make out the cot next to his, and the shadowed form of his wife. It stimulated him; he wanted her very much. Nonetheless he waited; there were men all around them, not yet asleep.

He lay there for half an hour anticipating, not sleepy at all despite the long day. Then, leaning half out of bed on his left hand, he reached toward her with his right and touched her arm. She flinched out of sleep as if burned, sat half up, then saw her husband's arm, and rested her hand on his. He swung his legs out of bed, and stood. She stood too. For pajamas, the troops wore short, dull-green summer drawers, Jael with a dull-green T-shirt. Esau paused, and from his locker took his poncho. Jael did the same, and they padded very carefully out of the hut. Keeping to the shadows, Esau led her through the night to the latrine building, and around behind it. There was the water heater room, its door without a lock; he'd done some advance scouting. They didn't speak till they were inside with the door closed, and didn't leave for nearly an hour.

Back in bed, Esau thought about how he might get a mattress—something for padding—and stash it behind the large water heater. Jael, for her part, thought about what might happen if she got pregnant. She hadn't in six months of trying back home. What a cruel thing it would be to get pregnant now.

The Wesleys weren't the last recruits to get to sleep that night. Not by a long shot. It was 0255 hours when Isaiah Vernon settled groaning onto his cot. He'd discovered one form that company punishment could take. Under the occasional eye of the Charge of Quarters, he'd dug a hole some six feet long, six wide, and six deep. In loamy clay, while water seeped in around his feet. Then, when the hole had met with the CQ's approval, he was ordered to climb out, urinate into it, and fill it up again.

He'd been careful not to ask why.

Chapter 19

Another Shortage

In the Office of Military Resource Planning, Captain Bruno Horvath scanned a message on his screen. "It seems we have a shortage, Colonel," he said laconically. "A *critical* shortage."

Colonel Wiktor Kobayashi raised a graying bushy eyebrow and grunted. There were endless shortages, most of them flagged critical. "Is that so? What's this one?"

"Nothing new. An old one getting more urgent." The captain flicked it to the colonel's screen. "With three red flags now," he added.

Kobayashi looked. It was the shortage of qualified warbot volunteers again. Warbots carried the cyborg concept to the ultimate, and lots of them were needed, but qualifying was tough. You needed to have lost at least three limbs, including both arms, or two limbs and your eyes, or be dying from incurable injury or illness, or be serving a life term in prison. The central nervous system had to be functional, intelligence normal or above, and personality profile acceptable. Thus most quadriplegics, amputees and convicts were ineligible, as well as older invalids with significant decline in CNS function.

"Nothing to it," the colonel said wryly. "We'll assign a regiment to meet the evacuation ships with swords, and cut both arms and one leg off everyone on board."

"Sorry, Colonel, but we've got a serious shortage of swords. Would laser saws be all right?"

Kobayashi was rarely sarcastic, and didn't like it when he was. And the shortage of warbots was real and serious; sarcasm wouldn't reduce it. It directly and seriously affected the combat readiness of all infantry divisions, of which 63 were now in training. Some of those divisions had begun or were approaching interactive tactical training—so-called unit training. Within five months, the plans called for a total of 300 divisions in service or training. And tactics—even strategy—called for each to have a "normal" contingent of warbots.

He was well-informed on the subject, and knew the arithmetic too well. Three hundred divisions, each with eight regiments, each regiment with two platoons of warbots. Forty-eight hundred warbot platoons; some 110,000 bots overall. But the latest figures showed only 4,400 qualified volunteers. If every one of them completed training successfully, that would still mean fewer than two bots, let alone platoons, per regiment. And for most warbot tasks and missions, "organics"—ordinary infantry—were not suitable substitutes.

Producing trained warbots took time and care. First the central nervous system had to be extracted from the body. Then came its painstaking neuro-electronic bottling. Installing the bottled CNS in a battle servo was similarly demanding. And finally a period of neurological, and sometimes psychological detraumatization and "breaking in" was required, before the individual was ready for warbot training.*

---

* A warbot consists of a mobile, electro-mechanical weapons system termed a "battle servo," or simply "servo," containing and controlled by a human central nervous system sometimes termed the "kiddo" to emphasize its humanness. The kiddo is installed in a life-support system termed a bioelectronic interface unit (BEIU, or "bottle") which is neuro-electronically interfaced with the servo. The composite constitutes the warbot. The individual kiddo is *never* called a warbot.

But the basic problem was the demanding legal qualifications for volunteers.

"Shit," the colonel muttered. The captain was tempted to answer "Yessir. I'll be right back, sir," but he sensed that just now, humor would not be appreciated. Certainly not that kind.

Kobayashi touched a pair of keys and began to dictate.

> I see no possibility of providing the necessary warbots without (a) modifying the legal qualifications for volunteers, and (b) promoting intensively. Therefore I STRONGLY RECOMMEND that the army:
> (1) Accept candidates with two useable limbs; volunteers with four useable limbs but who are blind; and volunteers with debilitating conditions, even though promising research is under way toward a cure. The latter limitation in particular permits all manner of opinions to block us.

It wasn't the first time Wiktor Kobayashi had proposed that. But previously he'd been rebuffed by government attorneys under political pressures. This time he would add to it. If he became sufficiently extreme—who knew? They might go along with his more moderate suggestions.

> (2) Attach recruiters to all hospitals, including emergency rooms, with access to candidates over the objections of hospital personnel.
> (3) Accept able-bodied volunteers—if they can pass appropriate mental and psychological tests—and to hell with family approvals.

Number three awed the captain. It seemed to him that reasonable mental and psychological tests would automatically eliminate able-bodied volunteers. And the part about attorneys and family approvals would offend a lot of politicians.

He hoped it wouldn't result in Kobayashi getting

transferred. If it did, he'd probably be named to replace
him, a dreadful thought.

> (4) Before long, we will start shipping divisions
> to combat sites. There they will suffer casual-
> ties, and some will become bot eligible. There-
> fore I ALSO STRONGLY RECOMMEND (a) that
> each division carry neuro-electronic conversion
> teams, and extra BEIUs and servos; (b) *that all
> organic trainees get effective virtuality train-
> ing on warbot operations and tactics.* The train-
> ing they already receive as organics will go a
> long way toward getting them ready. Let the
> motto be, "today's serious casualty, tomorrow's
> warbot."
>
> As it now stands, the warbot situation makes a
> charade of our entire defense program. If
> prompt and effective measures will not be taken
> to correct it, I recommend throwing in with the
> Peace Front and rolling out the red carpet for
> the invaders. It will save a lot of effort and
> money, and the result will be the same.
>
> (Signed) Colonel Wiktor Kobayashi, Assistant
> Director for Human Military Resources.

Captain Horvath stared aghast. Kobayashi scanned his
monitor, then pressed *SEND*. Thereby committing professional suicide.

Horvath blew softly through pursed lips. Maybe a suicide
was needed. Maybe somewhere up the line, someone would
pay attention. Maybe Lefty Sarruf would lay *his* neck on the
block; surely someone would pay attention then. *If it comes
down to it,* Horvath decided—*if they can Kobayashi and
promote me to the job, I'll send the same goddamn message
up lines, verbatim. And fuck the pettifogging, obfuscating,
political sons of bitches. It's the survival of the human species they're pissing around with.*

Chapter 20

A Day in the Life

B Company was gasping and staggering when it reached the top of the slope. And sweating profusely, although the sun was still low. This was only their third week, but already their morning run had been extended to thirty long Lüneburger minutes. And this was the first time it had been routed up what the Terrans had dubbed "Drag Ass Hill."

Despite their cadre, who'd snapped relentlessly at their heels, their ranks had strung out pretty badly on the hill. But once at the top, their pace firmed. Through stinging, sweat-blurred eyes they could see the regimental area some five hundred yards ahead, and their company hutment with its orderly rows of small gray buildings.

Almost there, thought Esau Wesley. Grimly. He'd never liked taking orders, even as a boy from his father. And looking back, his father's orders had mostly made sense. But where was the sense of running uphill? Or running at all, if you weren't in a hurry? For toughness, they'd been told. For physical conditioning. He had no doubt he was tougher than anyone in their cadre.

"Hup, hup, hup two three four!" The voice was Sergeant Fossberg's, and seemingly effortless, though he was sweating as much as any. Esau didn't notice. He was too busy being angry. Then, some three hundred yards from the company area, Fossberg shouted, "You're on your own! The last ones to reach the mess hall and slap the wall get punishment!"

Esau snarled his anger—wanted to shout it. Lowering his head, he ran hard. Too hard. With a hundred yards to go, his legs began to fail. He fought it, eyes slitted with effort, his gait increasingly heavy-legged. 2nd Platoon had been second in the column, yet without being aware of it, Esau had fought nearly to the front of the now badly strung-out company. Anyone in his way, he'd elbowed aside. But he staggered the last twenty yards, barely keeping his feet. When he'd slapped the wall, he stumbled aside and fell gasping to the ground.

After eight or ten seconds he looked back. Most of the company was still coming. Some had slowed to a walk, alternating with a staggering trot to avoid being last.

Jael was not one of the very last. Perhaps fifteen or twenty were farther back, most of them from 3rd and 4th Platoons, who'd started out in the rear. Wobbling, she staggered through the fallen and touched the wall.

A few had given up the struggle entirely, and knelt or lay in the dirt along the way. It was their names the cadre spoke into their belt recorders. Esau could hear someone retching—more than one—their heaving dry; the company hadn't eaten breakfast yet.

Although they didn't know it, B Company's trainees had just been through a test. Less of themselves than of the training pace. Was it too hard? How much could they tolerate?

Fossberg didn't let them stay collapsed for long. "Company!" he bellowed. "On your feet! Fall in and stand at attention!"

Their platoon sergeants and ensigns herded them into ranks, where they stood, still breathing hard, facing the company commander and field sergeant. It was Captain Mulvaney who addressed them. "All right, B Company," he said, "stand at ease." As always his voice was effortless but easily heard. "You're making progress. You've got a long way to go, but you've started out nicely. Some not as well as others, but you'll catch up. We'll see to that. It's our job."

He paused, scanning the ranks in front of him. Esau noticed resentfully that the captain wasn't sweating. He hadn't run, just strolled out of his office to watch them arrive.

"Now," Mulvaney continued, "everyone on the ground." To a man, the trainees dropped to their bellies, knowing what followed but not how many. "Give me—twenty-five!" Up from twenty; that was new. The captain began to count, and the ranks of trainees pumped pushups to match—in strict form; they'd already learned the penalties for cheating. Besides, for most, even in Lüneburger's 1.25 gees, twenty-five pushups were readily doable. Farm work or other hard labor in New Jerusalem's gravity had given them abundant strength.

For a few, including Jael, twenty-five were only marginally or not quite doable. But they were young, and with company punishment and New Jerusalem's work ethic, they did their best. And they did at least twenty sets of pushups a day; they were gaining.

" . . . twenty-four, twenty-five. All right, on your feet!" Mulvaney said, and the trainees stood. "The mess hall opens for breakfast at 0730 hours. You will fall out for muster at 0815 in field uniform. Company dismissed!"

The ranks dispersed, the trainees hurrying to their huts for towels and soap. Captain Martin Mulvaney Singh and Field Sergeant Kirpal Fossberg Singh watched them go. "How is recruit Jael Wesley doing?" Mulvaney asked.

"According to Sergeant Hawkins, sir, she asked if she could go to the dispensary. When he asked her if she was pregnant, she blushed bright red and told him no. And that she didn't intend to be. I'd say she's smart and responsible."

"Or hoping perhaps to be promiscuous?" It occurred to Mulvaney that some of his trainees, removed from their straitlaced culture, might cast off its inhibitions. Though Jael Wesley didn't seem like a rebel.

"Hawkins doesn't think so, sir. He doesn't think she'd find many takers if she was. Her husband is the dominant recruit in their squad. One of the two or three most dominant in their platoon."

"Apparently they've found a way to have intercourse."

"Apparently, sir." Sergeant to sergeant, Hawkins had told

Fossberg they snuck off to the water heater room, but
Fossberg didn't volunteer the information. Though if
Mulvaney had asked, he'd have told him.

"Tell Sergeant Hawkins to be alert for any undesirable
effects in their hut. The briefing we received on the Jerries
was long on generalities but short on details."

"Yessir, Captain."

Fossberg headed for the noncommissioned cadre's
latrine. The captain's questions had inspired one of his
own. *How did a young girl like her, from a primitive
fundamentalist planet like New Jerusalem, learn about birth
control pills?* He decided to ask Recruit Spieler, as circum-
spectly as he could. These Jerries were turning out to be
an interesting experience.

Esau had gotten over having to shepherd his wife to
the latrine, though he still hovered watchfully near her
in the shower. And as usual, they used adjacent washbowls.
This morning while they washed, he murmured to her:
"You fell way behind this morning on the run." His tone
was accusatory.

"Not till the last," she countered. "When we had to
sprint."

"That's what I meant, in the sprint. You embarrassed me."

"I did the best I could." She said it quietly, without
apology.

"Your best?" he muttered. "You were way back near the
end of 4th Platoon."

She said nothing, and avoided looking at him.

"Let's see if you can do better on the chin-ups this
morning."

She didn't answer that, either.

At the head of the mess line were several chinning bars.
Each trainee was required to do all the chins he could
before going inside to eat, monitored critically by two or
more cadre. This time Esau did thirty-nine, and Jael
struggled out eleven, with Corporal Fong watching.

"Good work, Recruit Wesley," the corporal said. "That's
up from four the first day." The number identified which
Wesley he was talking to.

"Thank you, Corporal," she said.

As the couple entered the mess hall, Esau jostled her. "Don't you have any sense of decency?" he hissed.

"What?"

"You know what I mean," he murmured. "Fong telling you 'good work.' For eleven puny chin-ups! I did thirty-nine, and he didn't say a thing to me. He wants you to commit adultery with him."

He'd turned his face to her when he said it, and without thinking or speaking, she slugged him in the left eye, almost knocking him down. The 1st cook had been standing with a spatula, serving scrambled eggs, and saw the exchange.

"YOU TWO!" he bellowed, pointing with the spatula. "WHAT'RE YOUR NAMES?"

Esau spoke for them both, glaring at Jael, who stood red-faced but without visible repentence.

"Report to Sergeant Henkel at the orderly room, both of you! Now! And tell him you're not getting back in here till I have his okay. In writing. Now out! OUT!"

They hurried out, aware that everyone in the mess hall had heard and seen their ejection. Esau was about to berate Jael some more, when Lance Corporal Fong called after them.

"Where do you think you're going?"

"The cook just sent us to the orderly room," Esau answered.

Fong pointed at the chinning bars. "You know the orders. Trainees do exit chin-ups when they leave the mess hall."

Esau made no move to comply. "We didn't eat."

Fong's reply was not particularly loud, but it was prompt, and strong with intention. "Recruit, that was backflash. Let's see those chin-ups. *Now!* And they'd better be good." Esau turned to the bars, pivoting violently enough, it seemed to Fong he almost screwed his boot into the ground. The Jerrie homesteader snapped off forty-two chin-ups this time; the corporal was impressed in spite of himself. Fong had trained with the 4th Terran Infantry, and some of these Jerries were already stronger than most of his buddies had been when they finished their training. And *their* cadre had been Masadans!

By the time Esau had finished and was free to leave, his wife was out of sight on her way to the orderly room. Her twelve hadn't taken a third as long as his forty-two, and when Esau had finished his chin-ups, Fong had ordered him to do fifty pushups for the backflash.

At the orderly room, Esau found Jael standing before Master Sergeant Gerritt Henkel, who clearly had been waiting for him. "What kept you, recruit?" Henkel asked.

Asked it like a cat, Esau thought, waiting for the mouse to move. He told the master sergeant how many chin-ups he'd done, and about the fifty pushups, not withholding what they'd been for.

The ex-marine looked at the couple appraisingly. "That's quite an eye you've got there, Recruit."

Esau said nothing. He looked like he could chew rocks.

"What happened? I'm asking *you*, Recruit Esau Wesley."

"My wife was disrespectful, Sergeant. So I upbraided her, and she struck me."

"Disrespectful? Really! And upbraided! My my!" The mockery was thick. "Tell me what you said, as exactly as you can."

Esau did. The sergeant turned his eyes to Jael. "Is that the way you remember it, Recruit Jael Wesley?"

She nodded. "Yes, Sergeant," she said quietly, and Henkel turned again to Esau.

"Where exactly did this happen?"

"In the mess hall, Sergeant. In line, by the tray stack. Then the cook kicked us out without breakfast."

"Um-hmm. You're in 2nd Platoon, right?"

"Yessir."

"Recruit Esau Wesley, go sit in that chair." He pointed. "Recruit Jael Wesley, you sit in that one." He pointed at the opposite end of the row, then turned to the company clerk who'd been watching with half a grin. "Corporal, go tell Sergeant Hawkins what we've got here. This is his problem. For now, anyway."

The clerk left briskly, and was back in five minutes. Hawkins, on the other hand, didn't hurry. He finished his breakfast first. If Henkel had wanted him right away, he'd have said so.

Meanwhile, for the most part Esau avoided looking at

his wife. But he was angry. His left eye was swollen half shut. It would be black, too, and everyone would be talking about it. He shot an occasional, resentful glance at Jael, but she never returned it, simply faced straight ahead, her expression stony. It struck him then how pretty she was in profile. And how strong her character, even if she was in the wrong. His anger softened.

When Hawkins arrived, he took them both outside, without berating them at all. "Esau Wesley," he said, "drop down and give me forty. On my count." As Esau got down, Hawkins continued. "Jael Wesley, drop down and give me twenty-five."

"What!?" Esau demanded, looking up. "Me forty and her twenty-five? That's unfair!"

"And that, Recruit Esau Wesley, is backflash," Hawkins said calmly. "Which will cost you. But not now. Later. And for her, twenty-five is as hard as forty is for you. Harder. Now, on my count . . ."

When they'd finished and stood before him, Hawkins told them their idiocy had cost them breakfast, because they had less than ten minutes before muster. "Report to me at the orderly room this evening, both of you, at 2030 hours. Among other things, I will tell you then what your punishment is. You, Esau Wesley, for repeated backflash. And you, Jael Wesley, for striking another recruit."

Then Hawkins turned and walked away. They needed more than punishment, he told himself, but he wasn't sure what.

From muster, where the trainees gave their cadre twenty-five more pushups, B Company jogged three quarters of a mile to a lecture shed, where they dropped down and did another twenty-five before entering. Then they filed inside and took their seats on wooden benches, benches hard enough, the trainees were less likely to fall asleep, despite their heavy exercise regimen.

The presenter was a major from Division, who stood before them in a clean, pressed field uniform. He also wore a crimson turban, instead of the field caps of the company cadre.

"What you're about to watch on the screen," he began, "is a presentation of regimental and small unit tactics. While you watch it, try to spot just what's going on. The better you understand it, the better fighting men you'll be, and the less likely you'll be killed. Afterward we'll go over it again.

"Incidentally, it is *not* a recording of actual fighting. So far as we know, there hasn't *been* any actual fighting with the invaders. They've attacked only undefended colonies. But the animated visuals you'll see"—he gestured at the large wall screen—"are as realistic as they can be made. Realistic enough to be mistaken for real."

The entire company cadre was there, including Captain Mulvaney and Master Sergeant Henkel. The cube was one of a set newly arrived from Terra, via pod, and none of the company staff had seen it before. The major had, the night previous. It had its own audio, but he had a list of questions to expect, and tips on how to deal with them.

The audience watched the whole forty-five-minute first run-through without a pause. Captain Mulvaney would have bet that none of them dozed. Then they got a fifteen-minute break that began and ended with pushups for the trainees, with time to rassle around or use a field latrine in between. Afterward the same cubeage was shown again, but this time with numerous built-in pauses where a voice-over discussed the tactics they were watching. When that run-through was finished, there was another break like the first—pushups, latrine, and more pushups.

Afterward the major took questions, almost all of them from the cadre. That went on till it was time to leave for lunch. Outside, the trainees gave their cadre a quick twenty-five, then double-timed briskly in a column of fours to the company area, where there was just time for another twenty-five and to wash up before their noon meal—broiled ground beef, mashed potatoes and gravy, crisp green beans, bread and butter with apple sauce, rich bread pudding, and coffee.

The 1st cook didn't say a word to Esau and Jael, and they said nothing to each other. They simply ate as if they hadn't eaten for a day. Actually it had been eighteen hours.

❖   ❖   ❖

After the noon meal and the break that followed, the company mustered, did pushups, then jogged to the regiment's physical training area. 2nd Platoon began its workout on "the log yard." Each five-man fire team had its own log, which massed roughly two hundred and fifty pounds, Terran. Working together, they lifted it to their collective right shoulders, then to arms' length overhead, then down onto their left shoulders, and back onto the ground. From there they repeated the sequence in \reverse, and again, and again, until they had to fight it up. Esau was the leader of his five-man fire team, a team that unfortunately included not only Jael, but Isaiah Vernon, two of the weakest in the platoon. Esau had put himself in the middle, between Jael and Isaiah, to make up for their lack of strength. Before they were done, he was gritting his teeth, partly from exhaustion, partly exasperation.

That done, they did twenty-five pushups. Then, driven by barking second-tier cadre, they ran hard to the chin-up bars, a bar per man, where they alternated between sets of ten chin-ups, fifteen pushups, and thirty side-straddle hops, each exercise serving as rest from the one before. After six rounds of those, they jogged to the obstacle course and ran it, climbing walls on knotted ropes, shinnying up rough-textured poles, vaulting or bellying over low fences, crawling through culverts, and ending with a hard, sixty-yard sprint.

They finished on what the Terran trainees had termed "the junkyard." The name had been passed on by the second-tier cadre. It had rows of stout iron pipes, the ends of which had been stuck in tins of concrete before it hardened. Each crude barbell massed roughly seventy pounds Terran, hefting about eighty-eight on Lüneburger's World. The exercises were led by a husky second-tier cadreman, a corporal, who'd finished twenty-six weeks of training only three weeks earlier, and was in superb condition. Mostly they did high repetition cleans and jerks. To rest between sets, they lay on the ground and did leg raises, pushups, and situps.

They'd been in the PT area every day since they'd been

at Camp Mudhole (which so far had been more of a dust
hole), but never had they been pushed as they were this
day. It was in the junkyard that Isaiah Vernon collapsed
in the sun. Two cadremen helped him into the shade until
an ambulance arrived.

From the PT area, the company ran to "the pond"—a
long, dozed-out depression covered with a foot of sand, then
flooded by damming a creek. It was new to them. They
ran toward it at a good lope, waiting for their cadre to halt
them. No one did, and to their own astonishment, the
trainees ran fully clothed into the water. Only when the
last of them was in did Fossberg bellow "COMPANY
HALT! REST!"

For the next twenty minutes they sported in the
water. There was a lot of laughter, splashing, wrestling,
some holding under, and a few brief fistfights that were
broken up by cadre. When it was over, there were no
pushups. Instead they marched back to the company area
in their soggy boots and socks, the clothes drying on their
bodies. They were even dismissed without further pushups.

They changed clothes before supper, which was preceded
and followed by the usual chin-ups. At 1845 hours they
mustered again, and marched to a lecture shed where they
viewed another cube. This one was an assemblage of
preinvasion scenes from worlds since captured by the
invaders. Presumably the people shown, those who'd
declined evacuation, were dead now. The trainees left
more soberly than usual.

Captain Martin Mulvaney Singh, Ensign Erik Berg
Singh, and Sergeant First Class Arjan Hawkins Singh didn't
go with them. They were in Mulvaney's office, discussing the case of Recruit Isaiah Vernon, and whether they'd
cranked up the physical demands on the trainees too rapidly. War House wanted them pushed hard, and Division
had provided guidelines and schedules, but the company
cadre retained considerable latitude. Berg pointed out that
most of the trainees were meeting the demands very well.
They were not only heavyworlders, and young; they'd also

worked at farming or other heavy labor. And Hawkins pointed out that the amount of running would soon stabilize. At midweek they'd be issued weapons and pack frames, and march to more distant field locations, carrying sandbags on the march.

They were interrupted by the Charge of Quarters knocking on the door. "Recruit Isaiah Vernon is here, Captain. They just brought him back from the infirmary."

"Good," Mulvaney answered. "Just a minute." He looked at the others. "I'll have him sent in, and question him. It may cast light on the subject." He looked toward the CQ. "Send him in, Corporal."

The CQ ushered a subdued Isaiah Vernon into the room, then closed the door behind him. The commanding officer looked the trainee over. "At ease, Vernon," Mulvaney said. "Let me see your medical release."

Vernon stepped over and handed a sheet of paper to him. Mulvaney scanned it. "Simple exhaustion," he read, and looked up at the young Jerrie. "Not heat exhaustion. Good." He paused, holding the youth with his eyes. "You've been having a harder time of it than the others. Tell me about that."

Vernon didn't hesitate. "The others—lived differently back home than I did," he said. "My father's a speaker of the books, and I was to be one, too. So when other boys were working in the field or the woods with their fathers, or in the tannery or sawmill or whatever, I studied scripture. Instead of lifting and carrying, grubbing stumps and ditching swales, I read and memorized. I did barn chores and cut and brought in firewood, but that was about it. And I never cared much for games or footraces or wrestling. So I wasn't properly ready for training to be a soldier."

The frown had left Mulvaney's eyes. "I see," he said thoughtfully, then made a decision. The abler trainees shouldn't be held back for the least able. "Recruit Vernon, I'll see about getting you transferred to administrative duties in Regiment or Division. Meanwhile—"

Remarkably the young man interrupted. "Sir?"

Mulvaney frowned. "What is it, Recruit?"

"Sir, I can do this training. I can! I quit this afternoon.

I just up and quit! I could have kept on. I thought I couldn't, but really I could have. I know that now. I'm learning that when I feel like I haven't got anything left, I've still got a little. And I'm getting tougher and stronger every day."

Mulvaney glanced at Berg and Hawkins, then looked back at the Jerrie. "Very well, Recruit Vernon, I'll leave things as they stand, and give you a chance to show what you can do." He handed the paper back to the young man. "Give this to Corporal Rodin." He paused. "I presume they fed you supper at the infirmary?"

"Yessir."

"Good. The company is at Lecture Shed Four. Do you know where that is?"

"Yessir."

"Go there and report to Sergeant Fossberg. They'll just be starting to show the cube now. You'll see most of it." He clapped his hands. "Now RUN!"

Vernon turned and fled, barely taking time to close the door behind him. Mulvaney grinned at the others. "'Just up and quit!' Hmph! I hope he makes it through. I like his self-honesty. Also, he answered my uncertainty about the pace of training. We'll proceed as we have been."

At 2015 hours, B Company was back in the hutment, where the trainees showered and lazed around a bit. Some went early to bed.

But not Esau and Jael. Sergeant Hawkins had reminded them before the company was dismissed; they had a date with him at 2030 hours. They walked to the orderly room together, not knowing what to expect. Somehow their mutual hostility had died. They didn't know why, and didn't wonder. It was simply gone.

They arrived several minutes early. The Charge of Quarters told them to sit down and wait, then returned to his novel. Hawkins walked in on the dot. "Recruits," he said, "we need privacy. Captain Mulvaney said to use his office." He opened the door to it, held it while they entered, then closed it behind them.

He pulled two folding chairs side by side, so he could see their occupants at the same time. "Sit," he ordered.

They sat. He examined them quietly, ordering his thoughts. "I'm going to call you by your given names," he began, "to save time and confusion. I'll ask questions, and tell you who's to answer." He paused, then spoke more loudly, for emphasis. "The other one will remain silent until called on."

His calm eyes examined Jael. "Jael, why did you punch Esau?"

"Because he said I was playing up to Corporal Fong, and that Corporal Fong had said what he did because he . . . wanted to commit adultery with me."

Hawkins eyebrows rose, and he turned to Esau. "What did Fong say that made you think that?"

"He congratulated her on her chin-ups. She did eleven. But he didn't say a thing to me, and I did thirty-nine! And I didn't say she played up to him!"

"Hmm. Jael, why do you think Fong congratulated you on your chin-ups?"

"Because when we started doing chin-ups two weeks ago, I could barely do four."

"I see." He turned back to Esau. "None of that sounds very lascivious to me. Has Jael flirted with anyone since you've been here?"

"Not that I've seen."

"Not that you've seen. Do you think she might have when you weren't around?"

Esau didn't meet his eyes. "No, sir," he said.

"All right. Jael, you claimed that Esau said you'd played up to Corporal Fong. Esau claims he didn't say that. Which is it?"

"He never said it in so many words, but that's what he meant. Otherwise why would he have said anything at all?"

"Um." The sergeant examined the situation. "What— Jael, I'm asking you this question. What were you and Esau talking about just before that?"

She gestured slightly toward her husband. "He was upbraiding me because I didn't run fast enough this morning."

"Um-hm. Esau, do you think she could have run faster?"

"Most of 3rd Platoon and half of 4th finished ahead of her. And they started out behind!"

"You avoided the question, Esau. Now answer me. Do you think she could have run faster?"

"She should have."

Hawkins' tone sharpened. "Recruit Esau Wesley, I asked you a question twice, and twice you've avoided answering it. Now . . ."

Esau interrupted. "But she lied! She said I accused her of playing up to him!"

"That doesn't answer my question. It's backflash, Recruit Esau Wesley, and it's earned you a six-by pit to dig before you go to bed tonight. You've got to break that habit. Another backflash tonight and you'll go without breakfast again in the morning."

Esau seemed to shrink, but his expression was bitter and obstinate.

Hawkins' voice was mild again. "Now, I'll ask you once more. Your last chance. Do you think she could have run faster this morning? Or is it just a matter of she couldn't run as fast as most of the others?" Esau didn't answer at once. "The answer, Esau," Hawkins prompted, his voice soft but ominous. "The answer. Nothing else."

"No, sir. It seems to me she ran as fast as she could."

"Thank you, Esau, for your honest answer. So why did you, ah, upbraid her for her late finish?"

Esau looked at his hands, folded on his lap. "I'm the leader of our fire team. I'm responsible for it. And her and Isaiah Vernon are both in it."

"And?"

He looked at Hawkins now, frustrated and upset. "They can't run as fast as the others, and they're weaker!"

"I know that. But do they do as well as they can?"

Esau deflated. "I guess."

"You have some doubts, do you?"

There was a brief lag, then Esau answered. "No. No doubts. She tries all right, hard as she can. And I suspect he does too."

"Are they improving?"

Grudgingly, "Yessir."

"Good. That's what we want them to do. What we want all of you to do. And you Jerries are doing well. You were strong to start with, and you try hard. Your corporals just completed their training here, and they tell us how impressed they are with you all. Jael in particular, because she's a woman. And most young women don't get the kind of physical exercise young men get. Even on New Jerusalem I suspect."

He paused, sizing up Esau, who seemed to be coming out of his black pit. "Tell me, Esau: have you said anything to Isaiah about his running? And his strength?"

"Once or twice."

"Did you ever upbraid him the way you did Jael?"

Esau relapsed a bit. "No, sir."

"Why is that?"

"He's not my wife."

"Do you think your wife's running, and her strength, reflect on you personally?"

He met Hawkins' gaze now, and his voice turned monotone. "It's not that. But I'm our fire team leader, and because of them, my team is the weakest in the platoon. I'll never make squad leader, or recruit platoon leader."

"Ahh! So you want to be squad leader. At least. Why?"

The question took Esau by surprise. "Why, so things'll be done right, and folks'll give it all they've got. Captain Mulvaney said it himself: we'll have to give it all we've got to win the war."

Hawkins nodded slowly. "Those are good reasons. So let me tell you how that works. You start with the people assigned to you, whoever and whatever they are. Some will be strong, some not so strong, some smart, some not so smart. Some able, some not so able. A leader's job is to work with what he's got, and make them an effective team. To do it with fairness, and a minimum of turmoil and resentment. A fire team and squad live together, work together, defend each other. They're closer and more loyal to each other than brothers.

"We senior cadre will base our final decisions on leadership on how well you lead. On your ability to handle the personnel you have." He paused meaningfully. "Including your fairness.

"You, Esau, are physically strong. And fast and smart. But those aren't enough by themselves. Just now, Ensign

Berg and I have misgivings about your suitability for leadership. You've shown excellent potential, but you have two major weaknesses. One, you are sometimes surly, and take your frustrations out on others. In this case your wife, which is seriously unfair.

"The other is your backflashing. You backflash more than anyone else in the platoon. When given orders, carry them out! Don't answer back, or argue or discuss—except when invited to. You can't be given authority to order others, when you take orders so poorly yourself."

Hawkins got to his feet. "Now. About your punishments— Recruit Jael, for punching Esau in the eye, you will dig a pit tonight, six feet long, six wide and six deep. After lights out. Recruit Esau, you will also dig one, for backflash. The CQ will supervise you. Report to him in the orderly room at 2200 hours.

"You are now dismissed."

Jael and Esau didn't go directly to their hut. Instead they strolled silently along the road that framed the battalion area. Esau's hand found hers, and she accepted it. After a bit he spoke. "At school once, Speaker Farnham chided me for bullying other kids. I denied it, didn't think I did it, till he gave me instances." He stopped, turned her to him, and held her two hands gently. "And this morning I was bullying you. The onliest one here that means much to me. I'm truly sorry, Jael, and I hope you'll forgive me." His voice broke then, taking him by surprise, and he took her in his arms, his tears falling on her hair and upturned face.

"Oh Esau, I do forgive you, I truly do. And I hope you'll forgive me for striking you. That was bullying, too. I'm not sure I'd have done it, if I hadn't known inside that you wouldn't hit me back. So that makes me a bully."

They clung to each other in the unlighted street until Esau could speak again. "Sweetheart," he husked, "I'm not sure but what I might slip up and talk like that again sometime. I'll surely try not to, but man is a weak vessel, and I might could slip up. So if ever I bully you again, just punch me in the eye. To remind me." His composure slipped again, and again his tears fell on her.

"Honey," she answered without smiling, "I'll pray not to. Because I do love you so."

They embraced again, this time their lips joining.

When the couple had left the orderly room, Sergeant Hawkins went to the hut and told Recruit Isaiah Vernon to come with him, that he had questions he wanted to ask. Then he took him to the dayroom, looking for privacy. At Hawkins' suggestion, they both drew a cup of coffee from the small urn there, before sitting down on opposite sides of a cribbage table. Isaiah had never been in the dayroom before. A sort of recreation room, it was part of a company's normal setup, but the recruits' training schedule left them almost no time to use it. Most had literally forgotten it was there.

"Vernon," Hawkins began, "you said you were being educated as a speaker of the books. I suppose by now you realize that we Sikhs don't know much about the Church of the Testaments. As children we're taught the basics of all the major religions, but we don't get down much into the, um, subdivisions. So I may ask you questions from time to time, to give me a better sense of your beliefs." He paused. "Does it bother you that we refer to you as Jerries?"

"No sir, Sergeant. Not me at least, and I've never heard anyone complain of it. It seems like a natural thing to do." He hesitated. "We are not a people greatly given to complaint. And in *The Book of Contemplations*, Elder Hofer taught that we should tolerate and respect . . . unbelievers."

Hawkins nodded solemnly. Their briefing had mentioned that a North American named Albert Hofer had founded the Jerrie church. "Ah," he said, "we have tolerance in common at least. "Guru Nanak founded the Sikh religion on the philosophy of religious tolerance." He raised an eyebrow. "How do you get along with other religions on New Jerusalem?"

Hawkins knew the answer, but he wanted to learn how frank this youth would be with him. The question didn't faze Isaiah. "Sir, there are no other religions on New Jerusalem. Other religions have their own worlds, or at least a place on Terra, and we respect that. But we keep our planet for ourselves. It's in our charter with the Commonwealth."

He paused. "From *The Book of Origins*, we know that long ago on Terra different religions fought each other, even massacred each other. Do they still?"

Hawkins smiled. "There's still some intolerance, but Terra got over most of it during the Troubles, eight hundred years ago. There hasn't been any serious violence since then. An occasional fistfight maybe. Intolerance tended to grow out of fear, and when a sect had the freedom to leave Terra and colonize a planet of their own, that fear became less. And the Commonwealth tries hard not to be overbearing toward the colonies."

He sipped the somewhat bitter Lüneburgian "coffee" he'd learned to like. "I want to talk about the platoon now. You grew up differently than the other men. Do they ever give you a bad time about that?"

"Not really, Sergeant. Esau's commented a few times, as the fire team leader, that I need to be stronger and tougher. But he's never been mean about it. When someone's as strong as Esau, and runs as fast, they might not understand why others can't."

"Ah. That brings up another question: How do you feel about Jael Wesley showering with the men?"

Isaiah's face showed no embarrassment. "I've never heard anyone say anything about it. Though they might, a few of them, if it wasn't for Esau. I'm pretty sure they were troubled by it, early on. But what Captain Mulvaney said made sense. As boys we used to sport together in the river, naked as newborns, and hardly anyone fretted about that. We boys didn't." He spoke more slowly now, as if feeling his way into the subject. "But that *is* different from swimming naked with girls or women, because sight of their flesh can make you think about having carnal knowledge of them. Maybe *want* to have carnal knowledge of them. The thing is, here there's no choice. She's a soldier and part of the company, so she should have the same rights. Like I said, I've never heard any of the others talk about it, but I suspect that's pretty much how they look at it."

Hawkins sipped thoughtfully, then nodded. "Thank you,

Vernon. You've helped me understand you people better."
He got to his feet. "We seem to be done now. You can
return to your hut. I may have more questions some other
time."

Isaiah got up too. "Yes, Sergeant." He paused. "Sergeant,
may I ask you a question?"

"Ask away."

"Do you Sikhs believe in Jesus?"

"Believe in Jesus? Yes, we do."

The trainee looked at his sergeant for a long second or
two, his eye contact mild. "Thank you, Sergeant," he said,
then turned and left.

Hawkins watched the door close, and smiled. *You almost
asked me whether we believe he's the Son of God, then
thought better of it.* The young Jerrie could have followed
his answer—he was abundantly intelligent. But that very
question, or rather Gopal Singh's reply to it, had split
Sikhism even before the Troubles, the better part of a
millennium earlier. Split it into the Orthodox and the Gopal
Singh Dispensation. For Gopal Singh's answer had posited
something akin to the Hindu *avtarvad,* which Guru Nanak
himself had rejected in the *Mul Mantra.* Gopal Singh had
tried to reconcile his belief with Orthodox leaders, but the
split remained.

Shortly before lights out, it began to rain. Not a storm
rain, but a steady soaker muttering on roof and walls, now
and then intensifying briefly. At 2200 hours, Esau and Jael
reported to the orderly room, wearing ponchos. The CQ
issued each of them a shovel, a short crude ladder, and a
six-foot measuring stick. And digging sites some fifteen
yards apart. "No talking," he warned. "Just dig. I'll be
checking on you out the window." Then he returned to the
orderly room.

They dug as rapidly as they could sustain, if only to get
more sleep time. Meanwhile the rain continued, and the
CQ wasn't eager to come out in it. So when Esau's measuring rod indicated he was done, he tossed out his shovel,
climbed wetly from the pit, and went over to Jael's. It wasn't
quite as deep yet as she was tall. Without a word he jumped
in. As in his, the water was about a foot deep.

"What are you doing?" she asked.

He kissed her. She tasted like rain. "Come to help out," he said.

"The CQ—he'll see. You'll get in trouble."

"To heck with that. We're not only husband and wife, we're comrades in war. Besides, we're eight or ten rods from the orderly room, and it's darker than the inside of a black bull." Then he turned and began to dig. When they'd finished, the CQ still hadn't reappeared, so Esau climbed out and went to the orderly room to get him. The man lay his book aside. "That was quick," he said. "You sure you're done?"

"I'm sure *I* am," Esau answered. "I can't speak for anyone else."

The CQ donned his poncho and they went out to Esau's pit. Esau jumped in. Nearby, Jael's continued to emit shovelfuls of dirt and slop. Taking Esau's measuring stick, the Terran measured height, width, and depth.

"Looks good," he said. "You're done." Then bypassing the ladder, the corporal squatted, reached down a hand, and hauled him out. Esau was impressed. *Stronger than I thought,* he told himself.

They headed for Jael's pit. "Quit throwing a minute," the CQ called. "It may be deep enough." He measured. "Good job both of you. Fill them and tramp them, and you're done. Tramp them every foot or so the whole way. I'll know if you don't, and you don't want to do the whole thing over again tomorrow night."

She came up on her ladder, to see the corporal striding off toward the orderly room. Filling the pits was far easier than digging them had been, and they worked hard and fast. When both pits were full and well tramped, the rain-sodden couple went to the orderly room together.

"All done," Esau announced.

The corporal donned his poncho again, went out with them to inspect the sites, then dismissed them to their hut.

On their way, Esau spoke. "You know," he said innocently, "we've already lost half our sleep time. We might as well lose another half hour, and go shower off."

She pulled his face down to hers and kissed him thoroughly. "That's a wonderful idea," she said.

In their hut, they hung their wet things on the drying rack—the clothes from the pond were already dry—put their cold wet ponchos on their bare bodies, and ran to the latrine. After a shower, a hot one, they turned the water off and made joyous love on the duck boards before scurrying back to the hut for three hours of sleep.

Chapter 21

Contract

Dr. Deborah Coonoor arrived at Bangui International Aerospaceport with zero fanfare, her visit and its possible importance publically unknown. Her welcoming committee consisted of one very tall person, Dr. Issa Libengi, who stood in the air-conditioned reception area holding a sign with her name on it. His grin was an expanse of white in a truly black face.

Weaving her way through the crowd, Dr. Coonoor herself was dark enough not to be conspicuous: a glowing mahogany. Her raven-black hair, however, was simply wavy. Her father was from Mysore State, in the south of India; her caramel-colored mother was "black English": Celto-Saxon/Caribbean/Brazilian.

When she reached Dr. Libengi, she extended a slender hand, which he carefully wrapped in his much larger one. "Ms. Coonoor, I presume," he rumbled. "I hope your flight was agreeable."

She laughed. "It was. Although I confess to being mystified by lunch. I'm unfamiliar with African cuisines."

He took her bag; emergency items in case of delay. She expected to be on her way back to Kunming before evening. Away from the gate area, they followed the flow toward the rotunda. "I was impressed by the flight," she said. "I'd never seen Central Africa before. Even from five thousand feet, your rainforest looks impressive. I grew up in Brazil you know."

"Seen from within the forest, it is even more remarkable. An invertebrate zoologist like yourself would find your interest quite stimulated, as mine was by your call—more by what you didn't say than by what you did."

Her eyes met his, and she laughed. "Perhaps we can discuss it in your car. Depending on your driver."

"You can trust his prudence absolutely. I drive myself."

Actually, she'd assumed that. Universities which originated as agricultural colleges were seldom pretentious, even after centuries of distinction. From the rotunda, they took a trackway to the four-story parking tower, then a lift tube to the third level, and walked to the coupé floater he'd driven, with the Bangui University logo on its door. Libengi held her door for her, a provincialism she found attractive. Then he stepped around to the other side, got in, and let the cybervalet move them to the floater exit, from which Libengi gently launched the vehicle into the midday air.

"So," he said, "what possible interest can Kunming have in a geneticist specializing in Central African species of Apoidea?"

She detected neither diffidence nor false modesty in the question. He simply wanted to know. "Because that is precisely what we need," she said, "a geneticist specializing in Central African species of Apoidea." She laughed without humor. "Particularly one who knows more about the genome of *Apis mellifera scutella* than anyone else. Which narrows it down to you."

Four hours later, Issa Libengi returned his guest to the aerospaceport. By then he knew Kunming's proposal in detail. The confidentiality was not from any fear that the enemy might have spies on Terra. Rather, it was to avoid stirring up the Peace Front, which would be upset by it.

Like a swarm of Apis mellifera *var.* scutella *stirred with a stick,* Libengi told himself, savoring the metaphor. The project was abundantly challenging, which was why he was so pleased with it. And the potential professional and public recognition were pleasant to contemplate. Even allowing for the multi-project nature of the program, its success could eventually mean prestige, salary increases, grants . . . And meanwhile, ah the challenges! Dr. Coonoor was well aware of them; her professional bona fides were substantial. "Take it as far as you can," she'd answered. "Interaction among projects should help."

What she hadn't said, and in fact didn't know, was that this was a contingency backup project. The equally vital other half of the program was quite uncertain.

Chapter 22

Close Encounter

The debris zone outside Henry Morgan's bolt hole changed from one trip to the next, and the change had become conspicuous. Shoots had sprouted from the base of many broken tree stubs, and were growing vigorously. Some were already more than ten feet tall: the place was beginning to heal. *Wait till the real rains arrive,* Morgan thought. *I'll need a machete.*

Actually he was carrying one on this trip, but not for clearing trail.

He'd been coming topside every week, spending a day hiking out and another back, and from one to three days spying. Among other things, he'd seen and reported several—foals? cubs? Small playful Wyzhñyñy juveniles, accompanying and occasionally nursing on adults at work in the clearing.

The previous time up, it had occurred to him that the stream flowing through the clearing was much too small to provide water for the invaders on the site. So he'd hiked to the bluff northwest of the clearing, and out onto a point he knew. From there his binoculars verified his suspicion: the invaders had installed what had to be a desalinization plant above the beach. Not large, but presumably adequate, no doubt powered by a geogravitic power converter.

May it be visited by a tsunami, he thought.

But it seemed to him his observations were trivial, except for the hornets. From that had grown two specific hopes: that it would (1) contribute a weapon, and (2) result in rescue. Robert and Connie would surely not be charged with piracy, while he himself . . . It seemed to him a pardon might be in order.

Terra had been in no hurry to reply to his offer. Then, at his last contact, had come the hoped-for word: "Captain Morgan, we agree on the potential of your proposal. Please capture a number of the hornets of which you spoke. Capture some from several separate nests, and if there is more than one species, some of each. Store them alive in stasis, if any of your stasis equipment has survived. Otherwise frozen, or failing that, dried thoroughly at low heat."

Not for breeding then, he thought. With disappointment but also relief. He had no idea how to recognize breeding pairs, if there were such things.

There'd been more to the instructions than that, and questions as well, but the best part they'd saved till last. "Last week we sent a long-range courier to pick you up, along with your brother and his attendant. And of course the hornets. We'll be in touch with the craft from time to time. At some point it will get in touch with you, via your savant, to discuss how and where to meet you. They cannot arrive for forty-nine Standard weeks. We wish, perhaps more than you, that it could be sooner."

Morgan seriously doubted the "more than you" part.

That had been three days past. On the first of them he'd returned to the hangar, where various useful material remained, along with tools. Using fiberglass mesh and aluminum, he built a hornet trap he thought would work. The next day he made three of them, modified to serve as cages for transportation, as well.

His limited experience with hornets had been in or near glades—small forest openings created when a large tree had fallen. A base keeper, Pat Kajimoto, had once said they came out of holes in the ground. With the increased light, the undergrowth thickened, and apparently the hornets preferred to dig their nests in the thickets. In a few months the debris zone might serve, but so far he hadn't seen any hornets there. Probably the shock of heavy blaster pulses had destroyed any preexisting nests.

So he headed for the clearing. Its south side was near the old resort, and hadn't been extended much. The plateau shelved off there, forming forested slump benches before dropping to sea level. Wisely the invaders hadn't built there. The forest fringe and the slump benches were thick with undergrowth.

Hopefully he wouldn't need to go that far. If he kept his eyes open, it seemed to him he'd encounter hornets along the way, and discover where they emerged from the ground. Then he'd hang around till they holed up for the night, swamp any vegetation out of the way with his machete, set the trap over the entrance/exit, and see how things looked in the morning. And if that strategy failed, there was no hurry. He had most of a year to develop a good capture system.

He hoped, though, that it wouldn't involve getting stung a lot. Tagus hornets packed a wallop.

It was afternoon before he even saw one. Then it was gone, to where, Morgan didn't know. He began to circle, spiraling outward, hoping to find the nest, checking a few thickets as he went. But found no more hornets.

Dusk was just beginning when he arrived at the foot of the knob. After hanging his net hammock between two slender, light-starved trees, he once more took his scope from beneath its log and lugged it up the knob. There was still enough light to scan the clearing by. The invaders' crop of whatever it was looked about three feet high, and was fenced. He recognized the fence generators.

The breeze was pleasant on the knob's exposed top. He took time to sit down and eat his supper—an airtight container of fruit-sweetened tapioca in rich cream, accompanied by hardtack with peanut butter. Connie had shuddered at the combination, but Morgan liked it, and it was quick, simple, and nourishing.

As he ate, he wondered if panthers had discovered the fence. The "panthers" of Tagus were black, lightly dappled with tan-yellow. They were also smart and wary, and had learned quickly that humans, with their beamguns, should be avoided. It was as if they shared knowledge with one another over a distance. But there was always the risk that some hungry yearling, driven from its mother's range, might make bold. It occurred to Morgan that in none of his spy missions had he heard a panther's moaning, far-carrying cry, and he wondered if the aliens hunted them. There was a lot of jungle. They could easily have hunters out patrolling without his knowing it. He hoped not.

He stayed on the knob till the stars were out, then moved the scope into the open and aimed it at the sky. In its narrow field of view, the stars stared coldly, unseeingly back at him. *Coldly*, he thought. *A strange word to apply to stars. Coldly in the sense of no emotions.* He wondered what emotions the invaders felt, looking at the sky, and what star or stars they'd come from. It didn't occur to him they might have come from another galaxy.

He covered the tube of his scope, shouldered it, and picked his way down the knob. Beneath the forest's dense roof, the darkness was utter, impenetrable. Shielded by jungle and the knob, he used his belt torch to find his hammock. Once in it, he activated the repellent on his belt. Its power output was low enough, it seemed highly unlikely to be noticed.

In scant minutes he slept.

He awoke to the dawn chorus of jungle birds and lemur-like "monkeys." Breakfast was like supper, except for an apple preserved "like fresh." After eating, he climbed the knob again for a brief scan of the clearing—with binoculars; they were enough for the purpose. There was little activity; too early, he supposed. Climbing back down, he shouldered his pack frame with its load of collapsible hornet traps, and set off, circling southwestward through the forest to approach the clearing's south edge.

When he was near enough to detect it, he slowed. The south edge had not been cut back at all, and was only about a quarter mile from the invaders' main building. This was

by far his nearest approach. Carefully he slipped forward
to the thick undergrowth of the fringe, where he lay down
and slowly crawled, making no sudden move.

He'd almost reached the edge when he made out
movement ahead: two aliens together, less than a hundred
yards out in the clearing. Seen through the screening
foliage, they seemed almost stationary. Briefly he heard a
small tapping sound, then the two moved a short distance.
He backed away till he couldn't see them at all, then angled
toward a large tree at the very verge. Reaching the tree,
he rose slowly upright, keeping the trunk between himself and the invaders.

Carefully he peered around it till he could see them
again. They had something on a tripod. One of them was
peering through it toward the forest—right toward him!—
and he realized what they must be doing: laying out some
engineering project.

He didn't notice their sidearms till one of the invaders, the one at the instrument, drew his, raising its muzzle
toward him. Withdrawing his head, Morgan turned and fled
into the jungle. There was no shot. How good a look had
they gotten? Hardly enough to know what they'd seen,
seventy or eighty yards away.

He slowed to a strong striding walk, not routing himself by the knob, glad his spying trips had gotten him into
good physical shape. He'd stay away from the clearing for
a while—or for good; find hornets closer to home. It had
been foolish to approach so near the clearing. Perhaps he'd
stay underground for a few weeks.

It was late afternoon when he reached the debris zone
and headed for his bolt hole. When he stepped into its
narrow irregular opening, the last thing he did was turn
and look back. *To see a floater hovering above the edge
of green forest! They'd followed him!* His heart nearly
stopped, and slowly he backed into the tunnel, out of the
light. There he activated the alarm, then the booby trap,
then closed the door and ran down the long tunnel, activating the other booby traps as he came to them. They
wouldn't bring the tunnel down, but they'd slow intruders and reduce their numbers.

The survey instrument, he realized now, had been telescopic, and the instrument man had realized what he'd seen. He'd radioed his headquarters, and a scout, no doubt on standby, had been sent up. Knowing his approximate location, it had gotten an infrared fix on him through the forest roof. They could have sent a gunship then, blasted the jungle where he was and almost surely killed him. But they'd wanted to know where he'd go. Now they knew.

Stupid! he thought as he ran. *You stupid, self-destructive sonofabitch!*

In little more than a minute he reached the steel door to the living area, unlocked and spun the wheel, then entered and locked it behind him. For a moment he leaned on it. Connie had heard him, and stepped into the entryway. She started to speak, perhaps to ask him how it had gone, then saw his face and stopped, eyes widening, one hand moving to her mouth.

"What?" she whispered.

He didn't answer at once, just shook his head. Setting his harness and pack aside, he got his pistol from a drawer and put it in his waistband. Connie followed, watching, seeming not to breathe.

"I was seen at the forest edge," he said quietly, "and slipped back into the jungle. I didn't think they knew what they'd seen." He put a hand on her arm. "When I got to the entrance, I turned and looked back. And saw it—a military floater hovering above the jungle's edge. They'd followed me." He stepped past her, speaking more softly now. "They'll have called for a troop carrier."

"What will we do?"

"Let them know on Terra."

She stared up at him; she was barely five feet tall.

"We don't have much time," he said. "Get Robert ready."

She nodded soberly, and followed him into what served now as the family room. Robert was at the computer, browsing star charts, unaware that anyone had entered. "Robert," she said, "it's time for you to go to work."

Her voice was wooden, but Robert's response was deeply conditioned. Already in trance, he got up, walked to the divan and lay down, folding his hands on his chest while

Connie moved a chair beside him and sat. After the connections were made, Morgan began to dictate.

He'd just finished when the alarm buzzed. His final words to Terra were, "They're here." Then he stepped to the alarm and turned it off. The first booby trap was small and distant; he neither heard nor felt the explosion. "I'm done now, Connie," he said. "Waken him."

He waited while she and Robert went through the brief withdrawal ritual. Robert sat up, saw his older brother, and grinned. "Hi, Henry," he chirped. "Did you bring me any flowers?"

"No, no I didn't. But I brought you a new story." A scenario was forming in his mind even as he spoke, rooted in an ancient movie, one that had touched him deeply. Initially, in pretechnological times, it had been shot on film, and since then copied and recopied in other media.

"Sit on your computer chair," he said, "and turn off the computer." He watched Robert comply. "Now look at the screen. Keep your eyes on it, and imagine you're seeing what I tell you. Seeing it like a movie."

His order sent his brother into a near-hypnotic revery. "Do you remember where we lived in Colorado? After father died?"

Robert nodded. "Yes," he said.

"Remember the garden behind the house. With all the flowers, and the lilac bushes. Do you see it?"

He'd made it all up years before, part of an imaginary past to help bury the ugly reality. Robert's head bobbed eagerly. "I see it."

Morgan heard or felt a booby trap explode, a small, dull, distant thump. Whether the second, or the last, or one in between, he wasn't sure.

"All right. Now see mother there. Do you see her?"

"Uh huh."

"Tell me what she's wearing."

The savant didn't hesitate. As Morgan drew his pistol from his belt, Robert answered. "She's wearing her white dress with the blue and yellow flowers." He chuckled. "And she's barefoot. She used to say it let her feet be friends with the grass."

Connie choked back a sob.

Morgan raised the pistol and put the muzzle almost against Robert's head. It wavered, and he gripped it with both hands to steady it. "All right," he continued, "now you and Connie and I are going there to see her. We'll be there in just a second."

He pulled the trigger, the explosion loud in the small room. Connie screamed and lowered her head, covering it with her hands as if knowing. He'd saved Robert once before by killing their father. Now he'd saved him again. Small tight sobs, like little chuckles, burned his throat, and his free hand wiped away tears. A much more powerful explosion roared from the other side of the steel door, knocking things from shelves. Morgan held the muzzle close to Connie's head and pulled the trigger again.

Tears blinded him. Then he heard alien voices; the safety door had been dislodged. A blaster pulse struck the family room door, sending a spray of Tuffboard fragments across the room. Morgan put the muzzle in his mouth and pulled the trigger a final time.

Chapter 23
Interrogation

Qonits' ranking bodyguard rapped sharply on the door, but not with the butt of his blaster, as he had at first.

Even that had been an improvement. In an early session, a half-hour charade with the chief scholar, David and Yukiko had managed to communicate that they didn't want guards, or even Qonits himself, walking in on them without permission. That it showed lack of respect, and they would not cooperate without respect.

Not that privacy was the point. Video cameras monitored them endlessly. The point they hoped to make was that they had rights. Of course if their captors disagreed, pain was always available to inspire cooperation. Neither David nor Yukiko imagined they could withstand serious torture. But the Wyzhñyñy didn't know that, and might prefer not to risk their deaths, or possibly inspire unbreakable resistance.

When Qonits had left that time, they hadn't known whether he'd understood. But beginning the next day, the guard who'd brought their meals had knocked. And so had Qonits' bodyguard, all without apparent resentment.

"Who is it?" David called.

"It is Qonits."

As far as it went, Qonits' Terran was quite understandable. On the other hand, the Wyzhñyñyç the humans had learned was negligible. For a while the exchanges had been fairly even, but apparently the Wyzhñyñy had changed their minds and decided not to teach them. At any rate the humans had no artificial intelligence to run endless cross-references, refining and expanding on meanings and nuances.

As shipsmind acquired a working vocabulary, sessions had more and more been built around lists—requests for the meanings of words recorded during earlier interrogations and the prisoners' personal conversations. Words presumably chosen by shipsmind. Qonits' efforts to speak became less halting and uncertain. His main difficulty was understanding what was said to him.

"Come in!" Yukiko called back. She and David made a point of neither being the prime spokesperson. Let the Wyzhñyñy consider them equal to each other in rank.

As always, Qonits' entrance showed what the two Terrans read as dignity without arrogance. They still didn't know whether that dignity and apparent lack of arrogance were idiosyncrasies of Qonits, or shared by other ranking Wyzhñyñy. But they'd come to *like* the chief scholar.

"Good morning," Qonits said carefully. "I wish you feel well now."

"We feel very well, thank you," David said, "and we wish the same to you."

The Terrans sat on a couch. Yukiko had sketched one for Qonits, and he'd had it made. His own people had such things, and Qonits could understand that humans might have greater need for them. It must, he'd told himself, be tiresome standing on just two legs. He'd wondered at first why they didn't fall over.

"You are welcome," Qonits replied, then paused. "I have—more questions."

David raised an eyebrow at Yukiko; the knowledge master's delivery suggested this might be a different sort of session.

"We are interested," Yukiko answered.

They almost always say that, Qonits thought, *and I never know why. What might they be learning from us?* He wondered how long it would be before he began to actually understand these aliens. Until he did, knowing their words and sentences would be inadequate to understanding their meanings or intentions. What went on in the privacy of those round alien skulls?

"We wonder what is the kind of your empire," he said.

"Ah," said David, and spread his hands. "It is—an empire."

Qonits looked at him warily. "Please tell me more about it."

Yukiko spoke next. "It is many worlds united to permit, and provide for, the separate and mutual satisfaction of each and all worlds."

The focus of Qonits' eyes slanted off into left field, a response the Terrans had learned to recognize: he'd gotten no real notion of what her statement meant. His fingers tapped something into the small key pad hanging from his neck. Presumably he was listening to what shipsmind made of it.

After a few moments, his gaze returned to the two Terrans. "Thank you," he said. *This session,* he told himself, *promises to require much work by shipsmind before I understand their answers. I wish I understood now. My subsequent questions could be more to the point.*

"And what is this empire's government?" he asked.

It was David and Yukiko who felt uncertain now. They suspected the monitoring they were subjected to was more than visual, and they preferred to keep the Wyzhñyñy guessing, uncertain. It was David who answered. "It is a commercial union, to facilitate the members buying from and selling to each other."

As he'd spoken, he began to see where this could take him, and felt a touch of excitement. Meanwhile something was obviously going on with Qonits. Disbelief? Concept overwhelm? David tried another tack. "We call it a commonwealth." He tapped his head as he went on. "Think of it as many self-governing worlds united for their separate individual good. And also for their mutual good—their joint good, their together good."

Qonits' eyes had lost their unfocused look. He was intent

now. "Then there will be no effective defense," he said. Even in the Wyzhñyñy's non-human voice, David could hear the mental wheels turning. And sense the distrust.

"That is not correct," David said. "There will be defense." *God, there'd better be!* "Defense is one of the primary functions of commonwealth government. Defense, the enforcement of valid contracts, and overall record-keeping."

Qonits' nictitating membranes slid over his eyes in a reflex the Terrans had yet to understand. "What is the kind of defense?" the Wyzhñyñy asked. "What kind of things is done by that defense?"

David wasn't thinking his way through the situation now. He was running on creative intuition, winging it. "My wife and I are not informed on defense. We are research scientists. We learn about the seas on new worlds." The nictitating membranes were back again. *This will give his shipsmind something to chew on,* David thought. *He'll be back with a monster word list tomorrow.* "We know the basic principle though," he continued. "Design the defense, or select the defense, which most damages and frustrates the enemy. Keeps them off balance."

Qonits' long tongue licked air. David and Yukiko hadn't figured that one out yet, either. It took a long moment before the chief scholar responded, speaking very slowly, very deliberately. "Then why have we not met such defense? We have now eleven of your planets. Still no defense. Why?"

There was no sense of challenge in the question. *He simply wants to know,* Yukiko thought. "We are a very numerous people," she answered. "In recent centuries—hundreds of years—we have colonized many new worlds. We are a very diverse species, with many different peoples having different wants. They go out beyond the older colonies, find new worlds and colonize them."

The answer stopped Qonits dead in the water. It seemed to her he was about to go catatonic, whether because he couldn't grasp what she'd said, or because he could. She wished she knew what he was hearing on the earphone he wore. "And," she went on, "apparently the newer, farther colonies are being sacrificed." She turned to David. "Wouldn't you say so, dear?"

He nodded. "It seems obvious," he answered.

"Sacrificed," she continued, "while our fleets and armies are being concentrated or distributed, I have no idea which. Preparing to defend our core worlds, with their vast populations."

Qonits mind was signalling overload. He bobbed a nod. "Thank you for valuable information. I now leave you, return at later time." Then he said something to his bodyguards, and they left together.

Quanshûk had witnessed the brief interrogation via monitor, and had understood the key questions; he'd helped define them. What had mystified him were the answers, even though, like Qonits, he was plugged into the ship's growing translation program. Too much of what the prisoners said had made no sense to him, while some had been disturbing. Qonits' physical responses he'd understood well enough.

His own tongue licked air. *We must sort this out,* he told himself. *As quickly as possible.*

Yukiko put her arms around Annika and rocked her, feeling her snuggle in response. *Poor kid,* she thought, then retracted it, as if the savant might read it and be troubled by it. *For you,* she amended, *a stupor is probably best. You don't suffer, you don't worry. It's the next best thing to sleeping through it.*

Then she decided she wasn't sure about that either. Did Annika, in her mind, revisit the events in the *Cousteau?*— the undoubtedly violent deaths of Ju-Li and Dennis? She leaned back to better comprehend the child. *Probably not,* she decided. *When the Wyzhñyñy gave her to us, she was deeply in coma. But since then . . .* Yukiko shook her head. *Within that stupor, there's something like serenity.* "Annika," she breathed, "I wish you could tell me what goes on with you."

David's eyes had been closed, but he hadn't been sleeping. Now they opened. "What?" he whispered.

She whispered back. "I was talking to Annika. I told her I'd like to know what she thinks about."

"Nothing very exciting I'll bet," he said, and closed his eyes again.

❖   ❖   ❖

Chang Lung-Chi sat beside the prime minister, watching Ramesh on the wall screen. Foster Peixoto had viewed either the complete or selected cubeage of almost every language session. This had been more like interrogation. He wasn't surprised at how much communication had taken place. Actually he assumed it had gone better than it had. He didn't realize how much Qonits had understood only vaguely or not at all.

After they'd listened to the complete session a second time, Chang frowned thoughtfully. "Remarkable. Those two are playing a game with the aliens. The question is what good it will do."

"I have the same impression. Perhaps they have enough sense of the alien psychology to accomplish something. Hopefully we will get a better sense of it as it continues. Weintraub and Li are studying the sessions carefully. When they have gained some insights, they will share them with us."

Chang was less optimistic. *When? Or if? One can but hope,* he told himself. *At any rate we must monitor this closely.* "And the child," he said, "the savant. Has she shown any sign of shutting down, and depriving us of this remarkable contact?"

"None. And Bekr is optimistic now. Gavaldon has commented to her husband on how much better the child seems. Yet she continues to send. Bekr suspects the condition may be effectively permanent."

"Good! Good! It may be that this will prove truly important." *We were optimistic about Morgan the pirate,* Chang reminded himself, *and now he is lost to us. May he rest in the Tao. He served his species well in his weeks of spying.*

Chapter 24

Hard Facts, Hard Decisions

Captain Martin Mulvaney Singh had spent most of the day at Division, being briefed on a duty he hadn't expected. As a training company commander, his main role was executive; to actually train troops was someone else's function. The company's noncommissioned cadre did the hands-on training—notably the platoon sergeants—with the platoon leader a step removed. While lectures, with or without video cubes podded out from Terra, were a function of Division staff. The training schedule came from Division, too, based on a plan from far-off War House. There were open periods in which the company commander could insert whatever he thought best, but his main role was to track the progress of training and the trainees, turning the intensity up or down, and dealing with problems.

A company commander addressed the trainees daily, at morning muster and often at other musters. This kept his presence and authority in their consciousness, and hopefully inspired them from time to time. But lectures? Lectures were delivered by Division staff.

Except for this particular, newly conceived lecture. War House had foreseen possible troublesome effects, and wanted the company commanders to deliver it. If a CO was doing his job properly, his trainees knew and trusted him. Division concurred, and Mulvaney didn't doubt they were right. Major General Pak—he'd been promoted from brigadier—took it a step further; he wanted each platoon sergeant to talk it out afterward with his trainees. If the sergeants had been doing their job properly—and Mulvaney was confident his had—they'd have bonded with their Jerrie youths, like experienced and respected older brothers.

Jerries were about as close to homogeneous as a human culture gets, and tended to accept authority. According to the ethnology report, the Jerrie religion was narrow, but persuasive more than restrictive. Its defining book, *Contemplations on the Testaments,* said that wise leaders led by example, gentle teaching, and mild admonition. And, like God, exercised "tolerance of the imperfections that are a part of being human."

Gopal Singh would have applauded that, Mulvaney told himself.

He got back to the company area in time for supper; his driver let him off outside the mess hall in a light but steady rain. Sixty feet away, the trainees were doing their pre-supper chin-ups before going in, callused fists gripping wet bars without a sign of slippage. Even with the enforcement of strict form, they were doing so many chins now, he'd tripled the number of bars, to keep the serving line moving.

He watched them for a moment before entering the officers' mess. He'd developed a real fondness and respect for his trainees. This evening he would brief his platoon leaders and platoon sergeants on what tomorrow held. Meanwhile Bremer and Fossberg could take the trainees on a sixty-minute speed march with sandbags, then let them off early.

The next day's training began with the usual run before breakfast. After six weeks they weren't grueling anymore. It was the one part of physical training that wasn't being intensified. Drag Ass Hill seemed neither so steep nor so long as it had. At the end of Week 4 their runs had been lengthened to forty of Lüneburger's long minutes, and would stay at that, neither lengthening nor speeding up. Nor did they end with any more "suicide races."

After breakfast the trainees fell out wearing fighting gear, complete with armored jackets and battle helmets. And of course with the blasters they'd been issued in Week 4. In Week 5 they'd learned to fire them, and had qualified for single-shot firing, set for soft pulses, for safety's sake. But they'd been shown what a hard pulse did to a dummy in a flak jacket. A jacket and helmet might help against shrapnel, or spent or grazing blaster pulses, but that was all.

This morning they marched four miles, burdened not only with their gear, but with forty-pound sandbags to build strength. Then spent an hour and a half moving carefully through forest, senses alert, firing short bursts at wooden targets that popped up for two seconds from unexpected places. Fired from the hip while walking. Failure to hit your target earned gigs, which, they were told, they'd pay for on their next day off. In Week 5, on slow fire, Jael had scored "excellent." But on quick fire she'd been charged four straight gigs before she'd gotten fast enough, and a couple since when she'd missed in her haste. On this day—Fourday—she got none.

The body armor didn't help, nor did the sandbag. But on the other hand, Esau hadn't missed yet; a number of young frontiersmen hadn't. He'd been hunting with a breech-loading single-shot rifle since boyhood, had learned marksmanship at an age when the reflexes channel readily and deeply. And New Jerusalem's version of squirrels didn't hold still longer than a second. "Shooting blasters in bursts, you can't hardly miss," he'd told Jael, "once you get the hang of it. There's no recoil nor windage, and the trajectory's flat. Durn energy pulse would travel around the world and hit you in the back, if it held together good enough."

It wouldn't, of course, and Esau knew it. It would head into space on a tangent. Lieutenant Bremer, the company XO, had told them that. Nor did the pulses fall to earth. They simply lost integrity after a mile or so, and died—"unraveled" was how he'd put it.

At 1100 hours the company ground out another fifteen pushups—all they were asked for, wearing flak jackets, sandbag and helmet—and headed back to camp. They had no notion of what the afternoon held for them. But there'd be something; there always was.

Pastor Lüneburger's World grew a lot of barley, so the trainees ate a lot of it as a frequent substitute for potatoes and rice. At the noon meal this day they found roast pork waiting for them, with barley, savory pork gravy, thick slices of hot, buttered whole-grain bread, crisp green beans, and a cobbler of some Lüneburgian fruit. And Lüneburger coffee. All with seconds if wanted.

Afterward they had thirty minutes to recover. Most napped on their cots. Then whistles brought them out in field uniforms for muster, and afterward they had the rare experience of marching to lecture with Captain Mulvaney leading them. Arriving at the lecture shed, they pumped out the now customary thirty pushups, then filed in. Captain Mulvaney was standing in front, at the lectern. When they were seated, his big voice barked, "At ease!" and the trainee chatter cut abruptly off.

"Men," he said, "today you're going to see something you've only heard about till now. You'll see cubeage of warbots in realistic simulated combat, coordinating with organic troops like ourselves. You'll find the warbots very interesting. After that you'll see cubeage of how they're constructed, and how they operate. You'll even see one of them interviewed." He paused, turning. "Corporal, begin the program."

The shed lights dimmed and the wall screen lit up. The presentation resembled a full-fledged dramatic production, opening with an interior shot of forest that had not been fought through. Artillery thundered in the distance. Squads of infantry trotted through in fighting gear, blasters in hand. Along with several seven-foot warbots roughly humanoid in form, their movements as smoothly articulated as an athlete's, though a bit different. Their laminated ceramic-steel surfaces were protected by camouflage fields whose color patterns fluctuated as they strode, mimicking the immediate surroundings. It was very effective.

A voice-over narration accompanied the visuals. A few weeks earlier the Jerries would have had serious problems with its language, but they'd been immersed in military life, and had already learned a lot.

Now the point of view followed close behind one of the infantry squads, till the organics reached the forest edge and began digging in. "This organic battalion," said the narrator, "has been bivouacked several miles back in the forest, hidden from aerial detection by a concealment field. Meanwhile, seek-and-engage actions have seriously reduced the capacity of both sides to launch aerial attacks."

When Mulvaney had first seen the cube during the briefing the day before, mention of a concealment field had troubled him. The last he'd heard, back on Terra, concealment fields were only theory. But the PR was, science was as fully mobilized as industry, and who knew what might be available by the time they left for New Jerusalem.

As far as that was concerned, who knew what weaponry the Wyzhñyñy had?

The Wyzhñyñy. *How,* he wondered, *had War House learned what they called themselves?*

The camera view cut to panoramic. Ahead of the troops lay farmland, with forest close to a mile away on the other side. A road ran across the middle of the open ground. Now, from the forest on the far side, a wave of armored personnel carriers emerged, supported by armored fighting vehicles. Behind them came another wave, and another— a whole series of them. "The enemy forces are shown in animation," the narrator was saying, "as realistically as technology can portray them."

Mulvaney wondered how close to reality that was. They had to be almost wholly imaginary. But the production was excellent. Neither the animation nor the battle choreography could be faulted. Trashers began to rip the Wyzhñyñy as soon as they appeared, but the infantry held their fire until the Wyzhñyñy had crossed the road, then began to lay intense fire on them with slammers and blasters. Immediately the Wyzhñyñy returned the fire, and the fight became a melee within which Mulvaney's trained eyes could see the basic drilled-in tactics and creative responses of the troops on both sides.

Even the casualties were convincing, though it seemed to him the Wyzhñyñy might be dying in unreasonable

numbers. Then Wyzhñyñy APFs—armored personnel flyers—
sliced across the field at perhaps two hundred feet. Not
a lot of them. The script writers, he recalled, had deci-
mated them during the aerial preliminaries.

The picture cut to an oblique overhead view a few
hundred yards back from the forest edge. The Wyzhñyñy
APFs hovered close above the trees, lowering troops on
individual slings, from doors with short, stout, drop booms.
Then it cut to a view within the forest. As the airborne
Wyzhñyñy landed, they triggered their sling releases and
began forming up squads.

Suddenly warbots hit them, greatly outnumbered, but
fighting with astonishing speed and power. The Wyzhñyñy
were slaughtered. The warbots seemed too heavily armored
to be harmed by their shoulder-fired blasters. And bots,
Mulvaney knew, had a backup "torso" sensorium in case
their eyes and ears were knocked out.

Briefly the trainees witnessed special effects sufficient
to impress even Terrans. For Jerries who'd never seen
dramatic video before—or video at all till they'd come to
Camp Stenders—it had to be a truly powerful experience.

The airborne Wyzhñyñy were shown as effectively wiped
out, the few survivors dispersed and routed. Only a handful
of warbots had gone down. The remaining bots did not
linger. As if on command, perhaps received by built-in
radio, they turned and loped off among the trees. Mulvaney
was skeptical that machines on two legs could move so
smoothly.

As the final bots disappeared, the viewpoint changed
again, to the close-range fighting in the forest fringe.
Wyzhñyñy bodies were abundant, but many humans also
lay "dead." *Not as many as you'd expect,* Mulvaney thought.
*I suppose War House doesn't want to shock the trainees
too badly.* Then the warbots entered the fighting there, too,
striking swiftly and powerfully. The Wyzhñyñy gave way and,
after a brief desperate moment, broke and fled across a
welter of bodies. Three warbots lay disabled, presumably
by heavy slammers. The camera watched the surviving
Wyzhñyñy gallop all the way across the fields to the forest
on the far side, impelled by human fire that added more
bodies to those already sprawled.

As the final Wyzhñyñy disappeared into the far woods, the scene froze on the field, and music cut in, restrained but powerful. Mulvaney recognized it as "The Arrival of Alp Arslan," by the Egyptian composer Ibrahim Hakim, in his orchestral suite *Manzikert*. It ended with a dark and powerful closing phrase, as the visual faded and disappeared.

Then the shed's lights came on, and the recorded narration resumed. "This cube was made to show you the basic function—and the great importance!—of warbots in modern warfare. For every regiment, the table of organization calls for two warbot platoons. Without them, no infantry regiment is complete, or fully prepared for combat. You will learn much more about warbots as your training progresses."

The voice stopped. Mulvaney got to his feet and stepped again to the lectern. *Well, Martin,* he thought, scanning his Jerries, *it's time to earn your pay.* "All right, men, stand up in place, and stretch. Really stretch, so you feel it."

They did, with a chorus of groans.

Mulvaney grinned. "Now stamp your feet!"

Boots drummed on the plank floor.

"All right, now turn to the men around you; tell them hello, and shake hands with them." After half a minute of confusion and laughter, everyone had been included. "Good. Now tell them you're glad they're here. And mean it." He paused to let the chatter play out. "All right, at ease. Sit down." They stilled and sat. "We have something very important to talk about."

He paused a long moment, letting them wait. "Who of you," he asked, "will tell us why you're here, instead of back home on New Jerusalem?"

A hand shot up. "Recruit Isaiah Vernon," Mulvaney said, "tell us about it."

"Captain, sir, it's because invaders have come, invaders not made in the image of God. They're conquering human worlds, and killing the people on them. If we stayed, we'd be killed, too. Here we're learning to drive them away."

"Right," Mulvaney said. "At last report they'd definitely captured fourteen human worlds, and probably two others. Those we've heard from say the Wyzhñyñy"—he paused, pronouncing the name carefully again—"the Wyzhñyñy were killing everyone they came to, including those who tried to surrender."

Mulvaney scanned his audience again, his eyes stopping on Esau. "Recruit Esau Wesley, suppose we don't get back to New Jerusalem soon enough, and the Wyzhñyñy take it. What then?"

"Then we'll drive them off, sir."

Mulvaney frowned. "Why not leave in—say a month from now? That should get us there in time."

"Fine, if we're ready. But if we're not, and we go, the Wyzhñyñy will beat us."

"Exactly right. And believe me, you're a long way from ready. You're coming along well, *very* well, but you're far from ready." His gaze found his religious advisor. "Recruit Spieler, you trainees are all from New Jerusalem, so it's obvious why you should return there to defend it. Or regain it. But I'm a Terran. All your cadre are. Why should we go there to fight?"

The somber Spieler got to his feet. As recruits went, he was old, twenty-seven Terran years. "Captain Mulvaney, sir, long ago, God put Adam and Eve on Terra, and they were fruitful, and multiplied. Then, in His own good time for His own good reasons, He shepherded folks out to the stars. But all of Adam's progeny are God's children, created in His own image and saved by the sacrifice of His own son. It is the duty of us all to drive out these"—he paused, struggling with the pronunciation—"these Wiz-nin-ee."

"Well said, Spieler." Once more Mulvaney scanned his audience, making them wait. He was no orator, but he knew how to communicate. "So," he said, changing directions on them, "what did you think of the cube? Anyone?"

"Exciting, sir," someone called. Someone else followed with "We've got some idea now of what fighting will be like."

"Recruit Jael Wesley, what did you think of it?"

"Sir, it made me realize the cost of being in this war. If we lose, we'll all die. But even winning, lots of us will."

"Good observation. Recruit Spieler, what about death?"

"Sir, we'll all die sometime. If not on the battlefield, then maybe in bed. But death isn't the thing to fear. Hell is, and next after Hell, the destruction of the human race."

Spieler paused, then went on. "Most of us here—maybe all of us—when we die, we'll go to Heaven and be with the Lord."

"Thank you, Recruit Spieler." Another hand rose as he said it. "Recruit Esau Wesley, what have you got to add?"

"Sir, I was wondering about the warbots. The cube said every regiment was supposed to have them. And those folks it showed would have been in bad trouble if it wasn't for warbots. But I haven't seen or heard of any in our whole division."

Mulvaney stood tall, sure of himself. He made them wait again, tightening their attention. "I was coming to that, Wesley," he said, "but I'm glad you brought it up. What do you suppose a warbot is?"

"Sir, it's a kind of machine."

"Ah. That's right, as far as it goes. But they're more than that." Again he pointed. "Recruit Vernon, do machines have souls?"

"No, sir. Only people have souls."

"And brains?"

"I suppose they have artificial brains, sir."

Mulvaney nodded. "You certainly might think that. But actually a bot has both a soul and a human brain."

There wasn't a sound from his audience, but it seemed to Mulvaney he sensed doubt, resistance. "I have a sister who's a bot," he went on. "A different model than shown in the cube. She's a medic bot."

Esau hadn't sat back down yet. "Sir," he said, "your *sister*?"

"My sister. She was a nurse, until she came down with a condition called 'cascade syndrome'—the breakdown of one body part after another. By age thirty she was expected to die at any time. The last time I heard from her was since we arrived here on Lüneburger's World. She'd volunteered to have her central nervous system—that's her brain, her spinal cord and nerve connections—removed from her body and put into what's called a 'bottle.' Then the bottle was put into a machine called a 'servo'—the sort of machine you saw in the cube. Without the human central nervous system, and the soul associated with it, the servo is a useless piece of machinery. It's the combination—the servo, the

central nervous system and the soul—that makes a warbot.
Or in Audrey's case a battlefield medic bot.

"And therein lies the reason the 1st New Jerusalem Division has no warbots yet; why no division has anything like as many as it should. People don't get converted into warbots unless they're badly crippled, or they're dying of something.

"Because becoming a bot is final. If someone becomes a bot, and later wishes he hadn't, it can't be undone. So even severely disabled people, who may feel tempted, often can't bring themselves to take that final step. And until the past month, many people who were willing weren't sufficiently disabled to qualify. Now recruitment for what is called 'bottling' has picked up. So the 1st New Jerusalem Division should have at least a partial contingent of warbots when we leave."

There Mulvaney stopped and simply stood, the silence longer than before, as if he were looking for the words to continue. Finally he nodded, as if to himself. "When we get to New Jerusalem, we cannot expect replacements for our casualties. You noticed in the cube that not all the casualties were Wyzhñyñy; not even close. We'll have a medical battalion to treat our wounded; Indis—people from another heavyworld called Epsilon Indi Prime."

Again he paused. "There will also be damaged warbots. We'll have spare servos—warbot bodies—and bottles can be transferred from damaged servos to replacement servos. But in some of the damaged servos, the human inside will have been killed. And we'll need to replace them if we can.

"So—" This was the hard part. His new pause was not for effect; he was groping. "So what we need," he said carefully, "are volunteers. People like you and me, who'll agree in writing that if we're disabled or mortally wounded, our central nervous system—our brain and spinal cord—can be bottled and installed in a warbot. Division will have specialists to do the job."

Once more he paused, sensing his audience was ill at ease with this. "We don't know now which of you will receive such wounds," he went on. "So beginning next week we'll start training all of you in how to operate as a warbot. The training modules are expected to arrive next Twoday.

The same ship is also bringing a platoon of real warbots to continue their training here. Later you'll do tactical exercises with them."

A hand shot up. "Yes, Recruit Arvet?"

"Sir, how can we learn to operate as a warbot if we're not—bottled?"

"You'll find out. You'll probably enjoy it." He grinned. "It won't require running up Drag Ass Hill."

He pointed at another hand. "Yes, Recruit Harrison?"

The young man's voice was subdued and tentative. "Where do we, uh, sign the agreement, sir? To get bottled if we're crippled or dying?"

"Right after supper, at the orderly room. Sergeant Henkel or Corporal Tsinijinnie will sign you up." He scanned the room and saw no sign of enthusiasm. "Or at some later time. The sooner we know, the better." Again he looked around. "Any more questions? Cochran?"

"Sir, you said we'd see cubeage of how warbots are made, and watch one of them get interviewed."

"Right. That comes next. Corporal Cavalieri, continue with the cube."

B Company was introverted when it left the lecture shed, but the condition was not allowed to persist. Captain Mulvaney had prearranged for that. Outside, they were ordered to drop down and this time pump out thirty-five. Even Recruit Vernon managed thirty-two. Then Sergeant Fossberg led them on a gallop to the Physical Training Area, where they spent a long Lüneburgian hour and forty minutes deeply in touch with the physical universe—gravity, dirt, fatigue and pain. Afterward they trotted back to the company area by a roundabout, nearly hour-long route, chanting from time to time, to disrupt their breathing cadence. They arrived at their hutment sweating profusely, and were dismissed for showers, dry clothes, and a layabout before supper, mostly napping.

After supper but before evening muster, exactly five trainees showed up at the orderly room to sign agreements. If they were severely disabled or mortally injured, and unconscious, the army was authorized to "extract the undersigned's central nervous system, and install it into an interfacing module for installation in a servomechanism, to serve as a cyborg of a model, and in a military unit, deemed appropriate by the army."

B Company's platoon sergeants had been allowed to choose their own site for their evening session. Sergeant First Class Arjin Hawkins Singh had chosen a field training site less than a mile from their hutment. There they found a platoon-size bleachers, with trees shading it from the lowering sun. Some second-level cadreman had delivered a folding chair to the site, for Hawkins, to help this seem like a conversation instead of a lecture.

The Jerries had been brought up to disdain war, and according to the briefing handbook on Jerrie ethnology, they put great stock in showing respect to the bodies of the dead, who presumably would be watching. On the other hand, the afternoon's training cube had rubbed their noses in their mortality, and the prospects of being killed or maimed would be more real now. And if five volunteers fell short of a landslide, it seemed to Hawkins that the bonding among the trainees, and their psychological identification with their regiments, would strengthen with time, and make a difference. A shortage of agreements now didn't necessarily mean they'd be lacking when the casualties began on New Jerusalem.

At any rate, Division, Regiment, and Mulvaney wanted this to be a relaxed and intimate discussion.

The trainees sensed that this would not be another training lecture. For one thing, their sergeant hadn't ordered them to give him thirty or thirty-five pushups before seating them.

Hawkins didn't begin with the usual "at ease" to shut them up. He simply asked, "What did you think of the training cube this afternoon?" When no one volunteered a comment, he pointed. "How about you, Abner?"

It took Abner McReynolds a moment to react. No cadreman had ever addressed him by his given name before. It distracted him enough, he even forgot to address Hawkins as "sergeant."

"Those warbots were something to watch," he said. "I can see why the army wants us to volunteer."

Hawkins nodded. McReynolds didn't sound like someone deeply perturbed by the request. "I'm signing up myself," Hawkins told them. "As soon as we get back in." He looked around, then pointed at Esau Wesley. "Esau, what did you think about the training cube?"

"Sergeant, the thing that struck me most was all the bodies, all the dead and wounded. I knew all along a person could get killed fighting in a war, but seeing it like that made it a lot more real to me. Those pulses don't pick and choose. If you're in the way, you're a deader. Wounded at least. It doesn't matter if you're the toughest man in the company."

"Good observation. Isaiah, what have you got to say?"

"Sergeant, it's well to be in good standing with the Lord before you go into battle. Of course, it's well to be in good standing with Him anyway, on general principles and for your own soul. As Jesus said in the Book of Mark: We don't know the time when death will come." He shrugged. "Although a battlefield seems a lot more dangerous than being home in bed."

"True. Unless you're home in bed when the Wyzhñyñy arrive." Hawkins paused. "What about death, Isaiah? What can you tell us about that?"

"In *Contemplations on the Testaments,* Elder Hofer wrote that 'death is the door to Heaven and Hell, and each of us chooses in life which one it will be.' So I'm prepared to die defending humankind."

"How about you, Hosea?"

"Well, Sergeant, say you're out deadening timber. And your hound's laid up hurt, so you're out there alone. You hear something and turn, and there's a big old tiger ten foot away, and you'd just set aside your ringing ax. My bet is, you'd be too scared to spit, even if you were spotless as the Lamb of God. The soul might go to Heaven, but the body? It'd stay behind for tiger feed, and don't no way like the prospect."

"Ah! Now there's a good way of putting it. Thank you, Hosea." Hawkins scanned and pointed. "Jael, you look as if you have something to say."

"Yessir, Sergeant. I'm a lot more scared of great pain than of dying. I suspect that lying out there in terrible pain, with maybe my innards ripped open and the flies buzzing, I'd be crying out to God to take me fast as he can."

"Good point," Hawkins said, thinking he'd as soon it hadn't come up. "But if it comes down to it, in combat you'll all have something in your aid kit that will greatly deaden the pain."

Jael continued before Hawkins could call on someone else. "And something else, Sergeant. There are things I want to do before I die. Have children, bring them up, watch them grow. Maybe even be a grandmother."

Hawkins nodded. "A good wish to have; a good ambition. But to enjoy it, it helps to have a safe place to live. There are lots of people who chose to stay on New Jerusalem—many with children—and they're a lot more likely to see their children murdered than grow up. While those who left with children . . . a labor camp's a hard place to raise a family. But when the war is over, and if we win it, things will work out for them.

"The fact is, the invaders have changed everything for us. I have a wife and two children back in North America. In a city called Madison, by a large beautiful lake. There's a good chance I'll never see them again, but I'll be doing what I can to keep them safe."

"Sergeant Hawkins?" It was Isaiah Vernon again.

"Yes, Isaiah?"

"Where do Sikhs believe they go when they die?"

Don't get into that, Arjan, Hawkins warned himself. *It'll dilute the subject we're here for, and maybe generate contention.* He would, he decided, give them a generality, something uncomplicated but basically valid. "Isaiah," he said, "think of it as returning to the loving arms of God."

When 2nd Platoon got back to the company area, there wasn't any real discussion about their evening. A few comments, but no actual discussion. In fact, the hut was more quiet than usual.

Jael Wesley was the first to take her toiletries bag and head for the latrine to brush her teeth. When she was almost there, she met Isaiah Vernon on his way to the hut. On impulse she stopped him.

"Isaiah," she said, "can we talk? Privately somewhere?"

His eyes widened. "What about?" he asked cautiously.

"I don't want to stand out here and talk about it. Where can we go that's private?"

For a long moment he stood silently. What would Esau think? Jael was so pretty and so nice, more than once he'd caught himself drifting into a fantasy about her. A guilty fantasy. It was well, he'd told himself, that they trained so hard and had so little time to think. "The dayroom," he said at last. "That might be all right."

She knew where it was, though she'd never been inside it. She led off, Isaiah following. No one else was there, and they sat down opposite each other at a reading table.

"It's about agreeing to be turned into a warbot," she said. "If someone's badly wounded and going to die."

He stared at her, then realizing he needed to respond, he nodded.

"I'm thinking about signing," she said.

His mouth opened slightly, but nothing came out for several seconds. "That's something you need to talk to Esau about, not me."

"I will. Before I make any decision anyway. The reason I want to talk to you is, you were studying to be a speaker. So you must have read and reread all the books, and thought about them a lot. And the first thing I need to know is . . ."

She groped, clarifying her thoughts. "Like I told Sergeant Hawkins, I'm afraid of great pain. And I don't trust myself to be signing for the right reason: to help out in the war. I might just want to be rescued from great pain, or not spend the rest of my life all crippled up. You see. But God might want me to experience those things. To suffer in those ways."

Isaiah's expression changed, showing not worry now, but focus, and his answer, when it came, was expressed as a speaker might have phrased it. "Jael," he answered, "you've read that sometimes God tests people, as in the case of Job, and Abraham. But there's no sign that he'd have punished them if they'd failed."

"But what about suicide?"

"Suicide?"

"If I caused my crippled body to die, on purpose and

ahead of its time, would that be suicide? And if my brain got cut out and bottled, then when God gathers the blessed to rise, and if I qualified, would I be resurrected as a warbot, or a person?"

Isaiah frowned not in disapproval but in thought, then shook his head. "First of all, all I can tell you is how it seems to me. The Testaments don't speak of that, nor does Elder Hofer's *Contemplations*. But it seems to me a warbot *is* a person. Because it has a soul. And as for resurrection— If a person gets eaten by a tiger, his flesh becomes tiger flesh, but he won't be resurrected as a tiger." Jael shook her head at that, rejecting. Isaiah continued. "And martyrs that were burned at the stake won't be resurrected as smoke and ashes. Nor cripples as cripples. God wouldn't resurrect them all humped over or twisted, or short an arm or leg."

He watched her thoughtful eyes. She was even prettier than he'd allowed himself to notice before. Finally she nodded. "Thank you, Isaiah," she said. "You've been a big help." Then she got up and left, leaving him sitting there.

Feeling guilty, because he hadn't been entirely honest with her. It seemed to him they wouldn't be resurrected in a body at all. He'd thought that when he was a child, and had gradually come to believe that when the time came, folks would have no interest in bodies. They'd just be souls.

Which of course brought up a lot of questions about the Testaments themselves. That was why he seldom let himself think about such things. The thing to do was trust in the Lord, and hope God would forgive his errors. Elder Hofer—and his own father—had always stressed that God was love.

Three more trainees of 2nd Platoon went to the orderly room that evening and signed warbot agreements. Jael Wesley was not one of them; she wasn't ready yet, if she'd ever be. The company as a whole signed 10 more; given those who'd signed earlier, that made 15. *Now*, Mulvaney thought, *if we can get the other 145 signed up . . .*

Chapter 25

Status Review

The mahogany table and wall panels glowed with golden sunlight, the ten-foot-tall window fields adjusting both the intensity and the blend of wavelengths. The entire Commonwealth cabinet was there, along with several high-ranking officials of War House and the Office of War Mobilization. Elsewhere, selected others watched on live, closed-circuit video. Whether in person or electronically, attendance was by invitation only. For some, this cabinet meeting was their first.

Prime Minister Foster Peixoto presided, with Chang Lung-Chi beside him; since the invasion, the president invariably attended.

The prime minister began with a brief caveat. "First you must all remember—MUST ALL REMEMBER—that what you hear in this meeting is confidential. Repeating *any* of it without authorization can result in a charge of insubordination or even treason. The Ministry of Information decides what will be released and when, and clears those releases with myself, in consultation with the president."

He looked them over, allowing his injunction to sink in. "Most of you are well informed on one aspect or another of our plans and progress, but not on all of it. What I will do here is summarize major areas. Others may elaborate on them.

"Our central strategy is and must be to stop the alien advance. At some point we must defeat their armada in space, which requires a great fleet well crewed. Which of course we do not have. Meanwhile the aliens are not waiting for us to get ready, and the course of their advance will bring them here to Terra as surely as if they knew where we are."

High on each wall, a screen showed a diagram of the Commonwealth and the alien progress, the captive worlds glowing redly.

"So far we have not challenged them," Peixoto went on. "Until very recently we've had no force that could fight a meaningful action. Even to draw a small demonstration of their armaments, we depended on Morgan's refugee pirate squadron. It was like a mosquito annoying a man, and what we learned from it was very limited. But *very* important."

Amazing, Chang thought, *that he can sound so worried when he and I talk privately, yet so calm and assured when speaking to others. It is a gift from the Tao.*

"Now we do have a significant space force: the First Sol Provisional Battle Force, commanded by Admiral Alvaro Soong. It is *far* smaller than the enemy's, but powerful enough to draw a broad display of alien armaments and tactics, and inflict significant damage.

"Soong's ships are ready. What remains is to finish training their crews. The crews of battleships have all handled battleships in test runs. Those on cruisers have flown actual cruisers. Every officer and man has carried out his flight duties and manned his battle stations and damage stations, in a ship of the kind he's assigned to.

"But they have not flown them through battle evolutions; not in reality. What they have done is fight numerous actions in simulation drills—actions in virtual F-space and virtual warpspace. And every officer has manned his station in war games against every tactic and combination of tactics that generations of officers could think of. Against the weapons we know the enemy has, and others we think he might have, given what is known of physics."

He picked up a glass and sipped, then scanned his audience, the president watching beside him. *Part of the impression he makes,* Chang decided, *is due to his height. And his eyebrows, like crows' wings! But mostly it is his intelligence and honesty. He speaks the truth, so far as he knows it.*

"Within days," Peixoto said, "Soong's force—they call themselves the 'Provos'—will generate warpspace and fly to the outer fringe of the Sol System. There its officers and men will carry out every sort of battle evolution in reality. And when Soong feels they are ready, but no later than four weeks after leaving the vicinity of Terra, they will journey outward to meet the enemy.

"The progress of alien conquests is direct and predictable. The flagship's savant will be in touch with ours, and we will keep the admiral informed of the enemy's progress, world by unfortunate world. At some point, when the alien armada emerges from hyperspace, Soong's force will be waiting for it."

A hand raised.

"Yes, Mister Bawadin?"

"Suppose the alien armada breaks up into separate task forces. What then?"

"At present we know little about alien psychology, but the possibility has been considered." He didn't mention the human prisoners on the Wyzhñyñy flagship. It would be a distraction. The few who needed to know already did. And at any rate, though what had been learned was interesting, it was of limited use. "The aliens haven't subdivided so far, except to establish colonies on the captured worlds. And of course, this sector of the galaxy is unknown to them. They don't know what they may encounter. And if they lack instantaneous communication, they'll be very effectively out of touch with each other."

"Suppose they do have instantaneous communication," Bawadin said. "What then?"

"There is every reason to believe they do not. That we have it ourselves grew out of fortuitous observations in unlikely research on unpromising subjects."

Another hand had raised, and Peixoto pointed. "Yes, Ms. Syrkin?"

"Why a Sol battle force? Why not a force more broadly integrated?"

"The answer is time and shipyards. Shipyards here in the Sol System were able to begin large-scale production of warships more quickly. Also, the majority of available training cadre were here, thus the Sol System has been able to produce crews earlier than the other core worlds. Construction and training in the Indi and Eridani Systems are well under way now, but their trainees aren't ready yet. In a few weeks that situation will have changed."

"What makes this force 'provisional'? Why not simply call it a fleet?" Syrkin asked. "Do you have misgivings about it?"

"We could call it a fleet. But what we learn from the first action may dictate major changes in force makeup, organization, and tactics. Thus it seemed appropriate to call it a provisional force."

"You said 'action,' not 'battle.' Why?"

"'Battle' suggests sustained fighting. This is expected to be a short series of hit-and-run actions. Lasting just long enough to record a spectrum of alien responses. You'll have an opportunity to ask Admiralty Chief Tischendorf about it later."

Again Peixoto paused to sip. "We are also preparing an action of another sort, to be fought very largely by far-worlders: the 1st New Jerusalem Infantry Division, supported by the 3rd Indi Armored Regiment with attached Ground Support Wing, and the 5th Lüneburger Engineers. All heavyworlders; all training on Pastor Lüneburger's World. Their commander, a Sikh of the Gopal Singh Dispensation, reports that training is on schedule. And . . ."

Another hand had risen. "Yes, Dr. Corneille?"

"The people of New Jerusalem are pacifist Christians. What makes you think they'll fight?"

"The question has been considered. The *founders* of New Jerusalem were firm pacifists, and their descendants have been inculcated with the beliefs of the founders, as filtered and adulterated by time and frontier living. But until the alien invasion, war was only a concept on New Jerusalem. And their most holy book, the Christian Bible, is replete with descriptions of patriotic wars and warrior folk heroes of the remote past. Intrinsic cracks in their pacifism.

"True, many on New Jerusalem stayed behind. Some refused to believe that aliens were coming. Others believe that God will protect them. But seventy-seven thousand adults, with their children, left farms and often family behind, and fled here. Those who volunteered for military service were well aware that it meant fighting a war.

"There is no indication that their cultural pacifism will prevent them from fighting. Certainly it has not interfered with their training. General Pak is confident of their willingness and toughness."

He didn't stop with that. "The Sikhs themselves, under their founder, Guru Nanak, began as fervent pacifists, but in time became notorious warriors as a matter of survival. While in his time, Gopal Singh was a peacemaker, if not quite a pacifist." Peixoto grimaced. "During the Troubles, many of Gopal Singh's followers resigned their positions in the military, on the basis that it was an unethical war. And spent years in prison for that dedication to what they regarded as right. But there have been no—*no* Sikh resignations in this war. Not one."

It occurred to Chang that his friend had never mentioned his own spiritual persuasion. *Probably deist,* he thought. Flavored by other doctrines, deism predominated on Terra.

"In about fifteen weeks," Peixoto went on, "when the troops are ready, the New Jerusalem Liberation Force will begin a five-month voyage to New Jerusalem. By the time they arrive, it will have been in alien hands for some time. And besides the ground and air units, there will be a space force, under Admiral Apraxin-DaCosta, to deal with whatever space force the alien armada left in the system."

He then described Apraxin's Liberation Task Force. When he'd finished, a hand thrust up, and Peixoto pointed. "Yes, Doctor?"

"Mr. Prime Minister, that is a rather modest force. What makes you think it can do the job?"

"Most of the conquered planets informed us of the number of alien emergence loci, so we know how many fewer they have been from world to world. Some of the

ships left behind with the conquering colonists are undoubtedly transports, and supply vessels left to support the
conquerors until they can support themselves. But others
are warships; Morgan's squadron provided information on
how many to expect."

Peixoto's gaze had been on the people in the room.
Now he scanned the faces on the monitors. He had their
attention.

"Also, judging from the elapsed time between worlds,
the armada remains in the system's fringe for about a
Standard week.

"We also assume that they expect us to make a stand
farther within the Commonwealth. If so, they probably
leave behind no more fighting ships than they consider
necessary."

He scanned the people in the chamber. "We've had to
make numerous assumptions, and add modest safety mar-
gins. While keeping in mind that the ships of the Liberation Task Force will not be available to Admiral Soong's
Provos."

He pointed at an upthrust hand. "Yes, Senator Bomboulis?"

"Why send a liberation force to New Jerusalem? At this
time, I mean. Why not send Apraxin's force with Soong's?
And hold the New Jerusalem division to help defend some
other world?"

"We have two reasons. One, we lack knowledge of how
the enemy fights. The ground units we land on New Jerusalem will be accompanied by several savants, as will Apraxin's
and Soong's space forces. They should give us very important information on how the alien fights. And two, if we
undertake to defend a world on the ground, the alien can
send in more and more forces to overwhelm our own.
While if we land a liberation force well after he's left, the
alien defense is unlikely to receive reinforcements. As I
pointed out earlier, we have compelling reason to believe
that they do not have instantaneous communication."

More hands had popped up; the prime minister waved
them off. "Now we will hear from our director of industrial mobilization, and our minister of war. Please jot down
any further questions; I will invite them afterward. Our time

is limited, and Mr. Shin and Mr. Stavrianos will no doubt anticipate many of them in their presentations."

The director of industrial mobilization spoke first, followed by the minister of war. When the meeting was again opened to questions, the first hand raised belonged to the chief of Senate Liaison. The prime minister pointed. "Senator Bomboulis," he said.

"Wouldn't it be simpler and less expensive to make warbots in the form of floaters? Because human soldiers walk upright on their hind limbs doesn't make it the optimum design strategy."

"A perceptive question, Senator," Peixoto said, "but I believe you'll find it *is* the best design strategy. General Kulikov, why don't you explain."

The general rose; he preferred to speak on his feet. "The human nervous system," he answered, "evolved to operate an erect, bipedal body with upper appendages which manipulate objects. And beginning in infancy, each of us spends years mastering their function. The warbot servo is designed to operate using those same neural circuits in the manner for which they evolved, and in which the person learned to use them.

"In the late 28th century, when warbots became feasible, alternative design strategies were tested. All but the bipeds presented serious training problems, while biped servo design proved less difficult than expected.

"So when the present emergency struck, we went with a biped design. Plans already existed for large-scale production. Have I answered your question?" Kulikov finished.

Senator Bomboulis nodded. "You have, General. Before my election, I was a professor of history at the University of Kaunas. So I am well aware how little appreciation and support your peacetime defense efforts received—both your predecessors' efforts and your own. You have my sincere admiration and gratitude for your dedication, foresight and ingenuity." He paused, then chuckled wryly. "Not to mention your thick skin."

When the meeting was over, the president walked to his office, briskly as always. He was thinking about something

Kulikov had failed to mention. A bot design, loosely speaking, only recently in production, and not bipedal at all. Not a fighting bot in the conventional sense, though in its way, military. But it wasn't time yet to make it known, even to the cabinet. A leak would result in problems he would gladly do without.

Chapter 26

Warbots

On their way to various training areas, B Company's trainees had seen the new building grow from bare, bulldozed earth to a completed structure in under four weeks. The largest in the regimental area, it even had two stories. They'd wondered what it was for. Now, obviously, they were about to find out.

Entering it, they filed into a small lecture hall and sat down on its benches. It smelled like newly-sawn lumber and fresh paint. Then someone, *something* entered and stepped to the lectern. "I am Lieutenant Mei-Li Huygens-Gurejian," she said, "from New Netherlands, in Spain. That's on Terra. I have two children, and for four years I was a lecturer in history at the University of Barcelona. Until I was afflicted—and I do mean afflicted—by cascade syndrome, the major killer of young adults on Terra." She spread her arms. "So when I had a chance to contribute to the defense of my species and my children, I took it. Without hesitation."

A mother! thought Jael Wesley. *More than seven feet tall, and steel! Here to protect her babies.* A thrill ran through her. Glancing sideways at Esau, she laid her hand on his.

Huygens continued. "Two years ago I was five feet four and weighed one hundred twenty-five pounds. In secondary school I was a competitive gymnast. It developed excellent balance and coordination, very useful for warbots. Now I'm seven feet three, and weigh four hundred forty-seven pounds; perhaps less than you thought. In the Core Worlds, materials engineering is quite advanced."

Jael didn't understand everything the warbot said, but she got a sense of it. And she was impressed by the bot's clear female voice. She'd expected a baritone, a voice like the bot's on the cube they'd watched.

"I see one of you is female," Huygens added, and Jael felt herself blushing. "As I still am in all but body. My viewpoint remains essentially female—a female soldier's—and my feelings are still female, though in some respects different than before." Her fingertips passed down her body almost to the knees; her arms were long. "Obviously I'll have no more children, but I've had my quota, and with cascade syndrome I couldn't have had more anyway. Nor could I have mothered the two I had much longer; I was expected to die within weeks at most. But now, if I survive this war, I can be with them. I may very well not survive, but if we lose the war, my children would die."

She paused, then laughed. "They've seen me like this, incidentally. I had five days leave before I shipped here. They're eight and five years old, a girl and a boy, and at first they were very shy with me. But within a couple of hours, the shyness was gone, replaced by curiosity. Argop loved using my arm for a chinning bar. We did some hugging and kissing, too," she added chuckling. Jael found herself loving this seven-foot metal woman. "Kissing went better for me than for them. My sensorial package—the senses built into this servo—includes a good sense of touch and being touched. And my brain translates it into familiar feelings. But touching *me*? I'm afraid I'm not the best for snuggling with." Her audience laughed nervously. "Krikor, my husband, says he'll be glad to get used to it, but I told him he should find a female companion anyway. One who'll be a good surrogate mother for our kids, and whom I can get along with when the war is over."

She sounded almost serene as she said it. It struck Jael

that this woman had needed to examine her feelings and make adjustments fast. But then, having a deadly disease, she must have gotten used to doing that. And now she had a life again, and a purpose.

It also occurred to Jael that she herself might never have had those thoughts if she hadn't left New Jerusalem, and the life and farm they'd had there. The realization took her by surprise.

Mei-Li Huygens-Gurejian hadn't been killing time, talking about herself. Part of her job was to make herself human for her listeners. That accomplished, she went on to prepare them briefly for the training they'd begin when she'd finished.

They could not, she told them, learn to operate a servo—a bot body—while still organics. What they could do, though, was learn and get used to what warbots did in combat, especially individual and small-unit tactics.

"Some of it," she said, "is much like the things you already do. Every day, while training as organics, you learn things that warbots need to know. And most of the time, in combat, warbots work with organics, and need to know what you know and do. So those of you who make yourselves available for warbot service—in case you're ever maimed or fatally injured—will already know much of what you need to know. You'll have it stored in your brains. And what you learn in the training you begin tonight will teach you the rest.

"The main thing you'll need to do, after being bottled and installed, is learn to operate your new body, the servo. And that's not so much learning as it is simply practice. You'll find that your arms and legs will work very much like they always have. Intend them to do something and they'll do it. But your center of gravity will be higher, so your sense of balance will feel a little off at first. Also your arms will be considerably longer, and you'll have to get used to that. You'll weigh a lot more, so it will be harder to dodge. And you'll be a lot faster, a *lot* stronger, and a lot more durable. Meanwhile, some things you'll have to be more careful about, till you get used to doing them in your new body. And some things you can be less careful about."

A lecturer is a kind of teacher, Jael thought. *No wonder she's good at explaining.* She wished she could get to really know this woman, this giantess.

"What you'll begin here this evening," Huygens went on, "is called 'virtuality training.' You'll wear a special helmet, and sit in a little room, seeing and hearing a realistic video scene all around you. Seeing it as if through bot eyes, hearing it as if through bot ears. The sounds that go with the scenes will be partly the sounds of battle, including orders from officers. And partly it will be the voices of your trainer and your coach, telling you what's going on and what to do. As an imaginary warbot, you'll seem to move around and fight within that scene, but without ever leaving your module. Your coach will be seeing the same things you see, and talk to you through your earphones. It'll be awkward at first, but that will soon pass."

Abruptly she went from being a professor to being a sergeant or whatever. "And that," she said, "is it. End of lecture. On your feet! Sergeant Burlingham will take you to the training section."

Burlingham was another bot. As the company followed him down a corridor, Jael had a nervous stomach.

Chapter 27

Messages

Encrypted pulse OSPCO
2912.07.13/14:16G
Bloemfontein to all AMS program labs
Subject(s): venom studies
We have what appears to be the appropriate insertion loci to work from, to increase broad-spectrum venom virulence in AMS. Exploratory work is under way. Suggestions?
— Marijka V.
(Issa, can you send me 12 of your best clone for some exploratory work? MV)

Encrypted pulse OSPCO
2912.07.13/14:46G
Lusaka to Bloemfontein AMS; copy all AMS program labs
Subject(s): venom studies
Suggest *Selenarctos thibetanus* as a test species. They are reportedly less venom-sensitive than any other Ursidae, even the honey bear. Availability of test material may be a problem. Check with

Institute of Biosystem Research @ Dehra Dun. If
they can't advise you, no one can.
— Jabari H.

Encrypted pulse OSPCO
2912.07.13/16:03G
Bangui to all AMS program labs
Subject(s): 1. reproductive enhancement (fecundity
of queens); 2. security break.

1. We have an enhanced clone whose queens,
under Hesselink B conditions, averaged 3,873
viable inseminated eggs per day over 14 days.
A busy lady! See attachment.
2. Minutes ago, university received E threats from
"Peace Front" re program, so the cat is out of the
bag. You will be hearing from the Bureau soonest,
if you haven't already.
— Issa L.
(Marijka, 12 princesses are on their way to you. IL)

Encrypted pulse OSPCO
2912.07.13/16:27G
OSP to AMS Nairobi; copy all AMS program labs
Subject(s): Foulbrood project
Kanika, given the update by Marijka on the venom
project (shudder), and by Issa on the fecundity
project (shiver), I certainly hope you folks are
making good progress.
— Benny

Encrypted pulse OSPCO
2912.07.14/03:23G
OSP to all AMS program labs
Subject(s): NSS 12
At 03:05G this date, NSS 12 reported passing the
halfway point (eccentricity 1.06) to Tagus. Looks
good so far, but don't depend on it.
— Debbie C.

❖   ❖   ❖

"Excuse me," said Major General Pyong Pak Singh, and took the call on his privacy receiver. "Pak," he said.

"Sir, this is WO-3 Kiefer." Yolanda Kiefer sounded very young, something he hadn't gotten used to. She was older than he was. "Dierdre just brought a message from War House," she went on. "About two minutes' worth. I can read it to you if you'd like."

A savanted message. "Just a moment, Kiefer," he said, and turned to his visitor, Mayor Ritala of nearby North Fork. "This will take perhaps two minutes."

The Lüneburgian nodded.

"Read it to me," Pak said. "I'm ready."

"From Lieutenant General Titu Cioculescu, deputy chief of staff, Commonwealth Army." *Cioculescu,* Pak thought, impressed. *Lefty Sarruf's right hand.* "To Major General Pyong Pak Singh, commander, New Jerusalem Liberation Corps. Greeting. When you have reached New Jerusalem, you will provide War House with three Wyzhñyñy prisoners alive and unwounded. Do not rely on serendipity. Develop a plan, and train teams accordingly. You will be informed later on how the prisoners are to be processed. Personnel will be provided to handle and transport them. You will be further informed as appropriate.

"(signed) Cioculescu."

Frowning, Pak pursed thin lips. "Thank you, Kiefer. Is that it?"

"Yes, General."

"I'll answer him when I've seen it in writing."

Reaching, the general disconnected, wondering what War House wanted with prisoners. It seemed highly improbable they had a translation program for whatever language the Wyzhñyñy spoke, or whistled, or gestured, or however they did it. It didn't occur to him that the questions might have originated from an agency he'd never heard of: the Office of Special Projects. And that the answers would come not from questioning, but from chromatographs and other tests.

He turned to his visitor. "Mayor Ritala, I appreciate that your merchants would like my troops to come into town more often, and I'm glad their behavior meets with your approval. But we are on Pastor Lüneburger's World to train, preparing to fight a very dangerous foe. The present schedule of passes on alternate Sevendays will have to suffice, and at any rate it's about as often as their very modest pay permits." He paused. "Is there anything else?"

The general's voice held a tone of dismissal; his closing question was clearly rhetorical, a courtesy. A thought passed through the mayor's mind: to invite the general to his home for Sevenday dinner. But somehow he didn't. This soldier was too single-minded for that.

It also occurred to him that single-mindedness was desirable in generals, given the circumstances the human species found itself in.

Chapter 28

Qonits Answers Questions

Instead of answering, Yukiko Gavaldon got calmly to her feet and faced him. "Qonits," she said, "it is not appropriate that you ask all the questions. Now it is time for us to ask questions, and for you to answer."

David had learned to conceal his surprise at his wife's sometimes off-the-wall responses. "Yes," he said, backing her. "It is disrespectful that we are not given a reasonable chance to question you. It becomes increasingly so as the imbalance grows."

Qonits stood for several long seconds without responding. This was something new from the captives. When at last he replied, it was slowly. "But we are the victors. You are our captives. You are obliged to do as we order."

Yukiko shook her head firmly. "That is incorrect. There are two categories of victors. One is barbarians. The other consists of civilized beings. Barbarians are inferior sophonts who do not care whether they behave properly or not. Civilized beings do care. And you have shown yourself to be civilized."

She stood with arms folded, her features firm.

The two Terrans had learned to read Qonits somewhat.

It seemed to David that the chief scholar was unsure of himself now. "There should be balance in all things," he added. His voice was mild, even kind. "Not absolute balance; that is hardly possible. But sufficient to show respect."

Qonits looked at him warily. "What questions would you ask?"

It was Yukiko who began. "Where in the galaxy are you from?"

Qonits' head jerked three times, as if with Tourette's syndrome—a reaction that seemed too extreme for the question. But he answered it. "Shipsmind says this not our galaxy. We jumped here in—no elapsed time."

David frowned; this had to be a language problem. "Not from this galaxy? How can that be?"

"We do not know. We crossed from our old spiral arm to another—very far voyage, eleven years—then emerged from hyperspace. At that time, shipsmind knew exactly what place we were, and where our home sector was. Then we entered a star system to explore . . . and suddenly . . ."

He stopped, his hide twitching weirdly, alarmingly. Yukiko got quickly to her feet and placed a hand on Qonits' arm. "It's all right," she said softly. "It's all right. You are with friends."

Qonits didn't answer for a full minute while his twitching subsided, but he remained agitated. "Suddenly," he went on, "the view, the stars, all things was different. And the ship's . . ." He gestured frantically, as if digging for the word with his hands. "Numbers that appear."

"Readouts," David suggested.

Qonits seemed not to hear. "Ship said we were in different galaxy—*and no time had passed!*" He paused. The twitching had begun again, and he breathed heavily, seeming to hyperventilate. More than his nictitating membranes had closed. His eyelids had clenched shut, and he stood without saying anything more until he'd calmed somewhat. Finally, eyes open again, he continued. "Ship was searching for known objects in space, as fastly it could. And was recognizing nothing.

"Some of our people lost . . ." Again his hands pawed as if digging. "Some even died."

The chief scholar's reaction stunned David. Granted the experience must have been a shock, it seemed to him that humans—certainly spacers—wouldn't have reacted so strongly.

"I'm sorry my question led to painful memories," Yukiko said. "I had no wish to distress you. I was simply interested in the world on which your people originated. Is that where you're from?"

The question seemed to calm Qonits somewhat. He stood as if digesting it. "Wyzhñyñy began on a world whose name would have not meaning to you, and hard for you to speak. We say Kryzhgon. My tribe would start long later, on different world. Kryzhgon had hard history to live with. Much danger. Much fighting."

"Fighting?" said David.

"Kryzhgon had three sapient life-forms, each on different part, with ocean between. One already had water ships. Came to our land on them. Two-leggers like you; we do not say their name. Had better weapons than Wyzhñyñy, but Wyzhñyñy more numbers." Qonits had begun to shiver again. "They tried to kill us, have all land for themselves. War was a very long time. Gradually, enemy grew more. But as they grew more, we made weapons like theirs. Better weapons. Our . . . old fathers?"

"We say 'forefathers,'" Yukiko told him, guessing.

Qonits picked it up without comment, as if deeply into the story he'd begun. "Our beforefathers fought hard, tried to kill them all, be safe from them."

Yukiko thought of pointing out the parallel between that ancient invasion and what the Wyzhñyñy were doing in the Commonwealth, but decided not to.

"For long time," he went on, "more enemy came across ocean, but beforefathers grew stronger. Finally no more enemy came, and Wyzhñyñy killed all that were there. Hunted them down till all were dead. Then beforefathers built water ships—explored, learned where enemy came from. Built fleet and went there. After many generations, and many many Wyzhñyñy killed, Wyzhñyñy killed last one of enemy. That enemy.

"But Wyzhñyñy still not safe. On another land was third sapient life-form. Small." He gestured, indicating a height of perhaps twenty inches. "Six limbs, like us, and very quick, very fierce. Very clever." Qonits tapped his cranium. "Our long-time enemy had gone also to small one's land. Then small ones came to ours."

"At first they fought old enemy, and us only when we met. After old enemy all dead, we fought small ones a long time; many generations. Both sides learned explosives. Wyzhñyñy became much more numerous than them, but it took very long time before killed the last one." Qonits paused, gestured a sigh. "Over many lifetimes, the small ones ate Wyzhñyñy. But not since a very long time now."

With that, Qonits stopped talking. He looked emotionally drained. Yukiko patted his arm. "The Wyzhñyñy had a very difficult history," she said. "I am glad our life-form is not so savage as the enemies of your past. We will not try to destroy you, but I don't expect you to believe that. Not after the long suffering of your people."

David nodded emphatically. "Now you have balanced your relationship with us," he said. "It is time for you to ask us questions again, before we must exercise Annika."

Qonits bobbed his upper body. After consulting with shipsmind through the speaker in his ear, he began.

Nine hyperspace months away, Chang Lung-Chi and Foster Peixoto sat awed by what they'd heard. "Amazing!" said the president. "Two oceanographers, prisoners of the enemy, yet they are providing us with information beyond anything we could have hoped for. Seemingly without realizing it."

The prime minister's nod was subdued. "Two oceanographers and a traumatized idiot savant." He paused. "What do you make of the alien's statement that their ship inadvertently jumped between galaxies?"

Normally Chang Lung-Chi answered questions quickly and with certainty. This time he lagged. "It seems to me . . ." he began, "it seems to me the creature told what he thought was the truth; I have never sensed subterfuge in anything he's said. And his grammar and pronunciations became poorer. As if he were strongly agitated."

Either that or the chief scholar is a good actor, Foster Peixoto thought. But that made no sense; the alien had no apparent reason to mislead his two captives in that. "I wish I could have seen him as he spoke," he said.

Chang nodded agreement, and for a moment the two men sat silent. Finally Peixoto spoke. "Wyzhñyñy history makes it psychologically more difficult to exterminate them. What we plan for them is much like what they did to their enemies, long ago."

Chang grunted. Humanity was the likelier candidate for extermination. "But if they had not attacked us," he said, "we would have accepted them peacefully. And even after they'd attacked us, if they hadn't been so focused on extermination, we could have negotiated."

Peixoto examined that. They'd become so deeply involved in the war effort, they'd never followed through on the question of negotiations. "Negotiations?" he said.

"It was you who first suggested them," Chang reminded him.

"What terms would you offer, now they've done so much harm?"

"They must remove their colonies from the worlds they've captured, and leave this sector."

Peixoto nodded thoughtfully. "That willingness, that preference, is what makes us civilized. But given the experience of their forefathers, what would it take to get their agreement?"

"We will need to dominate their fleet first, and rout them from enough of their colonies that they know they cannot hold the rest. Then perhaps they'll agree to leave."

Peixoto sighed. Victory felt unreal to him, and so did Wyzhñyñy agreement. "Let us hope we can do it," he said quietly.

"We will," said Chang Lung-Chi. "We will." But saying it produced second thoughts. Could they trust such a life-form anywhere in this part of the galaxy? Even with a peace treaty? And they "knew" only one Wyzhñyñy. How representative was he?

Quanshûk watched the monitor screen as Qonits left the captives' room. The prisoners had been a major disappointment to the grand admiral, or their information had been. Even now, with shipsmind's knowledge of the human language growing rapidly, and Qonits' expanding proficiency in its use.

It would mean a lot simply to learn how large their empire was. A hyperspace year in diameter, one of the humans had said, but the body-field monitor insisted he'd lied. Obviously they wanted their empire to seem larger and more formidable than it really was.

In a way, the lie had been reassuring. It established that the monitor worked. And why make small lies? To that question anyway. So say they'd doubled the actual size, and the true diameter was half a hyperspace year. Considering how far his armada had already penetrated, that was conceivable, though barely.

It never occurred to Quanshûk, nor to Qonits, that the human, to make himself more believable, might have deliberately described the commonwealth as *half* its actual diameter, not twice. And that the volume of human space was roughly sixty-four times what he himself was assuming.

The watch officer's voice broke Quanshûk's preoccupation. "Lord Admiral, the F-space potentiality indicates another stellar gravity field coming into range."

Quanshûk's gaze moved to the red view screen. Perhaps two hours ahead and to starboard, a white gravitic isoline formed hesitantly, a segment at a time. So many stars, and so few suitable planets; detouring and emerging to examine them slowed his armada greatly. Fortunately, some could be dismissed without doing either. Like this one, which promised to be a white dwarf.

What he really wanted was to reach a system with a human defensive fleet, something he could deal with. Not an empire too vast for his capacity to subdue and occupy. *Quanshûk,* he chided himself, *you worry needlessly. No empire can be that large.*

Annika now had easily recognized cycles of sleep and waking. But her waking state was definitely not normal; mostly she lay on one side or the other in a fetal curl, her eyes open. From time to time she'd get up on her own to use the latrine, though it was Yukiko, or occasionally David, who cleaned her up. Or she'd sit up and repeat the single word "eat," until she was fed. Fortunately for her health, she'd stand up when Yukiko asked, and allow herself to be walked around their fifteen-by-twenty-foot chamber. Recently she'd even done simple exercises when led. But she was nothing like the happy child she'd been aboard the *Cousteau*.

Yukiko had been tempted to impose herself on Annika's odd state, and see if she could break her free of it, but the temptation was easily resisted. As David had said: what good would it do? The girl seemed content as she was.

He broke his wife's thought now with a whisper, breathy and without sibilance. They weren't sure whether the monitor picked up such whispers or not, but they needed *some* means of confidentiality. "What did you say?" she whispered back.

He repeated even more softly than before. "It was spooky, the way Qonits acted when he talked about the ship being jumped between galaxies. Do you think it actually happened?"

"I have no doubt at all." Yukiko barely breathed it.

Snuggled beside her, Annika neither doubted nor believed. She simply, unknowingly, passed it on to Kunming.

Chapter 29
Night Surprise

The night was moonless, the galaxy a banner of frost half seen through bare branches and twigs. Boots crunched recently-fallen leaves, loudly enough, it seemed to Esau, to be heard a hundred feet away. Until it rained again, there was no chance at all of slipping quietly through the woods.

His helmet gave him a choice of two night-vision enhancements. One provided positive night vision, which worked even in heavy forest and under thick clouds, but might be detected by an enemy. The other amplified natural starlight, moonlight if any, and whatever other light there might be. The army preferred the latter, when there was moonlight or enough starlight.

Isaiah Vernon had wondered aloud whether the Wyzhñyñy might have a way of detecting starlight vision, too. And of course no one knew, or would know till they fought.

At any rate Esau could see in the dark, could see Jonas Timmins ahead of him, it being Jonas's time to lead the squad. Off to the left, twenty yards or so, was a meadow, with thin wispy fog on it. *Odds are,* Esau thought, *it'll thicken through the night.*

Ahead of Timmins was the rest of the platoon, and ahead of it, Ensign Berg, Sergeant Hawkins, and the point man.

Esau was a little irked that Timmins was leading 4th Squad tonight. He considered himself the rightful squad leader. But the ensign was giving others the experience, which Esau realized made sense. And Timmins was probably the next best leader after himself. Timmins and Jael. His wife had surprised him with her willingness and ability to make decisions and give orders. And to his further surprise, he liked her even better that way.

Somewhere up ahead, the ensign or Sergeant Hawkins raised an arm, and the file of trainees stopped silently. This was a simplified problem, Esau realized, one suited to their training level. Somewhere on the other side of the meadow, the platoon's scouts had spotted the enemy outpost. The platoon was to capture it. The problem had no broader context, strategic or tactical.

An order spoke in their ears, and the file became a rank, slinking toward the meadow's edge. Halfway there they dropped to their bellies and stopped. To lie waiting, while Timmins and the other squad leaders moved forward in a low crawl, to examine the ground with Hawkins and the ensign.

After a couple of minutes, Timmins spoke to his squad on their own frequency, ordering them to the forest edge. When they'd reached it, he spoke again. "4th Squad, we'll start out crawling; the vegetation'll cover us. And don't bunch up. See that pointy-topped fir sticking up above the hardwoods?" On Lüneburger's, the Jerries called any evergreen a "fir." "I'll guide on that. If anything happens to me"—they were being as realistic as they knew how—"Esau takes command. When we come under fire, proceed by teams. The teams that are covering, really pour it on."

They'll have starlight vision, too, Esau thought. *They'll spot us by the way the weeds move when we crawl through them.*

Timmins continued. "That worm fence down the middle is the sticky part. If anyone's over there, that's where they'll spot us. If we haven't come under fire before we cross it, climb over. Anyone not over before they start shooting at us, pull the fence apart and advance by crawling. Everyone that's across, lay down covering fire."

It was, Esau judged, about a hundred yards to the fence. Where he saw a complication: pulling the fence down would be easier said than done. The meadow hadn't been grazed that spring and summer; that was obvious. The livestock had been removed when the area was made a military reservation; that's why the vegetation was so tall. Along the fence, he could make out a row of naked saplings—probably a row along each side. Unbrowsed they'd flourished. Many were six feet tall or more, he judged. They'd tend to hold the rails in place.

He wondered if Sergeant Hawkins had spotted that. It would be like him to see if they came up with it themselves. If they didn't, he'd point it out later. Or maybe not. From things he'd said, Hawkins had grown up a town boy. He might miss something like that.

"2nd Platoon, listen up." This voice was Ensign Berg's, activating the platoon command frequency. "When you reach the fence, stop. Squad leaders, tell me when your squad is there. Now move out."

Timmins moved out at once, on elbows and knees, his blaster cradled in his arms. The rest of the squad followed, almost even with him, losing themselves at once in the thick, falling-down meadow growth. From time to time Esau raised himself high enough to see the fir tree. *Either they're blind over there,* he told himself, *or they're waiting for us to reach the fence. We'll be better targets then, for sure.*

They were all good crawlers. They'd practiced a lot, and it didn't take long to cover a hundred yards. After a bit, 3rd Squad's leader announced his arrival at the fence. Almost at once, Timmins reported his. Esau and the rest of 4th Squad reached it at almost the same time. Then 1st and 2nd Squads reported.

"All right," the ensign said, "squad leaders send your squads."

"4th Squad," Timmins said, "1st Team over."

Esau got quickly to his feet, blaster in one hand, and bellied over the chest-high fence. He hadn't hit the ground

before firing came from the woods ahead, the staccato
popping and thumping of blasters and slammers, loud in
the aggregate, each kicking out soft pulses at several per
second. None had hit him; even soft pulses had an impact,
and except for their helmets, they weren't wearing armor
on this patrol. He took up a squat-firing position—the
vegetation was too tall for firing prone—and began to shoot
back. Near him on his right, Jael, the squad's grenadier,
was launching a series of dummy phosphorous grenades,
the butt of her launcher on the ground, braced against a
foot. Behind him he could hear obscenities as 2nd Team
struggled to pull the fence apart.

Ensign Berg ordered the platoon to move forward by
squads. Adding, "Keep low!" Crouching, Esau sprang forward, ran six strides, then dove for the ground, taking the
impact on the butt of his blaster. Rolled sideways, then
returned to the squat position to lay fire on the defenders. To his right, Timmins yelped—hit, Esau supposed. The
red warning light on his HUD, his heads-up display, told
him he needed to change his blaster's power slug. He did.
Then Timmins shouted "1st Team go!" and Esau was on
his feet again; he ran another six strides and hit the ground.
This time he remembered to squeeze off a burst while
running.

Their cycle of rush, give covering fire, and rush again
was repeated several times, and still he hadn't felt the
impact of a blaster pulse. He wondered how many had.
Surely if this was hard fire, some of them would be lying
bloody behind him.

They were almost to the forest when warbots attacked,
the weapons attached to their forearms pumping bursts of
energy pulses. From their seven-foot height, they could
easily target the trainees in the vegetation. Esau felt soft
pulses slap him in chest and thigh. Without thinking, he
fired a burst at the nearest bot, at the primary sensorium
on the head, then dove, wrapping thick-muscled arms
around its ankles. The bot crashed down, and he scrambled
over it, grabbing at the head, going for the sensors. But
stronger arms than his wrapped around him. "Gotcha," said
a voice. Instead of giving up, Esau struggled.

Then cadre whistles shrilled; the exercise was over. The

arms that pinioned him relaxed, and the warbot got up, rolling Esau off. For a moment he lay stunned, not from any blow, but by what he considered an unfair trick. Warbots! No one had said anything to them about the Wyzhñyñy having warbots!

The platoon leaders were taken back to the regimental area by floater, to evaluate the exercise. The trainees marched back, led by their platoon sergeants. They marched "at ease" (no talking), left to their own thoughts, double-timing once they reached the road.

It was a lecture shed they went to, and did fifty pushups before going inside. 1st Platoon was also there; it had been their adversary in the game. The two platoons sat on opposite sides of the center aisle. Four bots were also there, sitting farther to the rear. It was Captain Mulvaney who reviewed the exercise with them.

"All right, men," he said, "at ease." He looked them over. "Who here got hit, by any kind of weapon? I'm talking about before the warbots attacked."

Esau looked around. On 2nd Platoon's side of the aisle, nine hands raised. Considering all the shooting, he was surprised there weren't more. 1st Platoon had only four, but it had been dug in.

Mulvaney questioned everyone who'd raised their hand. Of the thirteen organics who'd raised theirs, eight would very probably have died.

"And who was hit during the warbot charge? Keep them up so I can count you."

Esau didn't try to count them. All four bots had been hit. They'd charged into the middle of it, been big targets and drawn lots of fire. "Seventeen," the CO said, "plus the bots. Okay, take them down. Your ensigns and Division's umpires all agree: 2nd Platoon, you carried out your approach and attack very professionally. 1st Platoon, you dug in effectively in the limited time you had, and fought a good defense."

He looked toward the bots. "Corporal Sciacca, where were you hit?"

"In the head, sir, by a blaster. A hard pulse would have ruined one of my ocular sensors. I also took hits on my chest and left leg, but even if they'd been hard pulses, neither one would have done damage."

"Thank you." Mulvaney paused, turning his gaze entirely on 2nd Platoon. "What did you think of the warbots?"

Esau's hand shot up. "Esau," the captain said.

"Sir, it wasn't fair to use warbots against us like that. No one told us the enemy had any. We didn't have a chance."

"War is seldom fair," Mulvaney answered, "and surprises are part of it. So far as we know, the Wyzhñyñy don't have warbots, but they'll have something dangerous we don't expect. When fighting an enemy we know so little about, we can expect more surprises than usual, mostly unpleasant. This evening you got some notion of what it can be like.

"Some of you responded very well, incidentally."

Mulvaney turned his attention to 1st Platoon. "1st Platoon, Division's umpires estimate you took twenty casualties from phosphorous burns. You've seen demonstrations of what that can mean, so you can be grateful this was an exercise, with dummy grenades."

He paused, scanning both platoons. "The reason we didn't have you feign death when hit was, we didn't want you to forego the complete action. In combat, of course, when you're hit, you're hit. When you're burned, you're burned." Another pause. "History tells us that many soldiers go through numerous actions without being wounded, but there are also actions where casualties are very heavy. The best chance you have of coming through, of winning and surviving, is by working as a team." Again he paused. "Let's hear you say it: 'We work as a team!'"

"We work as a team!" they answered.

"Say it like you mean it!"

This time they shouted: "WE WORK AS A TEAM!"

Mulvaney grinned. "Good. I got that. And there are other things: We keep the enemy under heavy fire. Say it!"

"WE KEEP THE ENEMY UNDER HEAVY FIRE!"

"We maintain contact with the enemy."

"WE MAINTAIN CONTACT WITH THE ENEMY!"

"We are aggressive."

"WE ARE AGGRESSIVE!"

"All right! You will learn more about all these things over the weeks to come, including when and where they *don't* apply. You will practice till doing the right thing is as natural as breathing. And when you first go into battle, you'll be as good as you can get, short of actual combat experience." He paused, raised his voice. "You want to know what surprise really is? Surprise . . . " He slowed, his voice softening, becoming confidential. "Surprised is what the Wyzhñyñy will be the first time they tangle with you. They're going to wish they'd stayed wherever they came from."

He hadn't anticipated the cheers he got. Inwardly it shook him. He'd have given his life to cancel this war and send his trainees home, but it wasn't an option. For anyone. The Wyzhñyñy had come, and there was nothing that would cause them to leave, short of defeat. And there was no reason to expect even defeat to drive them away. If they had to be hunted down and wiped out on each world they'd occupied, this would be a truly hellish war.

Chapter 30

" . . . and God Created Humankind in Her Own Image . . . "

Summer had shortened and cooled substantially as far south as the Dakota Prefecture, and the Keewatin Ice Sheet—actually the fifth-year firn line, deep in metamorphosed snow—had reached the north end of Canada's Reindeer Lake. The previous winter's snow had survived the summer southward almost to Lac La Ronge. Four hundred and fifty miles north of Reindeer Lake, near the heart of the ice sheet, soundings reported an average of more than eighty feet of ice, with plastic flow on slopes.

Not surprisingly, Saskatoon's population was less than a third that of 250 years earlier. Over the past two decades, a congregation of the Reformed Church of the Holy Mother (Gaean), had formed there, centering on the campus of a defunct Church of the Divine Liturgy. The long decline of real estate values had attracted members of the sect from all over Terra, making Saskatoon the RCHM capital of the world. One of its activities was the production of "The Daily Worldwide News Roundup," broadcast from warm and pleasant Oaxaca, Mexico, by Gaea Worldwide, an ecumenical network of Gaean sects. It claimed a listener base of 80 million—roughly point-zero-seven percent of the planetary population.

Gaea Worldwide was part of the Peace Front, but Jaromir Horvath and Paddy Davies seldom listened to their program. The Gaean sects had not been major players. But the two leaders had been notified that Gaea Worldwide would release a shocker on the roundup, at noon Greenwich and at intervals afterward. So both men were tuned in, Horvath in Kunming, and Davies in Sydney. They'd discuss afterward whether to follow through on it.

The roundup began with a summary of refugee labor battalions: their locations, projects, home worlds, and the number of refugees "enslaved." *Old stuff*, thought Horvath. Obviously not the promised bombshell.

Next was a report from "an anonymous source high within the government." Horvath's ears perked up; Gaea was trying to add authority to what came next.

A different voice read it, the accent British. "Kunming," it said, "has inaugurated a new and unspeakable outrage against humanity and the Holy Mother. This station has previously uncovered Kunming's unconscionable use of mentally handicapped persons as slaves for War House. Now the government has taken those vile, soul-corrupting acts a long and evil step further. They have conscripted a large number of severely handicapped children and have . . ." The voice stumbled, paused. "Have *murdered* them!—butchered them like animals, then ripped out their brains and spinal cords and transplanted them into what are termed . . . 'bottles'!" He almost choked on the word. "Bottled innocence! Human beings designed by Gaea's holy evolution as the ultimate life-form for Planet Terra. In bottling the pitiful shards of these sad creatures, Kunming, under the leadership of Chang Lung-Chi and Foster Peixoto, has not only enslaved the souls of these children, their very humanity has been stolen. They are being installed in guided missiles, and assigned to

Kunming's war fleet for use in the brutal war against our visitors from deep space.

"This incredible atrocity proves the utter depravity of our elected government. I urge everyone listening to waste no time in spreading the word, personally and electronically, to everyone you know."

Horvath's first reaction was how incredibly cliché-ridden the script was. It discredited the story, and would deflect uncommitted listeners. But he believed the underlying claim, and muting the audio, called Paddy Davies in Sydney.

Foster Peixoto's phone trilled. "Yes, Ilse?"

"You have a call from Director Al-Kathad, sir."

"I'll take it." It seemed to him that an unexpected call from the director of Internal Security would not bring good news. "Peixoto," he said.

"Mr. Prime Minister, this is Nabil Al-Kathad. I have a recorded radio broadcast you should hear, broadcast ten hours ago. It was just now brought to my attention. I recommend you record it."

Peixoto touched a switch. "Very well, the recorder is on. Let's hear it."

The director began with a brief rundown on Gaea Worldwide, and the Reformed Church of the Holy Mother (Gaean). Then he played the cube, his eyes on the prime minister's long thin face, reading annoyance in it.

When it was over, Peixoto thought for a moment. "I want you here in my office in thirty minutes," he said. "You and Chief Kumoyama."

In his office, thought Al-Kathad. *Unusual.* "Certainly, Your Excellency."

The prime minister disconnected at once, and his fingers rapped out another number, this one at Special Projects. "Dr. Franck," he said, "I need you here in thirty minutes, to meet with the president, myself, Director Al-Kathad, and his chief of investigations." He paused. "Meanwhile, I want you to hear a radio address, broadcast by a station in Oaxaca, Mexico. Please record it."

He gave her a moment to activate record mode, then turned on the cube with the director's comments and the Gaean broadcast. He listened again himself, while watching

Dr. Franck's slender brown face. When it was over, she switched off record mode and was about to speak. The prime minister cut her off. "Be in my office in twenty-five minutes," he said, and disconnected.

He could deal with this without the president, he told himself, but Chang would want to be involved. A long finger tapped a dedicated switch. They'd eaten lunch together half an hour earlier; the president would be at his desk now.

"President Chang's office."

"Good afternoon, Setsuko. This is the prime minister. I would like to speak with the president, please."

"I believe the president is indisposed for the moment. Shall I interrupt him?"

Chang, like himself, had a phone in the private bathroom off his office. But no. "I'll wait," Peixoto said.

"Thank you, sir. It shouldn't be long."

An anonymous source, Peixoto thought. *If we have a traitor, we need to know who.* From the comments it wasn't a highly placed source. Someone overheard something in the office, or at lunch, and made up the rest. *Installed in missiles for godsake!*

He became aware he was grinding his teeth, a habit he'd defeated years before. Stopping, he took three long breaths: in, one two three; hold, one two; out, one two three four . . . *Our first concern is to counter this attack,* he told himself. *It is not one we can ignore. Detecting the source comes second.* He fidgeted impatiently, his mind moving back to the leak. *The most direct approach would be to interrogate the Gaeans who obtained the story, but they are unlikely to inform.* An investigation of staff would distract from the many jobs at hand, but it would also tend to increase their awareness of the risks. On the other hand, if actual treason was uncovered . . .

His phone warbled again, and he reached for the switch, wondering what the president would say.

When their meeting was over, Peixoto was glad the president had attended, for the strategy they'd agreed on was Chang's. They would not attack the Gaeans. They would take the issue away from them. Broadcast a prime-time special, publicizing the project as giving dying children a chance at extended life in a—call it a "life module," or something like that. *Not* a "bottle." While at the same time filling a vital, nonviolent defense need. The truth would outweigh Peace Front ranting.

There was no need to feel apologetic about defense; the polls confirmed that regularly. A promotional video would be made, beginning with crippled, mentally retarded children declining toward death. Afterward they'd show newly "converted" savants functioning as communicators. And painting, doing mental computing, listening to music . . . whatever their personal play might be. Franck, at Special Projects, would assign and oversee production responsibility, and run quality control.

Chang was confident it would work with the public. Peixoto, on the other hand, could visualize it backfiring if it wasn't done well. Franck assured them it would work beautifully, and that she knew just the producer for the job. Al-Kathad and Kumoyama hadn't volunteered their opinions; they'd been there to discuss the security problem, and how the source might be found. But Al-Kathad's face suggested skepticism. He was skeptical by nature, of course; it went with his profession.

With some misgivings, the prime minister had given the go-ahead on the project. They'd know soon enough how successful it was.

Chapter 31

Airborne!

The sweat shed had had only the body heat of the trainees, initially twelve platoons, to warm it above the frosty morning. Twelve platoons, one selected from each company in the regiment. Captain Mulvaney had chosen 2nd Platoon.

The shed was large and strange, as well as cold, with no lecture platform and no "pulpit"—the Jerrie term for lectern. But Esau had gotten used to strangeness. By now he felt at home in the army, though it was a lot different from his favorite army in Scripture: Gideon's, whose warriors had lapped water like a dog.

He smiled inwardly, imagining Gideon's Hebrew warriors sitting crowded on benches, with parachutes strapped on their backs. A strange thought, even though Sergeant Hawkins had said their airborne trainers were themselves Hebrews, from a world called Masada. A world whose people still spoke the Hebrew tongue; now *that* was strange.

It was also strange to have their Sikh cadre—even Captain Mulvaney!—training with them, with Masadans as

229

instructors. The division's Sikhs had all been airborne trained, Hawkins had told them, but War House had decided they'd retake the training.

Esau's eyes focused on Hawkins a couple of benches ahead, and he wondered what his sergeant was thinking about.

Hawkins wasn't thinking; that is, he wasn't processing data. He was meditating. He'd begun by focusing on his breathing cadence, which from long experience produced a deepening calm. And a viewpoint exterior not only to events, but largely to his own personality. Nonetheless, he was aware of his surroundings. He saw a door open—the benches faced it—and a Masadan sergeant stepped in. Heard the man call for C and D Companies' platoons, and watched some eighty men get to their feet. Burdened with chute packs and hampered by harness, they sidled to the aisle and filed out. Most of the benches had already been empty; the Masadans had begun with K and L Companies' contingents, and were working their way toward A and B.

Despite his calm exterior, Hawkins could flip out of trance and into action instantly. In more profound trances, a meditator might be oblivious to physical events, but Sikhs didn't court oblivion or bliss. Gopal Singh had advocated meditation to enhance living, not avoid it.

Isaiah Vernon often sought to enhance his life by silent prayer. For the most part he'd lived life cautiously, and stepping out of floaters far above the ground was seriously out of character for him. But dedication and duty were very much in character, and he was determined to be a strong and effective soldier for God and humankind. To calm his fear of jumping into what he thought of as nothingness, he sat praying and reciting Scripture in the privacy of his mind. At the moment he was repeating: "The Lord is my shepherd; I shall not want. He makes me lie down in green pastures; he leads me beside still waters; he restores my soul . . ."

Jael Wesley dealt quite differently with her nerves. In her mind's eye, she'd been jumping from a floater—without a chute—and watching the ground rush up at her. At the last moment she snatched herself away, back inside the floater, then jumped again, and again, until she was bored with it. The technique was nothing she'd been taught; it had simply occurred to her.

Beside her, Esau sat calmly unconcerned. He thought about the briefing Captain Mulvaney had given them, on why they were being trained as paragliders. Paragliding was an ancient technique, something the Wyzhñyñy were unlikely to expect. So on New Jerusalem, paraglider platoons would come silently down into Wyzhñyñy positions at night, and with luck, wouldn't be detected till they were on the ground raising Cain.

He was glad that 2nd Platoon had been chosen. In his mind, paragliders were special.

Paraglider raids would be particularly dangerous, of course, but Division didn't intend they do a lot of them. The main reason for doing them at all was that War House wanted Wyzhñyñy prisoners. The Wyzhñyñy had rejected human surrenders, so they probably wouldn't surrender themselves. Getting prisoners would take special measures, and paragliders seemed the best bet.

The danger was something Esau knew mentally, but not yet viscerally. He couldn't recall ever being afraid for more than a moment; not in his entire life. His most intense emotion in life had been anger, and for whatever reason, during the course of military training his temper had grown more moderate and less frequent. Which pleased him. He'd wondered if daily contact with Sikhs had anything to do with it.

The shed door opened again, and a burly Masadan called in. "A and B Companies on your feet and file out!"

2nd Platoon, along with Captain Mulvaney and Lieutenant Bremer, shuffled to the nearest aisle and out into the autumn sunlight. There'd been a shower the day before, and this morning the ground was frozen. Only thinly though, Esau thought as they walked to the floater. No more than a crust. It hadn't been cold enough to freeze solid.

The transport floater was ten feet wide but low, a semi-cylinder flattened on the bottom, with a wide entry/exit at the rear, where a ramp was extruded for boarding. The troop compartment was a more solid version of the roughly-made stationary mock-ups they'd practiced in. There were two long benches, one down each side. When all the trainees were seated, the Masadan jump master murmured to the pilot via the microphone strapped to his wrist. A moment later, the seventy-foot armored floater lifted on its silent AG drive and they were on their way. Esau wished there were windows to look out of.

He ran through the jump drill in his mind. It was simple enough; no one was likely to screw up. Refuse to jump maybe, but not screw up. Captain Mulvaney had said that anyone who couldn't do it should stay in their seat and not interfere with the flow to the doors. Esau glanced at Jael beside him. It occurred to him that being a woman, this might be too much for her, and that if she couldn't jump, she might be transferred to a different platoon. But he reminded himself that when she decided to do something, she wasn't one to back down.

It was a ten-minute flight to the drop area. The word was, it had been plowed, then harrowed, to provide softer landings. Also, for safety, the trainees wore no equipment except their chutes. They'd been told that with the parachutes they wore today, they'd fall faster than with parasails—about twenty feet per second in Lüneburger's gravity. That seemed awfully fast, but they'd been assured that on mass jumps, these chutes were safer than parasails. There was less risk of tangling in each other's lines.

A buzzer sounded. "Stand up!" called the jump master. On both sides of Esau and across the aisle, trainees got to their feet—*but to his dismay, his own legs failed to obey the order!* For a horrified second, Esau couldn't move. Then Jael's hand was on his sleeve, pulling, and somehow he managed to stand, his mind a fog of utter shock and confusion. Upright, his knees felt watery, as if he might sink to the floor.

"Hook up."

It was all well-drilled. On its own, his hand unhooked the static-line snap from its D-ring, hooked it onto the jump cable overhead, and tugged sharply. His mind, however, was frozen. "Sound off for equipment check." Each jumper, including Esau, checked the chute pack of the man ahead of him, and reported. "Twelve okay!" he called hoarsely.

"Stand to the door!" The two files shuffled toward the ten-foot-wide exit, each jumper sliding his static line along his file's jump cable. Esau felt paralyzed; Jael's hand on his back helped him move. Now the first man in each file stood in the exit looking out, a jump master beside him, eddies of cold wind snapping at his trousers. The others crowded behind. Esau's guts churned, and it seemed to him he was suffocating. Actually he'd stopped breathing.

He didn't see the light flash above the exit, didn't even hear the buzzer. He knew only that Masadan voices were shouting "Go! Go! Go!" The men in the doors had stepped out, the trainees behind them following quickly. Jael's helping hand was pushing, and somehow Esau kept pace. Then 3rd Squad was out, and the exit's lip was at his feet—the exit and empty air. For just an instant he hesitated. His jump master's meaty hand slapped his shoulder, and his feet obeyed, his traitorous mouth wailing feebly. He felt the jolt as his chute opened . . . and suddenly he was floating beneath its mottled green canopy—with a sense not of fear but exultation! Beneath him—2,300 feet beneath him—was the ground. He laughed aloud. His mental paralysis of a moment before was gone as if it had never been.

He gave it no attention, simply looked around. Parachutes formed irregular twin lines in the chill air. Invigorating! *Pay attention*, he reminded himself. *You're supposed to be learning*. As if paragliding, he examined the field for nonexistent obstacles. As he approached the ground, it seemed to accelerate toward him, a false apparency they'd been warned about. *Don't reach for it*, he reminded himself. Landing straight-legged destroyed knees. At almost the last moment he looked ahead, then felt the impact, and reflexively did a proper landing roll. Coming to his feet, he pulled in his risers and suspension lines, collapsing his chute. It was over.

He'd have happily gone back up at once, and jumped again.

"At once" was not an option. The rest of the day they went back to the physical regimen of infantry training, harder than ever, as if to make up for an easy morning.

After supper, they did a ninety-minute speed march with sixty-pound sandbags and flak jackets. But at 2130 that evening, the platoon and its company CO and XO, were back in the sweat shed, waiting for the platoon's first night jump. No one had failed to jump that morning. Esau wondered if any of the others had felt as he had. It seemed to him he wouldn't have made it without Jael.

I sure as heck won't let that happen again, he thought, and behind the thought was total warrior intention.

This time the selected platoons from A and B Companies were tabbed to go first. As 2nd Platoon shuffled to its carrier, Esau noticed the brisk breeze. When they'd arrived twenty minutes earlier, it hadn't been half as strong, he was sure. They'd been told in their first lecture that for safety reasons, War House had decreed that no training jumps be made in wind stronger than 18 knots. On New Jerusalem there were no anemometers, and he had no real sense of what an 18-knot wind felt like, but it seemed to him this might be stronger.

Still, he told himself, the Masadans knew what they were doing. Aboard the floater, he felt as calm as he had that morning when he'd boarded. But this time, he knew, there would be no water-kneed paralysis. Reaching, he squeezed Jael's hand in reassurance. Eight minutes later, the jump master ordered them to stand, and they went through the drill again, Esau grinning widely. He literally dove from the exit, and with his head-down attitude, the opening shock jerked him viciously.

He hardly noticed. The night was clear, quiet, dark—*peaceful!*—and seemed more beautiful than any he'd ever seen before. The sky glittered with stars. The wind began oscillating him like a pendulum, and he reached the ground on the upswing, softening the landing. Then the wind in his chute was dragging him briskly on his side, and he half-twisted onto his belly, powerful arms pulling in his front risers and suspension lines, spilling the air from his canopy.

He stopped. Jerking the safety clip on his harness, he hit the release sharply, gathered chute and harness into a great wad of fabric and cords, then strode toward the headlights of the bus coming to pick them up. He felt big enough, powerful enough, to eat the world.

✧ ✧ ✧

The next day was Sevenday; for B Company, a pass Sevenday. They slept in till 0730 and there was no morning run. After breakfast, Speaker Spieler held a religious service for the trainees. An early lunch followed, then those who wanted to—Esau and Jael among them—rode trucks in to North Fork. Since week seven, when they'd become eligible for passes, they'd spent their free afternoons in a by-the-hour room at a small hotel. With so much night training, they hadn't been visiting the water heater room much.

When they'd spent themselves, they dressed again and went outside to walk, holding hands. Old wives' summer lay on the land. The air was still, the sun soft with autumn haze, and Riverfront Park was carpeted with fallen leaves.

"What was it like for you yesterday morning?" he asked. "Jumping and all."

"Not too bad," she said, "until I started toward the door. Then I felt really scared."

"Really?"

"Really."

"Not as scared as me, I'll bet. If you hadn't helped me, I couldn't have done it. My brain was froze, and my knees were like water. I wouldn't have been any scareder with a tiger chasing me." He paused. "But as soon as I was out the door—bang! No way can I tell you how great it felt! When I got down, I wanted to go up and do it again. Right away. And last night was just as good. Maybe better, because the sky was so beautiful."

"It was, wasn't it." Jael paused. "About being scared that first time, scared of going out the door— Remember what Hosea Innis said that night, when we talked about warbots with Sergeant Hawkins?"

"Remind me."

"He said if he'd ever come across a tiger and didn't have so much as his ax, why even innocent as the Lamb of God, he'd be scared to death. Because while the soul goes to heaven, the body knows it's going to get killed and eaten." She looked up at her husband. "It was our bodies were scared. They did *not* want to jump out that door! And when they found out it was all right, the relief was so big, we felt really really good."

Esau nodded thoughtfully, then stopped and kissed her. "You know what?" he said. "I'm married to the wisest woman in the world."

She chuckled. "How about the prettiest?"

"That too," he answered, and kissed her again. "You know something else I really really like?" he murmured. "Better than jumping out of a floater?"

This time she laughed out loud. "Let's go back to the hotel," she said.

Over the next two weeks, each of the paraglider platoons made three free-fall jumps with parasail chutes. The first was by daylight from 4,000 feet, wearing high-altitude jump suits. The trainees needed to get used to them, and even at only 4,000 feet, these autumn days were freezing, or close to it.

Combat jumps would be at night, but the Masadans, demanding though they were, knew the value of training gradients. The trainees had been given a target to hit, a hundred-yard circle a mile from the flight path. Every jumper in 2nd Platoon came down inside the circle. And they all liked the parasails, which set them down less hard than the mass-jump chutes they'd used before. The second parasail jump was at night from 12,000 feet, their target a ring of unlit cloth panels eight miles away, invisible till they were near it. Until close in, they'd been guided by passive gravitic matrix detectors, read as a heads-up display on the faceplate of their jump helmet. They'd done it in virtual training, but needed to experience it for real.

Two missed the target, and were taken back up immediately, to try again.

Meanwhile, of course, they continued their infantry training, which was extended two weeks to accommodate the addition of paraglide and warbot training.

On the following Oneday, 2nd Platoon made its graduation jump. By then, Camp Woldemars Stenders was no longer Camp Mudhole. Or Dusthole. Deep-freeze temperatures had arrived, hardening the ground like stone.

It had already been decided to run this exercise in the
subtropics. Their target would be an abandoned paddock,
on an artillery range five hours by floater from Stenders.
The operation was to be as realistic as feasible. There were
even unwilling prisoners to be captured. Meanwhile, an
enemy might very well have detected the floater, perhaps
even recognized it as hostile, but would hardly connect it
to the intended capture site. The floater would pass it
twenty miles to the west.

Forty miles short of the jump point, the carrier had
slowed to 200 mph, hopefully still fast enough not to draw
suspicion. The jump would be made at the same speed.
And until they were on the ground, the only electronic gear
the jumpers would activate was their heads-up displays.

They had run and rerun this mission on sand tables,
complete with imaginary enemy responses. But this was no
sand table. Now they sat on bench seats 30,000 feet above
the ground, in a nearly silent floater. Some stared at nothing, their attention inward. Some slumped, dozing. A buzzer
sounded, loud and coarse, jerking them alert.

"One minute to amber!" The voice was the pilot's.

This time they had no Masadan jump master. Ensign
Berg stood at one side of the exit, Sergeant Hawkins at
the other. The floater arrived at the ready location. Above
the door, the amber waiting light flashed on. The trainees
got to their feet and did an equipment check. Static lines
weren't used.

The amber light flicked off, and the green ready light
came on. The double doors spread, and the two files of
trainees shuffled toward them.

Exhilaration flowed through Esau Wesley; this was the
life! Again the buzzer sounded, the red light flashed and
the files moved, jumpers disappearing out the exit at a
measured pace, one of Ensign Berg's, followed by one of
Sergeant Hawkins'. Then Esau was at the lip, felt the
ensign's hand slap his shoulder, and stepped out. The slip-
stream snatched him, then released him, and for a moment
he seemed to hang suspended in the starry night. They'd
been warned of the illusion. He maneuvered his arms and
legs for a good opening position, then pulled his ripcord

and felt the fabric feed out. There was no shock; he simply swung forward. Even the oscillation quickly damped and disappeared.

He spoke the words "Activate HUD" to his helmet, and his heads-up display turned on, hair-thin lines lit against the backdrop of night. A red X showed near the top: the target. Near the bottom was a green arrow point, himself. The arrow pointed to the right, so he pulled lightly and evenly on his left control line until the arrow aimed at the X. Small numerals at bottom left read 29,612—his altitude, referenced to the landing site. Next to it was the wind vector, an unobtrusive arrow with a shaft, the windspeed indicated by the shaft length and small numerals. At his altitude, there wasn't much wind at the moment. Then he jettisoned his reserve chute and its weight.

They'd been forbidden to activate their comm headsets till they were on the ground, in case the electronic signature was too strong. Again two key words activated his night vision. Peering around, he could see other parasails, higher, lower, ahead, behind . . . Deactivating the night vision, he settled down for the long, slow glide to the target. He could already sense the cold around him.

Isaiah Vernon felt his usual pre-jump tension and post-jump exhilaration. Glancing up, he saw his black canopy against the stars, then unclipped his reserve chute and let it fall, just as he would on a combat jump. But he did it out of sequence; he hadn't checked his HUD. When he did check it, the position arrow was rotating, not pointing somewhere.

Pulling on a control line—either control line—made no difference. Something was seriously wrong! His first impulse was to radio his predicament, but this exercise was to simulate reality. Besides, there was nothing anyone could do for him, and once he was down, he could call for help.

Again he checked his canopy, this time with night vision. His problem was a lineover, presumably due to faulty packing. Two suspension lines had gotten across the canopy, and instead of one large airfoil, he had what amounted to three small airfoils. One was ejecting air sideways, producing the rotation. His HUD showed him falling much faster than he should.

He responded quickly, climbing a riser hand over hand. When the connector link was in his reach, he pulled on its suspension lines. His thickly gloved hands were clumsy and the lines thin, but he was strong, and under the circumstances, driven. He continued climbing, partly collapsing his parasail, his rate of fall increasing markedly. Reaching the skirt of the parasail, he struggled to dislodge what seemed to him the lineover most susceptible to dislodging. What he succeeded in doing was collapsing the canopy entirely.

He let go. A moment later the sail caught air and reopened, but still with the lineovers.

I am going to die, he told himself, then shook the thought off and looked again at his HUD. His rate of descent was sixty-seven feet per second. At that rate, he thought, he'd end up mush when he hit. They'd bring him in in his helmet. Then he remembered a Masadan officer telling them the nearer they got to the ground, the thicker the air would be. That should slow him, but would it be enough? It seemed highly unlikely.

His rate of fall slowed to 64 fps. Possibly, just possibly . . . On the elevation readout, the tens column was a blur. The hundreds were peeling off rapidly, and the thousands inexorably. He jettisoned his blaster, his rucksack, and everything else removable, slowing to 47 fps.

Speaking to his helmet, he switched off all displays and deactivated his night vision. "Father in heaven," he said quietly, "into your hands I commend my spirit." Briefly he looked downward. A few miles to the north was a town, electric lights in its windows. There were people there—families, children—living their lives and worshiping the same God he worshiped. For a moment he felt love swell in him for those unknown Lüneburgians. It seemed the most natural thing in the universe to do.

Then he turned his attention to David's most beloved psalm. " . . . Even though I walk through the valley of the shadow of death," he recited, "I fear no evil; for you are with me; your rod and your staff—they comfort me. You prepare a table before me . . ."

✧   ✧   ✧

Jael Wesley was intent on her HUD. She'd timed her forward speed well; she'd make the paddock nicely before she hit. Hopefully without having to spiral in.

Briefly she activated her night vision. Too far to see yet; she switched it off. The HUD gave horizontal distance to center target as 2.07 miles, and altitude 915 feet. At this level there was an eight-knot breeze, not enough to worry about, as long as she didn't have to buck it. The paddock was said to be about one acre. At one mile she slowed her forward speed, and at half a mile tried her night vision again. Now she could see the intended prisoners clearly, scattered but mostly near the fence. She'd hoped they'd be bunched up.

Deactivating her HUD to avoid distraction, she adjusted her speed and direction by night vision. Her job was to land at the far side of the paddock and suppress fire from outlying "enemy guard positions." She swung wide, sizing up the guard positions while button-hooking to use up altitude and avoid the fence. Somewhere out there, A Company should already have arrived, and be lying in support, ready to attack the guards.

But A Company made too much noise, and from the enemy outposts came blaster fire, directed not toward the paddock, but outward. In response, A Company's grenade launchers flashed, followed quickly by the pops of training grenades around the guard positions. No sooner had the grenades landed, then with blood-curdling shrieks, A Company's raiders rushed the enemy positions with fixed bayonets, blasters spewing soft pulses. Jael freed her rucksack and felt it jerk the dangle line.

She was almost down, and braked. Her feet touched lightly, three running steps using up her momentum. She hit her harness release, released her blaster tie-down, and crouched by the fence, ready to provide supporting fire as needed.

The capture teams were already in action. The intended prisoners consisted of twenty calves, each weighing about 250 pounds Terran. Unarmed though they were, the calves resisted, running madly to avoid would-be captors, and struggling when caught. One nearly trampled Jael. She fired a burst of soft pulses as it careened toward her, so that it fell skidding in its effort to turn. Someone grabbed it, threw it back down, and struggled to tie its hooves. After several minutes of running, wrestling, and whooping with laughter, the capture action ended with the landing of two floaters inside the paddock. Jerries dragged the "prisoners" to the ramps, then cut the ties and let them go. All that was left to do was muster, board the floaters and leave.

The mission was over.

It was at muster they learned that Isaiah Vernon was not with them, and no one had seen him since they'd jumped. Nor could anyone there pick up his transponder. Using one of the floaters' high-powered radios, Captain Mulvaney called Division.

Yes, he was told, Isaiah Vernon's transponder had activated, giving his geogravitic coordinate. An ambulance floater from the artillery range had already picked him up, and he was being rushed to the division hospital.

Why Division? Jael wondered. *Didn't the artillery training camp have a hospital? Or perhaps his injuries weren't so bad.* Somehow, though, it seemed to her they were.

They learned the next day how severe Isaiah's injuries were, when Captain Mulvaney reviewed their graduation exercise with the entire company. Division's umpires had given B Company's paragliders a grade of "very good." Then he told them about Isaiah. "Apparently Trainee Vernon's parasail malfunctioned," he said gravely, "after he'd jettisoned his reserve chute. He hit the ground very hard; his knees and leg bones were shattered. He also had broken lumbar vertebrae and critical internal injuries. The medics kept him alive with life support equipment and an injection of Stasis 1. They assured me there was no chance at all that he'd have lived long in that devastated body."

Mulvaney paused, and when he continued, used the trainee's given name. "Isaiah signed a warbot agreement last Sixmonth, so he's been bottled. When the sedative has worn off, he'll undergo therapy for neural trauma and be tested for neural functionality. But the conversion team doubts that he can function as a warbot."

After the CO had finished, Speaker Spieler led the company in a prayer for Isaiah—not simply for his survival, but beseeching God that their brother could fight as a warbot.

Afterward, more than thirty new agreements were signed by B Company trainees.

Esau considered signing, and talked to Jael about it. "That's fine, if you want to," she answered. "But I've decided not to. I want to have babies if I possibly can, whether I'm crippled or not."

Esau nodded. "Well then," he said firmly, "I won't either." And chuckled. "Because if you have babies, I want to be the father."

Chapter 32

The War at Home

"Mr. Garmisch, Supervisor Reinholdt will see you now."

Paul Garmisch got uneasily to his feet. He didn't know what this was about, but a guilty conscience had made him wary. The production supervisor's receptionist was indicating a door. It had opened, and a neatly-dressed, athletic-looking man waited by it. He was not Supervisor Reinholdt, but neither was he an office assistant. He looked too hard, too sure.

"Come in, Mr. Garmisch," the man said.

The words, the tone were mild, but to Paul Garmisch they sounded sinister. Garmisch was addicted to adventure cubes, and now he realized what this man reminded him of. He looked like the CIS men on shows about crime detection.

Garmisch entered the office. It was not Production Supervisor Reinholdt who sat behind the desk. It was a woman, someone Garmisch had never seen before. Reinholdt stood to her left, somewhat removed. "Please sit down, Mr. Garmisch," the woman said, and beckoned toward a chair. To her right, also not close, was another man, seated in a chair with a monitor arm and key pad.

A small, brown, wiry man with probing, deep-seeing eyes; inwardly Garmisch squirmed, trying to escape them. *A foreign immigrant,* he thought. Perhaps a Malay. He'd known a Malay family once. The parents had looked somewhat like this man.

The woman repeated herself. "Please be seated, Mr. Garmisch. I am Ms. Sriharan."

She did not identify her function. The omission troubled Garmisch, and so did the chair she'd indicated. He'd never seen one like it before. It stood apart, on a low, apparently portable platform. He stayed where he was. "What is this about?" he asked. His tone was neither challenging nor indignant. It was wary. Frightened.

"I am about to tell you. But first, please sit down." She still sounded affable, looked affable. Her name was foreign, perhaps Asian he thought, but from her blond hair and blue eyes, she could be pure German. Garmisch did not consider himself hostile to non-Germans. "Let them live here, work here, vote here." He'd said it more than once. But he regretted genetic mixing, certainly with non-Nordics.

It was, he knew, much too late to be prevented. Non-Nordics had been trickling in for centuries. Perhaps as far back as the Troubles. (In school, history hadn't taken with him.) After a few generations, little remained of their origins except foreign surnames, sometimes dark skin. African hair. He himself was of mixed origin; it was hardly avoidable. But in his case, so far as he knew, his non-German ancestors were Aryan: Moldavian, Polish, and Croat. In school he had even taken German as one of his electives, learning it well enough to carry on limited conversations.

"Mr. Garmisch," she said. Her voice was still mild. "If you do not sit down, I must arrest you."

Garmisch looked at her, then at "the CIS man," then the Malay. *What is a Malay doing here?* he wondered. *And what is he thinking?* Hesitantly he stepped to the chair and sat. Perhaps, he told himself, the questions would not be about what he feared. Perhaps he had no reason to worry.

"Thank you, Mr. Garmisch. Let me complete the introductions." She gestured toward the supposed Malay. "This is Forensic Technologist Balaug, and the gentleman who admitted you is Senior Investigator VerDoorn. Both are of the Commonwealth Internal Security Directorate. You already know Supervisor Reinholdt, of course. He was kind enough to let us use his office."

The security directorate! The confirmation added weight to the stone in Garmisch's belly. He looked from one to the other. Ms. Sriharan leaned back in her chair like someone who'd just eaten a very fine meal. "It has been brought to our attention," she said, "that military blasters assembled on your line have been found defective. The assembler program had been altered, and a small but essential component was omitted, converting each blaster to a small but quite deadly bomb. A man died testing one; it blew his head quite off, and his arms to the elbows. We trust you can enlighten us on how this came to be."

Garmisch looked at Production Supervisor Reinholdt, who looked back at him grimly. Garmisch's gaze turned to his knees, and stayed there. It seemed to him that at the very least he would be discharged from his position. It was a good position. In these days, of course, there were many good jobs, but if they decided that what he had done was deliberate . . .

"First though," she continued, "let me advise you that you are not required to answer our questions. What you tell us may be used against you in a court of justice. Or to exonerate you, as the case may be."

They know. They surely know. I prepared the assembler program. I am in charge of it. Perhaps if I help them . . . Otherwise, it seemed certain he would be put in prison, where there were dangerous people who might harm him, beat him up for pleasure, or stab him to death so he could never tell what he knew. Inwardly he shivered.

Ms. Sriharan was looking steadily at him, as was Supervisor Reinholdt. And the Malay, and the senior investigator, whose names had not registered with him. They were all looking at him, waiting for him to speak.

"I have a neighbor," he said softly, as if not wanting to be overheard. "Sometimes he asked me into his apartment, where we would drink beer together, and talk. It is very nice to drink beer with someone and talk. One time he asked me if I would like to go to a football game with him.

He had tickets. There is always a party afterward, he said. There will be women, some of them looking for a good man . . ."

The prime minister's office, five thousand miles from Leipzig, was considerably larger than Supervisor Reinholdt's. And the people gathered there were interested in the broad issue of sabotage, of which defective blasters were only a part.

"It may be time," the prime minister said, "to take the issue to the public. Saboteurs have presented us with several cases having the potential of great harm, including defective equipment in warships and armored floaters. Even defective stasis lockers on troopships. All potentially serious, and a drag on the defense effort.

"Now, from Lüneburger's World, we have a case in which several parachutes arrived from the Indonesian Autonomous Republic improperly packed. One of them was used in a training exercise, and a soldier nearly lost his life—a nineteen-year-old from New Jerusalem. His body was effectively destroyed; he would not have survived the day had he not signed a warbot agreement."

Foster looks worn out, the president thought, *and the day has little more than begun; he needs more sleep.* He would not, however, urge it on him. Defense of the human species took priority. Perhaps if his ability to function seemed threatened . . . But his friend would never agree to ease off. He'd argue that in Terran gravity, Lunies habitually looked tired.

"I have heretofore been reluctant to bring the sabotage problem to the public attention," Peixoto went on. "Publicizing crimes sometimes does more harm than good by stimulating others to commit similar acts. Especially political crimes by extremists. But numerous inflammatory Peace Front harangues on the Ether and the broadcast media make this consideration less compelling than it might be. And now we are able to give the issue a suitable human face, an earnest, nineteen-year-old face. While at the same time promoting the warbot program."

He scanned the faces around the table. "Any questions or comments at this point? Nabil?"

The director of internal security had thrust his hand up, like Thor raising his hammer. He stood to speak, his words emphatic. "Declare martial law," he said. "Outlaw the Peace Front, and imprison its leaders for sedition or treason. Hold them incommunicado in special prison camps. Charges such as leading or organizing a demonstration, or burning the flag, deserve imprisonment at hard labor for the duration of the war. The most severe crimes—sabotage, mutiny, or inciting to mutiny—should bring sentences of hanging."

He remained on his feet for two or three more seconds, all eyes on him. But the prime minister showed no sign of replying while Al-Kathad still stood, so the director sat down.

"Thank you, Nabil. Martial law is an option, one I hope will not become necessary." He gazed mildly but unblinkingly at the director. "Imprisonment is appropriate, but not the death sentence. Historically, many fanatics have embraced execution to promote their cause. Often effectively."

Peixoto's gaze moved to the minister of justice—a one-time senior jurist, and Al-Kathad's boss. "Bikel, how would you implement martial law from the viewpoint of justice?"

Bikel Wong remained seated while he spoke. "Let me begin by agreeing with Nabil that martial law is advisable," he said. "Peace Front activities are building momentum. Its leaders are determined; they will not give in short of success—or their removal from the social/political environment. By which I mean imprisonment. Incommunicado.

"Membership in Peace Front organizations, including subscribers to Peace Front talk groups and newsfaxes, is less than two percent of the Terran population, and even lower on the other Core Worlds. However, polls indicate that as many as fifteen percent have reservations about defending the Commonwealth. Mostly on the grounds that we cannot succeed, and might do better leaving it in the hands of the All-Soul. On Terra, fifteen percent means some one-point-two billion who are more or less susceptible to Peace Front propaganda.

"At the same time, however, punishments for obstructing defense activities must be moderate and judicious. I recommend the use of civil tribunals, each consisting of three prominent and respected judges, sitting in closed sessions to evaluate the charges and evidence. And to pass sentence where appropriate." He paused, seeming unhappy at the prospect. "Nabil agrees, we do not want imprisonment based on rumors, nor an open season on dissenters. Or witch hunts. And people must not be arrested, then simply disappear. As for being held incommunicado—approved representatives of humanitarian organizations should visit the camps regularly, and question whomever they please. But complaints must be taken only to Justice, not to the public.

"And finally," said the justice minister, "all sentences should be reevaluated at the end of the war, when the pressure is less and our perspective greater."

Chang Lung-Chi grunted to himself. *Justice delayed,* he thought wryly, *is better than no justice at all.* He got to his feet without asking to be recognized; he was, after all, the president. "I recommend against martial law," he said. "Though I may change my mind later, the lessons learned from the Troubles advise against it. It is enough that our prime minister has extraordinary wartime powers.

"Today's activists are not the seasoned, well-schooled insurgents of eight or ten centuries ago, and I do not believe they pose so serious a threat. Certainly not yet.

"And let me say this about martyrdom: Peace activists are innately self-righteous. True believers. They will condemn any sentence, whether passed in closed or open courts, and deny all evidence, however compelling. They will declare—they will trumpet!—that everyone sentenced is a martyr. They are already our dedicated enemies, regardless of what we do. So in dealing with saboteurs, we must have two goals: first, the supression of sabotage, and second, the winning of at least acquiescence by those who have misgivings about defense."

He paused long enough that Nabil took the opportunity to speak. "If we imprison their spokesmen . . ." he began.

"If we imprison their spokesmen simply for speaking, we create additional martyrs and new spokesmen," the president said, "which we cannot afford to do. Certainly not yet. Arrests and punishment should be limited to those who commit crimes widely recognized as such. Meanwhile, we must strengthen public recognition that sabotage, terrorism, and the destruction of property are felonies. And that it is destructive to pass them off as simply differences of opinion."

Again he paused. "This means a bluntly honest exposure of Peace Front fallacies and lies. It means promoting the validity of our defense activities, and establishing that they are necessary and efficacious. And these efforts need to be headed by someone whom the population as a whole trusts and respects."

With that the president sat down. From beneath arched brows, Foster Peixoto's eyes rested on him quizzically. "Indeed. And are you willing to *take* the job?—while seeing to your already existing responsibilities?"

"I am. Though you may very well come up with a better candidate. Meanwhile, I am the head of state, not the head of government. If I have difficulties handling it all, I will delegate my ceremonial and other less essential duties, and give priority to this more critical work. But we should not create a special office. It should be done within the existing structure of government."

Nabil Al-Kathad listened glumly. He recognized the factors the others had pointed out, but saw himself as ultimately responsible for enforcing the law and suppressing crime. *I'm damned if I do, and damned if I don't,* he thought. Meanwhile there remained the matter of appropriate and effective punishment.

This time he raised his hand, and the prime minister recognized him. "Yes, Nabil?"

"I still believe it is appropriate to execute criminals for high war crimes. It establishes their gravity in the public mind."

"Mr. Prime Minister," said Chang Lung-Chi, "if I may?"

"Go ahead, Mr. President."

"Nabil, my good friend, in cases sufficiently extreme, I would be willing to consider loading the guilty into a hyperspace courier and shipping them, without stasis, to a system in the path of the Wyzhñyñy advance. There they would be shuttled to the surface of an enemy-occupied planet to negotiate peace. The minimum terms being

Wyzhñyñy withdrawal from the world they have taken, and from the general bounds of the Commonwealth sector."

With that the prime minister asked for further comments. As these were people with strong demands on their time, within five minutes the meeting was adjourned.

Chapter 33
Camp Bosler Nafziger

The third oldest deep-space colony, Pastor Lüneburger's World began as an agrarian religious settlement. Over the centuries, its original Mennonite doctrines had blurred and weakened, but low-tech agrarianism persisted. About fifty percent of its people still lived on farms, about thirty percent in rural hamlets, and twenty percent in market and industrial towns. The only colleges were seminaries. Trades and professions were learned by apprenticeship, with professional and trade associations providing optional certification.

Technological introductions were further hampered by disinterest in products. Nonetheless, over recent centuries, technology on Lüneburger's had gradually, and more or less unintentionally, been upgraded. The slowness was largely a matter of cultural inertia, rather than Luddism. "Burgers" tended to like things as they were, and new things, to be successful, had to fit into the system. This was something the benign elected government considered very important in granting import licenses, especially the importation of technology.

On Lüneburger's World, railroads were thought of as

"new." Actually they'd been used there for centuries, but only during the past eighty years had they spread beyond the mining regions. While "trucks"—steam-driven rigs that burned coal or wood—were a phenomenon of recent decades, filling the newly felt need for hauling heavy freight to the expanding railroads.

Most Burgers with serious interest in technology migrated to the Sol, Epsilon Indi, or Epsilon Eridani systems. The Lüneburgian government had established a small trust to help finance their offworld education. (A trust quietly supplemented by the Commonwealth.) On Lüneburger's, this was considered Christian Kindness, not a means of developing a cadre of technicians and scientists. In fact, the expatriates were not encouraged to return.

Some did of course. Lüneburger's had a number of engineers who'd trained offworld, or apprenticed under someone who had.

Given the circumstances, Lüneburgian farmers and craftsmen, especially in frontier areas, tended to be innovatively practical with the materials at hand. They could drain a swamp, or build a house from scratch. A small crew of farm boys, using hand tools and a workhorse, could bridge a deeply-cut creek in an hour, and drive a loaded wagon over it. While those exposed to machinery quickly became decent jackleg mechanics. Thus given a handful of trained officers of whatever origin, Burgers were proving to make excellent engineering troops.

The threat of alien conquest had already brought changes. Most new military training camps, Camp Stenders for example, consisted of buildings whose prefabricated sections and modules were assembled on site by local entrepreneurs. Such practices would not have been accepted earlier. But in warmer climates, military camps were primarily tent camps. Administrative buildings and lecture sheds were prefab, but living accommodations consisted of acres of squad tents on raised wooden floors.

Camp Bosler Nafziger was sited in a region where winters were mild enough to live year-round in tents. The Lüneburgian government had condemned nearly 40 square miles of rural land there for military use, including a village which was left intact. The Commonwealth had compensated the landowners liberally, and leased an additional 440 square miles of adjacent forest.

When the Jerries finished their advanced training, they were sent to Camp Nafziger for twelve weeks of unit training: combat exercises on battalion, regimental—even divisional—scale. These were to be carried out in conjunction with the Indi 3rd Armored Regiment, camped six miles down the Bachelor River. The Lüneburgian 4th Infantry Division, camped ten miles upstream, would provide opposition forces in conjunction with its own unit training.

Major General Pyong Pak Singh had arrived by floater several days ahead of his division. He'd spent four days inspecting the camp and its facilities, getting acquainted with the Lüneburgian staff in charge of maintenance and other services, being briefed on the military reservation itself, and finally reviewing the training plan with his general staff, and the Masadan commander and staff of the Indi 3rd Armored Regiment.

They were four gray, chilly days, with sporadic, wind-driven showers. His division arrived on the third, fourth, and fifth days, mostly by rail. On the fifth afternoon and evening, Pak inspected each regiment separately in a cold drenching rain.

The Indi 3rd Armored, with its Masadan cadre, had also traveled mostly by rail. He'd inspected them, too, at their own encampment.

The sixth morning had dawned gratefully clear, with a temperature of 45°, and a predicted high of 63°—much warmer than the Jerries had been having at Stenders. At 0815, he started off in an open command car, gloved, jacketed, and capped, with a map book on his lap, and a driver behind the wheel beside him. Pak had developed his trip itinerary in consultation with a Captain Hippe, a Lüneburgian engineering officer. Hippe had assigned the driver, and Pak had given the man his itinerary.

As they drove through the encampment, Pak gave his attention to the infantry companies standing in ranks on their mustering grounds. Shortly they'd march to lecture sheds for a two-hour orientation on the Camp Nafziger military reservation—a video lecture with large-scale topographic/vegetation maps and aerial photos. That would be followed by a two-hour talk on unit training, with an upfront caveat that the specifics might be changed.

Just now Nafziger's roads were puddled and muddy, but the car rode an AG cushion at the default height of four inches—enough to buffer it against irregularities in the surface. There was no splashing, and of course no rutting. And at the camp speed limit of 25 mph, even the puddles were little disturbed by the vehicle's air wake. Another main road crossed the one they'd been on, and the driver turned south, passing a cluster of prefab buildings—a regimental headquarters.

Ahead, the Bachelor River flowed through a stepped, steep-sided channel, its terrace forest jutting winter-bare treetops above the terrain break. Moments later the car crossed the break and skimmed down the forest-bordered road to the terrace, and thence to the wooded floodplain.

The river itself was about two hundred feet wide, crossed by a timbered bridge whose stone piers jutted from murky swirling water. On the other side, the car crossed the same levels in reverse order, until both road and forest spilled over the rim onto the plain above. Pak examined the open map book, checking road designations, and watched to be sure his driver turned west at the first crossroads. Corporal Müller was unfamiliar to him—a Burger assigned from the camp's driver pool, and supposedly familiar with the reservation's roads.

The river was like a boundary. The south side was mostly forest, the farms in small clusters, their buildings abandoned intact. A mile or so to the south, high hills rose, with forest shown as unbroken, except by occasional wet meadows. The car took them past several junctions, with rutted spur roads leading southward at half-mile intervals. According to the map, the spurs didn't reach the hills. Then they came to another road, this one graded. Müller turned onto it. When they reached the first ridge, the road angled up its long slope.

Stumps, most of them large and old, were scattered

throughout the thick forest. Many of the remaining trees were quite large. Obviously the people here logged lightly, entering the forest now and then to harvest trees that met certain criteria, probably by species, size and condition. Here and there along the road were small openings, some overgrown by saplings, others with little more than coarse weeds matted down by winter's rains.

"What are the openings?" he asked the driver.

"Landings, sir."

"Landings?"

"Places where logs were decked, sir. Dragged out of the woods and piled. They load the logs on trucks there, and haul them to the railroad."

That, Pak thought, *helps explain the railroad coming here.* "Couldn't they float them down the river?" he asked.

"Most logs are sinkers, too heavy to float."

The forest changed little for several miles, then the road doubled back eastward. The driver surprised him by turning onto another spur road that went south, and the general unfolded another map.

"Where are we going now?" he asked.

"To the edge of the virgin reserves," said the corporal. "Captain Hippe said you'd ought to see it."

Hippe, Pak recalled, would be briefing officers today.

Half a mile later, the spur ended in a loop, a turnaround. The driver stopped, and they got out. "Everything south from here," Müller said, "is the reserve. That there," he added pointing, "is the boundary."

"That there" was an east-west line of blazes hacked on trees, apparently with an ax. South of it the forest had many large old trees. Slowly the two men strolled into it a short distance, their eyes exploring. *It would,* Pak thought, *be beautiful in summer: green with foliage, and no doubt bright with birdsong.*

"The number of people keeps growing," the corporal told him, "and the need for wood along with them." He gestured at the surrounding forest. "When it's needed, the government'll open it up for cutting, but for now it's wild; no farms, no roads, nothing but woods from here on. Folks hunt in here, of course, as much to keep down the wolves and lions and bears as for game." His right hand slapped his sidearm. "And boars; they're worser'n mean if you come across one. They can gut a man in a minute."

He pointed to a tree whose otherwise smooth bark was vertically scarred to about seven feet above the ground, as if by large claws. "That there is bear sign; made about two years back, judging by the callus. Some he-bear marked it to warn off others. Lions mark by spraying piss on things. Hasn't been a lion reported north of the river for ten, fifteen years; they don't much tolerate people. But they're in here. Folks hear one screech from time to time."

Wolves. Bears. Lions. Boar. Pak wondered what manner of beasts the Burgers applied those labels to. Nothing trivial, he supposed. He was surprised he hadn't been shown pictures of them. He'd have to correct that when they got back to camp.

"Hunting helps keep predators leery of folks," the young man went on, "and out of the livestock. It's rare that one of them jumps a person, but now and then they do raise Cain in a pasture or sheep pen, or paddock."

He grinned at the general. "Your Jerries need to be ready to switch their blasters to hard fire."

It occurred to Pak to wonder if Müller would dare pull a general's leg. It seemed unlikely. "Are you from around here?" he asked.

"Yessir, General. My family's steading was just about where division headquarters stands now."

"Ah. It must have hurt to have your land condemned for a military reservation."

The corporal shrugged big shoulders. "There's some folks sour over it. But if the Wyzhñyñy get this far, we'll lose it anyway, and worse. As it is, Terra paid us good money for it, more'n anyone else would've. And when the war is won, if it gets won, we get it back for free."

The young man had seemed to turn inward as he talked. Now his eyes met the general's again. "Pastor Lüneburger told us to care for the land, the planet, and treat it with respect. Not abuse it like our long-ago forefathers did on Terra." He shook his head. "But he never foretold any alien invasion."

Pak nodded. "Few did," he said. "Few did."

They walked back to the car in silence and continued

the tour, getting back to camp for lunch. Pak realized more
fully now how suitable a range of conditions Camp Bosler
Nafziger provided: forest, open farmland, rugged hills, small
and large streams, even swamps and marshes in the north.
And a sizeable section that was essentially virgin. All in all,
it resembled conditions described for New Jerusalem.

Chapter 34

Reunion

Esau Wesley lay still on sodden leaves, peering across a forested draw. *With the sun up,* he told himself, *they're not hard to see. Not this time of year, with the leaves down.*

Not all the leaves were down, of course. There were patches of evergreen shrubs whose stiff leathery leaves looked nearly black at a hundred yards. And some trees had kept their leaves, mostly dead and brown. He could hear them rustling dryly in the breeze overhead, a breeze that scarcely touched the ground.

Much of the hundred-yard separation between ridgetops was unobstructed, for the two ridges were steep, and looking across the draw was mostly looking through empty air. His narrowed eyes could make out folks dug in over there, obscured by undergrowth and not moving around. *If those are enemy,* he thought, *we could open fire and really play Tophet with them. Blasters, slammers . . . Heck, our grenade launchers would reach that far. The umpires would charge them heavy casualties.*

Friend or foe, that was the nub of it. *If this was for real, it'd be easy to tell. Something that walks on four legs with the top half of something like a man stuck on the front—that'd be easy to recognize.* But playing war against other humans would have to do.

Just think of them as the enemy, he told himself. Whoever, whatever they were, they were dug in. Esau wondered if the real Wyzhñyñy dug foxholes. *It would,* he thought, *be awkward for folks like them.* And how would they climb in and out?

"Can he get close enough without being noticed?" Ensign Berg murmured it from a corner of his mouth, as if for secrecy.

Hawkins too only murmured; a nod involved movement. "He scored higher than anyone on the stealth tests."

That didn't really answer the question, Berg thought, but visor magnification didn't fill the bill. Too much obscuring undergrowth. "All right," he said, and triggered his helmet mike with a syllable. "Esau," he murmured, "cross the draw farther up, and get close enough to see whether those are our people or enemy. Then back away and let me know. If they are enemy, and see you, cover yourself with a smoke grenade. Then we'll give them something else to worry about."

The Jerrie's voice answered in his ear. "Yessir."

Not yessir, Ensign, just yessir, Berg observed. *Terse. Good stealth discipline.* Even so tiny and short range a source of electronic activity as an ultra-short-range helmet transmission on low might be picked up at 200 yards. He'd risked their security himself, with so long an order, but delivering it in person was a greater risk.

Carefully he turned his head in the young man's direction, but couldn't see him. Some evergreen brush was in the way. He'd already learned, though, that to give Lance Corporal Esau Wesley an order was to start a prompt response chain. He decided to talk to the CO about promoting Esau to full corporal. And to buck sergeant when they left Lüneburger's, unless he went sour along the way. And he wouldn't, not Wesley. Not seriously.

The first thing Esau did was crawl backward over the crest of the ridge. Slowly, with short pauses. Any movement might catch the eye. Protracted movement held the attention, with greater risk of recognition. Once behind the crest he arose, ran off to his left 200 yards, then crossed it again on his belly. When well below the skyline, he moved in a low crouch. Here the ridges were somewhat less steep, and the draw between them considerably less deep. Thus the forest provided a thicker screen than at the point from which he'd left.

He understood without being told why the ensign wanted him to identify the people on the other ridge. The draw opened into a grassy glen, a sort of natural travelway. Both 2nd Platoon and the force across the draw could lay down fire on armor or anything else using it.

He didn't think the fact. It was simply there, an operating datum. Once atop the other ridge, he'd need to get close; see whether those others wore gray-blue Burger armbands on their left sleeves, or yellow-brown Jerrie armbands like his own. He didn't intend to get close enough to hear their accents. Even though they'd shown no sign of having seen 2nd Platoon, any talking they did would likely be quiet.

His advances continued smooth and intermittent, even as far up the draw as he was. He moved from cover to cover, down the slope and up the other, taking advantage of evergreen shrubs. At every pause, his eyes scanned. The "enemy" would have sentries out: human sentries— electronic sentries were "noisier."

At one pause he peered long and carefully across the draw, toward where he'd come from. Spotted the outline of a helmet against an outcrop. Some folks had trouble getting it through their heads that the camouflage pattern on your uniform wasn't enough. A little brush, strategically attached, made a lot of difference. He'd mention it when this was over.

He still couldn't see the folks on this side. Some forty yards ahead, a rocky prominence hid them from view. It was a good place for a lookout, too, lying low beside a tree, watching for someone like himself. Esau didn't move again till he was satisfied with his surveillance. He couldn't afford carelessness. With backcountry like this, there'd be skilled hunters among the Burgers.

After seconds he moved on. The wet leaves on the

ground made effectively no noise, and the dry leaves rustling in the treetops helped cover the occasional wet twig breaking. When he reached the outcrop he paused again, then slipped past it on his belly. He spotted his first "enemy" thirty yards away, and stopped. He couldn't see an armband, but if he . . .

What caused him to look aside just then, he would never know. What he saw was something he'd only heard about, but he knew what it was, and it was looking right at him. It gathered itself, and for just a moment Esau froze mentally.

Then the lion rushed him, and Esau's paralysis transformed into action. Not to turn his blaster and fire. That would have taken too long, for he was prone, and the lion was to his right. Instead he twisted onto his back, coiling, interposing the weapon between himself and the predator, while loosing a shout at the top of his lungs. Then the 300-pound feloid was on him, and Esau jammed his blaster sideways into its mouth. He felt the front claws not as pain but as deadly threat. For a moment it tried to reach him with its jaws, but the blaster was in the way, and the young man's powerful arms held it off. Then it tried to move around him, flank him, and he pivoted on his back in desperation.

He didn't hear the popping of blasters across the ravine, firing soft pulses at the "enemy"; 2nd Platoon had misconstrued his shouts. He could only fight. Salvation came as unexpectedly as the lion. Steel fingers, numbingly powerful, penetrated the ruff, gripped the hide beneath, hauled the predator back, then swung it, slamming it hard against a tree, so quickly and overwhelmingly, the lion didn't have time to twist and fight back. Swung it again, and again, till it lay broken on the ground, hissing coarse bloody hisses at its metal assailant. The warbot set its right-arm blaster on full, and fired a single pulse, putting the lion out of its pain.

Esau stared up at the cyborg. It looked back down at him. "Hello, Esau," it said quietly. "You took us by surprise."

The "enemy" turned out to be 1st Platoon, E Company. Its ensign radioed 2nd Platoon B, and the firing stopped.

Meanwhile 1st Platoon E's medic cut off Esau's torn camos, poured antibiotic on his lacerations, bandaged him, gave him an injection, and wrapped him in a casualty blanket. Then Isaiah Vernon picked up his ex-squad leader and carried him down the slope to the meadowed glen as if Esau were a child. Within ten minutes an evac floater was there, and carried the injured man to the division hospital.

2nd Platoon was told that Esau's wounds weren't serious. Jael asked Sergeant Hawkins if she could go with her husband. He'd told her no, that she was a soldier, and this was part of war.

That evening Hawkins came to her while the platoon ate. The ensign had just gotten a message from Esau: he was fine, and expected to be back in two or three days.

The estimate was Esau's, not the doctor's. He rejoined the platoon and his wife five days later, when the regiment returned to camp. That was also the day Isaiah Vernon went to 2nd Battalion headquarters and asked to see the CO. He had the permission of Sergeant Henry Okinwobu, his squad leader, an ex-marine medically discharged for cascade syndrome.

The battalion sergeant major looked up at the towering metal-and-composites human standing in front of his desk. "What's this about, Vernon?"

"Sergeant Major, it's about my old platoon. I'd like a transfer to 1st Battalion, so I can work with it. I trained with it. I even jumped with it. My best friends . . . "

The sergeant major cut him off with a gesture. "Just a minute, Vernon," he said, and touched a key on his desk comm. "Major, a personnel matter has just come up, something not covered by policy. You might want to consider it." He listened to something Isaiah couldn't hear. "It's Corporal Vernon of the bot squad." Again he listened. "Yessir, that's him. He went through basic and part of advanced training with 2nd Platoon, B Company, before his chute malfunctioned. The guy he rescued from the lion is one of his old buds. Vernon would like to be swapped for one of 1st Battalion's bot squad . . . Yes, Major, that's the key to it. We're not likely to get a replacement with his level of infantry training, but . . . Yessir. Thank you, sir."

He jabbed the switch and looked back up at Isaiah. "Sit down, Private. I have another call to make."

Isaiah sat. In five minutes he had an answer. It wasn't all he'd hoped for, but it might work out. Technically, a warbot platoon was assigned to a regiment as a tactical reserve, which meant the regimental CO could use it any way he wanted. But Division had ordered them divvied out to the battalions. "So if you can find someone in 1st Battalion's bot squad willing to switch," the sergeant major said, "the major will take it up with the colonel." He paused. "But if you're going to do it, do it no later than tomorrow."

Isaiah got to his feet. "Yes, Sergeant," he said. "I'll get right on it."

Sergeant Major Pieter Fuentes Singh watched him leave. According to the grapevine, Captain Chatterjee, Division's technical specialist, had said that even bots weren't strong enough to swing 400-pound lions by the scruff, and beat them to death against trees. But this one did.

Fuentes shook his head. Apparently the adrenaline analog system built into them was more effective than the specialists had realized.

Meanwhile, Private Isaiah Vernon had laid to rest any reservations Fuentes might have harbored about the basic humanity of warbots. They felt the human bond. Certainly this one did.

wasn't in sight or hearing. On Lüneburger's World, schedules were casual.

Grunting, he rotated his shoulders. He'd gotten a job at the sawmill, stacking lumber, and was still a bit sore. In North Fork he'd found work as a free-lance engineer, but with eleven thousand inhabitants, North Fork was an important regional center. Sagenwerk's only excuse for existing was the sawmill that provided its name. Its population was said to be five hundred. Here a free-lance engineer would draw too much attention, and he'd make too little money to pay for the one-room shack he rented. The war had caused prices to rise.

When he'd left Lüneburger's, twenty years earlier at age sixteen, he'd intended never to come back. On Terra he would get an education and interesting work, and live in the 30th century instead of the 19th. And he had. Then this corrupt war had come along, an affront to the All-Soul, fouling the mother world with chauvinism and godless self-justification.

Actually, North Fork hadn't been so bad. It was civilized, with electricity, plumbing, green lawns, shrubs and flowerbeds. The streets were shaded by overhanging trees. Its main lack was people who could carry on a modern conversation; even the All-Soul congregation there was provincial. But the only language you heard was Terran, unless you hung around one of the dwindling old-order congregations.

Here in Sagenwerk, on the other hand, you were more likely to hear the old *Bauerndeutsch* than Terran, and got scowls if you didn't understand. *Bauerndeutsch!* A blend of 18th and 19th century peasant *Plattdeutsch, Switzerditsch, Volgadeutsch* . . . and old church German. Along with a sprinkling of recent Terran, and a mixture of archaic, germanized Anglic—words necessary to function in 19th and 20th century North America. Gawd! Even then, a millennium ago, *Bauerndeutsch* had been dying out. The early colonists had revived it as part of their blockheaded ethno-religious chauvinism, as if Jesus had spoken a broken-down peasant German! But gradually it had receded again.

And worse, Sagenwerk was a stagnant pool of bigots!

Mention the Church of the All-Soul and you risked a black eye. Say that being "born again" referred to reincarnation, and you'd lose your job before you could pick up your lunch pail. Refer to Jesus as an avatar of the All-Soul, and some ignorant fool on the green chain, who didn't know the meaning of "avatar," was likely to break your face in the name of God.

The town was changing—a result of the war—but even the changes weren't good. Greed was flourishing. The railway had brought in twenty coaches to shuttle soldiers on their days off, though the village was less a magnet than its people had hoped. The rundown old tavern faced competition from a new beer garden. There was a theater still smelling of fresh lumber and paint, and two large houses, refurbished, had been supplied with women and girls from Landfall and other "cities."

Joseph Switzer shook his head. It was his own fault he was here. The project had been his idea in the first place, and no one else in the organization was suited for the assignment. He knew Lüneburger's World, and he knew its people. With a little care, he still passed for one of them.

The wail of a train whistle jerked him from his revery, and he looked down the tracks. The train was in sight half a mile west, its locomotive spewing thick black smoke. Unconsciously he curled his nostrils. Instead of stepping out on the platform, he remained beside the depot door, well apart from the collection of young women who also waited. From there he'd be able to see if any of the Jerries he'd met at North Fork got off. Hopefully Wheeler, who'd been responsive and very promising.

Slowing, hissing, sighing, the train drew alongside the platform. Brakes squealed, couplings clashed, cylinders released steam. A conductor swung down from the first car, followed by a stream of uniformed soldiers. And there, the very first of them, was Wheeler, conspicuous by his height.

Instead of going out to him, Switzer waited. Wheeler was walking and talking with another soldier whom Switzer recalled. Elijah somebody. As they passed him, he spoke. "Good morning, Moses," he said. "Good morning, Elijah. Good to see you again."

Today he would get down to business.

Chapter 36

Charley Gordon

Admiral Alvaro "Spanish" Soong pressed the button beside the door and waited. *An admiral waiting to be let in!* he thought. *On business, on his own flagship! Ah, the universe we live in.*

There was no real irony in the thought. Courtesy was almost always appropriate, within the bounds of circumstance, and rare resources could require special treatment.

The door opened, and Ophelia Kennah looked out at him. As a savant's attendant, she was old-style: her personnel file said she was psychic. The briefing he'd been given on savants stated that many of the new savant attendants were simply empaths trained to act as nurse, hypnotechnician and companion. Also, Kennah was fifty-one years old, though slender and still graceful, with calm observant eyes.

She stepped back, and he entered. "Good morning, Ms. Kennah," he said.

"Good morning, Admiral."

The room was large for a ship's quarters, and impressed

him as the most aesthetic on the flagship. Though if asked, he couldn't have said why it seemed that way. Near one side stood a sort of wheeled stand, with a 30-inch-long module mounted on it. The module contained cube ports, and on its top a multisensor set. Just now only one of its sensory status lights was on.

"What's he listening to?" Soong asked.

"'Concierto de Aranjuez,'" she answered. "By Joaquin Rodrigo. It's quite old; 20th century."

Spanish, Soong thought. He didn't speak the language, beyond a few courtesies—family heirlooms. His mother's clan had long since abandoned both Spanish and Catalan.

He wondered if he'd ever heard the concerto. He enjoyed music when he had time, but seldom paid attention to who'd composed what. Probably Ophelia Kennah could set the player so she heard it too. She'd probably been listening when he'd rung, and switched off the room speaker before opening the door.

"I need his services," he told her.

"Of course." She stepped to the stand and touched switches. Two additional status lights flashed on. "Charley," she said quietly, "the admiral needs you."

Charley Gordon, that's the name. Presumably he'd been given it at the Institute. Soong wondered how that had happened. The savant's one-page personnel brief listed him as Male Infant Doe, followed by a registration number. A designation dating to when he was processed into the Institute.

"Ah! The admiral!" said Charley Gordon. "Good day, sir. I'm happy to be of service. Do we have a moment?"

The response astonished Soong. His impression had been that idiot savants were invariably retarded, by definition. And till now, Charley had never spoken in his presence except in trance, channeling messages from War House. Now this request for "a moment."

Soong answered solemnly: "A moment, yes. Then I must have your help."

"It is my privilege to serve." The statement sounded, and might well have been, sincere. Certainly Soong discerned no irony in it. "Meanwhile," the voice went on, "I shall take advantage of my moment." It paused. "You never visit me except for my services. Perhaps if I invite you, you will. Therefore, will you visit me? For friendly conversation, man to man?"

This question too took Soong off guard. "Why . . . If you'd like, yes. We'll soon enter hyperspace again, this time for an extended period. I'll visit you then."

"Thank you, Admiral. I will hold you to that." Again Charley Gordon paused. It seemed to Soong the savant had turned his gaze to his attendant, though the ocular sensors were immobile. There had to be a means of directing visual attention. "Ophelia," Charley Gordon said, "I am ready."

"Good," she replied, and paused. "We will now start. Begin the session." She looked expectantly at the admiral.

"Begin the session" was the standard formula that triggered Charley Gordon's trance. Soong began his message.

It had an unspoken context, one familiar to both himself, the prime minister, and War House. Soong had been given a four-week limit to finish training his battle force, then reluctantly granted a four-week extension. He was still not fully satisfied with its exercises in cross-dimensional combat. And it was entirely possible, if unlikely, for a battle to involve rapid transitions between warpspace and F-space. But his people had become basically competent, and three days earlier Admiral Tischendorf had told him there could be no further extension. The Commonwealth and the human species couldn't afford it.

Thus, Soong's message to War House and the prime minister was expected and succinct: "At 1100 hours Greenwich, this date, the 1st Sol Provisional Battle Force will generate hyperspace and proceed to the vicinity of the Nei Frieslân System. There we will determine what further jump seems appropriate for the effective interception and engagement of the enemy armada. Meanwhile I will contact you at appropriate intervals, and of course remain receptive of your orders and advices. Admiral Alvaro Soong, Commander."

A minute later, his message acknowledged, Soong left the savant's quarters. Thinking not of his responsibility, nor of his force's battle readiness, but of Charley Gordon, his strange power, and his seeming intelligence.

Soong often learned a great deal about people from their faces—their expressions and their eyes. But Charley Gordon? At least until very recently, savants had faces too. The only savant he'd seen before, he'd observed at War House before getting his present assignment. Chloë was tiny, deformed, and severely retarded, but her face, unexpressive though it had been, had permitted him to watch her consciousness shut down when her attendant spoke the brief hypnotic formula. Her features had fallen slack, and he'd known she was in trance.

Charley Gordon's apparent intelligence was far more interesting. *I'm glad he invited me to visit him,* Soong realized. *I would never have thought to invite myself.*

He decided to make his visit that evening, and calling Ophelia Kennah, arranged for a specific time. Then he asked a question: "Is Charley as intelligent as he seemed to be this morning?"

"Just a moment," she replied. He imagined her looking toward her charge, to see if he could overhear. Apparently he had his external sound sensor turned off, perhaps listening to music. "Charley's intelligence is an enigma," she answered. "He does—indifferently on intelligence tests which measure reasoning ability, though better than any other savant I'm aware of. But he does exceedingly well on rote memory tests, as do many other savants."

"Interesting. He memorizes things then."

"If by 'memorize' you mean an effort to imprint a visual or auditory experience, or to create a mnemonic to assist recall—no. He simply experiences things, then recalls them exactly. He can recite extensively and verbatim from biographies of great composers."

"So he reads."

"He does, but prefers audiobooks. He plays them at a rate incomprehensible to me—a high-pitched twittering. Faster than I can read them silently."

The admiral stared. She paused. "I haven't finished answering your first question. A test of intuitive intelligence was being circulated before we left Terra, a preliminary version for testing and professional critiques. I tried it on Charley. His score was nearly the highest possible. I sent a report on it to War House, but when we left, I hadn't had an answer. It seemed to me he might be of greater value there than here.

"Formal tests, of course, do not correlate perfectly with life performance. Charley sometimes produces marvelously logical replies to questions; produces them intuitively. If he is allowed a hand in directing your conversation with him, I do not doubt you'll be pleased and impressed. On the other hand, if you arrive with a list of questions, you may be disappointed. I recommend you simply open the conversation and let things develop as they may."

Soong wondered what Ophelia Kennah's intelligence score was.

She paused, then added: "Charley tires rather easily. The central nervous system tires; that's one reason students need rest and recreation. Channeling and other psychic activities tire it more than most. Typically, psychics hold up reasonably well during the activity, but if it's protracted, they may collapse afterward.

"Excitement may also tire Charley. He's not used to it, and having an actual visitor will be exciting for him."

Alvaro Soong's attention had been hooked by the mention of psychic activities. Like many people, he tended to respond skeptically to the word "psychic." The field of psychodynamics had risen above alchemy and Freudian psychology, to about the level of the phlogiston theory, but had yet to birth its Newton or Lavoisier. A few psychic applications had become routine in the world, but these were no longer thought of as "psychic." The term tended to be reserved for fringe activities and fakery.

But what the communication savants did was genuine enough. And the instructions on the management of savant communicators had warned against overworking them.

"Are there subjects I shouldn't bring up?" Soong asked.

"Charley is emotionally quite stable," Kennah answered. "I know of no subjects you should avoid. He is perfectly willing to discuss his condition and history. And yours, if it comes up."

❖   ❖   ❖

The admiral's appointment was for 2000 hours, and he was there on time. To find Charley not listening to a cube; he was waiting, ready. "Hello, Admiral," he said. Pleasure and anticipation were apparent in his voice.

Remarkable, Soong thought, *that his equipment reflects emotion so well.* "Hello, Charley," he answered. "Or would you prefer I call you Charles?"

"Charley, please. I have never been Charles, though it is a nice name. Please have a chair, Admiral, and be comfortable."

Soong pulled one to face Charley's sensorium.

"I've been studying your open file, sir," Charley said. Brightly. Eagerly. The announcement took Soong by surprise. *Kennah must have gotten it for him,* he decided. Meanwhile Charley continued. "It says almost nothing of your life before you attended the Space Academy. Born near Terrassa, in the Catalunya Prefecture, and attended the Space Academy in the Colorado Prefecture—twenty years in just a few lines!" He added the last almost merrily. "Then graduated with high honors; one more line! After that it summarizes your service record. Surely there is more to be told than that."

"Not really," Soong replied. Untruthfully of course, but it wouldn't be very interesting. Except possibly to a student of social and professional acculturation and family iconography. "I'll tell you what," he added. He was surprised at what he found himself saying. "I'll have some spare time for a while. Enough to sit down some day soon and record a few items of my childhood and youth for you. Things that may provide amusement, or insights."

He took a different tack then, to get his own questions answered. "You know more about me than I do of you. I read a bit on savants years ago. My impression was that most of them were children."

"*Idiot* savants you mean," Charley answered. "The adjective is apt, and typically accurate. Many of us are severely defective physically as well as mentally, and die as infants or children. Typically with our potentials undiscovered. Historically, especially before the Enlightenment, others were killed—sometimes burned—as being possessed by the devil. And later, many were put away, out of sight in institutions."

Charley sounded quite serene as he recited, as if he'd long since come to terms with the facts.

"As for me—I am thirty-three years old, and spent my life in an institution from perhaps two days of age until the War Mobilization Directorate learned of me."

"Was that when you were installed in a bioelectronic interface unit?"

"To understand that, you need to know my origins. As far as they *are* known. I was found abandoned in a trash bin, in Rio de Janeiro, in the Brazilian Autonomy. Seemingly in my first day of life. The police delivered me to a hospital, which passed me on to another, which forwarded me to the Sacred Heart Research Institute. Where I remained for more than thirty years."

Sent to a research institute at what? Five days of age? *There has to be an interesting story behind that,* Soong thought.

Charley paused. "As for being bottled . . . My early years involved a continuous struggle on the part of the Institute's personnel to keep me alive, because of the physiological imbalances that continually afflicted me. Finally they arranged with another research organization to extract my central nervous system and bottle it. An operation quite illegal then, even for research, and carrying severe penalties. But I was beginning to show signs of the hormonally driven syndrome referred to as adolescence, a period of powerful physiological changes. My staff guardians doubted I could survive it."

"They didn't call my bottle a bottle, of course, or even a bioelectronic interface unit. They called it a modularized life-support unit. It was hoped that that and being a monastic order would protect them, if the act came to the attention of the secular authorities. But it required extraction of a living central nervous system, which legally made it bottling."

Again he laughed. "And now, all these years later, here I am in my technological glory, and some would say middle-aged. Incidentally, what you see before you is my third module. The technology does progress, you know, albeit covertly."

The admiral sat without speaking. *I'll have to digest all*

this, he thought. *Sleep on it, see how it looks in the morning.* Meanwhile, Charley seemed to be waiting. "How did you go from being 'Male Infant Doe' to 'Charley Gordon'?" Soong found himself asking.

"Ho ho! You have opened a new area there! In the beginning it wasn't known that I was a savant. I was simply a medical challenge, not in the Savant Division at all. What set me apart from most critically defective infants was surviving my first day. Despite having been discarded. The neighborhood I was found in was quite degraded. I could easily have been eaten by rats.

"My savant status was first suspected before my third birthday, when I showed a love of good music, and recognized and asked for certain numbers. It was also determined that I could be educated to a higher level than supposed. The highest of any wards of the Institute, actually.

"Finally, at age twelve, my physical condition became quite precarious, and I was bottled."

Charley paused long enough that it seemed he'd finished. "You were about to tell the admiral how you came to be called Charley Gordon," Kennah said.

"Oh yes. Excuse me, Admiral. One of my mental weaknesses is a tendency to lose track of the subject. I have noticed that normal people sometimes do the same thing, but I excel in it. If I may use the word 'excel' in this sense.

"Now, where—oh yes. I was named Charley Gordon after a person in a story: a retarded man who became a genius."

He paused, then spoke again. "I really should tell you the rest. Otherwise it's not very meaningful.

"The study that discovered my ability to learn, was part of a project that became very important. Leading inadvertently to the discovery of savant-facilitated instantaneous communication."

Charley's fluency and apparent understanding awed the admiral.

"And as one of the study subjects, it was determined that I had 'the talent,' as it is called. I might then have been assigned to the Commonwealth Ministry, and sent to an embassy on some colony world. But because bottling was still a felony, I remained at the Institute, occasionally taking part in research projects as a subject or advisor."

Again he paused. "Admiral, I'm afraid I'm a poor host. I have not offered you food or drink. Ophelia, would you please?"

"Of course, Charley. Admiral, I do not have an alcoholic beverage to offer you, but I do have a mixed fruit drink, and some hors d'oeuvres."

"Thank you, Ms. Kennah," the admiral said gravely. "The fruit drink will be fine, and I'm sure I'll like the hors d'oeuvres as well. But I shouldn't stay long. I didn't tell the bridge where I'd be."

She saw the statement as an excuse. He could easily call the bridge and tell the officer of the watch where to reach him. "Of course," she replied. "Perhaps you could select your own hors d'oeuvres in the kitchenette."

The suggestion sparked his curiosity; it seemed lame. He wondered if Charley saw through it. Or didn't it matter to him? *Either way,* he thought. If she wanted privacy . . .

The kitchenette was small but not tiny. The door closed itself behind them. The hors d'oeuvres were on a tray. "Ms. Kennah . . . " he began quietly.

"Call me Ophelia if you'd like," she prompted. "Or Kennah without the miz. Or Ken; that's what they called me at the Institute. Actually, I prefer Kennah."

"Well then, Kennah it will be. How long have you known Charley?"

"Since he was only days old; as soon as he came out of intensive care. I was a seventeen-year-old apprentice nurse, assigned to watch him eight hours at a time, with a half-hour lunch break. It was then I learned to love him, when he was still a tiny baby. Before it was recognized how truly special he was. He *is* special, you know. The whole staff came to feel it. All the children are special, and loved, but Charley more than any. His fight to live was so brave. As if he knew he had a special gift to share." Again she shrugged. "And he was so cheerful! Did you know a sick infant can be cheerful? You can hardly imagine what he went through. For years! And his growth as a person and a personality have been equally outstanding."

Perhaps I can imagine, Soong thought. *Surely to some degree.* He took a tiny three-cornered sandwich and tasted it. Goose liver paste, he decided, its seasonings close to perfect. No doubt the makings came from the command officers' mess. "Was that why you wanted me to come into the kitchen?" he asked. "To give me that insight into Charley?"

She shook her head. "No," she said. "You need to know something he has done. He mentioned it just yesterday. You may not approve."

He frowned. "Yes?"

"He hasn't been listening to music as much as I'd thought. Playing it, yes, but quietly, as background. He'd . . . broken into the battlecomp system; he said it wasn't difficult. For weeks he's listened to your battle exercises. He told me it was the most interesting thing he'd ever done; much more interesting than battle dramas." She shrugged. "He's always liked battle dramas and histories, and war games when I smuggled them to him at the Institute. Patients were not supposed to have them, nor staff as far as that's concerned."

She paused, calmly accepting the admiral's eye contact.

Soong nodded slowly. "I see. Thank you for being forthright."

They returned to the living room, Charley's room, Soong carrying another sandwich and a glass of fruit punch. "Ophelia is quite skilled in the kitchen," he said, using the name Charley used for her.

"I'm sure she is," Charley answered. "Before you leave, I'd like you to have a cube. Of the early, magazine version of 'Flowers for Algernon,' translated from the original Anglic. It is the story of the original, fictional Charley Gordon. My dear Ophelia read it onto the cube for me. It is sad, but it is also beautiful. It is rich in love."

When Soong left the small apartment, it was soberly. It was not surprising that in Charley Gordon's mind, love was associated with sadness. Meanwhile he needed to have the battlecomp checked for anything Charley might have done to it.

❖   ❖   ❖

That evening, a careful rundown by Lieutenant Commander Bedi Chen, the flagship's senior computer specialist, found nothing out of order in the battlecomp. Chen was curious as to why the admiral had asked for the check; the system monitored itself constantly, and at frequent, random intervals ran all-inclusive scans. But he didn't ask, and Soong volunteered nothing.

The admiral was glad, in fact, that Charley had done what he'd done. What *he* needed to do now, he told himself, was find ways to (1) check his operating assumption, and (2) find a way to make use of it. While not allowing himself expectations. Hopes, yes, but not expectations.

Before he went to bed that night, Soong read "Flowers for Algernon." It *was* sad, and it *was* beautiful. Normally the admiral was not fond of sad, but in this case he made an exception. Perhaps because it seemed to him that Male Infant Doe, aka Charley Gordon, himself showed considerable love. And in the physical universe—the world Alvaro Soong knew—there could never be too much love.

Chapter 37
On a Different Flagship

Tension had worn on Grand Admiral Quanshûk, tension born of incongruities and enigmas—of a situation and life-form beyond comprehension.

Only a very potent life-form, powerful, vigorous, and technologically advanced, could have spawned so many colonies so far. A life-form strong enough, confident enough, smart and ruthless enough to have overcome and destroyed its sapient rivals on its world of origin. And on any other attractive world it found.

He didn't actually think the concept of ruthlessness. In the Wyzhñyñy world view, ruthlessness toward rival life-forms required no conceptualization. It was an underlying truth.

So far, his armada had penetrated only the outer zone of the human empire. That was obvious, despite the distance of that penetration. Somewhere ahead he would encounter the old, long-settled body of the Commonwealth, and there, if not sooner, meet resistance. The prisoners had admitted it.

He'd considered coercing more information from them, but Qonits had recommended against it, reminding his admiral that the two humans were simply marine scientists. Obviously most humans were not fighters. Their warrior gender, called "soldiers," seemed missing from their colonies. And clearly their other genders were untrained— probably unsuited—for war.

Quanshûk and Qonits had reviewed the situation repeatedly, particularly since the passage of time made it both clearer and more enigmatic. The landing forces had met essentially no resistance, and had already captured twenty-one planets. The human empire was truly vast. Humans must be bound together by unbreakable loyalty for such an empire to exist, a loyalty deep within the genes. The enormous volume of space involved, the time requirements even for hyperspace pod communication, the difficulty of effective policing—all made space empires impractical without such inborn loyalty.

But loyalty extended in both directions, from the ruled upward to the rulers, and from the rulers downward to the ruled. Quanshûk believed that implicitly. It was logical, and it was true to the experience of his species.

Over their long history, the Wyzhñyñy had known and destroyed a half-dozen, space-faring species. Two of which had created large empires, though neither with a radius that approached the distance he'd already traveled in this one. And both had responded to invasion with a united ferocity that could only grow out of such loyalty.

Yet the humans had not. Why had that loyalty not manifested? Or perhaps manifested so strangely?

From the very first human world his armada had reached—clearly a picket world—three, perhaps four craft had escaped. And beyond doubt had homed inward to warn their empire. They would have come out of hyperspace a day or so inbound, and launched message pods to the nearer inhabited worlds. Which in turn would have spread the message: invasion!

Pods were intrinsically faster, because they carried no life-forms. Nor did they need to detour and emerge, to examine systems for habitable planets. Nor cover an invasion flotilla when such a planet was found. So surely

the human core worlds knew by now. Should have known
months ago.

Unless their empire was vast beyond imagination! The
possibility gnawed on Quanshûk. What sort of empire had
he invaded? With how many core worlds? How many
fleets?

Yet he'd encountered no enemy force at all. None! And
clearly the humans had hyperdrive. Without it they could
not have begun to colonize so far.

This lack of resistance had to be a strategy. But what
strategy? Was a vast human warfleet being gathered, while
his armada was being sucked in as if by some enormous
singularity?

The thought squeezed his heart like a giant fist.

And on the other warships, his officers had surely
hatched and brooded those same fears.

The responsibility was his though, and it was taking its
toll. He was on medication now for arthritic hips and tarsal
joints. The ship's chief physician had advised him to stay
off his feet as much as possible, so he'd reduced his time
on the bridge, and worked more from his stateroom. Which,
after all, had full access to shipsmind, which meant to
everything on board.

A time or two he'd wondered if his anxiety was worsened
by the presence of humans on board. He'd even thought
of jettisoning them from an airlock, but his troubles and
fears would not die with them. And as Qonits had pointed
out, "We have learned much from the prisoners; to kill
them would be to throw away a resource. Soon we will
meet the humans in battle. It is unavoidable. Then further
questions will occur to us, and without our captives, we
would have no one to ask. They can make the difference
between success and failure."

And to that, Quanshûk reminded himself, *I had no
conclusive reply. Not then, not now. Shipsmind has found
no substantial inconsistencies in what they have told us.
I can only await what happens, and when the time comes,
fight skillfully and very hard.*

Fortunately the admiral's mood was not always so dark.
But never was it bright. It hadn't been since they'd

somehow been cast across intergalactic space, into this
galaxy so impossibly far from home. That such a thing
could happen . . . His view of the universe, and his confidence in himself, his fleet, his science—his reality!—
could never be the same.

Qonits quickstepped down the corridor, his bodyguards
close behind. The chief scholar shared Quanshûk's concerns,
but not his responsibilities. And in temperament he was
a scholar, not a master, driven by an urge to know, not to
rule.

Arriving at the prisoners' door, his senior guard knocked,
and Qonits identified himself.

"Come in," David answered. Qonits opened the door and
entered, his guards stopping just inside.

"My friends," said Qonits in Terran, "we will do something different today."

David's eyebrows rose. "Different? In what way?" Both
he and Yukiko had adjusted to the monotony, but Qonits'
visibly good spirits suggested that the change would be
pleasant. Or at least well intended.

"I shall take you to see more of the flagship. You shall
see the place of command and control, and the place where
the, um, the ship's workings are accomplished."

"Ah! The bridge and the engine room."

Qonits peered carefully at the human male. "Perhaps.
Where we go, I will show you things, and you will tell me
their names."

Yukiko spoke next. "Qonits, we would like very much
to do those things, but we cannot leave Annika alone. You
have seen how much better she is now than when we first
arrived. If we leave her, I'm afraid she will relapse—get
worse again. She might even die."

Qonits' expression changed into one they had not seen
before. A Wyzhñyñy grin? "I have," he told them, "foreseen the problem." Turning, he spoke in Wyzhñyñy toward
the open door, and in from the corridor came another
guard, pushing an AG seat large enough to accommodate
Annika. "You will bring her with us," he said. "On this."

Yukiko examined it, testing its stability, poking and
pushing on the cushions, inspecting the seat belt, its

adjustments, and the simple fastener. "Oh, Qonits!" she said. "A stroller! It's lovely! It should do beautifully!"

It wasn't "lovely," of course. It was strictly utilitarian. But her appreciation was genuine, and Qonits felt it. He and David waited while Yukiko took Annika to the potty stool they'd had made for her, and waited while the girl relieved her bladder. Then David buckled the savant into the stroller, and the humans left with the chief scholar.

They hadn't been outside the cell since they'd been put in it, nearly ten Terran months earlier. They'd eaten in it, slept in it, exercised and bathed—even on occasion made love in it. Told stories to each other and to Annika, to fill the time and amuse each other. By now they felt no discomfort at being nude among these people, these aliens who themselves wore no clothing.

First they visited the bridge, and for the first time saw a Wyzhñyñy master. Three of them, in fact—the grand admiral, the ship's master, and the watch officer, though the humans didn't know those identities. Like Qonits, all three were blue and red, but their crests were considerably larger and showier than any scholar's. They guessed Quanshûk's identity from his ornate harness. The bridge watch, to the best of their ability, pretended to ignore the visitation, but all managed a look. Almost none had seen the prisoners before, even on a monitor. Only Qonits and the prisoners spoke, and only to establish the Terran terms for the bridge's equipment and furnishings.

Next the Terrans were shown the engine department. Both thought they recognized some of what they saw, and by asking questions, were able to provide names, probably correct. Shipsmind, meanwhile, heard and saw everything, including the uncertainties. It stored, dissected, parsed, assigned tentative evaluations based on known roots and contexts, and ran correlations. Iteration was a major tool.

Next they visited a beamgun battery, then a torpedo battery, and finally the shield generator. Little guessing was needed.

The last technical visit was brief—the stasis section, where the equipment was even more unmistakable. Their final stop was the officers' galley, where a grinning (surely that was a Wyzhñyñy grin!) chief baker gave each of the

visitors what the baker regarded as a treat. It was crunchy
and dense—rather like something they often received at
meals. But this was also sweet, its flavor reminding them
of maple sugar. His eyes watched intently, expectantly, and
he spoke to them in Wyzhñyñyç.

"He asks if you like it," Qonits interpreted.

"Oh yes," Yukiko said. "Delicious," David added. Annika
gnawed silently, without cerebral response. The baker spoke
again, Qonits interpreting. "He says he will send some
special food to you each day."

Then they left the galley, and the chief scholar led them
back to their cell.

Afterward Qonits went to his own quarters. Shipsmind
would already have analyzed, organized, and formatted the
additions, but he was in no hurry to examine them. After
mid-meal would be soon enough. Meanwhile he would close
his eyes and nap briefly.

He felt good about the tour. The prisoners had benefited
from the change, and the ship's human vocabulary had
expanded in an important area, filling a hole. It seemed
to him there couldn't be many holes left. More and more
they'd worked on the nuances that separated synonyms.
Important work but less vital, for now at least.

The human language seemed more complex than
Wyzhñyñyç, but less so than either of the two exotic
languages previously deciphered. It was basically oral, and
many of the nuances were verbal, as in Wyzhñyñyç. But
even more than Wyzhñyñyç, the human language seemed
to him to have many visual nuances, including postures,
arm and hand movements, head movements, facial expressions, eye movements . . . Qonits wasn't sure how many of
those signals were deliberate and how many subliminal.

*If the time comes when we must negotiate with their
rulers,* he thought, *then the nuances will be critical.*

He hadn't voiced the thought of negotiation to Quanshûk.
It would be dreadfully inappropriate; circumstances would
have to do it. But with the translation program developing
so nicely—surely the possibility had occurred to the admiral. *We negotiate among ourselves,* Qonits thought. *Surely
we can negotiate with others. Even if we never have before.*

❖   ❖   ❖

On his closed command monitor, Quanshûk had watched the tour after it left the bridge, had seen Qonits say good-bye to the humans, and leave them in their prison. *Ships-mind will have analyzed the whole thing by now,* Quanshûk thought as he entered his quarters. As for the prisoners, none of it had surprised them—the bridge stations and their screens, the strange-space generator, the beamguns . . . which strongly suggested that human science and technology were much like his own. They'd hit the wall in much the same places.

He didn't know whether to feel relieved or disappointed.

The cube showed only the savant, Ramesh, lying in trance on his couch, with Burhan sitting attentively beside him, while words issued from the savant's lips in a variety of voices. As usual, the president and the prime minister viewed it in Peixoto's office, unedited except that the brief silences had been compressed. Now they viewed it again.

When the cube had played out, the two men looked long at one another. It was the president who broke the silence. "The Tao has been good to us, allowing us to hear that. And today I learned more than Wyzhñyñy technology. Those are people we must war against."

Peixoto pursed his lips. "But it does not change the situation. Alive or dead, they must leave the Common-wealth. And even if they were Eve's children, they would hardly leave unforced. They have too much invested, too much at stake."

"It seems so," Chang said. "But we agreed that if we could, we would negotiate. It was you who said it first. And the Tao is full of surprises."

Peixoto's inner reaction was bleak. *Full of surprises, yes,* he told himself, *but surprises fitting probability equations and natural laws. Some things simply do not happen.*

He kept the thought to himself though. There was no point in throwing negativity in anyone's face, certainly not his best friend's. And if an opportunity arose—if the Wyzhñyñy were willing to negotiate—he would approach the task honestly.

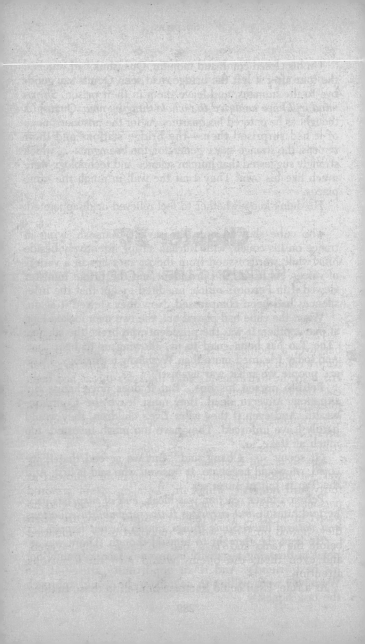

Chapter 38
Ruckus in the Morgue

Esau slogged forward, blaster in his hands and grenade bag over a shoulder. He hadn't slept for thirty hours— hadn't eaten for nearly twenty, except for an energy bar. His belly, he told himself, must think his throat had been cut. But his red-rimmed eyes moved constantly, from the forest half a mile ahead, to the farm woodlots that broke the croplands and pastures, to the Indi tanks moving ahead on their AG cushions. To both left and right stretched other 2nd Regiment companies.

Not all of 2nd Regiment was in his line. The lead rank was 1st Battalion; 2nd and 3rd Battalions followed at thirty-yard intervals, while 4th Battalion sat in armored personnel carriers as a tactical reserve. Esau was glad he wasn't in an APC. They tended to draw heavy fire when they showed up. They weren't supposed to be committed before the tanks and "legs" had the enemy fully engaged, and even then, the enemy would give them serious attention.

As a rule, Esau could immerse himself in these training

maneuvers as if they were the real thing. As he was supposed to. He never glanced back at the umpires on their grav scooters, following the action. The sight of them, even the thought of them, weakened the illusion.

No shots had been fired yet from the distant forest, nor from the building and woodlots nearer at hand. Which might mean no one was there, but that seemed unlikely. Surveillance buoys showed things like that. And if no one was there, 2nd Regiment would have crossed in APCs. Only if serious enemy fire was expected would they cross on foot like this.

At that moment, firing broke out from forest, woodlots and steadings—crackling, hissing, thumping—and a voice spoke sharply in his right ear: "Bogies from the rear! Bogies from the rear!" Esau flattened himself as low as he could, then hazarded a glance back past his shoulder. A rank of killer craft swept across the field, slammers flickering. Esau felt a soft pulse strike about at his tailbone, and obediently rolled over, playing casualty. The umpires' instruments recorded all hits, along with the victims' identities, the virtual force, and points of impact.

The assault craft swished by overhead, most of them. A few must have taken "crippling hits" themselves; they landed obediently as casualties. If they hadn't, and promptly, the "enemy" would have been penalized, and the pilots put on report.

The ground was cold but the sun bright, and Esau put a forearm over his eyes. He wondered if Jael had been hit, and if perhaps they should have signed up for bottling. If this had been a real fight, he told himself, and the hit he'd taken had been a hard pulse, signing wouldn't have made any difference. Because surely that had been a slammer. It would have blown his guts, lungs, heart and spine, all to Tophet.

He was aware of 2nd and 3rd Battalions passing him, trotting now. The sound of firing remained intense. It seemed odd to be lying there out of it. He was going to miss some of the action. It occurred to him to sit up and look around, see what was going on. Their own floaters should be up again, suppressing enemy fire.

But it was easier to just lie there with his eyes closed,

feeling himself drift into sleep. Then a medic gripped his arm, and he wakened.

"Where are you hit?"

"Tailbone, from behind. It would have been one of the killer craft. If it was real, I'd be deader'n Tophet."

"Okay. I'm going to give you a shot for the pain, just in case."

The man pretended to inject Esau in the side of the neck, then taped a fake syringe to his patient's field jacket and hurried on. Esau let his eyes close again. *Who knew,* he thought, *what would happen when they got into real combat, back home on New Jerusalem.* Wyzhñyñy weapons were thought to be pretty much the same as human weapons. "Physics is the same everywhere," Sergeant Hawkins had said. Jerries weren't taught physics, but Esau had gotten the basic idea; only certain things were possible. But the Wyzhñyñy had four legs under them, and might be stronger than him. Might all of them carry slammers.

"Esau," said Speaker Crosby, "they are way to heck stronger than you are." He patted his horse on the shoulder. "They're near as big as this fella, with arms in proportion."

Esau decided to keep Clancy with him for protection, and looked around for the big hound, but couldn't see him anywhere. Then realized he'd begun to dream. Clancy was a long long ways off, and so was Speaker Crosby. *It don't matter,* he told himself. *You're already dead anyway.*

Shortly afterward an armored ambulance landed a few yards away. Without speaking, two medics laid him carefully on an AG stretcher, then took him to the ambulance, where another medic secured the stretcher on brackets and turned on the "warm field."

Soon afterward they arrived at a field "hospital" in the forest, a complex of tents beneath the trees. It was supposed to be protected by a concealment screen so the enemy couldn't find it from the air. The tents were like shallow, upside-down bowls, protected by colors generated by their camouflage fields. The medics moved quickly and smoothly, transferring the casualties to a receiving tent.

Calling him dead on arrival, they put Esau in a body bag, and moved him to a morgue tent.

The activity had wakened him again, and because he actually was alive, the bag had been pressed shut only to his waist. He sat up and looked around. There were no attendants in this tent, but the trainee on the floor beside him was also looking around. "Well," the man said. His voice was quiet. "So this is what it's like to be dead."

"Not hardly," Esau answered.

"What's your company?"

"B, 2nd Platoon. Name is Esau Wesley. Yours?"

The other didn't answer at once, as if thinking about it. "Simon Justice," he said at last. "E Company, 3rd Platoon. Can you say bunch of foolishness?"

"What do you mean?"

The man's gesture took in the tent, perhaps the whole hospital, or planet. "All of this. Pretending to fight, pretending to get shot, pretending to be dead. All of it."

Esau decided he didn't like Simon Justice. Didn't like his tone of voice, didn't like his pretense of superiority. "It's not foolishness," Esau replied. He didn't expect to change the man's mind, but the statement required an answer. "We'll be glad we've gone through it when we get back to New Jerusalem."

"Huh! We'll never get to New Jerusalem. The government's going to send us somewhere else, to put down an uprising." His tone suggested scorn for anyone who didn't realize that.

"Where'd you get that notion?" Esau asked.

"Why, it's plain to see. A four-legged critter with a man stuck on the front?" He snorted his scorn.

"That's no more unlikely than what you said." Esau paused. "Are you calling Captain Mulvaney a liar? Or General Pak?"

"That's about right. Yeah."

Esau moved his hands to the open edge of his body bag, separating the closure all the way to his knees. And got up. "Get out of that bag and we'll talk about this," he said.

By that time others in the tent were watching, their eyes on Esau now. The man who called himself Simon Justice, on the other hand, had decided to lay back down again.

"What's the matter?" Esau demanded. "You were big on talk, with all that bullshit."

"It's against regulations to fight," the man answered. "Otherwise I'd get out of this bag and teach you a lesson."

With a single step, Esau was leaning over him, gripped him, pulled him to his feet and jerked him close, bag and all. "Simon Justice," he said, "you're a liar and a coward. And unless you take all that back . . . "

Another soldier was on his feet now. "A bigger liar'n you know," he said. "He's not Simon Justice. *I'm* Simon Justice. He's not even in 3rd Platoon. E Company, yes—I've seen him around—but not in 3rd Platoon. So if anybody beats him up, I'm the one ought to do it."

Esau's eyes widened, then he barked a laugh, and grinned at the real Simon Justice. "Well well! He's all yours. Have at it!" He let go the counterfeit, who dropped to the floor in self protection, gripping his body bag closed and yelling at the top of his lungs, "Help! Help! Murder!" waking whatever corpses weren't already awake.

Before either Esau or the real Simon Justice could decide what to do, a Terran medic stepped inside. His sleeves had sergeant's stripes, and above his jacket pocket the name "Sinisalo, Urho E." "What the hell's going on in here?" he barked. "You! And you! Get back in those body bags."

While they did, he murmured softly, as if to someone invisible beside him. Then he looked down at the false Simon Justice. "Are you the one who yelled?"

"Yes, sir," the liar answered softly. "They said they were going to beat me up." His voice was almost too faint to hear. He realized his situation. There were maybe a dozen—at least several others in the tent who'd heard the exchange. He'd never in the world lie his way out of this situation.

Sinisalo frowned, then looked around and pointed to a watching, listening corpse. "You," said the medic. "What happened in here?"

The man told him, closely enough.

Sinisalo looked down at the liar. "Give me your dog tags."

Only the liar's eyes moved.

"That's an order, soldier!"

The liar shook his head, encouraged by the apparency that he wouldn't be beaten up.

A lieutenant hurried in, a Sikh wearing a white turban and Medical Service insignia. "I'm the provost marshal," he said to Sinisalo. "What's going on here?" The provost marshal's post was only one of several he covered, the one he'd least expected to require his attention. His military police unit consisted of one man—himself. When he'd gotten the call, he'd grabbed a stunner, a belt recorder, and a set of handcuffs, and hurried to the morgue. But he was a Sikh, with five years' military experience, and a cram course in the basics of the provost marshal's job. He'd make it go right.

When Sinisalo had described what he'd found and heard, the provost marshal stood over the liar and reached down. "Your dog tags," he said.

Again the liar refused, clasping himself with his arms. The provost knew Jerrie strength, so he turned to Esau. "Sergeant, take his dog tags."

Esau crouched beside the liar, pulled open the body bag, grabbed the man's field jacket and hoisted him to his feet. Hurriedly the liar gave up his dog tags. Esau handed them to the provost marshal, who read them and scowled. "Private Thomas Crisp," he said.

He manacled the now compliant Crisp, then went around the morgue with his belt recorder and got the name, serial number, and unit of each "corpse" there.

"All right," he said, "Wesley, Justice, Crisp, come with me. You other casualties, continue in your roles." He turned to Sinisalo. "Sergeant, you come too."

As he herded his three corpses toward the hospital admin tent, the provost marshal drew his belt comm and called for an MP floater from Division. The hospital had no place to incarcerate anyone.

Before the lieutenant had finished questioning his three Jerries, two other things happened. The MP floater arrived, with six MPs led by a sergeant. And an orderly arrived to report a genuine casualty. A trainee in the maneuvers had been shot in the back with a hard pulse, a slammer pulse.

It had scrambled his innards—bones and organs. And all the power slugs used in the maneuvers, including those in the aircraft, had supposedly been for soft pulses.

Saboteurs again! the lieutenant thought, thinking of the parachute incident, the major ordnance and equipment-checking project that had grown out of it, and what was found. When the floater had taken off with the prisoner and the principal witnesses, the lieutenant returned to the morgue to get statements from the other corpses.

Esau fell asleep again even before the MP floater took off, almost as he buckled himself in. *Take advantage of your opportunities,* he'd thought as they'd walked out to it. He'd heard how it worked for "casualties," from guys who'd gone through it the past couple of days. In an hour or two he'd be reclassified from corpse to combat replacement, and flown to some company other than his own, to fit in as best he could till the exercise was finished. On New Jerusalem, of course, there'd be no replacements, but the general didn't want his casualties to miss out on the training.

Actually it was a dozen hours before he was reassigned. Division's provost marshal let him sleep for eight hours before questioning him. And learned nothing he didn't already have on cube.

Chapter 39
Digging for Roots

The weather had been pleasant for the Mühlbach maneuvers, with mostly sunny days, and temperatures reaching into the 60s. The nights had been near 40, with brilliant starscapes. The trainees might have enjoyed their five-day test, if they'd had enough to eat and at least a few hours a day of sleep. But the maneuvers were more than a test of tactics, leadership, and readiness. Their commanding general wanted them to discover their tenacity, and endurance of privation, so he'd cranked up the hardship factor.

They'd handled it well.

Maneuvers were the heart of unit training, and at least as vital for General Pyong Pak Singh as for his troops. Pak had never experienced actual combat, never directed a battle except in electronic games. So he lived maneuvers as realistically as he could. He directed his division from a floater; camped in the field, was often on the move, ate field rations, and caught catnaps when the situation allowed. Though he slept more than his men.

His alertness, or lack thereof, was important to every man in his "corps," his expanded division—Jerries, Indi Armored, air wings, and Lüneburger Engineers.

He'd delighted in the competition with his opposing counterpart, Major General Pauli Nachtigal of the Lüneburger 4th Infantry Division, and found strong satisfaction in his troops, who'd performed well—even E Company, 2nd Regiment which, with fifteen men in the stockade, was shorthanded, and perhaps a bit demoralized by the defections—while the opposing Burger infantry division was really good, Masadan trained.

Now that the Mühlbach maneuvers were over, and everyone had had a long night's sleep, the troops were enjoying a day off. In camp, for there'd be no passes till the matter of defections was sorted out. A day off with naps and base food: all the roast pork, the barley with pork gravy, freshly baked still-warm bread with butter and jam, pie with good cheese from Lüneburger's Mennonite dairies . . . and all the ice cream they could eat! Few if any of his Jerries had seen ice cream before they'd joined the army. Few had even heard of it. It had become their favorite, if infrequent, dessert.

If the troops had the day off, their general didn't. He was at his desk at 0730, working his way through his *In* basket. At 0930 he met with his division provost marshal, Captain Raymond Coyote Singh, and the CO of 2nd Regiment's 2nd Battalion, Major Amar Kalnins Singh. Of urgent necessity, the subject was the defections—the refusal by fifteen members of E Company to serve. Briefly the three officers reviewed the basic known facts, without speculating on the roots. Then Captain Coyote reported on E Company's Private Thomas Crisp, and his clumsy attempt to spread disaffection in the field hospital's morgue. He had his own cubes and those recorded by the hospital's provost marshal, with accounts provided by Sergeant Sinisalo, and by Wesley, Justice, and the bystanders. And by Crisp.

The meeting was interrupted by chirping from Pak's intercom. His monitor told him it was Administrative Sergeant Major Watanabe. Frowning, Pak spoke to his pickup. "What is it?" he asked.

The answer came via the pickup in his right ear. "General, Corporal Isaiah Vernon is here, with information that may be important to the defections matter. Vernon's a bot attached to 2nd Regiment, 1st Battalion. Would you like to see him now?"

Pak knew the name. "Bring him in, Sergeant," Pak said, then broke the connection and looked at Coyote. "Captain, record this. Apparently it's information on our problem."

The sergeant major opened the door. A seven-foot warbot stood behind him. "General," said Watanabe, "this is Corporal Vernon."

Vernon stepped inside and stopped. "Thank you, Sergeant Major," Pak said in dismissal, and the door closed. "What do you have for us, Corporal?"

"General, the night before we went on maneuvers, Private Jeremiah Spieler, *Speaker* Spieler, came to my hut and told me a story. He and I were friends. We'd been in B Company together, and back home I was a student speaker. He told me that the evening before, after lights out, some men came to his tent and woke him up. They told him they needed his advice. So he went outside with them. It turned out they didn't want advice. They wanted him to help them spread a message in B Company. Quietly, to men he trusted.

"The one that did the talking said the Wyzhñyñy were sent by God," Vernon went on, "to overthrow a corrupt and Godless Commonwealth government. And that God wants his people—all colonists and Terrans who follow his commandments and the leadership of Christ—to turn against the government. Refuse orders and stand against evil, even at the risk of their lives."

The Peace Front line all the way, Pak thought. "Why isn't Spieler telling me this himself?" he asked.

If there was a way of reading a warbot's reactions, comparable to reading an organic's face, Pak didn't know it. But the two or three-second lag suggested surprise. "Why, General, sir, Speaker Spieler was killed in the maneuvers. Someone shot him in the back with a hard pulse. From a slammer, I'm told."

The statement stunned Pak. He'd heard there'd been an accidental death, a shooting. This story made it seem deliberate. "Did they—the men who talked with Spieler—did they say who told them all that?"

"Jeremiah didn't say. They did tell him they were part of a group headed by speakers, but he was sure the man who did the talking wasn't one. Because when he tried to quote scripture, he got it all wrong."

"Hmm. This was—what then? A week ago?"

"Six nights ago he told me about it, sir."

"Why didn't Spieler, or you, inform your sergeants?"

"The speaker said he was afraid of them, sir. And he didn't know who they were. I asked. He couldn't see their names in the dark, nor their faces well enough. All he could say was, the one who did the talking sounded like us—like someone from New Jerusalem—but taller than just about any of us gets. As tall as Captain Mulvaney, he said."

Hmm. That would be more than six feet, Pak thought. "Afraid. Did they threaten him?"

"Not exactly. They told him to be careful not to say anything about it to anyone he didn't trust. They'd tell him when it was time. But Jeremy said it sounded like a warning."

"But Spieler told you."

"Yessir. I guess he needed to tell someone, and knew he could trust me."

"Why didn't you tell someone? Your sergeant."

"I should have. But we had breakfast at 0630 the next morning and left on maneuvers. And it seemed like just talk; I didn't suppose anything would come of it. Surely nothing like someone shooting Jeremiah. Or that anyone would quit the army. And we'll be leaving for home in another month; I told myself that when we got there, the facts would speak for themselves."

Pak nodded thoughtfully. "Thank you, Corporal. You've been very helpful. Say nothing to anyone about talking to us. And if you see anything, or remember anything that may help us identify the traitors, report it to your battalion commander promptly.

"You may go now."

A gentle giant, Pak thought as he watched the warbot leave. *I wonder how he'll do in combat.*

Well enough, he decided. Major Somphavanh Ruiz Singh,

CO of the division's bot contingent, was an excellent officer who'd given special attention to selecting his noncoms. But he'd ask him about Vernon and see what he said.

After Pak closed the meeting, Captain Coyote went to his computer and checked on several things. Near the end of advanced training, the various company commanders, in conference with their platoon leaders and platoon sergeants, had evaluated their troops for promotion. And Spieler had not made lance corporal. His platoon sergeant had characterized him as very conscientious, and hard-working, but passive. He'd probably make lance corporal at the end of unit training, and go no further.

He already knew that all fifteen men who'd "resigned" were in E Company, as Private Crisp was. The tallest man in E Company was a Private Moses Wheeler, who at five feet eleven was one of the tallest Jerries in the division. He was one of only four in his squad who hadn't defected. He was also 4th Squad's slammer man, and a troublemaker from the start. He'd done nothing extreme, at least not till now, but he led 2nd Battalion in the number of times on company punishment.

Coyote then called up the information on Spieler's death. The pulse had struck him in the left side of the left buttock, below the flak jacket, destroying the left pelvis. Overall the damage indicated an impact vector diagonally upward, out through the ribs on the right side, shattering the right humerus. The overall damage could only have been done by a slammer. It must have been after the troops had hit the dirt in response to the air attack, but the angle practically guaranteed it had not been fired by a killer craft. So. Something else then.

Coyote asked his computer for the regimental formation during the advance across the fields of Müller's Settlement. Spieler had been in B Company, 1st Platoon, 4th Squad. E Company had been about 30 yards behind B Company, and one position to its left. Wheeler had been in 4th Squad, 4th Platoon, but with almost all his squad locked in the stockade, he'd probably . . . Yes. He'd been attached as an augmentation to—2nd Squad, and from his position there, could easily have fired the pulse that killed

Spieler. Judging by the angle, the only one else who could have, given the high-powered weapon used, was 2nd Squad's slammer man. The provost marshal saw no clear way, yet, to prove that Wheeler was the murderer, but this established opportunity, and greatly reduced the apparent alternatives.

His next step, Coyote decided, would be to have Wheeler brought to him for questioning, and meanwhile have his belongings searched. If they were lucky enough to find an M-6 power slug . . . Then talk with E Company's 4th Platoon sergeant, and learn who were Wheeler's close associates. *They were probably in the stockade,* he thought. *I'll have them wired before I question them. See how they read. Maybe that'll lead somewhere.*

He was reaching for his comm switch when it occurred to him: *What was the source of this Peace Front line? Could some Jerrie have come up with it independently?* It seemed doubtful.

The good weather had broken near midday. Then Joseph Switzer had worked in the rain, piling slabs. The rain had turned to thick wet snow—a rarity at Sagenwerk—as wet as the rain but colder. Switzer's blanket-lined jacket had soaked up about five pounds of ice water, or so it seemed. At the end of the shift he headed home without stopping at the tavern. His nose had begun to run. His heavy work shoes were saturated. He'd have to dry them by the stove, and grease them in the morning. He'd stay home tomorrow, sleep, and nurse whatever he was coming down with.

He looked around him and grimaced. He had never, he'd decided, hated any place as much. Sagenwerk was a backwater without any backwater charms. In general, Mennonites liked flowers, liked to grow things, kept their buildings and yard fences painted. But Sagenwerk—ugly, weedy, and filled with truculent, narrow-minded people—Sagenwerk, he told himself, was where the mean and spiteful were reincarnated as punishment. Even sunny and warm he didn't like it. And in weather like this . . .

He shut out the surroundings he slopped through—rain, slush, weed-edged streets, slab fences . . . A chill shook him, and he wiped his runny nose on a sleeve. But as much as he'd like to, he didn't feel free to leave. Not yet. Private Moses Wheeler had arrived at their third meeting not only with his mind made up, he'd arrived with a plan! His own plan, and therefore the only plan he'd consider: work through the speakers. They had influence, and authority in religious matters.

Actually it made sense—except that Wheeler had telescoped it. He wanted to build Rome in a day.

Maybe he could. Joseph Switzer hoped devoutly that he could. If confidence—positive thinking—meant much, he might. For Moses Wheeler was a maverick, and a bomb waiting to go off. The problem was his fuse. Once lit, there was no way that he, Switzer, could do anything about it—control, guide, or even advise. If he'd realized, when they'd first met, what an arrogant asshole Wheeler was, he'd have made his pitch to someone else. But Wheeler made a good first impression. He was big, fearless, and had an aura of power. And he'd seen what Switzer was leading up to while Switzer was still feeling him out. Had taken over and made the mission his own.

In a way, Switzer told himself, he'd suffered from Wheeler's problem—one of Wheeler's problems—overconfidence. Now, though, he wasn't confident at all. Wheeler, on the other hand—he couldn't imagine Wheeler losing confidence. And if Wheeler showed more patience than seemed probable—if he let the speakers do their thing in their own time—the Jerrie army might be compromised enough that War House would be unwilling to send it to New Jerusalem. That was the theory. It was what he'd intended, and what the Front had financed him to do.

The only reason he was hanging around was to learn the results. The Front would expect him to. Word might well never get to North Fork, and almost certainly wouldn't surface on Terra except through him. And quite a few civilian workers at Camp Nafziger came into Sagenwerk on their days off, full of gossip.

Through gray rain and gray introspection, Switzer reached his shack near the tracks at the east edge of town. Stepping onto the rough stoop, he dug his house key from a pocket. With red trembling hands, he got it into the keyhole and turned it. Pushed the door open,

then closed and locked it behind him. That was another
thing about Sagenwerk: there were thefts.

Inside it was half warm. The single room was small
enough to heat with the cookstove, which he'd banked with
coal before work, then closed both damper and draft to
hold fire. After stripping off his sodden jacket, he dug coal
from a sack and put it on the embers.

Someone knocked on the door. Switzer's guts knotted;
he had no friends here. "Who is it?" he asked.

"Nockey Brant."

Brant? The constable? "What do you want?"

"You. You going to let me in, or do I kick the door
down?"

Switzer thought of the pistol in his bag. But if he shot
Brant, and they caught him . . . Maybe it was about that
tool theft at the sawmill. He was an outsider; maybe they
thought he'd done it. Brant would search the place, and
when he didn't find the tools, that would be the end of
it. Then he could fix his supper, eat and go to bed.

"Just a minute."

He stepped to the door, turned the key, then the knob,
and pushed. As it opened, Nockey Brant grabbed and held
it. He was broad and extremely strong, a veteran of the
green chain. Behind him were two MPs from Camp
Nafziger. Brant grinned a stained, spade-toothed grin.
"Couple of soldiers want to talk to you," he said. "About
conspiracy, and being an accomplice before the fact of
murder."

With his other hand, the constable gripped Joseph
Switzer by his wet shirt and pulled him out onto the stoop.
One of the MPs brought forth a pair of handcuffs and
secured Switzer's wrists behind his back. Then they pushed
him ahead of them in the direction of the depot. No one
locked his door. He supposed his stuff would be stolen
before the night was over.

Not, he realized, that it would make any difference.

Chapter 40

A Change of Plans

General Pyong Pak Singh finished reading the summary of evidence, then cleared it from the screen. The case was cut and dried, he told himself: simple, nicely tied together, and unbeatable. He'd send Switzer back to Terra tomorrow, via an embassy courier craft, for a civil trial in Kunming.

Ignorant, well-intentioned Switzer. In the "theology" of the Gopal Singh Dispensation, the evolution—genetic, social, and spiritual—of the human species grew from the interplay of individuals of every type. Remote interplay, and direct, immediate interplay. Joseph Switzer was part of it, and was not—was *not* faulted for that by THE ONE. Persons like Switzer were not only inevitable, but necessary to that evolution. But it was entirely valid for him to be tried and punished by social authority, also as part of that interplay.

Intellectually, Pyong Pak Singh knew and accepted all that. Emotionally, however, he felt offended by what he considered gratuitous troublemaking like Switzer's. He always had, he thought ruefully, and probably would throughout this lifetime.

The nature of the charges made Switzer subject to the court system on Terra. And when informed, the Lüneburgian chief magistrate had declined to claim him. Though born on Lüneburger's, Switzer held resident rights on Terra, and had come to his birth-world on a visitor's visa. He hadn't applied for more. On a world as loosely administered as Lüneburger's, a visitor's visa might be overstayed forever.

On Terra, according to Coyote, Switzer would almost surely be imprisoned but not executed.

Here on Lüneburger's, the courts-martial of the division's fifteen defectors would begin, and no doubt end, next Threeday, the day after the officers of the court returned from the Maple Mountain maneuvers. The trial of the five conspirators would have to wait till the day after, as three of them were among the defectors. That trial might require two, or possibly three days of argument and deliberation.

The murder trial would start the day after the conspirators' trial ended, because Wheeler was a defendant in both. Considered with other evidence, the used M-6 power slug found folded in a towel in Wheeler's footlocker would probably clinch a murder conviction, even if none of his coconspirators testified against him. Actually his mouth had killed any chance he had.

After the murder trial, Pak would ship the conspirators to Terra, because sentencing would have to consider the death penalty. And because Lüneburger's World was (1) not a war zone; and (2) had no military appeals authority. And where capital punishment was an option, a prompt, automatic appellate review was required before sentencing, except in a war zone.

The whole mess has been a distraction, Pak told himself. *I should be at Maple Mountain right now. Though Frosty's undoubtedly enjoying running the show. And it's good experience for him, so it's probably for the . . .*

His intercom chirped. "Pak here," he answered.

"Sir, the ambassador wants to speak with you. He's got a message from War House, via savant."

Pak frowned. "Switch him through."

The ambassador himself required only a minute. Then they both listened live to the embassy's savant, channeling

Lefty Sarruf—Sarruf's words in a remarkable mimicry of
Sarruf's voice. Altogether, the exchange took nearly thirty
minutes, followed by another twenty or so with Admiral
Apraxin-DaCosta of the Admiralty's Liberation Task Force.

There had been a change in the training schedule of
the New Jerusalem Liberation Corps. Apraxin's space force
had been engaged in battle exercises in the neighborhood
of Lüneburger's System for more than a week. Now War
House had decided they'd all trained enough—both the
admiral's force and Pak's soldiers. The invasion of New
Jerusalem had been moved up two weeks. After Pak's corps
had established itself on New Jerusalem, the task force was
to leave, to rendezvous with Soong's provos as soon as
possible after Soong's attack on the Wyzhñyñy armada.
Apraxin-DaCosta would leave an "adequate" force to back
up the troops on the surface.

The corps' transports would land on the Sixday following the Maple Mountain maneuvers, bringing several savants.
His troops would begin loading out at once.

When the conference was over, Pak half-whistled a
gusty sigh. He'd still send Switzer to Terra the next day,
but the courts-martial would have to wait till his corps
was outbound. The trial and sentencing would be held
aboard his flagship, in hyperspace; then the prisoners
would be stored in stasis as long as necessary.

He'd rather sentence them to service in a punishment
unit, assigned to high hazard duty. Let them experience
the Wyzhñyñy firsthand. It didn't seem right for them to
sleep in stasis while the men they'd betrayed put their lives
on the line. He decided to ask Captain Coyote about the
possibility. If the provost marshal sounded encouraging, he'd
run it past Lefty Sarruf, by savant. But he wasn't optimistic.

Chapter 41

Harvesting Trouble

Captain (Lieutenant Commander) Christiaan Weygand's handling of the Survey ship *Vitus Bering* reflected several astrogational facts of life. Warpspace differs from hyperspace in many ways besides the number of dimensions. For Weygand's purposes, four of those differences were decisive. (1) Hyperspace drive is far "faster" than warpdrive (which in turn is far "faster" than gravdrive). (2) In hyperspace, astrogation is approximate, with vagaries whose effects accumulate over the duration of a jump, while in warpspace, astrogation is quite precise. (3) In warpspace, the F-space potentiality is far less distorted by nearby planetary masses. With sufficient skill and care, one can venture minutely near a planetary mass. In hyperspace, approaching as near as a million miles to a planet no larger than Pluto would destroy the ship. And (4), warpdrive is suitable for covert encroachment, particularly since warpspace does not produce emergence waves in the warp-space potentiality.

Thus Weygand had first brought the *Bering* out of

hyperspace two weeks short of the Tagus System, after a forty-seven-week jump. It was time to locate himself in F-space—familiar space, "real" space—and take a new set of astrogational readings. It was common to think of it in golfing terms, as sizing up the "lie" before hitting the approach shot—the final hyperspace jump to the Tagus System.

Then he'd generated hyperspace again, to reemerge in the system's remote fringe—far enough out that the *Bering*'s hyperspace emergence waves would be undetectable on Tagus.

Theoretically of course, the Wyzhñyñy could surround the system with alarm buoys or picket boats parked twelve or fifteen billion miles out, in the cometary cloud. But given the enormous spherical surface that went with such a radius, to provide and place the necessary number of sentries would be impractical at best.

Survey ships had some drawbacks for such missions, but one decisive advantage: their superb instrumentation. Even from where she'd emerged, 29 billion miles from the primary, the *Bering* could plot the orbits of the system's planets and major satellites. And do it in a few hours, applying the mechanics of planetary systems to the tiny orbital segments observed. The info was necessary for the warpspace "chip shot" Weygand made next.

That chip shot—that warpspace jump—took more than a day to bring the *Bering* near enough to Tagus's sole moon to detect it in the F-space potentiality. But once in F-space, and so near to Tagus, the ship's electromagnetic output could quickly be detected from the planet's surface, or by ships in the vicinity. And Drago Draveç's experience had been that the Wyzhñyñy left a space force at their colonies. Something one might assume without evidence.

Weygand had known all that since he'd been given his first mission briefing, a year earlier. It hadn't troubled him then, and it didn't now. He ordered key personnel wakened from stasis, and still in warpspace, maneuvered into the lee of the moon before emerging. Hidden from the planet, less than a mile from the lunar surface. Which just now was the bright side, for on Tagus, the moon was near the "new" phase.

After a brief sensor scan, he landed.

Now come the real challenges, he told himself. Find the Wyzhñyñy colony at the old pirate base. Put down a team to collect hornets and bring them back to the *Bering,* which was to remain behind the moon. Then send marines down to take some Wyzhñyñy prisoners and bring them up. After that, he'd generate warpspace, the science team could start their examinations, and they'd all fly home.

Simple but not easy. The hornets alone sounded daunting; Weygand had had a lifelong aversion to stinging insects, and Morgan had said the Tagus hornets were as big as his thumb. But with decent luck they could capture their hornets and be gone without the Wyzhñyñy knowing they'd been there. Capturing Wyzhñyñy, on the other hand . . . that would bring them into physical contact with the enemy. He carried two squads of marine commandos in stasis, under a captain, with gunnery sergeants as squad leaders. Two squads! How many fighting personnel did the Wyzhñyñy have on Tagus? A division? Half a dozen divisions?

But War House wants those prisoners, he thought. *And what do I know? I'm a Survey skipper, not a general.*

A lot depended on how slack the Wyzhñyñy had become here, after a Standard year without anything resembling a threat. Because if any of them—the *Bering,* the scout, the collection boat—caught the Wyzhñyñy's attention, the prospect of getting away with prisoners would be nil.

"Captain, sir," said a man behind him, "the personnel you requested are being revived."

Weygand swiveled his command chair halfway around. "Thank you, Chief. And the steward?"

"The steward is preparing their meal."

"Good. Tell Captain Stoorvol I want to talk with him as soon as he's finished eating."

There was no rush, but the sooner done, the sooner gone.

They'd drilled the procedure back in the Sol System. The *Bering* had emerged off Luna's far side (and been snooped by a police craft from nearby Yerikalin Dome). The Tagus rainforest had been represented by the Marañon Ecological Benchmark Preserve, in Terra's Peruvian

Autonomy. And to make the drill complete, the hornet team had returned (illegally) with a bunch of outraged Terran hornets. None had been the size of a man's thumb, but they were big-time mean.

There too it had been Captain Paul Stoorvol who'd piloted the short-range scout, SRS 12/1. And beside him, as here, had been Alfhild Olavsdóttir, blond and perhaps forty years old, stocky and fit-looking. Now as then, Stoorvol guided the scout smoothly across the lunar gravitic field, veering around occasional topographic obstacles, then slowing as he approached the limb of the moon. He stopped when he'd cleared it, parking a bare hundred feet off the surface.

From there they got their first look at Tagus, a little less than 170,000 miles away. Alfhild Olavsdóttir inhaled sharply. "Holy Gaea!" she said. "It's gorgeous!"

Her oath annoyed Stoorvol; he disliked Gaeans. But the annoyance was remote; his feelings were often somewhat remote. Besides, lots of non-Gaeans used that oath, and somehow Alfhild Olavsdóttir didn't strike him as a Gaean. A deist maybe. Deism was supposed to be big among scientists.

At any rate she was right: Tagus *was* beautiful. Colonized worlds invariably were; it went with being Terra-like. At the moment, what dominated his view of Tagus was the world ocean—a vivid blue with white cyclonic swirls. The equatorial zone showed a modest continent whose predominant blue-green suggested heavy forest.

After perhaps ten seconds of planet gazing, Stoorvol called up his instrument display, checking for technical electronic activity. He found plenty, from a single south-coast locale. Two other sources appeared that the scout's shipsmind identified as surveillance buoys parked above the equator at an altitude of 4,600 miles. He marked their locations with icons, but just now his primary interest was the surface location. Centering it on his screen, he magnified the site. It was nearly rectangular, a six by eight-mile area cleared of forest—distinct enough to be measured by his scanner from 170,000 miles out. He marked it with another icon.

"That's probably the colony," he said. "Or one of them.

We'll have to check the other hemisphere, but except for size, this one fits Morgan's site description. It's equatorial and on a south-coast headland—an open block with forest on two sides, the ocean on a third, and an inlet on the fourth."

Olavsdóttir nodded. "It's hard to imagine a natural opening looking like that."

Stoorvol held the scout where it was, and they kept alternate, one-hour watches. Whoever wasn't on watch used the main cabin to nap, snack, exercise, or otherwise break the monotony. The scout's shipsmind didn't experience time in the same way humans do, and it also had external tasks. It assigned an arbitrary meridian to Tagus, bisecting the visible Wyzhñyñy settlement. With that and the equator as references, it mapped the gravitic matrix and what could be seen of the surface—topographic and water features, broad vegetation types—along with much that didn't show on the surface, including gravitic and magnetic gradients and anomalies.

And recorded the frequency bands of Wyzhñyñy radio traffic.

The humans, on the other hand, had no duties except to watch the sensor display and the planet itself. It was an invitation to drowse, so an alarm had been provided. The watch wore a communications earpiece, and when anything broke the slow and regular unfolding of the sensor pickups, an alarm ruptured any doze or inattention.

To ease the monotony, Alfhild Olavsdóttir recited, in a quiet voice, extensively from the Icelandic *sögúr*—the sagas. More than any other Europeans, even the Finns, the Icelanders had retained their old language as the primary domestic, social, and cultural idiom. Terran was their language of science, business, and the world at large. As for daydreaming—Olavsdóttir could be an enthusiastic, even a formidable lover, but she seldom fantasized sex. Except occasionally to compose erotic poetry about some lover in her past. But she did not do that here.

On his watches, Stoorvol's thoughts included women, Alfhild Olavsdóttir for one. She was a lot older than he—ten or so years—but interesting. According to the skipper, she was a Ph.D. planetologist with a bachelor's in invertebrate zoology. The academic degrees had made her eligible for this mission, but no more eligible than many others. What had made the difference, Weygand said, was her temperament, and her record as a field leader. "Those, and being smart as they get."

Smart, Stoorvol thought, *meant different things to different people*. But she'd made a good impression on him when they'd boarded the scout and she'd seen him stash his rucker in a locker. "Why the rucksack?" she'd asked. He'd always resented gratuitous requests to explain himself, certainly from people he didn't know well. So he'd simply said it held things he might need, and with a nod she'd let it go at that.

Besides thinking about women, he revisited old conflicts—fierce rivalries as a kid growing up; fistfights at boot camp and on pass; and later, one at the Academy, where fights were seriously frowned on. He'd almost always won, but the last had nearly gotten him expelled. He'd been young then, he told himself. He looked at things differently from the vantage of twenty-eight years.

And he thought about the collection missions—the collection of hornets and the collection of prisoners. (He was to protect the first mission and lead the second.) If everything went according to drill . . . Things seldom did, of course. It wasn't wise to rely on scripts. They were fine as a starting place, and even as a guide, but they weren't likely to survive a complete mission. Major Asahara had stressed that in Military Planning 202. Because others, notably the enemy, had their own scripts, and typically the physical universe added serious unforeseens. Things happened, and necessity often demanded snap decisions, with different people commonly responding differently. And in case his cadets didn't believe him, Asahara, as game master in their electronic war game labs, would throw in unforeseeables that required unexpected and often drastic improvisations: new tactics, new strategies, even new objectives.

Stoorvol could still quote the major, or nearly enough to make no difference: "Say you have a battle plan that will win this major battle for you. And a seriously chancy departure from it that, if successful, could win the war; but, if unsuccessful, would be a disaster. Discuss the factors in choosing, and create examples."

For days the class had gone round and round on that. It had been the most valuable discussion they'd had. And among the factors had been alien mentalities. Because if they ever fought a war—a real war, a serious war—it would be against alien invaders. None of them doubted it. It was the truism behind every plan War House made, everything it did. It had been for centuries.

In Stoorvol's ruminations, any verbalization was silent and in Terran. As with most Terrans, Terran was his only language. Olavsdóttir had commented that his surname looked Norwegian with an Americanized spelling, probably from the late 19th or early 20th century. That had been news to him. The Americas had been Terra's great ethnic melting pot; the rest of the world was only now catching up. He'd never wondered about his ancestry, which besides various European roots, included Dakotah, Ibo, Samoan and Kachin.

Hour by hour, the Wyzhñyñy settlement site crept across the face of Tagus, toward the terminator near the east limb of the visible hemisphere. Before the continent disappeared, a larger edged into sight. On the same watch, a settlement appeared on the new continent, and later a third, both marked by electronic activity. One was at a northern latitude, in what appeared to be a steppe. The other was in a large basin between two high, subtropical mountain ranges. Neither was at all like the tropical rainforest Morgan had described.

"So," Stoorvol said, "now the question is whether there's a fourth one down there somewhere."

Some hours later they were satisfied there wasn't. The first one was the right one. Meanwhile they'd learned the number of surveillance buoys parked off the planet— four of them, located to provide coverage of the colonized continents.

Their next task was to scout Tagus's surface. Stoorvol was about to generate warpdrive when they learned there were indeed Wyzhñyñy warships in the system. Their sensors picked up one of them a scant few hundred miles from where they watched in SRS 12/1. It was departing Tagus's single moon, and crossing to the planet in gravdrive. Why the Wyzhñyñy had been on the moon, or very near it, and whether others still lurked there, neither Terran knew.

So instead of generating warpspace and crossing invisibly to Tagus, Stoorvol backed away in gravdrive, then returned to the *Bering* with a short warp jump, to let the captain know about the Wyzhñyñy ship.

Captain Weygand promptly sent another two-man team out in SRS 12/2, to watch from the limb.

After listening to Stoorvol and Olavsdóttir, he decided to skip the surface scouting. With four Wyzhñyñy surveillance buoys, and possibly a space force on the moon's nearside, they might very well get only one chance before having to flee the system. So the first crossing would be for hornet collection—much the most feasible and least dangerous of their two missions.

The logic was inescapable, but it left Stoorvol ill at ease. In his heart of hearts, the most dangerous foray held priority, and at any rate, live Wyzhñyñy prisoners seemed more valuable than hornets to the war effort.

Some hours later, the hornet collection team boarded the 46-foot collection boat, the *Mei-Li*, sometimes termed "the nursing whale" because she was carried outboard. The hornet collection team consisted of Alfhild Olavsdóttir and two entomology techs, plus both squads of marine commandos for ground security. Paul Stoorvol would pilot the crossing, with PO1 Achmed Menges as copilot. Two weapons techs rode in the *Mei-Li*'s gun bubbles.

Slipping the magnetic tie that held the *Mei-Li* to the gangway lock, Stoorvol separated from the *Bering*. At 200 feet from the surface, he activated the strange-space generator for warpdrive. Then departed the vicinity of the *Bering* much faster than he would have in gravdrive, though not remotely approaching full warpspeed. Not this close to planetary bodies. Invisible from F-space, they quickly cleared the limb, and saw Tagus again on their screens. Not as a blue and white sphere against deep, star-strewn black, but a computer artifact—a featureless silver globe against utterly starless indigo blue. Shipsmind could mock up something very similar to the planet's F-space appearance, even dubbing in star images. But the Admiralty specified silver on indigo for simulations in warpspace, to remind the watch it wasn't real.

At the Marine Academy, Captain Esteron had shown them a screen full of mathematics, telling them it best represented the warpspace view of a planet. He hadn't expected them to sort it out. He'd simply been making a point. He went on to discuss warpspace in non-mathematical terms. In a sense, you couldn't be *in* warpspace; warpspace has no material content. A ship "in warpspace" actually occupied an anomaly. Before generating warpspace, you're in F-space—familiar space—which is "permeated by the warpspace potentiality." The strange-space generator generates what can be thought of as a "bubble" of warpspace, which is free to move within the warpspace potentiality at "speeds" greater than light in F-space. And that "carrier bubble" of warpspace contains an inclusion—a bubble of F-space intimately surrounding the scout and its contents. A ship within a bubble within a bubble.

According to Captain Esteron, it could be *understood* only through the appropriate mathematics, and even that depended on what's meant by "understood." The bottom line was, you can leave Terra in warpdrive and arrive at Alpha Centauri in far less time than a photon could. And without inertia. In warpspace you're not only exempt from the light-speed limitation, your ship is stationary within its own little universe—its "carrier bubble."

Stoorvol had decided then not to worry about it. Accept it, yes. Get used to it, sure. Learn to control it, damn right! He'd quickly done all three, and become a competent warpspace pilot—not very difficult in routine circumstances.

Especially with the safekeeps built into shipsminds, to constrain warpspeeds in the vicinity of planetary bodies. For there, the "interfacing" of F-space and warpspace is more or less distorted, and pseudo-speeds must be moderate. Otherwise distortion could rupture your carrier bubble. Which could leave you abruptly in F-space, with momentum a function of your warpdrive pseudo-speed. If that happens at a pseudo-speed greater than c, ship and contents are converted instantly into energy. The resulting explosion is terrific.

Even at only a few-score miles per minute, a ruptured carrier bubble would convert a crew into strawberry jam.

Thus the crossing to Tagus took twenty-eight careful minutes. But they were also twenty-eight invisible minutes. The odds of a Wyzhñyñy ship passing in warpspace near enough to detect your carrier bubble by chance were extremely low. While the prospect of being detected in warpspace by a ship in F-space was essentially nil.

The danger lay not in the crossing to Tagus. It lay in the fine maneuvering very close in. There, complex interface distortions made travel vectors tricky, and carelessness or clumsiness could easily be fatal.

So while the crossing took twenty-eight minutes, finding a suitable place to emerge required two hours of slow and careful sensor groping. Finally Stoorvol found what he wanted—a gorge. He recognized it by the nature of the grav-line distortions in the F-space potentiality, blurred though they were, and it was on the right part of the right continent. He groped his way almost to the bottom.

Emergence would cause a momentary surge of 80-kilocycle radio waves, a distinctive artifact that would hardly be misinterpreted. It was the primary reason he'd wanted to emerge deep in a gorge. A surge there would hardly be picked up by a ground installation, nor by any of the surveillance buoys, given their positions in space.

Once back in F-space, he keyed the gravitic matrix, and shipsmind gave him coordinates—0.65 degrees east of the Wyzhñyñy settlement. The gorge was visible on the map the scout had generated during its surveillance from the lunar limb. It was one of the larger gorges leading down from a broad basaltic plateau to the ocean, and the *Mei-Li* had emerged only thirty feet from the bottom.

He turned the helm over to PO-1 Menges, who raised the craft almost to the rim. Then two of the *Mei-Li*'s work scooters transferred the marines, plus Olavsdóttir and the two entomology techs, to the plateau top. Stoorvol flew one of the scooters.

He left most of the marines on the rim with Gunnery

Sergeant Gabaldon, to set up an inconspicuous defense
point. Then, with Olavsdóttir, two marines and a pair of
hornet traps, Stoorvol left on one scooter. Three other
marines and both entomology techs followed on the other,
with four more traps. The scouts' gravdrives were designed
to have a minimal EM signature, though even that might
be picked up if they rose much above the rainforest canopy.

"Just tell me where to go," Stoorvol said. Olavsdóttir
scanned across the forest roof. "Take me higher," she said.
"I can't see enough from here."

He glanced at the coordinate grid on his display, then
raised the scooter straight up, while the planetologist looked
around. At two hundred feet above the forest she spoke
again, pointing. "There," she said. "There's a pretty good
opening over there about half a mile."

He saw where she meant: a two-acre gap in the forest
canopy, probably a blowdown patch. "Right," he said, and
took the scooter down almost to the treetops before heading there, dodging the occasional emergent that loomed
above its leafy neighbors.

The gap proved unsuitable, filled with a dense growth
of young forest half as tall as the surrounding older stand.
They traveled several miles and checked four more gaps
before they crossed a long low ridge and saw what they
needed. A mile ahead, on the far side of a smaller gorge,
a sizeable area of forest had burned. As they drew near,
Olavsdóttir said, "That's it. Set her down there."

They landed near the center, away from the gorge.
Clearly the fire had been intense. It seemed to Stoorvol
he knew the place from Morgan's reports. This lesser gorge
was the approach to the old pirate base. And the fire? The
Wyzhñyñy had razed the forest there after they'd traced
Morgan to his bolt hole.

Olavsdóttir wasn't speculating on the burn's origin. She
was soaking in its ecology. The forest regrowth was still
patchy; much of the ground was covered with herbage and
low shrubs. Flowers were rampant, and "berries" abundant.
Insects in quantity visited both, probing blossoms or tapping
fruit juices with their proboscises. There would be hornets,
she was sure. And if they were nearly as large as Morgan had
described, they'd be predators, preying on other "insects."

She turned to the field entomologists. "This is it, people," she said. "Let's do it." From her small day pack she took something that, unfolded, proved to be a hat with a net rolled on its brim. Putting it on, she secured the net around her collar, then donned tough gloves. The techs did the same.

Then she turned to the scooters where the marines stood watching with their captain. "Stay here," she told Stoorvol, "and leave your repellent fields off. They disorient insect behavior over an area a lot larger than the repellent radius."

Stoorvol watched the hooded collectors walk off in different directions across the burn, heads swiveling slowly as they searched. Sergeant Haynes grunted. "She didn't need to tell us that. We know the drill."

"She's not used to the Corps," Stoorvol said, "and civilians generally need reminding. Otherwise no telling what they'd do."

He'd hardly said it when his radio beeped. He took it from his belt. Its transmitter was directional, so he pointed it east. "Stoorvol," he answered. "This had better be good. If I can read your signal, they can pick it up at the Wyzhñyñy base."

"Captain, a bogie just passed over!" The voice was Menges'. "Crossed the gorge about two hundred yards north, headed west! If anyone on board was looking our way, he'd have seen us. Or if they had their sensors on . . . They shouldn't pick up our radio traffic though. Way different wavelengths."

Unless they're scanning. "What kind of bogey?"

"A smallish craft of some sort, sir."

A smallish craft. That could be different things, some armed, some not. "Thanks, Boats. Gabaldon, are you on?"

Sergeant Gabaldon answered from the rim. "Right, Captain."

"Okay. Listen up both of you. They *probably* didn't see you. Otherwise they wouldn't have gone right on like they did." *I hope,* he added silently. "Gabaldon, get your people back aboard the *Mei-Li*, now! Boats, as soon as they're on board, fly south down the gorge, a mile at least, and even with the rim. Find a place where you can fit that frigging barge back into the forest, between the trees. Far enough back that you can't be seen from the gorge. Or from the air." *And let's hope the Wyzhñyñy don't scan the forest with grav sensors.* "Another thing: when you're in your hiding place, register your coordinates to four decimals. But don't send them till I ask. Keep radio silence. Got that?"

"Yessir," Menges said. "Radio silence. Are you coming back now, sir?"

"Hell no! We've got hornets to catch! Now remember: don't send again till I tell you. Stoorvol out."

He looked toward Olavsdóttir moving slowly across the burn, and clicked his helmet mike. "Doctor, a bogey may have spotted the *Mei-Li.* I'm moving both scooters under the trees. Continue as you are. If I trigger my alarm, crouch down and make yourselves as small as possible. And *don't*—repeat *don't*—flatten yourself on the ground."

"Thank you, Captain," she answered.

Thank you, Captain? For what? Doing my job? Stoorvol powered up his gravdrive. *Don't knock courtesy,* he chided himself. Sergeant Haynes started his scooter, too, and they headed for the burn's nearest edge. There, back beneath the trees, they set down about a hundred feet apart. From the burn came a pleased shout: an entomologist had found a hornet's nest. Stoorvol hoped to hell they'd get what they needed quickly. He wanted to get back to the *Mei-Li* and off the planet as soon as possible. The collection order called for six nests—for statistical reasons, he supposed. It could keep them out there till dark, which meant till morning. A disturbing possibility.

Achmed Menges found a suitable location, unloaded his marines again, and had two of them guide him between the trees until he saw a glade ahead. He stopped sixty or eighty feet short of it, with a clear shot to scram if he needed to. By that time the gorge was a hundred yards behind him, and marine lookouts at the rim could no longer see the boat. Menges shut down all systems except shipsmind, to reduce detection risks, then waited while the *Mei-Li* grew slowly hot and stuffy.

❖   ❖   ❖

On being relieved, Tech 1 Gortha turned his log over to the new watch officer. The Wyzhñyñy ensign glanced at it. "What is this?" he asked.

Gortha didn't need to look. He'd logged just one item that wasn't routine. "It's a call from the courier bringing Colonel Dorthût from Grasslands, sir. While crossing High Falls Gorge, the pilot spotted a wrecked alien craft in the bottom."

The ensign's hackles rose. "Wrecked alien craft? How did he know?"

"I suppose, sir, because none of ours is reported missing. And because there are no aliens left on the planet."

"You *suppose*?" The ensign's jaw muscles bulged like melon rinds along his cranial keel. The observation had been radioed in nearly five hours earlier. Such a lapse was intolerable. Reaching to the work station keyboard, he tapped three keys.

A voice issued from the desk speaker. "Dispatcher's station, Tech 1 Rrûnch."

"Rrûnch, this is the officer of the watch. The dispatcher you relieved—is he still there?"

"No, sir. He just left, sir."

"Get him! Now!"

"Yessir!"

The ensign heard the quick soft thudding of feet, and waited scowling, fists clenching and unclenching. There were more footfalls, then a voice. "Tech 3 Agthok, sir. How can I help you?"

"Who piloted the courier from Grasslands?"

"Tech 2 Kroliss, sir."

"How can he be found? Promptly?"

"Sir, I saw him enter the messroom about . . . forty minutes ago."

"Thank you." The ensign bit the words out and disconnected, then with an angry finger stabbed more keys. "This is the officer of the watch. I must speak to Tech 2 Kroliss at once."

"He just left, sir, carrying a mug of something."

"Go and get him! Tell him the watch officer wants him at the watch office NOW! And call me when you've done it!"

"Yessir!"

An unpleasant rumble issued from the watch officer's throat as he disconnected. *A mug of something!* he thought. *As if I had any interest in that!*

Tech 1 Gortha was glad Ensign Rrishnex wasn't on *his* watch. But he didn't ask permission to leave. He'd slip away after Kroliss arrived. He wondered why the ensign didn't just order someone else out to investigate. Probably, he decided, because Kroliss could find the place more surely.

Gosthodar Qishkûr, Governor of the Okaldei, lay on his AG couch with his torso upright. His eyes were obscured by their nictitating membranes, and his upper torso rocked back and forth like a dodderer's. *Not a reassuring sight,* thought General Gransatt.

"If it was mine to decide?" Gransatt asked. He was tempted to answer falsely, for it seemed to him the gosthodar would order the opposite of whatever he recommended. But he would not lie; not so blatantly.

"Lordship," he said, "I would order all scouts and all fighter craft to muster here. Then search the plateau between the Broken Hills and Long Inlet on the west, and the Green River on the east. Search it so that nothing living avoids detection. All attack squadrons to be on two-hour stepped alert, ready to destroy any aliens sighted. Until we find the alien and wipe him out, or are very very sure he does not exist."

The gosthodar's rocking increased, the sight transfixing his general. After a long moment the gosthodar spoke, his voice reflecting his age. "I thought we did all that a cycle ago," he said. "Was that not you in charge?"

Gransatt's hide heated; it required effort to avoid bristling. "That was not comparable. Then we needed to search the entire planet. A single region can be searched far more thoroughly."

The gosthodar ignored the general's omission of the honorific. "Mmmm. But that first scouring—did it not begin with an intensive search first of this very region, then that of Grasslands and Basin? And despite all that, was an alien not found reconnoitering this very settlement some weeks later?" Qishkûr had stopped rocking, and his eyes had cleared. "You

say you would make very very sure he is wiped out. That
he ceases to exist. But what does such certainty mean? You
were very sure before, and I accepted that. Until suddenly,
there came the alien who had hidden under the hill. Then
he died, and you were very *very* sure. But I was no longer
so sure anymore. Eh?"

The general's hide felt hot as fire. He did not reply.

"And now this. How can you have so much certainty
about what you will accomplish this time, and so little in
what you accomplished before?" Briefly his head swayed
from side to side in rejection. "I, on the other hand, believe
you did *well* before, you and your fliers. Not perfectly it
seems, but well. This was an alien outpost world, nothing
more. There were no towers. No ghats. Not even towns.
There were never more than a few sophonts here, and your
fighters killed most of them. The few survivors, those who
did not succeed in fleeing the planet, scattered to different regions, where they have hidden. In caverns no doubt.
It seems they have an affinity for caverns.

"But they cannot hide forever. They must surface, walk
beneath the sky, bath in the streams"—his words slowed
for emphasis—"and grow food. And when they do, our
surveillance buoys will find them. The aliens know this.
They are not ignorant primitives. This appearance today—
if it is real; if the report is not an aberration—this appearance is an act of desperation, perhaps to collect supplies
from some old cache."

The gosthodar repeated himself, as if savoring the apt-
ness of the phrase. "An act of desperation." He paused
thoughtfully. "There may be caverns behind the cliffs of
the High Falls Gorge, as there were behind the lesser. You
must seek them, and destroy any you find."

He straightened, his old voice sounding fuller, less aged.
"You will *not* gather the squadrons from Grasslands and
Basin. You will do your searching with what you have here.
If your fears reflect fact, and the aliens retain some little
potency, to gather the other squadrons here would expose
Grasslands and Basin to destructive raids."

The old head swayed again, side to side, side to side, and
for a moment the eyes closed entirely. "Go," the old voice
said, suddenly raspy again, "and heed what I have said."

The general backed away, arms spread, forelegs bent, belly low, trunk and head lowered in deference. "As you direct, your lordship, that shall I do. And as you enjoin, your lordship, that shall I not do."

The gosthodar was rocking again.

Tech 2 Kroliss had marked his approximate crossing point on Lieutenant Zalkôsh's map. Zalkôsh, piloting the armed scout, reached High Falls Gorge about two linear miles north of the marked point, at 5,000 feet local reference. He saw no alien craft below, nor did Kroliss, who sat beside him.

If there was an alien craft down there, they would probably have seen it. Nonetheless, Zalkôsh began descending on a gravitic vector. The gorge meandered sufficiently that one just might be concealed down there by a rock wall. And at any rate, he wanted to examine the bottom.

Tech 2 Kroliss could imagine serious personal problems if they found no alien craft. It would strongly suggest there'd been one, and that it had escaped. The obvious alternative conclusion would be that he'd hallucinated. So far, the lieutenant hadn't seemed to judge.

Zalkôsh paused some twenty feet from the bottom, then started southward along the curving gorge. Both he and Kroliss watched intently for any sign that an alien craft had been there. It was the dry season, and the stream level was low, exposing the larger rocks that had fallen from the walls. If an enemy ship had made a forced landing, it should either still be there, or have left signs of having been there.

It occurred to Kroliss that the alien ship might have been hovering just above the bottom when he'd seen it, and left no trace. Left because he, Kroliss, had flown over. That's what a Board of Investigation would think, and a court-martial.

Zalkôsh proceeded for more than a linear mile past the point where Kroliss reported crossing. Then he switched on his transmitter, accessing Security directly.

"Security, this is Lieutenant Zalkôsh, reporting on the alien sighting. I have examined more than three linear miles of gorge bottom, centered on Tech 2 Kroliss's reported crossing point, and have seen no sign of an alien craft. I suggest other scouts be sent to search this entire quadrangle, and that the surveillance buoys be instructed to intensify surveillance of this region. Unless otherwise instructed, I will continue south down the gorge to the ocean, or until I find an alien craft.

"Zalkôsh out."

Kroliss imagined himself assigned to the death platoon, making amends to the tribe.

Hours had passed when one of the marine lookouts trotted up to the *Mei-Li,* to report that a small alien craft had snooped the gorge from the north, just above the bottom, and passed out of sight southward. *A scout,* Menges thought. He felt extremely nervous. Other Wyzhñyñy might be flying a search pattern above the plateau, sensors scanning.

He'd heard that the Wyzhñyñy didn't take prisoners, and wondered what might happen to him if they did. He decided he'd prefer a pounding from energy bolts. A quick death. Meanwhile he wondered how the hornet hunters were doing. He wasn't about to break radio silence to ask.

While the entomologists and Olavsdóttir hunted for hornets' nests, and Captain Stoorvol's men napped, Stoorvol had scanned the known Wyzhñyñy radio frequencies. Hearing a lot of traffic but learning nothing, except what Wyzhñyñy sounded like on the radio. Finally, after five hours, Olavsdóttir collected her sixth colony of hornets. Stoorvol had seen no bogies, and had no idea what the situation was at the big gorge. When everyone and everything was loaded and secured, he took off, the second scooter close behind. He'd wait till he was nearer before radioing Menges and getting the new coordinates. Assuming the *Mei-Li* was still intact, and Menges alive and free.

Before the additional Wyzhñyñy scouts lifted from Seaside Base, their pilots were briefed. Among other things, they were given Tech 2 Kroliss's description of the alien craft: green, and about the size of a corvette. Actually, at eighty-three feet in length, a Wyzhñyñy corvette was seriously longer than the forty-six-foot *Mei-Li,* and proportionately broader. A corvette could hardly be maneuvered into the rainforest.

Stoorvol's two scooters had barely cleared the trees behind them when one of the marines shouted, "Bogies aft!" Both Stoorvol and Haynes accelerated, snapping heads back, then darted down into the pirate gorge, to career south together below the rim. They were quickly past the burn, then slowing sharply, lifted again to rim level, curved into the rainforest and proceeded eastward among the great trunks and dangling lianas. The whole sequence took perhaps fifteen seconds.

"Captain," said Olavsdóttir, "that was exciting!"

"I'm glad you liked it," he answered drily. "Now let's hope they don't find us with their sensors." He switched on his transmitter. "Menges," he said, "this is Stoorvol. What are your coordinates?"

He got no answer. *The forest damps transmission at both ends,* he told himself. Ten minutes later, in a glade, he lifted above the trees and tried again, using more power. The reply was brief and faint, but readable. He fed Menges' coordinates into his scooter's navcomp, acknowledged Menges' reply, then ducked into the trunk space again and continued eastward.

"I didn't see the bogies," Olavsdóttir told him.

"Right. They probably continued east when they lost us. But they'd sure as hell have reported us, which must have stirred things up considerably." *And they haven't found the Mei-Li yet. That's the hopeful part.*

He pushed as fast as he dared. The sun had been low when they'd left the burn, and once it set, this near the equator, it would get dark quickly. He didn't lift above the trees for a peek around. Didn't see the Wyzhñyñy scouts' ground support fighters and APCs posted above the big gorge, waiting for word from the surveillance buoys. He didn't need to. He assumed they'd be there, they and more.

"How's our cargo doing?" he asked.

"All right so far," Olavsdóttir answered. "But after a few more hours in those traps, they'll start dying."

Shit! "How much good will they be to us dead?"

"The composition of body fluids will begin to break down, probably including the venom. How much useful information we'd get then is impossible to tell. Some, possibly."

Stoorvol grunted. *So we'll push,* he thought. He stopped to rearrange personnel and transfer cargo, all the civilians and the hornets going to Haynes' sled. Stoorvol would haul the other four marines, in case a rearguard action was needed, or a fighting decoy, or someone to run interference. "If we run into trouble," he told Haynes, "don't hesitate to ditch the scooter and proceed on foot. Meanwhile load your belt nav from the navcomp right now, and be sure you take it if you ditch. And for godsake don't abandon the hornets!"

The two scooters went on again, side by side now. If they were detected beneath the trees, hopefully they'd read as a single unit. In the trunk space—the forest gallery— the light grew dimmer, more dusky. They were half a mile from the *Mei-Li* when bolts from a trasher ripped into and through the forest canopy, exploding overhead and on the ground. Broken branches and wood thudded and pattered behind him. Stoorvol shouted as if he had no helmet transmitter. "Set her down and run!" Then he darted upward through a gap in the foliage, evading branches as if by magic. In the air above, his marines poured blaster fire at the nearest Wyzhñyñy gunboat, targeting its sensor arrays. Then he dove through another gap, and zigzagged erratically away from the hornet scooter. An APC was firing into the jungle as if tracking him.

He landed skidding, 300 yards short of the *Mei-Li's* coordinates. "Off," he barked, then triggered the scooter's delayed destruction charge and sprinted sixty yards before it blew. For a few seconds he lay panting, then got to his feet. His commandos were unhurt. After orienting himself in the deep dusk, Stoorvol sent the others on to find the *Mei-Li.* Alone he paused, squatting by a fallen forest giant overgrown with lichens, moss, and toadstools. The firing had stopped when the scooter had blown. Now it began again, and he sprinted around the root disk to crouch behind the great log. More debris rained down.

Clicking his transmitter, he spoke. "Gunny, do you read me?"

"Loud and clear, sir."

"Boats, do you read me?"

"Loud and clear, sir."

"Good. Gunny, if you've got any men on board, get them off now, ready to fight.

"Boats, Haynes and the civilians should reach you with the hornets soon. On foot. As soon as they're secured, get the *Mei-Li* out of there, without lights if possible. Gunny's people will help you. Did you both hear that?"

"Loud and clear, sir."

"Loud and clear, sir."

"Good. And Boats, those hornets need to reach the *Bering* as fast as safely possible; otherwise they may die, and dead they won't be much good. Then we'll have come all this way for nothing. Do *not* wait for me; I'll be keeping the Wyzhñyñy distracted."

It seemed to him he'd already done a pretty good job of that. Otherwise they'd probably have found the *Mei-Li* and pounded hell out of her.

Meanwhile the trasher fire had stopped again. He suspected what that might mean, and getting to his knees peered over the log toward where the scooter had been. A minute later he saw Wyzhñyñy troopers lowering through the canopy in slings.

Crouching, he padded off into the gathering darkness.

With the help of his helmet's active night vision, Stoorvol found his way readily. Even with his belt nav, and knowing his own and the *Mei-Li*'s coordinates to four decimals, it would be easy to miss the boat in the jungle. Abruptly, gunfire sounded from multiple locations overhead: the rapid thumping of trashers, and the sizzling cracks of trasher bolts burning vacuum trails through the air. But without the tearing crashes of detonations in the forest roof, or the dull earthy whumps as they exploded against the ground. This continued for perhaps five long seconds, then cut off. The sound and its cessation told him what the target had been: the Wyzhñyñy had been firing at the *Mei-Li* as she accelerated outward. But there'd been no explosion as of the collection boat blowing up or crashing. Menges had gotten away into warpspace.

Which meant that Haynes and his civilians had run all the way, carrying their hornet traps . . . Either that or Menges hadn't waited. His fists curled at the thought.

At any rate the situation had changed. He was here until he either died or was picked up by the *Mei-Li*, when and if she returned for Wyzhñyñy prisoners. Stoorvol had ridden from Terra in stasis, and barely knew Weygand. Some commanders might justify leaving the system with what they had—the hornets. But there were others who'd try for the jackpot, especially since it seemed not to endanger the *Bering* herself. Weygand, it seemed to him, might be one of them.

As for himself, Stoorvol intended to get at least one Wyzhñyñy prisoner. Stash him somewhere, properly stunned, safe from rescue or escape. When they'd left Gabrovo Base in the Balkan Autonomy, every one of his commando carried a stunner, a gag, and a fifteen-foot roll of tape in his rucker.

As if on cue, he heard faint voices in the direction he'd come from, and maxxed his sound sensor. Alien speech, and not via radio. It sent a chill through him. How many times, as a boy, he'd daydreamed that!

In a perverse way it also irritated him. Their stealth discipline was lousy! They probably thought their quarry was out of reach in warpspace. They were also moving his way. Spotting a strategically situated liana, he tested it, then climbed thirty feet or so to the crotch of a tree.

Now the Wyzhñyñy angled off toward the gorge, perhaps to be picked up and returned to their base. Out of his reach. That would never do. Climbing back down, he trotted after them, blaster ready. Shortly he spotted a Wyzhñyñy soldier and shot him in the back, then dropped into a hole left by the uprooting of a mouldering, wind-thrown tree. Blaster pulses hissed, fired blindly into the darkness.

He stayed where he was for several long minutes, blaster ready. Probably they'd sent a squad back to look for him, and they'd missed his hole. Cautiously he raised his head, then screened by the log, crept toward another large tree a few yards away. A liana had rooted to its trunk, and he climbed it, to fit himself into a crotch forty feet up. It wasn't comfortable, but it mostly hid him. Minutes later a squad of Wyzhñyñy appeared—the searchers returning from hunting him. He shrunk behind one half of the fork, hoping the concept of an enemy who could climb trees hadn't occurred to them. As they passed, he got the closest look he'd had at one. *Centaurs? Not hardly*, he told himself. Leave off the necklike torso with its arms, and it looked like an oversized mastiff.

But beyond a doubt, they could run a lot faster than he could.

The warp jump from the gorge back to the *Bering* had been quick. Menges had reemerged in F-space above the lunar farside not far from the survey ship, then closed in gravdrive. Olavsdóttir and her techs had promptly disembarked with their winged captives.

Briefly Sergeant Gabaldon told the skipper what he wanted to do. The skipper never blinked. "Go for it," he said. So Gabaldon claimed the pilot's seat, and with Menges as his copilot, moved away from the *Bering*, generated warpspace, and headed back for Tagus.

This time he didn't need to grope for the gorge. As sensed from the F-space potentiality, the gravitic coordinate system was blurred, but he had a "sort of" fix on Menges' old hiding place.

His plan, such as it was, was based on two operational premises: (1) The Wyzhñyñy were already alerted; and (2) the mission now demanded quickness, not stealth, aggression, not caution. But not stupidity, either.

The immediate challenge promised to be finding a place to pull into the forest. He couldn't expect to find Menges' old hiding place; his fix wasn't that good. But his warrior muse smiled on him: he emerged above the gorge at close to rim level, within recognition distance of the gap between trees that Menges had used before. Jockeying the *Mei-Li* fully into the forest, he set her down.

His marines were already gathered at the gangway; he keyed it open and they moved out, taking defensive positions nearby. The naval gunners sat tense and ready

at their heavy weapons. Gabaldon opened his transmitter
and spoke. "Stoorvol, this is Gabaldon. We're parked
where Menges hid earlier, but close to the rim. Do you
read me? Over."

The message took Paul Stoorvol by surprise. "Gunny,"
he murmured, "there should be a platoon or so of aliens
very near you. Maybe just north, if you're where you say.
They seem to be waiting for a ride home, or maybe for
orders. They've given up hunting for me. I'd about decided
I needed to do something more to keep them around. Right
now I'm in a tree, a couple of hundred feet from . . . from
the rim."

He'd stumbled orally because the Wyzhñyñy on the
ground had opened fire, at either the *Mei-Li* or the
marines. He doubted that anything the Wyzhñyñy had on
the ground was adequate to breach her hull metal, but if
they concentrated on her sensor array . . . Or if a gunboat
was still hanging around . . .

From his perch he could make out two Wyzhñyñy,
eerie gold by night vision. He unslung his blaster and shot
them both, not to draw attention—the firefight with the
marines held that—but to help the odds. Then he climbed
down the liana, unslung his blaster again, and clicked his
helmet transmitter.

One of the *Mei-Li*'s guns began hammering heavy bolts
at the Wyzhñyñy, bolts crackling and thudding. Stoorvol
realized he could be killed by his own people.

"Gunny," he said, "I'm on the ground now. Their attention is on you. I've killed two more of them, and I'll take
out as many more as I can. We need to settle this now. Their
command is likely to pour support forces in quickly. Over."

"Received. Received. This is Miller in charge. Gunny's
out of touch; left the ship. Miller out."

Out of touch? "Got that. Stoorvol out." *Gunny knows
what he's doing,* Stoorvol told himself, and this was no time
for discussions. He found himself a new spot, a large tree
with a broadly buttressed base. He wished he had a bag
of grenades, instead of just the two on his harness. Taking
one off, he charged it, then peered around a buttress and
chose his next target—three Wyzhñyñy thirty yards away,

crouching together behind a fallen tree. He threw the grenade to land just behind the one in the middle, then ducked behind the buttress again, heard the explosion and peered out. All three seemed dead.

The firefight ahead of him went on as if he weren't there, so he darted forward in a low crouch to where his latest victims lay. There he raised up enough to peer over the log. Ahead as well as to the sides, he could see numerous Wyzhñyñy kneeling behind trees and the occasional fallen trunk. And he could see casualties. The marines weren't laying down much fire now though, as if there weren't many of them left. The thought flashed: *How many? Four? Five?* But the *Mei-Li's* starboard gunner, in his armored bubble, was still pumping out the heavy stuff.

With bursts of rotten wood, bolts blew through the log within ten feet of Stoorvol. To his right, a Wyzhñyñy he'd thought was dead, stood as if to flee, then stopped as if in freeze-frame, staring at the marine officer. Stoorvol shot him down, then turning, began to shoot at every Wyzhñyñy he could see.

It seemed the final straw. All along the Wyzhñyñy line, aliens rose to flee. Stoorvol crouched low again, and from his thigh pocket drew his stunner. To his left, a Wyzhñyñy cleared the log in a bound, so easily and gracefully it startled the marine. As it landed, Stoorvol thumbed the trigger. The Wyzhñyñy stumbled, pitched forward and lay still. Another followed, and it too fell.

The starboard gun hammered a dozen more trasher bolts after the fleeing Wyzhñyñy before it stopped. Then, heart in his mouth, Stoorvol stood and jumped onto the log, waving both arms overhead. The *Mei-Li's* gangway slid open, its ramp extruding. Three marines rode out on an AG freight sled, followed closely by two crewmen riding another.

"Over here!" Stoorvol shouted, again as if he didn't have a radio. "I've got two prisoners stunned." The marines veered to the north as if they hadn't heard. It was the crewmen who responded to Stoorvol, quickly setting down where he indicated. He helped them load an unconscious Wyzhñyñy on the sled. "Your gunner did good work with that heavy weapon," he said. "He broke them with it."

"Wasn't that," the older crewman grunted, lifting the second Wyzhñyñy's hindquarters.

"What, then?" It seemed to Stoorvol the man was going to give him the credit, for taking them from behind.

"Wyzhñyñy aircraft are on their way, sir. They'll be laying heavy fire in here." They finished getting the second Wyzhñyñy aboard, and as if that was a signal, an alarm horn blared from the *Mei-Li*.

"Come aboard, Captain," said the older. "That's Mr. Menges' twenty-tick warning."

Menges? Where was Gabaldon? And the marines with the other sled? He realized then; it was casualties, not prisoners they were collecting. Instead of getting on the sled, Stoorvol started toward the marines, but the senior crewman drew his stunner and thumbed the trigger. Quickly the two crewmen dumped the inert marine officer onto the sled with the prisoners, then sped to the gangway and inside the *Mei-Li*.

The marines, on the other hand, hadn't even looked toward the ship when the gangway slid shut. The senior crewman activated the sled's restraint field, felt it snug around him. "Jesus, Buddha, and Rama!" said the younger. "What's the matter with those marines? They should've come!"

Another alarm clamored through the boat, warning of imminent takeoff.

"They wouldn't leave their buds behind," the elder said.

"They were probably all dead!"

"Apparently it doesn't make any difference to them."

They felt the *Mei-Li* lift, pull backward from the forest edge, then swing about. At once it took flight, for five seconds of acceleration before warpspace generated. After a long moment's stillness, the senior crewman released the restraint field. Two others appeared, and helped transfer the inert prisoners onto AG litters, to be taken to a holding cell.

When the two Wyzhñyñy had been taken away, the younger crewman gestured toward the unconscious Stoorvol, still lying on the sled. "He was going to help them, wasn't he?"

"Yep. Who knows? Maybe those hyenas eat enemy casualties."

He said it absently. His mind was on the *Mei-Li*'s last
remaining scooter, with Gunnery Sergeant Gabaldon
piloting. It had left shortly after the *Mei-Li* landed. The
crewman had heard enough to know the strategy: the sergeant would drop into the depths of the gorge, speed north
a couple of miles, then climb a couple, to watch for
Wyzhñyñy aerial reinforcements. Finally he'd seen some
coming: gunboats and APCs. A lot of them.

Chapter 42

Moribund

"They are both moribund."

The *Bering* had left Tagus's moon less than two hours earlier, and Christiaan Weygand felt comfortable now about questioning the expedition's scientists working on the alien captives. The two Wyzhñyñy lay strapped on examination tables, wires and tubes leading from them to a life support system and a bank of readouts. If everything above the withers had been covered, and you overlooked the feet, they might have passed for some Terran mammal in a large-animal clinic.

"What actually does 'moribund' mean?" Weygand asked.

Dr. Maria Kalosgouros was a formidable, humorless woman, a vertebrate exobiologist of major professional status. "Captain Stoorvol's stunner had been set to render a two-hundred-fifty-pound human unconscious for a period of one to three hours," she answered wryly. "Unfortunately its effect on Wyzhñyñy of similar mass is far more profound. They are dying, and there is nothing I can do to prevent it. I doubt their own physicians could, working with their own life support system."

337

Weygand regarded the two Wyzhñyñy glumly. *And we paid eighteen marines for them, good men. Valiant* Not many, by the standards of war, but they'd been his, in a manner of speaking. "I presume you can still salvage information from them."

"Valuable information. Subcutaneous injection of minute quantities of African bee venom has resulted in encouraging tissue responses. But unfortunately their capillary circulation is virtually nil." She gestured at the bank of small monitor screens, where thin lines of colored light jittered microscopically, or sparsely, or flowed smooth as oil. Esoteric numbers showed occasional small changes. "I have injected the brain of one," she continued, "but that is not analogous to venom reaching the brain systemically. I could learn far more with studies on specimens functioning at something approaching normal.

"Still, we are learning far more than we knew before. And through Mädchen," she added, referring to the *Bering's* savant, "I am sharing our results with Dr. Minda Shiue, at the University of Baguio."

Weygand had heard of Dr. Shiue. The Nobel Committee might meet in Buenos Aires now, instead of Oslo, but its awards continued to shine. "Just now," Kalosgouros went on, "she is at War House, to help interpet our results. I believe they are sufficient that the African Bee Project will be continued."

"Thank you, Dr. Kalosgouros," Weygand said, bowing slightly. *We do what we can,* he added silently, recalling the cost.

Back on the bridge, he buzzed Dr. Clement and asked how the hornet venom chromatography was going. Her answer was gratifying. In important and surprising respects, Tagus hornet venom resembled that of *Apis mellifera scutella.* She was proceeding optimistically.

Chapter 43

Portal to Justice

The Peace Front's Kunming headquarters occupied the sixth and seventh floors of a building no longer stylish. Paddy Davies' corner office was not large, given his position, but it easily accommodated the five guest chairs with key-pad arms and monitors. Like the rest of the furnishings, they were not new, but in recent centuries, equipment had obsolesced slowly.

Two of the guest chairs were occupied, while Paddy sat at his modest desk. He and Jaromir Horvath were already familiar with the text on the wall screen. The third person, Perfeta Stolz, was reading it, "flipping pages" with her key-pad. Rapidly. She had a quick and practiced eye and mind. Occasionally she triggered a hypertext link for details.

The pages bore a header: "Summary of Charges and Evidence Against Joseph Steven Switzer."

Davies watched Stolz, not the screen. To him, her strongly-built body and broad face suggested Native American lineage. (Actually she was half Igorot on her mother's side, and a quarter Buryat on her father's.) When she'd finished the last page, she looked across at him.

"He doesn't stand a chance of acquittal," she said. "The

339

best anyone can do for Switzer is enter a guilty plea and ask for the mercy of the court. The government has generally handled Peace Front cases quite moderately." She paused, aware of what these men really wanted. They didn't like what she'd just said, and they'd reject what she'd say next, but it was necessary to say it. "A court-appointed attorney can do that as well as I, at no cost to you."

It was Horvath who answered, his voice dry and sour. "Leniency is not the objective," he said. "We want maximum mileage from the media."

"Mr. Horvath, I can guarantee lots of press, but it won't help the defendant, and it won't turn public opinion."

Paddy answered this time. "We know it won't turn the verdict. As for the public? It will be worthwhile if we can simply touch them. Touch their souls. Keep the shame of this war before their eyes."

He thinks in clichés, Stolz told herself. *They both do.* "What you want me to do will aggravate the court," she pointed out, knowing that wouldn't impress them either. "It could even result in a sentence more severe than it might otherwise be."

Horvath answered again, surlier than before. "There are other legal firms we can hire."

She locked eyes with him, his challenging, hers steady and unyielding. "And what of Switzer?"

Paddy stepped into the breach. "An appropriate question, Counselor. But I've talked with Joseph, and he agrees. He wants us to make the most of this. For the Front and for peace. Before we pass the point of no return."

Stolz examined her broad brown hands, their nails neat and strong but not pampered, then looked back up at Davies. "You realize that it's Mr. Switzer who must ask for the change of attorneys. I can propose it to him, but it is he who must request it of the court."

"Of course. Of course. And quite as it should be. I cleared it with him before calling you."

Once more Horvath broke in, drawing a grimace from Davies. "We don't pay your firm a retainer for arguments about what we want."

"Nor have I given you one," Stolz answered calmly. "You pay a retainer for our prompt attention and our professional opinion. I have given you both." Abruptly she stood. "I will talk with Mr. Switzer. If he agrees, I will represent him, but I will also inform him honestly of the prospects." She returned her gaze to Davies. "You will be paying the fees, and I will get you what you pay for: public attention. *With* Mr. Switzer's agreement."

Davies got to his feet and stepped from behind his desk, hand extended for hers. "That's exactly as we want it, Counselor. I have a copy of the cube for you . . . "

Stolz reviewed the cube in her office, looking for cracks in the case and finding none. *Hmh!* she thought. *He dreamed up the mission, knew the risks, and volunteered to carry it out. But knowing the risks, and having them crash down on you, are two different things,* she reminded herself. *He's lucky this isn't a vengeful, reactive government.*

The next morning, a slump-shouldered Joseph Switzer stepped into a small concrete room. He wore blue prison clothing, faded by many trips through the prison laundry. A guard gripped his arm. In the middle of the room, two chairs were bolted to the floor, facing each other five feet apart. His court-appointed defender stood by one of them. Switzer's gaze dropped to the floor again.

"Shall I leave now, Counselor?" the guard asked.

"Yes, thank you," the defender said. Without a word, the guard let go of Switzer's arm and left the room, closing the door behind him, then stood looking in through its thick glass window.

Switzer simply stood unmoving. The attorney was notably taller than he was. Her kinky brown hair was cut close as a cap. Her professional black pants suit emphasized her slimness, and made her caramel complexion seem light by contrast.

"Shall we sit down, Joseph?" she asked gesturing. He nodded, stepped to a chair, and they sat down facing each other.

"I'm told you've asked that I be replaced by another attorney, one hired by the Peace Front. If that's what you wish, I'm required to step aside."

His voice was low and husky. "That's how I want it."

"The Peace Front is less interested in minimizing your sentence than in making the Front look good. Do you realize that?"

He nodded, barely.

"Are you aware of how strong the evidence is against you?"

Again his nod was slight.

"Perfeta Stolz is an excellent attorney. But it is entirely possible that I can get you a lighter sentence than she can. Because leniency would be the entire thrust of my effort, while hers will be on getting the Front as much publicity as possible. Do you understand that also?"

"That's how I want it," he repeated.

She searched his face for some sign of defiance or stoicism, or perhaps nobility—the noble martyr. She found none of them. He looked defeated, his eyes avoiding hers. Not a promising hero for the Front. But Stolz had a reputation as a courtroom psychologist, with skill in preparing her clients.

"Well then," she said, getting to her feet, "my best wishes for a successful trial." *However you define success.*

Her blessing didn't sound entirely genuine. She was a competitor, a young soul, and didn't think much of surrender.

Arraignment took place in a small closed chamber. Journalists were not allowed, though the attorneys might well find the media waiting in the Justice Building courtyard.

Besides the panel of three judges, the chamber held Joseph Switzer, his counsel, the prosecutor, a bailiff, and two deputies flanking the accused. Switzer looked much better than he had three days past. He wore a business suit, stood straight, and looked not at the floor now, but at the chief justice. Though avoiding eye contact.

Chief Justice Gil Hafiz spoke mildly to him. "For the record," he said, "are you Joseph Steven Switzer?"

"Yes, sir."

"Have you been given a copy of the indictment?"

"Yes, sir."

"Have you read it?"

"Yes, sir."

"Do you understand the charges?"

"Yes, sir."

"Good. Do you wish to speak for yourself, or do you want your defender to speak for you?"

"I want my defender to speak for me."

All three judges turned their eyes to Perfeta Stolz. "Counselor," Hafiz said, "how does the accused plead?"

"Your Honor, as Mr. Switzer's counsel, I move that the indictment be set aside. The shooting took place on Lüneburger's World, not on Terra. My client was born on Lüneburger's World, grew up there, and has Lüneburgian citizenship. Also, the military reservation was not Commonwealth property. And per Commonwealth versus Patel, CE 2781/05/17. . ." She completed the citation, along with the Supreme Court decision. "Therefore, the accused should be remanded to Lüneburger's world, and tried there by the appropriate authorities."

The chief justice glanced at the other judges, who sat attentive and impassive, then he leafed through his notes before looking back at Stolz. "As you know, Counselor, the legal term is 'full rights of residency,' not citizenship. And your client had applied for and been granted full rights of Terran residency, with the accountability that accompanies it."

Hafiz cocked an eyebrow at Stolz; she knew her plea had no grounds. She was preparing to play to the public, and within minutes of leaving would be speaking to the cameras. In his view it degraded the law, but within broad limits it was her right. If her client agreed, and if he understood what he'd agreed to. Hafiz was tempted to query the accused, but held his peace. He'd do nothing that could be used as a basis for appeal.

Instead he continued to address Stolz. "Furthermore, at the moment of his injury and death, the victim was an employee of the Commonwealth government engaged in his governmental duties. The person who actually shot the victim was also an employee of the Commonwealth government, who at the time of the shooting was engaged in *his* governmental duties. Thus per Article 12, Section 3, of the Commonwealth Criminal Code, the crime unquestionably comes under Commonwealth jurisdiction. The murderer, a soldier, pleaded guilty as charged, before a court martial. His plea was accepted, and he has begun his sentence. Thus it is now appropriate for this court to try your client for the crime of contributing to murder."

Stolz stood for a long moment as if disappointed—as if the court's decision was unexpected. Then she spoke again. "In that case, Your Honor, I must request a jury trial for my client."

The judges had expected that, too. Jury trials were infrequent on Terra—three-judge panels were the norm—but in certain classes of crimes they could be granted. The chief justice turned to the prosecutor. "What say you to that, Mr. Prosecutor?"

Hafiz knew the answer to that as well. The Office of the President had sent down a policy that, if requested, jury trials would be granted members of the Front for alleged Crimes of the First Category. Basically Hafiz disliked the policy. As a rule, juries came to the same conclusions as a panel of judges would have, while requiring much more time, expense, and turmoil. But he appreciated the government's situation.

The prosecutor grimaced slightly; such a trial would turn into a Peace Front circus. "If the defense wants it so," he grumped, "we will not object."

"Very well, Counselor," Hafiz said. "Your client shall have a jury trial." She had, he knew, a reputation for being very good in jury trials.

She bobbed an almost bow in acknowledgement. "Thank you, Your Honor. Meanwhile, my client will not come to trial for a week or more. Therefore I respectfully request his release on bond."

The prosecutor's exhalation was more hiss than sigh. Obviously she intended to fight over every proposed juror, eating up all the time possible, and providing a magnet for public attention. A Peace Front circus indeed.

The chief justice smiled slightly. "Counselor, your request is denied."

"On what grounds, Your Honor?"

"On the grounds that whatever the outcome of his trial for contributing to the crime of murder, he will still face charges of inciting to mutiny."

Stolz frowned. "Your Honor, I do not see what that has

to do with my request. My client has complied with every order, responded to every request, without resistance." She appeared to grope for words, settling for "He is not a violent man. He decries violence, by persons as well as by governments."

"The trial should cast light on that," Hafiz answered wryly. "It is, of course, possible to contribute to the crime of murder without intending that it go that far. We'll see. Meanwhile, your client stands before this court accused of two Crimes of the First Category. In such cases, the court has full discretion with regard to bail. Mr. Switzer has much reason to fear the outcomes of his trials, and there is an entire social class who would willingly undertake to conceal him or help him flee."

Stolz's features had stiffened. "What social class, if you please, Your Honor?"

"Let me answer it this way, Counselor. Who is paying your fees?"

She answered indignantly. "The Peace Front, Your Honor. The party which more than any other decries this war and all violence."

"Exactly." *She plays her role well,* he thought, *for someone who belongs to the Center Party instead of the Front.* He'd respect her more, he told himself, if her first allegiance was to the accused. But there was little she could do for him at any rate, and if the Front wanted to use Switzer for propaganda . . . He hoped, though, that Switzer really understood what was going on.

She wasn't done yet. "Your Honor, I have one more request. A number of journalists have asked to interview my client." She took a small flat case from her pocket and held it out to him. "I told them to put their requests in writing, and that they might have to agree on one or two doing the interviews for all."

The chief justice declined to receive the data chips; they were irrelevant. *She took you by surprise on that one, Gil,* he told himself. *You're slowing down.* "Denied again, Counselor," he replied. "If the court granted such privileges to accused felons, activists would commit crimes simply for the pulpit they provided."

"Your Honor," Stolz said unhappily, "except for the jury

trial, you have denied every request I've made for my client."

"True. In fact, it seems to me you made those requests anticipating their denial. And I have no doubt you'll make good use of them after you leave this chamber."

He was right, of course. She spent half an hour standing before cameras in the plaza outside, speaking carefully, but airing all her complaints. The court would provide the media with recordings and transcripts of the proceedings, but meanwhile, she'd put her own spin on them.

Chapter 44

Battle Master

The CWS *Altai*, flagship of the 1st Sol Provisional Battle Force, was in hyperspace just seven days short of the Paraíso System. Its admiral, Alvaro Soong, lay propped on a pillow in his stateroom, hands cupped behind his head, reviewing. He was not a notable worrier. His usual style was to treat things matter-of-factly. But he'd made a decision—made and implemented it—that could wipe out whatever chance humanity had for survival. At least civilized survival.

His rationale was that the chance being risked was thin. And if his decision worked out, it could substantially improve.

If it worked out. He'd approached it on a gradient: "Just how good *are* you at battle games, Charley? Let me write a set of opening circumstances, and see what you can do with it."

Both men—the one who occupied 210 pounds of primate body, and the one who weighed only 58 pounds, most of it a "bottle" of metal and synthetics—both knew what lay in the back of the admiral's mind. *Are you good enough to direct a real battle with real warships? Are you really?*

Because the odds are heavily against us. I may be better at directing a space battle than any other officer in this battle force. At the Academy, my cumulative battle game score set a record. But if you can beat me decisively enough . . .

Basically he was praying for a true genius in war gaming. And Charley had passed the test with ease, even flair. And a second, and a third . . .

Soong himself was the default choice, but after extensive testing, he'd chosen Charley. For a while the choice had been reversible. Now it wasn't. Not if they were to engage the armada in the Paraíso System. They'd programmed too many changes into the *Altai*'s battlecomp, trying to take maximum advantage of Charley's talents.

Briefly the admiral turned his attention to his stateroom "window"—a large wall panel that in F-space usually gave a real-time view of the stars more clearly than an actual window could. But in hyperspace, the default view was of the F-space potentiality, as interpreted by the shipsmind, and it was neither esthetic nor ordinarily interesting. Usually it showed nothing at all. So he'd requested views of Terra. Terra, which he might never see again. Just now it showed the Swedish taiga—its trees sparse and stunted in the ever worsening climate. In the background was the great ice sheet of the Kjölen Range, intensely, painfully white in spring sunshine. It covered the fjelds as far north and south as the view permitted, and oozed slow white tongues of ice down the valleys toward the sea. A magnificent view, it also provided perspective. Many townsites and historical sites had been buried by the ice in this and many other valleys, leaving the region virtually abandoned. A few—a very few Sami had stayed, long since genetically more Swedish and Norwegian than Sami. They had relearned to herd reindeer, a valid lifestyle, given the climatic shift.

A thought surfaced: if the Wyzhñyñy prevailed, would they undertake to root out such tiny, harmless enclaves? That was what some of the colonies had been—small harmless enclaves in planetary wilderness. And seemingly the Wyzhñyñy had rooted them out. From the alien point of view, he supposed it made sense.

He pulled his attention away from the screen. In a week

he'd emerge in the Paraíso System—the first inhabited
system at which he could intercept the invader. How terrible, how overwhelming was that alien armada? How good
were his Provos—his 1st Sol Provisional Battle Force? What
chance did humanity have?

You'll be the first to know, Alvaro, he told himself.

He was not expected to win this battle, in the usual
sense. Thank the Tao. He was to attack the enemy, cause
as much damage as possible, then disappear into hyperspace
before the invader could destroy him. And in the process
learn as much as possible about enemy weaponry and tactics. Those were his orders. Engage, flee, and report.

The decisive part—the most dangerous moment—would
be just before escape into strange-space. That moment after
the shield generators had shut down, but before the shields
had sufficiently decayed to allow generation of a carrier
bubble.

War House deemed those waited-for reports so vital,
they'd invested five of a seriously limited resource to make
sure of them. In each battle group, the point battleship
carried a savant communicator, and through that savant,
a liaison officer was to give War House a running account
of the fight. Then, when the fleet had escaped into
hyperspace, the surviving commanders would debrief,
again via savant.

Though War House didn't know it in advance, the *Altai*
was the exception. Her savant would be far too busy
directing battle actions to give a running account. And
afterward he'd rest, as long as needed, before channeling
Soong's debrief.

Soong hadn't told Kunming about his new battle master.
War House might forbid following through on it. It seemed
to him he would himself, if he were admiralty chief.
Because War House hadn't personally tested Charley
Gordon. And the battle would involve most of the battle-
ready human warships and crews.

And if somehow Kunming found out before the fact, and
forbade it? Probably he'd ignore them. He'd spent weeks
as Charley's assistant, developing strategies and tactics,
modifying and remodifying procedures. But in simulation
tests, he'd been a spectator, while Charley interacted with

the *Altai* and the rest of the battle force in ways no one had thought of before.

Early on, the admiral had been visited by anxiety, but the weeks of development and tests had left him quietly confident. Not of victory, but of Charley's genius and skills, and the wisdom of his own decision. The limitations of ships and weapons remained, along with the unknown abilities and resources of the Wyzhñyñy.

And that two-edged sword known as Murphy's Law, which threatened both fleets. Soong wondered if the Wyzhñyñy recognized Murphy's Law. It seemed to him they must. It was inaccurate, of course. Murphy's Law— "Whatever can go wrong will go wrong"—had been predicated as humor. It was irony, not science. But by changing one word, you expressed a truth: "Whatever can go wrong *may* go wrong."

In any case you did what you could, and Charley could outdo anyone.

In normal gaming, a battle master gives the battlecomp a general strategy and a set of candidate tactics, via brief code words or phrases, very explicit. The battlecomp takes it from there, until that instruction is overridden by a new code word or phrase. Some gamers sometimes give a single such order. The secret to whatever success they have lies in evaluating the initial situation, and selecting or creating an effective strategy. The exercise itself is run entirely by the battlecomp.

Charley, however, had come to the job with major advantages. His response time was faster than any other human gamer's, perhaps because his responses were mediated by a shorter, faster neural system.

Charley knew the *entire* catalog of standard command codes, and had added numerous others of his own to make use of his special talents. And no one, to Soong's knowledge, was nearly so nimble with them. Charley could rattle off a sequence of appropriate commands, for a number of units, almost at the speed of thought. "Appropriate" involving the necessary allowances for unit momenta, signal time, equipment response times, and of course his own delivery rate in a command sequence.

The battlecomp could, of course, handle the command

function by default. But it could not know what Charley
usually knows: the event vectors of the moment. His central
genius.

Meanwhile, in simulation, every warship in the fleet was
carrying out battle actions bizarre and unimagined, even by
the centuries of tactical wizards who'd labored anonymously
at War House desks, programming, testing and gaming.

Because creative and imaginative though they'd been,
none of them had envisioned a resource like Charley
Gordon.

Estimated conservatively, the Provos would arrive in the
fringe of the system twelve days before the Wyzhñyñy's
projected date of arrival. With the short closing jump, and
a force no larger than Soong's, hours would be enough to
form opening battle formations. So far, Charley's fleet drills
had been in the virtual reality of the *Altai's* shipsmind. The
rest of the fleet didn't know there was a new battle master.
In the Paraíso System, the entire fleet would participate,
its ships coordinated under Charley Gordon's direction,
mediated by the *Altai's* shipsmind.

Soong was on the bridge four hours before scheduled
arrival. Already isogravs showed the system's primary, an
F9 star without a name of its own, unless you consider
catalog numbers. As soon as shipsmind had computed the
optimum emergence solution, the admiral ordered an
approach course and emergence tick, informing his battle
force via that awkward set of phenomena called hyperspace
radio.

When that order had been acknowledged, he sent
another: all hands were to be out of stasis before emergence, and ready to receive a live, all-hands briefing from
the admiral and his battle master. Because the battle plan,
tactics and protocols had changed greatly. The fleet's
officers and crews needed to be set up for that; informed
of what had happened, and how, reassured, and given
confidence in the new command situation.

On naval spacecraft, the signal for hyperspace emergence
is a gong, mellow and golden, repeated over five seconds.

Then the Provos popped into F-space scattered over a
significant period—more than a millisecond—to occupy a
million-cubic-mile volume of F-space shaped like a water-
melon seed. Against a scintillant backdrop of stars, cold in
aspect but hot, hot. The brightest, most vivid, being the
molten-yellow primary only four billion miles away.

The admiral gave his people thirty seconds to appreciate the sight. Then he began his all-hands address.

"Officers and crew of the First Provos. We are in the
fringe of the Paraíso System, and in a few minutes we'll
begin to form battle units. Not the formations we've formed
before, but something new. Something better. Something
that will enable us to truly raise hell with the enemy when
he appears.

"Eight weeks ago I made a discovery. I discovered that
one of us is a genius above all geniuses in battle gaming.
As a graduating midshipman, I set the Academy's official
all-time cumulative scoring record for space-battle games.
So I tested and retested this newly discovered genius, then
tested him some more. In every test he humbled me, and
as a result I've made him battle master. Given him the duty
I love best of all, because this will be no game. It will be
for real, for the future of humankind."

He paused, letting them absorb it.

"He improves our odds of victory by a factor of ten. So
I want to introduce this man to you, this supreme battle
master. You need to know him and hear him. He is a gift
from the Tao, and one of the finest human beings I have
ever known."

Up to this point, the camera had given the viewers a
close shot of their admiral, showing him from the waist up.
Now the viewpoint backed off, showing him standing beside
a wheeled, motorized stand.

"Our new battle master's name is Charley Gordon. Not
Admiral Gordon. Not Captain Gordon or Commander
Gordon. Charley Gordon, a civilian. He is also our flag-
ship savant."

The admiral's calm features seemed to gaze through the
screen at them, as they sat or stood, surprised or puzzled,
in messroom, wardroom, engine room, bridge, on battleship, cruiser, corvette . . . . He continued.

"A savant. 'Savant' is short for 'idiot savant,' because most of them aren't able to function mentally as we do. But all have talents that the rest of us do not.

"Charley Gordon is different. He has savant talents, *and* he reasons . . . superbly. He was born in the Brazilian Autonomy, in Rio de Janeiro. As a child he dwelt constantly at death's door, till at age twelve he was bottled, to save his life. Now . . . "

Their admiral waited again, then gestured at the cart, and the module on its top. "This is Charley Gordon," he said, then indicated the small sensor set that topped it. "He sees and hears his immediate surroundings with these. But through his connections with shipsmind, he sees much more. At will.

"And now I'll let him tell you more about what he does and how he does it."

Almost no one spoke, anywhere in the fleet. Inwardly Soong fidgeted. Because Charley had told him almost nothing about what he'd say. "One of my differences," he'd explained, "is that I function best when playing by ear."

Now Charley broke the silence, in a voice that was not in the least robotic. One might almost have called it merry. "I am Charley Gordon. I am thirty-three years old, and for most of those years I've been war gaming. It's as if I was born for it.

"My response to almost anything is an action. An action! Me, who lives in a box! I act electronically, via whatever mechanisms I'm connected with. Including my vocator, with which I'm speaking to you now, and by whatever artificial intelligence or other server I'm connected with. In this case shipsmind, especially its battlecomp function.

"As battle master I have certain innate and very important advantages. For example, I absorb books and other data sources like a sponge absorbs water. And none of it leaks out or evaporates. Instead it integrates, unifies, forms a coherent system. Where it harmonizes according to natural laws I can only sense, but use intuitively. Use in ways analogous to the ways I communicate with War House in real time, even though Kunming is hyperspace months away."

Soong had gotten used to talking with Charley Gordon; now he was listening to him with different ears, crew ears. *Great Tao!* he thought. *He's charismatic! How did I miss that? He positively radiates intelligence and assurance! This will work better than I'd hoped.*

"Some of what I tell you may sound strange," Charley went on. "But most of you have had technical training and games experience, so you will understand. If not at once, then when you've seen it in action.

"Equally important . . . " He paused. "Let me put it this way. Things happen in sequences. A cause results in an effect, which causes another effect. Et cetera. The causes may include a human decision, a weather incident, an argument, leaky plumbing . . . almost anything. Such cause/effect sequences I call vectors, and vectors often intersect, and interact.

"For example: Some geophysical incident—say a tidal wave resulting from a volcanic eruption—destroys a village in the Sulu Archipelago. As one result, a surviving villager migrates to Zamboanga, where he meets a stranger at a mosque. They talk, and decide to become robbers together. Ambushing a well-dressed man, they steal a message plaque he'd carried in a body wallet. The message is in a Tamil dialect which neither knows, but . . . " He paused. "One thing leads to another, and before long, one robber is dead at the hands of Han smugglers, and our ex-villager is hiding among pilgrims en route to Mecca."

His listeners could hear the calm and smiling competence in Charley's voice. "A vector in progress, you see. Now we Provos are on a vector which will soon intersect the vector of the Wyzhñyñy armada. And when those vectors intersect, they will result in a spray of new vectors.

"My greatest advantage as battle master is, I am able to sense the relevant vectors—*and their probabilistic futures*. Some vectors remain fixed over long periods of time: a planet in its orbit, a comet in its orbit. Eventually they may intersect, but very probably they will not. It would be useful to know in advance.

"Many other vectors are very erratic, like a spoiled child unrestrained in a toy store. Even those I can often foresee with some confidence. And while I do these things intu-itively, I know them consciously."

The admiral listened intently. Charley had never brought up these things to him, though by hindsight they'd been apparent in his gaming.

"Mostly," Charley continued, "I can't project them very far. Many intersect with too many other effective vectors. Human and alien choices, and of course chaos functions, can cause vectors to change, and give rise to new vectors. But I am generally a few steps ahead of events, and that is a very important advantage.

"Beyond that, I coordinate factors and data very very well. Not as precisely as a shipsmind, but on a higher level. For what is termed 'intuition' in an artificial intelligence is simply the use of stochastic processes to extrapolate beyond or around areas of weak or ambiguous data. Human intuition can go well beyond that."

Soong listened while Charley wrapped up his talk. Among other things, the savant knew when to stop. When he was done, the admiral added a few closing comments, then ended the session. It seemed to him they'd pulled it off. Or Charley had. Over the next day or so he'd know absolutely, one way or the other, by fleet performance.

Meanwhile *Altai*'s shipsmind had uploaded the contents of its upgraded battlecomp to the rest of the fleet. And when the all-hands session was over, the admiral called for a command conference on the closed command frequency. A few hours later, the force was ready to begin simulation drills.

The simdrills went so well that three days later the force began "steel drills." In these the battle groups moved physically in space while *Altai*'s battlecomp threw sequences of enemy responses at them. From his battle command station on the bridge, Charley rattled off rapid shorthand instructions to shipsmind, instructions forwarded by radio to the rest of the force, which fought as separate but coordinated battle groups.

In F-space, maneuvers were as limited as ever; one thing Charley couldn't do was cancel inertia. But by anticipating "enemy responses," he permitted individual battle groups to transit from F-space to warpspace with minimal losses. And his control and coordination of beam fire and torpedo attacks against enemy movements was deadly.

It was all pretend, of course, but the Provo crews had gained a large degree of optimism, and an enthusiasm that made the whole venture exciting. Even the "losses" of Provo warships did not greatly cool them. They were, they told each other, going to teach the Wyzhñyñy the cost of bringing war to human space.

Alvaro Soong was not as optimistic. The drills had been as realistic as possible, short of shooting at each other. But it was still a limited reality, because Wyzhñyñy weaponry, tactics, nerve—even the number of their warships—was unknown.

Which was, he reminded himself, the main reason he'd been sent there, he and his Provos. At the least, he needed to maintain engagement long enough to forward a definitive picture of Wyzhñyñy battle capacities to War House. To inflict substantive damage would be a bonus.

Chapter 45

A Time of Truth

The armada had emerged from hyperspace so often in this galaxy, it had become routine, and no longer drew Quanshûk to the bridge or to his feet. He watched from the AG couch in his quarters.

" . . . five, four, three, two, one . . . "

Stars exploded onto the screen, but their beauty no longer lifted him. Even the question—would one of its planets be habitable?—had long since become routine. The armada emerged every shipsday or two—at every star whose isogravs suggested any possibility of a habitable planet. Usually staying only long enough to discover there wasn't one. Sometimes five minutes was enough. Sometimes they sent a Survey ship for a closer look. When one seemed clearly habitable, they stayed several days, and left with a sense of accomplishment. But after so many, even that was routine now.

This emergence came during shipsnight, and Quanshûk closed his eyes again. The bridge would call him if . . .

His comm yammered, and he jerked wide awake. "This is the admiral," he answered.

"Your lordship, there is something you need to see. Perhaps on the bridge?"

The voice was that of Captain Krûts, the *Meadowlands'* master. "I'll be there momentarily," Quanshûk answered.

"Shall I notify Chief Scholar Qonits and Admiral Tualurog, your lordship?"

"At your discretion."

The admiral jabbed a key, then got stiffly to his feet, his arthritic joints complaining. He was medicated, always, but not so strongly as to banish pain. He was grand admiral, and would not risk dulling his mind.

At first, after getting up, he didn't walk well. He carried himself well—torso erect, long head high—but his steps were short and painful. Qonits caught up with him at the entry to the bridge, and they went in together.

Krûts was waiting for them, and pointed at the large screen centered in the monitor array on the bridge's forward bulkhead. It showed a compressed representation of the system, with the conventional armada icon, and other icons marking planets. Two others—flashing orange lights—marked detected sources of technical electronics.

Two sources. One was the second planet. The other was in the near fringe, its system azimuth 134 degrees from the armada's. Quanshûk stepped quickly to his admiral's station, and called for an enlarged view of the fringe source. Or cluster of sources, for that's how the monitor showed them. At nearly nine light-hours distance, there was no visual resolution. A sidebar numbered them, however: 230 individual sources—230 ships.

Quanshûk frowned. Two hundred thirty. Why were they here? They were far too few to do battle with him.

Then it struck him. Turning, he scanned the bridge crew. "An evacuation fleet," he said, then elaborated. "On most of the human worlds we've come to, much of the population had clearly been evacuated. Very probably we're looking at an evacuation fleet." He turned to his chief scholar. "Wouldn't you say, Qonits?"

"Indeed, my lord, that would explain them."

The chief scholar looked less than sure of it. But then, being skeptical was part of a scholar's job.

In the Provo force, an electronic bosun's pipe shrilled through the corridors and compartments of the *Altai* and

every other manned ship. Followed by shipsvoice: "Now
hear this! Now hear this! All hands report to mustering
stations by 1022 hours. All hands to mustering stations by
1022 hours." Then the sequence repeated. Every hand
knew; this was it: the time of truth. "All hands" calls were
infrequent. To repeat it like this . . .

Ten-twenty-two; in ten minutes.

To top it off, after a few seconds music began to issue
from the ships' speakers. Music! That was different. The
admiralty had established "instant tradition" for its new
fleet, including an "unofficial" fleet theme, dubbed "Spacing
Off to Dilly Doo." Dilly Doo being a planet in a very old,
off-color space tale—a sort of Valhalla where spacers supposedly went when they died, to binge and bawd. The
recording—by the pipes and drums of the Caledonian
Regimental Band—dated from before space flight. Its name
then had been "Scotland the Brave," something few spacers
were aware of.

By any name it was stirring. And when they'd finished
"Dilly Doo," the Caledonians continued without a break,
playing other martial music.

Meanwhile men in bunks swung their legs out, put feet
on the deck, and went to the head to relieve themselves
and splash cold water on their faces. Men in rec rooms
shut off books and games, officers in wardrooms finished
their coffee and rolls or set them aside. Something major
was up, and no one on board had any doubt what it was.

Most mustering stations were messrooms. Personnel on
duty could watch on their duty monitor. By 1022, every
man and woman aboard every ship was in front of a screen;
in sickbay perhaps a screen above the bed.

It was not the shipsvoice that spoke to them. They'd
have been surprised if it was. It was the "old man" himself, the admiral. A close shot of him—chest, shoulders, head.
Dark eyes dominating, jaw firm. "Men of the First Provos,"
he began. The thirty-one percent who were women took
no offense. The term "men" as a neuter collective had been
accepted for a long time.

"We have found the enemy. The Wyzhñyñy armada
arrived in this system at 1010 hours, only nine light-hours
away."

The admiral's face was replaced by a representation of the Paraíso System, showing the relative positions of the two fleets, as icons.

"By now they have surely read our electronic signature, and are wondering what in the Tao this small fleet is doing here. Knowing that we will have read their emergence waves, they will expect us to flee. They will expect that nine hours hence, our electronics will disappear from their sensors."

The admiral's face replaced the schematic. "At 1030 hours we will generate warpspace—and at 1230 hours emerge within the fringe of their armada." He paused, then spoke more loudly and sharply. "And show them what humans can do in a fight! Especialy with *our* battle master."

His voice resumed its usual even delivery. "Each of you knows your role in this. Your duty; what you are to do. I expect your best. We will shock the invader; we will bleed him; we will make him wish he'd never left home."

Then he raised his arms in closing, and "Dilly Doo"— "Scotland the Brave"—returned to the corridors and compartments of the 1st Provos.

Except on the "maces." Maces had no crews. They had the dimensions of cruisers, but beamguns as powerful as those on battleships. Built to stand accelerations up to 100 gees, they could accelerate and decelerate at rates that humans, and presumably Wyzhñyñy, could not remotely match. And they could fly high-speed evasion courses. Not extreme evasion courses, but courses that beamguns would have trouble getting locks on. At least beamguns on human warships.

"Flying guns" they'd been called. It would have been as accurate to call them flying generators, for those guns required great power. And more: the newer squadrons generated two-layered shields. Their interior design had been modified to accommodate not only larger power generators but larger shield generators.

As for their battle judgements and responses—the shipsminds aboard maces were second to none. And like every other Provo shipsmind, they'd been reprogrammed to respond to Charley Gordon's unique style of command.

✧   ✧   ✧

Rear Admiral Tualurog had taken over the grand
admiral's station on the bridge, allowing Quanshûk to
return to bed. It was easy duty. Shipsmind could manage
the re-forming of battle wings, and the even more numerous transport and supply ships. Cleansing the humans
from the habitable world was the colonizing tribe's responsibility. The Grand Fleet remained briefly on standby, to
lend support as necessary.

The tribe was already inbound in warpdrive, with its
regiments of shock warriors, its divisions of non-warrior
reservists, its integral ground support wing, and its own
insystem defense force: a flotilla of cruisers and corvettes.
The ground forces were supported by two bombards—
massive ships designed solely for ground bombardment—
assigned to the planetary guard flotilla. These would destroy
defense installations and troop concentrations, if any. And
all technical facilities and population centers. After that,
ground-support "hunters" helped "beat the bushes," guided
by surveillance buoys parked in near-space.

If the planet's defense forces turned out to be troublesome enough, the fleet could send down marines and
additional ground support squadrons. But that was undesirable. It meant delaying the armada's departure.

As for possible human incursions from space—the
departing armada would leave a pentagonal battle group
in the fringe: five battleships with a screen of cruisers
and corvettes, ready to move against any threat. While
a planetary guard flotilla was left insystem, to guard
against landings.

Like hideous trumpets, alarm horns blared through the
Meadowlands, jerking everyone awake. A single, eight-
second, ruff-raising discord that cut sharply to a voice,
strident but concise: "Battle stations! Battle stations! Battle
stations!"

Quanshûk was on his feet and into the executive corridor more quickly than he'd moved for months. The ship
was already fighting, its everpresent fine vibration amplified by the demands of heavy beamguns and the generation of her force shield. She jarred as a salvo of torpedos

exploded against her newly generated shield, throwing the admiral against a bulkhead. The corridor lights flickered, then held.

On the bridge, the only sound was quiet words spoken to closed-channel mikes. Quanshûk's practiced eyes took in the monitor array—diagrams; animations; live tracking shots, some foreshortened, others natural; enemy ships identified by pulsing red darts. Words flashed on the systems-status display. Beams of white light, war beams, crisscrossed screens, and not all ships were marked by the haloes indicating shields. Where war beams had locked on first, the shield generation process aborted.

Quanshûk's mind elaborated what his eyes could not: glowing red hull-metal puddling where a beam was locked, flowing and spattering away from the contact. Breached hulls, exploding, imploding. Torpedo salvos bursting on shields, disrupting some, blowing their generators. Where this happened, beams might find the hull for a coup de grâce. Then he was at his command station, jabbing keys, eyes snatching data from the thirty-inch station monitor. A diagram popped on, summarizing the firefight as it proceeded. Seemingly the attackers had not been picked up at once, for even as the sequence began, they'd reached substantial speeds from the standstill of warpspace emergence, and already had shields up.

The Grand Fleet's shipsminds were entirely in charge, coordinated so far as possible by the command shipsmind aboard *Meadowlands*. Once alerted, its response had been instantaneous, a reflex. The bridge watch could only try to catch up. Quanshûk's fingers stabbed keys, slid magnification tabs, his mind clearer and sharper than it had been for years, free of fear, anxiety and blame, watching patterns unfold in the action. Enemy fire control and coordination was superb. Almost solely they targeted fighting ships, the beams from several converging not only on one, but on the same part of its shield. Each battle group moved and fought as a vee through and out of its own sector of armada space, leaving a corridor of destruction.

A few of the ships destroyed or left derelict were attackers, but his battle formations were too incomplete for successful fire coordination. At twenty-eight seconds a few enemy shields thinned, then more in quick succession, to disappear before their ships blinked out of sight into warpspace. And somehow in their moment of vulnerability, few were found by beams. Then there was peace, marred by glowing broken hulls.

Quanshûk's brief battle high dissolved into shock. With an almost insolent dispassion, shipsmind informed him that the encounter had lasted thirty-four seconds, and presented him with a fleet losses report. Four battleships and eleven cruisers . . . Enemy losses, one battleship and three cruisers . . . The admiral stared blankly.

Then the next wave hit, as unexpectedly as the first. Alarm horns squalled. The *Meadowlands* was jarred by another salvo of torpedos. Again the lights flickered, and for a moment the bridge was lit only by the monitors, before the lights came back at half strength. This new wave accelerated impossibly, in randomized zigzags despite their momentum, while their bright war beams reached far forward. The admiral and bridge crew could do little but watch the monitors. Again the attackers' fire coordination was excellent. And far ahead, what seemed to be the first wave had emerged again from warpspace, sweeping through the still-mustering Fourth Battle Wing.

The second wave disappeared more quickly than the first. Then the reemerged first wave winked out again. Quanshûk sat dazed but upright, waiting for shipsmind to report losses. Even as the numbers appeared, shipsvoice reported new incursions, elsewhere within the armada. The admiral hardly reacted, leaving the battle to shipsmind.

Ophelia Kennah guided Charley Gordon off the bridge and into the corridor, Alvaro Soong following. With F-space and the Wyzhñyñy left behind, shipsmind, along with Soong's operations officer and the ship's captain, could tend shop very nicely. Soong would stay with Charley until the savant had settled down. Then, if Charley was in shape to channel, he'd report to War House.

In the corridor, Charley couldn't restrain himself. "Oh, Admiral," he said, "it was . . . marvelous! I am absolutely *wired*! *Wired!*" He paused just a second. "You do know the term, sir? It dates from the first drug era, before the

Troubles, and means intensely exhilarated. I have *never* felt like this before!" He laughed. "Did you hear that, Admiral? Laughter from a bottle! I'm like Ebenezer Scrooge, after awakening on Christmas morning! Like a drunken man! Isn't that remarkable? Even though I was just instrumental in destroying the biological housings of thousands of souls, sending them back to central casting, so to speak. And feel no guilt! No guilt at all! Isn't that remarkable? Oh! I'm even repeating myself! I don't usually do that. Do I, dear Ophelia? I don't think I do.

"And, Admiral, do you know why I feel no guilt? Because it is part of the great dance. Part of the great learning. And because . . . *We may have just saved the human species!* The vectors are distinctly encouraging now!" His voice lowered conspiratorially. "They are. We have not won yet, but we have crossed a watershed, believe me."

Charley fell silent then, and it seemed to Soong he should reply, at least acknowledge Charley's words. "I believe you, Charley," he found himself saying. "You did marvelously well."

They were at Charley's door before the savant spoke again. He was no longer wired. "How many enemy ships did we destroy, Admiral?" he asked.

"I don't recall. A lot more than we lost." Soong opened the door for Kennah, who guided Charley into their suite.

"Admiral, I am suddenly very tired," Charley said. "I'm not sure I can channel just now."

"That's fine, Charley. Take a nap. As long as you'd like. War House knows in general how the fighting went. I'll have one of the point ships let them know that you were the battle master, and that you need to rest now. I'll debrief to them later."

"Thank you, sir." Charley almost slurred the words. "Ophelia, dear, I think two hours will do. Two hours."

"Fine, Charley. Two hours."

Charley's sensor lights dimmed out.

"He's asleep now, Admiral," she said quietly. "I'll call you. Or if there is a need, you call me."

She paused, tipping her head to one side, then added: "I would not worry, Admiral, about Charley's stamina. I have never seen him unable to continue channeling. It is after he finishes that he—sometimes sags. I believe he could have conducted the battle as long as necessary, but once he disconnects, he must rest."

Soong nodded. "Thank you, Kennah," he said, then left. She'd looked and sounded tired herself. *I wonder,* he thought, *if she doesn't somehow lend energy to Charley when he needs it.*

Afterward, Alvaro Soong himself felt emotionally drained, and lay down intending to nap. But found himself reviewing, instead, sorting material for his debrief. His Provos' losses had been heaviest during the brief moments of shield decay, before strange-space could be generated. All told he'd lost five battleships out of twenty-five, twelve cruisers out of seventy-five, nine corvettes out of fifty. And only eleven maces out of sixty, despite high-risk assignments; they were hard to hit, and those with layered shields, hard to kill. War House would make something of that.

He also had good figures on Wyzhñyñy losses, give or take a very few. Fourteen battleships, forty-two ships seemingly equivalent to cruisers, and thirty-seven others he'd lumped in his mind as miscellaneous. Proportionately his own losses had been far heavier than the Wyzhñyñy's. But by the time he reached rendezvous, in the fringe of the Dinébikeyah System, the new battle units waiting to join him would more than make up his losses. Much more.

The Wyzhñyñy, by contrast, would get no replacements. Well, in a sense they would, because most of their warfleet hadn't actually been engaged in this fight. Call them on-site reserves; not potential future reinforcements like his own.

At any rate, his Provos, including Charley, had carried out their mission: they'd learned a lot about the Wyzhñyñy and done "substantive damage." The flip side of that being, the Wyzhñyñy had learned a lot about his Provos. He'd hardly catch them so unprepared again.

Tomorrow he and Charley would start work on how Charley might control a fleet several times as large as he'd managed today. With a sigh, Soong sat up. He really should nap on the battle experience, before debriefing to War House. Which meant stilling the thoughts that swirled in his consciousness. Buzzing sickbay, he arranged for a potent sleeping pill, then buzzed Ophelia Kennah. Let Charley sleep as long as he needed, he told her. A few extra hours shouldn't seriously dislocate War House.

Chapter 46

Wyzhñyñy Addendum

Grand Admiral Quanshûk had gathered himself sufficiently to lead Rear Admiral Tualurog and Chief Scholar
Qonits to his quarters. As always, his orderly had made
the bed, cleared and washed the counter, put things
away . . . Only his desk was as it had been, the orderly
being forbidden to touch it.

The three high-ranking Wyzhñyñy stepped inside.
Quanshûk closed the door behind them, then went to his
desk and triggered the recording system, before stepping
to his small bar. "Admiral Tualurog, what is your pleasure?"

The rear admiral named it, a product unadorned with
flavorings. A fighting man's taste. Quanshûk poured two of
them, the second for himself, then looked at Qonits. "The
usual?"

"If you please, Grand Admiral."

Quanshûk poured him a non-alcoholic beverage. "We
have finally met resistance," he said, "and I did not much
care for it. They stung us sorely. But we have learned from
it." He drummed clawed fingertips on the bartop.

Tualurog grunted. "The humans are cowards, afraid to
stand and fight."

"It served them well," Qonits said offhandedly. "In ancient times our ancestors used hit-and-run attacks. It enabled them to survive, and eventually prevail."

Tualurog scowled. In his opinion, Quanshûk greatly overrated his chief scholar. *Qonits is high aristocracy,* he told himself, *and Quanshûk, being a snob, gives his words too much weight.* Back in the empire, scholars were listened to for their knowledge, not their advice. But here the empire was beyond reach, and they were in the process of establishing a new empire. Which needed to maintain the integrity and honor that had made the old one great. In time it might prove necessary to take steps.

Quanshûk sipped, then sipped again. "What have we learned today, Tualurog?" he asked.

"One, that we must take nothing for granted. The enemy may strike when least expected. Two, in the future we must emerge and muster well out in the cometary cloud. At a distance from which our emergence waves will be too attenuated to read from the planets. Allowing us to form battle formations without disturbance. And three, we must take and hold the initiative whenever we detect the enemy."

Quanshûk nodded. "The first is self-evident. The second will slow our progress severely, but I will keep it in mind. As for the third—prepare a list of specific measures to be taken. In doing so, assume we will continue to re-form in the inner fringe. And let me know of any troublesome aspects that arise."

He turned to Qonits. "What do you have to say, Chief Scholar?"

Qonits bowed, bending forelegs and torso. "Grand Admiral, we need to review and revise our tactics in general. In past wars, fleets have tended to meet in close combat, sometimes no more than a mile apart, to pour war beams and torpedos at each other until one breaks. But it seems the humans do not fight that way."

Quanshûk's lids half closed, hooding his yellow eyes. "That is not necessarily so," he said. "This time we met only a small force. Their version of skirmishers perhaps, sent to test us. When we meet their main force, its situation and tactics may be different."

He paused, sipping again, not voicing the rest of his thought: that when they met next, the humans might have the advantage of numbers. So vast an empire! Then it would be to the humans' advantage to stand and slug.

"Nonetheless," he continued, "you are right. We must review our tactics, and be prepared to counter such hit-and-run attacks. Or use them if we are ever at a numerical disadvantage."

He looked at Tualurog. "Admiral, I leave it to you, to you and shipsmind, to review our tactics and recommend changes. I also want procedures for reorganizing formations more quickly after emergence. We need to provide a better-coordinated response." He turned back to Qonits then. "Chief Scholar, I want you to rethink everything we do. And have shipsmind make a complete analysis of human psychology, in the light of their language, and of their tactics to date."

A sigh hissed from the grand admiral's lipless mouth. "And now," he said, "you are both dismissed."

The two Wyzhñyñy nobles ignored each other as they left. *Analyze human psychology!* Tualurog thought. *What idiocy! We need to kill them, not analyze them.*

Analyze them, thought Qonits. *I should have done that earlier.* In fact, he realized, he had analyzed them to a degree, in conjunction with improving the translation program. But today had made it much more urgent.

David and Yukiko had been anticipating Qonits' arrival—his or someone's. Earlier they'd jumped half out of their skins at the battle alarm, and twice swallowed their hearts when the Wyzhñyñy flagship had been jarred by torpedo strikes. Meanwhile, the apparent firefight might have changed their situation. They might not be as well treated after this.

But Qonits knocked and identified himself as usual. "Come in!" they called, almost in unison.

Had Qonits been better able to read the nuances in human voices, he might have recognized relief. He entered, his bodyguards with blasters at port arms. *So far, so good,* David thought. To his eyes, Qonits seemed normal.

"Good day, humans," said the chief scholar. It had become his usual greeting. "I am sure you noticed the—uproar? The uproar earlier."

"It would have been impossible not to," David answered. "What happened?"

"Can you not guess?"

"There must have been a fight. Between your fleet and some of our warships. It was to be expected." Actually, only when it happened had he and Yukiko realized how little they'd expected it.

"What do you know about your people's warships?" Qonits asked.

This time Yukiko answered. "Very little. We are not of the soldier or spacer classes. Perhaps captives from one of them could tell you something."

"But you know about ships."

"Not warships," David said. "Not weapon systems."

Probably, Qonits told himself, *they actually are poorly informed on warfare*. They'd have some general knowledge of it, but clearly they were not of the warrior gender. Or "class" as they called it. He could not imagine people like these carrying out so daring and fierce an attack. *I may know more about their warships and tactics than they do.*

"You didn't tell us whether we were right," Yukiko put in. "Was it a small fight? It didn't seem long enough to be a full-scale battle."

"Quite small. Your people fought well, but there were far too few of them."

"Ah." David nodded thoughtfully. "A scout group, feeling you out."

"Feeling out? What is feeling out?" Qonits thought he understood, but preferred not to make assumptions.

"To feel out is to test. See how you respond; how easy you'll be, or how difficult."

Yukiko nodded. "If they learned enough this time, maybe next time they'll launch a fleet attack."

David looked around nervously. "Maybe it will come soon. Maybe the main fleet is nearby."

"Or perhaps . . . " Yukiko began, then stopped.

"Continue."

"Perhaps they plan to contest your conquest of this

system. I suppose you were in F-space during the fight. So you must have been in some star system."

"Yes, we were, we are, in F-space. But your ships have fled away. Those not destroyed."

"Perhaps the next system then," David suggested absently.

Qonits frowned. "Your rulers—" he said thoughtfully. "Are they elected by all the nobles? Or only by the high nobles?"

Yukiko actually laughed. "Neither," she said. "They're elected by all adults."

Loosely speaking, it was true.

Qonits didn't stay long, and left thoughtfully.

Chapter 47

Battlefield Proxies

Paddy Davies' corner office was too small for a quorum meeting of the Peace Council. So the utility room, used for coffee breaks, all-hands briefings, etc., had been cleaned up. Thermal coffee mugs had been set at twelve places, while cookies and assorted raw veggies occupied trays and bowls.

The council members were from several continents, and usually convened via the Ether. But not this time. Günther Genovesi, the Peace Front's attorney, treasury secretary, and sometime emergency financier, had called for this meeting, insisting it be live. And the entire suite boasted effective anti-snooping equipment. So the complete council was there except for Francesca Yoshinori, currently being held without bond on weapons charges, in Concepción, in the Chilean Autonomy. Her proxy on the council was Yolanda Guzman.

Jaromir Horvath rapped the gavel plate. "Günther asked for this meeting," Horvath said, "so I'll turn it over to him." He paused, then added drily, "He didn't confide in me, beyond telling me it has to do with membership and finances." Laying the gavel down, he turned to the heavy, Levantine-looking man to his left, the one council member who was truly wealthy. "The chair is yours, Günther."

Genovesi stood, and got down to business without acknowledging Horvath's comments. "I asked for this meeting for three reasons. First, you're aware that over the past eleven months, our membership has declined by eighteen percent. The reduction in income is troublesome, but even more troublesome is the weakening of leverage caused by our decline. Not that we've publicized it, but none of you is naive enough to suppose the government doesn't know.

"Second, and much more important, we've had no significant effect on the war plans of this government. We need to discuss changes in strategy. New ideas.

"And third—" Finally he looked at Horvath. "Third, we need a change of leadership. Yaro, you are the chairman and cofounder of the Peace Front, and more to the point, you've been our chief theorist and strategist. But when an organization needs to grow—in size, influence and results—and instead shrinks . . . " Genovesi shrugged. "It's time to change leaders."

He scanned the men and women sitting around the long table. No one shook their head, not even Horvath, who hadn't changed expression. "I will not," Genovesi continued, "propose someone for the chairmanship yet. But keep the matter in mind while we discuss this lamentable decline. This failure."

He turned to a stocky, militant-looking woman. "Kuei-Fei, give us your thoughts on the matter."

Kuei-Fei the complainer, Horvath told himself. He'd never gotten along with her. She wanted his chairmanship, and no doubt Moneybags would see that she got it. As for himself—he'd be better off rid of it.

He could taste the bile rising in his gorge.

She got to her feet and began. "The basic strategy has been wrong," she said, "based almost entirely on demonstrations that only a small fraction of the population could get to, take part in. Seen on the telly or holo, they draw attention. And sometimes new members, too many of whom later leave because there is no active role for them. No role most of them could afford."

Or because, Horvath thought, *between the media and the government, they end up convinced by stories of more and more human worlds conquered by murdering aliens.*

It was Paddy Davies who interrupted the woman. "And what would *you* have us do?" he asked. "Mind you, I'm not challenging what you say. I'm asking for examples."

She scowled, not trusting his disclaimer. "An example? We publicized the African Bee Project, and staged demonstrations against it in over forty cities. But few attended except for the demonstrators and the media. Those who watched, watched at home, safe from involvement. Most of them thought the bees were a good idea. Even most mainstream Gaians approved."

Horvath scowled. *What do you expect when a movement goes mainstream?* he thought. But beneath the thought lay a realization—that without the mainstream, their job was impossible. They needed to capture the mainstream, turn it against its government masters.

"But suppose . . ." Kuei-Fei went on, "suppose we'd arranged to have African bees collected? Whole colonies. And had them released in major cities here on Terra? Then people would have looked differently at the bee project."

When she paused, Horvath had his chance. "They'd have looked differently at *us,*" he growled. "We'd have multiplied our enemies tenfold, to no good purpose."

Coloring, she went grimly on. "Our demonstrations over capturing and murdering Wyzhñyñy colonists backfired; another poorly chosen issue. People considered the dead marines heroes, and resented our calling them murderous kidnappers who'd endangered any possible negotiations. And even though the dead Wyzhñyñy won't be seen on Terra for months, word that they're being brought here for display and study has weakened those of our allies who claim the invasion is a hoax. Meanwhile, Paddy's public proposal to negotiate—invite the Wyzhñyñy to settle on worlds not already colonized—was lost sight of in the bombast and furor of the demonstrations."

She turned to Paddy. "The media prefer a show to ideas, but without the show, it's the ideas they'd feature."

"And what would you think," Paddy said, "of printing fliers with our main arguments? Given in simple statements, catchy aphorisms. And passing them out to the demonstrators, with instructions to use them if questioned by the media. They always question demonstrators."

She nodded. Her face remained severe, but when she spoke again, her tone was milder. "That might be useful, if the ideas in the fliers are clearly tied to the matter being protested."

Horvath interrupted again, getting to his feet. His tone was domineering, but short of scornful. "You tell us our basic strategy is wrong, then you veer off into talking about tactics. What *strategy* should we follow?"

She locked eyes with him. "A strategy that grows out of one basic fact: We have nothing to lose, Horvath. Nothing except possibly our lives and liberty. If our goals are worthwhile—if *peace* is worthwhile!—we've got to go all out. Take risks! Considering the time factor, and the direction things are going, BIG risks!" Her words had been growing louder, more combative. Now they slowed, softened. "You've been a fighter all your life, Yaro. You led student rebels against university administrators before you were twenty, and got expelled. Four years later you led blue collar technicians against ISUTA schedule controls, and your people lost jobs. Then you learned to work within the system, learned to compromise without ever giving up. Learned to keep the pressure on, educating, politicking, building inside and outside support, but always pushing. Going for the best compromise possible, and more often than not getting more than anyone thought you could."

Horvath watched her narrowly. *What's your point, woman?* he wondered.

Her eyes had never given way as she spoke. Now she examined the nails on her right hand, fingers curled and palm up, like a man. Her voice became reflective. "You developed an operating style that worked for you." She paused. "And you brought it with you when you started the Front."

Again she met his eyes. "But this is not a labor dispute, or a political dispute, or an environmental or economic dispute." Her voice intensified. "It is a war against war, Yaro, and we need to fight it differently. Find the enemy's greatest weakness, and attack it. Regardless of risk, because the stakes are *so* great, and time is against us."

She looked around the table. "Many voices have urged the government to declare martial law, but Chang and Peixoto have refused. Because they're smarter and more farsighted than those who've pressed them for it. They appreciate that the people *hate* martial law. For more than ninety years our ancestors lived under it! Generations never knew anything else! Meanwhile they watched their technical infrastructure erode, saw their physical-biological environment degraded to a point where it seemed almost beyond recovery. After all these centuries it's still not completely recovered."

She stopped, standing silent, clenched jaw jutting, eyes hard, and let them wait till it seemed someone would surely burst out, demanding she finish. Then she spoke again. "We need to create a campaign that will force them to declare martial law. A campaign of acts by individuals and small groups. Of violence. Of destruction." She paused for emphasis. "And of assassinations. Aimed at the most egregious, or most heinous, or most corrupt government war action we can find. At the same time risking a backlash against us. And there *will* be one."

Then she sat down. No one applauded. No one even said "Hear hear!" For another dozen seconds the room was silent. Finally Genovesi spoke. "Well. That's said. Now we need to look at what issue or issues to use as a focus, a target, for that serious violence. Which is what it will take to bring about martial law."

Guzman suggested accusing the government of planning to use neutron bombs. The nuclear strikes in the Hitler War, the brief and suicidal nuclear religious war of the 21st century, and finally the cynical neutron bombings of the Troubles had made nuclear weapons—nuclear technology of any sort—anathema in the Commonwealth. It was the deadliest accusation possible.

Paddy Davies was adamantly against it. "If we make such a claim," he said, "we'll need plausible evidence. *Plausible* evidence! Considering the seriousness of the charge, the public will demand it. *I'd* demand it. And in all our gathering and winnowing of information and gossip, we've found no whiff of that or any other nuclear plans." Then Horvath stood, guaranteeing it would backfire, and Kuei-Fei pointed out that there wasn't even an infrastructure to provide the means for such a program. When Genovesi called the question, not even Guzman voted for it.

Afterward, discussion became listless, the proposals feeble and unpromising. Then Genovesi suggested that if crimes against Wyzhñyñy didn't seemed to resonate with the public, crimes against humans might.

"We've already plowed that ground," Horvath said.

"Not all of it," Kuei-Fei countered. "We can attack the newly leaked loosening in military bot agreements! Loosening designed to shanghai the wounded out of their bodies!" They were, she felt, nothing short of outrageous: reduced eligibility standards for the wounded. Battlefield proxies authorized to "speak for the unconscious wounded." The use of a stasis drug to prolong the survival of the mortally wounded till they could be bottled. Bottled and thrown back into the shame of battle, instead of peacefully joining with the All-Soul. And as an issue, it came with built-in support: some mainstream media had already criticized these changes as designed to allow abuses.

The discussion wasn't enthusiastic, but before lunch they'd approved the issue without dissent.

After lunch they discussed and voted on a change of leadership: previously, the chairman had worn the policy and planning hats, and the vice chairman the operations hat. That was now changed. Günther Genovesi was elected chief executive officer, which included chairing meetings. Kuei-Fei Wu became planning officer. Jaromir Horvath accepted the post of whip; he would make sure people did what they'd agreed to. And Paddy Davies would be public relations director.

Of the old "big three," only Fritjof Ignatiev continued in his previous post—the Voice of the Front. Its orator.

Chapter 48

New Jerusalem: Encounter In Space

Vice Admiral Carmen Apraxin-DaCosta had been born with more than her share of intellectual and leadership potential, and grew up in a family tradition of service in the fleet. Even as the fleet shrank to become a simulated fleet, existing in the real world as no more than light squadrons sent to hunt pirates. A remote ancestor had been Fleet Admiral Gavril Apraxin, who'd served during the Troubles. Hero of the Lesser Congeries, and postmortem scapegoat of the *President Akiro* disaster.

In childhood she'd pretended—believed?—she was that remote progenitor, reincarnated—the sort of thing children often play at mentally—but she never thought of it anymore. She was Carmen Apraxin-DaCosta, with her own life to live and her own career to fashion. Things she'd done conspicuously well.

On her flagship the *Uinta*, her attention was on something much more urgent. She'd just emerged from her closing jump to the New Jerusalem System, and shipsmind had promptly reported an alien pentagonal battle group—the Wyzhñyñy system defense force—also in the inner fringe, only 189 million miles away. At the same time, shipsmind tagged each enemy spacecraft by its complex electronic signature, each a composite of several system signatures. It wasn't as definitive as fingerprints, but between overhauls it was reliable.

Shipsmind had also registered the Wyzhñyñy's small planetary guard flotilla, parked only 90,000 miles off New Jerusalem. It was large enough to be seriously dangerous to a planetary assault, but far too small to threaten her task force. She'd ignore it till she'd dealt with the more potent system defense force.

Meanwhile she ordered the planetary assault force to generate warpspace and head insystem, getting it out of what she hoped would prove the primary danger zone. Sending one of her three battle groups as escort. She hardly considered moving against the system defense force. Almost surely it wasn't where it seemed to be, or wouldn't be for long. Because shipsmind hadn't registered it in real time; the finite speed of light got in the way. Given the distance, her current read showed it as it had been seventeen minutes earlier. So she would wait.

She was right; ten minutes later the aliens disappeared from her screens. They were nearly seven minutes under way, almost surely headed for either her main force or New Jerusalem, presumably the first.

She presumed correctly. In just six minutes they appeared abruptly in F-space, but not all in one place. Their commander realized he was seriously outnumbered, so his battle group emerged as five subgroups, in five locations around the human perimeter. Each subgroup consisted of a battleship, with a screen of what Apraxin thought of as cruisers and corvettes.

It was a far more favorable tactical situation than Spanish Soong had faced, and Apraxin was ready with more than shields. Six weeks earlier, via savant, Soong had sent Charley Gordon's detailed suggestions and instructions. Afterward she'd spent several days with her AI chief, programing and installing it all in *Uinta*'s shipsmind. That had been followed by weeks of simdrills, as she rode hyperspace toward the New Jerusalem system. They'd emerged in F-space 280 billion miles from New Jerusalem, for an astrogational read and to re-form formations. While there she'd uploaded Charley's "export" system to her fighting ships; it was designed for use without Charley at the helm. Then they'd done simdrills together.

Everyone was enthused with the new battle system, with the admiral less expectant than most. Simulation was simulation. Reality was reality.

Almost at the instant they emerged from warpspace, the Wyzhñyñy launched an all-out attack. But except for selecting their opening gambit, they left their actions entirely to their battlecomps, coordinated by their flagship's battlecomp. Even against Apraxin's superior force, that opening gambit provided an initial advantage. But the twists and turns of battle required better extrapolations and coordination than the Wyzhñyñy flagship provided. Apraxin's Liberation Task Force won decisively. Of the ten battleships she'd committed, seven survived, along with twenty-three of thirty cruisers and thirteen of twenty corvettes.

During the battle, several Wyzhñyñy ships had ducked back into warpspace, and not all had returned to resume action. When it was over, *Uinta*'s shipsmind "accounted" for them all, based on their signatures. When last seen, those not definitely accounted for had already been rated seriously damaged, and were probably no longer functional, lost irretrieveably in hyperspace.

It appeared to be a wipeout, but Apraxin accepted her success guardedly. The purpose of the Wyzhñyñy's system defense force had surely been to protect their colony from incursions. And given that purpose, if she'd been the Wyzhñyñy admiral, she'd have broken off contact as soon as it became apparent her force would otherwise be wiped out. She'd have disappeared into warpspace with what she had left, to begin a guerrilla campaign, harassing and bleeding the human invaders. In fact, that kind of warfare had been her greatest worry—hers and War House's.

That the Wyzhñyñy admiral had pressed his attack till

his force had been destroyed was suspicious. What had she missed? What ace had he hidden under the table? Or did he simply lack flexibility? She'd keep her force alert.

Meanwhile her principal concern had to be a successful planetary assault. Commodore Kereenyaga, in charge of the assault flotilla, had been a classmate of hers at the Academy, and graduated with honors. While Vice Admiral Ver Hoeven, in charge of the escort, was an excellent officer. Each knew his job. She knew next to nothing about the Sikh general in charge of the ground forces, but she had confidence in War House's personnel judgements. He'd at least be competent.

She turned her attention to the real-time view on the bridge's central screen: myriads of stars against bottomless black. *Serenely beautiful and utterly deadly,* she told herself, *a sort of Uma and Kali dichotomy.* But the dangers of the universe tended to be passive: vacuum, stellar temperatures, abrupt gravitational gradients were predictable and avoidable to varying degrees. Sophonts like *Homo sapiens,* using observation and imagination, developed systems of avoidances and protections within which they could live, grow, and explore quite nicely. Most of the time.

But within those safeguards, the powers of imagination and knowledge that provided them could also spring all sorts of deadly surprises on competing or disliked sophonts—of one's own life-form or others.

Jilchûk shu-Tosk was both gosthodar and commanding general on what had been New Jerusalem. Just now he was peering intently at his wall screen, which showed a representation of the local solar system. Orbits were indicated by fine lines. The primary was near the bottom, and several planets were shown at various removes. All out of scale, the separations greatly reduced. "Jiluursôk"—the name the Wyzhñyñy had given New Jerusalem—was centered near the bottom.

"There, my lord," said his aide. Near the top, where the captain's light arrow pointed, a redness pulsed. *It looks like a small red cloud,* thought the gosthodar, *a spray of blood.*

The aide thumbed a projection, and a small window framed the redness, then expanded to occupy the entire screen. The spray of blood became a ragged formation of ships, 127 of them according to the readout. Reducing the separations further showed each ship marked by the icon of a Wyzhñyñy warship class appropriate to its mass.

The gosthodar did not for a moment doubt what he was looking at: an alien task force, outnumbering and presumably outgunning the system defense force. *Humans* they called themselves, according to the grand admiral's chief scholar. It was satisfying to have a name for them.

"When did they emerge?" he asked.

The pointer indicated a digital event time posted unchangingly in a lower corner. "There, sir: 023.61."

The gosthodar looked, then moved his gaze to the familiar real-time read in an upper corner. "Hmm. Less than five minutes ago. Well done, Captain." He pressed a key, and his amplified voice boomed unexpectedly from every speaker in every office, barracks, barn, workplace, vehicle, infirmary, armory . . . on the planet. "An unidentified fleet has arrived in the near fringe," he announced. "It is presumed hostile. All personnel will carry out their Procedure One duties immediately."

In his mind he imagined the groans. Most would think it a needless drill. "Supervisors will ensure full compliance," he continued. "Anyone who fails to properly complete their checklist on schedule will be assigned to a penal platoon." *There,* he thought. *Now they'll take it seriously.*

He'd visited the great limestone caves right after they'd been discovered, and had seen their potential at once. As soon as their refugees had been rooted out, he'd assigned the necessary resources to make them accessible and habitable. "Captain," he said, "see to the transfer of my personal goods. I will stay here till my emergency headquarters has been activated."

The captain saluted sharply. "Yes, General!" he said, and left. *This,* thought Jilchûk, *will be interesting.*

Like all his tribe, he'd never fought in a battle. Now he would command one. The cleansing of this world had been quick and easy, and his warriors had been disappointed. Not that they'd complained; that would be inappropriate. But he knew his genders and their psychology, the warriors especially. Now they'd get their wish.

The gosthodar didn't worry about the enemy war fleet 900 million miles away. That was Admiral Zhokdos's responsibility. His immediate concern was the enemy's bombards that even now must be moving insystem in warpdrive. When they emerged, of course, they'd have to deal with Commodore Xarsku's planetary defense group, but even so, the humans might have a bombard overhead by nightfall. His defense forces needed to be underground or widely dispersed by then.

To prepare for a possible counterinvasion was standard procedure, and he'd begun while his warriors were still mopping up the scattered surviving natives. With the swarm still in the planning stage, he'd requested a full division of warriors. They'd given him a brigade; in times of swarming, warriors of fighting age were always in short supply. If he'd asked for a brigade, they'd have given him two battalions, three at most, and reminded him he'd have some 65,000 colonists of other genders, all of military age, all well-trained for war.

But they were not warriors.

On the other hand, he doubted the humans even had a warrior gender. If they did, there'd have been some sign of them. And while the sophonts here had been enduring and elusive, they'd also been primitive, and definitely not warriors.

Major General Pyong Pak Singh, and his operations aide, Major Etienne Stuart Singh, watched the action from sixteen miles up. The command compartment of the HQC-1—his armored command floater—had split-screen monitors showing the New Jerusalem surface. One window displayed a real view, magnified to show the details he wanted. The other showed a military map, generated by his shipsmind from real-time sensor data, with a window locating the real-view scene on the map.

So far his own people were not involved. His troops— even his aerial units—were still aboard their transports, parked some four hundred miles out. Apraxin's main force had destroyed the Wyzhñyñy system defense force in the near fringe, and one of her battle groups provided cover against a small planetary defense flotilla hiding in warpspace.

The planetary assault force had already begun pounding the Wyzhñyñy on the ground. Pak could see where a "Dragon"—a heavy bombardment ship—had stomped what once had been major Wyzhñyñy installations. Leaving fine rubble and bare ground, churned in places, seared in others. That phase was over now. Two marine "wolf packs"—squadrons of heavy, "Dire Wolf" ground-support floaters—were down there raising hell with Wyzhñyñy armor hiding in the woods, plus whatever Wyzhñyñy aircraft they could find.

He'd locked the real-view scene on one of the wolf packs, following it. It was guided by two newly placed surveillance buoys 360 miles out, protected from ordinary target locks by electronic gnomes, and from ground-launched rockets by riding constantly changing, randomly generated coordinates. (The Wyzhñyñy buoys had been clinkered, to sink, then free-fall as they lost their residual AG.)

He'd seen one Dire Wolf destroyed by ground fire. Radio traffic reported two others downed. The marines' good services came at a price.

His waiting troops, he supposed, were getting restless. Some no doubt eager to experience action, use their hard-earned skills. They *were* young. Others just wanting to get the waiting over with. He was in no hurry to land them. Let the wolf packs finish off all the Wyzhñyñy armor and air units they could find. Apparently the Wyzhñyñy didn't have concealment screens. His own concealment-screen generator had been delivered barely before he'd left Lüneburger's World.

It had occurred to him that military technology was restricted by more than the limits of science. Culture and history entered in—what your philosophies allowed, especially religious philosophies; to what degree creative imagination and innovation were given play; who you'd fought, and when, and under what circumstances.

If there's a technological mismatch down there, he thought, *I hope it's in our favor.* He especially hoped the aliens didn't have nuclear weapons. He was reasonably sure Admiral Apraxin didn't. That even the Commonwealth didn't.

Chapter 49

The Ground War Begins

"We'll let them come to us, and show us what they've got." That's what General Pak was supposed to have said, or words to that effect.

1st Battalion had moved into position in the middle of the night, and the Jerries, with their trenching tools, had dug like badgers. (What Jerries knew as "badgers" weighed upwards of forty pounds and dug out any whelping dens they found, whatever lived there.) In the forest edge, the top two feet of soil was thick with tree roots that had to be cut first, but once through that, Esau and Jael had really made the dirt fly. Made a foxhole to be proud of! Eight feet long and six deep, with the required firing step. Then he'd built a little roof over one end—sections of young trees, overlaid with bark he'd stripped from a large tree, covering it all with dirt from the hole. At the other end were three dirt steps they could use to get out in a hurry. He'd driven long stakes into the bottom, to keep the steps from breaking down.

Now they stood on the firing step, waiting. Behind him,

wilderness stretched all the way to the Ice Sea. He'd seen it on a monitor, while riding down in the shuttle; a view he'd never imagined when he'd lived on this world. In front of him was a broad field, way bigger than any he'd seen before on New Jerusalem. Green with some crop he didn't recognize—something the Wyzhñyñy had brought with them. About knee-high just now.

The Wyzhñyñy didn't farm the way his people had, who needed lots of woods for each farm. In the older settled districts the rule was at least one acre of woods for every three or four acres of field and pasture, depending on fertility. Enough to grow back, each year, all the wood you cut that year. Trees needed for building-logs, and for splitting out planks, roof shakes, and everything else needed. But especially for firewood, to take you through the long winters—a pile the size of the house. And logs and poles for fence rails. His dad had said about 8,000 rails for forty acres, plus replacements.

Esau didn't doubt the number. He'd sawed and chopped and split enough just in his own few years. But the Wyzhñyñy had cleared away the farm woodlots. Didn't need them, apparently. Seemed they liked open ground best.

Ordinarily, Esau preferred to meet trouble at least halfway, but it was a mile or so across to the next good cover. It was hilly over there—maybe sinkhole country—not suited for farming. They'd been told it was where the Wyzhñyñy would attack from. He sure as heck wouldn't want to cross a half mile of open ground with people shooting at him.

What he and his folks were waiting for was a whole new level of trouble. And a chance to learn what they were up against before they went charging into something. Even after Pastor Lüneburger's World, where they'd trained and trained, supposedly doing everything they'd do here. Done it by day and by night, in heat and in cold, hungry, wet, and sleepless.

But two main things were different: on Lüneburger's they hadn't killed anyone, and nobody'd tried to kill them.

Excepting Moses Wheeler, who'd murdered poor Spieler—shot him from behind—and the miserable dog turds back on Terra that'd sabotaged batches of stuff.

Grenade detonators, power slugs . . . and parasails, particularly Isaiah Vernon's. "Sabotage." It'd been a new word to Esau. Sergeant Hawkins said it was supposed to be done with now. Things got inspected in the making, the packing, and the shipping, and the "saboteurs"—the people to blame—got caught and put in jail.

Now the getting ready was over. Somewhere off across that field was a whole army of Wyzhñyñy, wanting to kill all the human beings they could. Including himself. They'd already disappeared the seventy percent of the human beings that chose to stay. They'd included just about all the older folks, and most of the younger with families of children.

And not satisfied with killing everyone, they'd knocked down and burnt every building, their foundation stones cracked and scattered. Or so the army said.

When he'd been a child, Speaker Motley had taught them the Testaments. And one thing he'd stressed was that the Lord God claimed all vengeance for himself alone. *Which doesn't leave much for us,* Esau told himself. But it seemed to him the Lord wouldn't hold it against him for feeling satisfaction whenever his blaster cut down a Wyzhñyñy. And he intended to cut down a lot of them.

Standing beside her husband, Jael Wesley thought not of killing but of dying. Not morbidly or fearfully though. In his *Contemplations on the Testaments,* Elder Hofer had described Heaven as a place of perfect justice and grace and love. In the lowest realm of Heaven—what some called Purgatory—angels helped the newly dead confront the wrongs they'd done, and those done to them. Helped them learn to truly forgive, themselves as well as others, with complete responsibility and love, till they became angels themselves. Then they moved higher, learning from more experienced angels of the splendors of Heaven's higher realms, growing in godliness, readying themselves to join the archangels.

She'd never been able to envision what it would be like, but it seemed fitting, and she had no doubt it was true. Some did doubt. She'd had it in strictest confidence from a girlhood friend who'd doubted. Miriam had stayed behind during the evacuation, and was almost surely long-since murdered. Doubt had been a burden to Miriam, but Jael was sure her friend was in Heaven. Knew it without question. Miriam had always treated people with love, except sometimes her wretched brother, who bedemoned her whenever the notion took him. He'd be dead now too, unless he left in one of the evacuation ships.

It'll be interesting to die, Jael thought. But she was in no hurry. A person was born to live their life as best they could. Live it through, and die when it came time. She smiled. Her time was not yet. She and Esau were supposed to have children, bring them up in love, send them on their way with joy, and see her grandchildren through their childhood. Being a man, Esau had the advantage there. On New Jerusalem, pregnancy and childbirth taxed a woman sorely, and not many lived to see their grandchildren grow up. She would though; loving and spoiling them. She felt sure of it.

Isaiah Vernon waited in the forest shade. The day was warm, and the breeze that rustled the leaves overhead didn't visit down among the trunks. Sitting in the shade meant his cooling system didn't have to work hard.

They'd arrived near the end of the season known as "greening," when the new growth was burgeoning, and thunder showers were most frequent. *We're lucky the weather was good when the marine squadrons were doing their work,* he told himself. The rumor was, today would be the day the Wyzhñyñy would attack. Then he'd learn what war was really like, and whether they—organics, bots, the army—were as good as they needed to be.

Probably more than anyone in the division, it seemed to him, he had a perspective on being killed. Been tested, proved, and come through cleanly, to be reprieved almost after the fact.

He looked back to their first months in training. The prospect of killing had begun troubling him sorely. He'd known the stories of Joshua, David, Judas Maccabaeus and others who'd won victories for the Lord. Fighting, killing, being killed. Without them, the worship of Jehovah probably would have died out, and the Hebrews as a people might easily have disappeared, ceased to exist. Then there'd have been no Jesus. But at least *some* of those Hebrew heroes had been harsh ruthless men, lacking the love that Jesus came to teach. Strange men to serve the Lord. And what of the sixth commandment? "Thou shalt not kill!"

Some said that didn't apply to the Wyzhñyñy; that they had no souls. Isaiah didn't believe that for a minute. Except for the number of limbs, they were too much like human beings. Like the Assyrians and Romans—human beings who didn't know Jesus.

He could have asked his questions of Speaker Spieler, but it had seemed to him the speaker would only tell him what he already knew, resolving nothing.

One hazy autumn evening at Camp Stenders, he'd taken his misgivings to Sergeant Hawkins, who'd told them to let him know if they had problems. The Sikh would have a non-Christian perspective, but Isaiah couldn't doubt his Christian compassion. And it seemed to him that what Hawkins had to say might fit with the teaching of the Lamb of God.

He could remember that evening clearly and in detail. It wasn't so far back, if you didn't count the time in stasis on the way to New Jerusalem, but it seemed longer than it was. That was before his body'd been killed—before he'd wakened in a bot body. There'd been a knee-high railing protecting the little patch of lawn in front of the orderly room. He and Sergeant Hawkins had sat down on it in the thickening dusk, and he'd described his problem.

After he'd finished, he'd waited. Sergeant Hawkins had sat gazing northwestward, where the dark gray sky was smudged with the last dusky red of sunset. Had sat there for perhaps a minute without talking. When finally he spoke, it was quietly. "Yeah, I can see how that might trouble you. Try this out for fit. The human species has all kinds of people, right?"

"Yessir."

"Some of them are pretty good people, but don't have much tolerance for those who openly disagree with them. They might be good friends—even fiercely loyal friends—but they're intolerant. Do you know people like that?"

Isaiah had smiled. "It sounds like my older brother.

Father was at wit's end sometimes, when Peter got in fights. Started fights! All in the service of what he thought of as right. Peter must have averaged a fight a week. I don't think Father had ever been in a fight in his life."

He hadn't been in one himself, he realized. Not even close. He'd never thought about that before.

"So your father was more—Christlike than your brother?"

Isaiah chuckled ruefully. "I'd say so. Yes."

"So if the Lord was going to choose one of them to fight a battle . . . "

"But the Lord doesn't *need* someone to fight for him! He's God! He can do whatever he pleases." Even as he said it though, Isaiah realized how many Bible stories—Old Testament stories—told of God sending men to fight his battles.

"True, as far as it goes," Hawkins replied. "But I'm thirty-one years old, and I haven't seen much evidence of God taking direct personal action in human conflicts. Looking back at history, I can name a number of powerful rulers—let alone other people—who did terrible things over many years. In the twentieth century alone there were two rulers each of whom executed millions of people, or starved them to death. And caused the deaths of millions more in what came to be called the Hitler War. If God was inclined to act personally, surely he'd have stopped them. Sent down a bolt of lightning to fry them, or just not let them choose to do such things.

"Instead, one of them, named Hitler, decided he wanted to conquer the other one, named Stalin. So he invaded Stalin's country, the biggest country on Terra. And Stalin gradually wore him down. It was a worldwide war, with most nations involved on one side or the other, but Hitler couldn't have been stopped if it hadn't been for Stalin, who was probably as evil as he was."

Hawkins paused, pursing his lips thoughtfully. It seemed to Isaiah his sergeant wasn't really sorting his thoughts. More like he was figuring how to put them.

"So I don't think God acts directly," the sergeant said at last. "I think he lets humans of good will work things out the best they can. At least that's what Gopal Singh taught. In the case of Hitler and Stalin, there were two

other powerful rulers, named Churchill and Roosevelt, who
helped Stalin when he most needed it. Even though they
both knew and feared Stalin, too. But stopping Hitler
seemed more urgent."

The names had meant nothing to Isaiah. Terran history
hadn't been taught on New Jerusalem, only some of the
lessons learned from it. He wondered if Elder Hofer had
learned some of them from the Hitler War. He must have
known about it; he'd lived back in the 21st and 22nd
centuries. Back before ever his people emigrated.

Sergeant Hawkins had grinned at him then. "I got carried away talking," he said. "What was your question again?"

"Uh . . . about killing. It feels like a sin to me, war or
not, and I'm supposed to do a lot of it when we get back
to New Jerusalem." He'd paused. "And I'm not sure I can
do it."

"Umm. As a child, did you ever do anything wrong?"

"Yes I did, but mostly in my mind. I got angry more
often than anyone suspected. A time or two I even cursed.
Within the privacy of my mind, I even did acts of violence
and lust. But never in physical action, except the sin of
Onan, and even in my mind probably not as much as lots
of folks. I believe I was born with a softness of spirit."

Again the sergeant had chuckled. "In Sikh schools we're
taught that Jesus of Nazareth said 'You must be born again'
to see the kingdom of God. In the Gopal Singh Dispensation, we believe that people really are born again. Again
and again, mostly not recalling our earlier lives. Born again
to live in all kinds of circumstances, good and bad. Male
and female. Sometimes doing really cruel things, and gradually developing a sense of responsibility for them. Until in
time we learn not to do them anymore. Except in extreme
situations, like some wars." He grinned at Isaiah. "It's my
impression that you're an old experienced soul, who just
now happens to be wearing a young body."

Isaiah's thoughts returned to the now, and he looked
down at his new body. His bot body: large, hard, and
fearfully strong. If he were inclined to violence, it would
be a terrible body. But maybe violence *was* all right, in
the service of God.

That wasn't what Sergeant Hawkins had been leading

up to though, because he'd gone on speaking. "There are souls of all ages," he'd said. "All a part of the One, some call it the Tao, others the All-Soul. You say God. And mostly, I suspect—mostly it's younger souls who take up the sword, for good or bad. During the Hitler War, I suspect the generals on both sides were mostly souls who'd lived enough lives to feel sure of themselves, but not enough to be seriously troubled by killing. Bad men and good men, but none of them Christlike."

Isaiah had frowned thoughtfully. "Jesus got mad once," he said. "Violent. He shouted at the money changers in the temple, tipped their tables over and ran them out."

"Well then," the sergeant had said, "you've answered your question yourself, haven't you?"

He'd nodded, but not very confidently. It had seemed—still seemed—there was more to it than that. "I guess I pretty much have," he'd answered.

Hawkins had laughed, a friendly, sympathetic sound. "We're human beings. Strictly speaking, there's not too much we *can* be entirely sure of. Not even those of us who feel absolutely sure. But the One doesn't hate us or punish us for making mistakes. We do what seems right to us, make our mistakes as many times as necessary, and learn from them."

The sergeant had gotten up then. "I guess we've looked at your question about as well as we can right now," he'd said. "Sooner or later we'll get it solved, maybe on New Jerusalem, or maybe between lives."

They'd separated then, Isaiah going to the hut. He'd told Sergeant Hawkins things he couldn't have dreamed of telling anyone before. When he'd been eleven New Jerusalem years old, his father had taken him aside and spoke to him about the sin of Onan, and told him that in God's eyes it was a very small transgression, when done privately. As if to set his mind at ease. But he'd never expected to tell anyone about it; surely not till he had a son of his own.

Maybe the sergeant didn't know what the sin of Onan was; probably he didn't. But even if he did, it had seemed to Isaiah the sergeant wouldn't think ill of him for it.

He remained a little uncomfortable with what his sergeant had said about living a whole string of lives though.

It seemed—heretical. But Jesus *had* said, "You must be born again." It seemed there was more than one way of taking that. And in a way, it kind of fitted with some of the things Elder Hofer had taught. Though he didn't think Elder Hofer would much like the idea.

During the months since then, it seemed to Isaiah that somehow or other that conversation had defanged the issue of killing Wyzhñyñy, because it no longer really troubled him. He still wondered now and then—maybe feeling a little discomfort—but it didn't *plague* him now.

A sudden booming snagged his attention. Artillery fire. The surveillance buoys had reported that the Wyzhñyñy had quite a bit of artillery left, here and there. Probably hidden from the Dragons. The army didn't much use artillery, unless you counted field mortars and tanks. Mostly it depended on aerial attack to deliver destruction behind hills and the like. He wondered if War House was going to regret that.

Then his lieutenant's voice spoke in his sensorium. "Load up, men. Time to get your feet wet."

To Isaiah, the command produced a sensation like he'd felt when they'd loaded on the floater for their first parachute jump: a sinking feeling in the belly, even though he didn't have a belly any longer. As his long metallic legs strode up the ramp of an APF, he heard the artillery's followup sound: the crashing of shells much nearer than the guns that fired them.

Lord God, he prayed silently, *let me do what is right in your eyes.*

When the booming reached Esau Wesley, he knew what to expect. Actually he knew and he didn't. Live fire exercises, with the rush of rounds passing overhead, and buried explosives simulating shell bursts, had given them a notion of it, but they weren't the same thing. He realized that before the first rounds struck. Stepping down from the firing step, he crouched in the bottom of the foxhole, Jael beside him. *This is it!* he thought. *The games are over!* The thunder of howitzers told him—that and Jael's wide eyes, and Captain Mulvaney's calm voice in his ears.

Then the shells arrived, the noise indescribable. Many exploded in the treetops. Wood and shell fragments whirred and whistled, thudded and slapped. Dirt flew, hissing. The couple ducked under their little roof. The ground shook, and now Esau was glad for all the tough woody roots; they helped keep their foxhole from caving in on them. Jael's eyes were no longer wide. They squinted, perhaps against flying dirt, perhaps in response to the noise, the violence.

He read her lips. "Blessed Jesus," she murmured, then said nothing more. The shells kept arriving, roaring. After the first salvo, they arrived more irregularly. Along the line, the sound was a steady roar, but the nearer explosions were sometimes overlapping, sometimes single. Esau spit dirt. Heard a scream. A tree crashed down. "Medic!" someone cried. Captain Mulvaney's voice spoke in his ear, in his skull: "Listen up, B Company. They're sending out armor—tanks and APCs. Stay down, ready on my command. Blastermen, fix bayonets."

As squad leader, Esau was no longer its slammerman. He slipped his bayonet over the studs of his blaster barrel and clamped it firmly. Then, unable to resist, he stepped out and popped a peek over the berm. What he saw riveted his attention. The tanks, those still coming, were already halfway across, riding their AG cushions, their antipersonnel slammer pulses invisible in the sunlight. Other tanks had stopped, more or less askew. He saw one take a heavy trasher pulse and hit the ground skidding, plowing dirt. No one emerged from it. Close behind came the APCs. He became aware of Jael tugging at him, and ducked down again, staring at her. "Good lord!" he said. "What a sight!"

She did not rise up to see, simply looked anxious. Captain Mulvaney's voice spoke in their ears again. "B Company, on your firing steps!" Esau stepped onto the firing step again, hardly able to restrain himself, wishing he still carried a slammer instead of just a blaster. The line of tanks, much thinned, was about a hundred yards short of the forest. An angled file of killer craft swept across the field, armored belly turrets laying trasher fire on the tanks. Which kept coming, those that could.

Another file of aircraft followed. Not many tanks were left, and a number of APCs sat smoking.

"B Company, fire!" Mulvaney almost shouted it, excitement in his voice. "Give 'em hell! Wipe 'em out!"

Esau rested his blaster on the berm and sought targets. The artillery had stopped, but Wyzhñyñy tanks continued to pump heavy trasher bolts into the forest. Wood still flew; branches and treetops still crashed down. The APCs had also thinned, and as if on signal, stopped sixty to eighty yards away. Wyzhñyñy poured from them—real Wyzhñyñy! Others, from crippled APCs, were already coming on foot, running at speeds a human couldn't hope to match, firing their blasters with a sweeping motion from what might be thought of as their waists. Esau had set his for semiautomatic. He fired aimed fire, almost every shot a mortal hit. When he paused to insert a fresh power slug, he saw Jael firing aimed fire too. She'd become skilled with the blaster—not as good as he was, but good.

All along the line, Wyzhñyñy kept coming. A running Wyzhñyñy launched himself to clear the Wesleys' foxhole, his blaster muzzle swinging toward them. It had no bayonet. Esau squeezed off a bolt that tore the Wyzhñyñy open, spraying them with fluids and tissue. The alien landed behind them in a heap. Another lay on its belly—blood flowed from its neck, red blood!—its torso upright, swinging its blaster toward them. Too high; Esau fired back as pulses passed barely overhead.

They kept coming, coming. Another flight of friendly aircraft swept the field, and another, and another, killing, but the attackers did not pause. Esau half heard fighting behind him. Those who'd broken through had been engaged by reserves.

"Trasher crews! Trasher crews!" This in a voice new to Esau. "Our own armor is moving in from the north, with camouflage fields and red pennants. Don't shoot the good guys! More Wyzhñyñy armor is coming, all of it tan."

That was nothing Esau needed to worry about. He kept firing, glad he'd started with a full bandoleer of power slugs. This wasn't likely to stop for a while.

❖   ❖   ❖

The bot APF had settled through a hole in the canopy about three hundred yards back from the forest edge, and unloaded its five-bot squad. They were somewhat back from where the shells were landing, except for the occasional long round. Their built-in radios told them the first wave of Wyzhñyñy was halfway across the field. The bots didn't immediately run to engage them. No foxholes waited to shelter them—bot tactics centered on high mobility—and they were too few to waste.

Instead they waited till the barrage stopped, then started toward the fighting at a lope. Their camouflage fields hid them better than any fabric could. Again they paused, near the end of 1st Battalion's battle line, but still back within the woods. The line was anchored by a battery of antiarmor trashers, themselves well armored. They'd waited to fire till the barrage lifted, to avoid the special attention they'd otherwise have drawn. Now they were firing trasher pulses at Wyzhñyñy tanks and APCs.

The bots stayed where they were. Sergeant Ali Al-Daiyeen was in touch with the battery CO, and with Division's G-2B, which monitored constantly the input from the surveillance buoys. The order to move would come from them.

And come it did. The battery had been flanked, with Wyzhñyñy in the woods behind it. Now the bots moved, running smoothly. A dozen or more Wyzhñyñy had sheltered behind standing and fallen trees, and were shooting at the battery, suppressing protective fire from its dug-in blastermen. Another twenty or more had begun moving along behind the Jerrie defense line, attacking foxholes with blasters and grenades.

"We'll handle them," Al-Daiyeen radioed back. "Tell your people to keep firing. We'll be fine." Then, to his squad, "Podelsky, you and I'll take the skirmish line. Vernon, you three take out the Wyz moving west. Go!"

Isaiah and his two loped off, eyes seeking. Seconds later they saw the other Wyzhñyñy, kneeling behind trees, firing at the foxholes, forcing their occupants to keep their heads down while grenadiers moved in, crawling on their bellies like dogs.

"Get 'em!" Isaiah said. They moved in, firing both

clamp-ons: the right-arm blaster, and the left-arm, short-barreled slammer. The Wyzhñyñy who survived that first burst of fire responded sharply and violently. Isaiah felt pulses strike his armored body, and ignored them, striding along the line, pumping short bursts, unaimed but accurate. Shortly the Wyzhñyñy were all dead or dying.

"Anyone damaged?" he called. None were. "Ali," he said, "we're done here. Where next?"

"Back where we were before. I'll let G-3 know we're available."

Running to rendezvous, Isaiah felt a sense of accomplishment. He'd killed half a dozen at least, and it felt right.

General Pak's HQC-1 had lifted to thirty miles. He'd asked Tech how high he'd need to be to keep from being spotted by Wyzhñyñy on the ground. Assuming their fixed flak installations had been taken out by the Dragons. Fifteen miles ought to do it, Tech had answered, depending on how good Wyzhñyñy field equipment was, and how much they had on their minds. It turned out that fifteen miles wasn't enough, but given the power of his viewing equipment, Pak could see well enough from thirty.

Watching had taught him a lot. The Wyzhñyñy had impressed him with their relentlessness in the teeth of heavy fire, heavy casualties. The amount of armor they'd used also surprised him. He hadn't thought so much of it would escape the Dragons and wolf packs.

In the ground fighting, his own air squadrons, armor, and antiarmor batteries, had reduced it seriously, though at greater cost than he liked to see. But War House had established the opening strategy: draw the Wyzhñyñy into battle—the Wyzhñyñy had taken care of that for them—and destroy their capacity to make an air and armor war of it. Turn the campaign into an infantry war, and keep War House informed in detail.

The Wyzhñyñy had been onworld long enough to make major inroads in the supplies they'd brought with them. Reports from Tagus had indicated they'd begun growing crops there almost at once. That fitted his observations here. They were concentrating on self-sufficiency.

One of the Dragons had destroyed two Wyzhñyñy cargo ships parked above a range of forested hills, lightering down cargo. Thick smoke had risen from the wreckage, as if they'd held something like grain and it was burning. Where were their cargos being stashed? He'd seen no buildings. Caves, perhaps? He'd look into that. And surely there'd been more than two cargo ships. Perhaps the others were hiding in warpspace.

How many supplies had been stored in the buildings the Dragons had destroyed? Hopefully the Wyzhñyñy were in poor shape to fight a long ground war. At any rate they were a lot of parsecs away from their supply source, the Armada, presumably with no way to communicate with it. As for his own supply ships—hopefully they were safe.

If not . . . He'd handle his assignments, and hope that others handled theirs. But there were no promises.

It seemed to Esau he was a different person than he'd been when he and Jael had finished their foxhole that morning. Since then they'd fought off four attacks, each one lasting what seemed like hours. The last had come at dusk, and it was different from the earlier attacks. This time the Wyzhñyñy hadn't used tanks and APCs. It was as if they'd run out. But they obviously had plenty of howitzers. Shells had come raining down on the forest's mangled edge, tons and tons of them, and everyone stayed hunkered down. Captain Mulvaney would tell them what was happening.

Mulvaney got updates from his platoon officers, and from Battalion. Battalion was in constant touch with HQC-1's all-seeing, automated command surveillance system. Which had separate channels to all regimental, battalion, and wing commands on the ground.

Esau knew none of that. He knew only what Captain Mulvaney said in his ear. Wyzhñyñy infantry were coming, lots of them, on foot. No tanks, no APCs, just troops at a trot. "Six hundred yards . . . " Mulvaney had said. "Five hundred . . . Four hundred . . . Their artillery's quit firing! Be ready!" The roar of shells arriving cut off just after Mulvaney said two hundred. Then Esau and Jael stepped onto the firing step, spare power slugs held in their teeth for quick reloading. He barely had time to think, *My God!*

The Wyzhñyñy were coming at a hard run, a solid rank of
them, unthinned by aerial attack. Neither Wesley used
aimed fire now, just shifted their shoulders from side to
side, pouring out deadly streams of pulsed energy in the
dusk.

The Wyzhñyñy had fallen like wheat before a scythe.
But behind that first wave was another, and even with spare
power slugs in their teeth, it took a moment to seat one.

The Wyzhñyñy broke through, really broke through,
because even having had replacements, quite a few foxholes were down to one man, or none at all. There were
enemies on all sides, and 1st Battalion clambered out of
their holes to fight. When a power slug burned out, they
fought with bayonets. But not *that* many Wyzhñyñy got
through, and reserves had come up. Then some of the
oncoming Wyzhñyñy turned and ran, and in minutes only
humans were left.

Then the reserve battalion took over the foxholes. 1st
Battalion pulled back and mustered, then marched an hour
northward through the forest, to where their sleeping bags
and shelter tents had been stacked. The company cooks
had a hot meal ready. The survivors ate, set up their shelter
tents, crawled exhausted into their sacks and went to sleep.

Esau stayed awake long enough to wonder how many
in B Company had died and how many were wounded. 2nd
Platoon hadn't come off too badly, and he'd lost only three
of ten in his squad.

Only! Give us another couple days like this, he told
himself, *and there won't be any 1st Battalion.*

He looked at Jael, curled up already asleep. She always
looked so pretty, sleeping—pretty face, sweet lips—but in
the dark he could only remember them.

For the first time since childhood Esau Wesley prayed
outside of church. "Oh, blessed Lord," he murmured, "don't
let her get killed. If it's got to be one of us, take me. She's
twice as good a person as I am, and if I lose her, I'm afraid
I won't be worth shit."

Then he slept.

and disinclined to keep himself fit. At the top, he walked along the crest till he came to a promontory overlooking the countryside. A place where he could sit beneath the sky while the forest behind him kept the sun off his back. There his orderly inflated the gosthodar's field mattress—high-ranking persons were not expected to sit or lie on the hard ground—and arranged it in the shade. Then watched dutifully while his ruler adjusted it slightly.

"Can I be of further service, your lordship?" he asked.

"No, Ethkars. Depart. I'll call if I need you."

Ethkars left, picking his joyless way down through the forest, paying no heed to the esthetics around him. He had an infant in the nursery, and while parents were less given to worry than the nanny gender, it was his firstborn. And given the gravity on this world, the pregnancy had been difficult. He was glad his mate would carry the next one. Meanwhile the tribe was isolated on this world, and yesterday's slaughter had depressed morale.

On his promontory, Jilchûk gazed across a landscape of broad fields—croplands and domesticated pastures. Still surrounded by forest, but his people were making progress. Or had been before the enemy bombards visited.

Until his people had applied their civilizing touch, the settled districts had consisted of small fields and primitive dwellings, mingled with woodlands. What kind of history, what kind of culture must these humans have had to prefer such an arrangement? Clearly they were socially fragmented. Until the day before, he would not have expected such unity of action from them in battle, nor such hard-bitten dedication. Apparently this *was* a warrior gender he faced. His previous evaluation had been in error.

It was not a painful conclusion. Jilchûk's stoic, practical personality was well-suited to military command. And mistakes were easily made when dealing with unfamiliar life-forms. The point was not to repeat them. It had been an error—natural but an error—to depend so heavily on his warrior brigade. The first attack should have told him that. But it had so nearly succeeded! Surely the next charge . . .

Until he'd lost more than half his warriors: killed, missing, and disabled.

I should have used my reserves in the first attacks—let the humans expend their air and armor on them—and then sent my warriors. The humans could never have withstood them then. We'd have chewed them up. Like most two-leggers, the humans had mobility problems. Break them—make them run—and they were doomed. They simply couldn't run fast enough.

Fortunately, they too had lost more of their aircraft and armor than they could afford. They'd fought off that last attack with infantry. *Best not to take too much for granted though,* he told himself. *They had plenty of air strength earlier. It's a good thing you moved most of your armor into caves before their bombards arrived.*

In the second phase, the humans' heavy ground-support fighters had almost surely been aerospace craft. While those used later appeared to have been simply aircraft. Had the human space force pulled out already, leaving their ground forces on their own? It seemed unlikely, but . . . He thumbed the mike on his harness. Intelligence would know if the space force was still in the system.

Vice Admiral Carmen Apraxin-DaCosta didn't have a hilltop, nor at the moment the luxury of solitude. She sat on a chair beside her bottled savant, Melody Boo'tsa, who lay in trance. According to the records, Melody was fifteen years old, with a mental age of four. Just now she was in receiving mode, channeling the deputy chief of space operations, Admiral Kaidu Ghazan. Her vocator provided an excellent copy of Ghazan's strong baritone, his delivery, and the modest accent Apraxin had always supposed came from a childhood in a traditional community.

"Carmen," he was saying, "I appreciate your concern. But you need to leave the Jerrie system no later than Terran 31.08.15, at 2400 hours. That gives you approximately twenty-nine hours. You need to rendezvous with Soong in the fringe of Dinébikeyah at system coordinates 2700/1700/00, no later than Terran 31.11.28. He'll need you."

Apraxin considered. "The Wyzhñyñy planetary defense

flotilla here still hasn't poked its head out of warpspace to show us what it has in the way of firepower. And it may include remnants of the system defense force. I'd like to leave Ver Hoeven's battle group, just in case."

"What evidence do you have that it's actually needed there? That it would be more than just a source of comfort?" Before she could respond, he went on. "Judging from your brief observations of their original planetary guard force, it looks as if Kereenyaga can handle it without Ver Hoeven's help. So. How many functional remnants of their system defense force do you think might show up?"

She hesitated. "The maximum and the minimum," he added.

"The maximum would be all five of them: two cruisers and three corvettes. The minimum would be none, zero."

It took him four seconds to respond. "You may leave three cruisers and four corvettes of Admiral Ver Hoeven's group."

"Thank you, sir." She pushed on quickly. "What about the marine mother ship? In case the Jerries on the ground need the squadrons. They're short squadrons now, and anyway they'd be of no use to Soong."

This time there was a long pause. When finally Ghazan spoke again, he sounded like someone who'd about reached his limit. "Admiral," he said, "I have checked with Marshal Kulikov. He says you can leave the mother ship on one condition: her squadrons are to be used only if the troops on the ground are faced with extermination. The Jerries' primary purpose is to find out for us how the Wyzhñyñy fight on the ground: weapons, tactics, psychology . . . all of it. And the force size Pak was given is the baseline in the study. It's not to be fooled with. If he scrubs the Wyzhñyñy, great. The government may even name a Day for him. But . . . "

"But his people are expendable," Apraxin said matter-of-factly. "I understand."

Ghazan didn't reply immediately. *You needn't have put it so bluntly,* she chided herself. Finally he spoke. "That's right, Carmen. That's how it is. That's how it will be at Shakti, too. And at Terra, if it comes to that. Resources can't be wasted. Invested but not wasted."

*Old Hard Head Kaidu. But he called you Carmen to
soften the message.* "Right, Admiral," she said. "I understand."

"Fine. Anything else, Admiral?"

"No, sir. I'll be at Dinébikeyah on time and ready."

"Very well. And I repeat—everyone here is pleased with
your results. Yours and Pak's both. Ghazan out."

"Apraxin out."

She nodded at the savant's attendant, then watched
while the young woman spoke the brief formula that
brought the savant out of her trance. A matted photo,
presumably of Melody Boo'tsa, had been neatly taped to
her module. The eyes were pink, the broad white face
faintly so. *An albino,* Apraxin thought. Albinism had
become avoidable, and extremely rare. Now Melody
Boo'tsa no longer had a face of any color. Just a bottled
CNS, a soul, and a unique sort of mind. With the unknown
energies, and access to strange dimensions, that enabled
two human beings to communicate across scores of parsecs, instantaneously.

"Thank you, Melody," she said quietly, then to the
savant's attendant, "and thank you, Sofi. You may not fully
appreciate it, but without teams like you two, humankind
would have no hope in this war. None at all."

She paused. "I have a personal question for you. I
presume your briefing on Melody was much more thorough than my own, and there's something in her file that
sparked my curiosity. Either she has a long compound
middle name, or several middle names. Can you clarify that
for me?"

Even as she asked, it seemed to her a pointless question.

"Yes, Admiral, I do know. I'm her cousin."

The comment startled Apraxin. Sofi's complexion was a
rich brown. *Hmh. And why not? Any racial stock can have
albinos.*

Sofi had paused, as if waiting for Apraxin's attention
again. When she had it, she continued. "She was named
Melody when she was born. But our community is quite
traditional. It retains many of the old customs, including
giving another name later on. One that tells something
about the person."

Sofi's gaze had slid aside and downward. After a moment though, it met the admiral's again, briefly.

"It is not customary to tell it outside the community, but I will tell you. You may find it—significant to our needs."

Apraxin's eyebrows rose slightly.

"Melody didn't speak sentences until she was four. Some of her first clear sentences were about things that hadn't happened yet. But later they would. Most of the family thought they were coincidences, but her aunt—my mother—and also her father, thought they were prophecies. Because when she said them, she spoke better than usual. So Melody was given another name: *Naan' voh ti' ta ka.* Because she has knowledge of the future.

"It is how she came to be here. She has an uncle who teaches mineralogy at the University of Northern Arizona, and he told the chairman of the parapsychology faculty about her. So she was sent there for study, and I was sent to be with her. To take care of her. And then the war started."

Apraxin exhaled through pursed lips, and nodded slowly. "I *am* glad you told me, Sofi. If you ask her questions about the future, does she tell you things?"

"I have tried a few times. She never answered. When she predicted in the past, it was always—whatever it was. Not something asked about."

The admiral frowned thoughtfully. "Will you work on it with her, Sofi?"

"Yes, Admiral. You know, sir, most people think of Melody as something empty, with very little mind. But she is—in there, sir. She listens. Hears. She hears what we hear, and she hears things we don't hear. I don't think of her as mentally deficient. I think of her as *Naan' voh ti' ta ka.*"

The admiral stepped back. "Thank you, Sofi. This could be quite important." She started to turn away.

"Admiral?"

"Yes?"

"You said that teams like Melody and myself are all that give humankind hope in this war. But without people like you, there could be no hope at all. It is the people like yourself—the fighting people—who are primary in this time."

❖   ❖   ❖

When Apraxin left the savant's suite, she headed for the wardroom, and a snack. While thinking about Melody's supposed talent for predictions, and whether they grew out of something like Charley Gordon's vectors.

She'd wait a bit, she decided, let Melody rest, then visit her again. Meanwhile saying nothing about it to War House. Let Sofi work with her, and define the possibilities.

Smoke from Kunming's many fires hung in the air. Stinking smoke, of half-burned, retardant-soaked fabrics, charred wood, melted synthetics. And perhaps burned bodies, though that could have been the product of their poisoned moods.

An hour earlier, when it was still dark, fires could still be seen from the prime minister's balcony. Chang and Peixoto had watched together. They'd been watching, on the telly or from the balcony, since the previous day, when the first fires were reported. Had seen them grow, while the over-extended fire department did its best. Sirens had ululated in every part of the city. There had even been fires within the government complex—one in the Palace of Worlds itself—despite the surrounding force shield.

The word was, most had been set in warehouses and retail stores, at least some by small teams of arsonists protected by gunmen, all masked.

Just now the two leaders were closer to arguing than they'd ever been. "We have no choice!" Chang said. "Tirades on the talk channels, demonstrations in the squares, slander and libel of ourselves and others—those could be borne. But arson and murder? They have gone too far now! Martial law is the only answer we have, for the short term!"

Peixoto's bleak eyes scanned the half of the city visible from his balcony. He thought what such a campaign of destruction could have done a thousand years earlier, when so much more was flammable. When every vehicle carried within itself a large quantity of explosively flammable liquid.

And at last report, what had happened here had happened in 137 other cities, to some degree or other. And worse, 183 assassinations and a number of assaults had been reported, mostly on military personnel.

A leak had triggered it, and when he discovered who . . . Peixoto shook his head. *You'd have released it yourself, if the victory had been greater. Big enough to blunt the Wyzhñyñy advance.*

He'd never imagined the Peace Front would do something like this. What was left of the Peace Front. Probably not more than one percent of the population remained members. But of Kunming's 2.7 million, that came to 27,000. Of which perhaps a thousand had been actively involved in this night of shame.

He looked down at the much shorter president. He'd almost forgotten Chang's demand. Now he shook his head again. "I cannot agree to it. Not yet."

He sensed the almost voiced response: Then I will resign. Unvoiced because Chang Lung-Chi would never abandon him in a dilemma. Never. Instead what the president said was, "When, then?"

"I'm not sure, good friend. But it's what their council wants us to do. We both know that. And we both know why."

A rumor passed through the city later that morning: a counterdemonstration would be held that evening at Wellesley Square, to defend humanity's right to defend itself. By noon the story was on the newscasts, the talk shows; and everywhere in the city you could *feel* the energy growing, swelling.

It shook the Peace Front's ruling council. They'd expected a public backlash, but this . . . ? Paddy Davies made a call, and Günther Genovesi's luxurious limo picked them up from the roof of their building.

By nightfall, demonstrators were packed into Wellesley Square and the streets feeding into it, far outnumbering anything the Peace Front had mustered. Among them, carrying a child on his shoulders, was a very tall, strongly built man with the lantern jaw and strong cheekbones common among the Goloks of Tibet. Carrying the child had not been entirely a good idea. The boy's short legs had rubbed off some of the Golok brownness from the man's jaw and ears. But it was night, a man carrying a child was surely benign, and as long as the child remained on his shoulders, the break in his camouflage was unlikely to be noticed. Besides, the crowd's attention was on the top of Martyr's Hill, where a large bonfire lit the night. It would damage the concrete slab on top, but that could be repaired.

There was no orator, nor any martyr. Instead, at the brow of the hill stood a cheerleader, capering like a court jester. It was no longer possible to hear him, even with his hand-held bullhorn. Once he'd begun shouting, the crowd—more than half a million—had picked up his chant and drowned him out: "MAR-TIAL LAW! MAR-TIAL LAW! MAR-TIAL LAW!"

A mile away, Foster Peixoto stood on his balcony, watching and listening. From so far away it was simply an immense roar, but he knew the words. A minute earlier, before the crowd joined in, he'd been watching on the telly, on a closed police channel, and had heard the chant begin.

Rumor and security reports had prepared the president and himself, and they'd perceived both opportunity and danger. But now, facing the reality alone, Peixoto feared, truly feared, a mob psychosis. He'd never imagined this volcanic potential in the people. What might happen next? An explosion of violence? A stampede, killing scores? Hundreds . . . ? Lynchings? The beating to death of anyone pointed out as a Fronter, whether accurately or not? And however moderate?

As usual, the response was to be Chang's. A response prepared late and hurriedly, and based on faulty assumptions. They'd expected self-appointed spokesmen to make speeches or pep talks, not this primal chant. *Chang will have to rethink his speech as he gives it,* Peixoto told himself. Otherwise the crowd might start to move, to act. Fists clenched, he gestured. "Now!" He spoke his urgency aloud. "Now!"

The Golok wasn't aware he'd joined in the chant. Also he'd forgotten the child on his shoulders. His body knew it was there, and subliminally allowed for its presence, but his conscious awareness had been swallowed by the flames, the man cavorting so near them, the crowd consciousness, and above all, "MAR-TIAL LAW! MAR-TIAL LAW! MAR-TIAL LAW!"

The spell had no power of its own. It was a manifestation of the half million human beings in the crowd. Overhead, police floaters kept the hovering news floaters outside the "eighty-up, eighty-out limit." But one floater moved inside the limits unmolested, and began to circle the mound not greatly above it, at about the diameter of its base. On a spar projecting beneath, a powerful light now strobed. Not painfully, but the chant began to unravel, weakening, as more and more eyes followed the light. Then the cheerleader stopped; the chant staggered and died; and a great stillness spread through the crowd.

As if suddenly aware of the heat, the cheerleader moved partway down the grassy slope, farther from the flames. And from the floater, a voice issued. Boomed! After the great chant, it did not seem so loud, but in fact it was very loud. The entire crowd could hear it. The voice was one they all knew, from numerous public addresses over the years by Chang Lung-Chi as candidate, senator, cabinet minister, and eventually president. The most trusted and admired public figure of recent decades, at least.

With the death of their chant, the crowd's minds focused on the president's words.

"Citizens and friends," he said. "We have come together here to rescue our species and our commonwealth from a dual threat. A *dual* threat! A powerful, ruthless invader . . . and our own hard-won hatred of war and violence."

For several seconds the voice stopped, but the floater continued circling, the light still strobing.

"A hatred of war, a hatred that turned into a war against ourselves. A war by the Peace Front against its own species.

"But I have not come to you to declare war against the Peace Front. My hands—all our hands—are fully occupied with saving the human species from the invader. We will capture and prosecute the criminals who set the fires and committed the murders, also those who helped them, and those who directed them. But we must not—we *must not* kill the spirit of peace, the spirit of pacifism within us! If it were not for human pacifism, we'd have destroyed our civilization centuries ago, with nuclear war, or biological war, or some other depravity. Centuries ago! With the survivors, if any, driven back to the caves and hovels, to the fear, and ignorance, and superstition, and famine, and *brutality* from which our ancestors struggled."

The circling continued, but the strobing had stopped.

"The prime minister and I have not been open with you. There are matters we've kept from you, hoping to avoid the kind of violence that happened yesterday. But tonight you have opened our eyes and our minds to your awareness. Your readiness.

"A few weeks ago our new warfleet, under Admiral Soong, fought its first real battle with the Wyzhñyñy armada. The Front was correct about that, though they got the details all wrong. Our fleet was greatly outnumbered, and the fight was brief and costly—a test of ships, weapons and tactics. But the Wyzhñyñy losses were much greater than ours. And our losses have been more than made up in the weeks since the battle.

"And just days ago, a small fleet under Admiral Apraxin-DaCosta arrived in the New Jerusalem System. There it destroyed a smaller Wyzhñyñy fleet." Again the president paused. "Then the New Jerusalem Liberation Corps was landed on its home world, and fought—*and won!*—the first human ground battle against the Wyzhñyñy invaders.

"These victories were far from decisive. Overall, our forces are still severely outnumbered. But they are growing, and we can now say that things look hopeful. Not favorable yet, but hopeful."

Another pause. "You came here this evening and demanded martial law. Something our species came to hate and fear centuries ago, for good reason. But now you've decided it's necessary for the survival of humankind. So under the extraordinary powers granted by parliament for the pursuit of this war, and with the agreement—the pained, grieved agreement—of Prime Minister Foster Peixoto, I herewith proclaim—martial law!"

Remarkably there were no cheers.

"We avoided it as long as we could, and will continue

it no longer than necessary. If we should continue it too long, we'll depend on you to let us know. But I do not imagine it will come to that."

Again a pause. Loosely the spell still held the crowd, the spell that had grown out of their mutual, deeply felt need, but quiet now.

"And now I have a request to make of you. I want you to do something further, for yourselves, your government, and your species. Do it as honestly as you know how." Again he paused, and when he spoke once more, it was slowly, deliberately, and less loudly. "If you believe you know someone who may have been involved in the terrorism of yesterday and last night, do not undertake to punish them. Instead, notify CLUES/TERRORISM on the Ether. Someone will investigate as soon as possible.

"Now I am going home to bed. You may want to do the same."

Most of the crowd left quietly. Others hung around talking, also quietly. The tall Golok left with the child, who slept now, draped over one broad shoulder. The man said nothing to anyone, but his long face looked thoughtful.

Chapter 51
Killing and Dying

Four days had passed, three of them on patrol, since the Battle of the First Days. APFs took platoons to designated map coordinates, and picked them up six or eight hours later, somewhere else. The patrols were to watch for any sign of Wyzhñyñy activities, but mainly they were keeping sharp, and getting a better sense of the wilderness fringe that was their stronghold. Meanwhile their platoon leaders checked out uncertainties on the detailed, large-scale maps Division had brought from Terra. Maps from high altitude photographs, made years earlier by Terra's foreign ministry, which on worlds like New Jerusalem had little to do, and cooked up unobtrusive, hopefully useful projects to pass the time.

Patrolling also served to integrate the replacements. There could be no replacements from offworld, of course. So the platoons with the heaviest losses had been deactivated, and their remaining personnel distributed to others to fill the holes. 2nd Platoon's replacements had come from 3rd Platoon, A Company, which had also been airborne qualified.

They were all Jerries, of course, had been trained alike,

and their limited combat experience had been similar. But their unit folklores had different characters and stories. Still, a couple of days was all it took to become brothers. The many casualties had made them more conscious of their mortality and brotherhood.

After breakfast on the morning of the fifth day, Ensign Berg mustered 2nd Platoon in a light rain. "Men," he said, "today we're going to do something different. The surveillance buoys report what seem to be four small groups of fugitives hiding out from the Wyzhñyñy. You may possibly know some of them. The general's sending us out in four armored personnel floaters, each with a squad, to pick up the fugitives and bring them in." He looked at his men expectantly. "How does that sound?"

Their response was not the enthusiasm he'd anticipated. It was Esau who finally answered. "Sounds fine to me, sir." This brought a circle of nods. "But we may hear some things that won't exactly warm our hearts. A lot of folks that stayed weren't kindly disposed to those of us that decided to leave. Called us deserters; said we lacked faith in God. It turned out they spurned God's offer of escape, instead. Some of them'll hate us for that, too. Hate us for being right."

Berg nodded slowly. "I expect some may at that," he said, then briefed them on policies and procedures.

By the time they took off, the rain had stopped and the sun had come out; steam rose from the forest roof. Esau knelt beside the copilot. He'd called up the regional orientation map in his map book. An X marked the reported location of the group he was to pick up, while the floater's location was a tiny moving icon. But mostly it was the ground he watched, the Milk River Hills. The only good orientation feature was the Milk River, named for its milky tinge. These hills were not rich in streams. Except for the Milk, they tended to be short, appearing from springs as full-grown creeks, then disappearing into the ground. All of them were a milky green.

The forest was heavy. Some of the species he could recognize from the air. Scattered whitewood, with large pale leaves, its wood light in weight, favored for sawing or splitting out boards; dense groves of "cedar," narrow-crowned and with lanceolate leaves, the best of all for building logs; here and there steelwood, some of them towering, its hard and heavy wood slow to decay; and "redwood," with roseate wood and red-tinged leaves, a favorite for cabinets and other dressy things. Jael had had a redwood hutch, crafted by her grampa as a wedding gift.

Esau pulled his mind away from that, and back to the hills they flew over. Hills not fit for farms, he told himself. *Best left to God's livestock, not man's.*

They were getting close now. The floater icon almost touched the X. Down there were folks who'd stayed behind. He wondered how they'd fared the past year, and how they felt now about those who'd left. *Not that it matters greatly,* he told himself. *Leastways it shouldn't.* As Speaker Crosby had said: "God made diversity amongst his people for a reason. They *will* disagree, but He loves them all." Speaker Crosby had stayed, but he'd wished them well. "I'm too old to go flying off to the stars," he'd said. "And my flock needs me."

Some of that flock had already condemned him for "encouraging desertions."

Esau called up a quadrangle page, its much larger scale showing considerable detail, including a second, smaller X. He guessed the larger was a camp, and the smaller a hunting party, now about a mile west of it. The smaller X moved slightly while he watched, still westward toward a meadow. "Go to the smaller X first," he told the pilot. "Before they get any more separated than they are."

"Right," the pilot said. Esau went aft to the open hatch, hooked his safety line, then knelt, leaning out. He'd already keyed the speech output of his helmet comm to the floater's bullhorn. Below, all he could see was treetops.

"Helloo!" he called. "You down there! An army's come to clean out the Wyzhñyñy—the aliens. If you hear me, fire a gun. We can pick you up at that meadow off west."

He heard no gunshot, and the APF's gravdrive produced only a low hum; if there'd been a shot, he'd have heard it. *Maybe,* he thought, *they've run out of powder.* There'd always been folks, a few, who preferred a crossbow or longbow for hunting. They'd have an advantage now.

"Fine," he called. "We'll go to your camp and wait there."

The pilot heard, and swinging the floater in an easy curve, headed for the larger X, where the map showed a creek along the foot of a ridge. Trees overhung it, but in places the water was visible from overhead, milky green like the river. *Probably*, Esau thought, *there was a cave there*.

He tried the bullhorn again. "Helloo! You down there! An army's come to clean out the aliens. I'm coming down to talk with you. If you want, we can take you to camp with us. Feed you up proper. Fix you up with shoes, and new clothes."

He could imagine what they looked like after hiding out in the wilderness all that time. They'd hardly have a shoe between the lot of them. Maybe moccasins. He disconnected from the bullhorn and spoke to his squad.

"Talbott, I'm leaving you in charge. Turner, you'll come down with me."

Turner nodded, and Esau turned to the pilot. "Sergeant Pindal," he said to the Indi flyer, "find a place close by, where we can let down."

The pilot glanced back, nodding. "Right, Sergeant," he answered, and in a few seconds had parked his aircraft over a small blowdown gap. "Will that do?"

The two Jerries were snapping on letdown harnesses as Esau looked down. "Yup. Good enough." There wasn't much visibility through the gap; branch growth was filling it. But it would do. Two letdown spars had emerged from their housings, one on each side of the floater, above the door. Esau stepped out backward and began his descent, controlling it by voice while signaling with his arms to refine the centering. It was something they'd all done before at Camp Nafziger. Then he was through the gap and into the trunk space. No one was waiting. When his feet touched the ground, he pulled the safety clip and slapped the release. "All clear," he said.

His harness disappeared upward on its cable; meanwhile Turner had landed beside him. They were about a hundred feet upslope of the stream, and seventy or eighty yards downstream from the X. "We'd better take our helmets off,"

Esau said. "Otherwise no telling what these folks will think
we are."

Both men tipped their helmets back, letting them rest
on their light field packs. Then they went downslope to
the creek. From there they could see a young boy waiting
a couple hundred feet upstream on the far bank. Esau
started toward him, waving. "Howdy!" he called. "I'm Esau
Wesley, from Sycamore Parish. This here's Malachi Turner,
from Tanner's Run."

The boy didn't answer, just watched their approach, his
eyes feral in a thin face. He wore only a loin cloth; his
wide frame all sinew and bone. Too much bone. *About ten
years old,* Esau decided, thinking in New Jerusalem years.
Perhaps thirteen in Terran years. *Hasn't been eating any
too good. Looks like a string of eels hung on a rack.*

Esau stopped. "Malachi," he muttered, "get me a couple
rations out of my pack." Turner gave them to him, and they
went on. When they reached the boy, they could see he
was frightened. Esau reached a hand to him. "My name's
Esau," he said. "What's yours?"

"Zekial. Zekial Butters."

"That hunting party off west—I talked to them from the,
uh, the airboat that brought us. Told them I was coming
here. They should be along directly. You're not here alone,
are you?"

A quick headshake.

"Is your mamma here? Or your grampa?"

He began to tremble! "My mamma—and my sisters."

Esau frowned. "What's the matter, Zekial?"

"We don't have no hunting party out. Some men came
here yesterday. They . . . " He choked, his face writhing like
a nest of snakes. "They . . . " Abruptly, unexpectedly, he
burst into tears and fled up the slope, disappearing behind
a laurel brake. Esau had backed off a step, glanced
thunderstruck at Turner, then looked around. A footpath
angled upslope from the stream toward a bluff, and the
two troopers strode up it. Soon Esau saw a wide opening
in the rock face. Without slowing he called.

"Helloo! No need to worry! Help's acoming!" From
behind him, Malachi could hear what else he said, half
under his breath. "This better not be what I'm afraid it is."

The cave began as a sort of open-sided gallery that narrowed inward. A small mound of embers glowed beneath the overhanging rock shelf. There were sleeping furs, and on the ground, a patch of dried blood three feet across. Esau swore again, and gestured toward the narrow gap that led deeper into the limestone. "They must have gone farther back in, scared spitless." *If they're still alive.* "Go back in there a little ways and see if you can talk them out. I'm going to call Sergeant Pindal, and find out where those others are."

He seated his helmet again. He didn't need it to radio the floater—his throat mike would serve—but he wanted its HUD. "Sergeant Pindal," he said, "this is Sergeant Wesley. We've got a situation here, but I'm not entirely sure what it is. Where's that party I talked to first? What way are they going now? Over."

"They're about a quarter mile west-northwest of where they were before. They're bypassing the meadow, as if they didn't want to be picked up. Over."

"So they're still headed away from here. All right. Jael, do you read? Over."

"I read. Over."

"I may need a woman's help here. I'm not sure, but I'm afraid I do. I want Sergeant Pindal to let you down by the creek, just below the big X. I'll be there to meet you. Pindal, are you still reading? Over."

"Still reading. Over."

"After you put Corporal Wesley down, I want you to follow those sons of bitches that took off. Corporal Talbott, do you read? Over."

"I read. Over."

"When Sergeant Pindal catches up to them that ran off, talk to them with the bullhorn. Tell them if they don't stop and give themselves up, you're going to blow them to bits from the air. Got that?"

"Got it, Sarge." He paused. "Do you really want us to kill them?"

Esau hadn't thought it through. Now he hesitated. "No, but don't let them get away. Tell them twice, and if they keep going, I want Sergeant Pindal to shoot ahead of them. Close as he dares. You still reading, Pindal? Over."

"I read. But I don't like what you're telling me. Over."

"Just shoot ahead of them. And if they veer off, do it again. I'm afraid they may be murderers, and worse. Worse than the Wyzhñyñy, because they're doing it to their own people. Over."

"I still don't like it. There's nothing in our orders that covers shooting at locals. Look. I'm just about over the creek. You down there yet? Over."

"I'm on my way. Ten seconds will do it. Turner, keep trying to talk them out of the cave. I'm going after Jael."

It was Jael—her woman's voice—that talked the mother and her two daughters out of the darkness. They pointed out where the renegades had dragged off her husband's body, and her oldest son's. While she talked, the younger son showed up again. He too had seen his father killed, and had fled back into the cave, where his baby sister had gone. The two had spent the night hidden well back in the darkness, but they'd heard the screams and crying. When the renegades had left, their mother and older sister crept back in with them, to huddle there without speaking. But Zekial had heard their attackers say they'd be back when they had meat. Finally he'd crept out, intending to find some other people, and ask for help. He'd barely emerged when Esau had called down on the bullhorn.

Esau radioed the floater again. Yes, they were still following the hunting party. No, Talbott hadn't hailed them. He'd been afraid it might make them scatter. Esau told him that was good thinking. "Pindal, stay after them, but not close. They'll stop somewhere. When they do, I want the squad to let down a ways off, and move in. Surround them if you can, then use your stunners if you can get close enough. I'm going to radio Division about this. I suspect General Pak will want them alive."

The floater dropped back a few hundred yards, following the X on the pilot's HUD. Esau called Division and was referred to the senior sergeant major, who was perturbed by a squad leader bypassing the whole divisional chain of command. But when Esau explained the situation, the sergeant major patched him through to General Pak, who ordered out a platoon, to make sure the renegades didn't escape.

They succeeded in capturing only two. The other two suicided before they could be stunned.

That wasn't the only ugly situation that 2nd Platoon, B Company ran into that day. The other three fugitive groups were all extremely glad to be found, and all three reported seeing or hearing about Wyzhñyñy soldiers eating humans. One group had found the remains of a feast by a Wyzhñyñy patrol. The victims had been neatly dismembered, and some of the bones were charred. The crania had been opened and the brains removed, maybe as a delicacy. Along with the human remains were plastic packages, apparently from Wyzhñyñy ration cases.

Word spread like a grassfire not only through the Jerrie division, but through the Indi armored regiment and air squadrons, and the Burger engineers.

Pak was concerned that his troops might commit atrocities of their own, as retribution, which would harm morale and discipline. So on his closed command channel, he ordered his company commanders to speak to their troops about it.

In camp the troops ate standing up, in company mess tents with high tables. It was in B Company's mess tent that Captain Martin Mulvaney Singh spoke to his four platoons. The rumor was, he was going to brief them on their next action, so there was considerable tension in the mess tent. More than before the battle they'd already fought, because now they knew what to expect. Or thought they did.

The rumor was wrong. "I suppose you've all heard about the Wyzhñyñy having eaten people here," Mulvaney said.

The reply wasn't loud, but it was ugly.

"Obviously they're meat eaters, and we look enough different, they may have considered humans to be nothing more than animals. Meat for the larder. I suspect we cured them of that notion the other day, when we killed so many of them."

His soldiers muttered agreement, sounding not quite as ugly as they had.

"In combat," he went on, "a soldier—human or Wyzhñyñy—is apt to be too busy, or at too much risk, to eat or mutilate dead enemies. Even if he was inclined to, which you and I aren't. His attention is on destroying live enemies and staying alive himself. But at other times some people might be tempted to mutilate an enemy.

"I can't imagine any of you doing something like that; it's as contrary to your religion as it is to mine." He scanned them again. "So that makes it between you and God. But in this world it's also between you and the army. Because mutilation is strictly against regulations, and the penalties are severe.

"Any questions?"

No hand raised. No one spoke.

"Good. Enough said then. And speaking of eating, Sergeant Ferraro is serving apple pie with brown sugar for dessert at supper. Make sure you save room for it."

Returning to his office, Mulvaney looked back at the event. He could understand Pak's concern. But at the same time, he felt that in bringing the matter up, he'd insulted his Jerries, just a little.

Jael, on the other hand, wondered about the difference between mutilation with a knife, and mutilation with, say, a grenade in combat. Probably, she decided, it was the difference between meanness of spirit and necessity.

Gosthodar Jilchûk scowled at his staff. They'd told him all they knew, and given him their opinions on everything he'd asked about, but he still knew too little for effective planning. There was no real border, no defined front, and he could choose his area of operation. The enemy, on the other hand, knew everything he did above ground as soon as he did it, and responded. They no doubt had reconnaissance buoys, an intelligence staff, and a high-powered AI working up contingency plans twenty-four hours a day.

Abruptly he slammed a fist on his worktable, making his staff flinch. It was that or shoot the map on his wall screen.

The cursed thing was dead as a stone. No movement. No life. It didn't even flinch at his temper the way his staff had. It showed things as they'd been when his surveillance buoys had been destroyed, except for changes made by Intelligence, none of them in real time.

Most numerous were the approximate locations where he'd lost recon floaters and their escorts to enemy action. The humans responded quickly to invasion of their airspace. Obviously their buoys picked up and monitored his own aircraft as soon as they emerged, and had interceptors up promptly. As if their duty crews waited in their aircraft.

They seemed willing to lose aircraft, certainly over their own territory, as long as they shot down his. And his scouts were at a disadvantage; their missions required more-or-less predictable flight behavior. He couldn't continue losing aircraft at the rate he had been, and he had no way of knowing what the enemy had left.

His Intelligence chief had pointed out that the humans seemed more interested in shooting down the escorting fighters than they did the scouts—in bleeding his fighting strength than in denying him information. Though they were doing a good job of that too.

Seemingly the human commander was leaving the initiative to him. But they were planning something. They hadn't invaded just to lie around.

He scowled, big jaws chewing on nothing. Back in the forest, his expensive aerial scouting showed a poorly defined "blind area" of something between twelve and twenty square miles. Probably circular. His Tech chief believed the humans had some kind of concealment screen, unlikely as it seemed. At any rate the "blind area" showed nothing at all in the way of humans, or of any mobile life-forms large enough—or in large enough groups—to register. But they were there. Something had to be. Large mobile objects could be detected outside of it, some of it wildlife, some clearly military. And the humans were thinning areas of forest, possibly preparing defensive positions of some sort.

Jilchûk shook his head. He'd have to settle for a ground reconnaissance in force. Meanwhile, one thing seemed definite: the humans had landed in inferior numbers. Perhaps to be supplied from space, for a war of harassment and attrition.

Attrition. He could play that game, he told himself, information or not.

B Company, 2nd Regiment, had set out on foot through the forest. B Company plus a platoon from C Company, because the mission required five platoons. One augmented infantry company to take out a tank battalion. Sergeant Esau Wesley felt proud that B Company had been chosen. He thought of it as the best in the division.

His wife looked at it differently: someone had to get the mission, and B Company was it.

To carry out their mission, they needed to penetrate twelve miles into what the Jerries were calling Wyz Country. Twelve miles through open country with nearly flat terrain. Twelve *straight-line* miles from the wilderness edge, but by the meandering Mickle's River, it was more like twenty.

The tank battalion was parked in the narrow band of floodplain woods that stretched along the Mickle's banks. Actually at a place where the woods were wider than anywhere else for miles. There, according to the buoys, they'd find not only the battalion's tanks, but its headquarters, trucks, repair and overhaul facilities . . . all of it.

At each corner of the encampment stood a newly-erected flak tower. The Indi assault pilots knew all they wanted to about those. Enough to guess the specifics: a swivel-based, multi-barreled, look-and-fire trasher on each tower, powerful enough to bring down an armored attack floater with a single burst. Or one pulse suitably placed.

Though B Company didn't know it, surveillance buoys had observed the tower construction in progress, but hadn't reported it. Regionwide, the buoys saw far more than humans could hope to deal with, so back on Terra, programmers had designed perception sets to notify Intelligence of opportunities and dangers. But inevitably the programs overlooked some things.

Thus when four thick concrete slabs were poured in a

nondescript stand of trees on a minor river, no relevance was perceived. Then four assembly floaters began assembling four tripod towers on the slabs. The buoys registered and tagged this internally, while awaiting further observations. Then some unrecognizable equipment was installed on the towers, and a pseudo-organic data processor, 360 miles out, notified Division that something was going on.

But it was an Indi scout pilot who said, "Huh! Those are weapons! Gotta be." So he reported it, then left his planned flight path for a closer look. But the Wyzhñyñy didn't respond; there was nothing else peculiar about the place, and whatever might be perched atop the towers was concealed in a cab.

And there was nothing else on the site but trees. And only hours later, Intelligence had their attention on something else: a Wyzhñyñy tank battalion, with its attendant ground transport, had appeared beside a limestone ridge deep within Wyz Country. Almost certainly it had been concealed in a cave. And they were promptly joined by a floater escort, which along with the antiaircraft armament of the tanks demanded caution.

So Operations decided to let be for the moment. They'd wait and see where the tanks were going. In less than two hours they knew. As for why . . . for one thing they were a lot closer to prospective battle sites.

General Pak wondered if they were simply bait, because by then he suspected what those towers were. Though he'd never heard of flak towers.

Then he learned how good the Wyzhñyñy ordnance was. He sent two flights of armored attack floaters to rip up the tank park—and lost six of the eight aircraft! Next he sent a flight of rocket-armed standoff floaters, and discovered the potency of Wyzhñyñy electronic countermeasures.

So he turned to infantry and inflatable boats.

B Company reached Mickle's River by twilight, in the forest three miles outside Wyz Country. The Mickle's was not very large there: forty to fifty feet wide and four to eight feet deep in the main channel. What made the mission feasible was, even in Wyz Country the Mickel's floodplain was wooded. That was one similarity between

Jerrie and Wyzhñyñy land-use practices: neither culture farmed floodplains, even along rivers that didn't often flood during the growing season. Here and there the buoys showed a break in the woods, where convergence between some meander and the bordering terrace pinched out the floodplain on one side or the other. But except for those infrequent breaks, the buoys showed woods along both banks for all twenty meandering miles through Wyz Country.

The troops unloaded their boats, demolitions, etc. on the river bank, then Captain Mulvaney ordered the grav sleds back to Division with their Burger crews. He watched the squads inflate their boats and put them in the water. Then troopers held them by the handlines while their gear was loaded. The current would carry them along, and the eight paddles with each boat would speed them. They'd had two training sessions with rubber boats back at Camp Stenders. Not much. But the three wilderness miles before they reached Wyz Country would give them the feel of boats, paddles and river.

The number one boat was smaller, the scout, with only five paddlers and a bow lookout. Mulvaney strode to the number two boat, where seven staff noncoms, including the medics, sat waiting with paddles. Corporal Jensen stood in water over his knees, steadying the boat. Crouching, Mulvaney boarded, settled on his seat in the bow, and looked back while his troopers boarded the other boats. Lieutenant Bremer had settled in the stern, holding the steering oar. Mulvaney raised an arm and gestured. "Let's go, men!" he called. With that, Jensen clambered aboard, took the eighth paddle, and they were on their way.

They suspected what this night might hold for them, but they didn't dwell on it. It wasn't real to them yet.

Isaiah Vernon's camo field was not only black at night, it also obscured his electronic image. Nonetheless, he waited quietly behind a tree trunk. They'd been told to use cover when they could.

He didn't wait alone. The entire regimental bot platoon was there: 22 bots against a Wyzhñyñy incursion thought to be of company strength. The Wyzhñyñy were getting close. On Isaiah's HUD, their linear icon had almost reached his platoon icon. Even from his east-end position he couldn't see them yet, but he could hear them. He'd maxed his sonic sensitivity. *They're trotting,* he thought. "Lieutenant," he whispered, "this is Sergeant Vernon. I hear them now."

Koshi answered from the other end of the ambush line. "On my command," he murmured. "Not before. Unless they see us and open fire first."

The Wyzhñyñy were skirting a tangled patch of old tornado blowdown, thick with fallen trees, brush and saplings. The platoon waited along its edge, Koshi at the west end. By the time the Wyzhñyñy reached him, they should all be exposed, or almost all. There was no cleared field of fire, but by opening fire together, they should be able to take out much of the enemy force in the first seconds. Then they'd rush the rest; take them out while they were shocked and confused. Those that fled, they'd let go; even bots couldn't catch them. Let them tell what had happened to them as best they knew. See what that did for morale back in Wyz Country.

The first Wyzhñyñy who trotted into view was the point man, followed by two other scouts. The nearest passed perhaps six feet in front of Isaiah, who'd have held his breath if he'd had lungs. The rest of the Wyzhñyñy followed in single file, Isaiah counting them.

He'd gotten to 143 when Koshi said, "NOW!" Then the entire platoon opened fire with both arms—blaster and slammer. There were screams and roars as Wyzhñyñy fell, kicking, thrashing, or simply dying. The first return fire was almost immediate, homing on muzzle pulses. Isaiah took a hit; his camouflage field flashing from the energy received. They'd all been shot with hard pulses before, deliberately in training, to prepare them. So he ignored it, looking for more targets. Knocked down another, and another . . . The Wyzhñyñy didn't go prone to fire, but stayed on their feet. After a few seconds, those still standing paused to reload. Isaiah had exhausted the power slugs in his clamp-ons, and jacked in replacements.

"TAKE THEM!" Koshi ordered, and the bots charged, juiced by an electronic analog of adrenaline. The Wyzhñyñy hadn't expected this. Those who'd reloaded fired. The others

ran. Two slammer pulses jarred Isaiah, his camouflage
field flaring strongly, reflecting from the visor of the
Wyzhñyñy who'd fired. Isaiah grabbed him by the head,
jerked, twisted, and threw the Wyzhñyñy violently to the
side, off his feet, before shooting him.

He paused, and saw no Wyzhñyñy standing. The order
was to kill the conscious wounded; a safety measure that
was also a merciful act, with no Wyzhñyñy medics on hand.
Unconscious enemy wounded were to be taken prisoner,
but no one had told them how to distinguish the unconscious wounded from one playing possum. And at any rate,
slammer and blaster wounds were typically fatal.

A few minutes later, when the platoon gathered
around Lieutenant Koshi, there were no prisoners. Only
a Wyzhñyñy body tally: 119. There'd probably be more
scattered along the path to Wyz Country, dead of
wounds. Courtesy of a buoy, Isaiah's HUD showed icons
moving rapidly east-southeastward.

The platoon started back to camp at an easy lope, Isaiah
feeling embarrassment along with exhilaration. It had been
almost too easy, killing so many with so little injury to
themselves. Then he wondered if the Wyzhñyñy had felt
that way when they'd wiped out the local humans who'd
declined evacuation. The thought didn't entirely erase his
discomfort, but it allowed him to dismiss it.

It had been Esau who'd suggested it, when Ensign Berg
gave the platoon its first briefing on the mission. "We ought
to paddle along close to the edge," he'd said. "Trees hang
over the water there. Cover, in case some Wyz scout flies
over. And generally, the outside of a meander is better than
the inside. The current cuts deeper, so we can stay close
to the bank, under the trees, and be harder to see. The
inside of a meander is likely to be shallow, so we'd have
to keep farther to the middle."

Afterward, Ensign Berg ran it past Captain Mulvaney,
who mentioned it to General Pak at a planning review.
"What's the young man's name again?" the general asked.

"Esau Wesley, sir."

Pak remembered the name now; that was the young
sergeant who'd unearthed the renegade fugitives. "Keep an

eye on that young man, Captain. He sounds like promotion material: smart, and takes responsibility."

Mulvaney had grinned. "We've made a project out of him, General, since early on. Especially his platoon sergeant."

Back at B Company, Berg told Hawkins what Pak had said, but the sergeant didn't tell Esau. It seemed to him it might make the Jerrie self-conscious; make him try too hard. What he did tell him was that Mulvaney had told the general, giving *him*, Esau, the credit.

From the time they started downstream, noise discipline was absolute. The buoys had been ordered to give special attention to the Mickle's and its vicinity, but you couldn't know for sure. There was Wyzhñyñy livestock here and there, and probably Wyzhñyñy herdsmen, indistinguishable by buoy imagery.

Esau's advice was heeded: They stayed mostly near the riverbank, and on the curves, favored the outside. Once Captain Mulvaney's HUD showed a Wyzhñyñy floater pass over, more or less in line with the river where they were, but it didn't react.

They moved rather briskly, without seeing or hearing anything threatening. The major moon—"Elder Hofer's Lamp"—rose at about 2330 hours, so during the last hour of their river trip, the visibility was better than earlier. That increased the tension level, but not drastically except during one interval when there was no woods along the east bank, and direct moonlight reached the water.

For several minutes, Captain Mulvaney had been paying more attention to his HUD than to the river. The icon of his sole scout was nearing the tank park. "Almost there, men," he murmured. "Easy now. Quietly. Quietly." He rounded a bend. Ahead lay a straightaway about a hundred and fifty yards long. "It's just before the next bend," he whispered. Then added, "Kill your HUDs." The lines on the HUDs were hair-thin, but even so, they were a needless risk now.

This was far the most dangerous stage of the operation yet. Mulvaney felt a focus and acuity of senses greater than anything he'd experienced before in his thirty-three years.

❖   ❖   ❖

As squad leader, Esau rode in the bow of his boat, watching the riverbanks, the woods, and the boats ahead, his senses as focused and acute as his captain's. The inside of the last bend had been on their left, the side they wanted, and they could have run right up on the mudbank there. It would have made for easier unloading. But then they'd have had to approach through the woods, and riding the current was quieter.

He'd glimpsed one of the flak towers, its platform and cab—turret actually—not much above the treetops. He ignored it; he had more immediate things to pay attention to. On the straightaway he saw no good place to land. The east bank was a natural levee about five feet high, about the highest he'd seen. And abrupt; almost impossible to pull the boats up. This hadn't been apparent in the images from the buoys. They'd either have to leave men behind to hold the boats, or struggle them up onto the levee, making a certain amount of noise. Or let them float on unoccupied, which would leave the company stranded.

But it didn't come to that. Just before the next curve, the high bank had been dozed—sloped and smoothed for easy access to the water. As boat by boat they reached the bend, the bow man slipped into the water close to shore, water waist to chest deep, and guided his boat to the sloped-down bank. Their gear on their backs, shoulders, and harness, the rest also slipped over the side, and transferred demolitions and other gear to shore. Then quickly but quietly they raised the boats from the water, carried them ashore, and very quietly stacked them four high. As soon as a squad had landed their boat, they moved up the bank, weapons in hand, and formed a defense line at the brow while others landed behind them.

Captain Mulvaney had been the first. Wet to the hips, he crawled to the top of the bank, and with night vision examined the Wyzhñyñy encampment. From time to time he raised his visor and used his night binoculars to pick up details. Trees obscured the view, but he saw enough to put the scene together.

The buoys had given him the basic layout, subject to uncertainties. There were definitely no tanks on the side toward the river. They were lined up along the other three sides, well spaced, forming a box several acres in size. Inside the box lay almost everything else—mainly shedlike prefab buildings that no doubt served as battalion and company headquarters, mess halls, machine shops, and probably officers' quarters. And mounds that had to be bunkers; probably concrete, covered with earth. *They couldn't be deep,* Mulvaney thought, *the water table couldn't be more than six feet below the surface.* By each tank was a tent large enough for its crew to live in. Outside the "tank box," at least on the far side, were more tents. Probably squad tents for the battalion's infantry company or companies. Except for them and the flak towers, everything seemed to be inside the box.

The only activity Mulvaney saw was one Wyzhñyñy soldier walking to what had to be a latrine. When the Wyzhñyñy opened the door, subdued light shone out until it closed again. He saw no sentry, not one, though there had to be some. Even here, miles and miles from known human forces, and no indigenous population that might snoop or steal. Inwardly Mulvaney shook his head. It was hard to conceive of a military installation with no sentries out, especially at night.

Only after several minutes of careful scanning and listening did he give up on spotting the sentries. Keying one of his command switches, he whispered to his platoon leaders, confirming sectors and objectives, and giving orders.

Ensign Berg had led 2nd Platoon through the woods as quietly he could, keeping well outside the three-sided tank box. He'd sent scouts ahead and off his right flank, and they'd reported two sentries. They'd reached the edge of the woods on the east side, the side farthest from the river. Now they lay in pasture grass, facing the woods, waiting for Captain Mulvaney's command.

Not far inside the woods, but outside the tank box, two flak towers rose above the trees, marking the southeast and northeast corners. If the towers opened fire on them, the platoon's orders were to run for the woods as hard as they could, firing as they went, regardless of what awaited them there. Though hopefully the flak gunners couldn't depress their guns enough to target them. Nearby, livestock grazed, mostly "calves." Remarkably placid, they hardly reacted to the strange bipeds. The long row of squad tents—almost surely the battalion's infantry bivouac—lay just within the edge of the trees.

The platoon lay in a line, ten or fifteen feet apart. Behind it, Elder Hofer's Lamp rode the sky. *Hopefully*, Esau thought, *if some Wyzhñyñy infantryman left his tent to take a leak, and looked to the east, his eyes would lift skyward, rather than studying the pasture.*

2nd Platoon had had the farthest to move, and it seemed to Esau that everyone else should already have been in position. But Berg had radioed their readiness three minutes earlier, and nothing had happened yet. When the captain was ready, he'd let them know. Then 2nd Platoon was to pour heavy fire into the tents, drawing Wyzhñyñy attention for a critical half minute or so, hopefully starting an eastward reaction.

Apparently things were hung up somewhere.

Esau didn't fidget, physically or mentally. Back on Lüneburger's World, he'd become good at waiting, despite his sometimes impatient disposition. Especially during the maneuvers at Camp Nafziger, he'd developed an absolute focus in ambush situations, like a tiger waiting to rush a heifer. For him, time became little more than sequence, its durations known but muted. Now his implacable gaze was on his personal sector of fire. Irrelevant thoughts did not visit his mind.

Finally Berg whispered in their helmets. "Fire on my command. Five. Four . . . " From somewhere in the woods came a premature burst of blaster fire. "Fire!" Berg snapped.

Each 2nd Platoon trooper began spraying long bursts through the tents in his sector of fire. The Wyzhñyñy response was prompt, survivors spilling out, blasters in hand, running for the nearest sizeable tree. *No foxholes or breastworks,* Esau realized, offended by the lack. Danged Wyz took too much for granted.

2nd Platoon's muzzle pulses and visible trajectories guided the Wyzhñyñy return fire. But they weren't used to the low target profile of prone humans, and the platoon's lack of cover wasn't as costly as it might have been. The firefight settled to a more measured exchange, the Jerries firing short bursts now, rolling sideways for target disruption, seating fresh slugs as needed.

Their job was not to suppress the Wyzhñyñy infantry—they lacked the necessary firepower—but to inflict maximum casualties, while distracting it from the defense of the tanks and flak towers. Meanwhile the whole base was in uproar. Firing seemed everywhere. Magnesium charges flashed brilliantly, and armor petards roared, as 3rd Platoon's Jerries worked and fought, destroying and dying along the rows of tanks.

It was Sergeant Hawkins' voice that spoke next in 2nd Platoon's helmets. "1st and 4th Squads, move into the woods and support 3rd Platoon. 2nd and 3rd Squads spread out and continue firing."

"Let's go, 4th Squad!" Esau said, and springing to his feet, darted to his left in a series of sprints and dives, his people following. They'd already been at the south end of 2nd Platoon's skirmish line, and despite Wyzhñyñy night vision, they quickly ceased drawing fire. Wyzhñyñy attention seemed focused on those humans still shooting at them.

So Esau shifted from sprint-and-dive to a crouching run, swerving more and more westward, guiding on firefights in the woods. At the same time he clicked his helmet comm to the command channel. 4th Squad was to suppress Wyzhñyñy tankers protecting their vehicles from 3rd Platoon demolitionists.

As he ran, he glanced back at his squad. Their spacing discipline was good, and remarkably, most of them seemed to be there. "Work with your fire team," he warned. "Teamwork!" Then they were in the woods. In the eruptive, roaring flashing chaos, teamwork tended to dissolve, troopers responding to the moment, firing, taking cover, throwing grenades, even bayoneting. The blaster racket was punctuated by the sharper sounds of gunfire. The Wyzhñyñy tankers carried only projectile weapons—pistols and carbines. Tankers who climbed into still intact tanks, initiated their AG engines. Demolitionists darted up to tanks and clambered onto them: slammed petards against access panels, or magnesium charges into shaper muzzles or air

intakes, triggered charges and time fuses, then moved on
if they could.

Esau and Jael kept aware of one another, less by conscious intent than by something deeper. Captain Mulvaney's
voice spoke on the command channel. "4th Squad, 2nd
Platoon, are you near the southeast tower?"

Esau crouched beside a tree. His answer was a rush of
words. "Sir, this is Esau. I'm not far from it, and Jael's with
me. The rest of the squad's close by, but I don't know how
many's left. There's fighting all around, like things were
stirred with a spoon."

"The southeast tower demolition team can't get up the
tower," Mulvaney said. "They're under heavy fire. Take your
squad and suppress it. We *must* take out that tower!"

"Yessir." Esau changed channels. "4th Squad, 2nd Platoon, move to the southeast tower. We need to take out
enemy fire that's holding down the demolition team there.
Otherwise we may not have a ride home. And give me your
names while you're on your way, so I know how many of
us there are."

Then he started, his stocky body darting from tree to
tree. Behind one he stumbled on a trooper with his head
blown half off. Behind another stood a wounded Wyzhñyñy,
guts dangling, looking the other way and firing a carbine.
They're tough! Esau thought. With superb night accuracy,
he snapped off a single pulse that blew out the Wyzhñyñy's
brain. He could die himself in the next second, but his
warrior muse wasn't entertaining thoughts like that.

Now he saw the tower, a thick-legged tripod in a clearing
some eighty or ninety feet across. Jerries lay on its slab,
at least two still alive, returning fire from behind tripod
legs. He could see several sources of the Wyzhñyñy fire
that kept them on the ground. Pointing, he growled. "Jael,
that one's yours." Then he moved toward another, whose
attention was on its target. Someone else loosed a short
burst, putting that one down. Esau found a third almost
hidden from view, threw a grenade behind the Wyzhñyñy
and dropped to the ground.

After it blew, he took stock, then opened the command
channel again. "Captain," he said, "this is Esau, 2nd Platoon, 4th Squad. We seem to have cleaned out the folks

shooting at the southeast tower team, but no one's going up the tower. I don't think they know it's cleared yet."

"Good work, Esau. I'll tell them. They're hung up at the southwest tower, too. Go help."

Esau ordered 4th Squad, then started himself, glancing at the southeast tower as he left. They'd gotten lines up earlier. Now two people were climbing them.

Intense fighting continued around the parked tanks. Bolts passed within feet of him, and he dove for the ground behind a tree. Jael's voice spoke in his helmet. "I got him!" she said, and Esau was back on his feet, running again for the southwest tower. He approached the Wyzhñyñy harassers from behind, shot one, then came under fire from another. Hit the dirt behind a tree, legs protruding on one side, head on the other. Fragments of bark and wood flew, and he scrabbled on his belly to better conceal himself. No further pulses struck, and cautiously he looked around the base. Saw a Jerrie kneeling behind a fallen Wyzhñyñy, peering toward the southwest tower, blaster ready.

Gathering himself, Esau darted to the man and knelt beside him. One of 4th Squad, a replacement, Tom Clark. "You know if any of the others are around?" Esau asked.

"I've seen Joash Steele and a couple others. That's all. I've been keeping track of you, best I could, you and Jael. Helps she's so small."

Jael trotted toward them, then something heavy, a slammer, cut loose at them, and she scrambled for shelter while Clark and Esau hit the dirt in opposite directions. Esau belly flopped, and kicked around into a prone firing position. The enemy weapon fired another burst, and Esau fired back. The enemy fire stopped, and they saw a large powerful body thrashing on the ground.

"Clark," Esau said, "I'm going to see if anyone's still alive over there." He thumbed toward the tower. "You folks keep anyone from plugging me."

"Right, Sarge."

Esau got to his feet and ran to the tower, briskly but not sprinting. Five Jerries lay dead there. Now Jael sprinted across to him and flopped prone. "I wish you'd get down," she said. "You're too good a target, standing like that."

He knelt. "And I wish you'd have stayed over there," he answered.

Ignoring the comment, she pointed toward the trees. "Someone over there's firing at the top of the tower," she said. "I think he's one of ours."

Esau peered where she'd pointed. At the moment there wasn't much blaster fire close by, though someone was banging away with a pistol. Slowly and deliberately, probably short on ammunition. "You stay here and cover me," Esau said. "I'll check it out."

Part of a large tree lay on the ground, cut to make room for the tower, and not cleaned up. He ran over to it, and finding two Jerries kneeling in a large fork, joined them.

"What are you men doing here?"

The one who answered never took his gaze from the top of the tower. "We were sent to give covering fire to the tower team, but they all got shot. Now he's covering me, and I'm covering the grapples."

"Grapples?"

"The team fired two grapples at the tower platform, and they both caught on the railing. Then two guys tried to climb it, on those little seats that ratchet up when you pull on the rope. They both got shot. They're hanging up there in their harness."

Esau hadn't noticed them before, one almost to the top, the other some ten feet lower. The blasterman raised his weapon and fired another burst at the top of the tower. "One of the Wyz just came out," the man said. "The way he dropped, I think I got him. They can crawl along the platform without us seeing, but they have to get up to free the grapple. I'm hoping I can kill enough of them, they can't man their guns."

They're probably worried about that themselves, Esau thought.

"The team had three grapple throwers," the blasterman said, looking at Esau for the first time, a quick glance. "There should be another one out there among the bodies. With a climbing seat," he added suggestively.

Esau squinted, then decided, and ran back to the tower in a crouch. Among the bodies, he saw what he needed: a satchel charge with shoulder straps, and a sort of drum with handles. On top of the drum lay something resembling a grenade launcher. A three-hooked grapple was seated in it, and from a slot below the muzzle, rope led to a hole in the top of the drum. Beside it lay a harness, with a little seat, and an attachment. He knew how it worked; 2nd Platoon had been introduced to them, though they hadn't tried them out.

The heaviest fighting was near the center of the woods now, as if the demolitions teams had finished their work or been killed. No one seemed to be shooting at him for the moment, but that couldn't last. And there was more gunfire than blaster fire now—a bad sign. He dismissed it; he still had work to do. The satchel charge had a detonator in place, with a short length of fuse taped on the side, and an igniter. Taking off his combat pack, he removed a phosphorus grenade and hooked it on his harness next to his remaining fragmentation grenades. Finally he lay his blaster by his pack and slipped his arms through the straps on the satchel charge.

Picking up the grapple gun, he handed it to Jael. "Bring this," he said. Then he carried the drum to the edge of the slab, took the grapple gun from Jael, and eyed the platform atop the tower. "Well," he muttered, "here goes nothing." Raising the gun, he pulled the trigger. The recoil almost separated his shoulder, and the blast hurt his right ear like a knife thrust. The grapple flew upward while the launch shank flew free. Rope sped from the drum; the grapple struck the turret, then clattered to the platform.

Jerking on the rope, he felt no resistance. The grapple popped from the platform and caught on the pipe atop the bulwark.

He turned to Jael. "This is an order," he said, pointing. "Go back there and shoot at any movement on top that's not me. I don't want some sonofabitch unhooking this, or shooting down at me. Then, if our folks start getting pushed out of the woods, I want you with them. I'll get out all right."

She nodded soberly and ran toward the trees. As she did, Esau saw the blasterman in the fallen tree fire another burst at the top of the tower. The clatter of the third grapple had stirred them up overhead.

Carrying the now-depleted drum, he went to where the seat lay, and attached the ratchet to the rope. Then he buckled himself into the harnesslike seat, located himself beneath the grapple, and after a deep breath began to climb hand over hand, the ratchet securing every gain. He got the rhythm of it at once, climbing as rapidly as his short arms allowed. Thinking that if an energy pulse hit the satchel charge on his back, there'd be nothing left of him for a Wyzhñyñy to eat.

Just below the platform he paused, removed a fragmentation grenade, pulled the safety clip, thumbed the plunger, then lobbed the grenade over the railing. It roared. With quick strong movements he reached the railing and bellied over it, releasing his seat harness almost before hitting the platform. A Wyzhñyñy body lay there. Rising to a crouch, he moved to his right, came to the open gunport, and removed the phosphorous grenade from his harness. As he activated it, he realized the gunport shield was sliding shut, but he had only one phosphorous grenade, so he tossed it anyway. If it had struck the shield, he'd have died horribly.

Ignoring the screams from inside, he scuttled to the door, shrugged out of the satchel charge, then tried the latch. Unlocked! Bullets smacked the turret near him. He depressed the igniter, stepped behind the edge of the armorsteel door, and opened it. Someone inside fired blindly, bullets spanging on the bulwark behind him. He slung the thirty-pound charge in by a shoulder strap, slammed the door and fled in a crouch, around the curve of the turret to the grapple and over the railing, not bothering with the seat. He started down hand over hand. *I should have thrown a fragmentation grenade in ahead of the charge,* he thought. *Someone in there's still alive and fighting. If he brings the charge out and throws it over the railing, I'm a goner.*

He heard the roar, and knew he'd pulled it off, but had no time to exult. Still thirty feet up, a burst of blaster fire passed too near. He slid—would have let go and free-fallen if it weren't for the concrete slab beneath him. Almost at the bottom, he gripped the rope hard again, braking, felt searing pain in his palms, and hit the slab

hard enough his knees buckled, aware that another burst
of blaster fire had missed him as he'd dropped. He
sprinted for the trees.

"Here!" Jael almost screamed it as she stepped into sight,
and he veered toward her. "Folks are pulling back!" He
realized he'd heard that on his helmet comm, and ignored
it. Together they ran, Jael leading. Not northward toward
where the company had landed, but westward, toward the
curving river. Northward would take them into a no-man's-
land.

Ensign Kemau Zenawi Singh arrived in a staggering
run, carrying a man who weighed more than he did.
Wyzhñyñy weapons racketed behind him. Crossing the
break of the bulldozed bank, Zenawi hit the sandy slope
on his butt, sliding feetfirst. Company medics were working on wounded. He rolled the body off his shoulder. "It's
Captain Mulvaney!" he gasped, then lay back heaving for
breath. "Somebody get Lieutenant Bremer!"

He'd passed Bremer and hadn't noticed. Now the lieutenant appeared beside him. "What? Captain Mulvaney?"

"Yessir. Hit by a bullet. It exited through his face, his
mouth. We were heading back here and suddenly he went
down. I think he was hit again, while I was carrying him."

"Blessed Gopal!"

"You're in charge now, sir."

Bremer turned to look at Mulvaney, but a kneeling
medic was in the way. "Sir," the medic said without looking back, "the captain is dead. Bullet through the brain."

Bremer sounded unbelieving. "Don't just . . . " He
groped for an appropriate word. "Just *kneel* there! Give
him something!"

"I have, sir. Stasis 1. But it's too late, believe me." He
rose to a crouch and started back to the wounded.

Bremer turned again to Zenawi. "Kemau," he said, "what
do I *do*?" His eyes looked large, desperate.

"Sir, you know the situation better than I do. But I
presume we have a defense perimeter covering the beach."

Bremer's head bobbed rapidly. "Yes. Of course. Of
course."

"I'd hole up here on the beach and give the rest of the

men time to get here. Then take to the boats and go
downstream."

"*Downstream?* Good lord, man! Downstream is the
wrong direction." Bremer sounded close to panic.

"Downstream," Zenawi repeated calmly. "It's in the plan.
That's where they're supposed to pick us up. Unload on
the other side, far enough away that hopefully the evacuation floaters can get in safely and land. The last I knew,
the enemy still held the southwest tower."

Bremer was breathing hard now, hyperventilating. "We
have men in the park here. We can't leave them. We'll
simply have to charge! Clear the Wyzhñyñy from the park
and bring out the casualties."

Zenawi's hand gripped his wrist. "Don't order it, sir.
Every man in your company will die. You'll carry the weight
of it on your soul forever."

Forever was how long Bremer's stricken expression
would stay with Zenawi; the XO was over the edge. "Let
me take care of it for you, sir," Zenawi said, and clicked
his all-personnel channel. "B Company, this is Zenawi for
the company commander. Perimeter, hold fast. The rest
of you retreat to the beach in an orderly manner!" He
repeated it. "In three minutes we begin evacuation. In
three minutes we begin evacuation. Perimeter, don't shoot
anything on two legs!"

Jael and Esau reached the river downstream from where
the Wyzhñyñy had bulldozed the riverbank. Going over the
levee top, they picked their way along the steep sideslope,
gripping brush on the levee brow to keep from sliding into
the water. Esau wasn't even aware now of his torn palms.
In two or three minutes they were within the Jerrie
perimeter undetected. Overhead, bullets popped, ricochets
sang, blaster pulses hissed. It was then they heard Zenawi's
order. Ahead they saw men kneeling on the smoothed-down
beach. A moment later they reached it, and crouching,
trotted to the officers they could see.

"I need to report to Captain Mulvaney," Esau said.

Lieutenant Bremer, the tallest man in the company, rose
abruptly, as if there were no hostile fire. His face twisted.
"Wesley!" he snapped, "where's your rifle? And your pack?"

"Sir, they're back under the southwest tower. I . . . "

"GO GET IT, SOLDIER! RIGHT NOW!" His face swelled with sudden rage. "GET THAT SONOFABITCH OR I'LL SHOOT YOU FOR COWARDICE!"

Esau stepped backward as if slapped.

A black hand gripped Bremer by a sleeve, pulling him down, and the XO went suddenly slack. "Sir," Zenawi said, "Captain Mulvaney *ordered* Wesley to the southwest tower. Let's hear what he has to report." Zenawi's black face turned to Esau. "Captain Mulvaney is dead, soldier. Is the southwest tower disabled?"

Esau was still in shock at Bremer's outburst. It was Jael who answered. "Yessir. Esau disabled it, sir. That's why he doesn't have his blaster. The tower team was all dead, but there was a grapple gun laying there, and a satchel charge, so he went up alone, all that way. Threw a phosporous grenade in the window where the guns shoot out; I could hear them screaming up there, clear from where I was. Then he threw the satchel charge in and came back over the railing, and slid down the rope. And the turret blew up! The steel door flew off the hinges, off into the trees, and Wyz on the ground were shooting at Esau, so's he fell the last ways. And lit on his feet! Then we ran!" She paused. "And now here we are."

Zenawi peered at her, then looked at Esau again. "Good work, Wesley!" he said. "Now you better get your head down. Be a shame to get killed before you even get your medal." Still stunned, Esau squatted, and Zenawi reached out. They shook hands. The officer felt the wet stickiness, different than the feel of blood, and retrieving his own hand, glanced at it before turning to Bremer again. "What Wesley did was worth a medal, wouldn't you say so, sir?"

Bremer's nods were like twitches, the sight penetrating Esau's shock. The XO had lost his mind!

While they'd talked, the Wyzñyñy fire had slackened. Now it stopped entirely. The silence was eerie. The only voice Esau could hear was Lieutenant Zenawi reporting to Division: "The flak towers have been taken out. Send medivacs, APFs and fighter cover."

The group on the beach looked at each other, then at the woods. Along the Jerrie perimeter, men lay or knelt, holding their breath. Those who hadn't already fixed bayonets, did so. Surely the enemy was about to charge. It seemed to Esau that if they tried to evacuate, they'd be overrun while loading the wounded on the boats.

An interminable minute passed. Two. Abruptly the woods in front of them erupted with crashes of exploding antipersonnel rockets, and the formless roar of multibarrelled slammers sounding from the sky. Zenawi reacted at once, his words broadcast wide band. "Everyone to the boats! Head downstream! That's *down*stream. Fighter command, we're under air attack. APFs, pick us up at rendezvous, half a mile downstream, on the west bank where the woods pinch out!"

Torn palms still ignored, Esau had already run to the nearest pile of boats, Jael with him. Alone they manhandled a top boat into the water, where he stood holding it. Others grabbed a second. Soldiers were spilling onto the beach, a small flood. More boats were launched, and wounded were loaded into them. For some reason the Wyzhñyñy air attack was focused on the woods instead of the beach. Zenawi helped Bremer into a boat, the XO like a doddering old man, then jumped in with him.

The escape hardly used half the boats, and some of them weren't full. Some had still not gotten under way when Indi fighters hit the Wyzhñyñy attack floaters.

The rendezvous beach had no place to land, so the troops went over the side, towing or carrying casualties, then boosting and pulling them and each other up the bank. Floaters were waiting, with medics, who helped first at the cutbank, then at the floaters.

By that time a group of antiarmor floaters hovered over the tank park. These too were Indis, and their fire was not antipersonnel. They wanted to make sure no tanks remained fit for renovation.

Chapter 52

Afterward

Seven large APFs had landed in the Wyzhñyñy pasture, only twenty to fifty yards from the cutbank—an APF for each platoon, and two medivac versions for casualties. The unwounded had already pretty much sorted themselves by squads and platoons—their "families and extended families." Crew chiefs called out the names of the platoons they'd come for, and the surviving officers and senior sergeants began loading their people, recording who was there.

Blood had darkened Jael's right sleeve when Sergeant Hawkins stopped her. "You're hurt," he said. "Go get on a medivac."

"Yessir," she answered. As she left, Esau started after her, but Hawkins put a restraining hand on his arm. "The medivacs are just for the wounded," he said. "You'll go back with us."

Jael called back without stopping. "Show him your hands, Esau."

Esau held them out; Hawkins looked. "Go with her," he

ordered. "Yessir," Esau said, and left, moving sluggishly, the adrenaline worn off.

Hawkins continued loading what remained of his platoon. *Jerries!* he thought. *They're not used to having medical treatment available. They don't expect it, don't seek it. Add that to the warrior trait of ignoring illness and pain, and you get people like those two.*

He'd long ago decided that Jael was as much a warrior as Esau, simply less aggressive.

The platoon APFs were ready, but the two medivac APFs were still being loaded. They'd leave together as a convoy, escorted by fighters waiting protectively overhead.

Jael and Esau were examined briefly, injected with painkiller, directed to seats, and strapped in. Except for painkiller, only Jael received treatment. A medic had cut off her right sleeve at the shoulder seam, exposing a ragged laceration of the right deltoid, apparently by a rocket fragment. She'd felt it when it hit, but they'd been busy launching boats. The medic cleaned her wound, then bandaged it. It was hard to tell how much blood she'd lost. A significant amount, he decided, but not dangerous. The water had been deep at the cutbank, and most of the blood had washed away in the current.

Esau's hands were ignored. They threatened no blood loss, and the medics gave priority to cases that might be serious. Most were. There'd been screams when casualties were manhandled off the boats and up the steep bank, but aboard the medivac, the sounds were muted groans, mutterings, and occasional cries.

A warning sounded, and the medics grabbed stanchions while the medivac first lifted, then accelerated. Then they continued treating wounded. Plasma injections were begun. Stasis 1 was injected where the wounds seemed mortal, and the dog tags had been stamped to indicate a bot agreement. Or where there was no stamp, but death was imminent, or limbs were ruined beyond repair. It wasn't all according to regs, but the surgeons could decide what to follow up on.

Tom Clark, one of 4th Squad's replacements, was aboard with a bullet wound through the belly. He'd been

doped for the pain, but not too doped to accost a
medic. "How about some of that stuff you give the bot
cases?" he said. He fumbled for his dog tags. "I signed
the agreement."

"Sorry, soldier," the Terran medic said, "but you're going
to live and be good as new in the body you've got."

"Don't matter. With so many worlds to run the Wyzhñyñy off, this war's going to last a long time. So I'm bound
to get killed sooner or later. I might better get my iron
suit now. The more bots we have, the sooner we'll get it
over with. And that way, who knows: I just might come
through it all alive." His chuckle was a weak, dry sound.
"Spend my old age rusting in the sun."

"Take it up with the doc," the medic told him, then
patted his shoulder and went on.

Esau had watched, listening. The painkiller had taken
hold; things seemed a bit remote and disjointed. But one
thing was clear: there was a lot of hurting going on. All
of it because some Wyzhñyñy decided to take away other
folks' worlds. He'd known that much all along. He just
hadn't realized everything that went with it.

Speaker Farnham had it right, he thought, *or the book
did.* A lot of the time Esau hadn't been sure when a
speaker was speaking his own words, and when they were
the Lord's, or some prophet's, or Elder Hofer's. But what
it amounted to was, when we have a task, we need to carry
it through the best we can, and trust in the Lord. And it
seemed to Esau that was the situation the army was in.

Shortly he felt the medivac settling downward. A minute
later they were on the ground, and the rear doors opened.
More medics came aboard, and within a few minutes, all the
wounded had been unloaded. Esau and Jael were among the
last—the least wounded—and walked to reception.

Brigadier Consuela Hagopian clicked her video control,
and the wall screen went blank. Despite her salt-and-pepper
hair and the lines in her face, to Chang Lung-Chi she
looked more than smart and confident. She looked combat-
trained and fit.

"As you see," she said, "it was an informative night. We
are *very* pleased with the performance of our Jerrie troops,

their auxiliaries, corps command . . . all of them. Less
happily, we're also impressed with the toughness of the
Wyzhñyñy troops. But General Pak suspects our experience
has been very largely with the Wyzhñyñy main force, their
regulars, and he's probably right. I hope so, because they
have lots of soldiers. Most of them second string, we think.
Call them reserves. We suspect their entire adult population is armed and trained."

What she says matches what Olausson says, Chang
thought. *And Kulikov had spoken well of her. But what
impressed Chang as much as anything was the way she
pointed out errors and uncertainties without being slippery.*

"After the Battle of the First Days," she went on, "both
sides have used their armor and air squadrons cautiously.
We seem to have an advantage in the air, so we've been
a little bolder with our air units. The Wyzhñyñy have been
bolder with their tanks, but with the destruction of the
battalion in the tank park, that may change.

"Meanwhile they have a large advantage in troop numbers. And a lot of artillery, while we . . . had to make difficult resource decisions in preparing for the ground war.
And decided to rely on airpower as our main bombardment
force. We intended our initial softening-up phase to largely
destroy the Wyzhñyñy armor and air units, but we'd overlooked something. Our principal colonized region on New
Jerusalem, now the Wyzhñyñy colonized region, has areas
of karst terrain. With caves—something we'd overlooked.
Wyzhñyñy command was foresighted; they modified some
of them to shelter armor and air squadrons, and for backup
base installations."

She gestured a shrug, a graceful movement. "One might
wonder that they felt the need to, but unfortunately they
did."

"So," said Foster Peixoto, "what is the upshot of all this?"

"I'm getting to that, sir. But first I want to point out
our advantages there. Our surveillance buoys above all—
no pun intended. And our concealment screen seems to
be quite effective against Wyzhñyñy aerial observation. Thus
we know a lot about what they're doing, and they know
rather less about what we're doing. In fact, in our own
domain, our troops have the forest to cover their movements,

while Wyzhñyñy aerial reconnaissance is harassed, hurried, and costly.

"The Wyzhñyñy have penetrated our concealment area with what appear to have been two-man ground recon teams, that in the forest tend to be missed by our buoys. But that hasn't seriously compromised our concealment.

"Another long-term Wyzhñyñy disadvantage is supplies. They've been depending on supplies they brought with them, of course, and seemingly had been using the supply ships for storage. Though we don't know how much they may have transferred into cave storage. The two supply ships we caught on or near the ground, we destroyed. Others escaped into warpspace."

"Are you suggesting we can starve them out?"

"I doubt it will come to that. We believe the Wyzhñyñy will take desperate measures to avoid it."

"Suicide attacks?"

"In time, perhaps. But we expect the Wyzhñyñy force in warpspace to make efforts to supply their people on the ground. Though the odds of their succeeding aren't good. Our offplanet flotilla is alert to possible emergences by Wyzhñyñy ships. Also we have Dragons and a marine mother ship standing by in near-space, for critical onworld emergencies."

She stopped expectantly. For long seconds the prime minister gazed thoughtfully at her before speaking. "I take it, then, that we need feel no concern about events on New Jerusalem, at least for the time being."

"I wouldn't go that far. The Wyzhñyñy remain a potent force there, but our successes so far are encouraging."

Now the president spoke. "Brigadier, you said nothing about Wyzhñyñy prisoners."

"Marshal Kulikov brought that up with General Pak this morning, when they discussed Pak's report. Pak had hoped to capture some live Wyzhñyñy prisoners in conjunction with other missions, but Wyzhñyñy do not surrender. Threatened with capture, their wounded suicide, preferably with a grenade, taking some of our people with them. Seemingly unconscious Wyzhñyñy are apt to be shamming, hoping to entice someone close enough. These things were learned in the first days of fighting. General Pak is now preparing a mission tailored specifically to capture and transport prisoners."

The prime minister sighed audibly. "Tell General Kulikov that both the president and I put a high priority on this."

They ended their meeting then, and the brigadier left. *Pak's capture mission!* she thought. *God, to be young again!* She'd have bucked for airborne training and an assignment on New Jerusalem. *Ah well,* she mused, *I'm lucky just to be in the military at a time like this. Interesting that I chose the military in this life, instead of business or music or child rearing. This life, when the military has meaning.*

Some personnel didn't like living and working underground, but Gosthodar Jilchûk was comfortable with it. He'd grown up in a cool damp region, and was not claustrophobic. And his quarters were comfortable, luxurious even. His walls, where not occupied with video windows, were hung with expensive tapestries from his old home world, and luxurious furs from the subpolar regions of this new home world.

Just now, though, none of that impinged on him. He was busy digesting and assimilating what had happened the night before. He'd absorbed the available information and opinions, then dismissed his staff. Now he lay at a low writing table, torso upright, jotting and doodling as he thought, using a stylus on a jotting glass. Sometimes he used them to make notes. Tonight he used them mainly to bleed off pressure.

The bottom line was he'd lost an entire tank battalion. Of fifty-four tanks, just six were repairable; ten at most. The day before, he'd been confident that despite the Battle of the First Days, he'd retained clear superiority in armor. *Getting so much of my armor underground before the human bombards attacked was the smartest thing I've done. No, the only smart thing I've done. I've been trading armor, aircraft and warriors for knowledge, and I've come out sadly short on the exchange.*

(Scribble scribble!)

When the bombards had left, he'd sent out his aircraft to challenge the enemy aerospace attack craft. Which unfortunately had proven more heavily armed and armored, and very well crewed. Now the question was: *why haven't the humans used them since? What are they saving them for? Or is there a rivalry between the humans' space commander and their ground commander? Perhaps even between the services themselves?*

He shook off the question. There was no way to know. He only knew he was overdue for some good luck.

(Scribble scribble! Jot jot!)

His latest rude surprise was that the humans had battle robots! Robots with responses more intelligent and nuanced than anyone could have imagined. They'd been reported on the Battle of the First Days—radioed reports from the confusion of close combat. But there'd been no verification, and no one had taken it seriously. The assumption had been that some of the humans, perhaps their master gender, wore full body armor. But the descriptions they now had seemed to repudiate that.

(His stylus had nearly stopped moving.)

So. Battle robots. That meant that humans had much more advanced artificial intelligence technology. But they couldn't have many robots. If they did, they'd have used them more extensively. Perhaps these were prototypes, or test models.

Don't talk yourself into any assumptions, he chided. Go about your business. Plan. Execute. Adjust. Exterminate. In the imperial dialect, the initials had long since become an acronym meaning victory.

Meanwhile he'd reduced one area of uncertainty. Seventeen two-man recon teams had penetrated the blind area at various points, and radioed when they'd done it. Eleven radioed additional observations from inside, and five had returned and been debriefed. None of what they'd seen had seemed noteworthy, but even that was worth knowing, and he knew now that the concealment field was not also a force shield. That had been predicted, but having it verified was vitally important.

(His stylus had speeded up. Now it moved furiously, in a sort of automatic writing.)

Especially in conjunction with something even more important: from the penetration points, Intelligence had mapped a decent approximation of the overall perimeter.

It was circular! Which suggested a single, centrally located field generator. Laying heavy artillery fire on the center might very well knock it out, depriving the humans of their concealment. It might also cut off the head of their command structure.

But before I do that, I'll plan the ground attack to overrun them. With their concealment broken, I can commit aircraft for effective reconnaissance, and air support for the ground forces.

He looked at his jotting glass, where his stylus had been so busy while he cogitated. In the middle he'd scrawled undisciplined spirals and swirls, with scattered small ritual sunbursts. Taken together they formed a circular mass. And into the heart of it were arrows, as if into the center of a target.

A shiver rucked his fur from scalp to sacrum. It seemed to him this was going to work. He began to decipher the tightly scrawled notes he'd written.

On the second day after the raid, Arjan Hawkins Singh walked into a patients' dayroom—a squad tent, with board floors on timber foundations. Courtesy of the Burger engineering regiment and its small but efficient sawmill. Only Esau and Jael were there; few of the wounded were well enough to use a dayroom. They sat watching a documentary on defense industries of the Core Worlds. It was a year out of date, of course, but interesting. Enlightening. Gave an outworlder a notion of how things were done on the Core Worlds, and how all this *stuff*—ships, weapons, equipment—came to be.

Jael clicked off the player as Hawkins sat down beside them. "Hello, Sergeant . . ." she began, then stopped. What caught her attention was the dark place on each sleeve, where chevrons had been removed. Then she saw his collar tabs. "You're wearing an ensign's bar!" she said. "You've gotten promoted! Congratulations!"

There's an interesting change, Hawkins thought. *When I first knew them, she wouldn't have spoken first like that. Not with Esau present. She'd have waited for him to talk.*

"Does that mean Ensign Berg is dead?" Esau asked.

"I'm afraid so. Killed in the first minutes."

Jael blushed. She'd overlooked how promotions came about in battle. Suddenly congratulations didn't seem proper.

"And you're replacing him," Esau said. "I figured he might be dead when I heard you giving orders he'd usually give." He paused. "Does this mean B Company's not getting shut down? Even after all the casualties?"

"Yep. We're still in business. We've been reorganized, of course. We're down to three platoons of three squads each, with most of the squads down to eight men for now. But we'll get first call on replacements, as the wounded recover and do rehab."

That'll be awhile, Esau thought. From what he'd seen and heard, most wounds were a lot worse than his and Jael's.

"I could fight right now if I had to," Jael said. "I don't hurt much, and I didn't lose that much blood. Esau's hampered a lot worse with his hands than I am with my shoulder."

Esau held up his bandaged hands and looked at them wryly. Only fingertips projected. "At least Jael doesn't have to tell me not to pick my nose now," he said.

Hawkins laughed. He'd never heard Esau say anything remotely humorous before. "There you are!" he answered. "Every cloud has a silver lining."

"Captain Fong tells me I'll be back on duty in a week."

"That's what I heard, too. Good thing. I need you." He held out a pair of sleeve patches. "Ensign Zenawi is Lieutenant Zenawi now, our new company commander. He told me to give you these; you're 2nd Platoon's new sergeant. If you're nice, maybe you can get Corporal Wesley to sew them on for you."

Jael laughed. "Might be she would." She took the patches from the ensign. They were a staff sergeant's stripes: three chevrons and a rocker. *There ought to be two rockers,* she told herself. *The other platoon sergeants have two.* Probably, she decided, the army didn't like to jump someone two grades.

"And while you're sewing on chevrons," Hawkins added, "these are yours." He handed her a pair of buck sergeant's chevrons. "You're in charge of 3rd Squad now. There isn't any 4th Squad yet. Maybe later."

She took them without hesitating. "Thank you, Ensign Hawkins," she answered. "I'll do the best I can."

Hawkins went on to tell them that 2nd Platoon's fit-for-action were on R&R, with Jonas Timmins as acting platoon sergeant. They'd ridden AG sleds to the upper reaches of their old friend the Mickle's, for a day's fishing. General Pak had foreseen the desirability of such days, and requisitioned abundant fishing equipment before they'd left Terra. Nothing fancy—gear you could use without instruction.

Esau had gone grim. "How's Lieutenant Bremer?" he asked.

"He's under—medical treatment. Had you heard something?"

"On the beach he said he was going to shoot me for a coward if I didn't go back and get my blaster."

Jael took command then, telling what had happened, and how Zenawi had stepped in. The story took Hawkins by surprise. He turned to Esau. "How did you feel when he said those things?"

"I couldn't believe I was hearing them. I felt . . . betrayed. Killed. Stabbed in the heart. Then Jael . . ." He described what she'd said, and what Lieutenant Zenawi had said. "And Lieutenant Bremer just sort of . . . caved in. Then I realized he'd lost his mind, and that he knew it. But I still felt . . . dirty, from what he'd said."

Hawkins nodded soberly. "Lieutenant Bremer's body wasn't wounded. His soul was, by all the killing. It was more than he could deal with. That's how some people are. He's in convalescence now. Major Ranavati is his doctor—a psychiatrist and Gopal Singh healer. The rumor is, when the lieutenant returns to duty, he'll be assigned to General Pak's staff, as assistant to Major Pelletier. Where he won't have responsibility for men in combat."

He grinned then, taking both Jerries by surprise. "As for you two—you did very well out there. Lieutenant Zenawi said in his debrief that you saved a lot of lives. If that tower had been in operation when our floaters came, it would have cost us dearly."

Esau nodded. "We could see that, Jael and me. No ride home probably."

Hawkins got casually to his feet, as if nothing heavier had been talked about than 2nd Platoon's fishing trip. "Well, I've got more wounded to visit. You two get well quick. Especially you, Esau, because a platoon leader's nothing without a good platoon sergeant to pass all the hard work to."

Then he was gone. Jael got up from her inflatable chair, knelt beside her husband and kissed him. "I'm proud of you, Esau," she said. Then she too grinned. "We've got to get well quick, so's we can slip off together behind a thicket."

He half grinned back at her. "You sure know what to say to a man. That'll about cut my healing time in half."

Before supper, Isaiah Vernon stopped to visit. He was wearing a new servo. The old one's cooling system had needed work, and they'd decided to install his bottle in an improved model.

"Division got hundreds of them before we left Lüneburger's," he said. "In case enough people signed agreements and were injured badly enough to qualify. And for replacements like mine.

"From the beginning my old one hadn't worked as well as it should," he went on. "The robotics tech said I should have complained then, but I didn't know. I thought that's just the way they were. Then, when we ambushed the Wyzhñyñy patrol, I took some slammer hits, and coming back in, I started to heat up pretty badly. Lieutenant Koshi told me to lie down, and radioed for an AG sled to come get me. Me and two others with damage.

"It made it more real to us—to me, anyway—that bot or not, you can get hurt or killed in those fights. But none of us did. We killed one hundred nineteen Wyzhñyñy, by count, but none of us died. These servos are really good."

Briefly then they talked of other things, mainly things that had happened on Lüneburger's World. They said nothing at all about their families or where they'd grown up. Maybe later. Meanwhile, those places, those people, didn't exist anymore.

❖   ❖   ❖

In adjacent cots after lights out, Esau whispered to his wife. "I've been thinking."

"What about?" she murmured sleepily

"About Isaiah, and what Tom Clark said to the medic on the medivac. I think maybe I *will* sign a bot agreement. If it's all right with you."

She didn't answer at once. Then, "That's up to you, not me," she said.

But she didn't sound as if she really meant it. More as if she thought it was what she should say. And at any rate, in the morning he had other things on his mind.

Chapter 53

Petition to Kulikov

It was late afternoon. General Pak was reading staff reports when his Intelligence chief rang. "General, the buoys have something you need to see. Corporal Chen has it framed for you."

Frowning, Pak looked at his screen and touched a key. He recognized at once what he was looking at: a column of tanks, or perhaps artillery, moving out of a forested, hilly area. Limestone hills. Magnification was set low, allowing him to see the column's full length. He zoomed in to examine a single vehicle—an armored, self-propelled howitzer—then backed off a bit. A whole unit of howitzers. Judging by Wyzhñyñy standing in open hatches, they were heavy stuff—perhaps eight-inchers.

Zooming back, he counted. A battalion of three batteries, each battery with sixteen howitzers, three squad APCs, an armored battery command wagon, a heavy salvage vehicle, and two ugly-looking flakwagons. He whistled silently. Forty-eight heavy howitzers in all! There was also a battalion command and support company with, among other vehicles, six flakwagons, and four of what could only be large, heavily armored caissons to replenish the ammunition carried by the howitzers themselves.

All of it loaded with bad intentions.

A total of twelve flakwagons! To send attack squadrons . . . He shook his head, thinking of the floaters lost against the flak towers.

He also thought of the Dragon parked 300 miles overhead, unavailable to him.

"Thank you, Captain," Pak said, and disconnected.

Request the Dragon, he told himself. *The worst they can do is say no.* He touched another switch, and in a second had Commodore Kereenyaga's yeoman on the radio, some hundred thousand miles out. "This is General Pak. I need to speak with the commodore at once."

In twenty seconds the commodore was on.

"Commodore, I'm afraid you have all the heavy ground bombardment capacity in the system. Except for the heavy artillery the Wyzhñyñy commander down here is moving against us. I need a visit from a friendly Dragon."

He listened to the commodore's reply, then answered, "I'm aware of that. I was on the planning group. But our assumption was that forces like I face now would be destroyed before we landed . . . .

"I understand. But the planning group didn't allow for the caves. If we had, your rules of engagement would read differently. . . .

"Thank you. Tell them to call me if they have questions. And keep in mind that the clock is running on us down here."

He disconnected, glowering. War House wasn't going to like this, and they'd probably say no. But damned if he'd let the possibility pass without trying.

The artillery that had shelled his line in the Battle of the First Days had been organic to the Wyzhñyñy infantry units. This appeared to be additional. It was hard to imagine the Wyzhñyñy leaving so much artillery on a world whose land surface was 99.9 percent wilderness and had no military at all, or any weapons beyond single-shot hunting arms.

He called the column's speed onto the screen. If it kept on that road, it could deploy for firing in under three hours. And surely they'd have tanks and infantry on hand to protect it, more than his forces could deal with in the open.

He touched a key that would boom his voice into every headquarters and orderly room in the base. "Urgent! Urgent! All units," he said. "This is your general. Evacuate base on Plan C. Evacuate base on Plan C. Beginning *now*!" Then he keyed Air Ops. "You're aware of the Wyzhñyñy artillery on the road? . . . Good. I don't want any enemy in our airspace for the rest of the day. None! We're going to have a lot of people and equipment moving outside the concealment field soon, with only the trees to hide them. Questions? . . . Good."

He disconnected and allowed himself a gusty, "Whew!" The order was given. If this was a false alarm, he'd look like a complete and utter ass. He grunted. *Better that than destruction, heavy casualties and regret.* At best his force couldn't all be moved out in time. But Plan C's priorities were set partly in order of replaceability, and partly for movement to a backup area that had only first-order infrastructure in place—little more than wells and unactivated biosumps.

Only then did he call in his general staff, and begin to sort things out. How would Wyzhñyñy command determine targets? Presumably they couldn't see through the concealment screen, and even that much artillery, firing blind into an area of twenty square miles . . . Ah. The Wyzhñyñy scouting parties. They'd been reported from a number of locations inside the perimeter. Their radioed reports would have allowed a decent map of the circumference, and Wyzhñyñy command would target the center.

Plan C allowed for that too. Headquarters Battalion would be moved first. All but his command center—a modified, platoon-sized APF that held his office and briefing room, along with emergency quarters for himself, his aide, his savant team, the corps sergeant major and two clerks.

The staff meeting was interrupted by the savant's attendant. "General," she said, "Genevieve has a call for you, from Marshal Kulikov at War House."

"Excuse me, gentlemen," Pak said, and walked to a room near the aft of the floater. Genevieve, who like Charley Gordon was bottled, was already in trance. When Pak had seated himself, the attendant nodded, and he began dictating. "This is Pak," he said.

The reply was immediate and to the point. "Explain to me, General Pak, why I should change the rules of engagement," the savant said. Very nearly in Kulikov's voice.

"General Pak" instead of Pyong. Not promising. Pak repeated the brief argument he'd made to Commodore Kereenyaga. He was operating more on intuition than analysis, and it seemed best to avoid specifics, except when answering questions that required them.

"So," Kulikov said, "you are not currently threatened with destruction."

Pak was not intimidated. "Not at present. If I was, the commodore would have acted without referring my request to you. But the farther my base is from open country, the less I'll be able to react to Wyzhñyñy encroachment. They'll establish bases within the forest, where my fields of fire will be much more restricted, and my new base will be subject to attacks from any point the Wyzhñyñy choose. I'll have to move my Operations Command and air units deep in-country, disperse my combat units to fight a guerrilla war, then try to supply them by air. And direct and coordinate them based almost entirely on data from the buoys. If that's what you want, we'll do our best, and keep you informed."

There was a pause of some seconds. "That's a remarkably pessimistic view," said Kulikov. Even via Genevieve, the words carried a sense less of accusation than contemplation.

"Not pessimistic. Realistic. It all comes down to your purpose for sending us here. We were to provide the missing database on Wyzhñyñy onworld tactics, potentials, and psychology. And we've already provided major data on all three.

"Whatever decision you make on this, we'll learn more for you. But data on fighting the Wyzhñyñy from something like an equal footing should be more useful than fighting a guerrilla war. And guerrilla wars are seldom successful without the covert support of a civilian population. Here there is none, and if you don't destroy this artillery threat, you'll have to bail us out later."

Another thought struck him. "Or maybe we've gotten all the information you need from here. Maybe it's time to stomp the Wyzhñyñy and let us mop up the remains. With all the—what? Terabits? Petabits?—of data from buoys, windscreens, helmet visors, the electronic communications of men and aircraft, all beamed live to Kereenyaga's shipsmind for sorting, selecting, sequencing—whatever it does with it . . . " His shrug was lost on Kulikov. "Eventually you'll get it by pod, though maybe not in time to be useful."

I wonder, Kulikov thought, *what he'd say if I told him Ari Geltman's been on Kereenyaga's flagship all along, sending us summaries via savant. Best let him learn about that later.* "No chance, General," he said. "We've invested a lot in your Jerrie force. You're there for the long haul."

"It was a thought," Pak said, and got back on track. "As guerrillas we can give the Wyzhñyñy a bloody game. But if you send down a Dragon, we stand a very good chance of winning down here, and the data should be more useful."

Kulikov was seldom slow to decide; this was no exception. "I'll do this much," he said. "I'll have Kereenyaga send the marine wolfpacks. They won't exterminate the howitzer battalion, but they'll club the hell out of it: destroy a lot of equipment, and probably prevent the barrage.

"But I will not authorize a Dragon. Not now. A visit by a Dragon is like an act of the old Hebrew deity, Yahweh: a force beyond human will—or Wyzhñyñy will—to resist. Early on, the Wyzhñyñy probably wondered what had happened to the Dragons that hit them initially, but by now they've more or less convinced themselves they'll never see them again.

"If I send it now, and it leaves after simply destroying an artillery battalion, it will seem to the Wyzhñyñy we're toying with them. It would break their will, and what we learned after that wouldn't be worth much.

"The wolf packs are a much lower order of deity. The flakwagons will bring down some of them, and some of the artillery will escape. A trade-off that will favor us, but still a trade-off. And they'll assume we don't use them more than we do because we don't like the losses. Which we don't.

"Any questions or comments?"

"One comment, sir. The sun is low here now: about thirty degrees above the horizon. If the wolf packs get here soon enough, and attack from the northwest, the flak gunners will have the sun in their eyes."

"I'll tell them. And, Pyong, this request hasn't hurt your reputation here. You've been doing a fine job, and we respect your opinions." Kulikov paused. "Just don't overdraw your account. Now I've got to end this session and get those squadrons on their way. Kulikov out."

Pak stared at the box on a cart. "Thank you, Marshal. Pak out."

He looked at the clock readout on the screen. The marines, it seemed to him, would make it in time.

Pak put the evacuation on hold as soon as the wolf packs entered the atmosphere. Then he watched the attack. It was he who'd brought the marine crews into harm's way; the least he could do was watch and root for them.

The Wyzhñyñy hadn't anticipated them, and the marines took full advantage of the sun, and surprise. Their first sweep focused on the flakwagons, and they destroyed about half of them. But given the volume of fire, a number of howitzers were also hit, some with hatches open. There were some splendid explosions. The second sweep followed closely, benefiting from the confusion. They killed three of the remaining flakwagons.

Before the third sweep hit, the remaining howitzers were fleeing for the refuge of the forest a mile away, drawing the Dire Wolves like magnets draw ball bearings. The howitzers' AA slammers were too light to mean much. Only ten howitzers made it to the trees. Not one was undamaged, and there were no operational flakwagons left at all. Three of the armored AG caissons were disabled. The fourth, despite the very heavy armor, had blown sky high, taking the battalion command wagon with it.

The field looked like an armor cemetery.

Briefly the marines hung around, dumping HE on the howitzers their sensors found beneath the forest roof. By then Wyzhñyñy fighters were arriving, and per mission

orders, the marines left. Six of the large-bore behemoths
never left the forest. The remaining four limped for home.

A traumatized Jilchûk took heart from two facts. The
first was hard to understand: He'd had a complete heavy
infantry division only a few miles away, ready to move into
the forest during the shelling, and attack the human base
soon afterward. The human attack craft had ignored it, as
if they'd failed to see it.

And five of the attack craft had been destroyed. Five
of the twenty-four; he'd made the humans pay. Perhaps the
remaining nineteen were all there were. He wasn't about
to take it for granted, but he could hope.

Pak, on the other hand, knew. He also knew that three
other Dire Wolves had been damaged, though they
remained spaceworthy. Everything considered, that was a
bargain, but it wasn't one he rejoiced over.

Briefly he considered sending a squadron of his own
fighters to harass the withdrawing infantry, but thought
better of it. After the marine heavyweights, his craft would
be a weak anticlimax. Not the right note to close on.

The evacuated units en route to the backup base location were ordered to return. News of the marine raid and
the destruction of the howitzer battalion more than made
up for the rush and hard work of packing and unpacking
gear.

Chapter 54
The Pecan Orchard

Pak stood in his somewhat crowded briefing room, speaking. In a dual role: as Liberation Corps commander, and chief of airborne planning. His listeners were his general staff; several officers of B Company, 2nd Regiment; and the leaders of three platoons belonging to other companies. The wall screen showed a map, and Pak held a pointer in his hand, moving an arrow on the screen.

"The buoys gave us several candidate targets," he was saying. "The one I've chosen is a harvest camp, in a cultivated lacustrine plain fifty-six miles east-southeast of here. The crop resembles grain, and since most of their harvest machinery was destroyed, they have a large crew harvesting with hand tools. It's one of a number of such operations scattered around the colony."

The window changed from a map to a live view from 360 miles up, greatly enlarged. It showed a large field centered on an orchard. Lines of minute figures could be discerned, advancing slowly. The arrow pointed, and magnification jumped, showing a segment of one line, with

Wyzhñyñy swinging harvest implements. In front of them, the crop stood higher than their withers. Behind them lay swaths of cut grain, with another line of Wyzhñyñy wielding what had to be large, long-tined rakes. "A count shows two hundred twenty workers, almost surely soldiers," Pak said.

Again the picture changed. Now the orchard occupied most of the screen. "Notice the three openings where trees have been removed. The object in the center opening is a rather small floater, parked, and almost certainly serves as the command center. The other two hold what seem to be mess tents." Again the magnification jumped, and the arrow pointed. "If you look carefully, you can discern what appear to be smaller tents beneath the trees, probably squad tents and latrines."

The focus and magnification changed. Around the orchard was a band of stubble field where the grain had been cut. The arrow pointed again, and again. "These are two flakwagons, two hundred feet from the orchard, one at each of two diagonally opposite corners. They can target any air attack—or ground attack—from any side. But you will notice"—the focus moved to one of the flakwagons and enlarged it—"that they are not presently manned. Presumably their crews have duties within the orchard, perhaps in the kitchen—somewhere from which they can run to their guns quickly.

"Presumably the work crew has weapons, but they do not carry them in the field. Probably they're kept in their tents. But you've seen Wyzhñyñy run. Even in New Jerusalem's gravity, they can be armed and fighting within a minute or so.

"They muster each morning at 0911 hours to begin cutting." He gestured at his science officer. "Major Pelletier suggests the lateness is to let the sun dry the dew off the grain before they start cutting it. At 1308 they take a fifty-minute meal break, then return to the field and work until 1722. After another meal, most of them work until 2107."

Pak looked his people over. "That's a long day, and the work is clearly hard labor. They should sleep heavily."

He paused. "You're all aware that there are three different Wyzhñyñy physical types, one larger, with blue fur, another reddish-brown and not so large, and a smaller, dun-colored type." The blues were few, and apparently high-ranking, while the reds seemed to be elite troops. Though experience showed reds in formations of the duns, perhaps as officers.

He went on. "Major Naguib says he hasn't spotted any blues with the harvest crews, but he can distinguish both reds and duns down there. They're on separate work crews. There are somewhat fewer reds, and they don't work after supper. It's been asked why elite troops would be assigned to a harvest crew. They don't appear to be a punishment detail; their hours are shorter, and their work supervisors go unarmed. They may simply be undergoing reconditioning, after wounds or other injuries, or illness.

"I told War House about this last night, and this morning they told me they want six prisoners of each type. That may complicate collection, but there are plenty of both kinds available, so it shouldn't be a serious problem."

Actually Pak didn't like it; his audience read it in his face. The mission didn't need added complications. "Any questions so far?" he asked. "Comments? All right, let's look at the action plan. . . ."

Jerrie troops were excellent squatters, as Jerrie farmers had been, when there were Jerrie farmers. Their legs were thick and strong, the knees and muscles limber and enduring. And at Forest Base there were no benches, so 2nd Platoon squatted a lot. Squatted during occasional field lectures and while yakking on breaks. Just now they squatted for a talk from their ensign.

With replacements drawn from other companies, 2nd Platoon was back at full strength, the only full-strength platoon in B Company. Nearly half of them were unfamiliar to Esau Wesley, who stood, not squatted, in front to one side, facing them. His hands were no longer bandaged. The new skin on his palms was bright pink.

"You may wonder why 2nd Platoon has been brought to full strength," said now-Ensign Hawkins, "when the rest of B Company is so shorthanded. And you new men may wonder why you were pulled out of your old companies. Last evening, Division gave us their reasons, to share with you.

"But first I want to introduce someone to the new people." He gestured at Esau. "Staff Sergeant Esau Wesley has replaced me as your platoon sergeant."

Esau colored visibly. It occurred to him he didn't look like a platoon sergeant. B Company's senior noncoms were of every human pigmentation, but all of them, the survivors and the dead—were or had been tall. At least taller than his own five-eight. He nodded acknowledgement of the introduction, telling himself the Sikhs had chosen him for the job. That should be enough for anyone. And it was a job he'd wanted from the beginning, though he hadn't envisioned someone dying to make it available.

"Esau's here to meet you, and to hear what I'm about to say," Hawkins went on. "Then he's going back to rehab. He'll be with us for good in two or three days. For you newcomers, Sergeant Esau got his job the hard way. He excelled throughout training, was my senior squad leader . . . *and* . . . at the tank park he took out the southwest flak tower single-handed. With covering fire from Corporal Jael Wesley and an unidentified trooper from another platoon. He climbed a rope ninety feet under fire, threw a phosphorous grenade in the firing port to suppress defense, and then, to make sure the guns would be out of service when our floaters arrived, he opened the turret door and threw in a thirty-pound satchel charge he'd carried up the rope on his back. Then he came back down." Hawkins grinned. "Fast, because he was being shot at. Left the skin from his palms and fingers on the rope, when he gripped it to keep from splattering on the concrete ground slab. It's hard to imagine anyone tough enough to do that on purpose. Great job, Sergeant."

Hawkins paused. He'd learned delivery by watching and listening to Captain Mulvaney, unconsciously adding a dash of theatrics. "Now," he said, "down to business. 2nd Platoon has a new mission; that's why it was brought to full strength. You'll get a complete briefing on it after lunch, from the division briefing officer. I'm just giving you an introduction."

He looked his troops over. "Back at Stenders, airborne platoons were trained for a special mission, one we've had in the back of our minds ever since. General Pak has chosen 2nd Platoon, B Company to *lead* a company-strength jump force to take Wyzhñyñy prisoners. The other platoons will be from C, D, and E Companies."

Hawkins didn't tell them the general's staff had had misgivings. B Company, it was pointed out, was by far the most shot-up in the division, and if brought to strength, 2nd Platoon would be half replacements. It would "lack unit cohesion." But he did tell them the general's reasons. It was the only airborne-qualified platoon with experience in raiding deep inside Wyz Country. The only platoon with combat experience in the desperate, helter-skelter situations that historically too often developed in airborne operations. Murphy's Law in action. Every replacement assigned to Hawkins' platoon was airborne qualified, while its veterans had distinguished themselves in the chaos, and extreme and immediate danger, of the Tank Park Raid.

"It's not that other platoons couldn't lead," Hawkins went on. "They could. But the entire force can feel more confident because of B Company's performance at the tank park.

"And there's a third reason. The general wants B Company's CO, Captain Zenawi, to command the raid, even though he's the newest company commander in the division.

"So you see the confidence the general has in him and in us."

B Company's veterans already knew, via the rumor line, how Zenawi, as Bremer's subordinate, had prevented B Company's extermination. And been awarded captain's bars to go with his new mission. Captain Mulvaney would never be replaced in their minds and hearts, but the troops liked what they knew of Zenawi, and his platoon swore by him.

"And that's it for now," Hawkins finished. "You'll learn the rest of it later, from Division's briefing officer."

He converted then from Hawkins the seasoned older brother, to Hawkins their commanding officer. "2nd Platoon!" he barked, "fall in!"

2nd Platoon got to its feet and formed ranks. There was no opportunity now to talk about it, but the excitement they felt as they trotted to the log yard had a definite mixture of nervous tension.

The general had had an additional reason for deciding on Zenawi as mission commander. He'd been impressed by reports, but before deciding, had called him in and asked how he'd prepare his diverse platoons, if he was in command. Zenawi's off-the-cuff reply had clinched the job.

Their real briefing came after lunch, from Major Naguib, Division's intelligence chief who often doubled as briefing officer. He showed them shots of the orchard. One of the Jerries commented that it looked like a "pecan" orchard, referring to a native species of nut trees. Afterward, all four platoons moved their gear from their own company areas to a new, temporary area with its own mess tent. For the two weeks of mission training, they'd live together, eat together, and train together. And play flag together in mixed teams.

For six days they trained on sand tables—squares laid out on the ground and covered with sand. Each platoon had its own table, each with a simulated orchard. Woody fruit stalks, from what the Jerries called "cedars," served as trees. Among the trees, numerous plastic cutouts simulated squad tents and latrines. Two larger cutouts were mess tents. In the center of the orchard was a small plastic box representing the command center, and at a little distance, off two diagonal corners, smaller boxes simulated flakwagons. Wooden pegs represented Jerrie troopers; each trooper was given his own peg, and wrote his service number on it. Everyone and every squad drilled their own roles.

Each platoon was labeled with its company designation: B, C, D or E.

When they'd drilled the mission to the satisfaction of their platoon leaders and squad leaders, Captain Zenawi threw in complications: troopers not reaching the drop zone, or the premature discovery of one squad or another. Or Esau being unable to fly the unfamiliar Wyzhñyñy floater.

On the very first day, Esau had asked three very basic questions: "How will we know how to fly their floater, and drive their flakwagons, and fire their flak guns?"

Grinning, Zenawi explained. "Indi ordnance specialists

flew to the howitzer cemetery almost before the hulls cooled. With salvage vehicles, and orders to bring in a howitzer and a flakwagon in the best shape they could find. They brought in three flakwagons, and cannibalized them to cobble together one that works. So you'll all get a chance to start it, and drive it a bit." The faces he looked at were very interested. "They also brought in two power drums that were only partly expended, so those who need to will get to fire a trasher."

Back on Lüneburger's they'd been quickied on driving light AG ground vehicles, and had loved it. Now the idea of driving a flakwagon, perhaps even firing its heavy weapons, really brightened their eyes. Most of them, he reminded himself, were in their late teens and early twenties. "As for the floater," he went on, "Sergeant Esau, you'll have to settle for learning to fly one of ours, you and your squad. An instructor will talk to you about some of the possible control differences you may encounter in a Wyzhñyñy machine. Then it will be up to you to fly it if you can."

For despite his promotion to platoon sergeant, in this raid Esau would wear another hat. He was regarded as the best stealth man in B Company, so he'd been assigned the most critical single job on the raid: to *steal* the Wyzhñyñy command center.

And as 4th Squad's sergeant—they had a 4th Squad again—Jael had one of the next two most critical jobs.

The next week they went over it all again, this time on a full-scale mock-up, with themselves in the action roles. Themselves and F Company, which played the Wyzhñyñy much more effectively than calves had. In the struggles, lips were inevitably split, eyes blackened, noses bloodied. But when wrists and ankles had been securely taped, the captives were dragged from the orchard no more roughly than necessary, to be loaded onto genuine cargo floaters. The injuries were minor, and gave the medics something real to do. They also "treated," and transferred to medivacs, jumpers designated as casualties by umpires from Division. After the second day they ran their drills at night, for realism, and slept late in the morning.

When each drill was over, the casualties were declared whole and sound again, the enemy ordained human, and they all attended a critique of the exercise by the Division referee and Captain Zenawi.

The mock-up had been prepared in advance by a company of Burger engineers, on a prairie area 380 miles from base. To serve as the orchard, they'd planted rows of stout, ten-foot posts at appropriate intervals. Among the posts they pitched actual squad tents in which the troops would live that week, along with two mess tents and canopied latrine pits. They also installed the two inoperable, partly stripped Wyzhñyñy flakwagons.

By the end of the second week, everyone had familiarized themselves with the operational third flakwagon, and dry-fired its light, four-barrelled trasher. Each member of 4th Squad had manuevered it around and live-fired its trasher.

Esau and his team had each flown a floater, with a certified pilot beside him. And, on each subsequent day a new floater was brought, each with the control system differently rigged, for them to figure out if they could. Only once did the Indi floater tech have to solve a problem for them.

And every raider became proficient with the short bola—a tough, slender, thirty-nine-inch cord with weights on both ends. Properly thrown, they tangled the legs of rustled Wyzhñyñy livestock. Coupled with a quick, aggressive, three-man follow-up, and tough plastic tape, the bola would hopefully serve in lieu of stunners.

On the last night at the prairie bivouac, Esau and Jael walked out of camp beneath a richness of stars that both beggared and lifted the soul. The Candle had set, and the Lamp wouldn't rise till near dawn. Esau had carried a poncho and an insect repellent field generator, and they'd gone to a cedar grove, to make love in the privacy of its deeper darkness.

Afterward they walked slowly back to camp, holding hands.

"Do you recall," Esau said, "what I asked you after the Tank Park Raid?"

She didn't answer at once. Not as if she didn't remember, but as if she was thinking about it. "I remember," she murmured at last.

"What do you think?"

Again her answer lagged, then finally she told him. "I'm still against it, for me. But if you want to, I won't complain or say you shouldn't, because in most ways, to sign up is a good thing."

His only reply was a nod, and after a moment she spoke again. "I read something when I was a child, in Elder Hofer's *Contemplations on the Testaments*. Even then it struck me as right, and I've reread it since. 'Beware what you set your mind on, lest you thereby create it in the world of phenomena.' He was writing about wishing ill on people you don't like, and the debt it might create for you in the eyes of God. But it seemed to me the meaning went beyond that.

"And I'm afraid if I sign a bot agreement, I might bring harm on myself, and maybe those around me, in order to fulfill it."

Esau frowned. He didn't find it convincing, but again said nothing. After a minute they made out the darkness of tents beneath the stars. "But if *you* want to," Jael repeated softly, "I won't say you shouldn't. Because . . . because I may be worrying about nothing."

He turned, gripped her shoulders. "I'll let be," he said, "for now at least. And if I change my mind, I'll tell you before I sign."

"Thank you, Esau," she said, and reaching up, pulled his face down and kissed him. "You're a good husband, a good person, and I love you dearly."

Two nights later, at 2350 hours, the Candle was well down, and high thin clouds screened the stars. Esau was planing in from the north, navigating by his HUDs. Now, by night vision, he could see the orchard itself.

What he didn't see were the sparks and vivid flashes far above.

As he drew nearer, he watched for the edge of the uncut grain. It wouldn't do to overshoot it. His night vision showed the standing crop darker than the stubble field.

Ensign Hawkins had explained it—something about dew and "evaporative cooling"—but it hadn't meant anything to Esau. He could also make out the broad path a crew had trod through the stubble, and steered so he'd land near it, but in the uncut crop. He could see two others who'd landed ahead of him. They were stuffing gear.

His encased blaster and stuffbag dangled on a line below his feet. The ground leaped upward, the 1.42 gees of gravity jarring him even as he rolled. Then he knelt and looked around. He was, he decided, about three hundred yards from the orchard. Looking back he saw two more jumpers incoming. Their chutes and thermal coveralls were black, but by night vision the coveralls shone faintly golden, barely perceptible.

After pulling in his blaster, stuffbag and chute, he shucked out of his coverall, removed his musette bag and gear, and stuffed chute and blaster case into the stuffbag. It took seconds. By then two more troopers were on the ground. Another was coming in fast, and still another was in sight.

He called up a time readout; keeping on schedule was more important than having the full team. "Bag your gear," he murmured into his helmet mike, "and be ready to move. And keep low." The ripe grain was pale. Their black night-fatigues would be conspicuous against it. Dismissing the no-show from his mind, he murmured, "I'm moving out. Keep twenty-yard intervals crossing the stubble." After two weeks of rehearsal they knew what to do, but reminders were standard.

He straightened just enough to locate the path through the stubble field again, then moved through the crop on all fours. Thirty yards brought him to the stubble's edge, where he paused, prone. The footpath didn't reach the uncut crop. He had twenty yards to go through pale stubble eight to ten inches high. There was no way to avoid it. Leaving his bulky stuffbag just within the crop, he began creeping, pulling with his elbows, pushing with his feet, blaster cradled on his forearms. Then he reached the footpath, where Wyzhñyñy feet had scuffed and trod the stubble down, baring dark earth.

Once more he paused, scanning for a sentry along the

orchard's edge, a sentry on four legs, with a muscular torso rising from the shoulders like a short-furred neck with arms. When he'd finished his scan, his night vision had found just one. The Wyzhñyñy stood unmoving, perhaps forty yards left of where the path led.

The sonofabitch could be looking at me right now, Esau thought. *If I was him, I'd let me crawl closer, wait till I was almost there.* Meanwhile, all he could do was keep crawling and watching, and if the Wyz raised his blaster, pot him first.

That was the first serious complication the captain had thrown into the drills: premature firing. If it happened, he'd have to change his team mission, and speed things up as much as possible. Until then, slow and easy were the key words.

Before he reached the orchard, he could see the sentry's head hanging. The sonofabitch was dozing on his feet! That was bound to be a bigger problem with four-legged sentries than with two.

Within the orchard's edge, Esau rose, moved ten yards to his right, then knelt waiting by a tree while Morris and Avery crossed, and spaced themselves. Only then did Esau start slowly through the orchard, threading his way among tents, avoiding tent ropes. He heard no sound, not even a Wyzhñyñy snore.

The control center, if that's what it actually was, sat in the middle of the orchard. Timbers had been set as a foundation, keeping the chassis twenty inches or so above the ground. No tents stood within ten yards. Its door was closed, but light shone weakly through the windscreen. There was no sentry. When Morris and Avery had reached the small opening and stopped, Esau lowered himself and crept slowly to the floater, belly to the ground. The floater was light-enough green, he didn't want his two-legged form outlined against it. When he reached the door, he looked around, then rose to one knee, slung his blaster, drew his stunner, and tried the external latch. It seemed to work like those on Terran floaters. Within the orchard there was no discernible breeze. Very slowly, very carefully, he opened the door half an inch. Dull light emerged. Quickly he stood, pulled it wide and stepped in.

The Wyzhñyñy charge of quarters had heard something. His torso turned, their eyes met, and Esau pressed the firing stud. The stunner's almost inaudible condenser hummed, the upright torso folded slowly, and the seated body fell sideways, toppling the low, padded chair.

Esau closed the door, and after a moment's fumbling, locked it. Less than ten seconds had elapsed since he'd entered. Judging from marine experience on Tagus, the stunned CQ would never waken. There'd been no alarm, and the control screen was serenely featureless. *So far, so good,* he thought. *Let's just hope no Wyzhñyñy radios in now.*

Using his helmet mike, he reported his progress on the command frequency. The others knew what to do next.

Jael's squad had landed east of the orchard. Its mission was to capture and hold the flakwagon that lay off the southeast corner, and with it, defend the raid from outside air or ground interference. Within four minutes of landing, she and her squad lay in the edge of the uncut crop, fifteen yards from the flakwagon. She could see no Wyzhñyñy on or inside the machine, but nonetheless they waited. They were not to move until either Esau had captured the control center, or there was shooting, or the tiny numerals of her HUD clock read 0030 hours— whichever came first.

They would not leave their stuffbags in the crop. The flakwagon controls were too far from the seat, even for a long-legged Sikh, let alone one of her people. So stuffbags would be used for seats.

She wasn't thinking about that, though. She was scanning the east edge of the orchard, and what she could see of the south edge. She'd found the eastside sentry, even laid her blaster sight on him. Southside was someone else's responsibility.

A voice in her helmet startled her. Esau's. "Raider command, I've taken the Wyz command center. Stunned the CQ. He's either dead or dying, and I've locked the door. So far as I know, no one knows we're here. Over."

"Acknowledged, Esau. Teams proceed with the mission."

❖   ❖   ❖

Jael looked around. She couldn't see any of her squad, but they'd all checked in. She crept across the intervening stubble to the flakwagon, Steven Tyler to her right, mirroring her move. Standing slowly, she peered into the cab, and saw only Tyler peering in on the other side. Her squad, she knew, was crouching in the standing grain, blasters ready. Stepping to the weapon platform, she pulled herself up to peer into the back. No one there, either. Smoothly she bellied over the armored side. A moment later, Tyler joined her. This flakwagon was a lighter-weight version of the one they'd practiced on. The armored sides were high enough to protect a Wyzhñyñy if he kept his head down, and the four-barreled heavy slammer had a gunner's shield.

She heard the cab doors open, a soft sound—Ambler and Hoke, as drilled. So far, so good. She felt calm as wash water. Stepping onto the gunner's platform, she activated the firing system. On the sighting screen, tiny lights showed traversing, elevation, and the power drum all engaged. The hum was louder than she'd expected, but according to the buoys, the wagon was 214 feet from the orchard. The gun swiveled, quick but smooth.

A Wyzhñyñy voice called, jerking her attention from the sighting screen. The eastside sentry was trotting toward her. Carefully she drew her stunner and knelt low, waiting. "Don't fire," she murmured into her mike. She wanted to avoid noise if possible. *Stun him as soon as his head appears,* she told herself, *and he'll never trigger his blaster.*

In her helmet, Jael heard one of C Company's people report the Wyzhñyñy's approach, body low, torso and head forward instead of upright. She expected its head to rise slowly. Instead it *reared*, blaster raised and ready. As she thumbed her stunner, she felt a monstrous pain in her belly, and lost consciousness.

In the control center, the first blaster fire was followed almost at once by a fusillade, some of it sounding like a flakwagon. Esau swore—something almost unthinkable before he'd left home. He'd pretty much figured out the controls while he'd waited. Now he tried powering up, hoping nothing heavy hit the floater, especially the windscreen in front of him. Windscreens were supposed to be blast resistant, but he didn't trust something he could see through.

The gravdrive growled softly, and a HUD came to life on the windscreen—concentric hair-thin rings of blue light with a pale yellow spot in the center. Quickly the spot turned blue. The joystick knob was obviously made to turn on the shaft, so he turned it. A new HUD appeared, and the floater rose. In seconds he was above the trees.

"Raider command," he said, "raider command! This is Esau! She flies! I'm above the trees now! Don't shoot me down!"

He turned the knob further, swiveled the stick and shoved it forward, sending the floater toward where Captain Zenawi's command post should be. In this contingency, his next job was to stand by as courier, bus driver, or whatever.

Almost at once, Steven Tyler had shouted, "Medic!" Then he saw the blood welling from Jael's lower abdomen. "God help us, it's Jael! And it's BAD!" Then the awakening blaster fire reminded him, and he mounted the gunner's seat, seeking targets.

Because the flakwagon teams would be outside the main action, an Indi medic had parachuted with each of them. At Tyler's cry, 4th Squad's medic had dashed to the flakwagon and clambered over the side. Now he crouched beside Jael. "Gentle Jesus!" he muttered. Blood flowed across the deck, spreading. In four seconds, with the fastest "scissors" on New Jerusalem, he'd cut away the ripped tatters of uniform; in two more seconds held a canister from which he sprayed a pressurized liquid into her abdomen, his other hand shifting her ruined intestines for better coverage.

In military jargon, the fluid was simply X-1. It would close the torn blood vessels within seconds, ending hemorrhage. After which surgical repair would be impossible in the division's field hospital. But without it . . .

Within a minute or so she'd be clinically dead, and soon afterward beyond CNS salvage. He checked a dog tag. Bot agreements were common these days, but her dog tag didn't show one. "Tyler," he asked, "do you know if she's said anything about a bot agreement?"

"I don't know of any."

The medic switched his comm to the platoon frequency. "Ensign Hawkins, this is Med Tech-1 Shinassi. I have a potential bot case here, Jael Wesley, but her tags don't show a bot agreement. Has she said anything orally? Over."

Esau stared at the radio, shocked. He broke in at once. "Shinassi, this is Esau. Just before we loaded out, she said she'd decided to do it. Shall I pick her up? Over."

He was shaking all over.

"Thanks, Esau, but she'll keep. I've given her X-1; now I'll give her Stasis 1. Med Tech Amud Shinassi out."

In time! In time! Esau stopped shaking, but now a different specter hung over him. What would Jael say when she awoke?

Though intense, the fighting in and about the orchard was brief and one-sided. The raiders were superbly prepared, attained total surprise, faced non-combat formations, removed the enemy's sole means of calling for help, and captured their heavy weapons before the Wyzhñyñy even knew they were there. Almost a textbook mission. When Wyzhñyñy APFs were sent, it was too late, and en route were attacked by strong Indi air units.

The bolas worked as hoped. In the confusion on the ground, the Jerries hadn't even tried to distinguish the larger, reddish-brown Wyzhñyñy—"the reds"—from the duns. They simply taped and loaded all they could before the order was given to pull out. And left with four more than War House had ordered—six reds and ten duns, as it turned out.

Early in the fighting, numerous duns fled the orchard, a major surprise. The flakwagons took a heavy toll on them. Except for a few who reached the standing crop and hid, all who weren't captured were killed.

By comparison, Jerrie casualties were moderate: seven died on the ground, and five more on the medivac or in the hospital. Only eight wounded survived, five of them bot cases. The high ratio of killed to wounded was normal for energy weapons, and in this fight, projectile weapons were not involved.

Two Jerries were injured when struck on the head by bolas being twirled or thrown by others.

Captain Zenawi made sure that all the stuffbags were evacuated with the troops. Hopefully the Wyzhñyñy would never know how this incursion was made.

not even bunkers. Instead they adapted modern tools to 16th and 17th century Scandinavian strategies. They should do nicely, if the Wyzhñyñy air support units were adequately suppressed.

The Battle of the First Days had taught the gosthodar that attacking the humans across open fields was unpromising and terribly costly. The Tank Park Raid established that the humans were aggressive and daring. The human surveillance buoys made stealth operations impractical, and the destruction of his heavy howitzer battalion limited the punishment he could inflict on the humans without closing with them.

Then had come the night of the Pecan Orchard Raid, and everything changed. Not because of the raid itself. Though insulting and mystifying, it had not been very damaging. But because of what else happened that night.

Commodore Xarsku had sent scouts into F-space to exchange radio messages with the gosthodar, who used the opportunity to describe his problems. He wanted—according to him, he needed—the destruction of the humans' wilderness base. And given the base's concealment screen, and the human surveillance buoys, he insisted that this required powerful intervention from space.

Xarsku didn't know as much as he'd have liked about the human space force remaining in the system, but he did know it was substantially more powerful than his own. Nonetheless, his function was to support the colony, so he'd scripted an attack. A bombard would approach the planet in warpdrive, and emerge in F-space some twenty miles out. Using triangulation, and data from Jilchûk, it would then pound the entire blind area—an action that would take about half an hour. At the same time, two marine hunter craft would take out the surveillance buoys. Meanwhile, two supply ships were to emerge as near to Jilchûk's main underground supply base as they dared, unload cargo as rapidly as possible, and leave.

Xarsku had no illusions; the supply ships would probably be destroyed before they finished unloading. But even so, they could easily make the difference between survival and starvation.

To cover these actions, Xarsku's planetary guard was to engage its alien opponent, holding its collective attention.

Jilchûk knew little about space warfare, so he'd awaited the action optimistically. His Intelligence section monitored Xarsku's radio communications throughout the action, and Jilchûk had followed it play by play.

Xarsku's plan was simple, and there was something to be said for simple plans. But this one had been predicted, so Kereenyaga was prepared. Even so, setting the place and time of engagement gave Xarsku an initial advantage, which cost the humans a cruiser and two corvettes. The gosthodar felt a swell of exultation. But the humans' greater numbers and firepower soon drove Xarsku back into warpspace.

Meanwhile, near the planetary surface, Xarsku's hunters had destroyed the two human surveillance buoys. His bombard, on the other hand, lay broken and smoking on a forest ridge. It had never gotten into position. Designed for punishing, not fighting, it had been attacked by four of Kereenyaga's corvettes, whose simultaneous torpedo salvos had disrupted its force shield, destroying generator and drives.

As if in retribution, the hunters that had destroyed the buoys then scorched two swaths across the blind area before Kereenyaga's corvettes could engage them. One escaped into warpspace. The other, crippled, careened into the forest miles away, and blew up.

The corvettes then caught the cargo ships in the act of unloading, and slammed torpedos into each of them before heading back into near-space.

When it was over, Jilchûk found solace in the destruction of the buoys. Also, substantial supplies had been transferred before the supply ships were attacked, and more after their fires had been controlled.

But the enemy on the ground had not been destroyed. Damaged, wounded, but not destroyed. Their destruction remained up to him. *Move quickly!* he thought. *Quickly and powerfully!* He'd told himself that before, he realized, but this time nothing would turn him. There'd be no hesitation, and no backing off. And with the buoys gone,

the enemy couldn't know or predict his actions as they
had before.

General Pak watched Wyzhñyñy infantry—a very long
column of fours—trotting easily down the road toward the
forest. The bulk of their equipment and supplies were
carried by AG trucks, and their speed of foot was sobering. He'd realized before he'd left Terra that this life-form
would run faster than humans, but actually watching
them . . . they and their guardian flakwagons, of which the
Wyzhñyñy seemed to have an endless supply.

At least he could watch them. Presumably the Wyzhñyñy
didn't know that Kereenyaga had replaced the lost buoys
with another. The Jerries had promptly nicknamed it "Lonesome Moses," which surprised the general when he heard
about it. It seemed irreverent for troops with their background.

Lonesome Moses provided less detail, less perspective,
and had far less versatility than the buoys the Wyzhñyñy
had destroyed, but it was infinitely better than no buoy at
all. Immediately after the fighting on the First Day, Xarsku
had sent a single daring Hunter to shoot down the first
two. Kereenyaga had quickly deployed his reserve pair, and
ordered his engineering section to cobble together a
backup. Shipsmind had provided the basic information, and
his engineers and technicians had provided parts and
ingenuity. And with it now in place, they'd begun on still
another, just in case.

Equally important was Colonel Schrager's Burger engineers, building defenses in the wilderness. The engineers
and the Jerries. The colonel had suggested that progress
would be faster with help, and that a battalion of resourceful backwoods infantry would be just the ticket. Pak had
complied. A Jerrie battalion had pitched in with beam saws,
AG sleds, and strong backs, felling trees and throwing up
breastworks. Pak had visited the work in progress, and been
impressed by the strength, energy and cheerfulness of the
Jerries at work. They treated it like a holiday, hard though
it was.

And urgent now, because Wyzhñyñy command was
moving troops into the forest at two points, one division

eighteen miles west of the howitzer cemetery, another thirty miles east of it. And strong reserves had been moved to several locations, with APFs. Obviously the Wyzhñyñy commander intended to attack at unpredictable points simultaneously. As soon as he'd made a breakthrough, his reserves would exploit it.

What Pak didn't know was, the key reserves were "reds"—what was left of the Wyzhñyñy warrior brigade.

Meanwhile Wyzhñyñy batteries were also on the roads, apparently detached from their infantry brigades. He wasn't sure what plans Wyzhñyñy command had for them, but he was sure he wouldn't like them. Lonesome Moses couldn't identify the caliber, but they seemed smaller than those destroyed by the marines. Five or six-inch bores, he guessed. They should have enough range to lay fire on the Wilderness Base, and on much of the defenses the Burgers had been building. It wouldn't be remotely comparable to what the Wyzhñyñy bombard would have done, but he was glad he'd moved his hospital and "bot shop" to the backup site, thirty-five miles north.

And the artillery were accompanied by tanks and flakwagons. Perhaps all the tanks the Wyzhñyñy had left. A simple count showed that the enemy had more tanks than he had. What was building here, he did not doubt, was a decisive showdown.

We'll see, Pak thought, *what Major Phayakapong accomplishes with our own modest project.*

Despite more than seven centuries of Commonwealth peace, the lineage of Major Patrick Feliks Phayakapong had kept and nourished a long military tradition. Privately for the most part. Eleven centuries earlier, an ancestor named McClintock had fought in the North American War of Secession. He'd been a private in J.E.B. Stuart's cavalry at the First Battle of Manassas, a sergeant at South Mountain, a lieutenant at Chancellorsville and Gettysburg, and finally a captain at Yellow Tavern. Where he lost his general to a Yankee bullet, and his shattered left leg to a surgeon's saw.

His experiences, pride, and storytelling began the tradition. Almost as far back, in various tributaries of the family line, others fought in the Crimean War, the Franco-Prussian War, the Boer War, the Moro Resistance, the European Great War . . . but either they were not story-tellers, or their stories were lost. Members of the family had compiled histories of their ancestors' units and campaigns, but those weren't the same as personal accounts.

Then a McClintock great-grandson fought in the Hitler War, serving as an armor officer under the fabled George Patton. A decade later he served as a senior officer under Walton Walker and Matthew Ridgeway in the Korean War. And described it all in his published memoirs, giving the tradition new life. Another forebear served as a sergeant in the U.S. Marine Corps in the Southeast Asian War, and another as an airborne ranger. The marine said he'd never have told his story if his grandfather hadn't passed his along. The ranger kept his memories to himself, but a buddy in his squad, in *his* memoirs, often referred to "Sergeant Walking Coyote," calling him a warrior's warrior.

All of this built and enriched the tradition. In yet another branch of the family, a British special forces officer had served throughout the difficult years of the guerrilla war in Malaysia. He'd shared none of it with his children, but a daughter assembled the basics from official sources, and interviewed aging veterans of her grandfather's unit. Another forebear fought, survived and escaped as a Shan guerrilla in the ill-fated Myanmar Revolution. His children recorded his reminiscences which, written down and translated, added fundamentally different material to the family lore.

Shortly before the Troubles, the core of the family went as colonists to Indi Prime, the first deep-space colony—one of only two sponsored by the government. During the Troubles, the deep-space colonies were lost track of. But after reconnection, in every generation some family member returned to Terra to join the fleet (such as it was), or its marines, or the Terran Planetary Defense Force, and kept the tradition alive. Despite the long centuries of low public esteem, little opportunity for advancement, and limited meaningful function beyond study, brainstorming, virtual warfare, and weapons design. They kept the faith. And when they retired, it was usually to Indi Prime, often bringing with them a wife and child, or children. Twice from families with a military tradition of their own.

But Major Phayakapong was the first in a very long time to ride a battle tank. Occasionally, mainly in the moments before sleep, he took time to savor what he thought of as the privilege, wondering now and then if he'd been a tanker in an earlier life.

Just now, however, his attention was on his mission, which so far had been uneventful. But that would soon change. His battalion had taken heavy losses during the Battle of the First Days, but in the reorganization that followed, it had been brought back nearly to full strength. On this mission, his infantry companies and their APCs had been left behind to help defend the base. His job was to strike deep within Wyz Country, and all he had with him were his forty-one battle tanks and eight flakwagons.

It was near midnight, and he rode in the turret of his command tank, its hatch open. The night smelled of damp soil and vegetation, for it had rained the day just past, then cleared, and now dew had formed. It occurred to him that the ancestor who'd ridden with Stuart would have smelled horse manure and urine instead, particularly near the rear of the column. Sometimes there'd have been the stink of black powder explosions, while the tanker who'd followed Patton and Walker would have smelled pungent fumes from internal combustion engines. And during combat? Probably the oxydation products of nitrocellulose. *Different times, different experiences*, he told himself. Tonight he'd smell ozone generated by heavy trasher pulses.

Via his visor HUDs, the jury-rigged Lonesome Moses kept him aware of where the Wyzhñyñy infantry columns were, where his target was, and where he was relative to both. The columns were coming together from various locations, merging on a few major routes. Several times he'd detoured to avoid discovery, for he was going south while the enemy was going north. And human tanks, like other human ground-proximity vehicles, looked different from Wyzhñyñy vehicles having the same function.

Just now the road ahead was clear. He stopped in a riverine woods, to let his men get out of their armored boxes, move around a bit, and relieve themselves. It was undesirable to enter action with a full bladder or colon.

According to his HUD he had just 1800 yards to go. Quietly he radioed orders. The column slowed, then deployed just behind the brow of a low rise, and a new HUD replaced the others all along the line. Just across the brow the ground dipped mildly, then rose again, becoming a steep ridge 1200 yards ahead. Less than 300 yards from where the tanks sat, forest began.

His tankers knew what to do. "On my count," the major said, then paused. "Ten, nine, eight . . ."

At zero the night flared. Penetration pulses slammed deeply into rock, and for the first few salvos it felt really good. Then the rug was pulled from beneath the major's feet. Prior to the arrival of the Liberation Corps, the Wyzhñyñy had cut gun emplacements into the bluff. And after a very brief delay—the crews had been sleeping—they'd returned fire. Lots of heavy fire. He lost thirteen of his forty-one tanks and four of his flakwagons before he reached the riverine woods again. In their cover he stopped, to throw off the enemy gunners' timing, and reorganize. And open his turret hatch again. His HUDs suggested it was safe for the moment, and he didn't like the stink of sweaty fear.

Pat, he told himself, *you really kicked the hornets' nest that time.* Still, his heavy trashers had sent tons of rock crashing down on the road—and presumably onto the entry to the Wyzhñyñy cavern complex. Pak, from surveillance information, had concluded it was the Wyzhñyñy headquarters base. Actually it wasn't. It was an important Wyzhñyñy supply base.

From the riverine woods, Major Phayakapong traveled mostly westward, targeted from time to time by Wyzhñyñy attack floaters, but unmolested by ground forces. The floater attacks were hit and run, directed mainly at his flakwagons, which gave as good as they got. And vice versa. He lost another tank, had two more with problems, and was down to two flakwagons. Then a flight of good guys arrived, and chased the bogies off. Shortly afterward his battered battalion reached the Mickle's, and turning north,

crossed on the first bridge they came to. They continued
mainly west then, jogging north from time to time at crossroads.

Shortly before dawn they reached the relative safety of
the forest, well away from any Wyzhñyñy. There the tankers
paused to heat and eat field rations. Then they lay down
on their fart sacks and slept in the open air. They could
hear distant fighting, back in the forest, but it didn't keep
them awake.

The woods were thick with the devil's music: the rapid
popping of blasters and slammers, the crackling of pulses
creating miniature vacuums through the air, the hard sound
of pulses striking trees.

Ensign Rrokiç spotted a source—humans behind a
breastwork of logs. "Up there!" he shouted, then sheltered
as well as he could behind a thick trunk. He hated to
gesture; it attracted enemy fire. "Don't just lie there!" he
snapped into his helmet mike. "Shoot, damn it! And don't
bunch up!"

Ensign Rrokiç was a nanny—as large as some warriors,
almost as strong—and protective. Genetically, protection
meant care and guarding of the young, but the master and
warrior genders massaged the nanny protective instinct and
extended it to cover defense of the species. The purpose
being to turn nannies into surrogate warriors when necessary. In fact, the nanny gender provided many reserve
unit noncoms.

Gender manipulation and noncom training worked about
as well with Rrokiç as it did with any nanny. He yelled well,
and could manhandle his troops when necessary. But the
hard authority of the warrior gender was never really
duplicated.

What was compelling was his rank, and the sense his
orders made. His platoon took cover as best it could, behind
tree trunks, or in the visual cover provided by the tops of
trees the humans had felled. From there they fought back.

All day they'd been moving slowly through the damned-
est mess Rrokiç had ever seen. The humans had felled
thousands on thousands of trees, in unpatterned bands
through the forest. Usually with the upper parts in your

face. The barriers weren't everywhere; that wouldn't have been practical. They'd been located to extend or connect natural terrain features, crowding the advancing Wyzhñyñy into whatever situations the humans wanted them. Or simply pinched the advance off, so they had to turn back to find a way around. Typically the barriers led into cleared fields of fire, and there was little anyone could do about it. *Little by little we advance,* Rrokiç told himself, *yet it seems we're always on the defensive.*

Now as before, when his platoon had taken what cover they could, the fight turned into a grenade exchange, delivered mostly by launchers. And his people were more exposed.

So he called for a flamethrower again.

Near one flank of C Company's position, Captain Freddie Bibesco Singh crouched in his command post, scanning with his small camouflaged periscope. His blastermen, slammermen and grenadiers were reaping well. As before, the Wyzhñyñy had moved into the visual cover of the abatis. Now they'd no doubt call in a flamethrower. Meanwhile, the Wyzhñyñy grenadiers and mortarmen were using timed fuses to produce airbursts, exploding above his troopers' improvised shelters.

It was time to deliver his new surprise. Setting his mike, he voiced the ignition command. Barely hidden by old leaves, ground vegetation, and the outermost foliage of the abatis, explosions erupted like a string of giant ladyfingers, as camouflaged shot-mines blew along a line of detcord. Debris rose, and cries of pain. Meanwhile, his people kept firing.

From where he crouched, he couldn't see the Wyzhñyñy flamethrower being brought up, but from treetops a little distance off, his camouflaged snipers could. They'd already been making things hot for Wyzhñyñy mortar crews. Though they paid; the Wyzhñyñy had learned that this enemy climbed.

A sniper spotted the flamethrower and felled the Wyzhñyñy carrying it, but another picked it up. Then some Wyzhñyñy threw smoke grenades, concealing both flamethrower and mortars. "B Company pull out!" Bibesco ordered. His own smoke bombs popped and billowed, his blastermen and grenadiers got to their feet, his snipers lowered themselves on ropes, and they all pulled back. Concealed a short distance to the rear, out of sight of the Wyzhñyñy, were their squad-size APCs. These would take them to their next ambush position much more quickly than they could manage on foot, and they needed to set up before the Wyzhñyñy arrived.

Not all of C Company would ride with their squad. The medics loaded some of them out to the hospital, or to the "bot shop," or simply to Graves Registration.

It was noon before Major Phayakapong ordered his crews back into their tanks. General Pak had given him his next assignment. Three battalions of Wyzhñyñy armored howitzers were on the move, four batteries in each. With tank escorts. It looked as if they planned to establish fire bases— probably three of them. It was unlikely they knew about Lonesome Moses, and Pak didn't want them to, so he hadn't started molesting them yet. Phayakapong was to continue westward, and be ready to hit them after nightfall.

The major decided to pick his way through the forest for a while. It would keep him out of sight. He hadn't mentioned that he now had only twenty-five battle-worthy tanks and two flakwagons. The general would already know that, or close enough, from Lonesome Moses, and anyway there was nothing to be done about it.

Normally, in the evening, Esau heard all the sounds of the forest. Fell asleep listening to the chirping of crickets, the peeping of tree lizards, the occasional grunting basso of a bull owl, or the warbling alto of a mouse owl. Even, barely audible, woodborers chewing tunnels inside a nearby fallen tree. And best of all, from above the trees, the thin piercing whistle of night hawks catching insects.

But this evening none of it registered.

Most of the division had been fighting all day, in the forest off both east and west. Far enough away, he hadn't heard any of it. And it seemed to Esau that tonight the war—their war, on New Jerusalem—would be won or lost. Not over, but won or lost. Weren't hardly any fighting units left on base, except the strategic reserve.

Which included the airborne qualified platoons, and now they were being sent out, trotting northward through the evening forest. There'd been no time to drill the mission— it was that urgent—but their briefing had been thorough, with a demo on the screen.

Probably it would work out all right. They were all veterans, and drilled or not, they had a clear sharp picture of what needed to be done.

He glanced at the man he trotted beside. He'd known Ensign Hawkins for—about a year he guessed. Esau wasn't someone who kept a mental calendar. But he had little idea of what the ensign thought about in the privacy of his mind. Didn't know all that much about him. He'd grown up in a Sikh neighborhood in a Terran town called Padstow, where it rained a lot; had a wife and children; and before the war he'd lived by a lake somewhere in North America. But what counted was, he was honest, and able, and treated people right. His platoon liked him and could depend on him.

Somewhere ahead were APFs: four of them, for four airborne platoons again. Tonight they were being called "A Company Airborne (temporary)," and 2nd Platoon simply "Hawkins' Platoon." But all four had jumped and fought together at the Pecan Orchard, and felt confident about each other.

Esau really didn't want to die yet, because he hadn't seen Jael since before her body had been killed. He needed to go visit her, so she could give him Tophet for lying to the medic, and maybe tell him she never wanted to see him again. He owed her that much, at least. When he'd got back from the Pecan Orchard, he'd gone off alone in the woods and wept hard bitter tears, with choking sobs that like to have torn him apart. But he'd have lied again if need be, because he couldn't just let her die, he loved her so.

Every day, floaters flew off north to the bot shop and the hospital, and he'd asked Captain Zenawi for a half day off. But the captain reminded him that after someone got bottled, they spent a few days in a kind of sleep. For what they called "neurological detraumatization," that helped them heal.

Remembering had started silent tears. Bottled. He hoped

it wasn't too bad. She could have been in the loving arms of God, if it hadn't been for him.

Now, courtesy of night vision, their APFs were visible among the trees, and his attention returned to real time. Above the forest roof there was probably a little twilight left, but down where they were it was dark night. The armored floaters were lined up in two ranks along a sizeable creek. From there they could lift through the slender break it made in the forest roof.

Major Chou was already there from Division, overseeing. He'd land afterward with E Company, to lead the demolitions follow-through.

They broke ranks to pick up their gear, which had been hauled there by AG cargo sleds. They wouldn't be jumping from high enough to require thermal coveralls. Gloves and winter underwear would do. They simply buckled on their chutes, snapped on their gear, checked each other out, then boarded their floaters and belted themselves onto their seats. Then the APFs rose carefully through the trees and into the young night sky.

Sergeant Isaiah Vernon sat on another APF, on a short hop east. As part of Pak's tactical reserve, all six bot platoons were going out together as a combat team—132 warbots plus 12 salvage bots and a command staff of four.

Their mission commander was Major Einer Arslanian Singh. The story was, Arslanian had been taking airborne training on Masada, got caught in a squall, and came down in a rock pile, tearing up his knees. Afterward, back on Terra, he'd specialized in bot tactics, even though there were no bots. That was before anyone had heard of the Wyzhñyñy.

Then had come the message from Tagus, and suddenly bots were dearer than diamonds. But at that time, having lost one's legs wasn't enough to qualify. Then Arslanian had another accident. Except the rumor was he'd set it up—had sacrificed his eyesight in order to be bottled. Isaiah didn't know if the story was true or not, but Arslanian ended up a major, commanding the 1st Jerrie bot contingent. He'd planned and led two different platoon actions. Now he'd lead a long company.

Isaiah, whose nature it was to like and accept people, was happy to have the major in command. Because this would be the most dangerous mission they'd been on. They'd be set down in the midst of a Wyzhñyñy operations headquarters, if they got that far.

The evening breeze was cool and clean, but Major Patrick Feliks Phayakapong's T-shirt was wet with sweat. They'd traveled buttoned up for a while, because after they'd left the forest they'd been shadowed by Wyzhñyñy floaters. Whether scouts or fighters he didn't know; Moses wasn't up to such distinctions. Then word came that a flight of Indi fighters were on the way, and he'd opened his turret hatch to watch. He didn't see much; most of it was out of his view. The Indi flight commander radioed that they'd shot down two of three, and the third had fled. The major appreciated that someone was looking out for him.

Meanwhile he was running low on time. His orders had been updated, and his HUD showed a Moses-eye view of the Wyzhñyñy force he was supposed to attack. Four batteries of howitzers—forty-eight guns in all—escorted by a company of tanks. Apparently they planned to set up a fire base to shell the Jerrie regiment manning the eastern forest defenses.

But the tanks had changed direction, apparently to attack his own battered force.

Eight additional batteries and another tank company were headed farther west on a different road, apparently to set up another fire base or bases. Probably to shell Headquarters Base.

According to Moses, the Wyzhñyñy no longer had scouts up, or out on the ground for that matter. Hard to believe, but if true, then neither enemy force knew what he was doing in real time. "Well crap," the major muttered, "it's now or forget about it." He keyed his mike and ordered twelve tanks, two groups of six, to diverge from his line of advance. Each group was to hit the Wyz tank force from the flank. To maximize surprise, he'd tell them when to fire, unless of course the Wyz fired first.

Then, if it looked doable, he'd take the rest of his force

through or around the Wyz tanks, and attack the east base howitzers. It looked like the best move he had available.

Calling Division command, he told them what he planned. "Fine. Do it," Pak said. "And, Pat, you need to know I've got airborne raiders scheduled to take out the central fire base. That's why I let the Wyzhñyñy scouts shadow you as long as I did. It fixed their attention on you.

"The jumpers will be in mortal jeopardy if the tanks from the east base show up there. So the more hell you raise, the better chance the airborne will have. They've got a very tough and dangerous job. Like yours."

The first salvo of 5.6-inch shells—forty-eight of them—was fired while the APFs were en route. To Arjin Hawkins it sounded like a distant thunderstorm. And the guns continued in unison, which struck him as peculiar.

If we'd gotten off half an hour sooner, he thought, *we might have prevented it.* But there hadn't been time, and at any rate, a half hour earlier it hadn't been dark enough.

For weeks the Burger engineers had worked their butts off day and night, building the base, abatises, and breastworks—and the backup base. Now they were working furiously, without Jerrie help, to move the more sensitive Headquarters Base installations there.

The flight was short, even though they bypassed the fire base and jumped six miles to the south—a subterfuge to avoid Wyzhñyñy suspicions. Now the troopers of Airborne A temp were planing back northward beneath their parasails. Even with night vision, Hawkins couldn't see most of his people. But they had their HUDs.

The salvos paled the darkness with great flashes of light, and as Hawkins planed nearer, the booming became less like thunder. It just sounded like artillery. His central HUD showed the fire base. Its layout seemed idiotic, though obviously the Wyzhñyñy didn't think so. The HUD was too small for detail, but Lonesome Moses had provided the essentials during the briefing, and Hawkins had imprinted them mentally. Six ranks of howitzers, eight in a rank, formed a compact square. Their spacing provided aisles, adequate for firing safety, and for howitzers to jockey in and out if necessary. Grav sleds would no doubt use the aisles to distribute ammo from the two massive caissons on the south edge. The border of dotlike icons along the east, south and west sides indicated squad APCs: twelve on the east and west, and eight on the south, where the center of the rank was occupied by the caissons and a heavy, armor-recovery vehicle. About twenty yards off each corner were two flakwagons, eight in all.

If a wolf pack were available, that compactness would make a marvelous target, but an airborne attack would have to suffice. His platoon's primary job was to take out the flakwagons at the two south corners, and the APCs along the south side. Dreiser's Platoon would take out the west-side APCs, along with the two northwest flakwagons. Castro's would handle the east side. Hussain's was the reserve, ready to defend the landers when they came in with Division's demolitions company.

The overall mission was etched clearly in Hawkins' mind. But if even two or three flakwagons escaped destruction, or most of the APCs survived, there'd be serious problems in carrying it out. Especially since it wasn't enough just to disrupt the barrage for the time being. The howitzers, or most of them, had to be destroyed. Which meant Demolitions' floaters needed to land safely.

He didn't consciously review all that. It was part of his mental database, not looked at. Just now, Hawkins was manipulating his black, night-jump parasail to set him down in his platoon's designated drop zone. When he reached 100 feet local altitude, he let his gear drop, felt it jerk the dangle line, felt its air drag, sensed the ground reaching for him. The strong gravity slammed him hard. He felt agonizing pain, and almost cried out. His left leg had broken below the knee. Broken badly. He knew it at once.

Fortunately the breeze was light, and his chute had collapsed. He released his harness, and hand over hand pulled in his combat pack, rocket gear, and blaster scabbard. Then he drew his combat knife, cut away his left pant leg, and stared. He'd already felt the blood. Now he could see a sharp end of broken bone protruding through skin and underwear, and shivered at the sight. Suppressing the reaction, he activated his casualty signal. *Get it tended to before the Wyz find out we're here,* he told himself. *The medics will have plenty to do then.*

He spoke to his helmet mike. "Hawkins' Platoon, this is Ensign Hawkins. I've broken a leg. Esau, you're in full charge of the platoon now. Proceed with the mission. The medics will pick me up." He was surprised at how normal he sounded. Taking his blaster out of its scabbard, he loaded it, then lay back to wait for a medic. And defend himself if necessary.

Esau was on the ground when he got Hawkins' order. *Foop!* he thought, then dismissed his chagrin. He'd already retrieved his gear. Now he slung his pack and blaster. At least to start with, his primary weapon would be his short-barrelled, antiarmor rocket launcher. One of its three light-weight rockets was already seated. The other two he'd snapped on his harness.

Esau had been the cleanup, the last jumper out, so he was pretty sure the others were all down. "Hawkins' Platoon," he said, "you heard the ensign. Squad leaders assemble your squads." Almost at once he saw their light wands signaling, visible via a wave-length window in their visors. Each squad leader had his own signal. He gave them half a minute, then called: "1st Squad report . . . 2nd Squad report . . ." One after another they responded, all alike: "All present and accounted for, Sergeant."

Only one man hurt or missing. I hope the other platoons are that lucky, he thought. Though to lose your leader . . .

He looked toward the artillery. All that noise—the Wyzhñyñy sentries should be numb by now. *We'll know soon enough,* he told himself. He saw no sign of their infantry. *Maybe they're all in their APCs. We can hope.* The nearest were less than 300 yards away, but hitting them needed to be synchronized with the attack on the flak-wagons all around the square. And Hawkins' Platoon was the key. The others were to start firing when it did.

"Hawkin's Platoon, any questions? Form up to attack." They did, counting off by pairs, one man with his launcher in hand, the other with his blaster to provide covering fire. When the launcherman had expended his rockets, they'd switch. Esau changed to Captain Zenawi's command channel. "Captain," he said, "Hawkin's Platoon is ready to move."

"Fine, Wesley. I'll tell you when."

Esau waited. *Any time now,* he thought.

Suddenly, midway between salvos came a premature burst of blaster fire from the Wyzhñyñy square, followed quickly by more. *"Hit 'em, Airborne A!"* Zenawi almost shouted it into his mike.

"Let's go, Hawkins' Platoon!" Esau said, and they started toward their targets at a lope. "Fire when you think you can hit your target!" Their rocket launchers were cheap and light, aimed simply by pointing. The briefing had specified not firing them at ranges beyond 50 yards on this mission, but that assumed they'd be able to approach that close before being discovered. So his troopers began firing at twice that range—when the first APC turret blaster began hammering slammer pulses in their direction. They took out both southwest flakwagons before either could fire, and rocket hits flashed at one, two, three, four APCs. One of the southeast flakwagons began firing at them before its guns were sufficiently depressed, the pulses angling skyward. But its controls were nimble. Its platform swiveled sharply, as the trajectory of its fire adjusted. In the instant before streams of trasher pulses swept toward them, troopers hit the dirt. If Esau had been able to squeeze between the grains of soil, he would have. He rolled his head to the side, to see without raising it. Pulses swept over him about knee-high, then he rolled to a knee and fired. The range exceeded 150 yards, but a second later his rocket struck the flakwagon, almost simultaneously with two others.

The remaining southeast flakwagon had busied itself with Castro's Platoon. "Hawkins up and at 'em!" Esau called, and the survivors were on their feet again, charging the south-edge APCs. A turret slammer didn't put out nearly the volume of fire a flakwagon did, but at least some had located their targets and were firing aimed bursts. Rockets impacted APCs, even as more APCs got their guns into action. And now the platoon was receiving blaster fire, as Wyzhñyñy emptied from troop compartments.

The surviving APCs were pulling out of line to evade trooper attacks, and to disperse themselves as targets. One came almost toward Esau, its turret slammer riveting the darkness with bright pulses, and he punched a rocket into its front armor panel, unsure if it could penetrate there. The vehicle swerved, careened, then lost its AG cushion and stopped, plowing a short broad furrow in the ground. Wyzhñyñy emerged from the rear, and firing, began to back toward the base's perimeter.

Esau sprinted to take cover against the front of the derelict APC, his partner staying behind, delivering covering fire. In the shelter of the APC, Esau paused for a second, receiving Zenawi's radio traffic along with his own platoon's. There was more of Zenawi's; Hawkins' Platoon was busy at a different level, fighting. The battle had become a melee.

The APC didn't have rungs to the top, like the human version did. He climbed to the roof via a front cowling and the top of the driver's compartment, then lay there. Saw an APC pass, separating itself from the chaos, fired his last rocket and saw it hit the troop compartment. The vehicle continued. He threw away his now useless launcher, and with blaster in hand, scanned for opportunities. He was some thirty yards outside the original row of APCs, now marked by wreckage. There was shooting everywhere. Soldiers were running around on two feet and four. "Hawkins' Platoon," he said, "when you unlimber your blasters, fix your bayonets!"

He fixed his own by feel, his eyes busy elsewhere. A flakwagon appeared around the southeast corner, a little distance outside the square, its multiple barrels hammering bursts of trasher fire in the direction of anything it saw on two legs. It would pass within ten feet. He rolled onto his side, his right hand freeing a fragmentation grenade from his harness, setting it to "impact" by feel, tossed it as the wagon passed, then jumped. The grenade roared and Esau sprinted, gripped the rim of the armored side with one hand and tossed his blaster over, running hard. He lost stride, and almost his hold, then pulled himself up and over, coming down on a Wyzhñyñy body. Another Wyzhñyñy hung slack in the gunner's harness, bleeding, eyes wide, jaws gaping as if for breath. Esau recovered his blaster and put him to rest.

In the cab, they'd felt and heard the explosion, suspected what had happened, and querying the gun crew, got no answer. The vehicle stopped, a door opened, and a Wyzhñyñy head peered over the side. Esau shot it, then vaulted out, losing his feet as he landed, recovered quickly and fired through the open door.

"4th Squad! 4th Squad! This is Esau! I've captured a flakwagon! About . . . thirty yards west of the west caisson. I need a driver or two, and a gunner! Respond!" As he said it, it occurred to him he didn't know whether anyone in 4th Squad was alive. "This is Tyler, on my way!" "This is Hoke. I'm a-coming." "This is Felspar, on my way!" The answers came almost simultaneously. Esau waited tensely.

Hoke was the first to arrive. He and Esau shifted the Wyzhñyñy body to serve as a driver's seat for Tyler. Tyler sat on it, and Esau climbed in back. Felspar had freed the Wyzhñyñy gunner from his gun harness, and with a little ingenuity had adjusted it for himself.

For a moment Esau hesitated. "Felspar, do you need me?" he asked.

"Be good to have someone to set a new power drum when I need it."

"Okay. I'm your man. Airborne A, Hawkins' Platoon now owns a flakwagon on the south side. For God's sake don't hole us. If anyone knows of a live Wyzhñyñy flakwagon, let us know. We'll see about taking it out."

He stepped onto the gunner's platform to see better.

"Wesley," Zenawi called, "there's one on the west side about a hundred yards out, stalled; I think her driver's hit. But the gunner's raising hell with Dreiser's Platoon, and it's got a couple of blastermen in back."

"I copy, Captain. We're on our way. Tyler, let's go. Felspar, don't fire at APCs now. I don't want to get tied up with fighting till we take out that other flakwagon."

"Wesley—" It was Zenawi. "That other flakwagon has a driver again. It's moving erratically toward the southwest corner, firing heavily."

"Copy, sir."

The reported flakwagon rounded the southwest corner and came toward them. "I see it, Esau!" Tyler shouted. Felspar said nothing. He swung his gun on target and at once fired a long burst. Like the APC, the Wyzhñyñy-manned flakwagon swerved and stopped, but it still directed its fire elsewhere. Apparently its gunner didn't know they'd been hit by one of their own.

"Pull past it, Tyler. Felspar, wait till you've got a clear shot at the rear end, then pump her again."

Felspar liked this machine. It was a heavy flakwagon, like the one they'd trained on. They passed the other on the outside, at ten yards, and he fired a long burst into the rear. There was a surprisingly powerful explosion. A trasher bolt must have hit the enemy's power drum.

"Tyler," Esau said, "stop a minute. I want to make sure the sonofabitch is totally out of action." Then he slung his blaster on a thick shoulder and turned his back on the gunner. "Get me a P grenade out of my pack," he said. Leaning, Felspar got it for him. Esau hooked it on his harness, vaulted over the side, ran the twenty yards back to the other vehicle, tossed a frag grenade into the rear for insurance, heard it roar, and peered over the side. It looked like a slaughter-house. The power drum that had blown had already been seated, and had torn the trasher's firing mechanism apart.

Esau opened the cab door then. Inside were two Wyzhñyñy almost certainly dead. He tossed in the phosphorus grenade anyway, and slammed the door. He never heard the P grenade pop. Felspar, watching from the back of the captured flakwagon, saw Esau fall, and called Tyler, who called for a medic while Hoke jumped from the cab and ran to Esau.

"Steve," Hoke called, "he's breathing, but there's lots of blood running from under his helmet."

"A medic's on his way," Tyler answered. "Now get your butt back here! In back, to help Felspar. The captain wants us to knock out APCs before the floaters get here."

"Right. I'm a-coming."

Hoke wouldn't have believed the fighting was less than ten minutes old.

Throughout it all, the howitzers continued to thunder. General Pak could hardly have been more pleased, despite the explosives raining down on his base, because it meant the howitzers were not pulling out. And he very much

wanted them to be there when the demolitions company
arrived.

They no longer fired in synch; it was as if the chaos
around their borders had spread inward. But the volume
of shells they threw across the miles remained as great.

Airborne A temp had done their job despite the fight's
premature beginning. When the demolitions platoons with
their petards and heavy rockets disembarked from the
APFs, the fire they faced was light. Briefly they lay low,
while Hussain's Platoon moved in ahead of them to help
finish off the Wyzhñyñy infantry. The other three jumper
platoons had been seriously reduced.

More than the demolitions platoons had landed. There
were two medivacs, and an APF with field medics and AG
sleds to bring in the wounded. Esau was one of the first
loaded. He was already on his way in, wobbly and on foot.
A medic sprayed his scalp to inhibit further bleeding.
Aboard the medivac, he'd refused to be installed on an evac
litter. Refused to be bandaged, because he wouldn't be able
to get his helmet back on. Refused to be injected, and
shoved an insistent medic hard enough that the man fell
on his butt. Tight-lipped, the Terran medical officer in
charge let Esau be. He had better things to do than coerce
some stubborn Jerrie. But when they got to the hospital,
he'd see him charged and disciplined.

Meanwhile Esau posted himself out of the way, just
inside the ramp, watching till it was nearly full. When the
last of the wounded was being brought up the ramp, the
doctor in charge again insisted to Esau that he lie down.
Instead he got off.

Because Ensign Hawkins hadn't been brought aboard.

He then went to the other medivac. It was loading the
dead while waiting for additional wounded. No, he was told,
they'd seen no Ensign Hawkins.

"Well, you got to go get him. I know where he is. I'll
take you. Not over there." He gestured toward the chaos
of the fire base three hundred yards west. "Over there, in
our drop zone. He broke his leg."

"How do you know that?"

"He radioed and told us. And turned his hat over to me."

"You people have casualty signals, right?"

"Maybe his didn't work."

This Terran major too was getting exasperated. He needed to finish loading and get his wounded to the hospital. But at the same time . . . "All right." Turning he called. "Corporal Chou, go with the sergeant here and pick up an Ensign Hawkins. The sergeant will show you where. And make it quick!"

Esau could have ridden on the AG sled, but he walked instead, leading off. He wasn't wobbling now. Not striding, but trudging purposefully. Having something to do had given him new strength. He didn't know exactly where the ensign was, but he'd be somewhere in the drop zone. *Ensign Hawkins*, he thought, *if you'll help me to find you, I'll surely appreciate it*. Then he repeated his appeal, this time to God.

Three hundred yards north of the drop zone, the thunder of howitzers had stopped. With the guns themselves under serious attack, the base commander had ordered them to cease fire and evacuate. But the evacuation wasn't happening. These howitzers were not only of lighter caliber, they were less heavily armored than those the wolf packs had savaged, and Demolitions was having their way with them. The initial spacing made orderly evacuation awkward, and the first howitzers destroyed were on the edges, where they were most in the way.

Esau paid all that no heed. He was busy. He spotted Hawkins from thirty yards away, lying in thigh-deep grass. The medic couldn't imagine how he saw him. The ensign's casualty signal was indeed not working. With the pant leg cut away, his wound was obvious, but more serious, he was in shock, and unconscious. With Esau's help the medic loaded Hawkins onto the AG sled and piloted it to the medivac.

They were the last loaded, and the medivac took off hastily. Esau gave up his damaged helmet and allowed himself to be treated, then lay down willingly, and quickly slept.

He had no idea—none of them did—of what was about to happen at the fire base.

Chapter 56
The Hospital

Casualties from the Fire Base Raid were only a small part of those received by the hospital over a forty-eight-hour span. The less seriously wounded were sedated, put in hastily set-up squad tents without floors, then largely ignored.

It was morning when Esau awoke, with a bad headache, and found himself on a folding cot with mattress. A mosquito bar was draped over it. Getting up he went outside, barefoot and in a hospital nightshirt, to find and use the latrine. He'd just settled down when another B Company trooper sat down next to him, a sergeant named Ferris, from 3rd Platoon. He had an arm in a sling.

"Morning, Esau," Ferris said. "What happened to your head? Jael hit you with a skillet?"

Esau might have scowled, but didn't. "Jael's in the bot shop," he said. "From the Pecan Orchard Raid. The Wyzhñyñy killed her body; she took a blaster pulse in the guts."

"Oh ... Gentle Jesus, Esau, I'm surely sorry. I shouldn't

have said that. War's no good place for jokes I guess. I was just wondering about your head being all bandaged up."

Esau nodded. Carefully. "The doctor says I took a fragment through my helmet, and it cut a groove across my skull. And scalps bleed pretty good; it looked worse than it was. I'll be back with the platoon in a day or two, if there's any of it left. We jumped the Wyzhñyñy fire base that was shelling headquarters base. I don't know how it finally worked out."

Before they left the latrine, Ferris told Esau there wasn't a whole lot left of the rest of B Company. They'd been in the breastworks, fighting all of yesterday and the night before, and even before that. The good part was, most of the casualties were wounded or bot cases. A lot of the fighting had been with grenades and mortars. People got hit with fragments, or lost arms or legs or hands. Or got burned; the Wyzhñyñy'd used flamethrowers.

Then in early evening, the Wyz had pulled back. Division figured that meant a heavy Wyzhñyñy barrage, so Colonel Leclerc pulled 2nd Regiment back, too. Then, with dusk thickening, the shells started roaring in. Sounded terrible, even from a ways off, and chewed up the forest pretty badly, but didn't really harm the abatises that much. Even most of the breastworks more or less survived.

The shelling stopped just when it had started creeping westward. The rumor was a bunch of Indi tanks had hit the artillery base and shot it up pretty bad. Leclerc had sent 2nd Regiment back in, but the Wyz didn't come back. "What happened to me is," Ferris added wryly, "a broken limb fell out of a shot-up tree. Broke my collarbone. Heh heh heh. A tree taking revenge! I guess trees don't distinguish people from Wyzhñyñy."

Esau nodded without smiling. It seemed like in war, there were all sorts of ways to get hurt or killed.

He wiped his butt and left. He felt hungry, a sign, he guessed, that he was getting back toward normal. When he got back to the tent, a clean uniform lay folded on the cot. He put it on; it didn't fit too badly.

At noon, the mess line buzzed with stories and rumors. A guy from Dreiser's Platoon, Mellon, was there with a bandaged face. He'd lost an ear to a grenade fragment, and

another had gashed his cheek and jaw to the bone. Best
he could do was mumble; Esau had to concentrate to
understand him. Mellon had gotten out later than he had,
when two more medivacs arrived at the fire base. One left
loaded. The other left only partly loaded; it had gotten too
dangerous to stay. A lot of Wyzhñyñy reds had arrived in
APCs—a battalion, he'd heard—and attacked what was left
of Airborne A and the demolitions company. Then a dozen
Indi tanks had arrived and pounded the Wyzhñyñy. Right
after that, an Indi air squadron had swooped in and shot
them up some more, but by then, Airborne A and Demolitions were pretty much used up. When the medivacs went
back again for casualties, about all they found were dead.

But the Artillery Base Raid wasn't the major topic.
Mostly Esau heard about the fighting in the forest. That's
where most of the casualties came from. It sounded pretty
bad.

After lunch, Esau went back to his tent and lay down,
but before he could get to sleep, a doctor came in, looking worn out. He told Esau he'd have to stay a few more
days. Esau was glad to hear it. He felt used up.

Esau told him about Jael. The doctor gave him a note,
saying he could go to the "Cyborg Processing Center" to
see his wife, if she was allowed to have visitors. So after
the doctor left, Esau did too.

He had no idea what to expect. The bot shop turned
out to be somewhat like the hospital but smaller—a long
low prefab building with several similar buildings attached
along the sides like hover-fly wings. It was as clean as you
could hope for; smelled like turpentine. Terrans in white
coats moved through the halls, and went in and out of
rooms.

He was directed to a desk, where he showed his note
to a woman and said he'd like to visit his wife, Jael Wesley.
Another woman, taller than he was, took him down a hall
to one of the wings, to a room, and went inside with him.

On a cart was a sort of cylinder, maybe two and a half
feet long, and eight inches across except at one end where
it was bigger. There were wires and tubes and dials, with
a couple of boxes attached. His heart sank.

"Jael," the woman said, "Esau is here to see you."

"Hello, Esau. I knew you'd come see me if you could. What happened to your head?"

The words came from one of the boxes. Esau's eyes welled up and ran over till they dripped on his clean shirt. It was almost like that night in the woods—the night he'd come back from the Pecan Orchard Raid—except this time he didn't sob, just moaned. Because the voice wasn't Jael's. The plastic cylinder wasn't Jael. Jael was dead, and he hadn't let her finish dying. "I'm sorry," he choked out. "I'm sorry. I just didn't want you to be dead."

"Oh, Esau, don't be sorry. I'm not." If the voice wasn't hers, the tone was. It reminded him of when she felt fond and loving. "And I'll have my new body pretty soon. Sergeant Boucher took me to see it. You'll be impressed."

He pulled himself together. "I . . . will." It began as a question and ended as affirmation. "Yes, I surely will . . . That is you in there, isn't it. The voice isn't yours, but it's you. I recognize . . . I recognize the soul."

Jael laughed quietly. It didn't exactly sound like a laugh, but he knew that's what it was. "That's right," she said, "when they take out the CNS, the soul comes with it. And the voice will come along. It takes practice, and I only just started day before yesterday. I didn't realize how poorly I'd laugh though. I hadn't tried it till just now."

It was only then he realized: she'd asked about his bandages. She could see as well as hear. The nurse said they had ten minutes, then left them alone. It turned out to be more like fifteen, and they got quite a bit of talking done. The best was Jael told him she'd rather be a bot than an invalid. "As for a bot agreement bringing bad luck," she finished, "I didn't sign one, and look what happened anyway."

Then the nurse returned and shooed Esau out. He found a place in the woods where he could sit alone and think, and weep some more, and talk to himself. Till after a while he felt pretty good. He even laughed at his own joke: grubbing stumps would be a lot easier, with a wife that was a warbot.

Not that he expected to farm after all this. Not really. He could, but he didn't expect to, even if they lived through this war. But there'd be something to do.

✧   ✧   ✧

That wasn't the end of Esau's day. He'd gone to the hospital to check on Ensign Hawkins, who turned out to be asleep, sedated, with his broken leg hoisted up. The nurse said he'd been in pretty bad shape from prolonged, untreated shock. But he'd heal all right. It would just take a while.

"How long?" Esau asked.

"His bones should heal fast. He should be ready for rehab in six weeks."

Six weeks! Esau left depressed. He didn't feel up to being platoon leader himself. During raids maybe, but not in the day-to-day activities between times. Or defensive fighting in foxholes, as in the first days, or in the breastworks he'd heard about that morning . . . He felt sure he didn't know enough to be platoon leader in those circumstances. He hadn't been platoon sergeant long enough. He'd make mistakes.

After supper, Isaiah Vernon looked him up. Isaiah was a staff sergeant now, too. When the bot cases from the Battle of the First Days finished their familiarization training, he'd been given a whole platoon of them, as their sergeant. He'd just hitched a ride north to see a couple of them, in the bot shop for repairs. An entire long company of bots had been in a firefight the evening before— been put down near a Wyzhñyñy field headquarters, moved in on it, and pretty much wiped it out. Then they'd made a fighting withdrawal, and been picked up by APFs that came down on a bald ridgetop.

"And while I was up here," Isaiah said, "I decided to see who was here from 2nd Platoon."

"Did you see Jael?"

"Jael? The hospital called up the names of B Company wounded on their records, and hers wasn't one of them."

"She's in the bot shop," Esau said, wishing a bot face showed expression.

"The bot shop? So she finally decided to sign."

"She didn't. She was unconscious, and I lied to the medic, so he shot her up with Stasis One. Afterward I was afraid she'd be really mad at me, but it turned out she's not."

Isaiah chuckled. *He does that pretty well,* Esau thought, *and his voice sounds like himself.* He guessed Jael's would too, with practice. It occurred to him how much Isaiah had changed personally; more than his body had got stronger. He wondered how different Jael would be, besides having a bot body. He'd just have to wait and see. *And get used to it,* he told himself.

Then he realized he still hadn't signed his own bot agreement, so when Isaiah left, Esau went to the hospital and signed one. They stamped out new dog tags for him on the spot, to verify it. *Now,* he thought, *if I get hit bad enough, we can be bots together, her and me.*

Chapter 57

The Battle of Shakti

Admiral Alvaro Soong's 1st Sol Provisional Battle Force had traveled three nonstop months in hyperspace to rendezvous with newly commissioned battle groups in the Dinébikeyah System. The result was a fleet with more than four times the number of manned ships that had fought at Paraíso. The new ships came not only from the Sol System, but from new shipyards in the Indi and Eridani Systems, with colonial crews. So it was renamed the "1st Commonwealth Fleet."

The number of maces, whose performance had been so impressive at Paraíso, was also more than quadrupled. They were quicker and easier to build than manned ships, and being drones, their destruction didn't cost trained crews.

And most of the new ships, manned or drones, had the improved shield generators.

Spanish Soong remained in command. To War House and the public, he was a hero second only to Charley Gordon. Before there was any fleet at all, he'd been judged the best qualified for command, based on temperament, gaming skills, and overall service record. And so far he'd disappointed no one.

While en route to the rendezvous, Soong, via Charley, had been updated on the new fleet units by Admiralty Chief Fedor Tischendorf himself. "And Alvaro," Tischendorf finished, "Axel Tisza is delivering the convoy from the Sol System. He's also commanding one of the new battle groups."

He paused meaningfully. "I've had him in mind as your command backup when he gets there, but I haven't told him yet. I know you two have had—a mixed relationship, so I wanted to run it by you first. What do you think of the idea?"

Think? Or feel? "Admiral, Ax is as able as anyone you could find for the job. Powerful mind. Quick. Aggressive. And basically we saw eye to eye for the most part, different though we are. As midshipmen we roomed together for four years and never came to blows. Loaned each other money on occasion, drank each other's scotch when one of us could afford it. And on pass in the Springs, we backed each other up in more than one scrap."

Yes, Tischendorf thought, *and you were rivals in almost everything, from the saber team to the classroom. And over Carmen Apraxin, when she came along; that's what spoiled it.* "I didn't bring this up idly," he said. "You two were the chief candidates for command of the Provos, and the difference in your grades and gaming scores was thin. But in your favor. And you had the best command temperament: more objective, and I've never known you to be abrasive."

Soong examined the words and found them true. "Not that gaming scores are so important with Charley Gordon available," he found himself saying.

"True. And there's another point in your favor. You discovered Charley's talent, and had the balls to stick your neck out and make him battle master. I doubt that Ax would have done either of them. I'm not at all sure I would have."

With the specifications in hand on the fleet additions, Charley Gordon plunged into reworking his strategies, tactics, protocols, and fleet organization. At the same time considering possible changes in Wyzhñyñy strategy and tactics. Charley claimed to have a good, if imperfect, sense of what those changes would be.

Soong felt uncomfortable with some of Charley's adjustments; they seemed too daring. Nonetheless he accepted Charley's new system *in toto*, showing no misgivings.

He'd always been stoic—his aunts and older cousins had commented on it—and rarely did that stoicism take the form of grim resignation. But now the situation was more urgent than at Paraíso. He'd also be risking much greater resources, and he needed to do even better than before. Because the Wyzhñyñy were getting closer, and time—the Commonwealth's most critical resource—was shrinking.

At the rendezvous, Charley's new battlecomp package was uploaded to the entire fleet. The battle groups remained the basic tactical units, but in the enlarged fleet, a new hierarchical level was added—the battle wing—to facilitate heavier concentrations of firepower. Instead of five battle groups, there were now four battle wings of five groups each, and part of a fifth. When Vice Admiral Carmen Apraxin-DaCosta's Liberation Task Force arrived, it would complete the fifth wing, with Apraxin in command. She'd bring two savants with her, one to be transferred to Soong on board the *Altai*, freeing Charley Gordon to function solely as battle master.

The maces were not organized into wings and groups. They would operate as coordinated triads, grouped into second-order triads—threes of threes. So far as Soong was aware, the concept was entirely new, and the enthusiastic Charley had big plans for them.

Large and technically upgraded though it was, Soong's fleet was still far smaller than the Wyzhñyñy battle fleet, which seemed to constitute about half the armada. But if Charley's assumptions didn't backfire, it seemed realistic to Soong that he could strike, maintain contact long enough to do serious damage, and get away without critical injury.

And possibly, hopefully, slow the invader; make him wary. Buy time to build enough more ships . . . and come up with new, hopefully decisive weapons.

❖   ❖   ❖

Three days after Soong's Provos had gathered with the reinforcements from the Core Worlds, Apraxin's New Jerusalem Liberation Force arrived, to begin at once the task of resupply and external maintenance. On the "evening" of the same day, immediately after supper, electronic bosuns' pipes shrilled aboard every manned vessel in the entire fleet, and shipsvoice ordered all hands to mustering stations in ten minutes. This was followed as before by the skirls of "Dilly Doo" and other Scottish martial music.

As at Paraíso, it was the admiral who spoke first. His real pep talk would come weeks in the future, not long before battle. But meanwhile, before the weeks of simdrills in hyperspace, a few words from the Old Man should help prepare them—provide context and perspective—and a sense of team, of family.

And the new people needed to meet Charley.

" . . . We are now the 1st Commonwealth Fleet," Soong said. "Commos for short. With the arrival of you newcomers, we are a much more powerful fleet than when we bushwhacked the Wyzhñyñy at Paraíso. A fleet with a toughness and assurance derived from a core of units with successful battle experience. *And* a fleet with the best battle master in the galaxy—Charley Gordon.

"You old hands know Charley's work. You know I don't exaggerate the advantages he gives us. When I've finished my own short spiel, Charley will speak to you himself. And during the next day or two you'll witness his ability personally, on cubes of the Battle of Paraíso.

"Still, some of you may remain skeptical. Few of you war-gamed till you entered the service, and you may not yet appreciate what Charley does, or what it takes. But we'll all be simdrilling his updated battlecomp programs all the way to Shakti. Perhaps even to Ivar Aasen. And if you're not convinced by then, you will be when you've experienced the cauldron."

He paused. "For those who don't know, a cauldron is a large iron kettle used in ancient times to boil things. You won't be *in* the cauldron; that's reserved for the Wyzhñyñy. Your job will be to help stoke the fire without falling in it."

Another pause. "Meanwhile, we all have things to do before we generate hyperspace again, so I'll let you hear Charley Gordon now. Welcome to the family."

Charley gave basically the same introductory talk he'd given in the Paraíso System, though he used a new example. It had much the same effect on the newcomers.

Minutes later, on a secure channel, Soong accepted a call from Vice Admiral Carmen Apraxin-DaCosta. "Hello, Admiral," he said. Presumably his wariness didn't show on the screen, but it seemed to him she'd know. "What can I do for you?"

"Not a thing, Admiral. May I call you Alvaro?"

"You may call me Al if you'd like." She still looked great. No longer young—forty-two? forty-four?—but great. She made him conscious of his thickened waist. She probably still practiced aikido.

Her laugh was not as light as it had been, but it seemed genuine. "I'll settle for Alvaro," she told him. "You're my commander now, and two grades above me. Is Charley Gordon as good as he sounds?"

"Every bit as good."

"I didn't know savants could be so . . . intelligent, in the usual sense. Or is articulate the word?"

"I don't know if 'the usual sense' applies to Charley. He's . . . superman in a box. But easy to work with. Likeable."

"Hmm. Maybe I'll have a chance to talk with him sometime."

For several seconds they sat without talking, looking at one another on their screens. "I suppose," Soong said at last, "you had something on your mind when you called."

"Yes, I did. I do. It's grown out of the life reviews some of us are guilty of in times like these." She paused, hesitated. "Not so many years ago you asked me to marry you. With good reason to expect a yes. But I had an opportunity to make a four-year patrol with B Squadron—as you had earlier, you'll recall. And I chose it over marriage."

Yes, you did, he thought. She'd been given command of a frigate, the largest class of warship the Admiralty boasted then. With Axel Tisza as senior captain—commodore—in charge of the squadron. He had no doubt Tisza and she had enjoyed each other's company on the occasional layovers.

"It was a great opportunity," he finished.

She looked at him mildly, but he had no doubt she saw through him.

"In a year this war will be over," she said. "One way or another. Then, assuming I'm still alive, I expect to leave the service. What about you?"

"I—hadn't thought about it." For a moment the realization surprised him, but it made sense. The prospect of surviving the war wasn't something he wanted to distract himself with. The odds seemed too poor.

"I can understand that," she said, and paused for a moment. "All I really called about was to invite you to ask me again when this is over."

He nodded slowly. "Thanks, Carmen. I'm surprised, and more than anything else, complimented. It's the nicest thing anyone ever said to me."

"Good. Now all we have to do is win the war." She paused. "We both have things to do. I'd better let us get at them."

Soong nodded. "Right. And Carmen, thank you *very* much for calling. I probably won't return this personal call till afterward."

They disconnected then, Soong wondering what he'd meant by "afterward." It had just popped out. He might survive the upcoming battle, but the war? He hadn't felt—and wouldn't feel—any concern at all about dying. His great fear was of losing, and associated with that, he feared that Charley Gordon might die. *That*, he told himself, would be a tragedy.

But if he did survive, and if Carmen did . . .

He resolved to lose weight.

The admiral seated himself in the chair indicated by Ophelia Kennah. It was always that chair, an AG chair set at 0.7 gee, large enough to accommodate his burly body comfortably. In front of him, the large wall window was set to a sky view within Terra's atmosphere. Judging from the elevation of Crux, it might be from somewhere near Rio de Janeiro, where Charley had lived most of his life.

Beside Soong's chair stood a small stand with several non-fattening hors d'oeuvres. No more goose-liver paste. Knowingly or not, Kennah was cooperating with his efforts to lose weight. Had she read his mind? With her that wasn't inconceivable, but more probably the command officers' chef had talked to her. He sampled one, washed it down with carbonated punch, then swiveled his seat slightly to face the life-support module and its occupant. "Good morning, Charley," the admiral said.

A tiny light-play danced briefly over Charley's sensorium, perhaps equivalent to an embodied human switching off a music or video cube, and swiveling his seat to face a visitor. "Ah, Admiral!" Charley said. "Since I completed our new battlecomp package, we seldom meet. What may I do for you?"

"I've called twice lately," Soong answered. "Each time, Kennah told me you were studying." Actually she'd said he was "studying deeply," whatever that meant. "And that unless it was urgent, she'd rather not waken you. But today when I called, she said you were listening to music, and suggested it was a good time to visit." He lifted an eyebrow. "And by now, of course, I'm curious about your studies."

"Ah." Charley paused as if considering how to put it. "I have been exploring another facet of my potentials, one I dabbled in occasionally when I was younger, without realizing I was merely dabbling. Actually I was being appropriately cautious. But now Ophelia acts as my security officer, an anchor to prevent my being . . . swept away. And though some risk remained, it seemed something I needed to do at this time. You see."

Risk? There was a pause of several seconds. He'd been jarred by Charley taking a needless risk, when his ability to function at a high level was so vitally important. "No, Charley," he said softly, "I don't see. You'll have to enlighten me."

Charley did, and he didn't. "I have," he said, "been visiting the Wyzhñyñy grand admiral. At the . . . soul level you might say. It is not a matter of telepathy, but of . . . call it integration. At the level of souls, that is. Something the grand admiral is not aware of at the physical or personality level. Though his essence is."

Soong stared. Uncertainties stirred in his belly like a nest of snakes wakening from hibernation. "Do you know his thoughts?" he asked.

"His thoughts belong to his personality, not his essence. My level of merging is not so strong that I sense them explicitly. But in a general sense I am aware of his fears, his hopes, his desires. Call it empathy in the fullest sense. The admiral is, of course, a product of his people—his culture and class—and I now understand him, and them, much more deeply than before. In fact, through him I have attained a degree of empathy with them as well."

Charley's answer did not assure the admiral. "Well then—" Soong found himself reluctant to ask the question, but reluctance seldom ruled him in matters of duty. "Can you influence him?"

"I have, Admiral, I have. Not to do some particular act, or assume some particular point of view. At the essence level, that is impossible. But he is influenced by the contact, and to an extent enabled by it."

"Enabled." Soong spoke the word cautiously. "Will he be more dangerous then?"

"Not dangerous. But he may break free of old acculturation and self-protective mechanisms. And do things he previously could not."

Soong looked troubled. After a moment Charley added, "Perhaps more to the point, I have a better sense of our joint vectors."

"Ah!" With relief. "So what you've done is beneficial to our cause. Our defense."

"Definitely, Admiral; definitely beneficial. This will be a costly battle, as you well know, but the vectors appear . . . not unpropitious."

Not unpropitious. From Charley, Soong would have preferred something more positive. "Good," he replied. "We need all the advantages we can have."

For a minute or so then, they spoke of trivia, until Soong was walking to the door. Then Charley added: "And, Alvaro. Do not worry if I seem changed. During my studies, I *have* changed. For the better. I discovered and dropped certain features of my personality that I am better off without."

❖   ❖   ❖

As the admiral walked back to his quarters, his discomfort persisted. And not just because of possible troubles growing out of Charley's "integration" with the Wyzhñyñy admiral. If it was real. Soong wondered if Charley might be less than sane, perhaps deluded by some experience in trance.

Meanwhile, he realized what the change had been in Charley's personality. Previously it had included a subtle sense of ingratiation that Soong assumed grew out of living under constant threats since infancy. Threats of equipment failure, a moment's carelessness by a caregiver ... even gossip or rumor. Being bottled, Charley's very existence had been illegal. And if the Institute had been shut down, what would have become of him? His only defense had lain in being liked and thought harmless. Yet today that ingratiation had been entirely absent. Remarkable, after so many years of conditioning by fear.

He'd talk about it with Kennah someday, he decided.

Meanwhile, there was one thing he did not doubt: Without Charley Gordon, the coming battle could not end well.

Admiral Axel Tisza had spoken with Soong previously since his arrival, their exchanges strictly business. Before supper, he called again.

"I was impressed with your battle master," said the Ax. "God! A damned tragedy he hasn't been cloned. One damned salvo of torpedos and he could be—gone! There might never be another like him."

The comment annoyed Soong. Cloning humans had become common in the 21st century, and again in the 23rd. More than enough to establish that much of what made a human valuable—beyond athletics and potential intelligence—the members of a clone were more or less different. Sometimes very different.

"Cloned?" he said. "You don't know what sort of body he had, or what he went through while he wore it."

Tisza examined his old roommate, and nodded. "I suppose. My savant reminds me of a frog. But he's worth his weight in anything you'd care to name, even if he's not a Charley Gordon." He shrugged. "Did Fedor appoint me your backup? Or did you?"

"Fedor. Conditionally."

"What condition?"

"That I agreed." *What the hell good is a conversation like this?* Soong thought. He was too old now to play power games.

"If he'd given you your choice, who would you have selected?"

"You. We were always neck and neck. You were always more hair-triggered than I was, and more abrasive when you felt the urge." *Or charming if you wanted to be.* He wished he had some of Tisza's charm. "But if the *Altai* gets cooked, or blown apart, and there's no more Charley Gordon and no more Alvaro Soong, this fleet might still have a chance, with you in command."

Tisza nodded slowly, thoughtful now. "I'd thought you might have chosen Carmen. She's had battle experience."

"I probably would have, if you were still at a desk in Kunming." He paused. "Ax, I've got some things to take care of before we generate hyperspace. Is there anything else we need to talk about?"

He'd put just a little emphasis on *need*.

"No, there isn't." It was Tisza's turn to pause. "Thanks, Spanish. But I do want to say I think Fedor appointed the right fleet admiral when he gave you the job. And it's assuring to know you approved me as your backup. Fedor thinks a lot of you. And while you may not know it, I do too. Always did. Ever since we were plebes."

And with that he disconnected, leaving Soong staring at his screen, wondering if he'd been petty.

Tisza too sat with his eyes on the now-blue screen. *Alvaro should have transfered his flag to one of the new battleships, with their two-layered shields,* he thought. For the sake of Charley Gordon, if nothing else. But it was late for that. And it might affect morale poorly, to trade the more vulnerable *Altai*, with its single-layer shield, for one of the better-protected new ships.

The Commo fleet didn't get to the Aasen System. The armada had reached Maitreya's World earlier than expected, and might arrive at Aasen before the Commos were ready.

Which would put the fleet at a needless and severe disadvantage. En route in hyperspace, simdrills would groove them all on Charley's revised program. But officers, crews, and Charley himself needed to follow the simdrills with adequate steel drills. So the Commos emerged in the fringe of the Shakti System. And there they waited, drilling until the Commos were fully confident of their skills, and even their fleet admiral was reasonably satisfied with their performance.

If my Commos had half—even a third—of the Wyzhñyñy firepower, Soong thought, *we'd win.* Unfortunately they had nowhere near that. But then, he reminded himself, they didn't need to *win* if they did well enough, then escaped with losses that weren't too severe.

When the klaxons sounded, and shipsvoice called, "Battle stations! Battle stations! Battle stations!" the tension generated was more anticipation than fear. Alvaro Soong had already suppressed his misgivings, and his fleet was as ready as it could be. The Tao would favor him or not.

Aboard the *Meadowlands,* the alarm was a six-second blast of raucous horns, scant seconds after emergence. This time the grand admiral was on the bridge, not in bed. A human fleet lay in the same octant of the local system as his own, but an hour's warp jump insystem. An hour.

This time, he told himself, the humans would not strike him by surprise. His warfleet had re-formed its formations only 11.38 hyperspace hours outsystem; they could be tightened quickly. "Shipsmind," he said calmly, "order all battle wings to generate warpspace on my count. We will move outsystem far enough to satisfy the parameters of Plan 1.3, then initiate Phase A. One minute and counting: ninety . . . eighty . . . ."

On zero his warfleet winked out of F-space.

Charley Gordon was on the bridge, his cart secured at the battle master's station. Alvaro Soong sat on his command seat, his hands resting loosely on its command board. For the moment his curved display screen was unsegmented, and inactive except for small analog and digital system displays.

Charley had predicted the Wyzhñyñy would generate warpspace, move farther outsystem, and set ambushes before emerging. In warpspace, ambushes usually weren't very practical, but facing Wyzhñyñy numbers, the risk was substantial. So the Commos would stay put. He predicted the Wyzhñyñy would then make a warp jump back insystem, and attack simultaneously from multiple surrounding points. He intended to meet them aggressively. His cool confidence had infected all the bridge watch, including his admiral, whose stoicism just now approached tranquility.

They waited, Charley in a trancelike calm, poised, alert, perfectly ready; a state in which durations registered with no sense of waiting. On his orders, shipsmind provided music chosen to calm without dulling. It began with Gustav Holst's *Planets Suite*, thence to Colin Jokisaari's *Uusisuomi Spring*, and others. After a while, a messman brought a lunch cart, and the bridge watch ate at their stations. All but Charley, who never ate and didn't seem to miss it.

Soong wondered how someone could get over wanting to eat. He'd always assumed it was hardwired.

Grand Admiral Quanshûk had emerged in his new, more distant location. Time passed, enough that electromagnetic evidence, poking along at 186,000 miles per second, had informed the human fleet where he now was. Then more time, enough to tell Quanshûk that the humans would not be baited. They were leaving the offensive to him. Clearly this human fleet had a different commander than he'd dueled with before.

"Very well," he muttered. "We'll give them more than they'll like." He spoke his next order with a feeling approaching confidence.

It was late in the following watch, midway through Aleksandr Borodin's *In the Steppes of Central Asia*, that klaxons clamored aboard the *Altai*, cutting off the music. Shipsvoice's strident "Battle Stations! Battle Stations!" was redundant. Officers and ranks were already there. Charley Gordon's Situation One was unfolding.

Twelve mighty wings of Wyzhñyñy warcraft had emerged
on the fringe of Soong's fleet. Beyond them, on a larger
perimeter, were twenty-four more. Outsystem a hundred
million miles, the armada's transports and support craft had
entered the relative security of warpspace.

The Wyzhñyñy wings were differently constituted than
the Commo wings, but comparable in power, and there
were far more of them. They began their attack at once,
accelerating in gravdrive, generating shields as they came.
The Commo wings in turn started toward the Wyzhñyñy.
The maces led, accelerating much faster than humans or
Wyzhñyñy could survive. In brief seconds they reached the
maximum speed at which they could carry out the intended
evasion maneuvers. Then, by triplicate triads—threes of
threes—they directed coordinated beam fire at selected
Wyzhñyñy battleships. While following evasion courses
designed to confound target locks.

Quanshûk stared, chagrined. He'd learned before, the
hard way, that certain human cruisers—presumably robots—
could maneuver at high speeds. But he'd overlooked the
acceleration potentials that implied. Nor had they previously shown him coordinated maneuvers on so large a scale.

His own ships responded promptly with both war
beams and torpedoes, the action swift and violent, with
too many craft over too large a volume of space for
organics to follow the action. But the battlecomps on both
sides took it all in, reacting with a quickness far beyond
human or Wyzhñyñy. Shields shimmered beneath the
onslaught of war beams, flared and collapsed from multiple
torpedo strikes. Hulls incandesced, exploded.

Then the surviving maces were through the Wyzhñyñy
formations. The Commo battle groups followed, their
battleships wielding heavy beamguns. Firing torpedoes
required complex shield topologies that made them more
susceptible to destruction, so it was their corvette and
cruiser outriders that wielded torpedoes. The smaller ships'
safety lay partly in numbers, and partly in the Wyzhñyñy
tactic of focusing on human battleships.

Concentrating on battleships was a sound strategy for
both sides. The Commos needed to destroy as many

Wyzhñyñy as possible, which meant maintaining fighting contact as long as they could—before the Wyzhñyñy could gang up on them. Inevitably they did gang up on some of them, of course. The trick then became to disrupt the Wyzhñyñy teamwork by throwing in maces. But meanwhile Commo ships were lost.

With the Wyzhñyñy concentrating on the manned wings, the maces dropped their shields, generated warp-space, and disappeared. Their battlecomps had their orders and knew the drill. So far their losses had been modest, and they'd disordered the Wyzhñyñy formations, disrupting their larger-scale coordination before the Commo battle groups struck. More ships died then, mostly Wyzhñyñy, while the Wyzhñyñy battle groups coordinated their fire as best they could.

From the bridge of the battleship *Pyrénées,* Axel Tisza saw the *Altai* caught in a crossfire from three Wyzhñyñy battleships, her shield shimmering strongly with intercepted energy; her shield generator would soon overload. With a quick touch he turned two war beams on one of the attackers; another touch simultaneously ordered torpedoes engaged. Automatically his shield reconfigured, the torpedoes fixing on targets, and launching. A moment later a salvo struck the *Pyrénées,* and her outer shield layer collapsed. On the bridge, the lights flickered. Systems display windows showed generator status red and pulsing. Damage Control cut off the war beam, lessening the stress on the matric tap, in order to regenerate the shield layer. But there was too little time; another salvo struck, and almost simultaneously another. The lights flared and died, returning almost instantly as the emergency backup system responded. Klaxons clamored briefly before two more salvos struck, and the *Pyrénées* died. Axel Tisza hadn't even had time to see if he'd succeeded in saving the *Altai* and Charley Gordon.

Soong had. The two battle groups had been keeping pace. He saw the torpedos flash against the *Pyrénées'* shield, which seemed to expand, then disappear, the instant almost too brief to register. Jabbing he locked a monitor on her. Almost simultaneously, another window showed one of the *Altai*'s three attackers lose her own overstressed shield, and her beam, as Tisza's first salvo struck; her generator, if not her matric tap, had blown. A second lost her shield a moment later, to torpedoes from the *Altai*'s cruiser escorts. The third, seeing the *Pyrénées* shieldless, turned its beams on her. Sprays of molten hull metal scintillated where the beams had locked. Then the final blow struck—two salvos, from two Wyzhñyñy cruisers—and the *Pyrénées* ripped apart.

For perhaps two seconds Soong stared, then he snapped out of it. He'd seen—at the Academy they'd all seen—just such episodes in virtuality many times, preparing for a moment like this. Which helped. But seeing it in reality, and knowing who commanded, the moment stabbed him deeply.

The Commo battle wings passed through the enemy ring, many of the Commo battleships with Wyzhñyñy target locks still attached. Then the maces returned. In self-defense the Wyzhñyñy turned their guns and torpedoes on them; the Commo wings dropped shields and escaped, most of them, into warpspace before the outer ring of Wyzhñyñy could engage them.

This time the maces continued outward, engaging the outer Wyzhñyñy ring, striking selected wings and ignoring others. And scarcely had they passed through the outer ring when the Commo battle groups reappeared in F-space at a distance, re-forming formations for their next assault—in which they would change tactics on the Wyzhñyñy, keep them guessing and off balance.

When the confusion had peaked again, the human formations, superbly synchronized, disappeared into strangespace. Quanshûk stared after them. The bridge of the *Meadowlands* stank with musk and sweat. Almost at once, status reports began to scroll. Watching them, Quanshûk's guts shriveled.

After several minutes it seemed apparent the humans would not return. But the grand admiral did not at once leave the bridge. It would amount to abandoning the watch in a time of trauma. Besides, who could be sure? The humans might suddenly reappear.

✧   ✧   ✧

This time, when the battle was over, Charley Gordon wasn't jubilant. Instead he "sagged" in sudden exhaustion. With the Commo escape into warpspace—that's what it had been, an escape—the battle master's bridge orderly wheeled him to his quarters, where Ophelia Kennah took charge. Ophelia: Charley's nurse, confidante, and best friend.

Alvaro Soong wasn't jubilant either, nor about to take his fleet back into that maelstrom. Reports were incomplete, of course. A host of data had been recorded by the *Altai*'s sensors, and more had been forwarded automatically in real time from his hundreds of other ships. All to be processed—compiled, analyzed and summarized. Only shipsmind could manage it, organizing and prioritizing, then scrolling at a rate his staff could deal with.

But what he did know was he'd lost about a third of his battleships and personnel, including the *Pyrénées* and Axel Tisza. The *Altai* herself had twice been in serious trouble, and been bailed out.

Inevitably his maces had taken the heaviest losses. About half were gone, despite their evasiveness and layered shields. They'd fought the most, where the risks were greatest. Without them, Charley could not have maintained battle contact with the Wyzhñyñy for nearly as long, nor done nearly the damage.

In numbers, Wyzhñyñy losses had been much greater, especially of crews. But again, in terms of percentages, Soong's Commos had gotten the worst of it. As expected.

Nonetheless, given the relative numbers and firepower, Charley had performed another miracle. Soong wondered what the Wyzhñyñy commander made of it. Was he shocked? Enraged? Dismayed? Or possibly pleased?

After ordering hot tea and honey for the bridge watch, he went to his channeling savant, to send a preliminary report to War House. A full debrief could wait. He'd emerge in F-space in the cometary cloud; F-space was a necessary intermediate between strange-spaces. Then, after pulsing updated orders to his fleet, he'd generate hyperspace, and debrief to Kunming. And tomorrow—next shipsday—they'd reemerge for a fleet review and memorial service.

❖   ❖   ❖

Finally Soong retired to his stateroom. He'd just closed the door, the lock engaging behind him, when it hit—the nervous exhaustion, the loss, the shock—all at once. He sank shaking onto a chair, put his face in his hands, and for the first time since he'd learned of his mother's death, he wept. *All those men. All those men.*

It lasted perhaps thirty seconds. After another minute he stripped and showered, then poured himself a brandy, read for a few minutes from Innocent XV's *Soul and Body,* and went to bed. Where his last thought was of Ax. *I wish,* he told himself, *there'd been time to get drunk together again, after so many years.* Then he fixed his attention on his old roommate and rival, and sent a thought. "Maybe next time," he murmured aloud. The prayer of a skeptic. He wondered if there was anyone, or anything, "out there" to hear it.

Chapter 58

Envoy

The grand admiral had recovered somewhat. The master gender, after all, were genetically warriors, who'd received cardinal nurture from birth to weaning, affecting the postnatal growth of the endocrine system, while setting up gender-unique memes.

He'd retired to his quarters before ordering his XO and chief scholar to meet there with him. This had given him time for a drink; an empty glass was the evidence. After pouring drinks for Tualurog and Qonits, he refilled his own. Masters typically held their liquor well, an interaction of the warrior gene and cardinal nurture.

Unfortunately for Qonits, liquor combined with the sage gene brought impulsiveness and poor judgement. Thus Qonits hadn't drunk alcohol since the evening he'd almost gotten himself expelled from the university. A disgrace for which, in his clan, atonement would have provided only limited rehabilitation.

"Well, Admiral," Quanshûk said to Tualurog, "it didn't work as we'd hoped."

The XO scowled sourly. He hated to be wrong, and hated more to have it known. "Their AI technology was better than we'd realized," he answered.

Quanshûk wasn't about to let him off the hook. "Enumerate for me, please, the things that went wrong."

Grimly, Tualurog listed them. There weren't so many, but they'd been costly. Qonits, who was less than fond of the XO, nonetheless sympathized—until Tualurog glanced at him and added: "Your chief scholar served you poorly."

"As did Operations and Planning," Quanshûk replied. "Surprises are to be expected when dealing with alien life-forms. And unfortunately, these humans are remarkably clever, as well as technically advanced."

He paused, smelling his XO's upset. "Meanwhile, my thanks, Admiral. You summarized the difficulties nicely. You may leave now. Please prepare a detailed review for me, with your recommendations." *For all the good they'll do. I have dug us a very deep hole.*

The two friends watched the XO leave, closing the door behind himself with icy control. "He is a surly fellow," Quanshûk said tiredly. "But competent."

Also jealous, spiteful, and self-justifying, Qonits added silently. Aloud he said, "All his life he's resented his clan's loss of status."

Quanshûk ignored the comment. "What do you think of our situation? Knowing what you know now."

"We are in serious trouble."

"Elaborate, Chief Scholar."

You already know my views, Qonits thought. *They are much the same as yours.* "Your lordship, easy gains enticed us down a flowered path, never imagining it led to such—unprecedented danger."

The admiral's close-cropped claws drummed on his small bar. "Self-evident, Chief Scholar. But what might I do now to—extricate us from that danger?"

Qonits met his gaze. It was not a time for easing into things, he decided. "Lord Admiral, I suggest we look at the possibility of negotiations with the humans. We have a working knowledge of the language, and a decent translation program. And a fleet powerful enough to provide leverage. We hold many of . . ."

Quanshûk raised a heavy hand, stilling him. "How can you say our translation program is decent? For me it is a confusion generator."

The grand admiral was avoiding the issue, but to Qonits his reply was encouraging; the idea had not been slapped down. "It is neither perfect nor complete," Qonits answered carefully, "but it has become quite functional."

The grand admiral's jaw jutted in thought. His gaze was on his richly patterned carpet, no doubt without seeing it. "As for negotiation," he said, "it has no precedent; the fleet would never accept it. To propose it would court rebellion. A coup."

Again Qonits answered carefully. "It might accept it, your lordship. One wonders sometimes if the human empire might not extend forever. Already the problems it presents seem overwhelming. We all go to bed worried, those of us who admit what we see."

But there were also those, Qonits reminded himself, who would roar with indignation at such a proposal, Tualurog the loudest. And might undertake rebellion; might even succeed in it. He thought of asking which was worse: the risk of a coup, or destruction by the humans. But all he could bring himself to say was, "It is Krûts who is master of this ship. Tualurog can order him only in your name, as your proxy, and Krûts doesn't like him. Many don't; he is abrasive. And I have seen the worry in Krûts's eyes. After today's battle, I believe many—possibly even enough— would support you."

He paused. "And there *are* precedents of a sort. Tribes negotiate with tribes, clans with clans, merchants with merchants. There are many examples of successful negotiations between groups unfriendly, even hostile to each other. It's a matter of incentive. And our prisoners have shown themselves logical and reasonable. They have deported themselves well." *A sample of two. Who knows what their rulers are like?* "I would be honored to serve as your negotiator."

Quanshûk did not raise his eyes, but his voice, when he replied, was contemplative. "Even aside from your proficiency with human speech," he said, "you are the only one I would consider sending."

Qonits peered carefully at him. The admiral had neglected his drink; now he downed it, poured himself another—and suddenly his chief scholar hardly dared breathe.

"If such a thing were to be done," Quanshûk continued slowly, "I would begin it covertly, then announce it after you were beyond recall, in hyperspace. To speak earlier would surely invite a coup, and our detention. At best.

"Meanwhile I will make a production of crushing the humans in this system. To strengthen both my image and fleet morale."

He said, I will, Qonits realized, and felt the resolve growing in his admiral's mind.

"I will hold the human mother and child hostage to ensure the reliability of the father," Quanshûk went on, and a rare glint of humor shone in his eyes. "Do you suppose he'll suddenly know how to find his way to their crown world after all?"

Qonits answered gravely. "If necessary, we will stop at some human-inhabited world, for guidance."

The next shipsday, Quanshûk sent scouts insystem, while the armada lay in the near fringe. The most recently-found human worlds tended to have extensive settled areas, more and larger towns, and relatively advanced industrial development. *And* much evacuation. On this one, the scouting report suggested an initial population in the hundreds of millions, judging by the extent and nature of settlement. How many had been evacuated was unclear, but at the edge of forest areas were thousands of abandoned vehicles. There was also evidence of many fugitive camps among the trees.

Quanshûk ordered all his bombards there, with three of his fleet's ground support wings assigned to follow up. Their job was to destroy the towns, the factories—everything that supported the human population there except for a few convenient reservoirs—then scathe the fugitives.

When the job was done, he would send down two tribes. The extensive farmlands would support a score of tribes, and there'd be more fugitives than usual to hunt down, but two tribes would have to do.

❖   ❖   ❖

It was late shipsnight, and the corridors were dim and
quiet. The bombards had started insystem to Shakti a few
hours earlier. Now a crewman guided an AG sled down a
portside corridor, followed by a larger Wyzhñyñy wearing
a lieutenant commander's insignia. From that and his color,
he was obviously of the master gender. His head was
bandaged, presumably injured during the battle, probably
when a torpedo salvo had jolted the *Meadowlands* severely.

The AG sled's cargo was covered by a tarp.

Shortly they stopped at the entrance to a scout hanger.
The crewman opened it but remained in the corridor. It
was the bandaged officer who guided the sled inside. Then
the crewman closed the hatch and returned quietly down
the corridor.

While shipsmind dogged the hatch firmly shut, the
officer unloaded the sled by himself. It wasn't much work,
and there was no injury beneath the bandage. Besides, the
largest item unloaded itself.

Chapter 59

Hearing Board

Within the Wyzhñyñy Admiralty, it had been customary, over the centuries, to convene a fitness board following a major command failure. Often these cleared the accused of malfeasance, but sometimes they uncovered previously unrecognized malfeasance, and found other contributive or ameliorative factors. Sometimes procedural changes were recommended.

But never before had so drastic a failure been addressed.

On the stand, Grand Admiral Quanshûk wore his finest red velvet military vest, with every Imperial decoration he owned. Most prestigious were the High Emperor's Medal of Service, the Medal of Military Accomplishment, and two Outstanding Cadet Medals. None were for valor in combat; there had been no combat for more than three centuries. Nor the rare Kôchasska, which protected the bearer from legal actions of any sort, civil or military. None of those had been awarded for nearly two millennia.

The presiding officer was Captain Krûts. As the ship's captain it was his job. The inquisitor was Rear Admiral

Tualurog. The fitness board consisted of six admirals, senior wing commanders. There were also the grand admiral's counselor and several officers of the court. The witnesses numbered eleven, including senior and junior officers, enlisted personnel, and two humans. The remaining seats were occupied by other senior officers, as mandatory spectators.

Just now, Tualurog was walking back and forth in front of the grand admiral, trying to upset him. It wasn't working. Instead of following the inquisitor's pacing, Quanshûk gazed calmly at the fitness board.

"Tell me, Grand Admiral," Tualurog said, "how many ships did you lose in the recent confrontation with the humans?"

"Objection, Lord President!" Quanshûk's counsel was a commander, a member of Quanshûk's own clan. "The inquisitor is implying that the grand admiral was responsible for the losses. Responsibility is for the hearing to decide."

"Sustained. Rephrase your question in a neutral manner, Inquisitor."

"Of course, Your Honor. I apologize to the court." He looked around. "Grand Admiral Quanshûk, how many ships were lost in the recent battle with the humans?"

"You know the number as well as I do, Lord Tualurog."

"I am asking *you*, Lord Admiral."

Quanshûk listed them by classes.

"Wouldn't you say that is a shockingly large number?"

"I would use the term sobering, Lord Tualurog."

"You weren't shocked by it?"

"Your Honor!" counsel cried.

"Inquisitor, restrict your questions to matters of evidence."

"I stand admonished, Your Honor. Grand Admiral Quanshûk, who was responsible for the decisions made in this war?"

"They have been my decisions."

"And the battle strategies?"

"In conjunction with shipsmind, I was."

"'In conjunction with shipsmind.' But shipsmind is an artificial intelligence. Are artificial intelligences responsible, legally or otherwise, for decisions?"

"Artificial intelligences bear no responsibility for anything, Inquisitor. They are a tool. As you well know."

Tualurog looked at Krûts, expecting him to admonish Quanshûk for his added comment. Krûts, however, gazed coldly back at him, saying nothing. *I will remember that, Captain,* Tualurog thought, *when I rule the armada.*

"A tool indeed, Grand Admiral," Tualurog said, "a tool indeed. And what do you propose we do next, to destroy these humans?"

"Objection, Your Honor!"

"Sustained. Admiral Tualurog, I am aware that you have never before acted as inquisitor. But let me make this clear: If you do not restrict your questions to inquisitorial protocol, I will have to replace you. Understood?"

Tualurog avoided eye contact with Krûts. He could easily blow up at the miserable gut picker, and ruin this whole case. "Indeed, Your Honor. I appreciate your forbearance." He delivered the line smoothly. "Let me try to rephrase my question, because . . . Your Honor, it opens up another, very important part of the investigation."

He looked again at Quanshûk. Having put it as he had, Krûts was obliged to give him greater leeway in questioning, at least so long as he was making apparent progress. "Grand Admiral," Tualurog said, "please give this hearing your best estimate of the volume of space occupied by the human empire when we first encountered it."

Quanshûk knew exactly what Tualurog was getting at. His answer was an estimate made by shipsmind on the day before, expressed as a probability range.

"And what percentage of that space have we swept?"

Quanshûk's estimate was relatively precise, but it was the sheer vastness of the first answer that made the spectators' hearts sink. They'd all known of course, in a general sense, but to have it laid before them like this . . .

Tualurog looked knowingly at the board, then back at Quanshûk. "And how many planets have we colonized here?"

"Forty-seven."

"Forty-seven. With how many tribes?"

"Fifty-six."

"How many tribes do we have left?"

"Sixty-four."

Quanshûk's counsel had been tapping notes on his neckpad. In his own questioning, he would have the grand admiral explain his decisions. They were convincing enough. Even compelling.

"Sixty-four tribes left," Tualurog echoed, making the number sound every bit as bad as it was. "And our warfleet now numbers?"

"Two thousand seven hundred and twelve fighting ships. The reduction has been due largely to leaving defense forces in the colonized systems, but losses to enemy action have also been substantial."

Tualurog looked meaningfully at the hearing board, then turned to Krûts. "Your Honor, I would like to leave that train of questioning for now, and open a new train, which I am confident will change the complexion of this hearing. I respectfully request your indulgence."

Krûts eyed him mistrustfully. "Proceed, Inquisitor."

Tualurog drew nearer to Quanshûk now, and his tone became almost confidential. "I have not seen your chief scholar for several days. Is he ill?"

"Your Honor!" counsel complained. "I seriously object!"

"Denied for now. Proceed, Inquisitor. But this had better lead somewhere."

"It will, Your Honor. I have witnesses. Lord Admiral, your answer please."

Quanshûk had known this was coming since he'd seen the two humans in the witness section. And there was no way to explain it except with the truth. It seemed to him he'd botched the whole affair—everything since they'd arrived in this galaxy—and there was no way in the universe to fix it. He would tell it as he knew it, and take whatever came.

"Lord Inquisitor," he said, "Chief Scholar Qonits is not ill, so far as I know. I have sent him on a mission."

"Sent him?"

"In a long-range scout."

If the courtroom had been quiet before, it was now quiet cubed. "With the human known as David?" Tualurog asked.

"With the human known as David."

Now Tualurog feigned reluctance. He'd guessed the

answer as soon as Qonits' absence had taken his attention. With that, uncovering witnesses had been easy. Then he'd requested a fitness board, proposing himself as inquisitor.

"And what, Grand Admiral, is that mission?" he asked slowly.

"I greatly underestimated the size of the human empire, Lord Inquisitor. As a result we are dangerously overextended, especially given the potency of the enemy fleets. However, our limited knowledge of humans suggests that while fierce, they are a life-form that can be—negotiated with."

A buzz filled the chamber. Krûts hammered it into silence.

"Proceed, Grand Admiral," he said.

"Of course, Captain. The mission, Lord Inquisitor, is to negotiate peace with the humans."

This time, instead of a buzz, there was an indignant hubbub. Krûts banged his gavel till the chamber stilled. "Lord Inquisitor, Lord Counselor, members of the fitness board," he said, "this hearing has grown to encompass far more than envisioned. I hereby adjourn the fitness hearing, and recommend that we deal first with this new development."

He scanned the gathering. "All spectators will leave the chamber until further notice. Security will escort the witnesses to the waiting room, except for the two humans, who will be taken to their quarters. Guards will remain with the humans to prevent suicide. Officers of the court, clear the chamber."

When spectators and witnesses had gone, the hearing board declared itself an emergency board, and elected Rear Admiral Tualurog as its chairman. Then work began on what to do about the predicament they were in.

Quanshûk, as a witness now, pointed out that no known empire except their own had exceeded twenty-eight habitable worlds. And their own had long since ceased to be an empire in its original sense. The second swarm had extended it to twenty-two worlds, and strained the power of the government to govern. The third swarm had set out with the understanding that it would form a sister empire, with loyalty to the same traditions, the Wyzhñyñy species, and the high emperor—the ruler of the parent empire. But the sister empire would rule itself.

Two millennia and six swarms had spread the Wyzhñyñy widely, but even so, the Wyzhñyñy Empire occupied an expanse only a small fraction as large as the human empire.

During the day's meeting, no consensus developed regarding the nature of the human empire. The remarkable lack of high technology on any of the worlds so far conquered seemed to rule out a group of sibling empires. And the long interval without military resistance, and the considerable gap between fleet encounters, suggested the human core worlds were not well prepared for invasion.

But there was consensus on a new strategy, and it did not involve anything so outrageous as negotiation. Speed was the key, and further colonization would be postponed. Strike for the imperial core. When a star was found within detection range in hyperspace, the armada would emerge promptly, and determine from the electronic signature whether the system held a core world. A *core* world. If not, they'd generate hyperspace at once and speed onward. In that way they'd advance far more rapidly.

If they encountered a human fleet waiting in other than a core world system, they would bypass it, generate hyperspace and speed on. The first priority was to destroy the core worlds, and particularly the crown world.

When finally they fought, it would be with the humans' main fleet, and the battle would decide once and for all which life-form would survive. If they won, and they must, then scouting forces would be sent to search out the remaining core worlds. The fleet could then be sent to destroy their technical infrastructures. The following mop-up might take generations, but bit by bit they would exterminate the human life-form.

Rear Admiral Tualurog was elected grand admiral by acclaim. Quanshûk was stripped of rank and privileges, and sentenced to death by suffocation, for treason. Tualurog's first act as grand admiral would be to question the human known as Yukiko—a parent fixated in female phase—and learn, if possible, the location of the crown world.

Then he intended to kill both humans. Evil was evil. It was probably contact with the prisoners that had corrupted Qonits, and through Qonits, Quanshûk. He would take no chances.

Chapter 60
Strange Message

"Blessed Buddha!" Foster Peixoto barely breathed the oath, while Chang Lung-Chi watched and listened silently. The screen showed only Ramesh lying in trance, but the words!

For many months, Annika Pedersen had channeled faithfully. And presumably accurately, Terran as Terran, and Wyzhñyñyç as Wyzhñyñyç. All seemingly without knowing what she did, or that she did anything at all. David MacDonald and Yukiko Gavaldon always spoke in Terran, except for a few, infrequent Wyzhñyñyç interjections. While Qonits' words . . . Seemingly they'd been channeled as faithfully as Ramesh's vocal apparatus allowed, whether slurred Terran from Qonits' lipless mouth, or Wyzhñyñyç muttered to his throat mike or spoken to his guards.

But now Annika and Yukiko were clearly in very different surroundings. David was either absent or silent, while Yukiko murmured only occasional soothing words to the savant. Everything else was in an incomprehensible

mixture of Terran and Wyzhñyñyç, in Wyzhñyñy voices
that differed in pitch, tone, and personality.

But the numerous intermixed Terran words included the
labial phonemes, all properly sounded! A Wyzhñyñy could
not have pronounced them that way. It was as if Annika
was mentally translating from Wyzhñyñyç into Terran, live,
so far as her mental database allowed. And what she could
not translate, sent in the original Wyzhñyñyç! At least that's
how it struck the president, and the prime minister agreed.

The proceedings seemed to be a legal hearing of some
kind.

Peixoto and Chang were listening for the second time.
When the chamber was cleared again by the—judge?—and
Yukiko and Annika had been sent to their cell, Peixoto
turned off the recorder/player. "This is incredible!" he said.
"Unimaginable!" Then switched on his desk comm. "Gisella,
connect me with the university. This is urgent!"

A page interrupted Professor Pelle Clough in class, with
a murmured, "The president and prime minister want to
speak with you at once." Puzzled and only half believing,
the professor took the call. It was brief, but extremely
exciting. After dismissing his students, he was picked up
on the roof by a security floater, and taken to the Palace
of Worlds.

Linguistics was a modest department in the Institute
of Antiquities, but within his specialty, Pelle Clough was
prominent worldwide. He taught and had written fascinating
books on the history and evolution of languages, was
reputedly expert in a dozen, and competent in perhaps
a dozen more. Which implied a rare, intuitive sense of
language.

He had, of course, never heard Wyzhñyñyç. But he and
the two leaders played and replayed the cube, and with the
help of the PM's artificial intelligence, wrung as much
understanding as they could from it. They quickly agreed
it was a courtroom proceeding, and Peixoto was a lawyer with
courtroom experience. Before they were done, they'd gotten
the sense of it. It seemed that Grand Admiral Quanshūk was
being tried for malfeasance, or treason, or both.

And what seemed almost certain—he'd sent an envoy,

Chief Scholar Qonits, as a negotiator to the Commonwealth, apparently with David MacDonald as an aide. The thought first dumbfounded, then excited the two statesmen.

They'd hardly finished—Clough hadn't left yet—when they were interrupted by Burhan Gokhale with another recorded channeling. This one was ugly, shocking, and very short. An apparent question was barked, repeatedly. Seemingly in Terran, but unintelligible, as if by someone who'd never tried to speak it before. Perhaps getting the words from the Wyzhñyñy's shipsmind via an ear button.

Clearly Yukiko understood it. She cried out as if in pain. "I don't know! God help me I don't! . . . Please don't hurt her! She's harmless! She can't . . . "

Abruptly the recording ended, leaving the eavesdroppers with no doubt at all. Annika was dead, and Yukiko either was or soon would be.

Ramesh had been deeply disturbed by what he'd channeled, though as always he remembered none of it. Afterward he sat at his piano and played somber music, until Burhan initiated a shallow trance—the attendant called them "healing reveries"—and put him to bed.

Then Burhan went to the prime minister's apartment, where the two leaders sat waiting.

"How," Peixoto asked, "could Annika have translated like that?"

"Sir, how do savants do any of what they do? We only know *what*, not how. But Annika was present at all the language lessons. She heard everything any of the others heard. And it all registered, perfectly and permanently. Somewhere in her mind it all registered.

"And how did she communicate to us over all those months? Instantly, in real time, from how many light years away? She simply did it, in the same way little Esko Rautasjaure can look at a star chart and tell you the travel time to anyplace you'd care to go. Or not go, including a supernova in Andromeda."

Listening, Chang marveled at this young man—no savant and with only an ordinary education. But his intelligence was obvious, and his humanity beautiful. The president was glad to belong to the same species.

Then Burhan Gokhale said something else. "Sirs, Charley Gordon may have useful comments on the courtroom material."

A savant in trance cannot ask or answer questions. He can only channel. Thus Charley heard the cube of Annika's courtroom account via Ramesh, through Admiral Soong's new savant. When it was over, the prime minister added: "We cannot expect anything further from Annika, and we very much want some idea of what to expect. Can you help us?"

"Sir," Charley said, "this brings two vectors to mind. I'd felt them both, but they were too vague to articulate. This clarifies them. I feel quite confident of them now. The Wyzhñyñy armada will postpone further colonization, and advance much more rapidly. Expect them among the Core Worlds in weeks instead of months, to destroy cities, industries, the entire infrastructure. And our fleet if they can pin it down. They particularly want to raze Terra. After that they will have all the time they need to root out the colonies. Decades. Centuries if necessary.

"Also, the Wyzhñyñy envoy will arrive at the Sol System somewhat sooner than the armada. He will have no diversions, and only astrogational stops. The Admiralty can approximate his arrival time for you, from his departure time from Shakti. Obviously his diplomatic accreditation is no longer in force, but he will have valuable knowledge.

"As for Annika and Yukiko—I agree, they are dead. The Wyzhñyñy commander wanted help in finding Terra, and Yukiko could not or would not help him."

It was the president who asked the final question: "Is there, then, any hope at all?"

"Oh yes, Mr. President, there is hope. But there is not much time."

When they'd finished, Peixoto gave himself a moment to recover, then looked at the president. "Whew! When I asked what to expect, I didn't imagine such detail. Now we have less time than ever." Keying his desk comm, he had his secretary call War House.

touched it. A HUD marked with three symbols—perhaps a Wyzhñyñy acronym—appeared on the "window." Looking at David, Qonits gestured at the mike. "Speak," he said softly.

David licked his lips. "War House, War House, War House." The words felt strange to him. At one time they'd been a mockery. It was said that in Proto-Terran—essentially Old Anglic—the words had meant a brothel. War House had long been regarded as a perverse waste of time, a place where grown men spent years in a universe of make believe. How that viewpoint must have changed!

"This is David MacDonald. David MacDonald. Research leader of the Maritimus Project. I am on an alien long-range scout in the vicinity of a pod beacon. On an alien long-range scout in the vicinity of a pod beacon.

"I've been a prisoner on the invaders' flagship for more than a year. I have come here with Lord Qonits of the Wyzhñyñy Empire. Lord Qonits of the Wyzhñyñy Empire. I am his guide and aide. Lord Qonits is the envoy of Grand Admiral Quanshûk, of the Wyzhñyñy armada. The grand admiral has sent him to discuss possible peace terms. Repeat: peace terms." He paused. "We will remain where we are, and await an escort. Repeat: We will remain where we are and await an escort."

He switched off the mike. It would take about six hours for the message to reach Terra, and the government would take—How long? A day? An hour? A minute?—to decide what to make of this, and respond. Or perhaps decide that someone was hoaxing them. Six hours after that would bring the reply. Unless a courier was sent via warpspace, or some system patrol craft intercepted his message and responded sooner.

He turned to Qonits. "Now we wait," he said.

Qonits nodded. They were used to waiting. They'd done long weeks of it. Long but not idle weeks. Most of their waking hours had been spent in the expansion and refinement of Qonits' Terran, until it seemed to David the chief scholar spoke it better than he did. Qonits had remarkable recall, and approximated human phonemes about as well as a Wyzhñyñy ever could, without electronic enhancement. Meanwhile their busyness minimized David's fretting about Yukiko, and Qonits' about what might have happened to Quanshûk when he'd announced what he'd done.

Now, while waiting for an escort, Qonits explained the seven Wyzhñyñy genders, which clarified a lot for the Terran. And David elaborated on Terran and Commonwealth history. After a bit they napped. David's dreams were strange but not troubling. Qonits's were troubling enough for both of them.

The long-range scout remained parked for ten hours, then its two occupants were picked up by a courier. On the trip insystem, both passengers, secured in their seats, slept again as if they'd been sleep deprived. The copilot wakened them when he emerged from warpspace above Kunming. Near enough that Qonits could appreciate the city's layout, but high enough to give it context. Looking southeast across 400 miles of grasslands and forests, they could see the Gulf of Tonkin. Northwestward, the view was dominated by the deep rugged gorges and towering snow-topped ridges and peaks of the Yun Ling Shan. To the east, spreading to the horizon, lay tawny farmland with intermittent woodlands.

To David MacDonald it was unbelieveably beautiful. He wished Yukiko were there to see it with him. For Qonits the view was interesting and aesthetic, and for the moment he forgot his mission—its responsibilities and dubious prospects.

The radio snatched their attention. Internal Security had further instructions for the pilot. They didn't want Qonits seen by the public. Not yet. His presence would no doubt leak, but let it seem only an unlikely rumor.

The city drew nearer, details multiplying, sharpening. Then they were above the Palace of Worlds, lowering quietly, unremarkably to its roofpad. There was no band, or red carpet, and the squad of marines who met them wore dress greens, not ceremonial whites. Looking hard and businesslike, if a bit distracted. They'd never seen a Wyzhñyñy before, of course, nor any sapient alien. To them, Qonits looked bizarre and dangerous.

If anyone imagines these people won't talk about this,

David thought, *they're crazy*. It seemed to him he got almost as many looks as Qonits. He wondered if they considered him a hero or a turncoat. *Try victim,* he suggested silently.

The president and prime minister waited in business clothes, without insignia. David had never, of course, seen either of them in person, but they were familiar from newscasts. It was to the much shorter, thicker-bodied human he gave precedence, ad-libbing. "Mr. President, Mr. Prime Minister," he said, "it is my honor to present to you Ambassador Qonits, chief scholar and personal envoy of Grand Admiral Quanshûk, Ruler of the Seventh Swarm."

David turned to Qonits then. "Mr. Ambassador," he said, "it is my honor to introduce to you the honorable Chang Lung-Chi, President of the Commonwealth of Worlds. And the honorable Foster Peixoto, his prime minister."

Qonits was surprised at Foster Peixoto's height, and wondered what gender he might be. Meanwhile he bowed slightly: David had coached him. "I am deeply honored," he said.

"I too am honored, Mr. Ambassador," the prime minister answered. It was the president's reply that surprised both Qonits and David: "It is good you come here," he said—in understandable Wyzhñyñyç! It suggested to them that somehow, somewhere, the government had had contact with other Wyzhñyñy. Actually, the recorded language lessons (as one-sided as most had been), the limited exchanges between Qonits and his bodyguards, and Annika's mixed channeling of the fitness hearing had been enough for the government's powerful artificial intelligence to create a partial and provisional translation program. And Chang Lung-Chi had taken the opportunity to learn this simple (and ungrammatical) phrase as a courtesy.

Chang and Peixoto, of course, knew what Qonits did not—that the armada was under a new regime, one not interested in negotiating. But Qonits could be a valuable information source, and at any rate, for the president, decency was natural. And judging from the hearing, Qonits was cut off forever from his own people.

❖   ❖   ❖

No time had been scheduled for resting or getting acquainted. The two human leaders felt strongly pressed by the oncoming armada. Thus, shortly after their introduction, Qonits and David were led through a private corridor to a sitting room in the president's wing. A luncheon had been set for four, and a seat hurriedly improvised for Qonits. He declined to use it, explaining that "persons with four legs commonly stand to eat."

Like bears, the Wyzhñyñy were omnivores despite their fighting teeth. For them, most human foods were digestible and nourishing. Most of them. But Qonits was uneasy. Like humans, the Wyzhñyñy had made a science of adapting to exotic worlds. They'd long since learned that if a planet fell within otherwise habitable parameters, they could usually eat many of its plants and most of its higher animals. Eat them safely and beneficially. But there were exceptions. So on a new world they ate rations they'd brought with them, while technicians analyzed and tested a broad spectrum of plants and animals for safety, digestibility and nutrient values. Without that sort of database, this meal involved a modest risk for the chief scholar.

When they'd finished dessert—*vaclava,* which Qonits found delicious—Foster Peixoto led them to a small conference room. Almost immediately, five humans from War House and the Commonwealth Ministry were ushered in, and the prime minister introduced them to Qonits. "Mr. Ambassador," he said, "we greatly appreciate your courage in coming here. And the courage Grand Admiral Quanshûk displayed in sending you. And finally, the desire for peace shown by you both.

"Before we discuss your mission further, however, there are things you need to know. Please interrupt if I say things you disagree with, or do not understand. Meanwhile I suggest you be seated." He gestured at a large cushion beside the conference table, and Qonits sat down on it like a huge ungainly dog.

"Since you left your flagship," Peixoto went on, "there have been very important developments you need to know about. They are described in a cube I'll play in just a moment." He looked at David. "Is he familiar with what I mean by cube?"

"Yes, sir. They have quite similar technology. And sir, we have cubes sent by Grand Admiral Quanshûk, with a player designed to play them. One of them contains the Terran/Wyzhñyñyç translation program. Another has a Wyzhñyñyç/Terran program based on it, which hasn't been tested. The third is a message to the president and yourself, recorded by the grand admiral, and translated by his shipsmind. If you'd take time to hear it . . . "

The prime minister cut him short. "Thank you, Mr. MacDonald. For now we'll proceed as I'd planned, and hear the grand admiral's message later." He looked at Qonits. "The reason will become clear." He glanced at the others around the table. "Now if you will put your attention on the wall screen, please."

The humans swiveled their chairs—Qonits already nearly faced it—and Peixoto touched his key pad. A freeze frame appeared on the screen, showing a dark-complected youth lying on a couch, seemingly asleep. "Mr. Ambassador," Peixoto said, "this young man is my savant communicator. When I run the recording, you will hear him speak. In several voices. He is analogous to a radio, but channels over interstellar distances"—he paused meaningfully—"over interstellar distances with no elapsed time. None. And what he will say is a duplication of conversations *on board your flagship.* Do you understand so far?"

Qonits nodded uncertainly. *Interstellar distances? No elapsed time?* The words seemed clear enough, but impossible.

"Good," Peixoto said, and pressed another key. Ramesh's mouth moved, and words came from the speaker—the fitness board proceedings, as hybridized and channeled by Annika Pedersen. None of the listeners spoke. David MacDonald's jaw went slack. He understood almost none of the Wyzhñyñyç, but the rest . . .

Initially Qonits stiffened, but as the hearing progressed, he wilted. When the replay was over, it was the president who spoke, his voice soft. "Mr. Ambassador," he said, "we realize what a shock this has been to you. You have my profound sympathy."

Again the chief scholar gave the Wyzhñyñy equivalent of a nod, saying nothing. Except for the first few seconds, he'd had little difficulty with its hybridized content. The Wyzhñyñyç diction, and the sense of speaker identity, had been reproduced surprisingly well.

When it was over, he simply sat, and after a long moment spoke, aware that the humans had been waiting.

"Is there more? There must be more."

Chang nodded. "Yes. We have no record of the later proceedings, but we do have a recording of something else that seems important." He paused, turning. "Those of you from War House and Cee Ministry, please go to the waiting room. What follows is personal. I'll call you back shortly."

David watched frowning as they left. What was this about? Qonits waited numbly. When they were alone with the president and prime minister, Chang nodded, and Peixoto played the next section, the one in which Yukiko was questioned. It left little doubt: Annika, and almost surely Yukiko, were dead. David MacDonald was pale and stony as marble.

"David, we are terribly sorry," Chang said quietly. Peixoto said nothing at all; didn't trust his control. David's nod was wooden. *I should have known it would come to that,* he thought. *It was inevitable. All of it. This mission was a charade, by an admiral trying to convince himself, and two fools who wanted to believe.*

After half a minute, the president spoke again. "I will call the others back in now. There are questions that must be looked at." The people from War House and the Commonwealth Ministry had heard the entire cube before. He'd sent them out as a courtesy to David, in case he broke down.

They did not question Qonits at length, but they did play Quanshûk's cube. Then they reviewed possibilities they'd discussed before, and the conclusions they'd drawn, asking Qonits for clarifications, and his opinions. The chief scholar's comments were brief but informative.

Peixoto's closing comment was to Qonits: "Mr. Ambassador, your grand admiral was correct in believing we prefer negotiation to war. We do not wish to destroy your people, nor be destroyed by them. When your fleet has been smashed, perhaps the survivors will agree to terms. Then you will have a major role in this."

Peixoto didn't actually lie, but he didn't imagine that terms could be agreed on, even assuming that Soong's Commos won the battle to come. For he knew things that Qonits still did not. The armada had stopped very briefly in the fringes of two more inhabited systems, departing quickly without attacking, leaving only their emergence signatures. Clearly, Charley had been right: They'd decided to postpone further conquests, and were inbound with the intention of forcing a showdown, a final battle. Given their new rate of progress, they'd reach the Eridani System in about three weeks. The Eridani System had a home-grown population of nearly two billion, a bevy of universities, burgeoning industries—and millions of colonial evacuees, armed and more or less trained.

Soong and his Commos would be there, waiting with reinforcements, and Charley Gordon was refining a strategy and tactics to include the new spook drones, whose functions were deception and confusion.

With the new weapons and Charley Gordon, there was still a chance. The Admiralty thought so and Soong thought so. The *Altai's* shipsmind rated it one in four, and War House's AI agreed. Charley Gordon rated it even. "Wait and see," he'd said. "If we survive the first phase, we will beat them."

Peixoto had never known Charley Gordon to fool himself, but in this situation he might. *Because this will be the final battle,* Peixoto told himself, *with everything at stake. And it is on Charley's shoulders. The pressure will not break him, but it might bend his judgement.*

Chang, on the other hand, believed the Tao wanted humanity to survive, and therefore that it would. And of course if all else failed, there was Project Noah.

David and Qonits sat in the palace guest suite they shared, neither speaking at first. Finally David suggested they have something to drink, something alcoholic, and diagrammed the ethanol molecule, elaborating. Qonits nodded. Ethanol was the active ingredient in most Wyzhñyñy liquors. Then David asked their marine orderly to send for dark rum.

The orderly, who wore a stunner and a lance corporal's

stripe, seemed a competent young man. Qonits assumed the stunner was a weapon, and the marine as much guard as orderly, but the chief scholar did not feel threatened. And rightly. The lance corporal had been warned that a stunner was lethal to Wyzhñyñy. He was there to *defend* his charges, and forbidden to use it on the ambassador under any circumstances, however desperate.

Another lance corporal delivered the bottle. Each "guest" took a drink; both marines declined. David took his straight. Qonits sipped his with water, but drank nonetheless.

"So it will only be a few weeks," David said. "Who do you suppose will win?"

"The grand admiral feared that you would, eventually," Qonits answered. "Your resources are enormous."

"But your fleet is enormous," David replied, "and we have not been a warlike species for a very long time."

"Perhaps not. But your battlecomps have proven much better than ours, and you have robot cruisers that can maneuver—" he failed to come up with the word "evasively," so he zigzagged a hand. "And obtaining target locks requires milliseconds—not an easy matter when a target moves erratically at such speeds." He paused, then added: "Also your shields are stronger."

David still had trouble imagining an effective Commonwealth fleet. Certainly not one so quickly constructed and trained. He peered thoughtfully at Qonits, who sipped his rum again.

"We lost many more fighting ships than you did," Qonits continued. "And a majority of our ships are not fighting ships."

It occurred to David that the chief scholar would be keeping those things to himself, if he thought there was any chance at all of meaningful negotiation. And the prime minister had told Qonits about the savants, which he wouldn't have done if he expected to negotiate.

"Many are colony ships, supply ships, factory ships," Qonits went on. "It is necessary that our colonies set up manufacturing industries, with different tribes having different industries."

"And therein lies a greater problem." He paused again to sip. "Agricultural tribes are landed first, to establish food production and a planetary database. And when shipsmind decides we have occupied as large a sector of space as we can administer, the tribes not yet landed are assigned by shipsmind to worlds already occupied. On the basis of planetary environments, tribal affinities, and an integrated, practical industrial program.

"Usually there is no technologically potent empire to destroy. And when there has been, it has never been too large to swallow. Until now."

He took another swallow himself, then fixed his bleak gaze on David again. "We never imagined an empire so large as yours. Not a hundredth as large. We were already badly overextended when we fought the first human fleet. We would not have enough tribes. And our industries would be so widely dispersed, they would not constitute a viable system."

"Then why . . . "

Qonits fist slammed the table top, making David jump. "Because we dared not stop! Not within the bounds of a technologically advanced empire! We would have been mortally exposed!"

He paused, staring ruefully at his fist. "I am sorry, David. I should not have committed violence, even against a table. The scholar gender does not tolerate ethanol well. And you are my friend. My only friend in this galaxy."

"In this galaxy," David echoed. "You've said that before, and I've assumed it was a figure of speech. Don't tell me the Wyzhñyñy are from another galaxy."

"We are." Qonits began to rock, forward and back. "We are," he repeated. Then he finished his drink and sat quietly.

Contemplating only the All-Soul knows what, David thought. "But surely you hadn't filled up your own galaxy. And how could you have gotten here from so far away?"

He'd never before heard Qonits laugh, but it seemed to him that's what this sound was. Probably an ironic laugh. The chief scholar refilled his glass himself, and drank. "We do not know," he said, then briefly described the experience. "Nor do we know which other one we came from. Not that it makes any difference. The nearest would be too far."

❖   ❖   ❖

Briefly they sipped without speaking. Then David, groping for a change of subject, asked what Qonits' home world
was like. They spent the next hour exchanging reminiscences of childhood and youth. And drinking. Finally Qonits
slumped onto his side and closed his eyes.

"You're drunk, old buddy," David said. And laughed.
"And so am I. How about that! We need to get ol' Pollywog or whatever his name is to get drunk with the president. What *is* his name? Pollywog."

Qonits eyes opened. He giggled. *That's what it is*,
David thought. *Giggling.* "I don' remember," Qonits said.
"Tooley Rooley." He frowned, trying to get it right.
"Toolarog. Thass it."

His eyes closed again. David wobbled to his bed and
flopped down on it. It promptly began to rotate on its
axis. He knew it was the alcohol, not the bed, but nonetheless tried physically to hold it still until the sensation
stopped. Then he nested his cheek in his pillow. "David,"
he mumbled, "you juss did something no human ever did
before. You know that? You got drunk with an alien."

It was the last thing he thought before sleeping.

Marine Lance Corporal Artemis Shaughnessy looked at
the two sleepers. What a story to tell his children and
grandchildren, when he had some. Surely the security
restrictions would be off by then.

It seemed to him he knew more about the aliens now
than even the president did.

He didn't, of course. The suite was bugged, and the two
leaders had all of it on cube. Including David waking later
from a dream of Yukiko, to soak his pillow with tears.

It was the last time he would grieve for her. It was done.

Chapter 62

The Battle of Epsilon Eridani

Abruptly, Alvaro Soong's command screen registered 221 radio sources, twittering code. He'd been expecting them: a corvette herding 220 spook drones, newly arrived in the Eridani System from Sol. They'd emerged sufficiently nearby that their emergence waves preceded their electromagnetic signature by only a few seconds. The corvette's captain, a lieutenant, had done an excellent job of delivering his herd.

A similar herd had arrived from the Indi System four days earlier and six days late, badly scattered, sixteen spooks short—and on the wrong side of the system. Far enough that the guide ship's signal lag was more then thirteen hours! What a mess. Gathering the spooks had been slow and frustrating, and the fifty-seven hours wasted would be time lost later from steel drills. As for the sixteen spooks lost in hyperspace—an admiral hates losing even unmanned ships.

The Indi guide ship had been a long-range scout, and her commander a mere ensign! Policy required a board of review, which took less than four hours to absolve the young officer of malfeasance. He'd had only introductory training in hyperspace radio—not nearly enough to reliably monitor and control the drones in hyperspace. As for gathering them for the closing jump—that accounted for most of the six-day delay.

The review board concluded he'd done well to lose so few.

Soong savanted a strongly worded message to War House, criticizing Indi Command for appointing someone so unqualified. It was Admiralty Chief Fedor Tischendorf himself who replied, very mildly. Ensign Fahzi had been at the head of his class when Indi Command had pulled him out of training, bestowed a premature commission, and *with Kunming's blessing* had given him the job. On Indi Prime, everyone of certified competence—short of Command and training staff—had already been sent with the 1st Indi Battle Wing. All they had left were midshipmen.

"Consider yourself well served, Alvaro," Tischendorf had finished. "Ensign Fahzi was the best available, and whatever spooks arrived are ships you wouldn't otherwise have. If he'd lost half of them, you'd still be better off than if they hadn't been sent. And if they hadn't been sent, they'd be meaningless. Because if you don't severely blunt the Wyzhñyñy advance at Eridani—and I stress *severely*—we're lost. All of us."

Soong had listened with chagrin. He'd popped his cork—rare for him—and the indignation that sprayed out had turned to rue. He didn't counter that Indi Command should have held back a qualified officer from the 1st Indi Battle Wing, then transferred him back to it on arrival. Fahzi *had* done the job. And historically, war was notorious for erroneous planning assumptions, pressure situations, decisions made under severe stress, and the need to use unqualified personnel. In fact, Soong told himself, a perspective review of this war would probably discover fewer and less critical foul-ups than in most historical wars. Because regardless of its other shortages, War House was rich in resourceful ingenuity. Not to mention long centuries of contingency planning and simulation testing.

And no one in War House had joined the military for prestige or benefits.

Now Soong's fleet was fully gathered. Since Shakti, it hadn't grown much in manned fighting ships: his losses had been made up, but he had only a single new battle wing. War House had decided to concentrate on drone production; he had nearly twice as many maces as before.

And now spooks, drones of quite another type. With the 220 from Sol, he totalled 404. Named "Ball Spooks" (for a fabled 21st century gamer and writer), they carried opaque-image generators which could disguise them as battleships, maces or cruisers. Spooks had long been part of science-fiction gaming, and a War House budget proposal for their development had been rejected by the government centuries earlier. Then the Wyzhñyñy had come, and industrial and research resources became the limiting factors, with maces and improved shield generators the Admiralty's top development priorities.

And properly so. Maces could kill enemy warships, layered shields could save ships and lives, and definitive research and development had already been done on them. But there was a role for sacrificial lambs—spook ships— that looked enough like lions to fool the enemy and occupy his efforts. So a project was also begun, small and exploratory at first, then more intensive.

When a spook-field generator had been successfully demonstrated, production began, because spooks could be produced quickly in quantities. Prospector hulls would serve, and could be mass-produced cheaply.

Prospector hulls had limited capacity, of course. And while spooks needed no crew facilities, they required lots of hardware, particularly generators of several kinds. Spook-field generators not only required hull space, they made serious energy demands, because ordinary holos were not enough. And of course there could be no skimping on strange-space generators; without them they couldn't travel. But limits could be set for other equipment. A spook without an energy shield would not fool enemy sensors, but their shield generators could be single-layer models, and needn't produce modified topologies.

As for "weapons" . . . Wyzhñyñy shipsminds would be dealing with great volumes of urgent sensory intake, thus spook "war beams" needed only to flouuresce a battleship's shield convincingly. They required far less hull space, and drew far less power than a cruiser's guns, for example. And they carried no torpedoes at all.

Soong had gotten the necessary performance and operating specs in advance, and Charley Gordon had considered them in reprogramming the battlecomps. The Wyzhñyñy would face a whole new set of Commonwealth Fleet tactics; the Commos had been sim drilling them for days. Now the *Altai's* shipsmind uploaded them to the newly arrived spooks from the Sol System.

Extrapolating, shipsmind had provided a probabilistic window of Wyzhñyñy arrival. It left only four days for steel drills, then Soong would have to order ready formations, and wait. Wait for the final and decisive fight. If they lost, snooze ships on Terra, Indi Prime, Lüneburger's World and Masada, there to load liberation forces, would instead embark women, children, and chosen specialists. None of whom knew yet the great and terrible secret. While cargo ships—so-called colony resettlement ships—loaded selected colonization equipment. They would rendezvous, then seek a new home, half a dozen hyperspace years distant.

But only a tiny fraction of one percent of humankind could be taken. Thus the iron-bound secrecy. The plan was too terrible to become known.

As for the rest of humankind—their future depended on the Battle of Eridani. If it was lost, they were lost. There'd be no opportunity, nor any meaningful force, to make a stand elsewhere.

In reviewing simdrills and coordinating steel drills, Alvaro Soong had occasionally spoken by radio with all his wing commanders. And on his secure, private channel, had twice spoken privately with Carmen Apraxin-DaCosta. Neither had mentioned marriage. This was neither the time nor place to discuss it.

❖   ❖   ❖

Less than four seconds after his armada emerged, the raucous blare of an alarm horn resounded through the Wyzhñyñy flagship. Grand Admiral Tualurog tensed. It was what he'd been hoping for, and he reacted with a mixture of eagerness and anxiety. His command screen showed several sources of technically produced radiation. The main source, very powerful, was the system's second planet, and there were numerous other sources farther outsystem— within an asteroid zone, and in the vicinity of a jovian giant. Their strength and distribution was far larger than in any system encountered since they'd left the Empire. Clearly a core world system—but hardly the crown system. The radio output wasn't that intense.

Also insystem, in the near fringe, was a source array that could only be a space fleet larger than any the armada had encountered before. Though still much smaller than his own. So. Not the Commonwealth's main fleet then. It was simply there to bleed him. That was the human strategy; had been all along.

That moment was pivotal, and even Charley had not foreseen it. For a moment, Tualurog considered generating hyperspace again and speeding onward. Find the human crown system, where their main fleet would be waiting. Defeat it and behead the enemy. But he rejected the idea almost at once. Because the fleet here would undoubtedly pursue him, and with his power advantage, it was better to deal with it now, by itself, rather than later, while engaged with their main fleet.

He voiced an order to shipsmind, and the armada, not greatly dispersed during the approach jump, began forming battle formations.

Alvaro Soong examined the pattern of emergence loci. A few yards away, Charley Gordon sat relaxed at his battle master's station, absorbing the displays on his screen, and no doubt much that was not on the screen. Calmly he began to give orders to shipsmind, the code words measured. Later they'd flow from him quick as pulses from a blaster. And this time he would not wait for the Wyzhñyñy to start the fight.

❖　　　❖　　　❖

The first strike was by an entire echelon of maces, doing something no one had imagined before: instead of emerging stationary from warpspace, they emerged with momentum—surged forth. There were no organisms aboard to be crushed by inertia, and shipsmind, on Charley's order, had computed an entry velocity the sturdy maces could withstand. At the instant of emergence they began accelerating, generating shields, and achieving target locks for war beams and torpedos.

The Wyzhñyñy had generated shields in advance, but still the concentration of fire wrought havoc, and within seconds the maces were deep inside the Wyzhñyñy formations. Nor did they pause. A second echelon followed, at the same unexpected speed. And a third. Meanwhile a human battle wing emerged a little distance out, stationary, then accelerated toward the enemy, firing both torpedo salvos and war beams, concentrating on individual targets.

The maces had charged all the way through the Wyzhñyñy battle fleet with modest losses, and dropped their shields on the run, the survivors winking into warpspace. And in warpspace, maneuvered promptly into a reverse vector, to emerge again on the fly, ripping through the same formations they'd already savaged.

By then the first-arrived human battle wing had closed with the Wyzhñyñy, the two sides fighting in a close-range slugging match. And of course the other wings replicated that behavior elsewhere within the Wyzhñyñy battle fleet. In those formations they attacked, less than one Wyzhñyñy battleship in three was targeted, but of those targeted, most died. A few survived derelict, their matric taps blown, maintaining life support systems on backups if at all. The human battle groups ignored them, concentrating on ships still dangerous.

This drew the Wyzhñyñy reserves, of course. It was their kind of fighting. Their mistake, foreseen by Charley Gordon, was to move cautiously. They'd been fooled too often. Thus the maces reached the dueling field ahead of many of them, sucker-punching and killing Wyzhñyñy duelists, winking back into warpspace, then charging out again toward the oncoming Wyzhñyñy intervention. And when the maces reemerged, Soong's battle groups used the opportunity to take refuge in warpspace themselves.

They did not stay there long. Warpspace was suitable for covert maneuvering, but poorly suited for actual fighting.

So far, Charley Gordon had not committed his spooks. He knew the circumstances he wanted them for, and it wasn't time yet.

The fighting continued, the Commos repeating the same tactics. Charley would change them when opportunities or difficulties required. In the vicinity of the *Altai*, the Wyzhñyñy had killed nearly a dozen human battleships, and twice as many lesser warships. And that was only one segment of the scene. Comparable scenarios played throughout the battle zone. Wyzhñyñy losses were gruesome. The *Meadowlands* bridge reeked with anxiety. Tualurog had chewed his cheeks bloody, and his eyes bulged wide and wild. *This cannot be allowed! Those cursed robots! Sixty-two tribes depend on us!* Torpedoes struck her shield, and the *Meadowlands* jarred. Her lights dimmed, then brightened again. The bridge screens, however, did not blink; shipsminds were powerfully buffered. Damage alarms jangled and systems checks ran. Her shield recovered, and her war beam generator rebooted.

Meanwhile another human battle wing reemerged in the vicinity. Tualurog decided, and barked a command to shipsmind, which passed it on. "All battle groups! All battle groups! This is your grand admiral! Your grand admiral! Do not allow the humans to run away! Choose a target, lock on and close! Attack, pursue and kill! Attack, pursue and kill! Do not be distracted! Do not disengage for any reason! Do not let them generate strange-space again!"

The order sounded on every Wyzhñyñy bridge, in every compartment, down every corridor. And whispered in Charley Gordon's mind in the form of an intuition: it was time to call in the spooks. On Charley's order, couriers generated warpspace and radioed the waiting spook groups, which emerged at the edge of action, and received explicit orders via the *Altai's* shipsmind. Then they winked into warpspace again, to emerge at rendezvous coordinates with battle groups and mace triads.

Meanwhile the battle wings fought in slow motion, to permit maneuver. The maces, with their heavy shields, repeatedly disrupted Wyzhñyñy contingents attempting to gang up on Commo battleships. Among the Commo battle groups, patterns of mutual support fluctuated with the need, their fire coordination adjusting constantly to threat and opportunity. And always the key was teamwork.

Most often the spooks mimicked battleships. And because they were less responsive than manned ships, they attracted much more than their share of Wyzhñyñy fire.

Mostly the Commos had the advantage of two-layered shields, but not the veteran *Altai*. She took a heavy torpedo salvo, the energy overload collapsing her shield. Her escort cruisers saved her, two of them deliberately intercepting war beams, breaking their target locks. "Generate warpspace!" Soong snapped, and after a long moment the *Altai* disappeared, her battlecomp automatically steering an avoidance course "on the other side," against the high probability that more torpedos had been launched at her. They would follow, but the transition would break their target locks, letting them pass into warpspace limbo.

Soong exhaled through rounded lips, half whistling. He had, he realized, very nearly lost both his ship and Charley Gordon.

"Admiral," Charley told him, "the battle vectors have evolved almost ideally. I expect your Commos will get by without us while Engineering repairs our shield generator."

Then he ordered the navcomp to take them to a location in the F-space potentiality, one from which they could emerge outside the battle zone. Meanwhile Soong watched the array of screens, which for the moment showed only systems rundowns.

Engineering required little more than five minutes to replace the *Altai*'s matric tap and breakers. Then she returned to F-space, somewhat removed from the fighting and unnoticed by the enemy. The battle had continued relentlessly. Few of the human ships with single-layer shields still lived, but many with two-layered shields fought on. This time Soong held the *Altai* clear of the fighting, and Charley began to issue directions to the fleet's battlecomps. Even during the *Altai*'s absence, his battle programs had been decisive. Some of his simdrills and steel drills had assumed the loss of the *Altai* and her battle master.

Most of the spooks had died, but they'd played a crucial role. Meanwhile the Wyzhñyñy could not waltz with the maces, which repeatedly disrupted Wyzhñyñy formations and fire coordination. The *Meadowlands* had been destroyed, and no one had taken command. Tualurog's "attack, pursue and kill" order had hampered teamwork, dispersed formations, and seriously reduced responses to opportunity and threat. Increasingly fragmented, his warfleet simply followed his final order, until teamwork had almost totally unraveled.

Now Charley's main attention was on directing disengaged Commo units to strategic locations. Finally a critical point was reached at which the Wyzhñyñy reactions became effectively suicidal, and their warships were overwhelmed.

The battle was over.

Soong remained on the bridge while the names of surviving ships scrolled. He had to know. When the list was complete, the *Uinta* was not on it. Even then he stayed, while shipsmind extracted and scrolled the identities of Commo ships destroyed.

Finally the *Uinta*'s name appeared. She'd been ruptured and melted down.

When the rundown was complete, he left the bridge, the victor of the most important battle in human history. His back was straight, his head high, and his eyes dry. When he reached his stateroom, he drank himself to sleep.

Chapter 63

Proposal

Morning sunlight slanted through ten-foot windows, causing the polished table and walls to glow a deep golden mahogany—a product of more than expensive veneer and thorough polishing. There were also the window fields. It had been years since David MacDonald had been exposed to advertising, but he recalled the trade name: Rich Light. *Because you have to be rich to own them,* he thought wryly. The light itself was free though: sunlight. But altered to order. The window fields controlled the intensity and wavelengths transmitted.

A gavel tapped lightly. The president had gotten to his feet. "We have asked you here," he said, "to help us through a dilemma. A situation much preferable to yesterday's, but . . . We have a choice to make that on the one hand threatens humanity with centuries of trouble and grief, and on the other, a burden of guilt very difficult to bear. We need a third alternative, one that avoids both.

"Under our Emergency War Powers, the prime minister and I have the authority to make that choice ourselves,

571

and in fact there is no time for parliamentary debate and clearance. So we especially want and need your counsel now."

Chang Lung-Chi scanned the assemblage: Admiral Fedor Tischendorf, Admiralty Chief; Dr. Arthur Shin, Minister of War; Melani Honghi, Commonwealth Minister; Dorje Lodro Tulku, Chaplain of the Office of the President; and Ambassador Qonits. With their principal aides, including David MacDonald.

Just now it was Qonits at whom Chang looked. "Mr. Ambassador, last night a great battle was fought in the Eridani System," he said. "A decisive battle. Analysis of battle recordings indicates that none of your warfleet survived, or even undertook to escape. They fought till the last was destroyed."

The words stunned Qonits; it was Quanshûk's vision realized.

"But that was the warfleet," Chang went on. "Your armada's noncombat ships—estimated at more than three thousand—still sit parked in warpspace, neither fleeing nor able to defend themselves. Experience suggests they even lack force shields. And we have the task of deciding how to deal with them."

He sipped honeyed tea, allowing Qonits a moment before he continued. "How many of your people do they carry? Ten million? Call it ten million in stasis. And their crews number what? Another quarter million? Along with the colonists you've set down, they are all the Wyzhñyñy that exist in this galaxy."

His gaze was on the mahogany table now, but his attention was on his thoughts. "Do we destroy them? If not, what *do* we do with them? A month ago, when the question was rhetorical, I would have said destroy them. Said it regretfully. But alive in this galaxy—certainly in this sector of it—they pose a threat to the human species. Already they've murdered some twenty million of us. Given another week or two, they'd have killed more than a billion on Eridani Prime. A billion! Why should we feel compassion for them?"

Why indeed? thought Qonits.

"The answer," Chang said, "is that you are a sapient

species. And in our various philosophies, almost without exception, the destruction of an ensouled life-form is a grave crime. We call it genocide. The word itself is considered obscene.

"And to commit it against your people is ugly to contemplate, although they—you—intended it for us."

Again he scanned his audience. "I will ask all of you to comment, but first I would like to hear Ambassador Qonits' thoughts. If you will, sir."

There was a long silence—twenty seconds at least—then Qonits swayed his head, a negative. "There is nothing I can say now. Perhaps after others have spoken."

David MacDonald exhaled softly. *Having Qonits here makes it harder to say "kill them."* He wondered at his own calm, his objectivity. Yukiko was lost to him, at least until he died himself. *Probably*, he thought, *it was Tualurog who killed her.* Tualurog himself was surely dead, and while that didn't lessen the loss, it had quenched the thirst for vengeance.

Chang's gaze moved to Admiral Tischendorf. "What do you have to say, Admiral?"

Frowning, Tischendorf pursed his broad mouth. "To stand off and fire torpedos at unarmed ships . . . ? If I order it, our people will do it. And for the life of me, I can't see any way around it. But doing it will . . . leave a scar on everyone's soul, even beyond this lifetime. As you said, we would carry it forever.

"On the other hand, if we start firing, I suspect that those not in the first target set will generate hyperspeed and leave. Then we'll have the long job of hunting them down; a long, unpleasant, unpromising job."

He sat back, finished.

"Dr. Shin," Chang said, "what do you have to say?"

"At this point, Mr. President, I can only echo Admiral Tischendorf. Perhaps next round." Shin knew Chang's style. The rounds of comments or questions would continue until he'd heard all he felt was needed.

"Ah. Ms. Honghi?"

"Mr. President, my concern is for the evacuees, and freeing their worlds of Wyzhñyñy occupation so they can go home again. Those who want to. Considering all the relatives and friends who died, and the farms and towns destroyed, many may not want to."

The president nodded gravely. "I'm sure that's true." His gaze paused on Qonits, then moved to Dorje Lodro. "Your Wisdom," he said, "what guidance do you have for us?"

"Guidance?" Her tone was mild. "You and the prime minister are quite able to make your decision on this without my input. But since you ask . . . Consider. The Wyzhñyñy are dangerous only if armed. Presumably they have weapons and munitions aboard their troopships and ordnance ships. If you can collect those, and launch them by gravdrive into the sun, the Wyzhñyñy are no longer dangerous."

You hope! David thought.

"Of course, if you spare them, you must decide what to do with them. They cannot go home. And if you do not spare them . . . " She paused. "As has been said: they are ensouled. You will bear great karma." She looked at Qonits. "Ambassador, within the Commonwealth boundaries, has your armada colonized planets which had no human occupants?"

Qonits looked at Dorje with the first glimmer of hope. "Three," he said.

"Ah." She turned to Chang. "If all the Wyzhñyñy in the armada were landed on one of them—perhaps the most favorable, or that nearest Terra—they would be relatively easy to monitor and police. Then the Wyzhñyñy colonists on other planets could be offered tranportation to that world."

She bowed slightly. "I have said enough."

Chang nodded, then looked at Qonits again. "Mr. Ambassador, you were sent to negotiate with us. Could you speak *for* us? Talk your people into surrendering, and settling on a world of their own? We of course would dictate the terms, but if those terms are not punitive . . . " He paused, waiting.

Dorje Lodro's words had revived Qonits. "I can try," he said quietly, "but I cannot guarantee success. It depends on who has taken command of the colonization fleet, if anyone has.

"The colonization fleet has no admiral of its own. It was

commanded by the grand admiral—Lord Quanshûk and then Lord Tualurog. Each of the colony tribes had a commanding general and a governor, both of the master gender, but—"

Foster Peixoto raised a hand and interrupted. "What do you mean by master gender?"

"Let me first finish answering the earlier question. Those generals should all be in stasis, and at any rate are unqualified to command a ship, let alone a fleet. It is unlikely they've been revived, but the possibility is worrisome: We could find ourselves dealing with a commander strong in pride but weak in understanding.

"Whomever I must negotiate with will probably, hopefully, be a warrior, not a master, and normally my status is superior to a warrior's. But they will distrust me. And with Lord Quanshûk dead, my status is . . ." He groped for the word "ambiguous," and settled for "unclear."

"On the other hand their situation is desperate, and I expect they will listen." He puffed a Wyzhñyñy sigh before finishing. "There is little more I can say about the prospects, until I know more about the terms you have in mind."

He gestured a shrug. "And now, Mr. Prime Minister, I shall explain the genders for you. It is important that you know; they are central to understanding us."

There are, he told them, four genetic genders and three nurture-actuated, "exalted" genders. One of the exalted genders—"matrons"—develops functional breasts, and if assigned a newborn, nurtures it. As a result, this "nurtured" infant develops distinctive anatomical, morphological and mental traits. That is, it becomes "exalted." With nurture, a genetic warrior becomes a master; a genetic artisan becomes a scholar; and a genetic nanny becomes a matron. Each quite distinct from the unnurtured phenotype.

Frowning, Chang said: "We were told by—another source that both sexes nurse the young."

"That requires clarification. We have only one parent gender. Each adult of the parent gender alternates between male and female sexual phases, and only the parent who carried the child nurses it. But the nonsexual nanny gender, which is larger, will also nurse any unweaned young in its care."

"You told us the matron gender nurses selected young."

"In a sense. But what the matrons produce is not what you might call 'milk.' They provide something quite different, and in smaller quantities."

"Seven genders," Tischendorf mused. "What percentage are warriors?"

David had asked the same question while they'd waited aboard the scout, to be picked up, so Qonits recognized Tischendorf's problem. "About twelve percent," Qonits said, "but the parent gender, and the nannies and artisans are also trained to fight. Masters, as exalted warriors, are physically the largest and most powerful, and well able to fight. But they are seldom called upon to physically participate in combat. Their command powers, and sense of responsibility, are too valuable."

The admiral regarded the information thoughtfully. "And only the parent gender has sexual intercourse?"

"Only the parent gender is appropriately equipped and hormonally inclined."

"What is the difference between a warrior and a—parent in uniform? On the battlefield that is?"

"Warriors are larger and stronger, and have more appropriate reactions. In fact, they are bolder and more aggressive in all matters, and in war, more ready to put their lives in danger. In peacetime, warriors both accept and seek responsibility more than any other gender excepting masters. In the military, the great majority of commissioned officers are warriors, but they do not attain the higher ranks. All elite units are made up of warriors."

Tischendorf nodded thoughtfully. "So then, all—citizens?—are trained as soldiers?"

"All but matrons. Matrons have seriously limited intelligence. Also they are very precious to the species, unique and uncommon. All the exalted genders are; nurturing a newborn for exalted status commonly results in the infant's death. We have a saying, half serious: 'Death by deranged morphogenesis is God's way of helping us appreciate the occasional success.'"

David wondered how such an odd system had ever evolved. And Qonits had mentioned God. Had he said it to mislead them, or was the proverb genuine?

"That is why," Qonits continued, "the exalted genders are exposed to actual combat no more than necessary. But matrons are especially precious. A warrior is most fierce when protecting a matron."

He bowed then, and the president reclaimed the floor. "Tell us about scholars, Mr. Ambassador."

"Ah, scholars. I have slighted my own kind, have I not? Scholars are exalted artisans. The artisan genotype in general absorbs information more easily than other genotypes. And artisans tend to apply information in practical ways. Scholars excel artisans in their affinity for information, but are less focused on its practical applications. Also we look more deeply, and analyze with greater facility."

He displayed what David knew was a grimace. "Unfortunately those strengths are not always accompanied by wisdom. They can give rise to overconfidence and vanity." He paused. "And it is a scholar weakness to become so engrossed in some area of interest—learning your language, for example—that we lose track of relative importances."

Chang regarded Qonits for a long moment. "Thank you, Mr. Ambassador," he said. "You've been very enlightening."

Chang led his de facto council through two additional rounds before he and his prime minister thanked and dismissed them. The last thing he said was that he would consult next with Charley Gordon, then perhaps talk further with them.

Leaving the council room, David felt relief at the direction the meeting had taken. For despite the death of Yukiko, he did not want the Wyzhñyñy eradicated. Qonits, who had become his friend, was a Wyzhñyñy. Also he remembered the pastry chef on the *Meadowlands*, who out of goodness of heart had been friendly to him and Yukiko and Annika. And who now was dead.

After lunch in their suite, Qonits napped, while David sat in one of the small roof gardens and read the Kunming *Daily Reporter* in detail. Later, Qonits also came up, accompanied by Lance Corporal Shaughnessy, who removed himself a dozen yards, as if to give them privacy. Nonetheless, David supposed the marine was bugged—surely something was—and that everything they might say would be recorded.

"Tell me about Wyzhñyñy history," he said to Qonits. "Not the details, but the broad features."

"The broad features? That is feasible, yes. I will begin at the beginning." Qonits also believed they were being recorded, and that David was leading him. Nonetheless he talked frankly, almost till supper.

Via Ramesh, the president and prime minister tried to consult with Charley Gordon after lunch. Admiral Soong, however, asked that they postpone it a couple of hours. Charley was still sleeping off the nervous exhaustion of the long battle. And the colonization fleet showed no sign of leaving. There was constant warp radio traffic between Wyzhñyñy ships, but while no one on the *Altai* had any idea of what was being discussed, it sounded desultory, rather than intense.

Chang and Peixoto gave him half an hour, then eavesdropped on the ambassador and David MacDonald, gaining useful insights.

Forty minutes later they called the *Altai* again, and counseled with Charley, and Alvaro Soong. When the armada had arrived in the system, Charley told them, the colonization fleet had obviously been ordered to park where they were, and wait. But they wouldn't wait forever. Their commanders were surely aware that their warfleet had been destroyed. His impression was, they'd been discussing the dangers of fleeing—of being dispersed and isolated, with the separate units lacking adequate technical-industrial equipment for long-range survival. Along with the probability that many would be torpedoed when they booted their drives. They were aware that a human fleet was standing by, also in warpspace, with target locks on Wyzhñyñy ships. And that survivors would almost certainly be hunted by the humans.

But they wouldn't wait forever. Unless something intervened soon, they'd leave, unless a peace proposal changed their minds.

An hour's discussion resulted in a plan. Half an hour later, Qonits, using a bottled savant in Cee Ministry, sent the basic features of an offer via Charley himself, who forwarded it using the Wyzhñyñy command frequency. The vocators of the bottled savants provided a much better approximation of Qonits' Wyzhñyñyç speech than any human vocal apparatus could.

The Wyzhñyñy commanders could expect an "imperial" ambassador in two Wyzhñyñy shipsweeks, to confer with them directly. Qonits would leave in a cruiser the next day, with David as his companion.

Chapter 64

Unfinished Business

Months had passed since the Wyzhñyñy offensive on New Jerusalem had been broken. The Burger engineers had worked diligently, transforming the army's base from a tent camp to prefabs, electrified for heat and light. The battalion officer's dayroom had a wooden frame and a subfloor of newly-sawn planks, provided by the Burgers' portable sawmill. Walls, ceiling, roof, and the floor itself were sheets of Plastosil brought from Pastor Lüneburger's World with the army.

The New Jerusalem Liberation Corps was ready for winter.

Which soon would be there. It was early ElevenMonth by the Jerrie calendar—dark, cold and wet—when Ensign Esau Wesley came in after supper. He'd brought his platoon back from patrol an hour and a half earlier, had cleaned up and eaten, then come to the dayroom to read. He'd never been much for loafing, and over the months had read, then reread the books Captain Zenawi had loaned him. He found them engrossing, full of facts and ideas— even wisdom—useful to a leader.

581

And that's what he'd become. The previous Sevenmonth he'd been officially posted as acting platoon leader. He'd never known or wondered why. In the army, orders came from on high—the company commander, Regiment, Division, or War House—and you went along with them.

He knew very well, of course, how he'd become *unofficial* acting platoon leader. Ensign Berg had been killed on the Tank Park Raid, then Ensign Hawkins had broken his leg on the Artillery Base Jump. But taking over in an emergency was one thing. Having the post on the company TO was something else.

There was a story behind it. It had been Sevenmonth. The entire corps had taken a lot of casualties, and the regimental commander, Colonel Leclerc, had called in his company commanders to work on reorganizing the regiment. They'd begun right after breakfast, and had pretty much wrapped it before lunch. Some companies had been deactivated—combined with other companies, or their personnel distributed within the regiment as replacements.

Division wanted airborne-qualified personnel kept in airborne-qualified platoons; something Leclerc would have done in any case. "Zenawi," he said, "your 2nd Platoon has the most distinguished record in the regiment. With a very fine commander. But according to Major Hatta, Hawkins won't be out of the hospital for eight weeks at the soonest. Add three weeks or more for rehab . . . " He shrugged. "And Hatta strongly recommends that Hawkins not jump again—not in this gravity.

"Fortunately Ensign Hussain is available. From 3rd Regiment; a good man. His platoon covered Demolitions while they'd wrecked the Wyz howitzers, and taken a lot of casualties. Including Major Chou, which left Hussain the senior officer, in charge of the rear guard action and evacuating the casualties. Then the Wyz elite hit. Hairy business, and he handled it well, all of it.

"I'm assigning him to you, to lead 2nd Platoon B."

Captain Kemau Zenawi Singh chewed a lip. "Colonel," Zenawi said, "2nd Platoon has a platoon sergeant who acted as platoon leader throughout the Artillery Base Raid. I'd hoped to see him get the job."

Leclerc frowned. "Esau Wesley? I reviewed his commendations last night, before okaying his promotion to sergeant first class. A remarkable young warrior. But he doesn't have anything like the training and the leadership experience Hussain has. Are you sure you don't prefer him because he's B Company, and you're loyal to your own people?"

Zenawi set his jaw. "That's part of it, sir. But on the other hand, I'm an old friend of Hussain. We were in the same cadet squad at the Academy. Went into Tehran together a few times, to sample the ethnic eating places.

"The thing is, young Wesley's a sort of icon in B Company, though I doubt he knows it. He's better than his official record, sir. For one thing he's got natural presence. Charisma. Berg, Hawkins, Captain Mulvaney, all made a project out of him early on, at Stenders, because of his leadership qualities. And he never disappointed them.

"On the Tank Park Raid, he took out the southwest tower by himself, with cover by a couple of blastermen. Then, at the Pecan Orchard, he led a stealth team into the middle of the Wyzhñyñy camp and stole their headquarters, a floater—took it from under their noses—which was vital to our success there. And . . ."

Leclerc interrupted. "Kemau," he said patiently, "I know those things. But his reputation stems from his individual exploits. Leadership's another matter."

"But not unrelated, Colonel. In that disorganized melee at the tank park, before he took out the southwest tower, he functioned effectively as a leader. He and his squad were one of two sent into an utterly chaotic melee to support 3rd Platoon when they were getting swamped. And it was Wesley that Mulvaney turned to to get the flak towers handled. And on the artillery base jump, Esau directed Hawkins' Platoon at the same time he . . ."

Leclerc cut him off. "All right. So he's a natural warrior and a *promising* leader. Hussain's another natural warrior, *and* a trained and proven leader. Where's Wesley's advantage?"

"You already identified it, sir." Zenawi showed no sign of backing off. "You wanted to keep units intact so far as possible; 'for morale and unity,' you said. Wesley's been 2nd Platoon from the beginning, and he's a legend in B

Company. In Airborne A Temp for that matter. He's got a reputation: they believe he can do anything, even salvage bad situations. He's smart, tough, fearless . . . and *lucky!* The men talk about it. The men of B Company, especially 2nd Platoon, would feel slighted, insulted, if he got passed over now."

Zenawi's expression was intense, his white eyes hard in his black face. "Hussain *is* a good man and he *is* a proven officer. In time, 2nd Platoon would forget their resentment, and like him. But it wouldn't be the same, and it would take awhile." He paused, and put his hand on his chest. "Speaking respectfully, sir, their company commander wants Esau Wesley, and so does his company!"

Leclerc pursed his lips, then grunted. "All right, you've made your case, Kemau. I'll post Wesley as commander of 2nd Platoon, B Company. But I want you to work with him. Help him with whatever he's short on. Give him some reading: *The Infantry Platoon Leader; Working with Men; The Challenge of Command* . . . And if he's willing, Gopal Singh's *The Wise Leader.* Then quiz him."

Zenawi relaxed. "Thank you, sir, I will. And sir, if you were the CO of B Company, I believe you'd have made the same request I did."

Leclerc stifled a smile. *You got the old man to back down, didn't you,* he thought. *And now you're rubbing a little oil on. Well, it's healthy to back down now and then, when the case is good enough. But pick your spots carefully, Kemau.*

That had been high summer. Now they were at winter's doorstep. Esau was rereading *The Infantry Platoon Leader* when Jael came in. For months they'd been in different units, quartered in different hutments, living different lives. He hadn't seen her for weeks; didn't often think about her anymore. So far as he knew, they were still married, but it felt remote.

"Hi, Esau," she said, walking over to him.

He laid down his book and stood up. "Howdy, Jael," he answered smiling. "It's been awhile."

Her voice sounded enough like her old voice now, Esau couldn't hear the difference. Normally, when a person signed a bot agreement, there were questions, the volunteer's answers were recorded, and they were asked to read selected lines. Then if they were bottled, they were given a cube of the recording, to help them learn their old voice again. Jael had learned without a cube, fitting her new voice to her personality, and to the "voice print" in her speech center.

"How're you liking your new servo?" Esau asked. Lamely, it seemed to her, as if he had trouble finding something to say. It was the same model as her old one, which had been damaged by a heavy slammer bolt two weeks earlier, on night reconnaissance deep inside Wyz Country. It had torn up her left knee.

"It's better than the old one," she answered. "It doesn't overheat." She paused to laugh. "The techs say that's because they've got them figured out. I told them it's the weather. Have you seen any action lately?"

He shook his head. "I've heard some a time or two, off in the distance a ways. Maybe things'll heat up when we get snow." He chuckled at the incongruity of terms. "Snow can come any time now, and Captain Zenawi said the last supply run brought down skis. If it gets belly deep, like sometimes, we ought to get around on foot better than the Wyz do."

"You folks still cutting timber every third week?"

He shook his head. "Haven't for . . . it'll be four weeks on Sixday. Things are getting dull around here." He half grinned. "Now if they'd let me start making a farm . . ." It had already occurred to him he didn't want to farm anymore, but the old thought patterns were still there, semiactive.

"If things keep going like they are," she said, "us and the Wyz might get so used to each other, we'll just say to Tophet with the war. You farm east of the river and we'll farm west of it." She didn't really want to farm anymore, either. Or live on New Jerusalem, where most women of childbearing age didn't live to see their thirtieth birthday (about thirty-nine Terran years). But she'd never thought of it as a cruel world. Most folks had been happy enough. And she'd accepted it—until she'd shared reminiscences with Terran women among the bots. Heard about their seventy-year-old grandmothers, even ninety-year-old great-grandmothers!

She'd wondered how long she'd live as a bot. A long time maybe. There were two main theories in the bot camp. The first was, your CNS would finally wear out. And the second—you'd live till you died of boredom. To her, the first seemed most likely.

Esau sat without saying anything, so she asked: "What're you reading?"

He held the book up—a paper book—showing her the cover. *"The Infantry Platoon Leader,"* he said. "This is the third time I've read it. Seems like there's stuff in it that wasn't there before. Like someone came in while I slept, and added new stuff to it. I've been reading others, too. Read three by Gopal Singh! Quite a lot different than the Testaments, but I suspect Elder Hofer wouldn't fuss too bad. Some of it—a lot of it—he'd probably like.

"What you said about us and the Wyz getting used to each other . . . Nearly nine hundred years ago—when folks still fought each other a lot—Gopal Singh wrote that humankind was learning little by little to live in peace. And afterward, for a long time, folks did live in peace. Wouldn't be fighting today if the Wyz hadn't come along."

Jael nodded. "To start farming here again, the womenfolk would have to come back. And might be lots of them wouldn't want to."

"Yeah."

There was silence for several long seconds before he added, "I sure do miss . . . some of the things you and me used to do together."

"Me too. But not as much as you do, I don't suppose. I don't have the juices I used to. I'd settle for being able to cuddle and nuzzle. But I'm afraid cuddling wouldn't do much for either of us anymore. The way I am now."

Esau rocked a little on his unmoving chair, before saying: "Sometimes I've wondered if we oughtn't have chosen a labor battalion, instead of the army. Then, when it was over, we could have been—still really married. Had those children we never got."

He looked and felt absolutely bleak now. *Not healed,* he thought. *Not healed. Just scabbed over.*

Reaching, Jael touched his arm as gently as if she were still flesh and blood. "Esau dear, don't regret. We always did the best we could, and had lots of good times. Back on the farm, and on Lüneburger's World, and even here in the war.

"And there are other girls besides me. Organic girls, flesh and blood. Indi girls in tanks and floaters, Burger girls wiring and carpentering. Terran nurses at the hospital."

The door opened and two Sikhs came in. Then Jael said she needed to go. "Even bots need their sleep," she told him, and left.

Her walk back to the bot hutment was five minutes of depression. That first time Esau had come to see her, at the bot shop, he'd been so sweet, and she'd been so happy to see him. It had seemed to her they'd get used to one another again, and if they lived, make a life together.

You were dreaming, Jael, she told herself. *The old Jael was killed at the Pecan Orchard. Now you've got a new life, and it's the one you've got to live, because you can't get the old one back.*

On the following Sixday, at evening muster, the troops were told that General Pak would speak to them at 1900 hours. There'd been no rumor of any plans, and the army had gotten used to relative peace and quiet. Something was bound to happen sooner or later, of course. They knew that. The Wyz were still there, and had to be rooted out.

With more time to reflect on matters, the Jerrie troops had come to realize how little New Jerusalem felt like home anymore. Too changed. Nearly every one of them had wondered if he could even find where he'd lived, so thoroughly had the Wyzhñyñy changed the face of the settled land. As if they'd deliberately undertaken to eradicate all signs of the humans who'd lived there before them.

Now it seemed as if they were going to be given another job to do. And at seven o'clock, they were in their mess halls, expecting to hear their general outline an offensive. The screen was rolled out; its power light glittering green. Captain Zenawi gave the order, "At ease, men," and the picture popped on, showing General Pak seated at his desk.

"Men and women of the New Jerusalem Liberation Corps, I have important news for you. And a confession. Eight days ago, I was informed that the 1st Commonwealth Fleet had destroyed the Wyzhñyñy fleet in battle." He paused. There wasn't a sound in B Company's mess hall. "The Wyzhñyñy warships fought till none were left." Again he paused. "My confession is that I kept the news from you until I knew what this meant to us out here.

"Their warfleet fought to the death, but that doesn't mean the Wyzhñyñy here will. Because the Wyzhñyñy's *non-fighting* ships surrendered. More than three thousand of them are parked in the fringe of the Eridani System, defenseless. Snooze ships, supply ships, factory ships—all of them. And they've signed a treaty of peace with the Commonwealth. They've turned over all their ordnance, and our fleet is in the process of sending it plunging into the sun.

"The Wyzhñyñy have colonies on forty-seven Commonwealth worlds, and the peace treaty agrees that those colonies are also to surrender. The question now is, will the colonies believe and accept that? Let's hope they do. If they don't, Commodore Kereenyaga is to send down both his Dragons to wreck the Wyzhñyñy caves here. Then any survivors will get another chance to surrender. If they don't, the war will not be over for us; we'll have to dig them out. But our enemy will be fewer, his firepower greatly reduced, and we'll have the support of the Marine wolfpacks. And winter will arrive any time now.

"For those of you who care to, I suggest you now pray silently with me that they do surrender."

After the prayer, the general announced a party at 2100 hours, to be held in all the army's mess halls. He'd heard of the Jerrie penchant for bachelor folk dancing, and the Indis and Burgers would have their own ideas about partying. He knew that Burger cooks had been fermenting mash, and distilling and stashing liquor.

B Company folded and stacked most of their tables, converting mess halls into dance halls. Other tables were placed strategically along the sides, and loaded with sandwiches, cookies, and urns of hot chocolate—something the Jerries had learned about in the army. At 2050, the company was already gathering. Two accordions, two fiddles and a harmonica had arrived, but so far not Captain Zenawi, with his bass guitar. Lieutenant Hawkins, now B Company's XO, was setting up his keyboard.

A bot ducked in—not surprisingly. Seven bots treated B Company as their other family. This bot was Jael; Esau and no doubt others knew her by the necklace of dried, orange-painted bank beans she'd put on. And who else would bring two female organics with her? They paused just inside the door, then Jael's eyes found Esau, and all three women started toward him.

Esau met them halfway, stopping before Jael. "Will you dance with me, ma'am?" he asked. From her elevation, he looked more dutiful than eager.

"I'd love to," she said. "I do believe you're the best-looking man here. But first I'd like to introduce my friends. This is Sergeant Ruta Mossland, Headquarters Company, 1st Indi Armored. And this is Ensign Björg Aribau, 12th General Hospital. Björg was born on Terra, but grew up on Indi Prime. She was Ensign Hawkins' nurse, and she wanted to meet the man who saved his life."

Blushing, Esau bowed and shook each young woman's hand in turn. Then Ensign Hawkins called out above the crowd buzz.

"Captain Zenawi will be here in a few minutes. He says don't wait." He gestured at the other musicians. "We've only played together a few times, so I don't know very much of the music they'll do. They'll start off, and I'll join in when I can. Consider the party officially started!"

Then a caller named the dance, and pairs of laughing soldiers walked to the middle of the floor. All were men, except for Jael and the two women she'd brought. Ruta and Björg had accepted eager partners.

When they'd formed lines, the caller and the music began. The dance was energetic, and the two women were totally unfamiliar with it. Do-si-do meant absolutely nothing to them. But the confusions created were treated as fun, not problems, and before the number ended, everyone was laughing and sweating.

Almost everyone. Esau had discovered how awkward it

was dancing with someone twenty inches taller and twice his mass. So before the next number began, they left the dance floor and went to one of the benches.

"Seems like we don't dance as well as we used to," Esau commented.

"It does, doesn't it? But we can still laugh together. And you can dance with Ruta and Björg. Actually I brought them for you."

The statement didn't surprise Esau. "I wish you wouldn't have," he said.

She nodded. "I thought you'd feel like that."

"Why then?" His voice was pained. "Why did you?"

"Honey, because I love you. And I want you to get used to touching other women. Organic women. I'm not trying to matchmake, although they're both heavyworlders, and very nice people. And pretty, don't you think?"

"Not as pretty as you."

"Why, Esau, what a nice thing to say! This model 7C warbot servo does look quite nice, and maybe in peacetime they'll let me polish it. But I never thought of it as pretty."

Esau had no reply. After a moment, Jael stood. "Let's go outside," she said quietly.

He didn't meet her gaze. Together they walked out into the now-freezing evening. "Esau," she said softly, gently, "please don't pout. It hurts me, especially when I'm trying hard to do what's right."

She stood with her hands on his thick shoulders, her *large* hands, larger than any organic human's, and crushingly strong. "This is a *party*, honey. It looks like the war may really be over, and the killing and dying done with. What I'd like best to do is sneak off with you somewhere—a water-heater room would be fine. But I can't . . . do . . ." Her voice broke unexpectedly, hitting him like a heavy punch in the chest, in the heart. "I can't do . . . the things we did any longer." She recovered herself quickly though. "I just can't *be* . . . your wife, your lover, any longer. No matter how much I'd like to. And I want you to find someone who can." Her fingers had tightened, and realizing it, she let her hands fall. Crouching, she peered earnestly, urgently into his eyes. "Do you see, honey?"

With that she broke entirely, sobbing and shaking despite having no tear glands. Esau watched silently dismayed, spilling enough tears of his own to do for both of them. Finding her hand, he led her farther from the mess hall, to the shelter of a large tree, where they embraced, metal against flesh. Without warning his control melted, grief surging out, grief he hadn't known was still there. Surged violently enough, bitterly enough, it snapped Jael out of her own grief. "It's all right," she murmured, a large hand patting him gently. "It's all right."

Half a minute sufficed him; then they separated. He discovered he didn't have a handkerchief, so he pulled out a shirttail, mopped his cheeks, then blew his juicy nose with his fingers, and wiped them on his pants, behind the thighs.

"There," he said, and surprised her with a shaky laugh. "I believe that's it. Sorry I was so messy. I still forget to carry a handkerchief sometimes." He smiled ruefully. "What d'you want to do?"

"We need to get an annulment. Not a divorce, an annulment. They're different. I talked to Sergeant Major Rinaldi and she checked with the chaplain." Jael paused. "But, honey, I want you to dance with those girls that came with me. I know them both. They're really nice. And if either of them makes a play for you—I'd feel so . . . " For a moment it seemed she might break again, but she rallied. "I'd feel so pleased if you'd go along with it."

Esau met her gaze. It was . . . metallic. There was a soul there, and goodness, and love, but the eyes weren't really eyes. He nodded. "I'll dance with them if you'll dance with Isaiah. He just now went in. I think it was him."

Now it was her turn to stand silent a moment. "All right," she said, "I will. But I need to tell you, dancing won't be the same wearing—this." She gestured at her body. "Not even with someone else my size. Now let's go back."

Esau danced with both women, several times during the next hour, but it was Ensign Aribau who made a pass at him. Ensign Gaughan, Esau's hutmate, saw them leave the mess hall, and told himself to stay away from the hut till the party was over.

Meanwhile, dancing with Isaiah was more enjoyable

Epilog

Soldiers has been the story of a war, and with the Treaty of Eridani Prime, the war and the story were over—officially, and pretty much in fact. But whether human or Wyzhñyñy, those who'd survived had futures, reset by the war itself, and by the treaty.

The war had never been named, officially or otherwise. It was just "the war." There was no other. There hadn't been since that earlier turning point, that long-ago fraternal conflict known as the Troubles. In his speech announcing the peace agreement, President Chang asked that it not be referred to as the Wyzhñyñy War. The surviving Wyzhñyñy would become part of the Commonwealth, and their integration would not be eased by naming the war after them. Describe it as it was, he said, but call it simply "the Invasion."

A millennium earlier he'd never have gotten away with a suggestion like that. But now, near the end of the third millennium, his request was very largely complied with. Gradually over the centuries, humankind had become increasingly civilized, with a civility beyond political correctness. A consensus civility. Without it, civilization and quite possibly humankind would not have survived in the Sol System long enough to meet the Wyzhñyñy. There was still significant and occasionally noisy social discord, but all in all, people were remarkably and comfortably civil.

Even on the hundreds of colony worlds settled by reclusive ethnic groups, and religious, political, and philosophical sects, civility tended to be the rule—at least as long as they were left alone, to live as they pleased.

Among the people of the forty-four human worlds conquered and depopulated by the Wyzhñyñy, cultural disruption had been extreme. But the people lacked the passion, the zeal of their expatriate forebears. Many of the evacuees harbored bitterness or grief, but few felt gnawed upon for revenge.

And most did go home, arriving to find it unrecognizable. With Core World help they rebuilt farms, villages, and towns, but it would never be the same. The genie didn't fit in the bottle anymore. Their cultural realities had been irreparably changed by the war and their brief exiles.

On Terra, a number of antiwar activists had already been tried for terrorism. A remarkable phenomenon: antiwar terrorists! And among the Terran public, zeal had become even more distasteful than before.

The Justice Ministry had aimed at penalties befitting the crimes. Thus Günther Genovesi and Kuei-Fei Wu, who'd conceived and planned the Night of Blood and Fire, were sentenced to visit every Wyzhñyñy-conquered world, and listen to the tales of nonevacuees who'd survived in hiding. Both were reprieved before completing the tour. President Chavez (Chang Lung-Chi had retired) felt that five years had been enough. The two spent the rest of their lives in tolerably comfortable exile, under house arrest on a colony world outside the invasion corridor.

Paddy Davies, Jaromir Horvath, and several other Peace Front kingpins had been sentenced to accompany the Terran 6th Infantry Division to New Miocene. It proved to be a Wyzhñyñy holdout world. Thus they experienced battle, loading wounded and dead onto grav sleds. Davies himself was mortally wounded, trying to help a wounded Wyzhñyñy. Always an idealist, he'd signed the agreement, and awoke as a medic bot. Back on Terra, Horvath became a sort of hermit, more misanthropic than ever.

Fritjof Ignatiev's role, on the other hand, had been little more than inspirational orator. And after the Night of Blood and Fire, he'd voluntarily come forward to work with the government in its terrorist roundup. Thus his sentence had been only thirty days on a work gang. But in his youth he'd been an emergency medical technician, and prevailed on the judge to send him to New Miocene with the others, as a battlefield medic. There he was wounded, and cited for bravery.

After his return, Ignatiev dictated his memoir of the Peace Front and his service on New Miocene. He'd always had an excellent memory, and his recounting fitted the known facts. It would become a useful source for historians of the war.

The New Jerusalem Liberation Corps saw no further combat. Commodore Kereenyaga's flagship had parked three hundred miles above New Jerusalem, and broadcast the peace treaty through Gosthodar Jilchûk's command channel. It was received in every Wyzhñyñy unit headquarters on the planet. The cube had been recorded by a savant bot—Melody Boo'tsa, whom Admiral Apraxin had left with the commodore when she'd departed for Dinébikeyah. Thus Qonits's cultivated Wyzhñyñyç was well reproduced and easily understood.

But still detectably foreign, so Jilchûk rejected it. Two days later, a Dragon parked above the limestone ridge in whose extensive caverns Jilchûk's headquarters was hidden. Along with what remained of his elite force, and other important units of his army, notably his two remaining tank companies. The earlier surveillance buoys had located the entrances and exits, and the Dragon thoroughly smashed them. It also pounded the ridge in general, and parts of the caverns collapsed. Elsewhere the Dragons hit the caverns sheltering most of the rest of the army. Little remained on the surface but patrols.

In the caverns, casualties had been moderate, and their geogravitic power converters continued to provide light, heat, and interior air circulation. But the air intake and waste air expulsion systems had been destroyed. Jilchûk reconsidered his refusal, and sent engineers to work their way through a collapse hole, to radio his acceptance to both the humans and his command.

This presented the Burger engineers with a new highly urgent project: to hastily set up secure, reasonably liveable POW stockades—tent camps. One for the Wyzhñyñy officers, another for the elite companies, and several others for everyone else. Meanwhile, many kilotons of key Wyzhñyñy military material were collected, and lightered into near-space. There they were magnetically bundled, and the bundles sent on trajectories that would plunge them into New Jerusalem's sun.

Four other Wyzhñyñy-occupied worlds had been invaded by liberation forces. Major fleet detachments were dispatched to visit the rest. The size of the forces tended to convince the local gosthodars. Those who were adamant had their colonies visited by Dragons and wolf packs. In several cases where a gosthodar still refused, coups or mutinies resulted in a more agreeable leader. On six planets that still held out, colonies of *Apis mellifera scutella* were widely introduced during the current or next growing season, and the colonies recontacted a few months later.

Only two had eventually to be liberated "the hard way," several years later. *After* being liberated from the African bees by the introduction of enhanced strains of American and European foulbrood. Then regiments were landed— with Wyzhñyñy interpretors—to root out the remaining Wyzhñyñy. Most of whom surrendered more or less readily.

Qonits zu-Kitku was appointed advisor to the president and prime minister. Later, in a sort of reverse appointment, the prime minister named him Wyzhñyñy ambassador to the Commonwealth.

In time, Qonits would also oversee the establishment of the Wyzhñyñy and human youth exchange programs, a School of Wyzhñyñy Studies at Kunming University, and a Department of Humanity at the Institute of Knowledge, on Wyzhuursôk, the world on which the Wyzhñyñy survivors were settled.

Twenty-three Terran years after the treaty was signed, Qonits died in his apartment on the Kunming University campus, of cardiac arrest.

David MacDonald worked with Qonits throughout the ambassador's career. After Qonits' death, he served for two years as advisor to the Wyzhñyñy's new ambassador. He then retired to the new Commonwealth-sponsored colony on Maritimus, referring to himself as "the ambassador to the dolphin republic." The dolphins were amused.

At the end of hostilities on New Jerusalem, Jael Wesley and Isaiah Vernon returned to Terra. By that time they'd become close friends, and married in Kunming—a union necessarily platonic. Meanwhile, rapid progress was being made on pseudo-organic civilian servos for ex-warbots. These were made as humanlike as feasible, and the couple was transferred to customized android servos. A meaningful sexual relationship resulted between these two who'd already developed a very considerate and affectionate relationship.

A few years after leaving military service, they joined the Gopal Singh Order of Compassion, and were trained to help the mentally afflicted. This period of relatively normal life, however, was rather short. Among ex-warbots, the peripheral nerves controlling the limbs began to deteriorate ten to twenty years after first installation. Use of the limbs was then lost within weeks or months. The only treatment was to rebottle the CNS for installation into a sensorially-equipped life-support system like those designed for savant bots. In any case, senile dementia set in, mainly at age sixty to seventy Terran. Persons inhabiting such life-support systems generally arranged for life support to be discontinued at some predefined point in their deterioration.

Jael and Isaiah died within seven weeks of each other.

Esau Wesley and Björg Aribau returned to Terra with the 1st New Jerusalem Division, and were married at Björg's family home in Tarragona, in the Catalunya Prefecture. Both converted to Sikhism (the Gopal Singh Dispensation), and remained in the military. They volunteered to serve in a New Jerusalem battalion assigned as the low-profile embassy garrison on Wyzhuursôk (*Wyzh*: root of Wyzhñyñy; *uur*: the seventh [swarm]; *sôk*: world).

After ten years they returned again to Terra, where they wrote a joint account of the war on New Jerusalem, from a soldier's and nurse's point of view. Its substantial success encouraged another book of their years on Wyzhuursôk. The experience there had been enriched by a powerful hypno-tutorial of the Wyzhñyñy language and culture. And by considerable involvement in Wyzhñyñy life, aided by friendship with several Wyzhñyñy of varied gender and status. The book's best-seller performance surprised them.

The marriage produced two sons and a daughter. One son was named Arjan, the other Isaiah. The daughter was named Jael. The family visited the senior Jael and Isaiah several times after returning from Wyzhuursôk.

Retiring from the military, Esau and Björg lived on Eridani Prime, to enjoy the 0.87 gee gravity. There they bought and resided on a small frontier "hobby farm," which Esau worked himself. They died in their nineties of natural causes.

The pirate ship *Minerva*, with Drago Draveç and his crew, showed up haggard and hungry in the Hart's Desire System. This was two days before, and most of a hyperspace year away from, the battle of Shakti. Draveç helped set up the planet's own "Project Noah," and a few weeks later married Ambassador Annalis Khai. After the peace, he managed a marginally legal import-export office for Harlan Cheregian, but seldom traveled offworld.

He is credited with having introduced war-gaming to Hart's Desire.

After the war, Male Infant Doe 731 had his name legally changed to Charley Gordon and, with Ophelia Kennah, left government service on liberal pensions, fortified by a very generous annuity to Charley, voted by parliament. Meanwhile, Alvaro Soong retired from the

Admiralty and married Ophelia Kennah. Charley "gave away" the bride. For several years the three shared a comfortable condominium, in an affluent retirement community in the mountains of the Chiapas Prefecture, in the Central American Autonomy.

During those years (with travel breaks to attend live concerts all over Terra), Charley's major activity was research on a unified field theory that included psionics. His mathematics was largely incomprehensible, however, except to a very few. More successful was the music he composed in odd moments. Strange, mostly beautiful music—some for instruments, some for voices, some for both. It was found therapeutic for many persons with physical as well as mental problems. (For still others it was psychologically addictive.)

Charley's research period led into what came to be known as "Charley Gordon's meditation phase," ending with three years spent mostly in silence, beneath a lovely canopy in a chán (zen) monastery garden near Kunming. There he was tended by monks, and visited by pilgrims not only from all over Terra, but from other worlds, including exchange youths from Wyzhuursôk.

Afterward Charley remained at the monastery, but treated himself to a well-accessoried artificial intelligence, and spent a year secluded with his new "toy." After programming it to suit his needs, he composed a musical work which he titled Opus Number One: *Logos for the Emotionally Centered.* It was premiered by the Melbourne Symphony Orchestra, to a video/holo audience estimated at 2.7 billion, and a live audience of 11,736. In a post-performance interview, Charley described it as an improved form of his unified field theory.

Following a brief period of CNS deterioration, Charley Gordon died at age 67, one of the best-known and most loved persons in the Commonwealth.

Ophelia Kennah, then 84 years old, dictated her best-selling *Memories of Charley,* and died shortly afterward.

EXPLORE OUR WEB SITE